The Son and The Heir

Robin Solomon grew up outside a village on the Norfolk-Suffolk border. He studied Politics at the University of Sheffield, focusing on international relations and development. After taking a gap year travelling and volunteering he returned to study International Development at Manchester University. Having focused on the political forces for driving development he became particularly interested in political agency. ***The Son and the Heir*** examines political developments in narrative form, exploring how different individuals seek to resist social and political forces that threaten to engulf them and instead engage in society through a path they find morally acceptable.

I would like to thank **Jenni Adams** for her
tireless efforts in proof-reading and giving a much-needed
second opinion on this novel

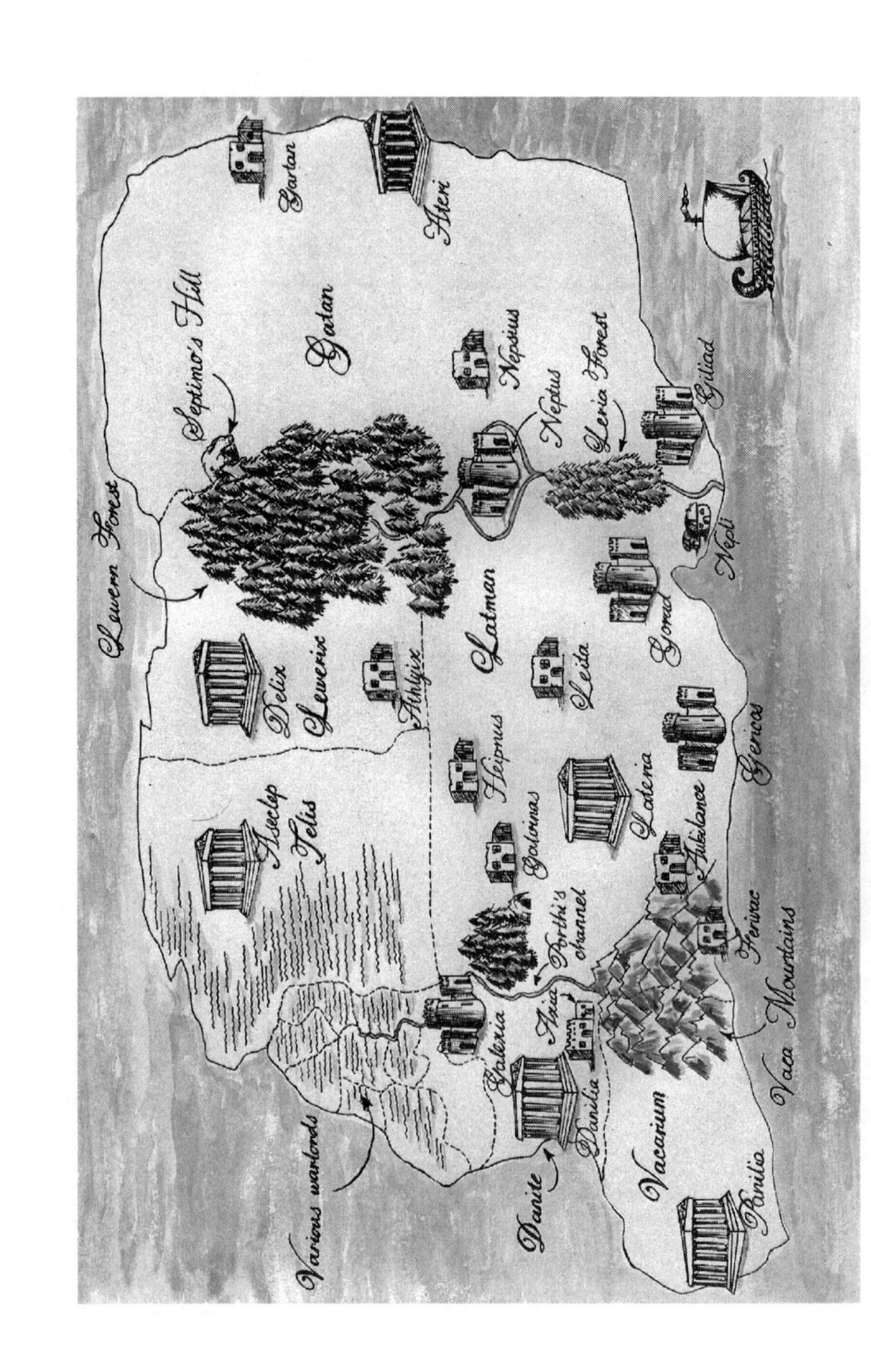

The Son and The Heir

Robin Solomon

Arena Books

Copyright © Robin Solomon 2010

The right of Robin Solomon to be identified as author of this book has been asserted in accordance with the Copyright, Designs and Patents Act 1988.

First published in 2010 by Arena Books

Arena Books
6 Southgate Green
Bury St. Edmunds
IP33 2BL

www.arenabooks.co.uk

All rights reserved. Except for the quotation of short passages for the purposes of criticism and review, no part of this publication may be reproduced, stored in a retrieval system, or transmitted, in any form or by any means, electronic, mechanical, photocopying, recording or otherwise, without the prior permission of the publisher.

Robin Solomon
The Son and The Heir
1. Island people – Fiction. 2. Interpersonal conflict - Fiction. 3. Political sociology – Fiction.
4. Individualism – Fiction.
I. Title
823.9'2-dc22

ISBN   978-1-906791-55-1

BIC categories:- FHP, FJM, FM.

Printed and bound by Lightning Source UK

Cover design
by Jason Anscomb

Typeset in
Times New Roman

The Son and The Heir

'There is no happiness like that of being loved by your fellow creatures, and feeling that your presence is an addition to their comfort.'
Charlotte Bronte, 1847

Chapter 1
The Moulding of a Crusader

The office walls were covered in banners of both patriotic and religious origin. Glorious paintings hung between the banners depicting Latman heroes, sword in hand declaring victory to the gods. Swirling auras of light and glistening stardust wrapped around the champions, spiralling down from the clouds. These were new additions. A mighty banner draped down from the back of the wall, covering the whole wall surface, the shining metal ringlets swaying joyously under the pressure. At the very bottom the toes of Thelus could be seen poking out from behind the banner. It was the only statue in the room, installed by the current lord's grandfather.

Lord Juscius Latman was a young man; indeed he was the youngest lord throughout Latman history, except for Lord Lysin who had been only ten when he ascended the throne. However, he had only theoretically been in control - his role had been entirely ceremonial. A court of advisors made up of noblemen at the highest echelons of trade and generalship, headed by the high priest, Xsedic, had openly ruled in his place. Sadly the young lord died before his eighteenth birthday, when he would have had a possible claim to assuming power. At the age of eighteen Juscius had caused much controversy when he became lord four years ago. Many nobles thought him too young, and therefore too brash and erratic to lead: they feared he may ignore his advisors, and, spurred on by the tragic death of his brother, may set about enacting his revenge with some irrational gallivant into Gatan. The Gatanese elite had been equally dubious; like their Latman counterparts, many had speculated war.

In fact, the young lord had lost much of his youthful vigour when his brother died. The tragic circumstances of his death had turned him against wars and military solutions, he had even lost much of his youthful sense of adventure, and instead he had turned to the moral guidance of religion. Rather than exploring the land and sea like he and his companion Ruperis had done until their teens, Juscius turned to spiritual exploration. This had pointed him towards the work of Zeuorox, a particularly contentious priest from the northern town of Galvina. He first came into contact with the cleric's teachings before he became Lord just under a year from his brothers' death.

Zeuorox's interpretation of the gods, as far as Juscius was concerned, achieved this: through endless examination of the myths and legends surrounding the gods the priest mapped out the relationship of the gods to each other and to man. He had managed to divide the gods into two factions, the true gods and the 'demonis', false gods. It is difficult to explain his whole theory at once. However, it can be briefly outlined. The true gods continued to uphold the principles of the mother and father of the gods; these were virtuous, good natured, pure beings. These gods were led by Thelus the King of the gods. Humans should not only strive to be like these gods but also have a duty to them as they protect them from the 'fallen'; the demonis gods who had betrayed the principles of old. Zeuorox's scriptures highlight that it was Septimo the god of the underworld that forced Thelus to aid him in the killing of their father. However, King Thelus was distraught with what he had done, and according to Zeuorox he had made his mother into the earth to hide her from her evil son, not to punish her. (He also noted that it was Septimo who lived in the underworld – cutting deep into mother earth and Thelus who lived above the clouds). Since man was created the fallen gods have constantly tried to harness them to their own evil plans and to wreak havoc on the world. This had left man in a confused state; the pollution of man's mind by the fallen beings had meant they worshipped them out of necessity, like Galex the war god, and Athyle, the goddess of war, fate and wisdom, when there was conflict. Man had to turn away from these evil gods and look to the true gods to minimise their evil taint.

Principally it had been the division of good and evil that had attracted Juscius, and their distinction, which put the most violent of the gods in the conception of evil, it had adhered to the very core of his distrust with his surroundings. The fact that it explained that evil things were caused by extra-human action by some misguided former-gods meant he had not lost his faith in the gods per se. And finally it offered a way of salvation for man. Man was not longer a helpless collective tool of the gods; man could align himself with the true gods and aspire to follow them towards development and virtue. This new interpretation breathed some meaning into the distressed heir.

By the time of his coronation the heir had become a total convert, yet had shielded it from the public. In the meantime Zeuorox was experiencing severe opposition from the other religious leaders. However, this ceased rather abruptly, when during the coronation ceremony Juscius broke into a rousing speech declaring his devotion to the New Interpretation, calling the Latman household the defender of the true gods; the Warriors of Thelus. With tears streaming down his face he passionately condemned the demonis gods, blaming them for the tragedies that had struck the people of Latman and the island's populace in general. He declared a new era in the history of the people of Rudia and attributed the enlightenment to Zeuorox. The pious young lord could never have comprehended the impact of such a speech, in fact he never really did learn of the extent to which this one speech had transformed the territory. In the weeks following the speech a theological shockwave swept the land. Some believed that the new Lord was directly in consultation with Thelus (some even went as far as to suggest he was actually the son of Thelus, conceived with Maritha when he was in the form of a particularly attractive bull), others merely embraced it out of fear of persecution. The most zealous converts set about destroying the condemned god's temples in fervent rituals before erecting new temples to the 'true gods'. Most Orthodox believers went underground although many rural areas remained openly hostile to the New Interpretation.

The conversion was remarkable; some would say miraculous, especially with respect to the immediate shift amongst the elite; however there were more factors than just the speech made by the nervous emotional adolescent. Crucially the religious elite instantly backed the New Interpretation; firstly they feared accusations that they were evil magi worshipping the demonis gods; secondly they observed (mainly through the speech) that Zeuorox was rising in power and influence and so they couldn't attack him. Finally many noticed that they were significant gains to the new religion; the sensational, evangelical style of actively preaching to a congregation not only brought in more crowds and donations but also influence among the populace. The priests were looked to for moral guidance and could shape peoples lives in a virtuous way.

Ironically, considering the role of pacifism in the conversion of Juscius, the military harnessed the good/bad distinction to their own ends, espousing ideas of a direct link between dedication to the true good gods though service to the Latman Household. It also enabled them utilise the orthodoxy of Gatan to degrade them to warriors of evil and inherent enemies of the virtuous soldiers of Latman, who were the vanguard of Thelus.

As for the economic elite, many embraced the new religion as though it was a new trend or fashion; nobles and traders looked upon the previous beliefs with a patronising sense of quaintness. Some deliberately changed company names in order to adopt acceptable gods or phrases (countless maritime trades must have been consternate when they discovered Neptus had been blacklisted).

For the general population it unleashed waves of conflict. In the south of the territory in particular there had been several rebellions after temples had been destroyed and orthodox magi executed. However, in the first few years, much of these reports had 'failed' to reach the Lord, thanks to the intervention of Zeuorox fearing it could have an adverse effect on his faith. Though Juscius himself had never enforced the new religion, this couldn't be said of Zeuorox, who had even visited Asclep, the Telis household capital, with considerable success. Juiscius' ignorance of the social conflict could never last, especially after the religious divide had reopened social wounds in the former Vacarium territory in the West.

Now in his fourth year as Lord, Juscius was totally enveloped in the new doctrine, spending much of his time talking with the High Priest; he often pondered to himself what the gods willed him to do. He found the metaphysical propositions so interesting, anything not related to this he relegated to triviality. Still, a sense of duty kept him dedicated to his responsibilities (Zeuorox often explained to him that every good report was a symbol of the satisfaction that Arminius had with him and every bad report was a test of his faith and resilience).

He shuffled through the various reports on his desk. All the reports from the Latman-Gatan border revealed that there had been only minor movements of troops. The Latman-Lewerix border was unsurprisingly uneventful; the only event reported was a cart breaking its wheel on the main pass between Heiphus and Athlyix.

The report that he longed for was one declaring the return of Ruperis Delvinius, the Lord's childhood friend who had left just over two years ago to explore beyond the island. The young man had never lost his sense for adventure and after amassing a small fortune through marine trade (undoubtedly aided by his close links to the lord's family) had decided to venture off on an expedition. Juscius hadn't even seen his companion much over the previous five years: when he was seventeen, Ruperis had begun to sail his father's ships all around the island meaning he was rarely in the capital at all. Juscius' mind wandered back to their childhood, when he and Ruperis used to spend so much time at the garrison of Gericos so they could watch the fishing ships and galleys soar across the water. It was then that Ruperis had become so obsessed with travelling and adventure. They would spend hours staring out at the deep shimmering sea studying the multicoloured patterns shift and twinkle with the sunlight. It always seemed so calm, yet apparently further out the currents became very strong and storms blew frequently all year round. They would always daydream of sailing off to sea and make up adventure stories. He smiled to himself when he recalled the time he and his companion had tried to live their dream and had hijacked a fishing boat and sailed off only to be caught as they struggled to control the sail.

To this day he knew they'd have made it much further if Ruperis' elder sister hadn't started screaming at them. Back then she could be so irritating, always screaming to their parents when they misbehaved; she had retained much of her headstrong character which Juscius now found charming.

Juscius silenced his thoughts and tried to return his attention to the coastal reports, although his mind wandered further into the depths of his conscience. He thought of his father, a stream of personal memories opening into the plains of professional recollection.

What had been his father's achievements? His father had created a highly disciplined full time army with proper position ranks, and superbly made scale mail armour, but all this was of little interest to the new lord. His household was already the largest and most powerful of the island households, only rivalled by house Gatan, and he had learned from his predecessors that war had achieved nothing, except the horrific death of his elder brother. The reforms to the military had been spectacular and they set an example of Latman being ahead of the other tribes. It also gave him a sense that his troops were the true guardians of Thelus. However, he had overcome the rage from that onslaught of the demonis false gods; their evil act had merely turned him into a buttress against their desire to destroy. The struggle was not over land and resources but good and evil; this was not an issue for man to make decisions over, it was man's role to worship those that were good and then truth would prevail.

Juscius returned to one of the reports in particular. It was from the garrison at Gorad, and informed him of yet another barbarian raid on a remote village. By the time the garrisons' squad had reached the village, the barbarians had gone. He pulled a contemplative expression then opened a drawer and began shifting through recent reports from elsewhere; over the past years there was a definite pattern. They always attacked at this time, when the villagers had the most food in store and when many travelling merchants stopped off at the coastal villages. His household was losing a considerable amount of valuable assets to these raiders, and with over half his army tied down in case any rival household attacks, he could defend barely any villages. Juscius looked around his room at the spectacular display of banners and paintings covered the walls. He leant back in his ornately carved throne-like chair and grasped the eagle's heads that emerged out of arm rests that were covered in a spectacular feather pattern. Juscius contemplated the dilemma he had: the barbarian attacks had begun towards the end of his father's reign, but then they were rare occurrences and little attention was paid to them; now they were a growing security problem. These savages had obviously come from the continent, further fuelling Lord Latman's desire to learn of it, what harsh, but possibly mineral rich land they must live on.

Just then his concentration was broken by the noise of the door to his room being thrust open. This meant only one person...Lord Juscius Latman's mother, Maritha.

The short plump figure of his mother half-waddled, half-strode into the room. She was red with rage and holding aloft a piece of paper; a report a she had snatched that had caught her eye no doubt.

"This is a disgrace; they are disgusting those pigs...ignorant pigs! They are worse than the savage barbarians!" she fumed. She waddled up and down the room in a rage shouting obscenities, Juscius quietly stood wandered over to his mother begging her to calm down. When she was in this state there was no point in trying to point out to her that the reports were confidential and for his eyes only.

He snatched the report off her and read it. As he read it he was horrified, it was from Gericos, it had been attacked by the Barbarians, the report stated that the attack had been at night but even more strangely it seemed the attackers had gone straight for the garrison to torch the barracks; apparently no slaves and little goods had been taken, the raiders had been in the largest numbers recorded so far: there was something too planned and un-barbarian-like about this attack. He felt disgusted at the acts of the unknown perpetrators, the thought of the brave Warriors of Thelus burning in a deluge of flame, murdered by cowards in their sleep. Anger flared up in him but he swallowed the bitter feeling of vengeance. He paused and looked up at his mother who had calmed down and was tapping her foot impatiently waiting for him to finish. Upon noticing he had finished she pointed to the offending article and muttered, "It was Gatan, I know it. It's much too savage and organised for the barbarians. You can't just let this go on, now's your chance, revenge them for this, they're murderers!" by the end of her speech she had reached a shriek.

"Mother, it isn't that simple. I know it seems like what you say makes sense, but I cannot prove it, besides now is not the time to fight, we are in a new era, I'm sure of it" reassured Juscius

"It's too late for that, stop living in your dream world, son. Remember, Gatan cannot be trusted. Your father learnt that and we lost your beloved brother!" Maritha replied passionately, enraged by the persistent naivety of her baby son. The anger soon surpassed, love for her remaining son prevailing.

Juscius lowered his head, memories of his brother flooded into his mind. Tears welled in his eyes; he wanted to weep, to embrace her as a son. He could not though; he was lord now, he had to be strong; resolute in the face of personal tragedy. Wiping the warm salty liquid from his eyes he looked up; the gaunt face of a bereaved brother slipped back behind the divine masking crown,

"Mother, we mustn't use him so." He whispered.

Maritha looked on distraught, was she losing him too?

Zealous dedication overwhelmed his emotions; the tests of the gods and the victories of the devils should not get to him. He had to try and move his house on from the dark times.

Adopting the blank expression for the espousal of doctrine, the surest defence against emotion, he declared, "Thelus will guide us to war if it is what he wills."

Seeing she was still distraught, Juscius loosely embraced his mother. In response she latched on tightly, muttering something,

"Don't worry, I'll make sure we find out what has happened," he announced coldly in an attempt to sound unemotional and professional.

Chapter 2
The Temple Visit

Lord Adonis Gatan of the Gatan Household stared into his ornately carved wine goblet and sighed; he was waiting for the reports on the harvest. In the gloominess of his chamber, the shimmering patterns of firelight illuminated patches of muscle and robe that constituted the numerous statues that glared into the centre of the room from their perimeter positions. The wrinkles and features glistened with the stroking of the orange flames. They waited, static, resolute like discarded chess pieces surrounding the chequered board of the stone floor.

Adonis glanced at the border reports again and ran his hand through his jet-black hair with striking streaks of almost pure white, then impatiently began scratching his full beard. He heard the enormous door creak open, being pushed by one of his guards. A slight figure entered the room and he looked up to see the wrinkled face and lanky figure of Gorax, his chief and only architect. He had no idea where this gangly old man got his skills from; he claimed it was because of these symbols and figures he used in his complex drawings. The prunish enigma had become quite a legend among his subjects and had attracted the intrigue of the other household lords. Adonis smiled to himself as he was reminded of the ingenious temple structure that had been erected three years back. Adonis wondered what it would be this time.

Gorax had sensed his lords' amusement but continued to walk gingerly up to his desk, he opened the large piece of paper he had tucked under his arm. "My Lord, this is my new idea," Gorax grinned nervously to himself.

Adonis squinted as he gazed over the complex scribbling, from his novice knowledge on such matters he could make out some kind of elaborate building with the usual bizarre figures and symbols littered beside the lines and angles.

"What actually is it?" asked Adonis, with a touch of impatience.

Gorax ignored his Lord's hint and continued. "It is a place of learning, where I can teach my trade to others, I am getting old, my lord, and with me will die my knowledge of construction and mechanisms."

"Yes, but why so elaborate?" asked Adonis.

"I thought my lord would want something spectacular to impress the other households."

Adonis nodded in agreement. "It depends on the harvest."

"My Lord, I have already heard that the harvest is very well and is to be ready early this year, which will give you the builders earlier, by about mid Juvian." answered Gorax.

Adonis frowned to himself; *how did this pioneering professional manage to find out news before me?* "Yes, fine, I'll think about it," he answered and shooed Gorax away.

The sprightly old inventor scampered for the exit. Just before leaving he looked up to his lord. "Oh, Lord Adonis, I have had some more ideas for contraptions that you may find useful in the future, I was wondering if you would allow me..." he began.

"Yes, yes take whatever you need," snapped Lord Adonis, not even bothering to look up from his goblet. He heard Gorax scamper off but when he didn't hear the door close he sighed out loud, wandered to the ornate oak door and slammed the door shut, muttering to himself.

Upon reaching his desk Adonis sighed again. The harvest reports were due this morning but for some reason were being held up and he needed them for the council he had summoned this evening. Many of the Commandants were deeply superstitious and looked upon the harvest as an omen showing how gracious the gods were towards them. For this reason every region would claim a good harvest no matter what so it was not seen as invoking a bad omen so it was up to Adonis to send out people to find out for himself. He couldn't just tell the Regional Commandants that he knew the harvests were fine because the eccentric old inventor randomly turned omnipresent and said so. He needed something they would trust; the only solution would be to go to Xsclepia the High Priest of the Grand Ateri Temple of Thelus.

Xsclepia was Adonis personal prophet; he could predict the outcome and they would believe his word. As a traditional man himself, Adonis followed the militaristic culture of the Gatan household strictly: like all his predecessors, he regularly spoke with his seer-priest advisor just as any true warrior-leader should.

Adonis slowly rose from his seat, walked over to his shelf and took up his golden helm (this particular helmet was more a symbol of his position than a military headdress). He opened the door out of his chamber, the tough bulkhead stretching his muscles to the limit, and stepped out into the corridor. It was a short passage that had no windows and was lit by two candles half way along it in little indents in the wall. The rest of the wall was bare, except for a battleaxe with the Gatan insignia on it at the far end where a doorway to the right led to the living room.

Outside Adonis' door were two of the lord's most trusted soldiers from his elite troop, who the lord made an effort to train with at least three times a week and he knew all by name.

Adonis nodded to the two on guard, "Alledic, Malki."

The guards stood stiff to attention for a split second then bowed graciously, "M'lord," they uttered in union with devotion.

"Do you know where my sons are?" Adonis asked.

"They are training with master Dephicos, m'lord," answered Alledic.

Adonis thanked the guards solemnly then departed down the corridor.

Adonis strode into the living room; it was decorated with furs and stuffed heads of various animals Adonis had hunted along with banners and almost relic status weapons of Adonis' predecessors. In one corner was an idol of Galex the god of war. It was a traditional artefact in the Gatan household and had been altered over the years to suit different lord's tastes. The effigy had its great plumed helmet donned upon its head. Interestingly, this particular statue was clean-shaven. Traditionally he had a beard and originally this one had done too but Adonis had preferred the idea that the god would resemble a young fresh warrior; brash, strong and fearless and so he had ordered it be changed. The idol used to hold aloft a broadsword but Adonis' father had decided this was too barbaric and had it re-sculpted into an ornate short sword. The well-muscled body had a light scale mail vest and traditional leather warrior skirt.

In the corner adjacent to it was a statue of the Goddess Angara, the goddess of love and fertility. Like the statue of Galex, which was for the lord, it was tradition to have an Angara for the lady. At the foot of the statue was Adonis' wife, Hierda, who knelt praying, no doubt for Angara to give her a baby girl. She had been the daughter of the previous Lord Danite. They had been married when he was young as part of a diplomatic tie with Danite household. Over the years their relationship barely extended beyond formalities. As a young heir he had usually been out hunting and training. These continued as he grew up, sometimes he would go on hunting expeditions that lasted months so they rarely came into contact, let alone spoke. It wasn't until Adonis was several years into his reign that they had their two sons in quick succession; Maximus and Claudix, who were 24 and 22 respectively. Adonis had paid little attention to them as they were growing up as boys, leaving the nurturing to Hierda. It wasn't that he didn't care, it was that he didn't know what to do and in the end decided it was acceptable to not get involved as it was the mother's job to nurture them when they were children. Now they were young men they were his responsibility and he had been with them as much as he could now they were doing things he knew.

He was proud of his two sons, as they were turning out to be fine warriors. He told himself he could never understand why Hierda was so upset that he had taken control of them now, *what could she do for them?* Adonis feigned ignorance, pretending he didn't realise that Hierda had enjoyed bringing the boys up, that the close bond they had formed had been a comforting respite from the lonely early years of their marriage. She felt she had lost them to Adonis and his warrior ways, and this was why she prayed daily to Angara for a daughter, who Adonis would never take away from her. Adonis didn't want to disturb her and so walked straight through the room, passing the giant statues of the King and Queen of the Gods Thelus and Helana. He left his elegant house and began to walk towards the temple.

Adonis did not feel threatened, he made a habit of walking unguarded in his capital town, and it was to show that not only he was in control but that he trusted his people and that he was in no danger from them.

As he neared the temple he could make out the exquisite pillars and gargoyles that covered the facade. Forty steps led up to the doorway that was headed by a statue of Thelus. Giant pillars rose from half way up the steps to support the outer porch, the inner porch itself had its own smaller pillars (this was so that the outer porch was above the inner porch and the porch roof would not be obscured from view whilst climbing the steps). The roof to the porch was a triangular prism, engraved with images of previous lords performing heroic deeds. On top of the porch, behind the statue of Thelus, was an ingenius invention of Gorax, a fountain that during prayer times was operated by a hand pump and a couple of junior priests. The main temple 'roof' was resting on triangular prisms much like that of the porch, but it also had its own roof and internal walls. It seemed magical that the roof could take all the weight, but Gorax had explained to Adonis it had been achieved by using chain supports from the side pillars on the roof that were concealed by certain walls to keep the method secret and add to the mysticism.

Adonis walked through the porch doorway. Two yards directly in front of the doorway was a wall, about the same width of the doorway itself, which stood between the porch doorway and the actual door into the temple. To reach the door you had to walk around either side of the wall. The reason for this being so that those inside were not disturbed by the sudden flood of light when the doorway was opened for a new visitor. The porch walls themselves were fairly plain; a few patterns trailed the edges of the walls, but other than that the bare blocks that made up each wall formed the only pattern.

When Adonis reached the door a middle-aged priest wearing a purple robe and a golden belt with an ornate curved scabbard opened it. After opening the door the bearded priest bowed courteously, then uttered, "Milord the High priest has been expecting you."

The guard priest always said that when Adonis approached; evidently Xsclepia told whoever was on guard to always say that if the Lord arrived. Adonis merely nodded and swiftly entered the temple, bowing his head slightly upon entry.

The room was very dark, lit only by the numerous candles that were littered throughout the hall. The walls were covered with banners, mosaics and scriptures depicting both legends of the gods and historical events in the Gatan history and all in some way praising Thelus. Columns of pillars rose to the ceiling with wonderful images carved and sculpted into them. Each had a unique base but symmetrical patterns to the rest from the tip of the base all the way to the ceiling. Adonis strode to the front altar, bowed to the gigantic statue of Thelus and began to pray.

Adonis' mind drifted away from his own uttering as he heard footsteps edging closer. He continued his prayer until he could almost feel Xsclepias presence just behind him; just being near the renowned priest gave off an aura of wisdom and holiness that sucked in one's thoughts. He heard the rustling of the high priest's robes as he came to a halt and loomed just behind him. He quickly finished his prayer then slowly rose and turned to Xsclepia. Xsclepia had been the high priest of the temple (and its predecessor) for thirty years. In that time he had barely aged, except that his beard was now almost totally grey, the few strands of black mingling almost unnoticeably in the grey mass. He, like all the other priests, wore purple robes, but his had the most ornate golden patterns all over them, rather than just on the cuff. He spoke in a deep, wise sounding voice and his prophecies were famous throughout the household.

"The chamber is ready, my lord," he uttered, turning to lead the way to the private chamber. They trudged along the familiar route to the room in silence, passing numerous priests who bowed nervously to the two solemn figures of Gatan high society, the warrior lord and the high priest. They walked to the back of the main altar room to a stairway leading down to a solid oak door. Xsclepia pushed the hefty door open and then continued down the narrow labrynthine warren of passageways. Most of the rooms were living quarters for the priests, but one passageway led to the catacombs below the site of the old temple that were just adjacent to the new temple. The passageways were dusty and gloomy; even though they had been built just over three years ago they seemed like an ancient warren of some long forgotten civilisation. The open flame torches flickered as the damp draft drifted down the corridors. Eventually they reached Xsclepia's chamber; the high priest produced a key from a pouch by his robe and unlocked the robust door. As soon as the door was opened a gust of warm, sweet-smelling air swept past Adonis, momentarily covering the musky smell of the passageway. They both stepped into the small room, a torch hung from the wall in front of the door and had obviously recently been put out as smoke still wafted from it. The room was being lit by a smoky fire in a massive plate-like tray in the centre of the room. The smoke however looked very clean and smelled of some exquisite sweet incense. The constant stream of smoke drifted about the room in swirling currents before departing eerily through a vent in the wall below the torch. Adonis knew the routine so sat on the small simple bench that rested beside the torch. Xsclepia took a candle lighter from a rack beside the door and prodded it into the flames and began uttering the language of the gods. He withdrew the short pole and approached the miniature altar that took up about a quarter of the room opposite the bench and torch. After lighting the two candles he bowed his head and muttered prayers to the gods, asking Athyle to grant him foresight.

"Re-light the torch," Xsclepia commanded.

Adonis heeded to instruction, taking a small bottle of incense that lay on the table beside the fire tray and pouring seven drops onto the torch then taking up the fresh torch lighter that had been ceremonially placed in a highly decorated container between the bench and the torch. Once the torch had been lit he gently blew out the lighting stick and placed it back in the rack then staring into the flames. Upon hearing the torch be lit, Xsclepia dropped to his knees in front of the altar and began whispering a prayer so quiet that Adonis could barely hear he was speaking. Suddenly he rose shouted something incomprehensible and quickly turned, cupping his hands before delving them into a bowl of water then thrusting the water over the flames. The flames instantly went

out with an abrupt fizz; the smouldering ashes were a multi-shaded grey with a nest of perfectly formed jet-black charcoal pieces of wood lying on top. Xsclepia drew out a small curved knife from its belt scabbard and cut a small slash on the palm of his hand. The cut was only light but his palm showed numerous scars from when it had accidentally been deeper. He rubbed his hands together, taking in deep breaths to inhale the incense, then he carefully took up a handful of the charcoal and once it was out of the tray crushed it in his fist then smeared marks on his face. Suddenly, without warning he plunged his hands into the grey ash. Underneath the smouldering grey were red-hot coals; he let out a shriek and began whispering. Adonis sank his face into his hands and began to whisper prayers himself. After a few minutes the ordeal was over and Xsclepia stood over the hunched lord, he was breathing heavily and upon hearing his breath Adonis lifted his head from the clasp of his hands.
His mouth was dry, "What did you learn?" he croaked.

The high priest was now back in his normal totally calm but uptight self, "This year much is at stake, great change is looming."

The word change resonated like a cursing spell in Adonis' belly.

"Great change? Is it the will of the gods? What is this change?"

"The will of the gods will prevail, but I do not know where they stand, I do not even know the issue. The eagle of Latman is high, but it could be tipped in the balance, the great change could make or break it. The visions showed a large fleet, with the Gatan banner."

Adonis was deeply troubled by this news, but pressed on for the information he needed urgently. "What of the harvest?"

If Xsclepia was surprised by such a trivial question he did not show it. "Arminius has blessed us with a fine harvest."

"So what do you suggest? Should I seek out allies? Danite and Vacarium are both sympathetic. If this is a matter of the Island's security I could get Lewerix on my side." Adonis' soldier mind was instantly thinking of how to tip the odds in his favour.

"My Lord, I can tell you no more. But it may not be that blood has to be spilt."

Xsclepia could see that the latter comment had been lost on Adonis.

"I must mention this at the council. Xsclepia, perhaps you should accompany me this evening as this may be the last gathering before this change you speak off begins."

"If it pleases you I will attend the council" came the sombre but loyal reply.

The Lord turned to the high priest, bowed, and thanked him, "I must depart now your holiness I must prepare for the council," then the lord left leaving Xsclepia in the prophesy chamber. Once the Lord was out of earshot the high priest muttered to himself shaking his head "He has the mind of a warrior, just like his father."

★

The torches flickered gloomily, momentarily shifting the minimal spread of yellow-orange light about the room, the dismalness of the lights adding to the sullen atmosphere in the room. Adonis always made sure he was first into the room, this not only gave a good impression of promptness but also ensured no bickering or inter-regional deals occurred before he entered. Some of Adonis' predecessors had preferred ceremonial entrances but to him such petty formality was just time wasting.

After Adonis had been seated for about five minutes Xsclepia arrived. He walked over to Adonis and performed a courteous bow. "Milord, I had feared I would be late but it seems that is not the case," the priest stated dryly, making an obvious observation at the lateness of the regional commandants.

He then took the seat next to Adonis; he sat perfectly upright, slowly moving his head as he began studying the room. Adonis watched him as he expressionlessly peered at the banners and canvasses that had been placed at uniform positions along the wood panelled walls. Suddenly he became aware that Adonis was watching him and snapped his head to face him with such speed that it almost made Adonis jump.

"Milord, seeing as I should not really be present I will try to limit my input to a minimum."

Adonis shook his head slowly. "No High Priest, if you have something to say, say it. Your opinion is just as valid as any others; in fact I trust your judgement more than them, I have no doubt of your wisdom but their position has been guaranteed by birth or closeness to my father."

At that moment the first regional commandants arrived. The attendance of the high priest came with mixed reception. Each bowed courteously to Adonis; some addressing the high priest with almost equal gratitude, others with a much frostier welcome. Last to enter was Racri Teritus, commandant for the far southwest region usually called South Neptia; he was the youngest present, being in his late twenties. The rest of the regional commandants were about Adonis' age and above, so there was quite a large age gap. The oldest was Marcus Meridius, the Commandant of the territory in the far northwest, who was almost eighty. This was Teritus' third council, so he had not quite grasped the council and at the last council was obviously getting frustrated by the squabbling and slow pace of the elder commandants. Adonis was interested to see how he reacted in this council. He had noted how Teritus seemed the pretty much indifferent with respect to the presence of the high priest, he had however been almost overwhelmed with nerves. Adonis had only one previous council to judge him properly (the first time he had been so nervous he had barely spoken) so he had little idea of what he thought, other than that he was highly sceptical of the superstitions of the older commandants.

As each commandant entered they tried to show immense gratitude and respect for Adonis but at the same time try to uphold their own respectability and nobility. None did this more effectively than General Hercela, perhaps the ideal epitome of the Gatanese Commandant. After the formalities both the General and the Lord grinned to one another, Adonis slapped his general and comrade on the back and whispered to Hercela that he should join him after the council.

His appearance was much like that of Adonis but more spectacular in form. He was middle aged, perhaps a few years senior to Adonis, a muscular stocky build and a streaky bushy beard, which like, Adonis' had retained its jet black colour with a few well defined streaks of almost pure white. He towered over Adonis, standing at six foot nine. The commandant wore a military uniform that was quite simply decorated but nevertheless impressive. The breastplate and each individual scale had been polished to almost mirror-like shine, making the plainness of the suit add to the spectacle by not disturbing the smooth shiny surface. The carapace was not just for show; any soldier could tell that this was a practical piece of equipment (even though it was merely for ceremonial purposes).

Hercela was the commandant for the North Neptus province. He was also effectively commander of the Gatan/Latman border forces, holding the former post for nine years and the latter for six. He was a formidable fighter, disciplined leader and a totally loyal subject.

Once the commandants had settled, Adonis struck the table with an ornamental wooden hammer to signal the beginning of the council.

Adonis rushed through the petty formalities and introduction to the council, and then ordered the servants to refill the wine goblets. Once this was done Adonis called for reports from each of the provinces. There was little to report except a few coastal incidents with the fair-haired barbarians that had begun to plunder the island coast for the past forty years. Even Hercela's spies in Latman territory reported little troop movement, except for increased watch posts along the coast and the usual rotation of troops on leave, although Adonis knew that Hercela would give him a more detailed brief on the covert operations in private after the meeting. Adonis was informed that Lewerix still had sparse garrisons on the borders, and the Danite household, whose current Lord looked to the Gatan house for protection, had barely any troops on the border.

Every province commander spoke of reported good harvests, as Adonis had expected, but gave very vague or no estimate of the quantities that were to be acquired. Adonis reinforced their reports, admitting that no total had been confirmed. It was then that the speculation began, Commandant Jarius started the 'discussion'. "That's a relief, the gods are pleased, maybe they shall end this cursed barbarian problem."

"More like the damned Latman's," contributed another.

"They have already granted us with good harvest. We should be thankful of that, and not start asking for more," added Meridius.

"Perhaps we should actually find out what the yield is before we start all your farcical speculations," cut in Hercela who disliked meddling in predictions and prophecies.

The council momentarily broke up into several arguments, as accusations over hoarding grain and stalling were flung, others arguing over the symbolism of it all. Adonis shook his head and shrugged. He was always intrigued by who accused who as it helped him make links over which commandants were in competition and revealed much of the behind-the-scenes politics of the commandants. Adonis glanced at the only other two who were silent, Xsclepia and young Teritus. The high priest was becoming increasingly agitated by the anarchy whilst Teritus sheepishly frowned to himself.

Suddenly the bickering was silenced by the deep piercing voice of the High Priest Xsclepia, "What makes you all think you are so adept at prophesy? How, Jarius, did you learn your skills in interpreting the will of the gods? I have lived a long life talking with the gods, vowing to serve them with devotion. Only through intense worship and ceremony can I become worthy of sharing in their knowledge, so how have you all acquired this ability to learn of the future through something as petty as harvests! Do you really think that the almighty gods confine their actions to the harvests like some struggling labourers toiling the dirt of this earth?" Xsclepia's booming voice had risen in volume as his anger brimmed.

All the Lords were instantly silent and embarrassed at their bickering. Some tried to hide frowns as their dislike of the presence of the priest increased.

Adonis took advantage of the situation to get onto the real issue at hand. "You are probably all wondering why the high priest is present. Well, I can tell you he has had a vision that holds prospects that will greatly effect the life of this great House. High Priest Xsclepia is the greatest prophet and divine link to the gods on this whole island, his wisdom and knowledge is beyond the comprehension of most people, indeed judging from your squabbling, beyond even your comprehension.

Suffice to say any vision he has must be taken as an incredible blessing and advantage to the House from the gods."

Adonis paused to see if anyone would answer or inquire into what had happened, but they all sat silently, paused, not even daring to flinch, so Adonis continued. "He has seen that a time of great change is upon us. Blood may be spilled; the balance of the houses is under threat. He has also seen the need for a great fleet of ships sailing under the Gatan banner."

Hercela frowned. "If blood is to be spilled we must be prepared, for great change and bloodshed must involve Latman."

Many of the commandants nodded in agreement.

"And if Latman is involved in bloodshed it will not be by our side that they stand," he added.

There was a cheer of agreement from the commandants.

The cheer was cut short by the booming voice of Xsclepia, "My vision did not show that bloodshed was inevitable. But Hercela is right; I saw the eagle of Latman as a key perpetrator in the events."

"I will intensify my spies in Latman, my lord," Hercela offered.

"Yes, I also want all troops taken off leave and at the garrisons or on patrol. I am going to send envoys to Danite and Vacarium to ensure good relations." Adonis informed the commandants.

The rest of the commandants barely held back their gasps of shock when Teritus began to speak. "My lord, may I suggest a degree of caution. If we leap into action it may cause an upset in the balance. This may not be about just the island, maybe it is about the barbarians, or another land. I say this in light of the High Priest mentioning of the fleet."

Most of the lords were in too much shock at his contribution to answer his doubt, Jarius however decided that the new commandant needed to be put in his place. "Young lad," he began patronisingly. "When there is talk of changes in the balance of power on the island and the soaring eagle of Latman, be it for better or worse, it must concern the island of Rudia, not some far off land inhabited by fair-haired beasts. Whatever the issue, it is going to be important to have allies in these troublesome times ahead. Besides, the boats could be for transporting our army."

The high priest was obviously about to object, but before he could, Adonis decided to settle the dispute. "No, the young commandant has a point, whatever is about to unfold I do not want to be seen as the aggressor trying to muster some kind of alliance. We must be cautious, otherwise we could find ourselves at war with not only Latman but also Telis and possibly even Lewerix. For this fleet fine wood is going to be needed and in great quantity, therefore an envoy must be sent to Lewerix as we will need to secure a deal to use their quality timber."

The council moved onto less pressing matters and continued for several hours. Little was resolved and most conversation was nostalgic reminiscing between the three older Commandants and their Lord. When the council came to a close Adonis beckoned Hercela over. The towering General obediently strode over to his Lord, and bowed slightly. By now the rest of the Commandants had departed, Xsclepia remained sitting as though in deep contemplation in the half-light. As Adonis turned to request for the high priest to retire, Xsclepia solemnly rose as though contemplating something and without looking at the Lord bowed and took his leave: "Sire, I must depart as I have important matters to attend to."

Adonis nodded authoritatively; once the high priest had left Hercela began to chuckle.

"Why!?" bellowed Hercela, shrugging jokingly.

Adonis tried to hide his desire to join Hercela in mocking the High Priest, casting a sombre expression over his face. "I needed him to convince the others about the harvest. Besides, it is our tradition to follow the wisdom of the High Priest, and he may have a point... I've long expected that new Latman whelp to do something."

He paused as the Hercela tried to cut short his laughter but still looked slightly bemused. "What about my 'wisdom'?" laughed Hercela, pointing to the hilt of his sword.

"Our forefathers did it and it bore them well," Adonis added, slightly offended by his comrades disdain.

"Yes, mil'ud but that doesn't mean they should decide policy! All those aromatic scents he's been burning have gone to your head!" Hercela chuckled.

Adonis could not stay annoyed with his brother-in-arms for long, especially as deep down, he shared his scepticism. "It's a necessary formality, my friend, and one which keeps Meridius and his cabal happy!" He let out a chuckle.

"And what about all that about war?" Hercela inquired.

"That's what you're here for, my friend. I'm not going to war just over that premonition. At the time I was really convinced, but now, now your 'wisdom'..." He laughed aloud as Hercela tapped his hilt grinning like a Cheshire cat, "can tell me what 'it' thinks!"

The joyousness disappeared from the General "Well, Mi'lud, that Latman lad's quite erratic, you never know. I've been training up a regiment so hard they could take Neptus single-handedly. These boys are the real stuff, rock hard infantry, they can take a heavy infantry charge just like that – and I don't mean hold ground, I mean *take them*, I should know, we tried it!"

Adonis looked impressed.

"We did a little practice with wooden weapons and the infantry just couldn't get at them. And when they tried, well we had some fatalities, on the infantry side! Some brigands from the Great Forest in Lewerix somehow found themselves in our territory, real hardened bunch they were. Well those that would join us did and the rest, well they made good practise opponents."

"You've got outlaws in our armed forces!" Adonis was alarmed but not annoyed.

"Lewerix outlaws, Lewerix outlaws," Hercela corrected. "Talking of outlaws, what's that Gorax up to these days?"

Adonis looked puzzled; he was sure the General knew something, "Something about a place to teach people".

Hercela paused, "Oh, well you should ask him about the other stuff. If were going to go to war, that stuff looks…interesting."

It was then that Adonis remembered. "Oh, yes, there were some other things he was talking about. Anyway, what of war? Should we strike? What about boats?"

"Just us versus them, it's a close call… we'd need allies to be certain."

"And if we were to attack suddenly we would never get the support of our potential allies."

Heites shook his head. "We would be the aggressor, we can't claim that we have to invade because sometime in the future we think we might be threatened by them."

"I just don't see why it would happen now."

"No, and if anything, our spies report the opposite; there are less troops on the Latman-Gatan border. But still…we're going to have to put them in their place at some point."

They sat solemnly not able to make eye contact, awaiting something to stir them into departing the drab room that was increasingly cloaked in darkness as the torches waned.

Chapter 3
A Coastal Encounter

The sun was beginning to set, signalling the end of the 12th day of Septmus. Sergeant Pluvius of the Gorad Light Infantry walked into the inn with his squad. They had been given five days leave from their post at the Gorad garrison. He looked around the musty room that had the aroma of salty fish mixed with bitter ale. Squinting in the dimness of the squalid alehouse, he and his comrades made their way to the bar.

The barman was bald and stocky, and slowly walked over to serve the newcomers with an eye of contempt, "what yew want 'ere?" he inquired abruptly.

"An ale for us each," answered Pluvius gesturing to his men.

"Yew do the counting boy," answered the barman disdainfully.

"That means he can't count himself!" bellowed Arios, chuckling to himself. The veteran stood at well over six feet tall, with a massive build, his black hair ending in a matted beard. Some of his comrades joined in, Pluvius tried to hide his smirk, but to little avail, then gazed around the room as he heard the sound of a chair being pushed back. A particularly burly sailor swaggered over to Arios, leaning his Neanderthal-like face within inches of the veteran's head so his foul ale-stenching breath engulfed Arios as he spoke. "What woz 'at?" he uttered slowly, staring straight into his eyes. Before Pluvius could stop him Arios was reaching for his sword. Instantly, at the sound of the sword being unsheathed, the rest of the sailors rose from their seats, grabbed bottles and stools and slowly edged closer to the soldiers. Arios got half way to unsheathing his mighty bastard sword before freezing and staring straight back at the sailor, menacingly.

Pluvius looked around. All his men had their hands on their short sword hilts. Geric the new member of the squad was nervously looking round in dismay. Then he looked down, to his own surprise he had done likewise, as a matter of habit. Pluvius quickly tried to get hold of the situation; Aros was always getting them into these situations. "Alright! Arios, stand down," he commanded, then turning to the barman "ten of your finest ale, and one for our friend here," gesturing to the burly sailor. He placed about a dozen gold coins on the bar, well more than the cost of the drinks.

The barman grinned at the sight of the gold, quickly scooped it up and, began pouring the drinks. The rest of the soldiers had relaxed and the pubs regulars had done likewise, Arios however was not satisfied and eyed the offending sailor cautiously. The sailor stared back and without moving slowly declared "These ain't no friends of mine," Arios was about to retort back, when Pluvius gave him a nudge to be silent; the barman was now on their side and so there was no point causing any more hassle.

The barman looked up, scowled at the two giants standing face to face and growled "Elbert, sit down, dis 'as bin sorted out. Dey were only 'aving a laugh, 'tis nuffin to do wiv yew," then he turned to the regulars who were still staring at the confrontation, "an dat goes for tha rest of yew."

Grudgingly Elbert the sailor returned to his seat with the freshly poured tankard.

Once the drinks had been served, the squad sat at a table in the corner. By now Pluvius' eyes had got used to the dinginess. He gazed around the room, the walls were littered with a variety of shipping tools. Various types of fishhooks, nets, rudders and oars were among the vast dusty collection which had been nailed to the dull brown walls with tarred-black wall and ceiling beams. On one wall were a number of sketches of ships and seabirds; at the centre of the wall was a considerably large sketch depicting some kind of sea creature. As a border to each wall were ship ropes, lining the edges. Like the other ornaments they had obviously not been dusted in years as they were littered with cobwebs. Larger ornaments were leant up against the corners of the walls; the corner that they sat in hosted a somewhat sinister statue of a goddess, which had once been the figurehead for a boat. Upon closer inspection Pluvius noticed the statue ended in simplistic but shapely scales meaning it was meant to represent the water goddess Neptu. Having this bulky wooden bust peering down at him, made Pluvius somewhat uneasy. This feeling was reinforced as he gazed at the rest of the tavern's occupants; the sombre mood was obvious from just looking at their faces as they spoke. Even when they chuckled to each other, there was an air of disquiet about it. He edged closer to his drink as an attempt to block out the smell that came from the fishing ships outside, and probably the numerous fishermen that sat in the pub bellowing at each other. He heard Arios talking about the Gatan border.

"Well I reckon they're gonna attack Neptus, I've heard there's some treasures there, and besides the neighbouring villages have good soil just what old Adonis wants," his face sneered as he spoke his household's rival's name; Arios had lost his older brother in a skirmish against Gatan raiders two years ago, and so had a particular enmity towards them, as so many veterans and widows did from this side of the territory. Pluvius had lost quite a few comrades in the thirty years he had been a soldier but had never let it get it to him. Pluvius thought back to his early days, his father had been a farmer on a small patch of land near Gorad, which he had bought with the money he had inherited from Pluvius' grandfather, who had been in the Latman army back in the days when it was more of a militia than the organised force it was now. He had fought in the war against Vacarium, driving them into the mountains. From an early age Pluvius had wanted to be a soldier, at a young age his father had given him his grandfather's spear, it had given him a fascination with the military and many times his father had confiscated it because he spent so much time playing with it. The neighbouring farmers would chuckle out loud when they saw the ten-year-old Pluvius trying to wield this hefty spear; one of them took pity on him and paid the local carpenter to make him a small wooden sword. His father, fearing that he would become a soldier, warned him of what his grandfather had said; how being a soldier was a waste of a life. Receiving a pittance of money and living a life of destruction of both others and oneself, as what little money a soldier gets would be spent on drink and women. However, he had seen how pitiful and pointless the life of the farmer was. Toiling in the fields to earn a reasonable keep, but what for? What had his father done with the excess money? Some was used to buy more land and eventually some labourers and the rest was spent in the tavern. So his father was spending money to create more work for himself and those who worked for him. His father had achieved nothing, now he was an old man being looked after by his sons and daughters who ran the farm for him. Pluvius had known from an early age, that to follow in his fathers footsteps was not enough, besides as Pluvius neared the time to recruitment the military modernisation and training schemes of Lord Octavius had begun and so being a soldier meant good pay. When he had declared that he was going to join the local garrison, at the age of fifteen, his father had tried to argue him out of it. Pluvius had got angry and told his father what he thought of the life of a farmer and had been banished from the house. He had not spoken to his parents since that day and only heard from his brothers and sisters through messages he had sent them via a friend. (Although Pluvius had been taught the basics of how to read and write at the garrison his fellow siblings had no way to learn). One day he was sure he would visit them all again and see how they had all grown and got children of their own.

  He remembered the wonder that overtook him when he went to the Vacarium border; the landscape was just as his grandfather had described it all those years ago. He had thought of his grandfather as a young soldier (as he was then) breaking the Vacarium line and venturing over the hills, pursuing the enemy; it had brought him back to his childhood days venturing into the grassland and plains near his home with his brothers.

  His dreaming was abruptly brought to a close when he felt someone shaking him; it was Heites, a seasoned comrade who had been in the squad for just over ten years. Heites had been transferred to his squad after his own was wiped out fighting a rebellion by occupied Vacarians in the west of the country. He was a reliable fighter who followed orders to the slightest detail in battle. "You okay Sergeant? You've been sitting there staring into your ale for the past ten minutes, smiling to yourself, which is probably a miracle in itself," he asked.

"What he means is, if you don't want your ale he'll have it," Arios jested.

"Speak for yourself, yours barely hit the table before you'd drained it," retorted Heites jokingly. The two of them had become close comrades over the years even though in battle they were the complete opposite. Whilst Heites was the disciplined soldier who ensured the shield wall was kept, Arios was as brash in battle as he was in conversation, cutting swathes in the enemy ranks with his bastard sword as he impetuously advanced. In fact, it was usually Heites that was trying to hold the hulking warrior back, or at least stop the rest of the squad from advancing (which was actually considerably easier!).

"Yeah, fine…just thinking about the old days," Pluvius replied once he had fully awoken from his thoughts.

"Well, I don't want to break your fantasies from when you were a strapping young lad, but could you spare a moment to solve an argument?" Heites paused even though it was a rhetorical question then continued, "Well Arios here seems adamant that the old temple of Neptu at Neptus castle holds some mysterious treasure. He reckons he saw some back in 550 when you were there!"

"He would!" Pluvius answered snorting. The rest of the squad laughed, loudest of all Arios, whose deep voice penetrated the solemn conversations of the pub regulars. They all briefly looked up then continued with their sombre chatter.

Pluvius looked puzzled, "So we left all those riches in the temple, on Gatans doorstep waiting for him to take, as his household did between 480 and 510 or whenever it was. Then he thought he'd leave it there for us to retake in the early 500's and then we thought that we'd just leave them there to goad them into retaking the castle again!"

Arios chuckled out loud, "You never know what could happen when politics, war and religion all mingle together. It's possible."

"Well it would explain why they keep trying to get it," acknowledged Heites.

Geric, the newcomer to the squad suddenly gained the courage to speak. "Sergeant so you were at Neptus when Raphel Latman, his lordships brother was killed!" he was so excited about such a thought he couldn't keep it to himself any longer.

"Yes, Arios and I were there, standing almost side by side his lordship when he took the arrow…" answered Pluvius recollecting in his mind what had happened.

"Took the arrow?" stammered Geric inquisitively; "I thought he died holding them off the wall?"

Aros chuckled. "Aye, that's how the story goes!"

"But they wouldn't just make it up would they?" Geric was getting confused and very embarrassed. The rest of the squad were silent, some sank their heads into their hands dramatically and Arios increased his bellowing chuckle, sighed, then also was silent. By now Geric was rapidly glowing red with embarrassment and fear. The sailors could be heard still muttering to each other, the relative silence was broken by Pluvius who asked who wanted another drink; unsurprisingly there were no objections, especially whilst the sergeant was paying. Arios rose to assist the sergeant in collecting the drinks, whilst the rest of the soldiers began their idle chatter. This had relieved the pressure from Geric who began to regain his normal colour.

Once he reached the bar Arios hunched next to Pluvius, glanced over his shoulder at the table that housed the squad, and then whispered to the sergeant. "That lad isn't gonna last five minutes in a battle if he doesn't lighten up."

Just then the door to the pub opened and about a dozen courtesans entered loudly, giggling to each other and making their way towards the table with the soldiers at it.

"Forget five minutes in battle; I'd give him two minutes from now!" Pluvius answered dryly. As they returned to the table Pluvius inspected the whores, they all seemed to be more dolled up than local prostitutes usually were (even for the ones that flocked around the garrison they were well presented). Obviously visitors were rare to the village and so when news of the arrival of soldiers reached them they saw it as a customer gold mine and so had donned their finest clothes to give them the edge in any competition. A number of them spotted Pluvius had sergeant stripes and so made a beeline for him; however, they were cut off by another courtesan, who grabbed his arm as soon as the drinks tray hit the table and half dragged him over to an empty table.

Pluvius took a glance at Geric, who was being engulfed by a somewhat stocky strumpet; he could just about make out his face, that had returned to its bright red state. He smiled to himself, and felt some pity for the boy, recalling his own first encounter that had horrified him as the young country boy he had been back then.

"Interested in someone else?" came the soft but stern voice of his courtesan. Pluvius snapped his head back to look at her; she was definitely attractive, verging on beautiful. Her long dark brown hair had been tied up; her brown eyes occasionally darted about the room energetically, giving an air of intelligence to her. She had a small slightly pointy nose, and similarly small lips, which widened only slightly by her delicate smile. When he gazed at her he could only smile as he answered her question, "no, no just checking Geric was okay, it's his first time I should think."

"I should think!" she laughed, "Aren't you meant to be his father figure in the squad? A great lot of good you're making of it," she added,

before taking a delicate sip out of a rather ornate goblet given the environment.
Pluvius smiled, "Well, my sergeant never gave me any advice on this sort of thing, and my father certainly didn't. Well, actually that's not true my sergeant told me…" Pluvius struggled to recall his exact words. At the same time he checked the courtesan wasn't losing interest. "He said to me, 'Lad' he said 'whatever you do when you encounter a strumpet' (sorry to use such an offensive term, but that's what he used)."

"Don't you worry I've been called worse, believe me," the courtesan interjected.

"Don't poison my innocent mind with them please," Pluvius pleaded jokingly, before continuing "Anyway he said to me 'lad, whatever you do when you encounter a strumpet, make sure you pay!'"

"And I hope you've kept to that advice," the courtesan concluded with a smile.

"Of course," Pluvius answered, "anyway, I'm sorry I haven't introduced myself, my name is Sergeant Pluvius and I'm from the 3rd regiment based at Gorad. What's your name?" The sergeant felt strange as he spoke the routine words that were usually more a tribute to his past self than for any interest in his company as he felt drawn in to converse with her.

"Huh, I'm not used to being introduced, or asked what my name is. Well, my name is Julia and I'm a courtesan, or whore, or strumpet or whatever you want to call me" she exclaimed.

"Sorry, it's just a little habit I have going back to my first time when I was as nervous as Geric"

"You! As nervous as Geric! Now that I would like to see! Tell me how young were you when you were evilly and savagely ravaged by one of us?" Julia exclaimed. Pluvius looked down at the table with embarrassment "When I was fifteen."

"That's not THAT early," Julia answered reassuringly.

"It was my first night away from home, the first night I reached the garrison!" Pluvius admitted looking embarrassed. Julia just smiled back and took his hand, holding it gently and rubbing her soft hand over Pluvius' rough scar-ridden hand.

Pluvius looked up and was met by Julia's smile; she looked down at his hand and inspected it. "So many scars," more to herself than to Pluvius "how long have you been a soldier?"

"Thirty years in about a months time" Pluvius answered sighing, "That's longer than you've been alive," he muttered

"Only just" she replied optimistically, "So what exciting stories can you tell me of your battles?" she added.

"Well… by exciting you mean bore you so much you fall asleep and then you and I can go upstairs and get the ordeal over and done with," Pluvius grunted.

"No, it's so dull here. I love to hear interesting stories about what people have really done outside this village. Any story you tell me about your adventures will be a godsend compared the drivel I get from the locals about fish shoals and harvest time!" protested Julia.

"Most of the time I'm just on border patrols. Not much happens. A few skirmishes. But the main thing I suppose is when I fought Gatan at the castle of Neptus seven years ago."

"What, you mean when the Lord's brother was killed?" Julia nearly jumped with excitement when she heard this.

"Yeah, well he was heir to the throne then. Yeah, I was at the wall when he took the arrow, of course I suppose you've heard a different story about how he died, but they had to make it up to make it sound more glorified." Pluvius fumbled in his pocket and took out a small medallion with inscription, "here, its what they gave each of the survivors." He handed Julia the medal. She held it close to her face as she tried to read the inscriptions.

"It says…" Pluvius began.

"I know, I can read…well, a bit," Julia answered softly, "Sergeant P-L-U-V-I-U-S – Pluvius?" okay I believe you, she smiled playfully back to him, then looked about the room. The rest of the soldiers had already gone. Pluvius looked back at Julia. "So where have all the others gone? Is the house nearby?" he inquired, looking confused, assuming they had gone to the whorehouse. "What? No, the barman will have sorted out rooms for us, they do if there's visitors," she answered. Then she led him upstairs.

★

Comfort comes.

★

Pluvius awoke with a shudder. He frowned to himself as he recalled the previous night; he couldn't remember Julia leaving. She had left to go to the latrine and Pluvius had felt totally exhausted so had placed the money on the side cabinet; he must have fallen asleep before she had returned. He glanced at the side cabinet to reassure himself, but to his horror the money was still there. Pluvius' heart sank, he felt forlorn and cheap, so low in fact that he had only felt like this on his first encounter with a courtesan. Pluvius was in shock, had he really unwittingly done the ultimate offence a client could do? A sweep of moral despair overwhelmed him, like when he had awoken after slinking off to the back of the garrison pub with a whore when he was fifteen. He recalled his feelings that morning thirty years ago when he had felt disgusted with himself and confused. Half of him felt like he had been a terrible user, exerting his lust on some stranger, the other half felt used and exploited. Over the years he had just come to accept it as part of life, up until this morning. For the past twenty-odd years he had just woken up in the morning feeling just as he did every morning; any moral opinions and objections had just worn off and it became part of the routine. Now he just felt like an evil exploiter. He sunk his head into his hands and let out a yelp of despair.

Suddenly he heard rustling next to him; he looked over to his side; for the second time in a matter of minutes of waking up his heart jumped. Lying next to him was Julia, still asleep. Pluvius tapped her on the shoulder and she dozily awoke, "What are you doing still here? You nearly gave me a heart attack!" whispered Pluvius still trying to recover from the shock.

"Uh, oh, morning" Julia replied croakily, she shook her head and rubbed her eyes "I hope you don't mind me staying," she paused then hurriedly began scrabbling to get up "I'm so sorry…please…its just…" she began stammering fearing the veteran sergeant was going to get angry,

"No it's ok, I thought I hadn't paid you. And you nearly gave me a heart attack! Why should I mind?" Pluvius inquired.

"Oh I did it once before with a client a few weeks ago, he'd lied about not being married in the sweet talk and he was scared his wife was going to turn up. He got violent." she replied.

"Well there's no chance of that," Pluvius informed her. "If you don't mind me asking, why do you do it?"

Julia showed signs of being deep in thought then finally concluded, "well, I got bored of the usual routine and I began to wonder how clients felt in the morning, and how they would react if I was still there. The results were not good." Julia then tried to change the subject. "So, you're not married then?"

Pluvius sensed that she didn't want to talk about it anymore so played along "No, not had the time, chance, or even desire too really. How could I look after a family, always travelling about the province? To be honest that's kind of why I decided to be a soldier; to avoid becoming a farmer like my father and brothers, settling down, having a family and never leaving the village. What about you?"

Julia had relaxed by now and lay back on the bed. When she looked up at Pluvius, he saw that she had her mouth open in astonishment.

"It's strange, I felt the same, I ran away from my family when I was thirteen because I was fed up of living my life by the harvests and hours of daylight. Also I knew my parents would marry me off to get more land or something. Somehow I ended up here."

"So are you glad you did it? Ran away, that is."

Julia paused, "Yes, I think so, I'd be doing pretty much the same thing as now, only with the same, dull old farmer. And I'd have to do all that dreaded farm work during the day and look after children." She looked up at Pluvius and smiled. "Whereas as I stand, sometimes an interesting client comes along."

"So am I an interesting client,?" Pluvius asked obviously.
Julia rolled her eyes and smiled with theatrical voluptuousness. "You were interesting, but I'm not sure if you were a client" came her awkward, baffling answer.

Pluvius grinned with disbelief and confusion, then shook his head.

"I'm sure you were better than my parallel self's husband." She added, "What would she be doing now?" referring to an alternative of herself.

Totally unprepared for how to deal with such a conversation Pluvius decided to let her radiant soliloquy continue uninterrupted, seeing as it was on such a roll.

"Rocking backwards and forwards in her filthy squalid bed as she hid from her sweaty feral mate who was stumbling around outside with a bottle of wine made from weeds mumbling about corn and the weather whilst he trips over the hordes of screaming brats that she has spewed forth for him!" As she spoke she seemed to be imagining the totally life-engulfing Bastille that she had avoided, jovially inventing a fate she had triumphantly escaped. After a contemplatory pause she burst out laughing, throwing her head forward onto the sheets with such force that her straggled hair flailed the bed and spread out like a clump of dark seaweed and swayed rhythmically in the sea breeze that wafted through the open window.

He felt intrigued by the energy that resounded in her. Unlike most courtesans who were either morose drones or even worse depressingly jovial, she seemed so genuine. She had shared information on her life and inquired about his with interest and cordiality.

Suddenly guilt engulfed him. Like a flood kept at bay for decades, the nervous teenager within him had burst out of the crack that her speech had made in his husk of a heart. All these years of being numbed into comfort through utilising women, all these years seeing them as a commodity, part of the deal. She seemed so alive, not like the emotionally insipid prostitutes of before. Immediately he began to ask himself: was this because of how he had treated her or was this because she was different; had she treated him differently and made him feel human and so he had reciprocated?

Pluvius then decided to ask a question that could make or break the guilt he had felt when he was fifteen. "So... I don't know how to say this, but please be honest, do I.... have I exploited you?"

"Or have I exploited you?" Julia replied instinctively without looking up from her concealed position amongst the matted clump of seaweed-hair that clung to the coral reef of the bed. Pluvius just nodded, slightly baffled.

She dramatically flung her head up, flicking her hair over the back of her head, "Well, I can't speak for the others of my profession, but I do this because I want to. I'm providing a service. Men want it." Julia continued, Pluvius couldn't argue with her, after all these years he felt disgusted that he had never talked to his courtesans other than to lure them to him.

"So you don't see your job as immoral? If you're choosing to do it then..." Pluvius trailed off.

"No, do you? As I said, I'm providing a service. If my job is immoral, what's yours? I'm providing people with pleasure; you're providing them with pain! I'm satisfying my clients, you're killing yours!"

"I suppose so. I mean, I was just expressing the stigma society puts on. I don't think it's that immoral, well not anymore, but I mean I wasn't sure if that was just because I'm just so used to it and I'm just being ignorant and not realising what I'm doing."

"Like when you kill," Julia added with an air of irony. Although fascinated by what the 'morning after' conversation was sparking up she decided to change the subject. "So tell me about your childhood, and your family".

"Well I haven't seen my family in thirty years, they disowned me when I joined the garrison, we lived on a farm near Gorad, in a village called Herik. You've probably never heard of it. You don't want to, believe me. Total dead end. I worked there until I was fifteen, then I left and joined the garrison."

"Huh, yeah, working on a farm is so mundane. I remember when I was a little girl having to get up at the crack of dawn to weed the fields and water the crops all day until was dark, my back would be killing me." Julia reminisced, laughing.

"Yeah and then in the spring we'd be toiling in the rain and mud thinking our feet were going to fall off or grow webbed toes," Pluvius added chuckling aloud.

"No wonder they were all so deformed in the countryside!" Julia exclaimed.

"No, I think that's because of all the inbreeding," joked Pluvius.

Julia could not help but burst out laughing, after a couple of minutes she began struggling to breathe and Pluvius began slapping her on the back to stop her from choking. Pluvius quietly shook his head as he did so, thinking about how amazing it was that the two of them were talking as though they had come from the same village and were reminiscing about some shared past time. Both of them had done pretty much the same thing, ran away from a dreary life of farming for a more exiting life in the most debauched professions of their genders.

After a few minutes Julia recovered from her fit and turned to Pluvius. "You said you've travelled; I'd love to travel. I want to see the mountains on the Vacarian border." Julia lay there smiling as though in some daydream high in the mountainside.

Pluvius smiled. "The most beautiful place I've been. The hills and mountains are so wonderful, not like the flat fields of this area. Mind you, I didn't get to see it much, not in its peaceful tranquillity."

"They say the reason why our household is so prosperous is because we have such a variety of land. What a shame so few of us gets to experience more than one."

"You should travel to a town, or the Gorad garrison. You'd get much more money then, and you could perhaps save up and go one day," Pluvius advised.

Julia quickly snapped her whole torso to face the veteran and grabbed him on the shoulder, leant close and uttered playfully, "Is that advice, or you just wanting me all to yourself?!" She leant in as though to kiss him but paused when she noticed his bewildered expression.

After a short pause Pluvius just grinned, got up and began getting dressed. Julia quickly got dressed, grabbed her stuff and made her way towards the door. "Maybe I'll see you some other time?" she said as she opened the door.

Pluvius was shocked by her sudden departure. "Well, I'm about for a few more days…maybe," he trailed off as she smiled, shrugged then disappeared out of the door.

Pluvius finished getting dressed then wandered out of onto the landing, he peered out of the window; it must have been mid morning as the sun was quite high in the sky.

It then occurred to Pluvius that he had just had the most philosophical conversation of his life over immorality with a prostitute! The irony of an aging soldier and a young whore finding that they were debating morality after a night of passion seemed overwhelming. It had been perhaps the most enlightening conversation he had ever had, and as he wandered down the stairs he found himself asking so many more questions. Had he really only now seen a prostitute as a human being?

What parallels could he think of between prostitution and his own profession?

The steps creaked horrendously as he descended the stairs. He stepped onto the ground floor and the groaning of the wooden steps ceased replaced instead by the loud but solid thumping of his boots on the wooden floorboards. The rest of his squad minus Geric were slumped at a table. Arios was obviously telling them some notorious (and probably untrue) story about his experiences on border patrol. His massive hands waved dramatically as he described various opponents and imitated his own manoeuvres. Pluvius took several steps towards the table and then Arios looked up and signalled to his sergeant, bellowing aloud, "ha ha, the stud himself!"

Pluvius hid his smile as he approached, then threw himself into a vacant seat that had probably been specially set-aside for him next to Arios. "You like to enlighten us over why a certain young damsel who had been at your abode has only just left the building?" Arios asked, chuckling out loud.

Pluvius just snorted to himself and stared at the table with a blank face; he felt the eyes of his entire squad bearing down on him in silence. Heites then broke the silence by asking Pluvius if he wanted a drink, "Water," Pluvius grunted sharply.

"Oh, so it was that much of a night, was it?" Arios exclaimed. The rest of the squad joined in the laughing.

Pluvius just stared at the table with a bewildered look, still trying to get his head around his conversation with Julia. A tankard of water was placed in front of him and he nodded appreciably then intensified his bewildered look into staring at the rippling liquid contained within the gigantic mug. The laughter had stopped, but as if on cue Arios' barrage of comments continued, "So was it per hour?" he mused "Or was it *lump* sum."

"Or *piece* rate!" interjected another comrade called Kilnos, Pluvius continued to stare into the cup without flinching; his mind was totally confused and was full of questions with no answers or any idea of where to start. The staring and sniggering of his comrades was certainly not helping.

Just then, Geric timidly scampered across the floorboards with barely a creak let alone a thump, then without a word slid a spare chair back and slumped in it. Immediately Arios looked up with a big grin and bellowed to the new recruit, "Ah hah, there you are lad, I was scared you'd been devoured by some sumptuous young harlot. Well you're a proper young gentleman now aren't you!"

Geric turned a spectacular red colour and remained silent.

Pluvius stopped listening to their interrogation of the poor young man and looked about the room; it was pretty much the same as the previous night, only with fewer sailors lolling about. His mind flashed with numerous questions that he struggled to answer: *'what had he been doing all these years? Was his job as a soldier as alike to her job as she made out? No, surely not. But why not? He was a professional. Was he? Wasn't she?* Pluvius snorted to himself, recalling what his trainer had told him, that he was entering the first profession. How wrong he had been! The courtesan had beaten the first professional soldier by years, no doubt centuries.

His comrades let out a sudden explosion of laughter, causing Pluvius to jump. He looked up and over to Arios, who was retorting to someone else's last comment, "Well for an inexperienced little rookie like you maybe, but I have an eye for precious whatnots and I know when someone's trying to guard it. I mean there's no point in putting a squad right over by the temple unless there's something special there," he explained with a chuckle. Pluvius let out a dramatical sigh. "You're not on about the treasure of Neptus again, are you Arios?" he asked semi-rhetorically.

"Yes, and unlike you unbelievers I stand by my beliefs!" Arios proclaimed proudly.

Pluvius had had this argument on countless occasions and he really didn't need it now. Pluvius' concentration sank away from the conversation and he began to peer through the heavily dusty and grime covered window that was behind the table where they sat. He could just make out a black blob in the morning mist; he squinted to try and make the ship out. He tried to judge its distance from the shore and the work out its size but he had no eye for measuring water. Pluvius was about to call over a sailor so they could confirm his suspicion when to inn door banged open and a large burly man dressed in sailor's trousers and shirt entered. Tucked in his belt was a vast array of knifes of many sizes.

"Barbarian raiders coming in, to your ships!" the brawny watchman bellowed.

The rabble of sailors wearily rose from their seats and stampeded out of the inn, Pluvius' men took one last swig of their drinks then rose as one; calmly they walked out of the inn. Pluvius noticed the barman scrabbling around trying to hide his valuables. Pluvius wished he had his scale armour, or preferably some of the light plated armour that some of the cavalry had been awarded. Luckily his men all had their short swords.

The streets were silent; some merchant's stalls had been deserted with the trinkets still on the stall tables. The raiding boat was closing in fast and the fishing ships were leaving the harbour and heading further down the coast. Pluvius surveyed the landscape. He had no idea how many raiders there would be but he guessed he would be outnumbered, so he needed to somehow get the upper hand. The village was on a mound above the small docking area, which had a small stretch of shore on which a storehouse was situated. By the storehouse was a patch of sparse trees and bushes. Pluvius came to the conclusion that that would be where he would attack. The mound may be a good defensive position but it was too open. He led his men down the steep drop to the storehouse; Pluvius sent six of his men into the building whilst the other three accompanied him outside concealed in the vegetation.

★

Pluvius stared out of his concealment; he could see the barbarians from across the sea heading straight for the storehouse, just as he had expected. Then the leader strode closer. The barbarian was very tall; Pluvius estimated about six foot four. His hair was long and a musty blonde, probably due to a rough sea life. He had blue eyes; a bizarre salty deep-sea blue caged in a weatherbeaten socket. His frame was built up even more by a heavy cloak that was attached around his shoulders with two long paws; the thick fur was a magnificent white from some kind of large foreign wolf or dog. Behind him strode similar warriors but none as magnificent. The leader reached the door and raised his gigantic barbaric double handed axe. In one mighty crushing blow the door was shattered into a spray of splinters. However, the mighty champion didn't have enough time to raise his axe for a swing at the men inside. As soon as Pluvius heard the giant scream, the Latman sergeant leapt from his position. The nearest barbarian was stabbed in the heart by the sergeant and fell clutching the wound and gurgling. Pluvius engaged the next fur-clad raider; blocking the slow but powerful attacks then quickly thrusting his short sword with routine accuracy through the barbarian's leather armour and into his heart, *if they actually are human* Pluvius thought as his mind went through the procedure his trainers had taught him years ago. The short sword slid out of the dying man as easily as it went in; he had been taught how far to thrust so the sword didn't get stuck inside the corpse. Pluvius glanced to his side in the swirling melee, he saw one of his men fall with a gash in his side, Pluvius couldn't make him out in the fog of battle and looked away just in time to dodge a spear that flew at his head. He saw an axe head glint in his direction and he blocked. Pluvius found himself ducking and stabbing completely out of the trained rhythm, he hated disorganised skirmishes; shield walls were much better. Something swept over his head and he could just make out a fur-clad figure in front of him. He lunged into what he guessed was the man's gut, a slow and bloody death. As soon as Pluvius withdrew the blade, blood poured from the wound. The scream that accompanied it was shattering; the man dropped his axe and collapsed groaning. Pluvius didn't have enough time to shorten the man's torment, and spun around stabbing aimlessly. *This is when I wish I had a long sword to slash people as I'm turning,* Pluvius thought as he found himself facing many raiders. He looked up just in time to a gigantic axe blade sweeping down on him. Instantly Pluvius dived to his side, knocking a raider over. Pluvius rolled over and was knocked into the mud where the waves just reached. He scrabbled to his feet and lunged out at his assailant, pushing the sword in and turning the blade. Hearing the man's ribs crack and his lung burst, then with one jerk his blade was free. Arios was attacking with his bastard sword, using both the point and the slashing edge to decapitate and skewer. Arios brought his blade slashing into a particularly large barbarian's collar bone then kicked him to the floor as he tried to wrench the weapon free. This was one of the problems with the weapon; also, slashing left you body open to attack.

A raider ran towards Pluvius; the sergeant lowered his weapon so he was ready for a blocking manoeuvre. Pluvius remembered a trick he had been told and side-stepped at the last moment whilst stabbing at the man's face. Although Pluvius hadn't put much force into the awkward attack, the spluttering raider lowered his weapon to wipe his eyes of the blood and as he did Pluvius stabbed him in the throat, leaving the barbarian spluttering and choking on blood. Pluvius saw the last raider fall grappling with a bloodied Latman. He rushed over to his men. Three were dead, and two more were quite badly wounded, the others had a few minor wounds. They began to inspect the bodies for valuables. Pluvius rushed over to the corpse of the leader. As he stood over the corpse he shouted to his men, "Who killed the beast?" pointing at the body, Geric scampered forward. "I did Sergeant, though he hadn't seen me so it wasn't really a kill."

"You can keep the gold, I just want the cloak, is that okay?" he asked rhetorically.

"Of course, Sergeant" came the timid reply.

"Good," concluded Pluvius, who hated timid warriors because they wouldn't be determined or proud of their squad. Still, he had held his nerve in his first skirmish so he had to be proud of him.

His men followed, all as exhausted as Pluvius, except Arios, who strode beside Pluvius talking, ignorant of his sergeant's fatigue.

When they reached the inn the squad slumped in their seats, the two wounded soldiers were immediately attended to by their comrades. When this was completed, most rested their heads on the table, whilst Pluvius tried to keep himself upright. All soldiers found this: that they were only tired when they stopped fighting. Pluvius swayed with weariness; he felt a burning sweat as the stuffiness of the pub made his already sweaty skin secrete more sweat to combat his rising temperature. He barely heard Arios' gigantic fist slam on the table as the giant rose effortlessly to get some ale. As he began to regain his breath the thought of despair washed over him, *what had happened to Julia?* As Pluvius became lost in his thought he could hear the barman scrabbling about behind the bar in the background. His concentration was broken by the sound of the barman slamming a tray full of ales on the table.

"Ere ya go Sirs," the barman bellowed cheerfully, "on behalf, ov tha whole village I wuld like ta thank ya'll," he added graciously.

Pluvius looked up at the table. On the tray were some simplistic glasses; even though they were hardly ornate glass containers were rare in any pub let alone a village local and by their condition Pluvius guessed they must be saved for special occasions. Pluvius glanced up appreciatively at the barman then picked up one of the glasses and took a massive gulp of its contents, before sinking back into his thoughts. He was trying to think about what the barbarians who had headed for village would have done. They didn't have any prisoners and very few, if any, valuables so they couldn't have got up too much. Still, he couldn't dispel the fear something had happened to Julia. Then he began to wonder why he even cared about what had happened to her anyway, they didn't have any connection, there was no reason why he was responsible for her, yet he couldn't stop himself from worrying about her. At this point he gave up thinking. His mind was racing in circles whipping up despair for no apparent reason, and he realised it was going nowhere; he also had work to do. He rose abruptly and announced their departure: they needed to return to Gorad and report the incident. Before leaving he strode over to the barman. "How much do we owe you?"

"Nuffin, ya've saved more than ya've cost," came the unusually jolly and thankful reply.

"We've just done our job, I insist we pay. Failure to act would have been a failure of profession," Pluvius protested, as he thrust some gold coins into the barman's hand and strode out of the pub. By the time Pluvius had mounted up and signalled for their departure, he was no longer worrying about Julia, he was a soldier again.

Chapter 4
Rabica's Introduction

Rabica Lewerix, son of Zenith Lewerix and heir to the Lewerix Household frowned as he read the House Lewerix Scriptures; these sacred texts were meant to explain how and why the house was so successful and why the Lewerix name was so important.

Rabica found it hard to understand. Rather than casting clarity on the subject it seemed to mystify the whole issue. Most of it was hypothetical metaphysics attempting to justify the family claim to power.

Rabica stroked his clean-shaven chin. "So let's get this straight, six hundred years ago, Lewern the God of hunting and the forest left his dwelling in the forests to seek out a virtuous and viable man to be ruler of the tribes of central-northern Rudia. On the outskirts of the great forest he found a priest called Nerix who was venturing into the forest to find penance with the forest god. He came to Nerix in a dream and instructed him to gather the tribes under his name. The druid, inspired by the spiritual encounter, called on the local tribes to unite as the Lewerix, combining his name with the god who had guided him. His speeches inspired all those he met and they fell to his feet with divine devotion. Huh! Never underestimate the stupidity of the common man!" He had been reading this story since he was a young child. Each time he heard it he became more sceptical.

He returned to reading the scripture, but was instantly repulsed by the content; the heir shook his head. "So, my hereditary right to power is because of some flagellant-druid having some mysterious dream in a wood."

It had been a long time since he had read this piece. As a child he used to read it to himself often, reciting it joyfully with a sense of pride. Now this written epitome of traditional hereditary prejudice seemed to the heir to be like some sick joke that had become fact. This superior bank of knowledge was supposed to be the foundations of stability and practical reason; however, the precocious Rabica saw it as mere romanticist propaganda.

His father was always telling him how important these manuscripts were to the household and any future lord. Rabica was grateful for the holy ordainment but he really couldn't imagine the gods, especially Lewern the god of nature, who spends so much time nurturing the land that man destroys, meddling so intricately in the politics of man. Why would Lewern call upon the northern tribes of Rudia to unite, supposedly to defend his Great Forest? The other households hadn't formed then, in fact the biggest threat to the Great Forest would have been from the very nation he was creating that would be in great need of resources such as timber.

Rabica had decided long ago that the story was probably half true, i.e. Nerix was some self-ordained prophet who had a vision while in the forest and managed to convince droves of people to his cause and consequently formed the first household.

His father had been Lord for twenty-eight years ascending the position at the age of thirty, so he was certainly a long-lived lord and was still totally capable of ruling. This Rabica was grateful of; it kept the burden of ruling away from him for quite a few years and was allowing him to think and learn properly before being plunged into the deep end, as he saw it.

Lewerix had always stayed neutral in inter-household disputes. Only once had it been in a considerably sized conflict, with Latman in 287, and even then it took the Lord of Lewerix a month to accept war had begun. The then Lord Falcia Lewerix was a young and indecisive lord who after the decisive defeat capitulated entirely and retreated into personal and diplomatic isolation. Whereas when he was younger he had learnt of these conflicts and been angry at the lack of aggression his house had taken, now Rabica was disappointed at how the house had shrunk away in isolation and not tried to assist in resolving the petty rivalries.

Rabica's thoughts were interrupted by a knock at his door, followed by the sound of someone clearing their throat as quietly as possible. Rabica sighed, looked to the door and croaked in a voice of someone who had not spoken a word in hours for the servant to come in.

It was Marcus, the middle aged senior servant. Rabica made an effort to treat all the servants as humans equal to him merely performing an occupation or duty that was to serve him, but with Marcus this was impossible. He was a very dutiful servant, who had worked in the lord's house all his life, and because of this he knew exactly what was expected of him. To Rabica he was too obedient, making him seem cold and totally emotionless (no doubt how he had been instructed): any attempts to engage in conversation, or indeed any act that may suggest equality and he would back away and shrug apologetically. This persistence to degrade himself annoyed Rabica unremittingly. Rabica tried not to blame Marcus for his behaviour, as it was entirely due to how he had been brought up.

Marcus bowed in a courteous but not too excessive fashion. Then, without raising his head to make eye contact (one of the many petty things he had been taught that infuriated Rabica), he told Rabica that dinner was about to be served.

Rabica entered the dining room. The candles had been ceremonially lit but as usuall were offering very little light despite their grandeur. The heir could just make out his father's stern face in the wavering candlelight,

"Father, do we have to go through all this petty candle-lit dinner rubbish? I can't see a thing," Rabica asked with a hint of annoyance.

"Yes, we do. That is because I say so, which seems fair enough, it being my house," came the severe reply. "Now sit down" he commanded. Rabica gave up the petty struggle and obeyed grudgingly.

The table was laden with assorted bread rolls, cheeses and slices of various meats.

Lord Zenith began whispering instructions to Marcus as to what he wanted on his plate; Lady Issetia did likewise to her servant, Yara. Rabica immediately began heaping the food on himself, much to 'his' servant's dismay and his parent's disapproval. Other than the occasional whisper of the lord and lady to the servants the occupants of the room were silent, quiet enough for the flickering of the candles in the evening draught to be heard.

Lady Issetia broke the virtual silence abruptly; as soon as she began to speak a shudder of annoyance ran through Rabica (the constant questioning by his mother and indifferent lectures from his father made dining a precarious and stressful event for Rabica, especially when he had been deep in thought).

"So what have you been up to today, dear?"

Rabica didn't even look up from his plate. "Me? Looking at that book," he grunted.

"Which book?" came the obvious reply.

"The Grand Chronicled History of the Lewerix foundation?" Lord Lewerix interjected.

"Yes."

"Good, that's an essential read for a budding lord," Lord Lewerix commented approvingly.

"It's laughable," Rabica objected "All that about Lewern and the flagellant."

Lord Lewerix snorted angrily. "Those stories are based on facts, besides that they are our heritage." Although he was not of particularly large build the aging lord could seem formidable when angered, especially in the half-light of the candles.

"But it just seems to imply that our position was created and held onto by a combination of a crazy nomadic priests and isolationist reactionaries. It's no wonder Gatan and Latman have surpassed us," Rabica protested.

"That is enough. You really need to learn a lot if you want to be lord," bellowed Lord Lewerix.

"What do you mean if? Thanks to Nerix and his abuse of dried mushrooms…" Rabica chuckled but was cut short by his father who had dropped the anger in replace of a deadly serious tone.

"If you act as you do now as lord then the nobles will not like it. Don't think that just because you're lord you can do as you please. Popularity amongst the nobles is essential."

"Oh, them and their petty formalities will try and bar the way, I have no doubt about it."

"The steady pace of House Lewerix has kept it one of the greatest houses on Rudia," countered Lord Lewerix.

"The steady pace of decline," Rabica retorted bitterly. "The aggression of Gatan and Latman may give them fortune for the short term, but now they are locked in a bi-polar struggle that has no end. Do you wish it was us wasting all this money arming and threatening because we are fearful of our neighbours?"

"Whereas where we stand now we are ignorant of our neighbours. Of course I don't want us to be some chauvinistic military power like Gatan, locked in a continuous rivalry, but don't you see how important Lewerix could be if it got involved. A third party to drive these two hulking beasts into co-operation and stop the ridiculous squabbling."

"Speaking of ridiculous squabbling will you two stop it?" interjected Lady Issetia, but too late as the war machine that was Lord Lewerix in argument had just picked a chink in the armour of his opponent: "someone needs to look at The Grand Chronicle more closely! Lewerix has intervened. It stopped the war of 369. And that was without the sword, I add,"

"In the short term that was good, but it hardly stopped the bloodshed forever. They are still at each others throats."

"Juscius is no warrior, and Adonis has little ambition."

"Juscius isn't a warlord, no, he's worse. He's a crusader. From what I've heard, if the high priest of Lateria told him to march on Ateri single-handed he would."

"He's been in power some four years now and he hasn't done anything of the sort," Zenith objected.

"Well, I don't know…"

With that submission the argument ceased and the table was returned to silence. This, however, was short-lived, "I do wish you two would stop all this nonsensical bickering, especially at the dinner table," Lady Lewerix commented. She did not shout as there was no need; they both knew she was right. Rabica muttered a grumbling apology and Zenith merely shrunk his posture, lowering his head closer to his meal.

The rest of the meal was conducted in silence. Rabica was first to finish. Pushing his plate forwards, he requested permission to be excused. His father grudgingly agreed in order to avoid another argument though the Lord believed it was polite to wait for all to finish before departing from the table. Besides, he knew that Rabica needed to prepare for the evening debate that was being held by a visiting sophist, Hiccopes.

Rabica left the darkened dining room and briskly returned to his chamber. With the ordeal of his parents over he set about preparing for the next. Hiccopes was a renowned travelling philosopher who preached about defining the moral codes and rights of citizens. The heir was extremely interested in this debate as although he had learnt much of inter-household politics his knowledge was considerably thin with respect to individual virtue politics. He had been looking forward to this evening for a long time; it was his first public debate and would serve as a refreshing change from the lectures from his tutor and his father. He had managed to extract fragments of Hiccopes' theories from his tutor; what little he had heard seemed quite strange. It was meant to be much more structured than the thoughts of other sophists, who merely pointed out what Rabica thought were fairly obvious separate traits for successful behaviour. Those were more like lessons on practical issues and citizenship than a debate, much like the tutoring he received. It was not so much what he had heard of the man's theories that intrigued him, for he had heard very little, indeed, it was the very fact that his tutor refused to tell him anything substantial that had captured the mind of the young heir.

  The evening was dry with a sweltering hot air that meant even the gentle breezes that occasionally picked up brought little comfort. Before venturing outdoors Rabica slipped on a creamy-white robe made from a very light material; not only was this the only dress that would enable him to survive the heat but wearing such traditional dress made him feel like a true philosopher. He selected the least substantial of his sandals, a very plain and simple pair that he wore loosely so the single strap did not stick to his feet in the blistering temperature. After ceremoniously tying the robe belt he nervously departed.

  The debate was taking place in the living room of a wealthy tradesman; the house was very grand for a merchant, with an ornately decorqated exterior adorned with numerous pillars and gargoyles. Inside the ornaments and furniture were spread out spaciously in the capacious rooms. Rabica was led into the living room, the broadest of the rooms, again with sparse decoration. The plain walls and lack of furniture gave a bleak chilling atmosphere that was echoed throughout the house. Those few ornaments that were on show were marvellous and eerie, proving that the apparent lack of decoration was deliberate.

  Upon entering, he was introduced by the servant. Some of the other guests looked up in surprise at the arrival of the heir. A chubby elderly man with a large woolly grey beard stood up from a seat positioned in the middle of the room, Rabica guessed this was Hiccopes. He waddled slightly as he walked to meet Rabica, greeting him with an almost theatrical hug and kiss on the cheek.

"Greetings, Your Highness, I am honoured to have your interest." Hiccopes bowed joyfully.

"Great Hiccopes, I am honoured to be able to listen to your wisdom. I have been looking forward to meeting you," Rabica answered, unable to hide his excitement.

"Really!" the philosopher exclaimed. "I didn't know I had a budding acolyte so high up in the Lewerix aristocracy." He turned to an aging man who stood beside him and grinned (Rabica guessed from his 'wise look' [and sour expression!] that he was a sophist of some kind), "Have I become so popular that even you talk of me and my theories, Ariston?"

The man grunted lazily, much to the delight of the philosopher; Rabica smiled, his attention was then brought to the owner of the house, a middle-aged man with a mean but hardworking face.

"Sire, You are most welcome to my humble abode. I am Articus Proconos; I own some stables just to the North of the city. It is most pleasing to have you here! I only wish you had sent word that you wished to come and I could have organised things to be more accommodating," he uttered, with the precision of someone who had perfect the art of appeasing important individuals.

Rabica could help but laugh at the man calling his mansion a 'humble abode', but hid his laughter in his happiness to be at the debate.

As more guests entered, the servants brought in more and more chairs to accommodate the huge numbers of nobles trying to cram into the room. Those present were of all sorts of ages, all wearing the traditional robe and sandals. The tradesman had positioned himself next to Rabica to ensure he could get his attention. Rabica turned to Proconos. "I never thought so many people would come. Have you had many debates before?"

Proconos smiled and bowed his head obediently. "I've had a few, but none as spectacular as Hiccopes. Have you never been to a debate before, milord? Oh, I shouldn't worry, some will only stay for about half an hour and get bored, they just come to look cultural but it's all over their head. Others will just listen to the speaker then leave. But then tonight may be different, Hiccopes has many controversial ideas so the debate could go on for hours."

The room had filled up fast and so Hiccopes prepared to begin.

"I would like to welcome you all to this meeting and I hope you will all join me in thanking Proconos for allowing us to meet in this fine residence of his. Seeing as I am the visitor, I propose that I begin the debate with a brief talk. Please, if you need clarity or disagree profoundly, intervene."

There were no objections so he began. "Many of you will be familiar with the teachings of the 'sophists,'" - at the use of the term sophist, especially with such a derogatory tone their were grumbles from the assembled audience - "who centre around practicality and citizenship. To them philosophy is the instilling of effective citizenship and tradition into the populace."

At this point there were several members of the group nodding in support of the sophists. "Well, as some of you are aware, I believe such talks are narrow and negligible compared to the volume of theoretical knowledge that awaits us."

Already some of the audience were looking disapprovingly at the philosopher. "Now, I do not deny that these are important for bringing young men into the adult world, but to call such common sense lectures philosophy is a farce."

There was a series of gasps from members of the audience. One red-faced objector stood to remonstrate. "Sir, how can you say this? These men teach us the fundamentals of being a citizen; their teachings are the essentials of working within the nation. You just wish us to believe that you have grasped something more than others; man needs to learn how to cope with the workings of his fellow man."

Hiccopes seemed slightly alarmed by the rapidity of the man's expression of hostility. "Dear sir, I beg to differ: learning how to deal with another man tells us nothing of fundamentals of life. They must be searched for, examined, tested and perfected over time. You cannot pass on the philosophy of politics like one would courtesy or a firm handshake. Such citizenship is merely a rudimentary basis for further knowledge. I am speaking of the search for the most virtuous and respectable leadership, not just some hastily cobbled-together governorship."

Members of the audience seemed puzzled so Hiccopes, after a brief pause continued, "Imagine political philosophy is a boat that needs constructing. Now, any citizen could construct a raft or even some simplistic boat. But it would be far from ideal; it may just about keep afloat but would not achieve its full potential unless crafted by a professional. That is why we have shipwrights to build ships, they have studied and practised and learned how to construct the most useful boat through dedication. Likewise, any educated man could use his common sense to make basic observations or indeed make decisions for a nation, but they would be limited."

The temperature of the room seemed to be combining with the heated atmosphere generated from the debate making Rabica very uncomfortable. His nerves had kicked in rendering him unable to move, let alone query Hiccopes. Everyone was silent, struck mute by the extreme tension in the room. Rabica searched the eyes of those present; all seemed to be searching within themselves, yearning to vent their views but not daring for fear of a ferocious counterattack. The room seemed to be permeating a reddish glow, sweat collected on the debater's brows; some seemed to be muttering to themselves, mouthing words that Rabica couldn't hear; he turned to Proconos, who seemed to be addressing him with an artificial look of concern. Rabica squinted tightly feeling the strain on his forehead sear around his brain. His ears felt like they were clogged with hot lead. He closed his eyes and buried his head in his hands. Silence.

    Rabica felt something jab into his waist; in his sluggish state it felt like a gnarled claw. Immediately his head shot up and he felt a cool breeze wash over his face. He suddenly felt awake, as awake as he had ever been. All around him was chaos; the men were shouting at one another, whilst Proconos tried to silence them. A serving girl had made her way through the raucous assemblance to hand him a glass of water; she had a hood covering most of her head, her face was pale and slightly chubby, and a few wisps of blondish hair protruded from the headdress. As he took the glass she smiled slightly and he nodded his thanks. He took a substantial gulp; he stared into the glass. Just looking at the shimmering ripples in the water seemed refreshing. Rabica snapped his head up. His eyes were wide open as though in a trance. "Silence!" the booming tone of his voice shocked himself as much, if not more than the 'debaters'; to Rabica's surprise they were all silent. Some bowed their heads in shame. He opened his mouth again; the surge seemed to have gone. "Sorry, what's going on?" instead of the authoritative voice of before he sounded relaxed and somewhat confused. Before anyone could answer he continued. "I thought this was supposed to be a civilised debate, between noble and courteous citizens. Not a bunch of rag tag slaves and peasants slavering over who can gobble the most of each other's dignity." (Rabica's heart felt as though it was on a high, satisfied with his speech so far, beating steadily, it urged him on). "Please may we return to what Hiccopes had said about the shipwright," he concluded.

    Before Hiccopes could begin, a flabby man, probably in his late fifties, cut in. He pointed a chubby finger at the philosopher accusingly. "This man is treasonous! He wishes to defy the rule of our Lords! He claims they cannot rule in virtue and instead learned men who have studied his 'art' should." There were nervous agreements, many pointing out the convenience that Hiccopes' theory suggested philosophers such as him would be best suited to rule.

The philosopher shook his head disappointed with the apparent lack of understanding, "My theories do nothing of the sort. I am not denying the lords of their right to rule, in fact I reinforce it. Virtue is a skill that can be perfected; yet all cannot perfect it. All may develop and improve their virtue but some will be able to do better. We cannot expect a slave to be able to gain the same level of virtue as a king; a slave may be virtuous to his master but no more than that. It is only a certain few who have the capacity to be virtuous as a leader of men."

"But what virtues should they have? Surely there are many ways to be virtuous, many paths of righteousness?" asked the sophist Ariston.

"Indeed, the 'path of righteousness' as you put it, is different depending on the path of life you take. For this we should look at what virtue is," came the philosophers' reply.

"Virtue is to live justly, to thrive and act courteously to others," answered Ariston.

"And what does one need for these qualities?"

"A good upbringing," suggested a middle-aged lean man.

"What is important for that as well as the previously mentioned things?"

"Stability?" offered a youngish man.

"Again that is important, but not the central issue. It is something less practical or physical." After a short pause Hiccopes continued. "It is love."

Nobody noticed the cynical snort that Rabica made.

"Not just love of one's family and friends, but love of man and finally love of one's occupation."

Some of the participants seemed confused.

"I will clarify. Too be virtuous is to develop; for if virtue did not make us improve then it would not make us better and so would not be virtuous. For a man to thrive he must have a successful livelihood, which he must be good at. To be best at his occupation he must wholeheartedly enjoy it, it must thrill him to do it, and in effect he must love his profession. So the shipwright must love the art of shipbuilding. And all of it at that, for a fussy eater would not make a good food taster."

"The same is true for rulers, they must love the 'art of politics', that is, knowledge and wisdom, for without these how can the ruler make wise decisions and avoid mistakes of the past? They must embrace all knowledge and search for truth, for it is the art of ruling, just as carpentry is the art of the carpenter."

By now Rabica was feeling uncertain about some of the arguments the philosopher had made. Hiccopes had paused for a moment so Rabica seized the chance. "But, with respect to the food taster, surely they must have likes and dislikes in food? Not only is it impossible to have someone who doesn't prefer certain types of food from others but also surely it is not desirable, for if they have no dislikes they will say they like everything and so their opinion on food would be worthless. So a ruler will have preferences and opinions, certain things will not appeal to them, principles that are passed on may be misleading and new ideas that are untested and not based on passed down knowledge but personal theory may be required."

"But a food taster should base their opinion on the quality of the food not the type, for if a food taster disliked cheese how could he give a valid opinion of it? The view would not be worthless, all tasters would follow the same criteria; all would say very much the same as that would be correct. This is the same for the ruler, one who has a love of wisdom and truth will discount the arguments that are invalid or flawed, the misleading and unappealing actions would not be taken by such individuals, it is those leaders without such virtue that make the mistakes. The mistakes, by definition are bad actions and so must be non-virtuous, the opposite of virtue. Those that are virtuous will survive the test of time and be successful."

Hiccopes reiterated his point, "So, virtue, and the path to righteousness is not about sophists teaching you how to be a citizen (although this is part) but it is through wholehearted love of one's occupation and only that occupation. No trader or shipwright should meddle in the affairs of the rulers, just as no carpenter should try to be a fisherman. For is it not so that a carpenter can construct a chair much better than a fisherman? Is it not also true that the best fisherman will be one who is exclusively a fisherman rather than one who is both a fisherman and a carpenter for he can learn and love one livelihood better if it is his only livelihood. Therefore each individual should stick to their profession."

It was Ariston who began to query the philosopher; "You claim that politics is for the lord and his philosophical advisors only, what of priests? And more importantly the Gods? The divine right of our Lord to rule over us seems missing in your analysis."

"Oh I knew you would bring that up, dear Ariston, you can disagree with me all you want but don't try and brand me as a heathen. Why the divine right slots into my theory almost perfectly, I really expected you of all people to be able to do likewise! Who are the Gods going to choose to be rulers of man, the wise and virtuous or the unwise and unvirtuous?"

"The wise and virtuous" came the reply from the group.

"There. The Gods have chosen those who are the most virtuous to be the rulers of man, therefore they have a divine right to rule as the gods are the epitome of virtue are they not?"

"So they can choose who will be the most virtuous".

"What of priests?" queried Ariston.

"Priests and other religious figures should not be involved."

There were widespread gasps in the room.

"If the Lord is ordained by the Gods then what need is there of religious leaders being involved? The Lord is the most virtuous of individuals as we have established and they have been hand picked by the Gods, so why would they need priests, who surely are not as close to the Gods as the Demi-Gods-on-earth that are the Lords. Religious leaders have a responsibility not to politics but to religion and its significance within the wider population. They should stick to their profession and keep the populace in good heart and faith. Similarly, the military should act as the auxiliary arm of the Lord, not as a political entity itself. The Lord needs no generals to make political decisions, only military strategy on the battlefield, which is their domain. You see they, religious and auxiliary, are just like the other professions and are best left to exclusively dealing with their domain."

"Then why does the Lord need philosophical nobles?"

"Simply because it would be impractical for the lord to deal with all his territory alone."

"So religious leaders and generals shouldn't get involved in politics?"

"No, their knowledge is in their fields, which may from time to time become part of politics. If a war breaks out then the generals should deal with strategic details."

"Does that mean Lords shouldn't learn strategy?"

Hiccopes winced at such detail, "They should know some basics as it is part of their responsibility as a ruler; how to conduct war, but not as far as battlefield specifics. Our rulers should be learning about the truths and knowledge of a virtuous society."

"But surely it is virtuous to be heroic and fight. By not fighting the Lord is being a coward, and so not being virtuous," Ariston declared.

"No. The ruler should ensure the cause is good as without a virtuous cause there can be no hero. The auxiliary therefore needs the wisdom of the ruler to ensure it acts virtuously and so can be heroic. For although a hero is virtuous, a fighter is only virtuous if his cause is good. A barbarian is a fighter, he can hardly be called a coward, but he is not virtuous as his cause is not good."

"They are cowards, they attack villages that are unprotected!" exclaimed the chubby man.

"Surely that is merely tactics and strategy," Rabica cut in dryly with a hint of sarcasm. He cautiously searched the room as the occupants fell silent at his somewhat flippant comment, Rabica suddenly noticed that many of the visitors had left already.

"Now that really puts us in a predicament!" Hiccopes exclaimed joyfully, "When do tactics, strategy and indeed security become irresponsible and unvirtuous? Would you care to share with us an answer, young sir?"

Rabica jumped, slightly startled, and fixed his eyes on the philosopher. "I'm sorry, I haven't given it much thought myself. I don't really know. I'd rather think about it, maybe some other time we could discuss it."

Hiccopes smiled "Why certainly, milord, if you would permit me. It would be most pleasing. I'm encouraged that you care to think things out before you speak, it is always a promising trait." When espousing the last part he grinned slightly at Ariston.

Rabica felt inspired to continue, "I have another query, what if war breaks out between two Households? Which is heroic and virtuous?"

Hiccopes laughed, it was loud, bellowing but still joyous. "Cannot both sides have a reason for war? If both sides are led by those that are wise then war will only occur when it is deemed justified by both sides, as neither would do something that is unvirtuous. Both Gatan and Latman have heroes from the same wars, Latman mourn their hero Raphel Latman, the current Lord's brother who died defending Neptus, as do Gatan celebrate their hero General Percis who conducted the very same assault. Both did their duty for their Household, they are not responsible for whether their leaders were correct in attacking or defending. Indeed, as it is impossible to know who rightfully owns the castle, neither side can be called unvirtuous, both were protecting their security."

Rabica was satisfied for the moment and nodded approvingly; he didn't especially want to cause any more trouble and thought it would be better to think about what had been said.

Hiccopes sighed and looked about the room, "are there any more queries or points?"

The room was silent, Proconos seized the moment, stood up courteously and wiped the sweat off his brow, "If anyone wishes to dine with me, supper will be served in about ten minutes." He pretended to look about the room at the remnants of his visitors, but everyone could see that he kept his eyes fixed on Rabica.

Rabica wriggled in his seat to wake his body up, he looked up at his host, beaming with gratitude. "Thank you for your hospitality, it is most appreciated, but I am tired and so will retire. Again, thank you."

Proconos attempted to hide his disappointment behind a wide grin and bowed as the heir stood up from his seat. The rest of guests rose to their feet as he stood and bowed.

Rabica felt a head rush as he stood. He winced slightly as it hit its peak, and fought off a yawn as he thought it would be impolite. Strangely the head rush didn't seem to be subsiding, so Rabica stiffened and decided he should depart immediately. He lazily began walking towards the door, bowing slightly as he passed his host.

★

The gatehouse to the Lewerix Palace was fairly recent and had replaced the wooden shack that had existed previously, although much of the wall that surrounded the grounds was still a palisade. It was only a brief patch near the front entrance that was walled by stone and this looked more like part of the grandeur of the gatehouse than any considerable attempt to embark on a universal replacement of the palisade. That is not to say that the palisade was disfunctional, on the contrary it was well maintained and looked quite staunch and somewhat macabre, with its tar coating to protect it from rain giving it an eerie darkness. Torches lined the wall all round at regular and as symmetrical as possible intervals and looked like well choreographed fireflies dotted in formation marking out the path of the wall in the darkness.

The palace itself was highly decorated: hefty pale limestone blocks with granite buttresses formed the basic structure, but over the years enclaves had been cut out to house statues, and patterns going back centuries lined various edges in no particular order, often colliding and even overlapping each other. The entire history of Lewerix architecture combined in this structure like a brickwork leviathan. Rabica had spent hours spotting the clear continuities in the patterns. He was also concerned about the seemingly thoughtless unstoppable excavation into the structure in order to house more and more frivolous statues depicting famous events in Lewerix history, a programme that to him seemed to be pursued without consideration of its implications for the stability of the building itself. Rabica thought it ironic that the Lewerix palace, the symbol of the Lewerix household, could be brought down by an excessive obsession with the celebration of its past.

The gatehouse was simplistically decorated, constructed from a darker stone. It seemed more robust than the palace, and it was constructed by the order of Lord Perscia Lewerix, Rabica's grandfather, who had brought in much of the professionalisation of the Lewerix military. It was manned by two guards, the first of which was tall and strong but not overly built; he stood staunch, not flinching at all despite the streams of perspiration covering his body. The other guard, who looked several years junior, squatted by the other side of the gate with his helmet between his knees and was gently rubbing his forehead with his hands. The senior guardsman must have warned the younger guard of Rabica's approach, as he scrabbled to his feet and began struggling with the chinstrap on his helmet. The senior guardsman stood to attention. "Sire, the Lord and Lady have retired, they request that you do not disturb them upon arrival, and they demand that you seek their audience in the morning," he bellowed robustly and obediently.

Rabica merely nodded acknowledgement and swiftly passed by.

He hurriedly wandered through the garden, occasionally staring up at the sky and gazing at the stars with intrigue. "What makes us so special?" he thought aloud. He snorted and gazed around at the beauty of the well-kept garden. The patchy torchlight gave a reddish/orange tinge to the vegetation; its shimmering shifting patterns of light combined with the gentle swaying of the branches in the light breeze to give it a sinister feel. Lost in the sinister splendour of his surroundings time flew by and he was soon at the doorway to the palace.

He knocked on the door twice quickly followed by a small pause and a loud slow knock, and then three quick knocks so that the doorman knew it wasn't an intruder. As the door opened Rabica saw a head peer around the door. He could only make out the outline and not the features of the face. "Evening sire, gosh you are late, if you don't mind me saying, sir," came the familiar and fatigued voice of Marcus.

Rabica was in no mood to answer and so deliberately kept his mouth clamped shut tight enough for it to be visible to the servant so he 'knew' not to ask questions. The heir walked straight through the porch and corridors in the half light hastily as though on a mission, swerving around the corners without flinching as he passed the various servants who scurried about putting out the lights behind him as he made his way to his room.

Rabica slammed the door to his room. The servants must have learned of his return from the Marcus as the torch had been lit on the far side from his bed. He rubbed his eyes as he gently staggered towards his bed and sat on it. He kept rubbing until his eyes began to ache, at which point he sunk his face into his hands and let his head drop into his lap. The heir's mind raced with thoughts and visions of the evening. He slowly straightened his back. He reached for the cupboard of his beside cabinet opening the door swiftly in order to minimise noise. Quietly he grasped a bottle of wine and slowly lifted it and navigated it out of its lair. After struggling with the cork for twenty seconds it popped out with a loud and somewhat satisfying noise. He froze as he contemplated how loud it had been. A shiver of fear ran through him, before he paused and frowned to himself as he confusedly wondered why he was being so quiet anyway. He shook the thought away with a self-disgusted shake of his head, and lazily placed the nib of the bottle to his lips and took a swig. As the liquid sloshed down his oesophagus he could feel the warmth sooth his throat, the emollient feeling diffused through all his neck, and spreading down into his chest and up into his head, numbing the ache in his brain.

Once the sensation had dissipated, he began to consider the seminar he had just been in. He immediately thought of the soldier dilemma:
'Could they both be Heroic, and therefore virtuous? What of the soldiers fighting at Neptus? Who was good? Was anyone bad?'

'Well they need a just cause. Latman...well that's easy, surely they were protecting their land and were fighting for the good of their nation. What of Gatan? Surely they are unjust aggressors?'

Rabica paused. He took another swig. It couldn't be that simple. Indeed it was not:
'But that isn't objective; I should consider it from their point of view. To them it is their land, or at least a strategic position required for the defence of their nation. It is strategic for their security: they need it as a defensive position to overlook Latman.'
'Also it is a holy shrine which they both have a right to.'
'hmm...yes.'
Rabica gulped down a few more mouthfuls of wine in the silence; suddenly he paused and frowned to himself, grasping the bottle tightly as he rested it on the bed.
'But what does it mean? ...The good of the nation? Prosperity? Security? Stability?'
'I suppose. With more land they will be prosperous, have a revered and feared military which will make them more secure and make the leaders more popular resulting in more stability.'
'But this is only in success. Gatan failed to take the castle. Neither is more stable, Gatan suffered defeat and Latman lost its heir. Where is the "good of the nation"? Who prospered? Land was wrecked, more so in the Great War where crops were deliberately destroyed. Men left widows to become paupers; taxation drained into mobilisation and enforced conscription ruined lives. How is this secure or stable? Indeed, surely by having to resort to violence the two sides must have been insecure and fearful of each other. All wars do is heighten tribal tensions and hatred...By resorting to politics of the muscle they are not developing. How can they be virtuous - they are killing over land, killing over personal gain?'

'Hang on. What am I saying? War is for pride, for one nation, for greatness, to thrive. A thriving lord will have a prosperous and content people. The development is not for the individual but the nation, which in turn will benefit the people.'

'How? How can it be? I have already established that it is not good for prosperity.'

'Not at the time, but later. Prosperity will come in victory'

'But who Prospers? Those that acquire the new land: the landowners and tradesmen, and those that arm the military. The soldiers, don't they just get pay for fighting (or they are killed? They don't benefit, they gain no virtue from killing fellow man for money.'

'But isn't that it? They become better at the job they love - they are the auxiliary - their virtue is their occupation, which is to defend and fight for their nation. They must become more effective killers and follow the orders of their leaders.'

'How is this development? What is the difference between them and a barbarian? Both fight for leaders, for prosperity. Or is it that the barbarians fight for their personnal gain that differentiates them? That means that what makes someone virtuous is killing for another, for a superior.

What is so heroic about fighting anyway? Surely it takes more courage to question one's "superiors"? Mindlessly following orders isn't virtuous it is irresponsible and dangerous to one's own moral well-being. If one cannot be responsible for one's actions then one cannot claim virtue (or disgrace) for them, they must be exempt from both. To be exempt from both is to cease being a human.'

'But it is for the good of the nation. The nation must stand tall and be proud; it is the essence of the people and is embodied by the lord.'

Rabica grinned to himself slyly.

'You're spouting textbook rubbish! What does that mean?...huh! NOTHING, "living embodiment"! ..."Essence of the people"! How is it the essence of the people? Those toiling the fields are more concerned with the next crop, not whether the lord instils pride and upholds the greatness of the household, (in fact, they hope he doesn't as then he'll conscript them into marching at a rival's castle).'

'Pride isn't enough to justify such loss of life. Neither stability nor security are secured by war: it causes instability, and conflict arises out of insecurity and fear of one's neighbour. Without such fear and insecurity would there be no war? Surely virtuous leaders would realise that it was not beneficial to instigate war; and with no attackers no one would need to defend, plus no one would want to break from their rule as they would bring the best society for all.'

'*So what makes them do it? Why would they cease to be "virtuous" and attack another?'*

'*...Prosperity...another love: greed.*

The elite prosper from expanded borders. The military gets to up its prestige and funding. Those that benefit from the lower social strata's misfortune, they are not being virtuous but pursuing personal gain.'

'*Love of greed? Surely that cannot be? It cannot be naturally intrinsic to human nature. Nor can it be love; love is about compassion, sharing, respect and so cannot be used in conjunction with greed?'*

'*huh... what do I know about love? What was...is...love?'* As he mouthed the word the image of Her emerged from his mind and into view. '*Why did he love Her?'* He found the words forming in his head yet despite his fear and mortification of the topic he was still whispering aloud. For some reason he had to.

'*Did he love Her? He?... I. Do I? How can I know if I do? I don't know what it is; How can I know what it is?'*

It had been so long, so long since he had told Her, so long since the fateful day. What could I do? I had to tell Her. I knew...oh come on... I knew She would say no... my life would have been so different... could I have coped?'

Rabica paused; a sarcastic, embittered smile cracked open on his face, turning his expression sour as emotion took him. He could feel himself surging towards breaking point, his throat was dry, and his lips were curling and twitching at the sides. He shook his head and wiped the contorted expression from his face.

'*I'm missing the point. For three years now I have been like this, a wreck. I may not be getting better but I'm not getting worse! Or am I? The gradual degeneration of festering rejection...I'm getting worse. It's disappeared from the surface but its burrowing into my inner core, my personality.'*

Rabica shook his head with irritation.

'*No, that's not important... well no, not unimportant but it's not the issue. Hiccopes talks of love as though it is dedication, a routine, almost as though it is a practical skill. One can 'love' their job as a carpenter and take joy in woodwork'*

'*That isn't love. Love is more than that; it's more than dedication, dedication is too controlling. Love is an interaction, a two way process. Love only occurs when, it's returned, like a cycle. One way love is needless desire and commitment to ones own subordination.'*

'*That means I cannot be in love. Love is two-way. She does not, and will not love me in return; therefore, by definition it is not love. It doesn't matter, and this is the crucial cause of pain, it doesn't matter what I do because no matter what I do for her, she won't love me. It is only if she loved me that I could be in love; and she does not. I'd do anything for her (indeed, exactly as with Hiccopes' carpenter, I have wholehearted commitment to a point that I am controlled by it, my 'love'), but my desire to please Her means nothing...'*

Rabica trailed off into silence, *'why do I bother?'* he thought. He shook his head and returned to whispering.

'All those years ago I saw Her. No matter how strongly I tried to deny it to myself I couldn't stop falling for Her; I had to abandon my reluctance and admit it. Everything about Her is so wonderful, Her beautiful round eyes that always seem to stare attentively and affectionately at me (and indeed everyone I should guess) when I see Her, that sparkle with energy and excitement when I talk to Her. The tone of Her voice, polite, calm, laid-back, soothing it always seems so concerned. The more I learn of her the more interested I become. She is so well-mannered. She seems so considerate, yet quiet and reserved. Sometimes it seems cold, yet really it's just her secretive, reluctant modesty.'

He paused and let out a sigh.

'Why did I tell her how I felt? Maybe if I'd waited...'

Rabica gave off another tremendous thoughtful sigh. He drained the bottle, slowly placing it on the floor, and curled up in his bed. As despair surged over him he retreated into more tightly curled up ball and clamped his eyes shut, bravely gritting his teeth for the emotional onslaught. His mind filled with words of despair, a never-ending stream of words bombarding his brain as if in an attempt to shatter what was left of his self-esteem. Eventually his mind slowed its self-inflicted showtrial as consciousness took the upper hand, spurred on by a sudden crackling coming from the torch that was now dimming. His eyelids released their iron grip until Rabica could just make out the patches of various shades of oranges where the dying torch was.

He nestled himself on top of his covers and lay still, feeling the surging sense of tiredness unwind his mind towards sleep. Rabica sensed the flames flicker their final wave goodbye…

Chapter 5
Problems in the Vaca Region

Juscius had been poring over the reports for the past two days, especially the event exactly two weeks ago at Gericos. As was often the case, there had been no report from the North Vacar region in the far south, but Juscius had given up being concerned as whenever reports came from there, they rarely had any important content. Vacarium was far from a hot spot; as far as Juscius was concerned, it was certainly not a threat to the vast Latman household.

Vacarium was often teetering on the brink of losing its national coherence as a sovereign body and becoming like the short-lasting borderless tribes of the northern territory. They barely had an active permanent military, and its small collection of semi-professional soldiers were too preoccupied maintaining a presence in the mountainous populations and patrolling the northern border to keep any of the northern tribes at bay. Spies often reported a sense of wariness towards keeping more than a minute garrison of troops on the Latman border for fear of being accused of aggression against Latman, as had happened frequently in the past (often resulting in Vacarium ceding Latman territory). All in all it was of little concern as the North Vaca region's own regiment could at least hold off if not defeat Vacarium without further assistance.

Despite Vacarium's lack of military threat, however, Latman policy towards the small principality had been kept quite severe, as there was a common fear that the nationalistic opposition towards Latman could spread to the northern tribes and even into areas of southern Latman and escalate into a serious threat. The Latman-Vacarium war (432-435) had been justified as protecting the nomadic mountainous inhabitants that had been persecuted by the Vacarium settlers who had united from both sides of the mountains of Vaca.

The northern side of the mountains and the surrounding plains constituted the North Vaca region (usually called just Vaca by Latman officials). It was governed by Hoppolies a distinguished, somewhat traditional, general from Juscius' father's day.

Juscius was more concerned about the events at Gericos. What worried him in particular, besides the horrific tactics, was the effect it had on his mother. Such concerns had been clouding his prioritisation of the main issue: whether Gatan had orchestrated it, and if it had, what was to be done? To solve this Lord Latman had summoned Zeuorox.

There was a sudden authoritative, but polite knock at the door. Without waiting for an answer Zeuorox entered and bowed courteously.
"Sire I came as soon as I could. I am deeply regretful, but I had a pressing matter with the Pontiff of Vaca." The High Pontiff silenced himself, dipping his head apologetically, but the lord motioned for him to continue.

"He had urgent issues to raise, which he pleaded that I pass on to you." He paused to see if the lord wanted to make a comment. When it became apparent he didn't, he continued. "It seems that the Orthodox believers have been persecuting the reformed believers. From what he said, this has been going on for a long time but not at a particularly significant level. However it seems to have escalated considerably, with the destruction of several temples and considerable numbers of deaths from vigilante rioting."

Juscius gasped.

"It gets worse sire, there have been reports that Vacarium may have been assisting the acts of terror."

Juscius was shocked. "Why has this only just come to my attention? As soon as there is any disturbance I wish to know about it."

"I do not know sir. Am I right in thinking that reports from the area are somewhat scarce? Because I have requested that Hoppolies seeks your audience to explain why."

"You say Vacarium has been involved, why?" Juscius was bewildered; he felt a frog of fear in his throat.

"It seems that Vacarium has latched onto the orthodoxy of many of the Vacarium descended peasantry in the region and are seeking to exploit that to cause an uprising. At least that is the only way I can see it. Perhaps they seek to take the mineral rich mountainous region off us by cutting it off with a rebellion." Zeuorox spoke with a deep authoritative voice, deadpan almost to a point of coldness.

"But why would they try that now? Surely they know how powerful our military is?" Juscius couldn't comprehend such behaviour from a tiny principality.

"No offence milord, but perhaps your eloquent peaceful speeches have been mistaken for reluctance to fight. Plus, they have opportunistically utilised some of the localised opposition to The New Interpretation, secretly sowing dissent amongst the general population."

"You say there is localised opposition? How deep does this go?"

"I wouldn't like to say, I doubt it goes far at all; most of it is probably Vacarian propaganda. Besides, not many of our citizens still follow the old ways; it is just a minority that don't seem to be able to adopt our way of life." The priest seemed unsure but decided to take an optimistic stance.

"I suppose, they just can't comprehend our world view. Still, it is just opportunism on the behalf of some backdated tribal thugs," Juscius shrugged.

Zeuorox gave the young lord a stern look, staring him straight in the eyes with his own bulging orbs. "I fear that they may have found an opportune factor that runs the risk of becoming entrenched, if indeed it is not already an inevitable cleavage that will set us apart."

"What do you mean?" Juscius was wide-eyed.

The Priest looked down dramatically to emphasise his point. "What I mean sire, is that I fear we and they may be incompatible. Those of the old belief just cannot live side by side with us, it is an inevitable clash..."

"No, a peaceful solution can be made," Juscius snapped angrily.

"Sire..." the High-Pontiff pleaded.

"I am sorry Zeuorox, you know how war makes me feel."

"Peace can only be achieved if you both follow a similar moral code, the Orthodox followers do not. They do not even recognise evil, some even revel in it. They cannot comprehend our compassion and tolerance."

"We cannot have traitors and terrorists within our territory whilst the heathen barbarians are sacking our garrisons and thieving our grain and gold."

"We need unity as a single whole; dissent and disagreement merely undermines our efforts," Zeuorox agreed. "Especially with Gatan looming over us," he added as an afterthought as he fiddled with the ringlets in his beard.

Juscius stood up, brushed himself down, and sighed profusely, before looking up to address the high-priest. "Did you say Hoppolies was here? I believe it may be necessary to talk to him."

Zeuorox nodded in confirmation and momentarily left the room to summon one of the servants and instruct him to find the ex-general. Once back in the room the high priest humbly asked if he was required to remain.

"I think that would definitely be a good idea, you have more knowledge of the area than I do."

The priest waved his hands in protest at the compliment. "I do not wish to give off such an impression sire. I am merely interpreting what I have heard."

"Perhaps we should include the pontiff?" Juscius queried.

"That is probably not a good idea sire. You see, the pontiff and Sir Hoppolies have not been on good terms recently."

Just then there was a knock at the door. The strikes were brief and sudden. Juscius called for Hoppolies to enter. After a short pause the door swung open slowly. In the doorway stood the huge frame of the veteran, who was wearing simply-decorated black studded leather body armour and matching black trousers. By his side was a long sword. Much of his hair had turned white and his face was gaunt, showing severe ageing. He strode up to the lord and priest and bowed uncomfortably, wincing slightly. "Sire... your holiness," he addressed the duo authoritatively, "I assume this is about the growing conflict between different denominations within North Vaca."

"Yes, why were we not told of this earlier?" demanded Zeuorox. "Why is it that the lord has to hear from the pontiff?"

The ex-general looked surprised. "Oh, so he finally came to tell you about it, did he? Now the tide has turned!"

"Yes he did, why have we not heard of this? We have hardly received report from you and when we have they have never mentioned this." Juscius remained calm as a sign of respect to the aged warrior.

"What do you mean? I have been sending reports regularly. But I received no reply so I have been trying to mediate." The aged-veteran looked puzzled, but a semi-concealed expression on his face gave the impression he was onto something.

"Well, in such a circumstance you should have sent an emissary or visited yourself," retorted Zeuorox. The lord nodded in agreement.

Hoppolies shrugged. "In hindsight I suppose I could have sent someone." His back stiffened. "I'm a soldier, I don't quit a conflict until it is resolved. I dread to think what could have happened if i had left to report to you in person. In fact, being here now is quite a risk."

The High Pontiff had admit to himself that the veteran was probably quite a stabilising factor, although he had failed to stop the disturbance and plundering of temples by a foreign-backed force. "What steps have you taken to rebuke the rebels?"

"What of the influences of Vacarium?" added Juscius.

Hoppolies' eyes bulged as he made a deep sigh and at the same time drew a vast volume of air into his lungs. "Rebels!" he exclaimed in a loud but controlled way, "which side, pray tell, do you refer to as rebels?" Both the lord and the priest grew bright red. "Why, this is preposterous…" began the high pontiff, believing the lord in too much shock to make his own objections.

"Sir, what do you mean? What are you insinuating?" Lord Latman inquired sharply.

Hoppolies reeled back from the onslaught. "So the pontiff didn't care to mention the 'new interpretation' priests rousing their supporters and looting then destroying the temples of 'condemned gods' as well as incidents of burning crops and seizing property of suspected orthodox followers. And some radical desecrating Neptus' temple in Ferivarc."

"Neptus?" Lord Juscius seemed confused; he turned to Zeuorox for an answer, yet he had drawn a blank.

"Apparently because she is half fish she is a beast and so cannot be a true god," came the sceptical answer from Hoppolies.

Zeuorox felt that the interrogation was not going well. Juscius and Hoppolies were arguing over some point, Juscius was using some semi-patriotic rhetoric about tolerance and virtue. Zeuorox needed to act quickly; otherwise Juscius would run out of things to say or even, worse begin to believe the traitor. Zeuorox reached for his lucky golden medallion and began praying to Thelus. Suddenly he spied a jackpot. Around the veteran soldier's neck was a necklace with an icon on it: it was the symbol of Galex. He cleared his throat commandingly and pointed a finger precisely at the offending article. "Hoppolies, may I inquire what that is around your neck?"

Hoppolies stopped and looked down, "This?" Completely devoid of emotion he lifted it preciously with his right hand. "This is an icon of Galex, patron-god for soldiers," he answered proudly.

"It is an icon of war and misery!" accused Zeuorox. "You wear that and wonder why there is rebellion in you region. That is just irresponsible."

"Pardon me, Pontiff, but that depends on your interpretation, doesn't it?"

Zeuorox opened his mouth to speak but was cut short.

"No that was a rhetorical question, Pontiff." The general still had his spirit.

"I am sorry Hoppolies, but such an icon should not be worn by someone of your position. The implications will only exacerbate conflict in the region if you are seen. If you are a follower of the war god then I find it hard to see how you can diplomatically resolve anything. Do you seek guidance from him?" Juscius looked very concerned.

"I seek protection, as does any soldier. This medallion saved me whilst I fought the Vacarians at Vayli."

"Still, your judgment could be clouded by the war god," concluded the lord.

Zeuorox turned to Juscius and whispered in his ear. "Sire, it does not look good domestically if the official in charge of the region in question seems more affiliated with the minority of rebels, foreign fighters and terrorists than the loyalists."

Juscius agreed. Whatever his previous glories, he wasn't suitable.

"Sir, it seems to me that you own personal position jeopardises your neutrality."

Hoppolies looked distraught. "Sire, I have been as impartial as possible, I have been trying to calm the orthodox revolts just as I tried to stop the burning of the temples."

"What of military action?" inquired Zeuorox.

"That would be counter-productive. The very worst that could happen would be a spreading of the disturbances about the province...at worst, it could lead to desertion or even fragmentation of the military."
"But what of the foreign invasion?" asked Juscius, losing his temper again.

"Vacarium? There are some militias that seem to have sneaked in. I doubt they are official, but then who knows with the Vacarium military. To be honest, after the new interpretation fanatics burnt down the village with strong Vacarium links where there was an orthodox priest, I can see why they might be annoyed."

"Are you welcoming paramilitary invasion?" exclaimed Juscius.

"No sire, not at all." Hoppolies felt the 'discussion' was spiralling so decided to change the subject onto something more productive. "I believe the way forward is to repair the villages and temples that were destroyed, step up the military presence on the border with Vacarium and keep a check on who is coming through."

"You mean the borders haven't been closed already?" Juscius looked disgusted.

"We have closed off the roads but there are countless paths and tracks across the mountains. Also as Vacarium is petrified that they will be invaded if they have more than a dozen squads on the border, we have no one to co-operate with," replied Hoppolies defensively.

"It's a bit late for negotiation, isn't it?" queried Zeuorox cynically.

Hoppolies shook his head at the priest. He wasn't going to see the Household descend into anarchy because of an inexperienced lord and a misguided theologist. "I think you misunderstand the situation. Violence on any sizable scale will not only disturb the population of the southern provinces - I really do not think either of you properly comprehend how high the composition of the population in the south are still orthodox - but it could spread to Vacarium and onto the rest of the island."

Juscius thought about what had been said and nodded slightly. *'Was this his first real test from Thelus?'* If the problem escalates then it could lead to war with Vacarium, which could request assistance from the other houses, in particular, Gatan.

"This really needs to be resolved diplomatically. If we are going to show that we stand for peace and prosperity, we at least need to try to negotiate with Vacarium. War should be used only as a last resort."

"But what of the insurgents?" asked Zeuorox.

Juscius looked down at the ground slowly, with a look of disgust. "They are rebels and so should be treated as such."

Hoppolies was about to object but was stopped short by a deathly serious stare from Juscius. "Also Hoppolies, as this is an issue of religion I believe it is unhelpful having you in the position of regional governor, now you have declared your theological inclination, so I will have to remove you from command." The lord seemed genuinely reluctant to give the honorary general such treatment. "You are dismissed, sir."

The general shook his head slowly in disgust. "I fought for your father for years. Decades of service to my beloved household and this is how I am treated. Whatever happened to honour, sire? The virtue of the honourable warrior...that is why I wear this medal!" The aging veteran was alive and young again, as he turned and stormed out. The thundering of his boots echoed down the corridor.

Juscius stumbled over to his chair, sat down, and planted his elbows on the desk for support. Shaking his head slightly he sank his face into his hands; the rigid elbow-based structure wobbled slightly. "Surely that was not the accepted way of doing such a thing."

The high pontiff remained silent; he slowly paced up and down in front of the desk, digging his heels into the floor like ice axes clawing up a mountain before bringing the rest of the sole of his boots slapping down onto the floorboards. After a long pause, he ceased pacing. "You did what was necessary, sire. It is a sad conclusion, but such is the affair in question."

"But we didn't give him a fair chance. Did we?" The lord was unsure and somewhat regretful.

"You were very patient, milord. If this problem has been festering beneath his nose for years and he did nothing, then that is bad enough, and that is what seems to have occurred. What is more, his attitude was most baffling - he virtually condoned the invasion of our country by terrorists!"

Juscius' conscience seemed to be lifted slightly, he looked up from his organic elbow fort, "his judgement did seem clouded; perhaps you are right about the incompatibility. He seemed to be protecting the rebels. It would be foolish to have someone like him in control of the region. He could easily become involved in the insurgency, or in the very least tacitly accepting of it to keep his religion alive in the region. Finally he was not willing to uphold the tactics that are necessary to restoring order."

"It is a shame that he couldn't join our ranks, but alas he is too stuck in the old ways to move through the transitory process towards the reformed style of living one's life. It is the religion that he believes in that has brought about this alliance of different parties and turned them against us." Zeuorox sounded genuinely disappointed.

"This is a new era. The old traditions are coming to an end and a new theologically enlightened society shall be born," Juscius announced proudly.

Zeuorox sensed Juscius needed some encouragement to drive him confidently on to Thelus' path, "a new society to bolster the social order, upholding the Latman dominance in the name of the true gods. You are the first of the ordained sons to be solely dedicated to Thelus and the true gods. You are here for a reason, The Reason: Thelus wills it. Your will is their will."

Juscius felt an uplifting feeling inside him, as though Thelus was surging through his spirit. He felt inspired. His mind raced, thinking about the events in Vaca. There seemed to be more to it than a localised problem.

Why was Vacarium such an enemy of Latman? It was because it was in league with Gatan. Gatan saw it as a vital mineral-rich reserve. Also its position meant Gatan had an ally in the rear of Latman. What if Gatan had something to do with this?

His heart sank. *Gericos!* The name echoed through his head. He grimaced.

"Sire, what troubles you?" asked the concerned priest.

"Have you heard about the incident at Gericos?" the lord answered weakly.

"Sire?" the pontiff feigned bewilderment.

"The event...the barbarous event. The one that we thought was by barbarian raiders, yet the actions were unlike them," Juscius explained.

"Oh, I heard something about it. Didn't the heathens burn down a barracks?" Zeuorox recalled.

"Yes, that was the despicable act. I can't help but feel that it was not the barbarians, or at least not their idea to do it. It seems too deliberately directed at our military...too tactical, for mere raiders."

"It really does beg the question why they would do such a thing. They wouldn't get any riches out of it," agreed the pontiff.

"Perhaps it wasn't barbarians at all, but troops pretending to be them," Juscius pondered.

"Did they capture or kill any of the attackers?" the pontiff was sceptical.

"No! Of course they didn't, it was a massacre, cold-blooded evil frenzy. Septimo and Galex are probably wallowing in the spilt blood of our brethren now." Juscius was highly emotional. He had images of the fur-clad impostors sneaking up and burning the barracks while soldiers with his brother's face slept. The flames licked through the thatched roof, dropping in clumps of flaming reed onto the straw floor and swarming around the bunks, sliding and darting up and between the legs to the bunks. Then simultaneously striking out at the sleeping warriors of virtue. As the hellish flames smothered the angelic figures they changed from multi-coloured oranges and yellows to a deep monotone red. A chorus of screams erupted as one, sending the hellish flames reeling down towards the earth, only to resurge more violently and sporadically, dispersing the saintly chant into erratic screams of agony. The once sturdy roof structure, totally ablaze, and losing its supporting beams fell upon the doomed compatriots within.

"So, this horrific act could have been perpetrated by Gatan? It's possible, but I doubt they would risk using their own troops. What if they promised riches for the barbarians if they did it?"

"That would make more sense," agreed the lord.

"But why would they do it?" Zeurorox subtly nudged him on.

"Because they want to take pressure off Vacarium, weaken our military, and what's more, make us mistake who the enemy really are. We would increase coastal defence and inevitably this would put a strain on our border defences. Plus Gericos is a perfect target; it is the closest military port to the Gatan border."

"What is to be done?"

"I fear that you are right about incompatibility. Gatan feels threatened by our moral code, they fear our virtue. We must be resolute. If you are right, conflict may be inevitable." Juscius was slightly worried about the daunting task ahead but he was sure that Thelus was on his side.

"If it is any relief, I believe it is likely that Telis would aid us. Much of the urban elite are very receptive to the new interpretation, and Lord Telis is eager to remain our ally," reassured Zeuorox. He paused as though weighing something up, his preparation unnoticed by the lord. "Sire, I am concerned. If these threats are true, and bearing in mind the loyalty issues of some of our generals, maybe we should be keeping more of an eye on them?"

Juscius furrowed his brow and winced distastefully.

"What I mean, sire, is that if this is as you predict - some theological war in the making then do we not need to ensure that our soldiers are true warriors of Thelus? It seems that some are orthodox and this divides their loyalty. This concerns me..." he trailed off. "...I believe that in such a time it is best that our soldiers are well prepared spiritually and that we have more of a connection with them..." The artificial spontaneity by which the high priest spoke these words passed unobserved by the lord. "That is why I propose that we assign one of the new interpretation priests to each garrison, I know I can trust them and they can ensure that we receive the truth."

Juscius nodded. He felt the spiritual vigour had dissipated within him. As the notion of impending war spread in his mind he could not help but deepen his frown. In such a state he could not continue the discussion. He told Zeuorox to leave him to his thoughts.

He sat cogitating his depressed state. What should he do? Surely diplomacy was the expected route forward, the correct way, the most virtuous. They had struck first but he had to hold the high ground and negotiate. Then the light of Thelus would shine upon him. His patience and resolute serenity in the face of the tides of barbarism would show his virtuous worthiness.

Or was it just weakness and indecision? Was he too scared to take serious action? Didn't he have a duty to avenge his brother? Wasn't his honour at stake? That was why his mother was so distraught. Honouring one's family was an essential part of the moral code of virtue, was it not? Surely this includes honouring their name in noble death? Revenge was a chivalrous deed, an obligation to one's family, and, most importantly in this case, to the Latman household. Both as institutions of divinity.

He was torn between which was the correct path; but perhaps he should try diplomacy first, it was worth a try. That doesn't necessarily signify defeat; negotiation can be just as steadfast as war. He still felt that his confidence was wavering; there was the larger picture to worry about, too. What if Zeuorox was correct with his prediction that the two belief systems were incompatible? That would make war inevitable, a struggle for survival between a spearhead of progress and the slow slumber of orthodoxy. The evil axis was forming: Vacarium, the rebels, the mountainous peoples and Gatan, he pondered about who else would join. Lewerix? Danite? Hopefully Telis would join the side of righteousness. Its youthful leader was forward-looking and progressive, much like its flourishing elite.

He decided it was unwise to speculate.

He should be prepared for war, but to say it was inevitable would be premature and unwise…but where would diplomacy get him?

Juscius decided that the only way to soothe his nerves would be to seek spiritual guidance. He lit a small tray of burning oil that sat, grubby and overused, beside the reports. The waft took a few second to reach his nostrils. It was reassuringly pleasant and familiar: already Juscius was feeling slightly more relaxed and so adjusted his posture, laying his hands palm down on the desk.

Closing his eyes lightly, he began to utter praise to Thelus. As he spoke the rites he felt a loosening within his mind. As the binds of nervousness, fear and hesitancy unshackled themselves his consciousness tried to drift free; he could almost feel the sense of harmony lingering on the very outer realm of his mental capacity. He continued whispering out to Thelus, feeling himself open up, ready for his guidance.

'What should I do?' came the crucial query, which the neophyte theologian asked repetitively until it ventured out of his lips *'What?…'*

As though this mental questioning had been the signal to some demonic horde, a flood of images forced themselves into the newly cleansed mind that was now free from restraint. The orange/black milieu created by the intense rays filtered through his eyelids blurred into a fiery backdrop. Instantly he thought of the barracks on fire, the screams of the fallen comrades. The images created a virulence in the waves of thoughts traversing the young lord's mind. The mental state of inordinate emotion created a cyclical sense of exacerbated anger, drawing in images of his deceased brother and the sadistic rebels.

He felt the anger rising in him, desire for revenge. The calmness that he had mastered was waning under the might of righteous fury. With his rational senses off guard, he was sure something spiritual was within him.

I can feel Him, the lord of lords; his spirit is rising within me. I sense his extensive power beckoning me to act. He is showing me the power of the enemy, their unyielding love of destruction. They desire to rape and pillage our lands, in unison with the barbarians. They rancour for our virtue, which they intend to seize by uncompromising force.

The images changed to Lateri, where the people were peacefully going about their business and thanking Thelus for protecting them from the evils of war and famine. In the centre of the projection was the Great Basilica of Virtue, the bastion of the celebrated ideal.

Yet such a state of mind can only be acquired through dedication to the new interpretation, to its teaching of virtue and forgiveness. While we promote content with what one already has, they are the opposite and wallow in a sea of avarice. There is no hope...

The feeling waned, and the once cogent argument dispersed into deep internal questioning. Again he felt drained and was left motionless, cogitating ferociously inside, yet with nothing decipherable taking form within his brain. It seemed like a blur of words.

There was a sudden timid but loud knock at the door, which made Juscius start. Similarly the spirits in his mind fled, leaving him dumbfounded.

"Juscius?" came a firm but concerned query from the other side of the door. "Are you ok?" continued the voice of Ruperis' sister, Torian, before the startled lord could muster a reply.

The door opened and she stood there in the doorway with such a presence that even the bewildered delirious young lord was stirred. He awoke slightly from his reverie.

"Torian!" His face cracked into a smile and his voice was full of ecstatic emotion. He returned to facing to the sidewall.

Such a greeting merely raised her concerns more. "You look awfully pale," she remarked.

The young lord barely reacted to her observation except a weak but friendly snort attempting to uphold that he was fine. He clumsily rubbed the tips of his fingers over his sticky brow.

"Anyway..." he attempted to sweep his physical disposition under the carpet and begin afresh, "what troubles you, dear Torian?" His voice wavered, wracked with his own concerns.

Torian eyed the lord apprehensively, but embarked on explaining her original reason for disturbing him. "I had come to inquire as to whether you had ascertained any news of my brother."

Juscius was focusing on something across the room and showed no signs of receptivity to what the young lady had said.

Torian felt her heart beating rapidly; time seemed stretched in the brief gap between her finishing and the lord shaking his head. Her concern rose to such a level that she strode forward. "Are you well?" she asked sharply.

The lord nodded, yet his expression revealed otherwise.

"I can see that you are not," the pertinacious young lady declared. The stern composure of how she spoke concealed much of the emotion and anxiety that she felt.

She reached over the desk and took his hands. Instantly the lord gave a start.

With a jerk, the lord came back to his senses. He instantly looked up at Torian, who was stooped over him. She smiled. He felt a coldness that would have been icy and uncomfortable had he not been burning up moments earlier. Her touch seemed to have revitalised him; refreshing and homely.

"I am so sorry Torian, please forgive me, I was in quite a mental predicament, and I feel you may have saved me," he explained amiably. "You spoke of Ruperis? I have not heard from your dear brother. I am sure he is well...and up to no good!" His serious face glided into a small cheerful smile.

Torian rolled her eyes in light-hearted embarrassment, "He won't recognise you at all when he gets back..."

"What is that supposed to mean?" Juscius asked.

"You used to be just like him," she replied.

The lord went red with embarrassment, rendering any comment unnecessary, then to add to his predicament he realised that his hand was still in contact with hers. He coughed to clear his throat then simultaneously rearranged his posture into a more upright position and slipped his hand free.

She laughed playfully at his discomfort then made a patronising "arr" as she straightened up and took a small step back from the desk. "You've changed a lot now."

After a short pause, Torian embarked on an attempt to establish what had been troubling him. "What is it that bothers you, Juscius?" she asked directly.

"I have quite a predicament, and it is of the highest level. I fear you would not understand the complexities," Juscius answered honestly.

The young woman seemed slightly offended. She may not know the complexities but from his morose state when she arrived she could see it was at least in part a moral dilemma. "I'm sure I can provide you with an opinion free from such complexities. One not tied to facts or theories of the past, or even to the material costs and benefits that no doubt preoccupies the experts. I can see from your distressed look that this must be a question of utmost importance and therefore, for you, not one that is personal or material, but spiritual and moral."

"Oh, it links all issues, it is so fundamental. Yet you are right, the priority must be spiritual. I must value my piety. It is the one thing we have over the others."

"It is, but what is the issue?" She seemed to be almost demanding to know, yet it was merely intrigue into how the young lord's mind worked that made her so determined.

"It concerns all... Vacarium has been assisting heretic rebels in the arson and plunder of the Vaca region and we believe there is some dark alliance emerging between them and Gatan, hell-bent on the conflagration of Latman. Yet I feel torn apart between riding out and vanquishing our foes and trying to negotiate."

Torian concealed her horror of the events and was instantly ready to provide her opinion. "Juscius, you must remember why you have become who you are. Ask yourself what makes you so different. What is it about you that has changed?" Before he could answer she answered for him. "Your dedication is matched only by your addiction to reason. Remember, tolerance and diplomacy, they were the two words that rang in my ears when you made that enchanting speech. It is your greatest virtue."

Juscius felt inspired. "Of course, how could I have been so deluded?"

"I don't know, but now you know what to do, you can lead the way. If you commence a council with all the leaders concerned, then you can resolve it like the nobleman you are." Torian was delighted to see the lord cheerful so quickly.

Now the devout idealist really believed that this was to be the decade of development towards a new order. He would resolve the inter-tribal rivalries and begin the unity of the island.

Chapter 6
The Sophist visits

Three days had gone since the debate, but it was the attributed nightmare that still trailed in Rabica's mind. The past days he had been moping about, lost in thought, preparing for the possible re-acquaintance with Hiccopes the philosopher.

However, so far there had been no news of the philosopher, which was beginning to drive the heir mad with anticipation. Rabica had thought often about what the elder had said, and had also examined and expanded all that he had been thinking. The apparent anti-religious undertones to his theory meant he was reluctant to share it with others, but he felt that Hiccopes was the only man, probably on the entire island, that he could express the views to. For this reason it was imperative that he got to talk to this man, as it was likely to be a once in a lifetime opportunity.

There was a knock at the door, which took Rabica by surprise. It was Marcus; he seemed to be smiling smugly to himself (Rabica was unsure as he had never seen the man show anything but the usual obedient look of non-emotion), which Rabica instinctively took as a bad sign. He bowed then addressed Rabica in the usual way, without looking at him directly.

"Sire, the great philosopher Hiccopes has arrived and requests your audience."

The heir's face lit up with sheer excitement. "Show him in, show him in immediately, thank you," he uttered hurriedly.

Marcus bowed and briefly left the room, entering a moment later with Hiccopes behind him.

Hiccopes was dressed in a plain robe which distinguished him as a scholar; he smiled warmly at the heir and winked.

Marcus asked if they required anything. They both replied in the negative, so he daintily removed himself from the room.

"I must apologise for not visiting you sooner, I wasn't sure how long you wanted to contemplate. I felt a cautious man such as yourself should be given as much time as he deemed necessary. Then I heard from your dear servant and I came as soon as possible," Hiccopes began. The heir smiled slightly. "That is very thoughtful of you... and my servant...he is very observant."

"I see that you are eager to begin, so I will not dawdle any further," said Hiccopes. "Tell me, what is it you wish to talk about?"

The heir didn't know where to start, so he guessed it was best to take advantage of the situation and show his appreciation. "Firstly may I thank you for your talk three days ago, it was most stimulating. It really opened my eyes and got me thinking. Even though I fear we may come to some disagreement, and you may end by thinking me an ungrateful, brash young man, I must express my deepest appreciation for your insight."
Hiccopes chuckled, shaking his head at the self-derogating remarks. "I really doubt I would think that of anyone, least of all you. Please go on."
The heir stumbled for words, unsure where to start. "Well, sir, I wish to begin with a continuation of our discussion about virtue and war... seeing as that is where we left off... and so to give you a chance to see my argument on lower levels first... you will have to bear with me, sir, as I have only scratched with the wondering of a ponderous mind."

The philosopher looked delighted, waiting for the heir to continue.

"Well, you claimed that the soldiers were virtuous, yet I find it hard to justify. You see I cannot see what the virtue is in killing another man in war. At face value, killing for one's nation and sacrificing oneself for their nation's pride seems virtuous, but what is the good that comes from it?"

"It is virtuous because they are performing their profession for the good of their society. That is, for the functioning of their society. That is where virtue is instilled, through being part of a harmonious, working society and performing your role within that union of people. A soldier who doesn't fight for his nation is not being virtuous."

"So where is the good?" Rabica seemed puzzled.

"It is in the well functioning of the society that occurs as a result of them performing their duty. Failure to do so is unvirtuous. In much the same way a carpenter who refuses to make a chair that he has promised to make. Both are betraying their society, letting it down in their obligation."

"But if we look at them separately the comparison is stretched. A soldier kills, it is his occupation. If he were to kill women or children it would not be virtuous." Rabica felt a lump rise in his throat and strike into his head, a sign that his conscience feared that he had overstepped the line.

"Of course not! Only when he kills by the order of the lord. When he is ordered into battle. Killing women and children is not his role!"

More than slightly embarrassed by his outburst the heir continued to press the point "But what if the lord demand that he kill for unjust reasons? Say a woman or a child?"

The philosopher looked perplexed for a second then shrugged, "Then the leader is being unvirtuous, he is misguided. A virtuous leader would not get his soldiers to do such a thing."

Rabica still wasn't going to give up. "Why not? It depends on the role of the leader. If it is to make his nation prosper surely he may do? Perhaps he will get resources for his carpenters by seizing a territory from his enemy and killing them all."

Hiccopes shook his head "A virtuous leader would not decree that a member of his society should break his role. If he will not allow a carpenter to be a fisherman, he will certainly not force a soldier to be a murderer. As for the issue of the leader's role, a virtuous society will be the most satisfying for the population as a whole, agreed?"

"Yes."

"And this will be prosperous."

"Obviously."

"Also a virtuous society would not kill women and children."

"No."

"So the situation would not arise. They would have to be prosperous without doing such a thing. Which would incidentally mean someone had to break from their role."

"But leaders do not act in such ways; both Latman and Gatan have burned villages, killing bystanders. What responsibility do the soldiers have?"

"I do not claim that Latman and Gatan have philosopher kings. They certainly do not espouse the virtues of such leaders. If they did I would not need to travel the land telling people of it. If there were virtuous leaders they would undoubtedly only have 'just' wars. As for the soldiers, they are not responsible for whether a war is 'just', they are just responsible for following orders and providing a military arm for the state."

"Surely it is demeaning the soldiers; they in effect have no responsibility for their actions. To me that means they cease to be human beings. It also seems that your conception of virtue is about control, about keeping people in their place in society!" Rabica blurted out.

"Firstly let me deal with what you declared about the responsibility of the soldier. I think you miss the point, sire. Soldiers can have no responsibility over that which they do not completely understand. Can they?"

The heir gestured for the philosopher to continue.

"A builder can lay bricks, but he leaves the design and planning to the architect,"

"But that is because the architect definitely knows more about the planning."

"Surely the virtuous leader knows more than a foot soldier; what constitutes a just war or action in a war. Therefore, logically speaking, the philosopher's opinion will be the better."

"But who is responsible?"

"Why is that so important to derive? If such an event occurs then there has been an error in the collective virtue and that would be the responsibility of the philosopher's guardians. The soldier merely did as he was ordered; he cannot be judged for whether it was correct, that is not within his sphere of responsibility."

Rabica did not look impressed.

"If the soldier refuses to do as the leader says then he will cause even more disruption, upsetting the harmony of the state-society further."

"May we move on to issues of conceptualising virtue?" the heir asked politely.

"Most certainly! I need to refute your comments, as apparently my conception of virtue is tyrannical!"

The heir smiled timidly but deep inside Rabica's mind he wanted scream in agreement.

The philosopher sighed. "To thrive, people need a society, do they not?"

"They do."

"Such a society will need a social order; it will need structure to keep it in a harmonious state."

"I guess so."

"Only in a stable situation can people develop, and achieve perfection. This means that those who rule should be the most knowledgeable, and they should be left to their own devices."

"Well, they shouldn't be swayed by elite interests."

"Exactly, now for someone to achieve their best attainment…which is the purpose of a society, you agree?"

"…Yes it is."

"Well for someone to achieve this they will need some kind of profession, that which they choose themselves. Which is most likely to be that which they are best at?"

"Probably, but not necessarily." Rabica waved reassuringly, "anyway, it doesn't really matter; we can assume that they will at least be competent at it and enjoy it."

"Ok. Well, they are not being forced to do anything; the state merely provides a cohesive unit that is harmonious and just, which makes such development attainable. They are able to slot into a role, being part of a socially constructed collective virtue. An all inclusive one-nation society, a community that is harmonious as they all put something in and get something out."

"I still think that your conception is flawed. Virtue is not so much about work but about personal decisions, assisting others. You don't have to be prosperous to be a good person, indeed the more prosperous you are the more capacity you have to do good, therefore more obligations you have. Your view makes peoples value nothing more than how efficient they are at their occupation. I fail to see how your conception makes someone, say a soldier, develop internally"

"Go on," the philosopher prompted. He had evidently realised that they were both grappling with completely different ideas of what virtue was.

"Well, the soldier neither develops mentally (through knowledge) nor physically (by that I mean improved standard of life). During war a soldier risks his life, yet when the war finishes he will not benefit, he will not prosper. If he dies, his widow will be punished with remorse; if he survives he will have to live with the mental scars from the horrors of war."

"He does not fight for personal gain, that would be unvirtuous. That is how a brigand, mercenary or barbarian is motivated, not the noble professional soldier. He performs his role to protect the harmonious society for all to share and participate in virtue. And for this the soldier receives respect and heroic status, as it is no easy task with many costs, but it is necessary."

"Exactly, war for personnel gain is unvirtuous. And who is it that gains from war? The nobles and lords, those who orchestrate and perpetuate the war and send young men to their deaths!" Rabica ranted.
"Wars are often for the greater good of the nation. The auxiliary performs its service, protecting the nation and promoting its interests, and some of the soldiers sacrifice themselves for this greater good."

"How is it a greater good? Only the rich benefit, from land they receive, contracts for military equipment and the raw materials that are used. It is the poor that bear the burdens, fighting, even have food requisitioned from them. And when the war is over, they receive no benefit from it. The conscripts return to the land, the soldiers go back to their barracks. Meanwhile, the landowners divide up the new territory and the armourers and large-scale blacksmiths shower themselves in gold. Often they hide behind the idea of security, remember in 287 when Lord Adonis Latman claimed that they had to invade Lewerix because it was a security threat when really it was just to get the fertile central plains. Apparently we were massing on the border, ready to strike! That's why we didn't actually put up a sizable defence until a month later!" The heir noticed he was getting sidetracked, "anyway, I feel that you treat society as a single entity with a single interest, furthermore you treat people as a means to an end."

"That is why the philosopher kings must not have vested interests. They must concentrate on the direction of the society and not get involved in the work of the other professions. Man is a political animal who thrives in society. You seem to forget that I outline an ideal society, one that has not been achieved by any of the households; a harmonious society would have one overlapping interest, disputes and conflicts of interest could be resolved by the rulers with their comprehension of wisdom and justice."

"But vested interests seem to be inevitable in any society of this layout. Tradesmen seek to expand markets and resources; religious leaders seek to dominate people's hearts and minds. And the Lords not only benefit from expanded territory and prosperity of the elite, but they rely upon the elites and their support to remain in power. They will have to accommodate and mediate between different interests to keep the elite on side otherwise they will be overthrown."

"That is why part of virtue is about knowing one's place, it is about sticking to your profession. Therefore tradesmen shouldn't interfere with the leaders... As a future leader perhaps you can lead the way?"

Rabica laughed at the idea that he was the heir. "But both the leader and tradesmen will find it in their interest, and in order to further their profession (which you call virtue) to squeeze those below them. And those below will, by your definition, have to take the pressure and work as hard as possible in order to be virtuous (i.e. fulfil their function to their leaders and masters as their role dictates)." Rabica's voice raised to a threatening level. "Your virtue amounts to control and exploitation," he charged. "It is about holding people in a hierarchical social order, whereby those at the bottom can only achieve a low level of virtue by lapping up their own alienation and performing menial tasks. Surely virtue should be enlightening for all? They will not become developed virtuous people, only slaves."

The philosopher sat motionless, his eyes wide open. "Was..." he seemed lost for words. "Was there anything else?" he uttered feebly, sounding more like a plea for the encounter to end than a question.

Rabica's face lit up in frenzy. Spurred on by the memory of the sophist disappointing him when he spoke approvingly of the gods, he could not restrain himself. "The gods are a farce, we do not need them, even if they do exist, we are able to differentiate between good and bad without them. They serve as role models for people's ignorance of the whole picture, merely serving their little role. Religion is a combination of superstition for the unexplained and a mystical justification of one's own power and a way of putting questions of legitimacy and requests for further explanation outside the bounds of mankind." By the end, Rabica was reduced to a babbling wreck, ironically much like he imagined a prophet.

Hiccopes was shocked. "You, Sire, you are misled...misguided..."

"Miscellaneous?" Shouted Rabica, chuckling to himself.

"You purport a set of beliefs that account to little more than blasphemy. You seek to deny the very institutions that you were born to protect and uphold. With such subversive, deranged perspectives I find it disturbing if not wholly impossible to see you as Lord."

The philosopher stormed out of the room. As soon as the door closed Rabica instantly ceased laughing, shaking his head slightly with glee. "Blasphemy! He's turning into a 'new interpretationist', or whatever they are called." He grunted a controlled laugh to himself. "Subversive... I like that. Maybe not deranged though." Looking up at his reflection in an empty bottle, he whispered, "what do you think?" then he continued sniggering for a few moments. Sighing, he surveyed the room slowly and shrugged. "I wonder if the heir left with him?"

Chapter 7
Reminiscing

Rabica suffered from severe capriciousness over the next day. He would be joyously celebrating the birth of his beliefs, his own critique of society, then suddenly he would be overcome by a most morose mental state. Uttering the most rigorous critiques of his beliefs, usually sliding into flippant remarks about his person. The acrimonious statements would eventually relent, countered by triumphant reminiscing of his victory over the philosopher. Neither side seemed to be gaining a particularly significant foothold in his troubled mind, and so inevitably the warring sides fell upon the vital ground: the hot spot.

'What would She think? Hmm…' (He had to be careful).

'Oh come on! A subversive! A radical. Surely she would approve; questioning the social order, she'd know I'm not just some idiot.'

He laughed at himself and the refutation began.

'How ridiculous! Well to begin with She certainly would not approve of my boisterous manner. It was disgraceful how I treated that old gentleman.'

'"Old Gentleman" indeed, he was a reactionary in revolutionary clothing…'

'Do they have specific distinct dress senses then?'

He snorted.

'Besides I got my point across…'

'I think.'

'Maybe I should have been more tolerant… like She is.'

'Ha Ha. Maybe you should just not bother!'

He felt as though he was getting side tracked.

'Anyway…what about the content?'

'What content?!'

'She would blatantly like the emancipatory aim of my beliefs. I think She'd be interested.'

'Maybe it's too idyllic? (Like when I thought she would like me). It's too utopian and dreamlike. It makes me seem crazy…'

'Why should she care? I mean does it really matter? She doesn't care. That is not to be critical as such, but there's no reason for her to. Even if it did matter, it's hardly as if it would make a significant, if any, effect on her perception of me. Ultimately this entire debate is meaningless and I should stop.' This interjection was somewhat confusing for the warring parties. Deep down he was concerned for the two sides. However, his dry dismissal of both factions was mistaken for impertinence.

'Where did that come from?' There was a short pause. *'I know what she is like (?) She is a very humanitarian kind of person. If only I had all this insight when last spoke to her properly...'*

★

It had been roughly two years prior to the current date; it was midsummer, a few weeks before she was due to leave Delix for Athlyix. There was a chariot race on in the fields to the north of the capital. It had been a bright and cheerful day, but Rabica had hardly been in an amicable mood. The fact that the young lady in question was soon to leave for an indefinite period was lulling at the back of his mind, although it had not quite yet taken precedence of his thoughts. The main reason for this was because something much more morose had struck him.

The previous night there had been a gathering of many of her associates as a farewell party. Rabica had long awaited this event as a last-ditch attempt to convey his feelings; hopefully in a more cordial way than before. His usual apprehension quashed his attempts to engage her in any conversation; eventually he retreated to his closest coterie of friends. Such hesitancy cost him dearly, as what he believed was the greatest chance he would have had became lost. In hindsight he often wondered how such an insignificant act by others could have such a profound effect on him.

The actual event that flew him into such a rage was simple enough; the travelling band that had been hired had begun to play a romantic song. Rabica, who was by and large ignorant of such symphonies, was beaten to his goal by another. This had instantly crushed his hopes, and to make matters worse the totally innocent couple seemed more than happy at each other's choosing. He instantly went from a jovial state to that of utter saturnine; whether others noticed such a rapid shift in deportment he would never know. None ever spoke of it, and he was certainly glad to never have to regurgitate it.

As he stormed home, he felt his rage consuming him. The sudden injection of anger and consternation resulting from the thwarting of his hopes, set his mind on the trail of who to blame. Instinct led him immediately to himself, yet he was also convinced that he had been mistreated. Had he been given a chance, it would have nullified much of his anger, even if he had been refused.

However, perhaps it was in fact a blessing smiling upon him: with a bitter twist of irony, had he been given the chance it would have concentrated the blame entirely upon himself and not partially on the misfortunes of fate.

Worse still, it enabled paranoia to establish itself out of a natural inkling towards pessimism. At first this was a remonstration against some nebulous spiritual overseer, hell-bent on causing him anguish.

However, his paranoid mind had quickly latched onto events of sheer circumstance and twisted them into evidence of a grand conspiracy. What he had originally merely declared to himself as a flippant remark whilst inebriated grew into a serious stab at those around him. He learnt that some of his acquaintances had been planning and encouraging the two for some time. This had fuelled his conviction that something was afoot. Like a blinded bloodhound trapped in a cemetery, his mind darted about in search of that which was not there. But once he had caught the smell of blood, nothing could stop him from carving deeper. Even the seating arrangements during the meal came under intense scrutiny; she had been seated opposite and one to the right of Rabica's rival, whilst Rabica had been sat two places to the right of her on her side. From such a position he could neither see her nor talk to her with ease, nor could he get involved in a conversation between the two, although he was close enough to be an inane spectator.

The next day he was wrought with guilt and embarrassment, only daring to venture to the race to see her for the last time. This was all he hoped for; it was not to reconcile and continue; indeed there was nothing to prolong. This was it, the end, his loss, his loss in a slanted mind-game totally devised by himself. The events of that day served as an epilogue to the death of his struggle. For some reason a sliver of his mind had tunnelled into an optimistic fantasy land, so deluded that somehow the circumstances were right for it all to end. As far as this component of him was concerned, he had survived the ordeal of last night, she was happy, and the farcical struggle had been revealed.

Rabica arrived and hurriedly sought out those he knew. They were all together, loosely spread out. Fear rose in him as he approached the flock. They were laughing and chatting. To any normal observer they seemed as usual.

This was not the case for Rabica; even the slightest chuckle from one of the number alerted his neurotic eyes, the result being that his eyes constantly darted amongst the various sub groups. The crowd of vultures skulked behind veils of vivacity and affability, but deep down Rabica was sure they were at least disdainful of him. Some saw him approach and eyed him with condescension.

As he ventured into their midst many greeted him to a varying degree: in reality, there was nothing particularly different to usual. Rabica blinked past the assorted greetings he received. He knew all the creatures were struggling to shroud their superciliousness. Many merely shouted his name and accompanied it with a grin. Forgetting that this was customary amongst the group, such interjections punched considerable holes in his now buckled mental carapace. Every greeting was treated with contempt by Rabica, who instinctively siphoned from them non-existent scorn and so retreated more within himself.

When he reached his closest circle they seemed to grimace as he approached. They let out falsely jovial greetings, and then engaged him on some unrelated matter. He grumbled unreceptive answers whilst occasionally surveying the pack for the young lady.

He began to panic after a few panoramic scours of the vicinity revealed she was nowhere to be seen. He must have given a visible start, as the circle had stopped and were staring at him in a befuddled manner. Whether they commented, he didn't know, as his mind was elsewhere. Even his vision was no longer receiving access to his brain, which had shrunk within itself and instinctively resorted to paranoia. His heart almost stopped when he noticed the young man was not present either.

The conspiracy began: they were out there somewhere, laughing and adoring each other's company, totally oblivious of his temperament. Concentration on the surroundings waned and his eyesight found itself disengaged from his brain; consequently the imagery of a daydream began to plague him. He saw *them* frolicking in the glorious summer sun. The landscape was a perfectly flat field enclosed in a valley. While the surrounding hills formed bastions of green. At the very top of the tallest were beautifully shaped rocks that had been smoothed by the refreshing breeze. The field was dotted with trees that shimmered gracefully; their bright juicy leaves were each perfectly shaped and blotless. The grass was lush and plump, slightly dampened by the morning dew that amplified its freshness. The radiant streaks of verdant blades elegantly wafted in the breeze. The couple seemed in a serious discussion, their expressions affectionate. They stopped and faced each other; she smiled with pleasant modesty, he grinned back like a primate.

Rabica felt sick; the edge of his lips rose into a sneer. He strode into the vision, kicking the short, rough, scratchy, greying grass. Clumps of dry cuttings flew from his reckless footsteps. He stumbled on a tuft, the anger rising in him. The glaring sun forced him to squint as he trudged through their utopia.

He glanced up at the trees; their leaves were cankerous and drying to a crisp. A flicker of delight came across him when he noticed the destruction. The couple seemed frozen in their iconic pose.

Rabica's heart stopped and with it went the image. The scrap of rationality had forged an alliance with a reformist section of self-cynicism, which saw such actions as extreme even for his irrational mind, and so sought to steer himself away. They were disgusted. He found himself in awe at how he could become so primitive.

Guilt attempted to revitalise some dignity, suggesting simply being pleasant, feigning happiness and accepting the relationship. Such pragmatism was the only viable action plan. Besides, he had to impose a radical self-reform programme if he were ever to stand a chance. The chauvinism was crushed; he was wholly disgusted with the macho temperament that had overcome him, believing such thoughts ribaldry. He thought, *'what right do I have to act in such a way? It is none of my business. And even if it were, that's an obscene way to act. In times of great strife one can surprise oneself at how low and uncivilised one can become.'*

The vision flickered like strobe as he neared them. The wind had picked up, and he had been focusing on the pair with such dedication that he had let the neglected landscape slip into a void and vanish.

As he approached he muttered under his breath *'I am sorry to interrupt.'*

They turned to look at him, the young man first, grinning maniacally as though he knew of Rabica's disposition and was preparing for confrontation. The young lady, on the surface at least, seemed oblivious and smiled pleasantly, although Rabica could sense that amongst the complexities of her mind there was some concern.

He felt himself being prodded back into reality. The vision vanished. Sartha was attempting to attract his attention and was calling his name with a pinch of frustrated anger. Turning to face her, he took a long blink to wipe his memory and focus on her. Rabica inspected her chubby face: pinkish cheeks, suggesting she was suffering from alcohol-induced illness, offset her pallid complexion. As she spoke an indignant sneer crept into her expression, meaning Rabica could guess she was talking of some short-term liaison. His concentration wafted in and out; he heard someone's name being mentioned abundantly (and often as an expletive), so he guessed it was indeed an account of her latest ordeal with a recent exploit (or exploiter).

In the situation that summer's day he was inundated with lethargic nonchalance. Nevertheless, he decided he needed to mobilise into action, and so under the feigned excuse of looking for somewhere to get a drink, Rabica departed on a quest to find her.

Rabica gathered up his strength then wheeled off nervously, his eyes darting from figure to figure as he stumbled along. Nobody seemed to recognise him, causing him to smile slyly: his clothing gave no signal of his importance. He wore a dark long plain tunic made of a quite stiff material that hung loosely and scruffily around his scrawny body. He calmly brushed at the creases to try and overcome the dishevelled tunic's form. Then he fiddled fretfully with the buttons, attempting to straighten them for when he saw her. The heat had drained what moisture was left in his parched throat, and under the rigid yurt-like tunic he felt uncomfortably sweaty. He fanned himself with the front of his tunic in a somewhat vain attempt to cool off.

The assemblance of people passed him by rapidly; hurrying to their destinations, they shot past his view without any significant presence, wandering in their own private worlds that were enclosed in a bubble of harmony through routine. Rabica searched for her. Then he paused to survey the nearby crowd. The people all seemed jovial and chattering like a swarm of swallows preparing for a great migration. They seemed so alive, so engrossed. Rabica searched for what he believed to be the source of this exuberance. Suddenly, his focus zoomed in on a familiar figure. There she was. The Young Lady. She seemed to suddenly materialise before him, her posture relaxed as though she had always been there. Rabica's heart stopped. His throat clenched tight and a searing pain emanated from where a hefty lump sat lodged within. His gut ached and his head spun.

★

They had spoken in a quiet cordial fashion, though Rabica had felt a lingering anxiety emanating from them both. He had found her every word soothing, but a soothing that he was immediately aware was a short-term relief, like rubbing a spot, that would cause greater irritation in the long-term. He fought to stave off his disgust at his actions the previous night and a petrifying fear of a bleak future without her. He sought to savour these last few moments in her presence. Her sweetness was like an addiction from which he suffered prolific withdrawal symptoms. It relieved his anguish whilst he was around her, but never offered any real remedy or defence. It merely kept the wound open, and exposed to his constant mental bombardment.

He had tried to apologise for his early departure, a coded apology for all his nervous actions in her presence over the previous years. She had glossed over this, perhaps embarrassed at the knowledge of its real cause, attributing it to drink. Unbeknownst to Rabica, when she had gently chided him for his excessive drinking it was an attempt to express a deeper concern.

They had attempted to move the conversation on to the destination of her departure. But Rabica had found any discussion of the beauty of this place a painful reminder of his vision of her with his rival. Even now he glowed red with embarrassment as he recalled his stuttered attempt to pronounce the word 'beautiful', eventually abandoning the word in favour of the more neutered 'wonderful'.

A dark cloud hovered over his mind, draining life and giving him the image of a barren landscape torn by the thrashing of the harsh weather. It had been summoned by a paranoid insecurity that felt he had spoken ridiculously, destroying his credibility. She must think of him as a bumbling idiot, devoid of any real conversational output. He felt alone and trapped on the barren landscape; a storm seemed to be brewing, yet it refused to come. Rabica felt his arms were stretched out ready to embrace the onslaught.

His mind raced. Suddenly he felt totally unprepared; flashes streaked the nightmarish sky, filling his mind with a sense of admiration for the powerful beauty. The mighty punishment that this environment both enacted and endured left him with a sense of awe. The arid air and archaistic power of this vision of natural magnificence was much to be admired. Parasitic creatures seemed to be darting across the jagged landscape; they scuttled to destinations far over the rugged horizon or else tried to hide in rocky crevices. Then, demons swooped down from the great titan of the cloud formation, their fortified abode of gigantean proportions. They hurled themselves irrationally at the scuttling creatures, lobbing misshapen stones and sticks at them; they swarmed over the dirt tracks and rocky tunnels for the pitiful creatures. The demons were a grey/blue more startling in colour than the colossus that floated above the rocks. Their bat like wings aided their swoops, which seemed terrifyingly graceful despite the carnage they wreaked. Although they looked inhuman, their otherworldliness was somewhat appealing, almost beautiful. The nervous creatures scuttled for cover.

He found himself looking positively upon the demons. Could they be some kind of saviour? Perhaps if they succeeded he could join their celestial body, in harmony. A blind anticipation had overwhelmed him.

As their conversation waned and his attempts to press her into continuing fell on unreceptive ears he began to fear she was merely enduring his presence out of modesty.

Rabica felt deceived; he was now horrified by the massacre of the creatures; it was no righteous crusade. The demons had no resting-place for him. Perhaps he had coaxed them out, desiring their divine inspiration, but now he was beginning to feel both angry and unworthy. He imagined the creatures scurrying about attempting to rally, small groups trying to light fires on the windswept crag using the sticks that had been thrown by the demons. Attempting to ward off the demons with the fires, and shed light on them.

Rabica recalled they had somehow begun to talk of a play she had been to see. As he listened tentatively to her description he was enraptured, his mind quaking in awe at her eloquence.

Sheet lightning had blanketed the sky; the clouds seemed like floating behemoths of beauty. The clouds rumbled a round of triumphalist thunder, cackling out mighty bellows of power. The energy from these mystical vessels turned the image into negative; even the craggy rocks seemed bleached by the radiance. A few crevices remained black, housing the remainder of the creatures seeking refuge and fearing to venture onto the surface. In the whitewash sky the winged spirits seemed like angels, soaring casually as they celebrated their victory. Tucked away in their covens in the caves the creatures were in disarray, planning how to restrain the new regime.

Her knowledge seemed a mighty shining citadel, to which his blind attempts to grasp were a mockery. He was a shallow incompetent husk in the face of her apparent perfection.

The forces of paranoia and insecurity had now turned on the invading presence, subversively trying to undermine the cloud hegemon. Yet their attempts were too late. The fixation had taken hold and paranoid speculation began to target the host rather than the root cause. Like a biting frost it swept across the barren landscape, the angel-demons flocking back to their unearthly lair. The rocks crackled and strained; some crumbled into an icy dust twinkling in the darkness and flashing brightly with each veil of lightning. The earthly creatures fled deeper into the caverns, desperately trying to salvage lighting material as the ice gave the bleached rocks a crystalline texture that highlighted the harshness of the landscape.

★

Rabica lay back on his bed as the images faded and the memory came to an end.

Despite her warmth and benevolence, to this day Rabica could not stop feeling that she was uncomfortable speaking with him. She had seemed reluctant to talk to him about anything, especially her destination. He believed this showed she wanted to hide much of herself from him. That she was not content with sharing even the most trivial things deeply depressed him. He felt as though this must mean that her true feelings towards him were untrusting and remote. Yet on the surface her attitude towards him seemed to not have changed; she still received him with cordiality.

He frequently found his thoughts following this cyclical tunnel; he would begin to think that she was not being candid with him and could even despise him. He would begin to question whether she had ever truly enjoyed his company and seen him in a positive light at all. He would suggest to himself that their entire friendship had been based on her benevolence and her tolerance of the strains of his character. Sometimes he wondered whether it was some perverse intention on her part to torture him more. Of course this was merely his extreme paranoia trying, as usual, to shift the blame elsewhere. He was sure that whatever their relationship prior to his confession to her, he was now trying her patience to the limit. Every conversation they had was evidence of her magnanimity.

Rabica did not fully understand her feelings. She was reluctant to talk of private issues, as it was not in her nature, being a modest, private person. Nor could she understand his interest in her day-to-day life; perhaps she was even slightly concerned by the force of his questions. She felt awkward when talking to him, not because of any bad feeling but because she knew how he felt (even if she did not comprehend the extent of its effect). At worst she felt some pity towards him or perhaps she blamed him for exacerbating his own problems and occasionally felt her patience tried.

It was unfair of Rabica to read so much into such trivial conversations, yet understandable as the nature of his infatuation meant it was necessary to try to acquire as much information about her and analyse anything she did, and from it, to try to establish her perception of him. His obsession had made all of her actions, no matter how petty, fundamental to his life, as they were his sources in determining her true thoughts, which had become the singular important factor in his life.

It is such a pity that infatuation degrades the infatuated to such levels, scrabbling for any scrap of information or even just a glimpse of their idol. Hungrily they devour the memories, picking at the leftovers and regurgitating it over and over again to keep themselves sustained. They ravage their senses pondering and predicting pivotal assertions of the object of their desire, often on the basis of speculation and with little or no bearing to reality.

The recipient of the infatuation is as much the victim, if not more, as they have no responsibility for the cause of the incident, nor can they directly influence or even be aware of those indirect consequences their actions have. Their only influence in causing the mess is perhaps to have been too pleasant to one of these obsessives. They find themselves under extreme pressure, as any of their actions could (in some circumstances inevitably will) be exaggerated and taken out of context by the obsessive. This is because those most prone to infatuation are very sensitive and this reaches its peak under such circumstances. It is their sensitivity that makes them so reluctant to confess how they feel, and when they do, it is because they wholeheartedly believe it. When relations break down, it will go straight to their hearts.

Chapter 8
Garrisoned

Sergeant Pluvius lay in his bunk; although he was physically exhausted, his mind was hyperactively sustaining him in a semi-delirious state of consciousness. They had arrived back at the garrison late that evening, after two days travelling, in a state of exhaustion that had been exacerbated by inanition. Their hasty departure from the hamlet had left them with few supplies and the frequent stops for the wounded had merely prolonged the agony for those who were well as they hurriedly saw to the casualties in the sweltering heat.

However, Pluvius was used to the physical strains. It was the mental confusion that was troubling him. The conversation he had had with Julia had shaken up his mind. Totally unused to such discussions, the veteran felt the quagmire of his consciousness disturbed. His dry resilient heart had been opened up and with it an inexperienced pink-flesh interior that had been totally secluded from the constant day-to-day battering of his hectic and somewhat savage life. This adolescent rawness had come into contact with the world around it now the casing that surrounded it had been cracked. Its softness was easily bruised by the memories of his past. Thousands of days of routine flashed before him. Death and debauchery surrounded his profession and recreation respectively; calculated non-emotion towards victims, opponents and even fellow loyalists, meriting them all with little more than strategic significance for objectives and duty.

Pluvius recalled three years ago in North Vaca. He had seen a green squad get run down by a mob of disgruntled serfs because they failed to stand firm when taking a charge. The uneasy youths had been assigned to the left flank to take the charge from the ragged group of rebels as a test of their nerve in battle. Suffice to say they failed their test and paid dearly. Pluvius had been ordered to guard the right flank from a suspected sneak attack through the woodland and only move up to catch the rebels in the flank.

Now Pluvius felt disgusted, and deep remorse for the fallen young men. Yet at the time, he recollected, that he had merely been angry with the foolish cowards and their idiotic leader as they fled a vast array of agrarian implements wielded by overworked dregs of society. His, ingrained, harsh instinct was trying to uphold his past judgement. However, this merely made his newly rediscovered sensitivity more disgusted with how he found himself reacting. Only now were the horrific scenes he had witnessed finally filtering through to his conscience: their screams, and the sprays of blood as crude implements viciously impacted on flesh. The stumbling adolescents tripped and slipped, only to be trampled into the dry earth as they disappeared into a cloud of dust that trailed the ground of the stampede. A particularly burly boy stumbled out of the melee with a pitchfork plunged into his side, a trickle of blood forming a reservoir in his mouth and spraying forth with each of his hoarse pants. Pluvius recalled the aftermath. *'Inefficient weapons lead to the most brutal deaths. No wonder once the first began to fall the rest fled,'* he thought. The bluntness and inadequacy of the tools at the rebel's disposal merely meant that they had to strike harder and more viciously to get the desired results. Whereas with a sword a single thrust will pierce one's organs; a spade or hoe needs excessive force to batter an organ into rupturing.

Veteran discipline tried to keep a check on his emotions. Perhaps it was good that he hadn't been so emotional at the time, as he would have been in such a vengeful mood. He could feel the desire for vigilante 'justice' rousing in him, wishing unwarranted destruction on the now vaguely conceptualised rebels for their atrocity. He then recalled how he and his comrades had flanked the bloodthirsty rebels and ridden them down to a man. "Justice was done that day, praise to Galex and Athyle," he whispered under his breath.

It seemed strange that even though so little had been said between him and Julia he found himself questioning his lifestyle. Had she opened him up to a fresh perspective? Or just reopened old concerns he had felt when a rookie?

His mind wandered, questioning why he had taken up his profession; deep in his heart he felt a loathing towards it. Reminiscent of his first kill, it was that ache in one's heart and throbbing in one's brain that made it feel surreal and painful, a trembling in the fingers from fear. People claimed that it dissipated after a few kills or bouts of death, but it did not. Most of one's conscience became numbed by the routine, adapting to the life. Yet part of one's inner core remained dubious. They say a soldier must shut it off if he is to stay sane (on the contrary, perhaps it is exactly this reluctance to accept that keeps most on a thread of sanity). Pluvius was pondering what price this sanity was if it involved removing the fundamental concerns and emotions of human life.

Soldiery latches onto the adaptability and the inertia of men to keep them from truly accounting for their actions. Nostalgia, which can normally be of formidable force, is undermined by snatching recruits early and with no prospects so that their 'previous life' is either so dull and depressing that they will not dwell on it, or can be dismissed as youthful idealism that ended when they 'became a man'. Locked in their barracks, a physical cage for their mentally drilled routine, kept apart from society and loved one's. A deprivation that means consolation can be reduced to drinking, gambling and prostitutes; it is also essential that they be kept in the company of their fellow like-minded comrades. An enclosed society that keeps them isolated and under control, shrouding their alienation in the company of those of similar disposition. By monitoring their life their anger can be switched on and off when required. In such an environment they will not dare to step out of line.

To Pluvius the world had become a series of factors to be utilised for systemic strategy. His life was a balance of routine war and comfort with no room for love towards a particular person or to fellow man. With no room for love, the only human interaction became that of short-term comfort to take his mind away from the war routine. Pluvius thought of what he and Julia had said. The weak voice of his compassion was adamant that he had been using her; despite her protest. The interaction had been to meet his sexual desire; she was a source to exercise this. He thought back through the years he had been participating in such debauchery; they seemed so empty of intimacy. His memory of the countless encounters merged into one unspecific mass of sweaty repressed flesh, bitterly writhing with bestial instincts. To his horror the recollection felt like a mechanical process blanketed by organic matter; it was as though the action was solely for the end release and nothing to do with the experience itself. Like a wolf driving itself through a chase, totally focused on the end result; savagely targeting itself on the goal, ignoring its own fatigue, using all of its anger, desire, bitterness, hunger and brutal instincts to keep itself wholeheartedly focused on the kill. Every encounter for over a decade had been the same.

Pluvius turned his attention to Julia. Had she not spoken to him so deeply she would have been an object just like the others. For a moment Pluvius wondered if all clients felt like him. An acidic nausea rose within him. He shook his head, twitching his neck muscles in an attempt to drive the perceived taste away. He could only describe his own feelings; surely many others were not like him. Though he was sure many of his profession used them for similar purposes; what of other frequent clients? Were they seeking to quench sexual desire? Or find intimate but brief compassion? Or just escape?

Pluvius began to be swayed by the idea that it was a source of relief from the pressures of life and society. Many clients no doubt had wives, surely if it was mere sexual desire they would have no need; unless they felt they needed to escape their lives? If it were for compassion then they would seek out a mistress to complete them where their spouse did not.

Pluvius shook his head as he lay in his bunk; the room was dark, virtually pitch-black, only an inconsistent flicker from torches outside the barrack window offered any light. This, rather than illuminating the room, merely made Pluvius' vision resemble a two dimensional patchwork of merging shades of grey, tarnished with a yellowish tinge. The familiar smell of leather drifted aimlessly in the room, mixing with the currents of sweat from the exhausted soldiers who occasionally rustled, sighed or groaned from within their reveries. Endless muttering and groans came from Arios' bunk; the veteran was having his reoccurring nightmare. The tortured giant never spoke of these nightmares that plagued him and no one dared to bring them up. Pluvius could only speculate at what horror it was, and in his current unsettled state he felt unwilling do delve into such conjecture. He knew it must be of the most horrific and bestial kind to fill the resolute veteran with such torment.

Pluvius glanced to where he imagined the bunk directly to his left would be; somewhere in the darkness Geric the novice lay. Pluvius had ensured that he was near him in case he had another panic attack. However, he seemed sound asleep. This provided some solace to the grizzled veteran who had suffered the rookies whimpering whilst they travelled. No doubt he slept only through exhaustion, a state of complete exhaustion that even lulled his subconscious into a nostalgic, idyllic dream of his childhood. Pluvius had seen the young adolescent sink further into nervousness. However much he and the other veterans had tried to keep his spirits high by congratulating him on killing the leader of the barbarians it seemed not to have broken through his gut moral instincts of denial and disgust. Pluvius thought of how privileged Geric was for his first kill being a lowly savage; a much easier opponent to dehumanise in order to cope. Pluvius wished that his first kill had been one of the Baresark raiders. Their salty feral stench and hairy limbs and torso wrapped up in crudely fashioned hides made their corpses resemble some sea faring beast of legends; twisted denizens warped by the underworld and then banished from this torturous resting place by Septimo, as Pluvius had been taught years ago. The sergeant could cut through swathes of these ungodly degenerates with little remorse at all. Yet Geric seemed more distraught about felling one of these beasts than Pluvius had been when he killed his first Gatan soldier. This worried the sergeant about the mental constitution of his recruit; it brought into doubt that he would ever be able to cope with the effects of killing a *civilised* man.

Pluvius thought back to his days on the Vacarium front. They had been the worst days of his life-absorbing career; he shuddered as he recalled the epoch in his life that had secured him firmly into the unique mental framework of a professional soldier. The kinship ties that found themselves set against each other, fragmented or simply and erratically cut down the middle by sheer chance or personal circumstance. Many of his comrades had been of partial Vacarium descent; some were tightly interwoven into a Vacarium based sub-culture that thrived in the region. Conflicting ties consumed these soldiers; the love of the royal household, or of their family. Many of the inhabitants were of Vacarium birth, and even those that weren't saw their land as truly belonging to Vacarium.

Pluvius was reminded of Arios, who had been present at a skirmish near a village called Delicia; the commander had made a blunder when he had sent a squad dominated by several soldiers from a neighbouring village that had been an early Latman settlement. Bitter tribal feuds dating back years had been vented that day; the solders had clashed with Vacarium descendent serfs from Delicia rebelling against their enforced serfdom who had united with mountainous natives and even some 'traitor-peasants' (Latman people who feared they would be incorporated into the feudal-serf system). Rumours of atrocities in the aftermath of the battle were horrifyingly likely, as a result of personal hatreds and cultural differences that had caused the breakdown in discipline.

Pluvius angrily tossed and turned, trying to shake off the contemplation. He fluttered his blanket to get a waft of stale sweaty air to sweep across his body as an artificial breeze, in an attempt to cool himself down. When this failed he slipped out of the blanket with silent caution and sprawled over the top of it. He grimaced as he tried to ignore the itches that erupted on his skin as a result of the new surface he lay on. The prickling merely hindered the veteran's efforts to calm the newly awakened disgust within him, further lengthening his tortuous lingering in the conscious realm. The tingling feeling that resonated throughout his body drummed out the internal pressures in his mind. Mimicking his mental twitches as though they were the root cause of the physical suffering. As his brain toyed with revived horror and anguish so too did his hardened skin feel extraordinarily sensitive to the harsh surroundings. The sticky environment and stale air all swarmed his senses to engulf both his mental and physical constitution. His resilience felt exposed. He felt his reanimated conscience on the brink of collapse, like an aborted foetus cruelly revitalised to live over the tortured life it had escaped.

Had he really become a heartless ogre?

The rise of youthful morality had left him with a deep resentment of his actions right up to the present, condemning his lifestyle to such an extent that he felt he was indeed a monstrous character. Yet his military reasoning remained in overall control and the youthful remonstrations, no matter what their true content or validity, were riveted with sensationalist rhetoric and panic, rendering them inadequate, merely troublesome and unfounded.

All these years he had merely obeyed. He had committed no offences against the vanquished foe. With utilitarian logic and efficiency he had dispatched wounded foes if it would minimise suffering. He treated them as he would desire himself to be treated.

With a toughness only residing in such experienced warriors he swept aside the emotional turmoil. He had followed the disciplines, duties and honours of a soldier, obeying the strategic logic and relative self-preservation as his profession's responsibilities required.

Whether killing was right or wrong, the sergeant defended his actions by asserting that he merely did as his household desired, protecting its citizens in whatever way those above him deemed necessary. He decided it was not for him to decide when war was justified; he was responsible only for the lives of his squad and himself. Such were the limits of his jurisdiction. Once on the battlefield he killed for defence, on the spur of the moment. He thought of someone who was about to be mugged and murdered, that they would use force against the assailant and possibly kill them. What difference was there for him? The victim of the mugging could legitimately kill in self-defence, why could he not? Granted, he searched for the assailants, but following this logic he was guilty of little more than vigilantism or entrapment.

He trusted that the Lord Latman would know what was best to suit the interests of the gods and their people. Wars were fought out to the will of the gods, so he should pay his respects to the relevant gods and they would look on him favourably. If Juscius Latman felt he had a connection with Thelus, then Pluvius had no reason to doubt him, and would obey him as both his profession and the gods determined.

Pluvius tossed and turned for a few stretched out minutes as the crux of his discomfort again trundled nearer: that which involved himself intimately. *'What of all the countless and nameless courtesans he had utilised in his travels?'*

Excessive guilt gripped him as images of vacuously smiling faces emerged in the gloom. Some looked dejected and sombre, pale ghoulish faces with tears running eerily down their cheeks; pink fleshy rings from years of fear and mistreatment encircled their beady eyes. Such gaunt faces were contrasted with colourful, false faces that crudely nodded and spasmodically rocked as they veiled their internal disquiet with laughter. Whether these ghostly faces were projections of real encounters plucked from his subconscious during the affairs, or whether they had been entirely contrived on the spot he could not tell. This merely exacerbated his self-disgust.

'They were all human beings with lives and loved ones' he whispered to himself internally.

'Or were they? These empty husks of humankind, deprived and drained of human life?'

He felt he had been part of their demise, selfishly utilising their bodies as objects. Until Julia he had never treated them as more. He surely did not speak for all of their clients, but he knew that was his disposition towards them.

Being a practical man he knew dispensing remorse now would do nothing, instead he knew he must change his actions from now on; shifting to apply some personal moral code in an attempt to regain some humanity. He would, if he felt the impulse, make sure that he engaged with them and attentively listened to their fore-chatter. He would try to respect them as he would expect citizens to respect him for his service. No matter what his discomfort and fatigue he would force himself to be attentive to them and if he could not manage that he would abstain, for the good of both him and them.

A creeping feeling trickled into his mind; it suggested that he would not be able to partake in such acts, that he would only be reminded of Julia: she whom, out of all in the world, he felt some affinity to. Not only had she revealed his despicable vice, but also she had replaced it with a flower. Perhaps this was an exaggeration on his part. For although the cankerous weed that had tunnelled deep into the soil had been burnt to a crisp, there was no vegetation visible in its place. Yet that did not make the (somewhat arid) soil free. There was something buried deep within it, a germinated seed that kept the earth fixated to nurturing. The wasteland felt it had nothing to give to this potentially bright young seedling. However, it was the only viable source of life for this patch of barren hinterland.

The analogy crumpled (further) into dust.

His mind raced over their encounter. Deep in his childlike heart he longed to see her again. She had engaged with him in a way that he had previously thought impossible. It seemed strange that he would have such feeling for a woman aside from physical atraction; indeed he did not experience any sexual stimulation from thinking of their encounter. This puzzled the veteran, as it implied an entirely different pattern to his relations with her compared to her predecessors. Suddenly he felt misled in his thinking: he began to question, 'was this right?'

Surely this was just as bad as his usual crime of exploiting the courtesans for the satisfaction of physical desire. He felt cheapened, disgusted. Had he exerted his sexual desires on his one true friend in his life? The one human being who could understand him, he had used.

He threw himself back on his bunk, lulling in self-disgust. 'I must see her again, talk to her, and learn of her, share and exchange interests and concerns.' He mouthed the words as he thought them, the soliloquy bursting into the physical realm.

Could she be his consolation?

★

Pluvius awoke with a start; the silence suggested that his comrades were still dead to the world, deep in a fatigue-induced slumber. He squinted at the window. The blue-stained rays from the sun suggested it was very early in the morning: the angle was virtually horizontal and there was a refreshing early morning air to the pure beams.

The sergeant inspected the room in the fledgling light. All of his squad were motionless, although on closer inspection some looked awake to varying degrees, and they stared at the rough beams towering above them with squat permanence. Pluvius heard some rustling to his left. A quick glance ascertained that Arios was fully awake, sitting on his bed inspecting his belt but obviously preoccupied with some deep soliloquy. The giant toyed slowly with the ornate but heavily weathered garment. He wore his night vest and long-johns, both of which were exceptionally grotty, stained with grime that had collected over the years. By his side on the bed was a plain but practical knife. It was a particularly broad and brutal looking exhibit with a wide blade.

Feeling exhausted, Pluvius gave up on his observations, but just as he abandoned consciousness and shut his eyelids the door slammed open and a voice bellowed with such sharp resonance that all in the room bolted upright. The only exceptions were Arios, who merely casually glanced upwards, and Geric, who froze in his prone position, totally petrified.

The drill sergeant who had just stormed into the room paced a few steps, then ordered that Sergeant Pluvius get dressed and go to the captain's quarters for debrief. In a slightly less harsh tone he informed the rest of the squad they were permitted to sleep in a couple of hours. Pluvius did not recognise the voice but he attributed this to his weary state. Like a flash, the drill sergeant disappeared, the door slamming shut with a pounding clap of thunder to signify his departure. Pluvius sighed deeply. This was just what he needed. Lazily he gathered his clothes that were messily strewn around him from when he had haphazardly thrown them off and collapsed the night before. The rest of the squad meanwhile had instantly fallen back into prone positions without a word, except Arios, who remained seated, concentrating on his belt. The giant seemed totally oblivious to his surroundings and ignored his sergeant-comrade as he fumbled for clothes. Pluvius concluded it was best to leave him to his thoughts.

Pluvius dressed quietly so not to disturb any of the soldiers, then with expert stealth, slipped out of the door, closing it with extreme care as he departed. He stepped off the porch of the barracks and onto the dry hard earth below. By now the sky was bright and cheerful, yet it was still early and so a chilly freshness lingered in the air. There was barely a cloud in the sky; save for a few sparse misty patches, the only white in the sky was the moon that was still hovering in a peculiar ghostly fashion.

As Pluvius walked the familiar route to the captain's office he passed several pairs of bleary-eyed guards uncomfortably grasping their wooden spear shafts with chilled, red-blemished hands. He nodded discreetly to each pair, who probably failed to register his gesture. The more optimistic ones seemed to be grinning to themselves that the shift was coming to a close.

Within a minute Pluvius found himself outside the captain's office facing the colour sergeant and two stiff guards. The veteran sergeant stared at the drill sergeant, expecting to recognise him now that he could see him properly. Confusingly, he did not; the failed identification must have registered on his face as the younger colour sergeant noticed a disappointment in his countenance.

"Something up Sergeant?" he barked. His voice was sharp, succinct and hostile, as was common with young soldiers in positions of authority. He was probably in his mid thirties. His face was compact and tough, yet his skin was perfectly smooth and shining healthily in the morning gleam. It had a highly tanned complexion no doubt from hours of continuous drilling and training of the unfortunate recruits. His darting eyes added to his air of fierceness. He was not particularly tall or stocky in build, although he had an aura of power about him.

Pluvius was certainly in no mood for conflict, and even in his somewhat drowsy state, he knew causing a fuss with such a character would be a serious mistake.

"I just didn't recognise you, Sergeant," he shrugged, dipping his head slightly to show he meant no disrespect.

"Well. I am new. You may enter," he snapped in short sharp bursts with minute pauses between each volley to allow the words to sink in before the next barrage.

Pluvius just nodded and hastily entered the office. The drill sergeant seemed to notice something as he passed him, as his lip quivered in preparation for the onslaught, however, he was not given time.

The room was as it always had been, the walls bare except for one, which displayed where a war-torn banner from the 3rd company when it had fought at Neptus, at which the captain had been present. Maps, scrolls and miscellaneous administrative and military objects were piled quite randomly in the cosy office. Over-used candles, mere puddles of crusty wax, donned the top of the military-administrative pillars of data. Some were strangely still alight, unwavering in the draft that plunged into the room when Pluvius entered. The candles gave off a waxy aroma, making the office seem both homely and studious.

Pluvius saluted the familiar seated figure of Captain Dummonius then paced over to the desk. The captain looked up from his report and smiled, he knew Pluvius well as they had fought together at Neptus. They were of similar age, though Dummonius a few years junior. They held some mutual respect for each other; the captain could rely on Pluvius to do his job, in return he treated him well and occasionally provided him with perks. Captain Dummonius was a kindly man once one got to know him, quite traditional and set in his ways but relaxed towards his men. He was a hard working administrator and dedicated commander, although he could get caught up when multi-tasking between fighting and keeping control of the strategic positions of all the troops. That was why he held Pluvius in such high regard, as he could use his own initiative.

"Morning Sergeant. How are we today?" he asked brightly.

Pluvius just groaned.

Captain Dummonius laughed. "Too early, huh?" He chuckled briefly. "Well, I would say I'm sorry, but I have to be up so why can't you!" He paused, hoping for a reply, but Pluvius was too exhausted for humour.

"Well anyway, to be honest I had no choice; we have a new priest, His Holiness Priest Vultai, he arrived a couple of days ago…" he paused as though counting days, "when was it… it must have been the fourteenth. Apparently Zeurox is assigning priests of 'the true faith' to each garrison. There've been some loyalty issues over in North Vaca…" he winced subtly, "I mean just Vaca." He was hurrying through the explanation and seemed somewhat confused. "There's been some changes… I suppose you have met Drill Sergeant Hari. He came with the priest. Anyway you can meet them later. Vultai will want to have a sermon with your men as you missed it yesterday. Anyway I will cut to the chase… Gatan has been dealing with the Barbarians. A new war is beginning…or something of the sort. Our faith is at stake."

The captain's tone seemed scripted as though he was talking in rhetoric; Pluvius' newfound scepticism was rooting deep into speculation about the abrupt and uneasy mannerisms of his superior. He seemed to share the sergeant's discomfort. He stopped the sound-bites, paused, looked down at his messy desk and sighed. After a few seconds he looked up from his reverie. "Please be seated, sergeant." He reached for a blank scroll. "So what happened?" he asked vaguely.

Pluvius collapsed into the seat opposite the captain, who was hunched behind his desk and accompanying stacks of reports. The sergeant was lost for words; for almost a full minute he murmured, rubbing his eyes, unsure where to begin. The captain waited patiently, his quill pressed forcefully against the paper. A lamp flickered aimlessly, unaware of its insignificance in the glaring light of the rising sun.

"Where do I start?" inquired the sergeant. "You know... what is there to say? The usual. We saw ships approaching; we ambushed them as they headed for the barns and dispatched them all. They were barbarians and they didn't expect us. It was mere chance."

"Was it? In these difficult times we need to question such coincidences. We hardly ever catch them. *Even I* must admit it seems too rare to be from chance."

"Well they were definitely surprised to be met by us," answered Pluvius.

The captain shrugged, as though he wanted to accept the answer but was compelled not to.

Pluvius laughed nervously. "What do you want me to say?" he asked.

Just then the door burst open. A tall man dressed in priestly attire stood beaming in the doorway; he looked excited, in a zealous ecstatic state between fury and glory. He had a well-trimmed beard, both short and tidy, which gave him an organised ruggedness. His features seemed quite charming and youthful but his current expression betrayed his mental state to declare this misleading. Without introduction he shot a question to the startled sergeant. "What was in the boat?" boomed the voice.

Pluvius nearly jumped out of his seat.

Captain Dummonius seemed unmoved by the dramatic entrance, neither shocked nor offended.

Pluvius glanced at the smouldering piles of wax. The flames had gone. They had capitulated, no doubt due to the rapid circulation of air from the priests' arrival. Suddenly he was brought back into the intense situation by the beady glare of the cleric. He shrugged, unsure what he was expected to say. "Well, it was definitely a baresark vessel. We... I left it to the sailors to deal with, I told them to keep any spoils but not damage the ship as it may need to be looked at."

"Well maybe you could explain this?" bellowed the priest. He had seemed to expect such an answer, and even though he sounded angry there seemed to be some twisted satisfaction on his face. With startling speed he drew his right hand out of his cassock; on his little finger was a coin, with his thumb he flicked it onto the table in front of the sergeant, who was astonished by his expert precision. The small exhibit gave off a painful ring as it impacted with the solid table.

Once he had recovered enough to open his eyes from a protective wince that had clamped his eyelids shut, Pluvius peered at it. It was a small gold coin that glittered brightly in the sunlight from the window. It had a very smooth face yet the edge was jagged, and from this Pluvius deduced that it was old.

"Pick it up," instructed the zealot.

Pluvius obeyed. He reached out for it slowly. He glanced at his fingers. Normally an unwavering steel set of digits, they shook nervously.

He touched it lightly with the tip of his finger; it felt unexpectedly cold (Pluvius had guessed that having been tucked away in the fiery-mannered priest's robe it would have been warm). Just as his hand began the reflex withdrawal action, he forced his hand forward and snatched it nervously. He clasped the coin in his sweaty palm and drew it to him. Once it was before his eyes he slowly opened his stiff digits. He squinted in to try and interpret the significance of the blasphemous item; the inscription struck straight into his heart: Maximus Gatan II. Pluvius was baffled. In the atmosphere of paranoia his mind filled with fearful questions, *is one of my men supposed to be a traitor? Am I supposed to be a traitor? Was this planted on my men in some attempt to remove them? What was this?*

Pluvius looked up at the gleaming saint-like figure and made an expression to plead for enlightenment.

The cleric seemed to sense the sergeant's distress, but rather than explain eyed him accusingly. "Why did you not show this to me?" he threw at the sergeant accusingly.

Completely out of his depth, Pluvius decided just to shrug and admit ignorance. Not daring to speak in the tense situation.

"You knew?" scolded the inquisitor. He thrust the question at the sergeant in such a way that failed to conceal the amusement that spewed around the edges of his mouth, curling his lips.

The cleric knew that the sergeant had nothing to do with it, but he needed to keep the subject on edge in case he would implicate others. Also, such vigorous interrogation would, theoretically, keep his mind racing and so jog his memory into something that he had missed at the time.

Pluvius was convinced that the man was a sadist, and a powerful one at that. "No, I knew nothing of it. Of course I didn't, if I had then I would have mentioned it. To me it suggests they have been raiding Gatan too…"

"Oh really, you are a master diplomat, tactician, and seer of baresark raiding patterns are you?" came a sneering virulent onslaught from the holy man.

Captain Dummonius coughed politely and shuffled slightly.

The priests gaze locked onto the captain, his beady glare attempting to transfix the captain. "Have you told the sergeant of the Baresark-Gatan alliance, a grand dark axis of heathens and orthodox?"

"I have told him that there have been suggestions of a possible deal between Gatan and a Baresark vessel," came a somewhat stern reply from the captain.

The priest threw his hands up in the air in disbelief. "Suggestions!" His disbelief rapidly transformed into a fiery disgust. "Two dozen of our heroes were burnt to a hellish crisp. Murdered by the devilish flames of evil, by those evil creatures under direction from the household of evil." With each utterance of the word 'evil' the cleric's zeal warped his disgusted face into one of acrimonious relish. After a short pause in which he suppressed his satisfaction at hearing the captain splutter apologies and excuses he continued. "How dare you devalue their sacrifice so readily? Who are you to judge?"

The captain, wallowing sulkily in ignorance, was silenced.

"Well, as I was saying to the captain..." Pluvius disrupted the deathly mien that the cleric had created; he paused as he reeled from the domineering glare of the priest that was thrust in his direction. "It was not some kind of attempt to ambush us, as they were truly shocked when we attacked them, nor did they seem as though they were embarking on a military sweep of the village... I am not denying that they have allied with Gatan. I know nothing of it, but in the skirmish we had I really see no reason to believe that they had been instructed to engage us."

"Well, you failed to notice that they were in possession of Gatan gold. The *fact* that they were inadequately prepared and that our troops valiantly vanquished them does not disqualify the probable *fact* that they were in Gatan's pay," the cleric retorted.

Pluvius shrugged; what could he say? No doubt the priest could report him for negligence if he so desired. He concluded that it was best to keep quiet.

Sensing victory, the priest turned back to Pluvius, "you have told us all that you know. I thank you on behalf of the Latman Household for your services and effective action in despatching the savages. The captain and I shall formulate the report from here." He turned to Captain Dummonius who sat transfixed, staring at one of the candles that valiantly let off an almost invisible wisp of smoke. The captain sensed that attention had been brought to him and instinctively dismissed Pluvius.

As the sergeant took his leave he noticed that the priest seemed to be eyeing his neck with a hungry look of elation. Upon opening the door to leave he heard a calm but stern voice tell him that a special service would be happening for his squad in two hours.

★

The barracks felt uncomfortably chilly. The musty warmth that had collected from the perspiring soldiers as they slept had dissipated and been replaced with an icy freshness that had swept away the comradely aroma, leaving the room with a frosty and unreceptive air.

Such a mood seemed to be shared by the squad, who held a collectively sombre mood, tense with a melancholy that Pluvius could tell was containing an inner torrent of sizzling rage.

Upon reaching his bunk and receiving no recognition from his men, Pluvius became increasingly concerned about their silence. Surely the priest hadn't got the better of them? Could that zealot have really silenced level-headed Heites? Surely even he feared the wrath of Arios?

Despite his fatigue which had suffered a net change for the worse since his ordeal with the cleric, and fear of how they would react, Pluvius took it upon himself to try and lighten the mood.

He began to open his mouth, then paused, cutting his vocal cords before they could warm themselves for the task. He felt that perhaps he should not take to jesting about such an issue. After all, he thought, was not the priest the effective envoy of both the King of the Gods *and* The Lord Latman? Surely it would break his code of conduct to undermine and ridicule a divine emissary. Questioning and upsetting the gods as well as defying a fundamental virtue of a soldier by rejecting the guidance of his superiors, he would be extending his personal responsibility into a realm that he neither deserved nor could truly comprehend. Such defiance would be opening him to scrutiny on a level of which he had no conception. By questioning the morality and authority of the priest, he was suggesting that he, a mere soldier, knew better and could take responsibility for his actions beyond a purely soldierly-strategic level. With such claims to responsibility for his actions would come the burden of guilt from any previous sins due to miscalculations of his superiors.

Pluvius shrugged, it was his job to allieviate his men's suffering how he saw fit; if he was barred from entering the priestly domain of activity then they were barred from his.

"My my, we are all jolly today!" the sergeant muttered deliberately loud enough to be heard.

Yet there was no reply, not even the slightest flinch in his direction.

Pluvius decided to step up the effort a notch and be more explicit. "So did that priest come and visit?" At first he intended an open question, but it rapidly became evident that he would be ignored, so he assigned it to the most likely to comply. "Heites?"

Heites looked up slowly from his depressed slouch. He stared straight into the sergeants' eyes, and his own pupils glistened slightly. His expression gave off a bittersweet impression, a combined grin and grimace. "Aye," he grumbled, drawing out the syllable slightly.

"So he came in here and started interrogating you all?" The question was rhetorical, not that it mattered as Pluvius would not have received an answer. "Something is changing around here. Who does he think he is?" he found himself muttering to himself.

Compassion seemed to override and shift Heites' grim countenance. He must have sensed that his sergeant had been put under just as much if not more intimidation and had the added burden of responsibility: they were no doubt trying to pin the blame on him. "So you got it bad too then sarge?"

"Yes, he stormed into the Captain's Office throwing this coin about, spouting all this fire and brimstone stuff."

"Sorry bout that sarge. It was mine…well, I nicked it off a baresark. Didn't think anything of it." The veteran now seemed both sympathetic and apologetic.

"Nor would any of us. What did he say to you?"

"Well, he was doing the whole inspirational speech stuff; you know it was quite nice. Congratulating us, welcoming us, nearly worshipping us. Then all of a sudden he starts on about the heathen and being in league with the orthodox Gatanese, then he gives the order and little Mr. Drill-Squirt starts shouting at us to show all the loot we had. They saw the coin… you should have seen that priest's face when he saw it, when he was in full swing I thought he'd have a heart attack. He lit up like he was possessed!"

"Then that priest went crazy at me, accusing me of this that and the other. Cursing me for negligence, heresy…whatever that is… I thought he was going to accuse me of being a spy or something. But despite all the shouting he seemed happy, deep down."

"It was lucky it was you that had it. Imagine if it had been Geric." Pluvius was astonished and struggling to control his anger.

"T'would have been worse if it had been Arios. I'm telling you…"

Pluvius leaned close to his unofficial deputy to whisper to him. "How is he?"

The clear-minded veteran looked concerned, and shrugged. "He's been like this all morning. Luckily that priest had enough sense to leave him alone… or else it could have got ugly…I wouldn't have even tried to hold him back."

Pluvius returned to his professional senses, and shook his head disapprovingly. "Whatever we think of this priest, he's here for a reason, and that reason is beyond anything we can comprehend. All this stuff about Gatan, there must be something in it. If he's been sent here something must be going on. They'd only be this strict if there really was a threat to the household. We certainly mustn't badmouth him, it could anger the gods, and he is our guide to them." Tradition had obviously arrived in his mind just in time to save him from falling, although he had been attempting to convince himself more than Heites. Again he was comfortably safe within the community. He was safely back within the familiar moral security, under the motherly wing of the soldiery.

The submissive and supposedly rational acceptance seemed to spread to Heites, restoring his tolerance and diplomatic temperament, as was symbolised by a gentle nodding of agreement.

Pluvius glanced around the room. The chill had been lifted but the air still felt heavy; the squad had slowed its pace in its menial tasks and was evidently listening attentively. Like minor body parts of a mastodon-whole they flexed and jerked about their business, ears trained in the direction of the leadership. Sensing that they were waiting for a signal, he decided to address them all. "Ok lads, you all know we have a job to do. It is our priority. It is our meaning. We are professionals. We obey. It is our duty. It is our virtue. It is our Truth…" Pluvius trailed off for a moment, aghast at how much he sounded like an ideologue. "We do not search for The Truths, we obey Our Truths. Those based in the tradition of society, those assigned to us. For this reason we cannot let personal dislike come before duty, our honour is at stake. Times are changing, but the politics are up to our superiors. We must adapt. Only then can our safety, through our dedication to the gods, be complete." Pluvius roused an inner zealousness never known to him, raising his hands above his head he proclaimed, "Athyle be praised!"

The squad seemed revitalised. Even Arios looked up from his buckle and enthusiastically raised his meaty fists in the air to chant to his beloved Goddess.

Just then, whilst the squad were roused in a cheerful praise of their beloved protector, the door swung open abruptly. Believing that the Priest would be pleased with his stirring banter to his men, Pluvius raised his fist so it was entirely vertical, and chanted the name of the Goddess once more.

Pluvius nearly jumped out of his skin when, with a flash of whirling metal, a small throwing axe sped past him and bit deeply into the bunk in front of him. Instantly the room hushed and the once abrasively charged squad sheepishly huddled together.

"What is going on here?" demanded the furious priest. Without waiting for a reply he cursed, "by the gods, may they be praised for their guiding of me to this place to cease this spiritual disease that has engulfed you! Colour sergeant: Treachery lurks in the air!" The speech was acted out in perfect dramatisation; Pluvius concluded that the squad would be satisfied and would repent. As the cleric paced up and down gesturing manically, a considerable amount of guilt was evident in their expressions, none more so than Pluvius himself. His countenance oozing culpability, he felt like both the ringleader and the negligent being who should be responsible for countering such dissent at the root level. He had not just failed in his duty but he had actively encouraged dissension. He didn't know why yet, but he knew he was about to find out.

Pluvius turned as he heard Heites protest. The usually level-headed veteran, adopting the the tone of the stereotypical intellectual who immerses himself too deeply in the movement, began the stubborn project of continuing dissent. "What were we doing wrong?"

This remonstration was met by a defensive posture from the righteous priest, that is, the often-declared best form of defence that is indeed attack. Accusations poured out of the cleric; however, he quickly realised this could not win him support amongst comrades of the rebel.

Pluvius cringed as at the critical moment, the brawn behind the movement, blundered demagogically into the fray. Arios had been shoved into reality by the unfolding events. "Yeah we were just trying to get protection. And with supposed holy men like you squirming between us and driving us all apart, we need it!"

"You are destroying our ability to be virtuous in our way! It is our freedom, as His Gracious Lordship Juscius Latman said at his inauguration," added Heites.

"Protection!" bellowed the cleric, and then following a brief pause, he calmed himself and adopted a more reconciliatory tone to counter the contumacious duo. Pluvius felt the cleansing nature of the spiritual emissary's words. Reassurance and acceptance was asserting itself, making Pluvius feel at ease; the order was mending.

"Yes, you deserve freedom, but as your colleague says, you...we all NEED protection. As it is your duty to protect us all from physical assault, I and my colleagues and his Lordship have a duty to defend and protect this nation's minds. We are under threat from uncivilised factions with roots in the past. Our order, that makes our defence so resolute, functions through co-operation, for this we need unity and uniform support. If you break the chain of support then the whole household will become much more susceptible to attack."

"This would be dire, for if we lose, then civilisation will go with us. These haters of virtue do not respect the ideals that we hold dear; they do not respect the virtue of the freedom of choice, the freedom of freedom. If they win there will be no freedom. That is why some sacrifices must be made now as they make us weak in the face of the enemy."

"Once we are victorious then it will no longer be a danger to diverge or EVEN believe in that, which is close to the enemy. But the twisting beliefs of the Gatans and the savages could easily influence us if we are not vigilant."

"Such practises as yours are in effect those of the enemy, and so would undermine your closeness to the Lord, for you need his trust, which cannot be total if you do not share with him... He has a vision of how the skies are ruled, who is fighting for us...and who is not... and it follows that those who They worship are not going to be any help to us. Athyle [his face twisted as he pronounced her name] is no help to us, she fuels Them."

There seemed to be general acceptance, a few uneasy grumbles, but most seemed to be reluctantly accepting the situation. Pluvius himself felt reassured. He had been offered the privilege of the 'whole picture', and he had to follow his duty and responsibility to protect this grand idea of his Lord.

But Heites surprised Pluvius; "So hang on, you want us to give up our freedoms in the name of freedom?"

"You simplify it and twist it... but in the short-term, freedoms have to be infringed upon to allow greater freedoms to thrive."

"What freedoms do we get?"

"You have many: occupation, property, arms, movement, religion... even what you see as curtailments are not; such so-called curtailments are actually freeing you from manipulations, manipulations that would have massive repercussions on you as an individual and on society as a whole. We need to protect you from your own mistakes, keep you away from decisions that will undermine all our security."

Heites still looked concerned but Pluvius guessed he had lost his appetite for conflict. He asked one last question; "Your holiness, how long will this conflict go on for?"

The priest shrugged sternly and gave a severe expression. "Who knows? This is ultimately a war of civilisation, freedom and the heavens. It could go on forever."

Pluvius noticed a spark of energy flicker through his comrade's brain; it lit up his eyes like they had just absorbed a lightening bolt. *'What is going on in his mind?'* queried Pluvius *'how can he be excited by such a reality?'* Whilst troublesome thoughts dominated the sergeants thought patterns, the priest was preparing for the next onslaught. Pluvius suddenly became aware of the beady frown of the priest sapping his self-esteem, yet the glare was not directed at his face. The purging pupils were fixated on his neck, or more accurately that which hung loosely around it. In a fearful bout of despair he glanced down, half expecting to see a shimmering tattoo of allegiance to the savages, burning hatred of virtue into his once pure soul. Yet he did not. All that offended the harbinger of righteousness was a poorly maintained, ill-shaped figurine of Athyle clinging to his sweating breast. The more he stared at the once sacred idol the more it burned into his heart. The crossbeam of his defence was creating a searing pain as it impacted with the glorifying power of the cleric, or so Pluvius believed.

"What heresy is this?" hissed the cleric, totally awestruck by the defiance, directing a stubby finger towards the offending article.

A babbling collection of mutterings spewed from the sheepish flock of once proud resolute fighters. They were silenced by divine intervention on the part of the cleric: "remove those figurines of heresy!" he exclaimed. "You have no need for that harlot. You answer directly to the almighty! Thelus!"

Something bit into the conscience of Pluvius; the poison disseminated and tried to instil dissidence in the old veteran. It attempted to question compliance with the righteous being. Thankfully, certainly for the short-term at least, the rebel infection was eliminated, destroyed by his sense of duty and responsibility. As he dramatically snapped the idol from its chain and flung it away he felt cleansed, seeming to have already forgotten the past decades of pledged allegiance to his beloved protector. She, the once pure ethereal being who had visited Pluvius in his sleep on the wake of battle, was no longer their protector. Like a queen of sirens she had posed as a nymph seducing warriors to her no-doubt twisted cause. She had indiscriminately protected all men of war to prolong and intensify their slaughter of each other, to serve her desires. She cared not for their cause; she cared only for war, death, destruction, perpetuating war for the sake of war. Now that Latman had a mission it had no need of her and her morally static ideals.

The sheep had followed suit: all seemed pleased, sharing the sense of cleanliness that Pluvius felt. All except Heites and Arios: the latter stood slightly irritated, passively doing as the others were, and the former imitated the others with a half-bemused, half-concerned expression.

With the troops rallied the cleric departed, feeling ecstatic and thankful to Thelus for guiding the lost flock.

In the brief time it took the priest to leave, Heites seemed to lose control of his amusement. He strode over to where he had flung his necklace, chuckling to himself. Kneeling down, he picked it up gently in his broad hands. His face was awestruck like a child returning to a butterfly it had mischievously flicked into the summer breeze. Holding it preciously like a delicate creature in his cupped palms, he rose ceremoniously and kissed the engraved face of his beloved protector. After a brief pause he turned to Pluvius as the grin cracked back from beneath the expression of solace. He swaggered over to Pluvius. "Well cop a load of that!" he exclaimed.

Pluvius spasmed slightly as he focused on the veteran now standing in his close vicinity. He felt his face muscles instinctively contort up into a concerned expression. "What?." he found himself answering sternly.

Heites slapped him playfully on his left shoulder. "Come on sergeant, you can't have bought all that!"

He sounded genuinely surprised. An uneasiness rose in the sergeant; however, he was unsure whether this was his own quivering remnant of resistance shaking back to life or if it was growing distrust of the dissenter who stood before him.

The veteran's sense of judgement had been hampered by the extremity of the situation, but it was finally kicking in. His diplomatic nature was, however, still reeling in shock. "Sergeant! You ain't believing it?"

"What do you mean? We've been told…"

"Naah!" He shook his head, his mind sandwiched precariously between disgust, disdain and pity. "Some crazed monk, probably from a secluded temple where they lived off dried 'shrooms, just came in here spouting new interp crap and told us to forget about Our Beloved Athyle because we need to fight to win a war that will never end. Well, I don't know about you, Sergeant, but Athyle has kept me alive through more than twenty years of service. I ain't forgetting about her like that."

"Times are changing, they are getting worse. He knows more about the big picture than us. We have a duty to follow orders, as he has a duty to pass on our orders."

"No he doesn't. Last I heard it was captains that tell us what to do, not zealots."

"But he knows the big picture better than any of us, and probably more than Dummonius. His orders come straight from Lord Latman, who we are here to serve."

Heites waved his hand in partial submission. "Ok, sergeant. He can give us orders, ok. Yeah, I'll obey him over where to fight. But I'm not worshipping who he says; he can't tell me how to think."

Pluvius shook his head. "But weren't you listening, this is a war of the heavens, one of our hearts not just our muscles. Unless we believe too, our contribution is meaningless."

Heites' face screwed up in disbelief. "That's clever," he congratulated, then added "no offence, not you sergeant." He brushed over his comments by quickly embarking on an explanation. "Don't you see, that's just new interpretation mumbo-jumbo to try and get us to think like them. We are soldiers, we fight in the dirt not the heavens. That's the job for zealots like him." He pre-empted Pluvius rebuttal. "Yeah yeah, whatever… all that shit about difficult times and him getting involved in our sphere so we should do the same for him. Well, bollocks to it. Maybe if he kept his nose out of military business and left it to professionals he could concentrate on winning the war in the heavens. I am not stepping out of my duty. Isn't that a bit hypocritical to say that we should help him in the quest to vanquish the afterlife or whatever, and poke his nose into military stuff, and then when we ask questions tell us to know our place?"

"But the gods affect us all," protested Pluvius.

"So does damn politics!" Heites exclaimed.

Pluvius began to remonstrate but was cut short.

"Sergeant, you do what you want, you think what you… I mean *they*…think and let me think what I want. You know you can trust me, hell, you know Lord Latman himself could trust me with that fine lady of his! I'll go along with this stuff passively and I'll protect my household to my last breath, but you aren't going to stop me from paying my respects to Athyle. And that is final."

Pluvius realised he wasn't going to win; in fact, he was beginning to wonder if he even wanted to.

Chapter 9
The third party

Rabica lay pondering on his bed. He was daydreaming about what he could achieve if, by some optimistic fluke, he found himself able to control the household. Even by ignoring the internal restraints and customs of his historical context, he would be stopped from pursuing his desire of reshaping the illogical world around him.

As the third power, what could his household do to stop the inevitable bickering that would render any real change impossible? What foreseeable role could the third party play in overcoming the digressive forces of bipolarity? He could not strike out a new dimension to the perpetual tug-of-war of inter-island conflict that stifled the possibility of progress. He needed to change the structure that inhibited them; it was not an issue of siding with one of these lesser evils. It was not even about creating a mediator; it was about a real alternative, something beyond the squabbling of nationalities: those farcical divisions that arbitrarily circumscribed humanity into separate, competing societies. Such partitions, forged out of petty squabbling from a primordial era that had never truly been overcome, were rendered more durable by the forging of dialects and languages that solidified divisions and perpetuated misunderstanding.

Rabica imagined some petty feud being created out of a mistaken grunt from a hairy nomad, to another equally mentally deficient being, causing a rift that would never be healed throughout the centuries up to this day.

His silent internal soliloquy was broken by an abrupt knocking on his door. He heard some recognisable giggling; that of someone with nervous temperament, it was Janyi. The knocking was Justian. No doubt Athlyian was there too.

The door swung open.

Cheerful but somewhat arbitrary greetings signalled their entrance. Rabica grunted an acknowledgement. Essentially meaningless inquiries into each other's health followed, more as a routine custom than any real concern. Justian and Athlyian had until recently been a couple, tensions between them were still high; the rejected deeply upset and the rejecter deeply unsure, and to an extent guilty. As was usual, they attempted to pretend to others that there were no issues to be resolved.

Rabica observed the actors for a few minutes, examining their positioning and posture towards each other. He closed his eyes and began to imagine their movements, their expressions by just listening. The mere closing of his eyes, the thin layer that his eyelids provided, was not enough. As he swayed slightly, he felt a draft render him part of the situation. It was not enough; he had to embed himself in the background. Collapsing onto the bed, lightly keeping his eyelids closed over his eyes (if they were clamped tightly the strain and effort made him too self-conscious), he slid his head under the pillow…

★

It was complete darkness under the pillow, a darkness that seemed devoid of any substance. Not the heavy daunting darkness that normally plagued our senses. Such a usual darkness feels chilling not for its drab nothingness but for its unobservable but evident weight, the sense that something is there, for if it were truly empty it would not scare people. This darkness was different. It felt like a blank page, waiting for the reality that surrounded it to make itself known.

"So did you enjoy the production?" inquired the rejected towards the rejecter. As the words were spoken the reality was projected. The familiarity of the room, combined with knowledge of the actors, who could be pin-pointed by the tone, origin and destination of that what was said enabled this projection to take place.

Both the rejected and rejecter were trying to conceal under a benevolent smile the impression that sought to betray them both.

"Yes, did you?" The rejecter upheld the cheerful ruse.

"If you did," replied the rejected; already the connotations were rising to the surface, teasing like a twitching tendon: silent but evident if one concentrates.

"Are you ok?" asked the rejecter, with genuine concern.

"I am if you are," replied the rejected, with tactical motives of binding their happiness as one.

The third party, who tried to rescue the situation from a timeless stagnation, broke the deathly silence that followed. "I thought it was ok. The costumes were a bit minimal though". I can imagine exactly how she said this, raising her eyebrows as she began, using her dark eyes to dart between the two key actors and finishing with a slight extension of her lower jaw as though into some erratic primitive pout, probably widening her eyes as she did so.

But the rejected was determined, "I suppose you liked the **minimal** costumes did you?" a cheerful expression would hide the serious emotional undertones.

"They did the job," answered the rejecter, with a strained and deliberate dead-pan tone, trying to avoid rising to the emotional challenge.

"And what job was that?" inquired the rejected with a splitting smirk. No doubt staring with wide eyes straight into the eyes of the rejecter, a slight (but obvious) sense of bitterness tinged the tone of the question.

The rejecter was getting irritated by the insinuation. "What job do you think?"

"I don't know. That's why I'm asking you!" The rejected feigned innocence.

The rejecter was not going to take any chances. "Well, they portrayed the character's major attributes and what you should associate with them. Does that make you happy?"

"It's ok if you are," came the awkward reply.

The rejecter sighed, clearly aggravated. "Yes, I am ok, but what's that got to do with it?"

"Well I'm sorry if I'm concerned with how you are!" The rejected retorted.

"I care about you too. You know I do."

The *'love-hate-bickering'* continued for a few minutes, down its torturously explicit path. I cringed with every word they spoke as they invited each other to take it in turns to perform open-heart surgery on themselves. I could picture their contorted faces as they ripped and scratched at their rapidly beating plump primary-organs; pulsating stretched-taut, shining with a smooth deep red as the arteries and veins connecting it to the body were ripped to tatters by marauding hands. I gritted my teeth as the spectacle was performed on the inside of my eyelids. The imaginary screams began to mingle with the true words spoken, acting as a revealer of background subtleties.

Finally, there was silence.

The third party tried to open a new conversation, one that would not be manipulated into the mutually self-torturous debates that went on both within and between the key actors. "Did you hear about Hiccopes visiting the city?"

Yet the question was ignored.

Deathly silence took over; in such a silence the imagery that this narrator was relying on began to slip. I, your temporary gaseous narrator, in a secluded state was losing his grip, his capacity to even imagine a reality.

Finally silence was broken. "So what are my 'major attributes' then? Except that I am horrible." The rejected lashed out with its most powerful tool, self-destruction of its own self-esteem.

The rejecter was hit hard by this erroneous assertion but rose above it with self-parody, "Yes I think that. I think that you are horrible." The rejecter paused, evidently deeply hurt. "Is that what you WANT to hear?"

Now the rejected was deeply hurt. "No" it whimpered.

I, the gaseous narrator, sighed in my solitude. 'Were people so obvious? They know it's not as bad as they implicitly make out, yet they conceal the pain behind triviality, which only exacerbates the issue, as they do not address the real problems.

They stood gazing into each other's eyes, with a tension that made the air heavy. The room seemed to only include them; the furniture had been shrunk under the pressure of the heavy air. Yet the third party was not shrunk: she seemed strong, resolute and prepared for the tensions.

The tenseness of the room was deadly. The silence seemed to be binding all in the room, locking it together like a crystal. I could sense everything; any slight twitch from the actors and the whole structure would jolt and resonate movement. Yet where was the Third Party? It had scurried off, scuttled up the wall or hidden in a crack. Then I sensed it, it still had a presence; it clung onto the wall like a fly. The once resolute bastion of reason had shrunk away, or had it merely tactically retreated, knowing that to get involved now would be foolish?

Like a rapidly freezing lake the frosty structure spread to engulf the entire room, locking the bed covers with the structural normality of stillness. I shivered as though a layer of icicles had sprung up on my back. They heard my rustling, reminded of my presence.

"What is Rabica doing?" the Third Party asked. She had seized the moment, the chance, to divert the interrelationship from conflict to co-operation.

The rejecter sighed. A misfire. Such a critical misfire...

"I don't know what he's doing?" the rejected answered, "let's just leave him."

Perfect, I was no longer there, the gaseous narrator had dissipated and spread to engulf the whole room, yet in such a dispersed form these heavy bubbles of air could not detect me. I was an anomaly, the freak noise that erupted in an untraceable cackle.

"Are you ok?" came a hoarse croak from the rejecter.

"I am if you are," replied a resolute rejected.

The pain was unbearable, again it harkened back to those golden days: their days of union. The rejecter felt like sobbing aloud, was it not lonely too? Was it not suffering too? Only it could not do anything: It could not even utter comforting words to the other actor without being guilty of egging them on in some cruel ploy. Is It not the victim, not the rejected? Surely the true victim is the one who merely existed in the wrong place at the wrong time and fell into a trap with this rejected being. It is the rejected that has brought them to this end; it is the rejected that withholds their feeling to further diminish itself and drain the rejecter/victim. Or expresses them in some rage that merely devalues its feelings and embarrasses the rejecter. What can the rejecter do? It can only be kind and friendly but this will be misinterpreted. Maybe it should be harsh. Blunt. Even exaggerate their discomfort to drive away the infective thoughts of the rejected, who spreads the infection to the rejecter.

The situation was descending, and rapidly. I heard the sound of someone emphatically slapping their thighs in a gripping shrug. It was followed by a gasping sigh that I instantly recognised as the rejecter.

Suddenly the bipolar world was split; the Third Party entered the fray, prepared to extend the spectrum of interaction beyond a single-dimensioned tug of war. Action of any significance depended on her. Her tweaking and guidance were the only things that could create anything new; otherwise there was only the stagnation of these grappling emotional wrecks trying to simultaneously incapacitate and captivate the other. Two emotionally-based desires combined into one: pure kindness and care for the other but at the same time a perceived need to beguile,

THE SON AND THE HEIR

entice, even mislead the other into recognising them and their benevolence towards the other. Was this love? An inherently contradictory emotion, something so true it just couldn't make sense, and could only be expressed through a paradoxical combination of tactical luring and innocent affection.

It was the Third Party who could bring more than a one-dimensional farce to the escapade: some substance beyond primordial instincts. Anything... anything at all. I was almost begging. Even the most mundane agenda would shift the spectrum out of this dichotomy of two stagnant ideals completely opposed to each other yet with the same ultimate goals. Just something grounded in the banality of day-to-day life, to give them a dose of reality. To shake them off their high horses of mysticism, their airy-fairy dreams and desires, and in the shattered remains of a dual-styled utopia of emotion (that was never truly realised until the moment was lost) pining for a return, yet at the same time resenting the other for shattering the pleasant normality that had been so comforting it had been rendered part of the natural scenery.

"Who wants another drink?" she asked.

Was this it? Was that it? The valiant attempt to sweep away the tensions?

"Oh, yes please," half whispered the rejected, who seemed to have perked up in the interlude.

"No." The rejecter waved away the offer, soothed but not devoid of all the acidity that had built up.

I could hear the abrupt (but still soothing) plop and pour of wine into two glasses. It was closely followed by the clink of the goblets being passed out and their contents daintily sipped.

Then followed some idle chatter, I must confess I was so delighted to hear it that it (at least the details) seems to have slipped my mind, so forgive me if I do not correctly represent the answers, queries or even topics assessed. The banter was customary, the usual jitter between friends, reminiscing (without denial or emotive longing).

At first it was just between the rejected and Third Party:

"Did you hear about Athis?"

"Oh with the milk cart?"

There were giggles and cackles of laughter, perhaps too much to be attributed to the issue at hand.

"With the..."

The petty rumours and ridicules were merged together with scheming bouts of chuckling. Swirling in a cauldron of pestilent anecdotes, stagnated with snide poignancy, an acidic kick numbed the senses ready for the ooze to pour slowly down my throat, surging and engulfing like a fetid glob of magma. I was disgusted by their...(my mind strains to find a suitable description). I felt sickened; was this it; the only way to avoid

conflict: the derogatory scorning of someone totally irrelevant to the situation; deflecting the issue elsewhere, to someone else's misery? Still, it did no harm. For the short term, at least, it could end the feud.
Then the rejecter began to chuckle aloud.
Yes, I guess it was it.
"Oh yeah, I remember that; he was meant to be going to the court afterwards to speak to the emissaries from the north." The rejecter had reached for the cauldron's murky contents and been sucked in. The victim's bitterness had been dispersed by the more viscous gluttony, washed away by the bile of jovial denial. Having become integrated, the rejecter-victim was furthering the incident's humorous unwinding:
"And when they saw the stains..." he continued. I shall not concern those trawling through this with this particularly unfortunate and childish antic.
Trust such populist notions to triumph in transforming the theme. I felt repulsed, not so much for the explicit content (I must confess - the gaseous entity managed to formulate a snigger as it swirled and mingled with the air between the pillows), but firstly for the poor subject of this predicament and secondly, I could not stop tasting the sickening flavour of totally artificial conversation, regurgitated reminiscing to cover the fetid corpse of true candour. No doubt the nostalgic pleasure drawn from such recollections was real. However, it was the contemporary falseness that had infected the stories' purpose, into an awkward conversation breaker in a crisis.
How quickly would I become part of this past? Or am I now? Not just this second, but have I been? That is, have I been a constant bearer of such delightful clownery? A continual source of amusement, a walking-talking bundle of mess-ups, ridiculous dares, failures, dogmatic-cynicism, foolish struggling and heartless-below-the-belt anecdotes? Just look at how quickly they have forgotten me! And I am only beneath a pillow, in the same room as them! I was even referred to in third person. Yet I am not the Third Party, I am the fourth. The fourth must not be relevant; anyone beyond the third party is treated as a non-entity.
My mind paused. Their aimless gibbering faded into background sounds, almost like a disjointed backing music drifting through the room without any true meaning or impact.
I tried to refocus:
"Do you remember the time he got drunk and threw up in the plant pot at Malphillie's?" queried the rejecter.
Obviously the poor Athis was still being used as a decoy to hide the true tensions.
They all chortled, but their loud laughter failed to disguise their nervous unease. The unnaturally forced volume merely revealed how

much of an exaggerated disposition their current state was. It seemed painfully obvious to me that if they were to express their true levels of amusement it would barely surmount to nervous giggling.

"...And there was the time he nearly got beaten up by that drunken commoner, you know the one with the huge straggly beard, with flecks of gods-know-what... some kind of carrion from his last victim that he'd stumbled upon and beaten into a pulp with a bottle... or his dogs fourth leg... You know the fucking scruffy half-starved flea-infested mutt; which actually had three legs...I'm surprised it didn't have a fucking patch or something...smoking an incense pipe... That beard though... god... I thought I was going to get sucked in...or dragged in by some multi-limbed mutant that's never seen the light of day cos it's caught in that hairy construction!" The rejecter actually sounded genuinely ecstatic with amusement, gasping between each word or so, performing his recollection like an eminent thespian.

I can imagine the theatrical expressions accompanying the hilarious account: eyes bulging with intense recollection. Adding to the comedic value, the rejecter would be thrusting limbs in overly emphatic gestures, sketching out the delinquents beard with its fingertips.

Such a powerful performance brought me into the room; I chuckled under the pillow as the image of the rejecter's performance mixed with reminiscing reflections on the event under assessment. It was a short emotional lapse though. I clamped my mouth shut, killing my internal amusement and concentrated on rebuilding my disdain for the trio. I then found myself mouthing words of superciliousness towards them to resist the pull of involvement in their petty convulsions that made a conversation.

'This was all pettiness,' I mouthed to myself ' I can rise above it...I can, my mind seemed unsure, ok, it's funny... but now is not the time' I conceded.

As I returned to my dispersed state of being a non-entity in the room I noticed that the subjects had gone quiet. Tension was rising, broken only by infrequent quiet chuckles from the rejecter.

The silence was abhorrent. Even in my nest-like enclave, the frosty air that had engulfed the room could be felt. The chilling environment created an irritating itching under the skin, much like when one plunges freezing cold hands into hot water, yet the other way around. The chilly atmosphere created a crystalline veil over the three furnaces of energy. Yet, this engulfing layer did not quench the burning heat; it merely encased it; pressurized it, and ultimately intensified it.

Under such conditions the heat was bubbling over in one of the receptacles; I could hear it whispering. The rejected was murmuring to the Third Party. Like an over-pressured, overheated test tube, the bung was failing under the pressure. Obviously the jovial attempts to cool the situation had backfired; the relaxed, chilled surface was merely causing greater contrast to the burning tension inside. Luckily the bung had not been a perfect fit; it had not created a sealed lid to the receptacle and so the pressure did not build up to breaking point. The bubbling contents was able to froth out around the rim and trickle down onto the Third Party container, which was ready to collect the undesired residue.

Sadly, I could not hear what it was uttering. But I could grasp the tone, and from that an idea of the content. The pressure had been too much; the rejected wanted depressurising frankness, it was sick of wrapping the tension up in supposedly neutral, unrelated stories, only to have them politicised and even corrupted to express the underlying tensions between the subjects. The rejected was upset, but hadn't cracked; it was attempting to relieve the tension before it got out of hand.

It all hinged on the Third Party; how would it react? What would she do? Could she uphold her neutrality? Would she seek to guide and support the rejected; rallying to the call, but hindering any neutrality? Would she try to bring the two parties together to compromise and negotiate; try to tone down the rejected's complaints; or separate and contain the two parties and talk to them separately?

I sensed the rejected was already distant, I heard the occasional slurping of a beverage being consumed. Obviously nervous and wary of the threatening possibility of collusion between the other two actors, the rejecter certainly felt alone. I began to share its unease. I breathed as lightly as possible and lay poised, straining my ears in preparation to hear the Third Party's response.

Yet when she replied it was loud in volume, matter-of-fact in tone and surprisingly blunt in content:

"Yes, well, what can you expect from h_. Don't worry **you** have done what you could."

Where had the neutrality of the third party gone? Like an angered subconscious of the rejected, buzzing around the confused subject's head, the Third Party had discarded any attempt to be a mediator and was egging the rejected on.

I was sick of it all. I was feeling angry at their flagrant disregard for someone who had been a close friend and for the rejected a lover. Should I intervene? I began to ask myself. Should the fourth party get involved? Was the action of the Third Party and rejected uncalled for? Was this a necessary process for separating the two?

But, it is supposed to be the mediator's role to keep them in check and to come up with alternatives that favour neither of the mainstream approaches (or is this just a farce?). The Third Party has taken a side, so I guess the fourth party must do too.

But then the fourth party is ending its unique outsider position. Being drawn in AND taking a side with part of the mainstream; which it mustn't do. The fourth party should critically analyse the actors and the rules of the game, like a narrator or critical spectator.

Oh screw all that! This isn't a social experiment; these are my friends. My friend is in need, abandoned and under attack from two closest friends and yet the next closest friend merely hides behind linen and analyses it. This short-term conflict can be counter balanced if only I can offer some support. I want to be a friend so I should act like one. The rejecter has done no wrong, no more than the rejected: they both feel as though they may love each other; what's more they are both torturing themselves over the other. There! As the analytical observer I have learnt my lesson: the rejecter suffers just as much, if not more, than the rejected. Now I must rally behind my comrade and offer some assistance for the one in most dire need...

Rabica emerged from under the pillow. He did so in silence, as though awaking from hibernation. A thin layer of moisture covered his face. This was not perspiration; it was the condensation of his breath that had formed a sticky layer of warmth, an extra layer to his cocoon. His vision was fuzzy, not used to the light. Still within his own bubble of silence, he blinked a few times as the rest of his body creaked towards standing position, like a dreadnaught being launched. Then he stretched with an accompanied yawn, striding forward as he did so to settle himself into his new environment.

Rabica seemed not to notice the lack of reception to his re-launch; he was too preoccupied with the sense of satisfaction that overcame him as he noticed the similarity between his imagined positioning of the actors and their real position and posture. Although their locations were incorrect, the likeness was more than evident. The rejected and Janyi were even sitting on the floor, tensely backed against the wall (they were in a corner whereas he had positioned them in the centre of the room for dramatic emphasis), leaning against each other slightly. The rejecter was isolated, but in the direct firing line of any eruptions of anguish flung at it from the overwrought duo. The rejecter was leaning against the wall almost exactly opposite them.

He examined the room before him. Several empty bottles of wine lay discarded in a pile in the middle of the otherwise desolate floor. They leant against one another like some picturesque diorama, standing in their wasteland proudly, knowing they defined the landscape. Rabica found himself staring at them as though he had just discovered alien architecture on another planet, the glass structures rising in the barren dunes like an ancient forgotten temple. He continued to scan the room; the Third Party was guarding a half opened bottle. She cradled it in her lap and fiddled with the spout whilst she talked. The shimmering lights flickered glimmering patterns of green on its surface. As Janyi's body moved so did the bottle, swaying as she leaned in to the rejecter. This in turn shifted the glittering patterns of reflection. Rabica found himself enchanted by the green tinted light.

Janyi glanced at the bottle and tapped it playfully; and so instinctively Rabica jerked his head away. However the sudden movement must have alerted the Third Party; Janyi smiled at him and asked if he was all right. Rabica was momentarily distracted by confusion. When the inter-fighting had ceased, he replied in the positive, "Oh yes, I'm fine. Thank you." He felt like he should have been summoning his reserve politeness yet he found himself feeling surprisingly piquant.

He shook his head again, as though to wrest his mind from demons. When he had finished the room seemed to reach absolute zero. They all seemed to freeze, physically it was from the neck down, socially it was complete; they gazed about as though oblivious of each other. No doubt their minds raced through their internal dilemmas. Like self automated components of a once dynamic whole their heads pivoted and swung, monitoring the ground about them. Whilst their centrally controlled torsos and limbs remained fused in lifeless positions, clamped by their sides defensively like mechanical crabs. In such situations of complete alienation, time tends to seem like it has virtually frozen.

Countless minutes passed with barely a breath. The absolute hold of the stasis was shattered by their attention being brought to concentrate on the torch that had begun to flicker as though failing. Its ability to illuminate was waning in the face of the mute, hibernating subjects. Perhaps it was the growing incommensurability of time that was making the flame not feel it was receiving its worthy respect. The subjects seemed content within a vapid surrounding. So why should the flame bother to remind them of sights of the universal reality too?

It was not nonchalance that perpetuated their inaction, but a mutually constructed fear and unease that had frozen them, made them fearful of each other. It was an awkward limbo, where the misconception that it was timeless kept them imprisoned. Only the flickering of the flame held the opportunity to escape the nihilistic mental prison. The need to keep the light alive spurred Rabica into action. The flame seemed to have thawed his throat of the icy reluctance. He no longer feared to speak out to end the torture that seemed to have earned acceptance.

As he held the torch, he turned to them in the new light, "How are we all?" he announced, like a closet-outing confession, turning to stare at each in turn until they answered. Their replies were neutered.

Placing the torch back on its holder, the room dimmed in his shadow. The patchy darkness concealed much of the occupants as they clung to the walls. Sidestepping to let the flame vanquish the dark ethereal shade that stymied attempts to reawaken his friends from their vacant states, Rabica was determined to revitalise and reunify the circle.

After a few minutes of silent contemplation, Justian had a revolutionary idea and ended the collective silence.

"Perhaps it is time to call it a night."

The trio stretched and straightened like spectres awakening from the long sleep. Slowly they picked themselves up from the floor, creeping from the shadows as though assembling for a sombre death-march. The destroyed remnants of an excursion into (or indeed out of) the underworld, trudging from the battleground, their morale a bitter memory like their dignity.

The two ghouls shuffled past, yet the third being, Janyi, flittered past Rabica like a banshee. They all nodded lazily as they passed him, though Janyi seemed in a reverie, dreamily smiling to her visions. Waddling shadows accompanied the ghoul's retreat and the swooning shadow of Janyi fluttered with a gothic air as she sauntered out. Just before Janyi slammed the door, they bemoaned his name and bid him farewell. He answered abruptly, thrusting himself back into reality just before the big bang.

From the other side he could hear their dazed bickering trailing off as they were unleashed on the earth: "Are you ok?" "I am if you are." "Yes... I am." "Ok." "Why do you have to say it like that?" "Like what?" "I'm sorry..."

Finally, they had departed. Now Rabica was truly alone. He sank his head into his hands and thought profusely about the spectacle he had just witnessed. He inadvertently let out a snigger. It felt releasing.

"What a bastard!" Rabica paused. He shook his head, and then looked up to the imaginary audience, staring them in the eye. *"Using my own friends to test my crackpot theories." "Oh come on, I wouldn't have been any use. They didn't miss or need me. What could I say to reassure them?"* Rabica protested back. He was silent as he pondered an answer. The monologue ceased and the battling sides retreated within his head.

Rabica paused in contemplation. Then he realised how selfish he was being. What had begun as a dispute about his friends had descended into the squalid homeland of his own issues. Fuming with shameful anger he threw his head and arms in the air in exasperation. Secretly he was glad they had ignored him, as, if pressured, he would have had no idea what to say. Could he really have told off the rejected for being too harsh about the rejecter, especially to his face? Would sticking up for the rejecter have helped or just created a dividing line? It really did seem to shape up like the unsolvable. He guessed only time could tell, either they would mend their differences and try again or they would recognise their incompatibility and shed their affections. The problem was that not only did the latter have to happen whilst they remained friends, but also that any vigorous friction did not necessarily dampen their affections, more bring them to the surface.

With a sudden capricious jolt he returned to the earlier soliloquy, a final remark to bury the banter deep in shame. *"Hang on. What was I supposed to have learnt from this experiment?"* he queried himself rhetorically. *"That she is just as much the victim, as I if not more. I sit here and lament like some martyr expecting the gods to shine down on me just to cradle my childish whimpering. It's bad enough with all this slanderous 'she hates me' and 'oh woe me' rubbish. She must have been shocked when I told her. It'll be more torturous for her to talk to me than vice versa. I mean, I only get a bit scared, and when she's not very responsive I get paranoid that I'm boring her. She has been forced to surrender a neutral friendship to a friend-pity-fear relationship."*

"Enough of this. What of the third party project? Did the Third Party fail?"

"It tried to mediate, with early success, but got drawn in. That's the problem with Third Party mediators; they have to work between the first and second parties. Within the first two's system. As it is not an agenda setter it could only try to smooth off the harshness, or as in this case take a side. Both the first and second parties had a point and needed a mediator, yet the mediator took an explicit side. It would be hard for her to steer them onto alternative routes, as she was a minor player. Normally it would be the most stable way to deal with a dispute, a mediator slightly supportive of both, with an incentive for a resolution that will last (i.e. one which is just). The third party can mop conflict up and calm nerves if both the parties are essentially enacting with a just cause. It is at most a Problem-Solver.

I guess this is where the analogy ceases, but I can see where it should go. While Third Party can act as a reserve or rally point for the disillusioned few, if it tries to move in and gain popularity it will increasingly have to obey the agenda set by the others, closing in on their ideas, trying to slip in between them. It acts like a protest puppet, a puppy yapping at the heel of the other two. It gives the spectrum a second dimension, so it does not seem like just a single plane decision. Without it the two prime actors can slide closer and closer as there is no comparable plane to realise how close they are getting. Yet it is unstable, as it is easy to notice there is another plane, an alternative: citizens could easily step off the line and be free to spectate. Without a third party the disillusioned citizens may be tempted to set up their own outsider 'Fourth Party': one that is not linked to the spectrum and system. Three actors are needed, a triangle: Threedom. The Third party can act as a short-term protest group. If the party is a nation then as it grows in strength it will merely begin to act like them and replace one, so Lewerix cannot be a force for good. The same applies to any other 'Third Party' household. They are all dissatisfied powers, protesters who are complaining only because they are disadvantaged, latching onto the real concerns of injustice of others and using them in order to gain support (or morale), but only so they can replace the current dominant groups and impose a system beneficial to them.

Within the system the reformist third parties are ready to capture the dissidents and ensure they are moderate or alienated from the mainstream disillusionment.

This is why the Fourth Party is key; it is the outside spectator. From its position it can criticise all the parties and more importantly it can condemn the system in which they function. Unlike the third party, which, like Janyi, cannot make long-term critical stances without succumbing to a side. Although they will achieve some reform they are ultimately a distraction from larger scale problems and are only relatively better.

In political situations the fourth party can mobilise and educate from outside. From this view it is more objective, obviously not totally impartial. It can truly direct and help those in need through mobilisation and education, without tumbling into demagoguery."

Rabica paused, lifting his head from his sweating palms; slightly baffled. "I got all that, but was it worth abandoning my friends?"...

Chapter 10
The Messenger

Adonis Gatan did not even flinch as the sudden thumping sound resonated from the solid door to his chamber. He calmly slipped out of his contemplatory state and focused on the robust oak door. Its ornate but sturdy iron studs formed a rigid structure with their shining iron struts that linked them in an unyielding framework. The door could withstand a heavy crossbow bolt from point blank with barely a dent.

"Enter," he growled authoritatively.

The heavy hinge creaked as the door slowly swung open. Arutha, Adonis' most trusted and fearsome bodyguard heaved with his mighty muscles as he drove the door open, like an ox pushing a mill wheel. The sturdy door stopped just short of striking the beam beside it. His impressive full beard stretched around his head into the mighty mane that crowned his scalp like a fearsome crest. His large facial features puffed slightly as he winced behind the weight of the door.

The beaming behemoth raised his head to look upon the equally staunch lord, who sat cowled in his mighty fur cloak.

"A messenger is here, sire," Arutha spoke softly but firmly. "…From the Latman household," he added cautiously.

At that moment a nervous boyish face peered around the door, at first Adonis thought it a mocking apparition of Juscius Latman. The messenger murmured something, clearly in a state of total intimidation.

"Let him in," Adonis answered.

Arutha, living barbican, instinctively leaned against the mighty bulkhead-door and thrust a glare at the messenger giving him a miniscule nod that was of military precision.

The messenger was very young, a slight boy of around thirteen. He stumbled into the room shaking and making furtive glances at the guardian statues that were draped with a silky black shadow in the eerie orange half-light. With each glance at either of the towering warriors, he would jerk his head towards a statue as though deflecting his fear of the two flesh-and-blood colossi to one of the dormant pieces. He slid forward on the square-slab floor, like a cornered pawn trying to rush the king at its ambling pace.

The image of the trembling messenger began to replace the obnoxious, strutting figure of Juscius Latman that haunted Adonis' imagination. Lord Gatan could not help but smile to himself.

Once the boy had approached the desk, he proceeded to bow right down so his head rested on his left knee, which was bent out as he lowered. In the moments whilst the messenger was concealed from Adonis' view, the Lord half suspected the jester-Lord Juscius to spring up from below the worktop horizon, and cackle jovially in his face. To Adonis' relief the same red-faced mewling child reappeared, convulsing profusely. Once upright the messenger extended a trembling hand that weakly clutched a sealed envelope.

"Your highness, Lord Latman sends his greetings and desires that you read the message as soon as you are willing," he reeled.

Adonis looked across into the boy's eyes with a slight look of bemusement. The paranoid messenger, believing he had unwittingly defied custom and held his head too high slouched sheepishly, darting his eyes down evasively. Adonis slowly outstretched his hand, testing the boy's nerves. As his hand neared he could feel the wet heat of the boy's fear perspiring off his body. A steam composed of evaporating confidence swirled as it was extracted by the fearsome authoritative glare of the Lord.

Then, with lightening reflexes, he snatched the envelope from the messenger's loose grip. The boy nearly jumped out of his skin and narrowly avoided shrieking aloud.

"You may go," Adonis ordered emotionlessly.

Quivering, the messenger boy bowed and fled the chamber.

With a nod and a slight upward turning of the right side of his mouth, Adonis signalled to Arutha to treat the messenger with the fullest of hospitality. The granting of such amiability was partially out of pity for the trembling boy's nerves, but mostly as a celebration of the death of the haunting demon-jester.

Obediently the hulking warrior closed the door with a slow, expressionless heave.

Beginning at just over 90° the face of the door momentarily disappeared before reappearing on the other side. At first, the whole face was dark as it hid behind its own shadow. With a mighty flash the first shimmering pattern appeared; a pure white reflection from the tips of the studs that contrasted tremendously with the dark frame. Arutha winced slightly at 70°. It was at precisely 62° that the glistening eruption of the torches reflection had spread across the entire face of the door. The iron frame shone like a mirror of white, whilst the wooden beams reflected a patchy gleam of orange.

The door slammed shut with a monumental crack.

Adonis smiled to himself as he briefly recollected the spectacle of light as though it had been the passing of a comet. The event had to be just right, with the glistening white shimmering like the sea, spreading across the iron bars like ripples in the water, engulfing the stretches of land in liquid light. Then celebrating the sweeping victory with an almighty crash.

He looked down at the scroll. It was sealed with the Latman eagle insignia stamped on wax. His nose instinctively wrinkled as he stroked the wax lightly with the tip of his index finger. His caressing got harsher as he thought of the first day his father had explained the Latman-Gatan situation. With a sudden flash, the youthful apparition of Juscius the jester-lord was back torturing his mind with its mischievous taunting. He had never met his adversary; he did not need to, this creature already plagued him in his head, daintily burrowing and tunnelling deep. He imagined a hedonistic crusader prancing around in shining polished armour (which had only been used for exquisite banquets and parades) eloquently pronouncing idealistic rhetoric of his new craze; 'the new interpretation'. Theatrical young swashbuckler-barons giggled and cheered at the darting darling, who grinned smugly as he fenced an imaginary combatant with a red rose. The thespian-lord cavorted about his golden chamber espousing meaningless but impressive aphorisms. The hall was a den of frolicking and debauchery, masquerading as a dedication to (half of the) gods. The adolescent demagogue skipped about as he threw malicious defamatory remarks about Galex. The puppy-barons lapped up the lords spewing, yelping and barking in pleasure, exalting and praising Thelus whilst damning Athyle.

Adonis shook off the visions. He took a last glance at the seal. The eagle had been scratched out of existence and the wax shone with a ruby glint, evidence that it had begun to melt under the onslaught of Adonis' fingers. The seal folded awkwardly then snapped, the semi-molten wax stretching out into strands. Like two intimately involved squids the stretching tendrils of the two halves resisted separation, desperately interlocking even as they were drawn apart.

Lord Gatan reached into the envelope and took out a scroll; he squinted to read the extravagant swirling scripture that elegantly decorated the page. He read it.

Most Exalted Lord Adonis Gatan,

My sincere greetings to you and your family and indeed your whole house. I hope that you will welcome my open courteous hand and forgive our houses' apparent lack of diplomatic contact. For too long we have grappled over petty inconveniences without truly seeking to deal with the underlying problems and more importantly the actual common ground that we share. We are both pioneers, sailing the same sea with our loyal crews. Searching for stable shores on which we could anchor. I write with a proposition for a council of all lords for discussion of the resolution of an issue which plagues my house, and which must be of prime importance of all the islands inhabitants. The lands of Latman Household have had marked encounters with the Baresark heathens, a growing problem of which I am sure you are aware. This infestation could be easily resolved with more co-operation. Additionally if any houses wish to deal with border issues, which seem to inflict our island, this may be a perfect opportunity. I believe that this is a time of progress, where united as one, we can end the unruly conundrum that afflicts this most worthy island. Your presence is of the utmost importance as the unity of our houses can be an example to the less civilised factions. I hope you will take the opportunity and trust your wisdom to make your decision the right one. Further, if you could bless this project with your support and make this known to the other houses, which would be inspired by your bravery and readiness (especially your noble and enduring ally Vacarium), it would service as a massive bolster to our success.

I thank you for your time and pray for your good health. May the eternal blessings of the mighty god Thelus be upon you.

His Royal Highness Lord Juscius Latman I

As he read the letter, the demon-jester-lord was squirming in his brain, wriggling joyfully as it bathed in the torrent of anger that swelled in his mind. Its bloated body inflated as it fed on his resentment. He felt a pain in his right ear; the jester-demon was writhing past his eardrum. There was a pop and the miniature of his nemesis was born; mincing about the room, scurrying over reports and kicking at them to scuff them with its curly shoes. It taunted him with its boisterous demeanour, pouring out mocking remarks.

Adonis snorted dismissively at the parading apparition, but could not help a growing feeling of inadequacy faced with the gleeful perfection, and the youthful delight of a young man in his prime. He stared down at his own wrinkled hands. They were thick and meaty, but crude, cracked and covered in worn skin. Hairs erroneously wisped out of the primeval digits. He looked up to locate the imaginary adolescent lord prancing about in total joy. With a single blink the lord was transformed into the innocent virgin-lord embracing his dearest mother, but the masquerade was instantly revealed for its true private self, the mother disappeared and was replaced by a horde of high-class strumpets and baronesses (they all seemed the same to the out-of-touch lord Gatan). Like bees hovering around a sweet sickly flower they followed the pansy-lord, who playfully caressed them with kisses, drawing them closer, willing them in.

Adonis was disgusted, yet enthralled, struck by a disturbing sense of virulent eroticism. His usually reserved virility found itself overcome with sexual greed. The more the lead apparition played with one of the wenches, the more the others wanted it. Suddenly the painted ladies disappeared, their laughter trailing in the air. Adonis blinked again; it wiped the 'screen' clean. He opened his eyes to see the baby-lord again cradled in his mother's arms. Like some messiah he muttered to the holy mother. Both were dressed in white, a bright, no doubt tainted, white. Juscius looked up at Adonis and a suggestive grin formed on the misleadingly boyish face. Adonis shivered. Nausea began to engulf him. He took a long blink.

Adonis thought of the eagle that adorned the seal; this pouting young pup made a mockery of the symbol; a sinister carnivorous dove masquerading as a graceful symbol of a change in leadership towards a thin veil of peace.

The torches flickered in the corners of the room. He felt frustrated, angered by his dreamy distractions. Once he had calmed himself Adonis found his normal level-headedness return. Trying to brush over the implicit snubs in the letter he decided it was best to accept the offer, call the bluff, he had nothing to hide. Not like this pip-squeak of a lord. This was *his* chance too. He could pull off a colossal stunt as he marched into Lateria with his bodyguards and some invention of Gorax's. He could command the lesser houses and ally the middle houses against this pompous crusader. Adonis could see right through that arrogant lord: he was a puppet to his own confused agenda. No doubt someone else was pressuring him for their own reasons.

No doubt the lord-boy was seeking to trick him into subordination through humiliation at this banquet. Well, Adonis would show him. Besides if he did not go, the thespian-lord would have a free rein.

"Now for the tone of my reply," Adonis pondered. "Should I be aggressive? Snide? Or feign ignorance of his little jibe?" He thought intently for a moment. "No, I should rise above it all. Send a cordial reply that is totally decent and proper. That saves me the disgrace of sinking to his childish tactics and will lull him into a false sense of security. If he wants a reaction, he will have to wait until the time comes, when I can do it in style and with household dignity, not worthless sniping with the quill."

Adonis set about writing the reply.

★

The messenger hungrily stuffed his face, whilst furtively glancing about the desolate room. It was stone, with an earthy damp feeling. It was well lit but not very inviting; cubby windows let in a pale vapid light, and the room had a musky, mossy aroma. His hands shook as he fiddled with the huge hunk of bread. As his trembling mouth tore chunks out and rapidly ground them into a rough pulp ready for abruptly swallowing. The messenger focused on the mosaic adjacent to him. It portrayed a Gatan Lord in battle with lots of squat Latman guards. The Lord's beaming face of bravery seemed emotionless and coolheaded in the onslaught, unlike the brutish features of the assailants that surrounded him.

It was then that the messenger heard the heavy thumping of boots and the laughter of some youngish men. He instinctively shrank into a hunched position like a startled rabbit, nibbling at the bread nervously. The noises got closer and the messenger froze, staring wide-eyed straight ahead. The door latch went and he bolted upright. Then the door began to creak open and he instantly shrank back down, poised like a cornered rat. He furtively glanced to his left, where the door was opening, without turning his head. In a desperate panic his head instinctively snapped towards the only possible escape (he had already decided the windows were too small): the door he had been let in by. A bellowing laugh echoed from behind the rapidly opening door, which caused the messenger to quiver transfixed by fear. The iron grip on his jaw loosened and it swung open weakly, revealing remnants of half-eaten bread.

Within seconds two men in their mid twenties stood proudly in the doorway. They were stocky in build though not excessive, their builds suggesting a near perfect balance of strength and agility. Straight away they noticed the hunched boy. One sported a small stubbly beard, the other was clean-shaven, and their hair was identical in colour, a piercing dark brown, which was virtually black. Both were clearly handsome and important.

The clean-shaven one laughed and approached the boy. "What have we here?" He turned to the other young man who grinned and chuckled slowly.

"What are you doing here, boy?" The clean-shaven one queried again, with a distinct mocking-harshness.

The messenger tried to stutter something incomprehensible.

"He's from Latman." The clean-shaven man seemed surprised, with a sense of bitter delight; he was now barely a metre from the messenger. "Taking our food."

The last statement was said in jest but the frightened messenger found it difficult to be sure and could not avoid trembling. He had never been prepared for this. He began to wonder if this was it. The end. Thelus had no use for a quivering wreck like him. He had been sent to his death because he was no use. Thrust into the pack of wolves to be devoured and fill the belly of the savages. To quench their ever-thirsting desire for blood.

"Hmm...what's Latman doing here?" pondered the bearded youth, stroking his facial hair thoughtfully as though in deep contemplation.

"I'm ...messenger," the boy stammered, though his breath was gone so it came only as a whisper in the dank air.

"Ooh..." exclaimed the clean-shaven man.

"We gathered that," answered the bearded one, in a matter-of-fact tone that was laced with loose sarcasm, but not acidic.

"Give us some cheese, boy," requested the clean-shaven man. His tone was not forceful but the petrified messenger was already intimidated. He handed the man some cheese, trying to minimise his trembling. It failed.

"Don't worry, boy. Not gonna hurt you, been knackering ourselves out beating each other in the training room. Plus don't reckon you'd be much of a fight anyway." He paused. "Well, not yet anyway...huh?" He laughed unthreateningly.

The boy nodded and tried to smile, though his frozen facial muscles merely contorted as though he was about to burst into tears. He struggled with the fear that constricted his face.

When he had regained his senses, he noticed the bearded man had approached him. "Hey, lad, don't worry. Cheer up." He reassured, tapping the messenger on the shoulder in a friendly if somewhat patronising way.

"We'd better go see what Father's got to say about all this," the clean shaven man announced.

"Unless you want another caning?" replied the bearded man, punching his brother lightly on the back.

"Yeah right. I was well ahead of you!" came the headstrong retort

"Catch you later," the bearded man shot at the messenger.

"Quite literally," laughed the clean-shaven one as they left.

They departed by the door that Arutha no doubt stood guard at on the other side.

The slam of the door resonated in the messenger's mind as he sat staring at the solid oak bulkhead, frozen stiff as though awaiting their sudden return. He imagined them storming back in with axes to cleave chunks of feeble flesh from his skimpy frame. With his exterior in frozen stasis he could feel every pulse in his veins, throbbing with the gurgling, thick liquid that circulated around him, keeping his mind red hot with syrupy fear. The pounding of his heart sent waves of energy through his arteries, pulsating like a lava flow that crashed into the solid block of a capped volcano. He could feel the pressure building up; the little organ was driving with such force he thought it was on the brink of exploding. As the warm liquid surged through the narrow passages of his body it itched against the icy sheet of hypnotic fear that had overcome his exterior and seized his muscles in a thorough deep-freeze.

Yet it was an external movement, namely the fiery entrance of Arutha, that shattered the grey ice of fear. As the beast approached, the messenger twitched, his muscles thawing and stretching out of their taut incarceration. Strangely, for some reason he no longer feared the hulking monstrosity, that now resembled a gentle giant who had stumbled upon the bewitched boy.

"Still munchin' away boy?" queried the hulk, in the patronising tone of a distant father.

The messenger boy resumed nibbling the bread, now with many tiny gnaws, his teeth chattering and scraping away at the remaining hunk like a startled rabbit. Still transfixed with fear, the young mammal contemplated scampering into the burrow hole it had created in the bread, the intimidation still associated with the size of the approaching beast shrinking him to a size that rendered the burrow large enough.

The peaceful ogre leaned into whispering distance of the messenger. "Don't worry about the boys; they were just having some harmless fun. They don't mean any of it. They're just being boys. They're like that with everyone. You'll be like that someday…" He looked the child up and down, "…well maybe you won't," he whispered, primarily to himself, as he withdrew.

Though the messenger found it comforting that Arutha had been listening through the door in case he needed protection, he was still scared and so had to feign a nod and smile.

Once fully upright, Arutha patted the messenger reassuringly on the shoulder.

"Your horse is fed too. Good luck young man," he declared earnestly.

★

Lord Gatan had finished the letter; he had been as cordial as possible, but at the same time retained his authoritative tone. He had refrained from mentioning Vacarium, for it was an issue he felt passionate (and extremely knowledgeable – something the young Juscius was most certainly in short supply of) about and though he wanted to make his position clear he feared he may overdo it and so would rather be present to be able to gauge the rat-lords squeaks and reveal its misconceptions. Besides, he did not want to ruin the banquet-council before it had even been organised.

As he sat back in his throne-like chair his mind drifted back to when he had been young and his father had sent him to Vacarium for training. It had been a secret operation, which had prepared him for suitability of office by making him the hardened and quick-witted fighter he was today. Perhaps it was ironic that the now deceased lord had sent his son to foreign lands to imprint him with the Gatanese military tradition, but nevertheless it was a success. Gatan's power and relative stability meant there was little in the way of experience on home soil, so he had been sent to the harsh mountainous region of the Gatan ally. The hardship of those days had made him. Living with the mountain people, he had learn micro-tactics, personal strategies of subsistence and general techniques of sustaining morale that surpassed any theorising or even practical experience of military training. Adonis had felt as though he had gone back centuries to the true Gatan roots. Such was the Gatan way, if times were relatively soft, an heir must travel to find those hardships or he will fail when they return. There was no relishing in good times for a lord; he must be responsible and capable, just like his ancestors. What is more, he had proved his worth amongst the generals, not just the top brass who were aware of his training but to all when they saw the outcome of the training in his strategic planning afterwards.

Roaming the mighty hills, raiding Latman outposts and scouting, he had felt truly free. Secretly he longed for a return to those days. It was then that he had proved his worth, not among aspiring generals, but amongst the men, side by side with comrades and trusted allies. He felt the uttmost respect for the tribesmen and Vacarium scouts alike, brothers in arms against the ambitious crusaders. The simple ideals of survival and protection combined with a well-disciplined nomadism that despite its hardship felt truly free. Every man and woman counted in those days; every member from top to bottom was significant, fulfilling an essential role, a component in the organic machine. In such a society the leaders were truly respected, truly needed. Those below them were compelled to co-operate, and obey.

Whatever his personal feelings, he knew the friendship between Gatan and Vacarium was still viable. But he was worried that his personal affinity to Vacarium, and more importantly, his private hatred of the arrogant Juscius Latman II; the flamboyant crusader-usurper, could cloud his judgement.

It was a concern, a looming fear that his association of the crusader lord with inconsiderate extravagance and ignorance, contrasted with his own grizzled experience, and love of the dirt, was creating such an intense personal hatred as to render him unable to assess the situation objectively.

His concerns turned to the apparition, not only did it cloud his judgment with personal animosity but its very appearance suggested he was losing his clear-headedness. It was a sign that he was failing himself and ultimately his household by succumbing to the influence of his own personal demons. He remembered that he should not judge his enemy as a person; instead, he should seek to appraise him as a political threat in an objective way. He was not judge of people; only the gods could do that.

Chapter 11
The Birth of an Epoch

Juscius smiled whilst Torian gently caressed his short hair. He turned to her and slowly stroked her peach-like cheek; she smiled back and let out a sigh. She looked around the garden. The paradise: the only suitable abode for their love. The well-kept grass waved in the soothing breeze, the sprout tips swaying as though in worship of her long hair that floated in the air like a shining black halo for her beaming face. Waxy petals glimmered in the glorious sunlight. Built in secrecy, this was their hideaway from the bustle of business and court; a retreat for them to be expressive without the beady eye of society. For some reason the earthly necessities of politics were determined to quash their celestial emotion and dedication to each other. The dirt of the epoch could not comprehend this spiritual bonding. Juscius felt it was preposterous that the mundane realm of man could restrain this perfect unity that the gods themselves praised.

Juscius had dug out a shrine below this gate to the heavens to shield it from the earthly evils that oozed out of the underworld to infect the realm of man. The barrier had become Zeuorox's abode, where he warded off the putrifications that sought to corrupt man and hold him in spiritual limbo; incarcerated in a horrific oubliette never to reach his destiny in the sky.

Here the sickening couple could express themselves without exposure to the raw harshness of the world. Here the innocent lovers could express their true feelings through words and float in each other's gentle candour.

"Why can't every day be like this?" asked Torian dreamily.

"Because Thelus has work for us both. But, my dear, one day we will be together. We will purge this island, and then we can have each other. Then they will understand our love."

She sighed and looked downwards gloomily; the sunlight seemed to wave with her:

"But your mother wants you to marry politically; to marry Telis' sister." She set her face in a sulky pout.

"I can't marry in such a way. You are a sign that I must continue in my fateful destiny: to be united with you. Heretics plague us, and she is from a people of heathens."

She glanced up to catch his eye; once adequately entranced she burst into a smile.

Enraptured, Juscius sat staring into her eyes: misty whirlpools that whirled gracefully and emitted the emotive gleam that his eyes could elicit.

"Surely the gods will save our love. Surely it means more than any earthly spat. It would be a sin to deny our emotions, leave them dormant. Our emotions for each other are rich with divinity; the prime goal of our ethical duty," Juscius drivelled.

She looked in feigned puzzlement, hiding the mischievous tease of an intelligent lover.

"The gods will decide. They will guide us to purity," beamed Juscius.

Torian giggled. The deep blue mists in the sky wafted and amalgamated with wisps of cotton-wool cloud; her eyes; the whirlpools of beauty seemed to freeze into a serious stare. "So how is it our duty?"

"If fate decides, how do we do anything?" she laughed.

His hurt expression was the true source of her amusement, though she felt compelled to conceal it behind giggling befuddlement.

"Because, they decide who is worthy in the earthly realm. Only those men who are obedient to their wish shall be blessed with their protection."

She laughed and the eye-beads became mists again as she swayed in rhythm to the wind. She held him under the chin and looked him in the eye playfully. "I see..." she smiled, and rubbed her nose lightly against his. "Well we had better be good *men* then hadn't we!"

Enraptured by her dainty look his face exploded into a smile of adoration.

"Once I have succeeded, once the earthly realm deserves our love, it shall have it. Then the island shall be Thelus' beacon in the earthly purgatory."

"Aaah, that's so romantic," Torian replied, in a slightly patronising tone. No doubt she recognised the sickening sweetness of their exchange. The sugary syrup was sickeningly saccharine; thankfully, for the sake of the human race, there were no onlookers to be overwhelmed with the vomit-worthy milieu. Such a sickly rich sensation would infect one's throat, eating at the neck and causing an uncomfortable throbbing itch in one's head as though from a sugar rush, pounding at the physical and mental support struts of the brain.

Yet they, the two lovers, did not retch.

Nor did the tweeting swallow that had perched like a feathery cherub on a blossoming sapling near them.

They smiled ecstatically at each other, overwhelmed by the moment.

Then they embraced. As Juscius leant forward and rested his neck on her shoulder, in a perfect setsquare-like fit, Torian turned her head, in a most vomit-inducing cliché, so she could look him in the eyes and press her middle finger to his lips. She then proceeded to complete the sickening display with a patronising kiss on the cheek. Then she fled, silently exiting through the trapdoor to the shrine.

Juscius sat alone, observing his paradise. In front of him a beautifully sculptured statue of Angara stood resolute and charming, just like Torian. Indeed, the resemblance was deliberate. Her outstretched hand was cupped and the little finger parted from the other fingers so a small stalk of a flower could be wedged between the little digit and the other fingers, securing it in a peaceful clasp. Her other hand rested calmly on her heart and supported the ethereal gown that was draped over her. The sculptor had perfected the shimmering look of the material as it rippled behind her as though flung out by a brisk breeze. Surrounding the idol was a moat of sparkling water.

The swallow landed on the statue's outstretched hand; it cocked its head, staring at the smooth surface of her face and chirped innocently. The sound was mellifluous to Juscius' ears. Then it hopped twice to perch on her wrist. Juscius grimaced as he found himself focusing on the tiny claws that griped the pale thin wrist. He whistled and the bird cocked its head the other way for a few seconds then launched off, swerving about the garden before disappearing into the perimeter hedge.

Suddenly the bell in the far corner by the trapdoor rang out. Juscius jumped at the unexpected intrusion of noise. It summoned him from the paradise; Zeuorox operated it from his shrine. Only he and a trusted servant knew of the utopia, each entrusted to guard an entrance.

Slowly and reluctantly the young lord rose from his sprawled position and brushed himself down. He picked up his cloak that had been laid on the fresh turf to keep her ladyship dry. Carefully, he draped it around his shoulders and clipped on the brooch around his neck. He daintily crossed the lush grass to the bell. It hung lifelessly from its wooden perch that was wedged between a two-pronged pillar that rose from the shrine concealed under the greenery.

Juscius reached for a handle that stuck out of the left face of the column. Grape vines twisted up the stones, elegantly winding up the brickwork like rigid tendrils. Individually they were swirling streaks of creativity; together they formed a giant root of rigidly gripping onto the structure.

With self-reassuring coolness the lord yanked on the mechanism of the hulking structure. The trapdoor to the shrine slowly arched upright, creaking with a revitalising sound of aged mysticism. Juscius eagerly bounded over to the trapdoor and hurriedly descended. He stepped into the shimmering ankle-depth pool before entering the temple. Ceremoniously he shook his feet of droplets, bowing before taking one of the dry towels. Once satisfactorily dry he pitter-pattered on into the main room of the shrine.

Compared to the seemingly endless green paradise of the garden, the shrine was small and dank, a crammed room of piled scrolls and incense. Yet it was surprisingly light, bearing in mind its submersion. Painted glass panels seemed to spread a spectacular blue aurora, and the startling haze contrasted starkly with the yellowish-white bulbs of light that floated above the numerous candlesticks. Bronze and copper cups and goblets seemed black but glistened with illuminated speckles of sky blue light that tarnished their silhouette on the blue background panes.

There, behind his desk, stood Zeuorox. His wiry frame concealed under extravagant robes and frills, and his beard was neatly trimmed into a small and fashionable moustache and goatee. Countless white candles that managed to offset the blueness of the rest of the room surrounded him. There was an unusual gleam of excitement in his typically emotionless face: a beady tranquillity in his gaunt eyes.

Juscius strode up to him.

"What is it, your Excellency?" Juscius asked with a pleasant calmness.

The robed cleric bowed stiffly. "You have a visitor sire... a very important visitor," he answered emotionlessly. The monotone words mirrored in his vacant eyes, the whites of which glimmered like beads in the light. A myriad pattern of veins in the eyeball gave the pearls a pinkish gleam.

The young lord's mind raced with excitement. Was it a messenger from Gatan or another minor house? It seemed too soon.

Zeuorox paused momentarily then slowly turned to the door and gestured. "This way, my lord?" The statement was masqueraded as a request.

They stepped into the corridor. Juscius followed the sombre cleric past the heavenly statues that stood to attention at each side. Just before the darkness engulfed them, Juscius glared at the finely chiselled face of a sculpture of Heric, the mischievous semi-bestial messenger of Thelus. In the degenerate light, Juscius saw how striking it looked, the few rays of light highlighting its most obvious and necessary grooves with bold black lines, and at the same time illuminating the white stone with pretence of blanketed purity. In the semi-light it seemed unblemished, with a startling contrast of well-defined furrows outlining a playful blithe creature forged from a shimmering radiant ore. The familiar face made him smile.

As Juscius blindly followed the swish of Zeuorox's robes he heard the clanking of keys and clicking of the lock mechanism followed by the screech of the bolt latch. The door creaked open into a startlingly well-lit small room. The shower of golden rays filled the young lord with zealous pride, illuminating the final stages of the path in a blinding light. Juscius did not look behind him to see the exposed deity, dappled and gnarled with shades of grey and cracks betraying the previous appearance of smoothness. It was as though the salient torchlight had burnt off the shadows that sought to embellish the statute's profile.

Juscius was instead in awe at the spectacle before him. Bright lamps were flooding the room with a divine all-engulfing light; it was such a luminous white that Juscius assumed it must be of celestial origin.

Of course in reality they were actually devised by the servant, Promana, using a special fuel that utilised a chalk-based lime residue and a metallic component that caused the first blinding sparks. Nevertheless, half-blinded by the sudden contrast in available light, to Juscius they were a relic to remind him of his first spiritual encounter with Zeuorox.

The high priest currently stood in the centre of the doorway like a silhouetted angel against a blessed bright backdrop. His robes draped either side of him, bulking his actually fragile frame into a mighty figure standing proud and steadfast in the ecclesiastical milieu of the room. The returning pilgrims entered the room, Zeuorox sidestepping to allow Juscius to approach the tiny rippling cleansing-pools. There were two of these 'pools', though they they were actually miniature streams that flowed endlessly through pipes that were concealed under the tiles opening out into these square patches that resembled pools. Adjacent to each pool were two patches of material, a brown mat of coarse hairs and a green softer rug-like segment. One pool was for entering the shrine, the other for leaving. This was determined by which mat was on which side of the pool, the brown always being the first. Towels hung on each side of the pools ready to try off the holy water.

The water was pure and transparent; wave currents rushed across the pool's depths like swirling tapeworms, wriggling with the man-made tide. A herbal aroma drifted from the streams, but was occasionally overcome by a faint waft of the burnt metal that was used to start the lamps.

Juscius stepped onto the bristly brown rug. The coarse hairs streaked out of the hard surface. The sudden pricks sent his foot nerves tingling. As he wriggled his toes the speckled mass flicked against his reddened sole. This was to awaken the senses and prepare them for the plunge out of his sanctuary.

Juscius raised his right foot then drove it forward before plunging it down into the pool, in a three-part series of perpendicular motion. It was followed by the left foot, mimicking the right exactly. The water was ice cold, a refreshing sensation of a newly exhaled breath from Weih, the wind creature tamed by Weihros the wind god. He shook his feet, daintily manoeuvring his feet with such precision as to ensure that not a single droplet rose out of the shimmering sheet of ripples. The ripples themselves lapped against the top of his ankles attempting to clamber up his shin. Then he stopped dead still so that the miniature waves could dance around his ankles. Satisfied, he stepped onto the soft green pad of cloth, and dabbed his numbed soles against its soothing surface. Ceremoniously, he took a towel and rubbed his feet dry, then put on the sandals that awaited him. Then he began the trek past the next door and out of the chamber. He stood still, perpendicular, in the corridor, where two passages met as crossroads.

Zeuorox had not followed and stood anxiously twiddling his thumbs. Gloomily he stared at the lord. After a brief pause of frozen-to-the-spot silence, Juscius slowly turned his head uneasily so he could make out the high priest's figure in the corner of his eye. The cleric cleared his throat abruptly in order to ensure he had captured the lord's attention. "The guest is in the left waiting chamber."

This meant it was somebody important. He strode over to the door to the room at a deliberately protracted pace, his flimsy sandals somehow mustering up resonating slapping clicks with each step. He opened the door rapidly, and marched in, head held high in pride. Looking down at the seat, he expected to see his visitor, yet it was empty. He noticed a bright puffy blob of cloth standing by the table with the decanter. It was accompanied by a sound: "Aye". This was followed up with a familiar sound. "Jus!"

Within a millisecond of recognition the two-year long glacier that had solidified around a section of Juscius' youthful heart shattered: It was Ruperis.

They embraced, gripping each other tightly. Juscius could smell the briny smell of sea-salt laced with a pungent spicy aroma that drifted into his nostrils sporadically. As the two companions separated they held each other's hands, smiling as though boys again. To Juscius it seemed dreamlike; finally he had returned. The swashbuckler, the merchant raider, the swindling quasi-pirate prince had returned from his seafaring gallivant to chart (and profit from) the unknown.
The plundering entrepreneur.

It was only now that Juscius first contemplated the danger his companion had been in. Not once had he even considered the possibility of peril for his comrade. Never did it cross his mind that Ruperis was pursuing a hazardous voyage, from which he could have never returned.

When he had left, Ruperis had been bouncing up and down the craft, dancing and waving like a youngster. He had acted so theatrically, like a child at play. It had seemed more like he was just racing fishing boats or searching for non-existent treasure, not sailing into the unknown.

Ruperis' hair was shoulder length and waxed back immaculately with animal fat that had been mixed with some flowery residue to give it a substantially more pleasant aroma. He was clean-shaven, except for a tiny square patch of beard, which had been perfectly placed in the exact centre of his chin. His left ear housed a sizeable earring. He was exquisitely dressed: medallions hung around his neck, flashing impressive beams of gold in the sunlight that shone in from the high windows. These were not a sailor's lucky charm, a humble offering to a god; they were symbolic icons of the self. A grand red and orange cloak swished with his attention-seeking poses and gestures. His white shirt was puffy and spotless; it was impossible to believe it had seen two years at sea. His trousers were black and tight, gripping onto the once spindly legs. Below these were well polished shoes.

This impressive deity was topped off with a vast array of jewels that glittered on the rings that covered his fingers like badges of import. This parade of multicoloured lights was only surpassed by the ornate belt that was littered with a rainbow of sequins. All in all, his appearance was remarkable, a well-preened hero returning from his adventure. However, who was he the hero of? This idol of heroism seemed characteristically un-Latman; it had the unique dynamism of something new: He was the fresh-faced entrepreneurial deity.

Yet his actual face was unusually pale, especially for a man out on deck in the blasting sunrays. Still, he seemed his usual chirpy self.

"So, what crazy antics have you been up to?" grinned the traveller. Juscius shrugged.

"How's Torian?" the merchant-swashbuckler winked.

Was this fraternal intuition wrapped up in a feigned innocent joke?

Lord Latman found the returning friend impossible to read.

He offered a silent prayer to Thelus for his boyhood friend's soul.

"More importantly, what '*crazy antics*' have *you* been up to?"

Ruperis laughed aloud. It began as a booming chortle, descending into a childish giggle. Every change in tone resonated at a more painful pitch in Juscius' heart. It took a good minute of cackling for Ruperis to notice the lack of humour on the lord's face.

For a moment there was silence. The first silence between these two in their long history. The two boyhood friends had returned to each other, reaching maturity in way constituted by surprisingly different lives. Commerce impacted upon the new world of the Ecclesiastical.
They probed each other for common cause.

The swift machete of information sliced the vapid but weighty atmosphere:

"The stuff we found out there! The opportunities for House Latman, the potential assets for us both are beyond belief."

"We sailed north of the island for over a month, our resources were low, but austerity prevailed and we found land. We found some inhabitants, who were most impressed. A simple folk, brown-haired peasants, their scalps the colour of an elk, actually I've got one if you want a look! Once we'd introduced ourselves with the just amount of vehemence they were quite docile settled farmers. Productive in their little way. They were not like the towering blond beasts; in fact they are plagued by those sea devils too." He changed the subject back to potential propitious accumulation. "Their land is fertile, ideal for agriculture, though they lack our techniques. That is what they need of course, they are begging for our colonisation of their land. There seems to be abundant and easy to access metal deposits as well, iron was commonplace."

"Well, we headed further north and struck upon many similar tribes, they were non-descript pale, brown-haired. Anyway there wasn't a lot there; simple beads and rocks... oh and plenty of fish. Even pink ones!"

"Well anyway, we braved the rough seas and headed north, battling against a strong southerly wind. It was becoming more and more bitterly cold, as though we were entering the icy reaches of hell."

Ruperis paused as though in contemplation.

"I know they say hell is fiery, but believe me, this desolate, inhospitable environment is the most harsh and torturous place known to man. It is truly bleak; the elements are all battering against you, and that one saving grace of an element, fire, cannot even get a wisp of warmth to you. The flames are torn from their roots in the embers and thrown into the maelstrom of squabbling wind currents and bombarding showers of precipitation. The storms and gales tossing our vessel about, thunder cackling out the laughter of the gods, the whistling wind luring us on with a sinister whine that must have been plucked from the seductive vocal cords of sirens. What is worse, so secluded is this land from the warmth of Thelus and Prometha that most of the day is blanketed with darkness, and even the daylight is not from the sun but a dreary haze of white, that is almost blinding in its intense blandness. It must be the brightest nothingness experienced by man. One cannot tell if it is a close up thick fog or a far distant sheet or screen of pure white offset by the howling winds into a hazy shroud. Personally, I believe it to be a mystical trick of Weihros."

Ruperis paused, half expecting Juscius to launch into a tirade about how Weihros was a 'good' god'. His mischievous temperament was disappointed, though.

"Unsurprisingly, this is the habitat of those hulking blond beasts. No doubt the harshness of the environment has warped them into the ferocious beings they have become. They spew forth from the frozen gates and border tundra wastelands of hell to wreak havoc on the emulations of the gods. They themselves have been weathered by the harsh environment into the savages they are. No doubt, they are sick of scrabbling in the snow-covered dirt of their own lands in search of grubs and so have chosen to plague us with their bloodlust... and if you think they are horrific, you should see their women. I use the term loosely, they are not women, they are merely classifiable as females. They are brutish, guttural hags. But then when you've been at sea all that time you aren't fussy!"

Juscius ignored the perverse twinkle in Ruperis' eye.

"Anyway they are pitiful as a society, these baresarks. No civilisation at all, they are like nomadic primates of the sea. Their land of banishment offers them little, yet they cannot leave it for good, their females stay in their shacks whilst the strongest men venture out to wreak disaster on mankind and return with spoils."

Ruperis paused dramatically. "Well anyway, we had an incident with some of their females so we never really got very far into their wasteland. We burnt the evidence... and yet somehow they caught up with us and scavenged our ship whilst most of us were out hunting." His face turned to a sour look of utter disgust. "Savages flayed and gutted our men like animals. Yet they must have been inspired by our civilisation, somehow civility managed to seep in between the cracks into their brutal lobes; they took the painting of Gericos. No doubt in total awe at our culture. They took most of our coinage too, but don't worry, it will not affect our coffers. Yet, no doubt they toyed enviously with the inferior craftsmanship of our enemy brethren, totally unknowing of the superior cultural beauty of even crude Gatanese forgings."

"Now I fear their awe has turned to envy as they attack us tenfold, angered and frustrated at their inability to mimic our supremacy. Yet now we know their home, their origins."

"And with it the gateway to the great enemy: Septimus!" Juiscius announced jubilantly. "Hurrah, Ruperis! The war against the evil ones can truly begin." His expression of utter excitement transformed to a cold vapidity only achievable when totally dedicated to the cause the statement purported.

"We have really got to get you away from that cleric!" Ruperis exclaimed patronisingly.

Juscius was too engrossed in his fervour to notice the vehement assault on his mentor.

Realising that he was lucky to slip through the ferocious spiritual defence mechanism, Ruperis tactfully steered the conversation back to his travels. "Basically there's nothing there. We have no need for it, though they could be a menace to trade. Luckily we salvaged a method of preserving meat from the barbarians; you strip the flesh and smoke it into a hard leathery substance with plenty of salt. They have had to learn that in order to survive the long winters. That stuff kept us alive. We headed southeast rather than up the giant river." Ruperis paused for a long time, as though cogitating over the events of their travels at sea. Deciding it was not worthy to disclose he skipped to their next land-based encounter. "Well, eventually we came across strange beings."

Juscius' face lit up and he leant in to pay special attention to the revelation.

"The opposite of those pallid behemoths; they were slender, oily, dark-skinned creatures. Their skin was scorched by Prometha, and weathered into a smooth sleekness by the fierce torrents of Weihros. Their sweltering land is like an ocean of sand with sparse oases that provide scant lifeblood to the land and peoples. Harsh winds howl across the desolate place, tearing away at the skin with flails of dust.

"The people seemed most hospitable at first, but one should not be fooled, they can be just as ferocious as the mountain people. Fiercely defensive, they will wreak revenge with the sweetest sense of relish, slashing sinew expertly with knives to maximise pain; assisting the endurance of their captives only to prolong their suffering." Ruperis noticed that he had diverged into a blood curdling-description, and so stopped.

Juscius was horrified; he seemed like a child. "Heathens!" He shook his head in disgust. "No civilisation. What can be done for such a despicable amalgamation of scorched infected flesh and putrid ideas?"

Ruperis seemed to be trailing far behind Juscius' purifying rhetoric. "Actually they had quite a remarkable civilisation, huge temples to their bestial gods," Ruperis trailed off quietly as he realised he had probably just condemned the entire dark-skinned race to holy purging. "It is most wondrous, their architecture. No doubt they worship the animal for they are so few in their inhospitable land. Yet that is not to say their land is worthless, for it is rich in other splendorous resources, gems, spices, the food stuffs they do have are most exotic, and crucially, most profitable."

Juscius remained sceptical; he did not want his household's powerful spirituality succumbing to avaricious, spiritually-putrefying gluttony. As Ruperis continued with detailed illustrations of the exquisite items to satisfy the upper classes (though he, as a new-entrepreneur, would never use such an 'old and dated term'), Juscius felt angered that such indulgent excess would expose those who held the house together to a malignance that would degenerate the entire population.

Sensing his companion's distrust, Ruperis attempted a final attempt to convince him; he would fling in a flippant comment concerning its urgent necessity, and over time the notion would grow on Juscius. "I hear the nobles are increasingly anxious to experience new things and need a diversion away from the trivialities."

The seed was planted.

"Anyway, after a bit of trouble and disagreement, mostly due to some mis-interpretations, we managed to do some deals." He paused to crack open a beaming grin.

The expression that had been welcomed with humour by the young lord, now only deepened the rift of sickened nonchalance that was laced with the scent of disgust.

"I guess it's time to introduce you to your present." Ruperis clapped his hands loudly.

Juscius became even more distressed.

The door opened very slowly. Juscius heard the pit-patting of bare feet on the cold stone floor; the sound was entrancing and beautiful. It contained a trace of the joyous innocence of a child yet also a graceful seductiveness of something beautiful in a totally different way. The lord had averted his eyes to the ground, partially in intrigue induced fear of looking at what was to stand before him but also because his eyes were drawn to the source of the noise. Two large, slender and hairless feet were lightly planted before him, they were dark-skinned, yet their pure blackness was offset by the shimmering glimmer that reflected off the smooth oily surface, underneath crystal clear nails, pinkish blimps spread out as though pressed against a glass pane. As his eyes trailed upwards his mind mapped out a woman-shaped column. She was coated all over in the shiny black layer that seemed to have been stained and polished onto her skin (Juscius could not believe this was a natural colour). Her face was tightly held together in nervous confusion; to Juscius her features were hard to fathom, giving her mystical appeal. A flat but wide nose sat on her face with a perfectionist's beauty; captivating brown bead-eyes flashed intelligently every half a second in a striking survey of the room. The dark pupil contrasted remarkably with the pure white watery ball in which it was enthroned. Her tall slender build still contained an athlete's muscles, most of which were revealed or poorly concealed by a skimpy two piece costume made of soft cloth. Juscius could not restrain his surging feeling of desire; he felt his soul be tainted with perversion. He silently set about internally suppressing it. It was unwanted, unnecessary, and wrong.

Ruperis had sensed the lord's unease and gave a wry smile. "She's meant to be mine, a gift, but I see it as only fitting that she be yours." He turned to her and spoke slowly and authoritatively. "Bow to the lord." He nodded his head down to demonstrate, then smiled patronisingly as she complied.

She offered the lord her hand. Juscius was confused and shifted with embarrassment; nervously he took her hand lightly. It was as soft as silk, so smooth that his fingers slid along it as though it was wet, though it was dry. Although the digits were stone cold he felt a tingling warmth that he rarely felt explode in his throat. He inspected the exquisite fingers and rubbed his thumb against the smooth skin of this angelic effigy. The colour was not a stain, but natural, or more likely supernatural. Was she not just a gift from a returning friend but a gift from the gods?

She stared forward emotionlessly. Unease had crept back to consume her mindset, this was transmitted to Juscius as his eyes met hers. The lord reeled back, awestruck. A fiery intelligence was revealed by the darting orbs. As fear rose in the poor girl her eyes erupted with a watery, pinkish tinge, the whites tainted with trepidation, but to the lord this merely confirmed her demi-god status as they resembled the renowned pearls that adorned Neptus' necklace of the sea. Were they the very pearls?

Surely not, how could something of such beauty belong to Neptus, how could such a thing exist in the dark dank depths of the sea?
Perhaps they were plucked from the depths and paraded on this dark-skinned nymph as a victory of Heric in the service of Thelus? Thelus probably did not specifically ask for the prize to be embedded in a woman, but that was the mischievous idea of Heric.
She was divine.

She smiled: remarkable white teeth glistened in the gaping but nervously controlled mouth. Juscius could not help but smile back with a sheepish blush.

"She is divine. Heavenly. When I touch her it is like when my hands contact..." he trailed off briefly as he wanted to say Torian, thankfully he was saved by her image in stone "...a smooth marble statue, an effigy of a deity, yet it is warm, as though more than a picturesque imitation of a goddess," he mumbled incomprehensibly.

'*Was she a prize from the gods?*' he pondered. As he admired her and her aura of beauty he dismissed the notion that this was a plundered artefact from Neptus. That would make her dangerous, which would mean Heric had been deceived and brought an uncontrollable menace to the Latman house. Could he be deceived? Why would Thelus allow it?

All of these questions filled the young lord with resolute but contradictory answers, all considered in total seriousness.

What if a force masqueraded as Thelus, a false speaker, a deceptive pedagogue, had led Heric astray? The cheeky god was easily conned into causing mayhem well beyond his own mischievous tendencies.

A sudden gust of rational dismissal wafted into his melting pot of erratic metaphysical speculation.

'*It's not Heric and Thelus anyway, not directly, it's Ruperis and Zeuorox. Ruperis went on the mission, and I know what he's like, so no wonder he brought this divine being back. And as for Zeuorox, he helped me plan it and I know he is the closest to Thelus of us all. And I have no reason to even suggest that Heric, the self-interested mischievous scallywag he is, has had anything to do with this.'*

With the winds of spirituality swirling vigorously within him again he concluded she must be a gift from Thelus and Prometha, an intermediate gift to encourage him to fulfil his destiny of unifying the island, and so bring together the peoples and bring together him and the gods. This meant it was a sign that he had performed Thelus' will and was edging closer to attainment.

Juscius looked her up and down cautiously, and spoke onto Ruperis, "I hope you treated and fed her well? And I trust that you have not let anyone befoul her." The last comment was passed to Ruperis sternly, with such weight that it ceased to be a question for he did not want to hear an answer.

Ruperis winced as he heard the remark. His surprisingly candid expression transformed into a momentary mask of confusion and concern, before settling uneasily on a plain smile of reassurance, yet the shockwaves undulating from the query had swamped the reassurance with inconvincibility. *'Note to self: Must make reassurances (esp. concerning sexual misconduct) more convincing. It was ok this time, but in a trading deal it would be much more crucial to uphold false pretences to avoid devastating economic costs.'*

Juscius chose not to recognise the blatant falseness of the assurance, deciding to believe that no mortal could truly defile a demi-goddess.

"Does she understand our language?"

"Very little."

"We must teach her, and we must learn her language: It must be a descendant language from Prometha." At this Ruperis rolled his eyes, unbeknownst to Juscius. "Zeuorox can help and provide the necessary spiritual enlightenment."

The merchant rolled his eyes again.

"Now we have taken her away from Prometha she will miss his guidance. We can bring her closer to the lord of gods. It will be an enlightenment to bring her in more direct contact with the divine."

"Yeah! Cut out the middleman. In business we call it streamlining," Ruperis commented dryly.

The sarcasm was lost on Juscius. "Really! We are 'Streamlining' her and teaching her of the true origins of her people... not some wolf-man, or whatever they worship in that lost place. In time she will come face-to-face with her Prometha in his true glory, our sun god, her creator!"

"Where do you learn it from, Jus?" a slightly worried Ruperis asked.

"It is not learnt, it is intuition, mental processing based on spiritual knowledge." He sought an illustration. "You see, it all makes sense now. She is the antithesis of the baresarks; they are the evil acolyte's of Neptus, as you suggested: spawned with her and Weihros, but banished from Neptus' realm deep under the sea adjacent to Septimo's fiery underworld hell, and Galex and Athyle's bloody realm of perpetual strife, and sent to roam the seas and huddle in mountain shacks to hide from Weihros' onslaught. They are excellent seafarers and you said their land was covered in snow; even their land is Neptus' territory! No doubt they stole fire and so were banished from their lair with the dark gods and sent to the barren lands where it would be needed."

"What is so dark about Neptus? That reminds me, why did the guards at Gericos seize my statue of her?" Ruperis' consternation was replaced by a more aggressive, offended querying.

"You had a statue of Neptus?! You really were tempting fate! Surely you know she has been found to be a dark one. She is a malicious demon, who is now ignominiously pandering to the evils of Septimo. You allowed her power over your vessel even though she already pounded that floating beacon of Thelus' light with her evil fists of brine!" His exclamations were ecstatic. Upon detecting Ruperis' ignorance he continued with a slightly bemused expression. "Isn't that ironic? Whilst you were sailing the gods backwaters with the supposed goal of enlightening us, civilisation itself has been revolutionised in your absence, new knowledge from the new interpretation has shed more light than your mighty escapade. You learn of peoples and products, whilst we have learned of the gods! Your alleged jaunt of exploration has made you miss the new epoch! The simplistic days of old, of routine bickering between ignorant but self-convinced fiefdoms is coming to a close. Stratified conflicts shall be shown to be dogmatic and non-existent. Instead we shall all embrace Thelus as one. The Latman household shall be the golden palace from which this asymmetric amalgamation of peoples can converge. For we of the new interpretation faith believe in moving forward, not back, in consensus amongst the many individual servants of Thelus. This is the goal of the new interpretation, as is it my destiny too. We need to draw a line under these squabbles, move on, and encourage Gatan and Vacarium to share our goal of peace... and prosperity."

The otherwise bored (and somewhat scared) Ruperis perked up upon hearing the multi-syllabic 'p' word.

Juscius stopped, realising he was in the meeting room, not the chapel. He felt uneasy: his words, his plans, had been uttered in unholy air. Juscius feared that the devil-like Septimo was present, lapping up the sweet serenity of the lord's planned crusade. The bestial false-god encircled him, swirling playfully in the breath-fumes that surrounded the creature in a thick cloud, which emanated from its gaping mouth and created an eerie shroud. The fetid stench ate away at his words, splicing them into morsels to be devoured effortlessly, swallowed in their fractioned hundredths and thousandths like plankton before a blue whale. Occasionally the beast's deformed chin spat out a spray of acidic solution, forming a residue that in turn reacted with the evil god's repugnant saliva.

As the frightening spectacle exploded before Juscius, Ruperis frowned with concern as he observed the sudden quivering and deathly silence that had overcome his friend. Ruperis decided that the best way to end this was to try to distract the lord and calm him simultaneously by talking candidly and with a squeeze of dry humour. "Juscius, calm down. What has that Zeuorox... what has he done to you?"

He longed for the return of his lost friend. He felt morose and forlorn, a feeling he thought he would have experienced whilst at sea but not upon returning (as it happened, he had been so busy whilst on his adventure that he was never lonely). He began to pity the serious being that had inhabited Juscius' form. *'But wasn't this Juscius grown up?'* Was this what he had to do? Stop being such a happy-go-lucky mischief maker and become a proper entrepreneur? Was this a reminder?

He tried a new tack. "Come on Jus, you must be strong and resolute."

Juscius seemed to wake from his tortuous reverie. He turned to Ruperis, this time taking up the invite for a casual 'sofa-style' debate. "Let's get a drink and reminisce."

Though the entrepreneur was startled by the sudden change of mood on the part of his friend, it came as a relief. "Let's..."

Juscius turned to the slave girl and a wave of refreshing admiration washed over him. To the awestruck lord, it was as though she had an inbuilt mechanism for spreading benevolence. She stood attentively, clearly waiting to obey his beckoning call, though not daring to raise herself to look at him directly.

Cautiously, the lord leant towards her and patronisingly took her hand. His attempt to retain his superior position was thwarted by the unavoidable quivering that undulated briskly over his body as his fingers touched her silk skin. The twitching irritant of prurience seemed to only emerge sulkily, wallowing in the depths of his stomach. He led her to the door and slowly lifted the door latch, seeming not to notice the sound of someone scurrying back on the other side.

Upon stepping through the doorway the trio were confronted by Zeuorox, who looked up with a perfectly convincing look of surprise that the door should open exactly when he was 'passing by'. He stopped mid stride and faced Juscius humbly. "Sire, am I needed?" he asked expectantly.

"No Zeuorox, not yet, me and Roo are going to talk a bit more."

"I'm glad the two of you still get on as when you were children" No doubt Zeuorox was hugging himself with joy internally, having heard Juscius' spiel through the door.

Juscius looked about the corridor in search of the absent guard.

Foreseeing the lords concern, Zeuorox launched into an explanation. "I assumed his lordship would want the slave girl to take his handmaidens quarters and so I sent the guard to tell your servant…"

"As usual you have had a brilliant idea! It will keep her safe and away from the rest of the servants, who might get a bit of a fright." He paused. "So you have met her before then?"

"Yes, it is such a wonderful gift; I could not have chosen a better one myself… still, what can you expect but the best from Thelus." Zeuorox replied confidently.

"You think it is a sign too?" the lord asked eagerly.

"Surely it must be. We are on the right path for sure; I believe she may be a nymph of Prometha, a gift from Thelus; may she be a guiding light to us all!"

"What made you get me a gift?" Juscius asked Ruperis.

"Well actually Zeuorox had suggested I get something, but I think he wouldn't expect something like this!" He grinned, with a mischievous look as though he had deliberately chosen something to offend the high-pontiff.

Zeuorox hid his sly grin. "Quite. Still, that means it must be a sign from Thelus," he conceded with fake reluctance.

Zeuorox turned towards his temple, briefly leaning back to the lord to bow before uttering that he needed to depart from their gathering. As they went their separate ways Juscius almost skipped, captivated by the slave girl. He was so enthralled that he did not hear Ruperis' thanks to the priest for providing the funds to take on the trip. On the venture down the corridor they met the returning guard, who, once he had overcome his consternate state at seeing the alien beauty, was able to take her off to Juscius' quarters.

As they continued down the passageways, Juscius explained to Ruperis the dangers of the divisive Latman trouble-makers in Vaca who were rebelling against serfdom, and how this was because they were servants of the 'old' gods that were worshiped by the dark 'old' Rudian nations. Along with their out-dated beliefs on the realm of the spiritual were their backdated old-fashioned somewhat selfish strata-specific demands. He stated that they missed whole picture; a consensus towards Thelus; one where they did not need to oppose those economic forces that they saw as oppressive. Instead they should embrace the dynamic power of wealth creation and co-operate, just as the gods would want.

Then he spoke of Gorax: "That intellectual conjurer, who builds in a vain attempt to compete with the gods. He is a heathen … he is the most distance from Thelus out of us all. He is like a Baresark seeking to steal fire. He should realise the gods do not allow us things for reasons (and that those reasons must remain mystical to us). See what happened to the baresarks when they stole from the gods! They were banished to their wasteland. He could condemn us all! At least the baresark beasts knew no better!"

Ruperis was confused, even frightened, that this was not just his friend but the most powerful man on the island. "So we shouldn't have fire?"

Juscius scowled in irritation. "Of course we should now! Just not back then. Now we use it with Prometha's blessing… but we must always fear fire, respect it but remember there are two fires: that of Prometha the shining light in the sky, and that deep red sulky licking flame that trails the underworld. There is this earthly fire that we are forced to utilise, and then there is the magical light and heat that emanates from Prometha mighty orb."

"Anyway as for Gorax, he is an engineer, and meddler in the fundamental laws that hold this world together, like those peasants that are trying to be social engineers: both of which are the job of gods… and their interpreters."

★

Eventually they reached the office. Before they entered, Juscius turned to Ruperis and embraced him warmly. His gesture cut through the uncomfortable mien that had re-emerged around them. "I have missed you so much, Roo," he exclaimed passionately. "You are like a brother to me, I knew you would return. My heart went out to you every day." He smiled as he reminisced the days of remembrance. "Though not for one second did I think you would be in peril. You're just not the sort!" Juscius smiled a true smile.

They parted from each other and entered the office. Inside, they were bombarded by the illumination emanating from bright canvases that shimmered in the torchlight. The array of colours rivalled the assortment of red and orange that coated Ruperis' figure. Ruperis closed the door with a dainty push. He then set about briefly admiring the wall decorations, passing his gaze over each and nodding at each with the otiose fakery of a yuppie pretending to 'get it'. Once he had finished this totally vacuous convention he looked up at Juscius with a grin. "Isn't she divine?"

Juscius was half way through pouring the wine when Ruperis' words snapped his imagination to her. His concentration seized up so that his wrist was left clasped as though in death around the bottle neck. The neurons in his limbs seemed preoccupied, siphoning all his energy to feed the image of her that burnt into his mind. The few expressions she had made whilst in his company seemed to have been embedded already. The image contorted slightly as though sent through a distorting lens, undulating as though reflected in a rippling pool. The lord was broken out of his reverie by the waft of sugary wine. While his mind disengaged from the trance, his limbs and senses went into automation and he found himself sniffing the rim of the bottle. He turned to face his companion, but was just reminded of the question that had set him off. He began to ponder what she should be called. To him she needed no name, yet she deserved an ecclesiastical name, one that would link her to her ancestry in the smokeless fires of Prometha's heavenly orb. After a few minutes Ruperis' eager grin began to droop. It was as this state of dismay spurred Ruperis into jerking forward, in preparation for an attempt to re-establish contact, that Juscius finally awoke and reconnected to his surroundings.

"Quite," Juscius boomed with uncontrolled assertion. He cleared his throat and attempted to draw the conversation away from the apparent personal taboo. "I have missed you so, yet I never doubted you would return. Only now do I find it strange. You were in real danger." Every word was spoken slowly and solemnly, yet this did not mean it was morose or insipid; quite the opposite, the lord felt so strongly about his companion that his vivacious joy had been overwhelmed by the strength of emotion to a point nearing lachrymose.

Ruperis sniffed, trying to conceal his own emotional state as supercilious snorting. Having relaxed his muscles from their tense emotive state he daintily took a sip of wine and nodded approvingly. With the relaxed male persona fully operational, he was ready to speak. "As if danger could stop me! You must remember our sailing days! How many times did I cheat death? How many close shaves!" He was smiling with the beaming grin reminiscent of the boyhood Ruperis.

It was the childish persona adopted by equally childish young adults; though not directly macho, it tapped into the handicap gene of stupidity in order to endure hardship.

"Those crazy days! How did you get away with it?" Juscius pondered light heartedly.

"How did WE get away with it you mean!" Ruperis corrected cheekily, "you only got away with it because Torian liked you and hated me... I can't think why!"

"Because you used to torment her!" Juscius laughed aloud.

"I used to torment HER! She used to torture me as a baby, I merely enacted revenge! Anyway it's not my fault she has no sense of humour!"

"She…" Juscius unwittingly launched into a remonstration, which he promptly sought to silence.

Too late.

Ruperis raised an eyebrow. "Come to think of it you two seemed pretty cosy when I left". A wry smile split across his face, crudely hanging open like a dry cracked cliff face. Juscius refused to respond.

Ruperis, having been stymied, attempted a less direct assault. "How is the old gal?" he inquired in reference to his sister.

"She is fine… well, she was the last time I saw her… which was a while ago". He attempted to cover up with a hail of three bursts of words.

"Oh it was, was it?" Ruperis commented with an evil grin, relishing the fact that his recently born-again companion had retained both the urges and the embarrassment at having them. "So when exactly was that?" he added, to catalyse the squirming of his friend.

Juscius could not lie to a friend; he looked at his left sandal and twiddled his right sandal in clockwise circles whilst the toes wriggled like keys on a piano being played at the height of a symphony. "This morning," he confessed in an embarrassed mumble.

Ruperis' boyhood grin broke open on his face again, a great crack of youthful angerless scorn. Then he laughed out loud. "Surely, you're not!" He shook his head in disappointment. "Surely you can do better! She's nice but… well… a bit dull."

Juscius should have been mortally offended; but he took pity; Ruperis could not ever understand their dynamic. Also, not that Juscius seemed to notice, his closest friend was doing what they do best, and showing him the lighter side of life, providing a true happiness of shared comfort and subliminally proving they added something to each other that made day to day life better and ultimately liveable.

'No, this was blasphemy!'

'Surely not! Boyhood innocence and camaraderie cannot be perverted, they are pure.'

'Yes pure and isolated, aged in a realm of youthful innocence, but not when set loose in the realm of adults. Responsibility and piety rules adults, it gives them those opportunities to prove themselves or fail at their tasks of attaining divinity.'

'Clearly, true friends of such high calibre can relax their zealous dedication; surely I can stoop to his antics in order to retain those links to the past we share.'

He should value what he and Ruperis had shared, like he valued what Torian and he had shared. They had been through so much together over the past two years; the mysticism of their love was solidified in their shared ecclesiastical aspirations.

This shared aspiration highlighted the beauty of their unity. What is more, it had come to epitomise to Juscius the epochal framework that constituted his thought.

Juscius was thrust back into the real world by an inquisitive remark from Ruperis. "So, what about Princess Telis? ..." The mischievous traveller grinned and winked cheekily. "Has she been given the pre-emptive proverbial boot yet?" he added with a raised eyebrow before continuing. "Cos your old lady Maritha ain't gonna like it!" he smirked. Allowing Juscius a split second to prepare for an immature addition, "Nor is Mister Peni!" he remarked predictably crudely, jerking his hand sloppily towards the young lord's crotch.

The lord smiled silently, barely hiding his disgust.

"I doubt if that item will dictate my actions." This was followed by a snide addition to incriminate the interrogator for asking an undesired question. "Maybe it does for you…"

Ruperis shook his head smiling with controlled annoyance. "Jus, don't give me that… I'm your friend, and I am Torian's brother, don't I have a right to know what's really going on?"

Still in politician mode, Juscius had to pause momentarily to think of a vaguely candid response. "I can't marry for just conventions and strategic reasons. Marriage should not be a mechanism to struggle with mankind's inevitable flaws in co-operation," he stated firmly.

"Surely you haven't told Maritha?" Ruperis sounded actually slightly concerned for the old crone's wellbeing.

"She will understand." Ruperis found Juscius' reply worryingly certain.

"But will her loathing for Gatan, and her obsession of uniting with Telis to crush them?"

Juscius did not answer.

"I take it she does not know about you and Torian?"

"Of course not, nobody knows."

What about his holy skeletonness'?" Ruperis queried, jerking his hand crudely towards the door.

Juscius paused to absorb and attempt to overcome the deluge of rage he felt at such a derogatory reference to his divine sophist. Calmly he uttered a stern warning for his companions soul. "Don't speak of him like that!" The disciplining over, he returned to the conversation, "Of course he knows, he had to. He has offered much advice."

Ruperis laughed aloud. "What does that puritanical old goon know about women?... or is that randy old goat not letting us in on something?!"

"Ruperis!" Juscius objected, disgusted to an extreme point of rising abhorrence for the creature that sat before him claiming to be a companion from his past. His face turned coldly serious. "If you speak in such a way in the presence of others... your boyhood friend will not be able to save you..."

"Hey, I'm sorry. You've changed. He's changed you. I worry he's sucking the life out of you and replacing it with a driven pomposity. I can't help but think there's something going on." Ruperis was unusually straight talking, which instinctively worried the young lord, whose memory of their childhood told him that he only did so when truly concerned. That is not to say that he was perceived as dishonest by Juscius, but more that he was cautious and strategic with true expressiveness.

"Well, something *is* going on. He *has* changed me, enlightened me, and shown me the path. The true path for improving current realities. We shall show the rest of the houses this path. A united path where we can fraternise, and trade in unison in combined ideals..."

Ruperis jumped eagerly at the word trade. Juscius noticed that he had hit a crucial cord and so pursued the entrepreneur spiel.

"Trade will be so much smoother, freer, and easier. No longer will backdated cleavages separate us. Instead we can all, all islanders unite and share commercial access across borders, and provide security for the island with a united front against the barbarians and internal insurgents with their ideals of plunder and destruction." The rhetoric slowed with choreographed timing, just enough to allow for (positive) reflections from the audience (though not enough for an objection).

"That sounds, most... opportunistic," the entrepreneur commented slyly, though he was confused by the lord suddenly glossing over his offence.

"Oh it will be, especially for you, you deserve a reward for your assistance in exploration. I promise spiritual-political and economic prosperity," agreed the lord.

"So, what is the plan then? How exactly are you going to get once, indeed still, great enemies to jump on the wagon together?" Ruperis' scepticism was embalmed in a skilful charm that enabled him to ask probing questions concerning crucial policy decisions without arising suspicion, they seemed just like a cheeky companion using fake mockery to tease an idealistic friend.

Juscius beamed with self-righteous pride. "I have proposed a banquet to be attended by my fellow lords. The first of its kind, a great opportunity for all to enjoy... provided the other factions use the opportunity we are providing. There we will, gods willing, set the legacy in stone."

Ruperis was unimpressed, but retained the pretence of a boyhood taunt. "Your legacy, you mean! You and your legacy!" He shook his head with a semi-disdainful, semi-joking sigh.

Juscius did not falter. "I must obey the quests set before me by Thelus."

Before Ruperis could make a wise-crack comment, Juscius had enticed him in. "Of course, you will invited, and you must come." He paused as though unsure if he should continue. "Princess Telis will be there." He raised an eyebrow at Ruperis, who looked positively shocked. "Me... and her... Would they accept non-royalty?"

Juscius smiled as his mind conjured up images of his own unison with Torian. "Semi-royalty... soon." This was posed in part as a request for Ruperis' sisters' hand.

"I suppose it's a necessity for diplomatic ties..." Ruperis eagerly conceded.

"Telis will be a key ally.... If others should resist... hopefully they won't."

Ruperis shook his head worriedly. "No, the dream won't work then." He shivered at the economic costs of such a tirade. "Trade routes blocked or rendered unsafe so you have to hire extra guards, workers drafted, usually unrest amongst the peasants."

"Although in the long-term you must understand it will be worth it, so if it is necessary we must be prepared," Juscius protested.

"As long as 'long-term' means it will end within my lifetime. There's no point in making concessions for the next generation, that's up to them to sort out."

Of course this was hypocritical coming from a man who was in his position solely because of his father's closeness to Juscius' father and prosperity he had reaped and passed on upon his retirement from day-to-day running of their family enterprise.

"Anyway, it won't come to that," Ruperis attempted to reassure himself.

"No, just think how profitable a Telis-Latman alliance would be! Your Latman based logistics and administration combined with Telis' vast labour... my economics is patchy," he added apologetically.

"No, you're right; you've been reading my mind!" Ruperis exclaimed. "Brotherly intuition!"

"Actually, Zeuorox pointed it out to me." Juscius seemed more proud that his pontiff had thought of something to impress his boyhood friend than if he had thought of it. His disposition resembled that of a child proudly boasting the greatness of his father.

"... though what I really fancy is some of those cheap Vacarium mineral deposits, and those Vacarium mountain people would make good labourers (they need little investment). Although I hear they have quaint (and unproductive) beliefs in balances and subsistence (not taking too much – which is essential to selling and profiteering) because they are 'close' to 'nature', oh how primitive superstitions seek to stifle our efforts!"

Juscius spat disdainfully. "Heretics, seeking to wallow in the dirt like animals, worshipping ethereal elements and not the gods that created them. Do they deliberately disobey the will of the gods for man to prosper, or are they just cretinous creatures hybridised between bestiality and humanity? Either way, we shall teach them our ways or put them to the sword. They shall no longer worship the soil, the sprawling bulwark to Septimo's lair; instead they will see the true guiding light of Thelus and join us in prosperity."

Ruperis smiled to himself.

"What?" queried Juscius, with pleasant intrigue.

Beaming, the entrepreneur looked directly into the lord's eyes, "I should meet this Zeuorox!"

Juscius smiled radiantly in return, pleased with the belief that he was on the way to converting Ruperis to the enlightened spiritual ideals.

★

Ruperis the entrepreneur left the office of his companion with a satisfying sense of expiation. However, he knew before could call this a success he had to meet this Zeuorox character again. The pact would only be solid once this shadowy figure of unknown power was more known to the entrepreneur. Ruperis retraced his steps down the winding corridors of the warren-like palace passageways. Occasionally he passed a veteran servant who recognised him and showered him with vivacious greeting and praise, ecstatically asking him of his travels. He politely gave the impression that he was listening attentively. He tried desperately to remember their non-descript menial lives, this was not just practise for the budding entrepreneur for when he pretended to care about his employees, the massed storing of uninteresting information for no reason except to give of the right impression, it was also crucial for building up contacts within the halls of power. Between each conversation he pondered to himself with irritation how much effort he had to go to, whilst all they had to do was live out these menial lives with their menial chores.

He met Zeuorox solemnly wandering the corridor near the visitor rooms that Ruperis and Juscius had been in previously. Though he feigned surprise, the brooding look betrayed to Ruperis that he had been pacing there for some time, which Ruperis assumed meant he was waiting for him.

Following a brief reintroduction, the high pontiff led the entrepreneur into the visitor room.

All bar the far corner torch were still alight, waving in solace to each other from their eternal distances. Providing their far-flung neighbour with relief in the darkness, each flickered a dance with a sudden passing draft that undulated across them as though they were warning beacons attempting to struggle against isolation from their brethren by relaying messages the length of the room, fearing that another would meet the fate of the corner torch.

Zeuorox was busying himself at the small table in the far corner. "I am glad you came and found me, Mr. Delvinius." Without turning to face the merchant he lit the torch before him. Then, without pausing, he strode quietly to the door and stuffed cloth in the gap between the door and the floor so the light did not show beneath. He then, without even turning to Ruperis, let alone consulting him, returned to the table to pour two drinks.

During this time Ruperis shuffled uneasily, tapping and scuffing his shoes as silently as possible before striding to a seat and politely sitting in it. He ensured his posture was that of a professional; upright, hands placed delicately on his knees (not gripping them, but loosely clenched to show the knuckles), eyes silently admiring the wall decoration. This sombre countenance expressed a relaxed alertness and calm interest in the arts, as his eyes critically inspected each article on the walls. Internally he desperately pondered what to expect; was he about to be preached to, shouted at, accused of treason, or asked to return the loan? He recalled his fathers' advice that one should always instigate a dispute concerning a loan, for it ensured you were prepared and a step ahead of them.

Anxiety built up to such a point that he could no longer contain it, though he retained his business-like cool. "So, the loan?"

Zeuorox did not even look away from the table, he merely waved his free hand in dismissal, "No, don't worry about that; think of that as payment for the journey."

Nervously Ruperis scratched the back of his neck, the fingers snugly hiding away under his hair. He looked humbly to the floor, mumbling, "good, it kind of got lost."

Zeuorox turned suddenly with a masterful look of utter surprise. "Oh?"

Ruperis stumbled verbally under the weight of the cleric's piercing, inquisitive eyes. "Some baresarks took it."

The mask of surprise that Zeuorox had donned was swiftly discarded in order not to alienate Ruperis and make too much out of this expected outcome. "It does not matter. Such things happen I suppose. Anyway I am not here to discuss missing money."

Ruperis sat silently in anticipation, waiting to hear what he had been brought in for. Yet the priest began lighting scented candles and showed no sign of expressing what the purpose of the meeting was. Confusion was flooding into his head. His mind floated in the deluge precariously, trying to stay on an even keel, but as with any real or metaphorical ship, with no sense of direction found focusing difficult.

Worse still, the high priest seemed to be waiting for Ruperis to make a comment; it was as though he was deliberately performing frivolous tasks in expectation of Ruperis beginning a conversation.

Fighting irrational intimidation, Ruperis tried to sound impressed: flattery would make a good start. "You seem to have made a strong impression on Juscius."

The trigger was activated; the chief spiritual advisor turned towards him with two glasses that seemed to have miraculously appeared in his hands, his face wrinkled awkwardly into a wry smile. "No doubt you do not approve."

Ruperis attempted an objection, but it was waved off with another slight hand gesture from the chief cleric (this patronisingly supercilious gesture was already irritating the merchant). "Don't worry; I haven't brought you here for a lecture... I think I understand why you have your differences."

Ruperis returned a much more adept smirk. "I suppose you do not approve of my gift," comforted by the promise not to give him a lecture. "I sincerely hope you were not offended, it's just that gold and riches Latman has a plenty," he added, as a sincere explanation verging on apology.

"Not at all," the Pontiff replied. Thankfully for Ruperis refraining from making the gesture, instead leaning in to give Ruperis his glass of wine. "It will do his lordship good." He leant back and turned away from Ruperis. "Besides, it is a sign there is a reason that she was brought to our shores; this nymph of Prometha." The cleric stood upright staring at the torch in the corner; he gazed into its flickering yellow orb of light.

"That was exactly what Juscius said," Ruperis muttered sullenly.

Zeuorox gave a slight scowl, angered by the merchant's apparent ignorance. "Obviously she is not a direct descendent of the gods, a more vague diluted descendent, as the Lewerix line are that of Lewern. She is a living symbol of them, an organic effigy if you please. Anyway, that is academic; I don't want to argue with you on this, you probably believe it is nonsense."

Ruperis just smirked in a sceptical manner.

Having said he would not, the High Priest then preceded to rant, more out of spite than a belief in achieving a conversion. "She is the antidote to the baresarks. You see, they were banished from the fiery gates of Septimo's Lair for stealing its smoky flame, they soaked themselves in this hellish concoction, inhaling its deadly inebriating aroma, its wafting prurience placing them into an itching, surfeit state that always desires more; it is this addiction that renders them so savage. Their banishment to the icy barren lands of tundra is a punishment for them; they became slaves to their inquisitiveness, left with so little light to force them to need their flickering drug."

Ruperis nodded. "We once witnessed their ceremonial to the fire spirit; they were truly crazed."

"Whereas she is scorched by the purifying rays of Prometha, her skin soaked by it so it gleams, reflecting its rays out to all. It must be divine; why else would something so dark radiate such brightness?"

"You say hell is fiery, but believe me the freezing glaciers and torrents of ice cold sea, frothed by the howling winds. The torrents and gales screech taunts and warnings that are yet intriguingly seductive, preventing those exposed to these noises from taking heed and fleeing. One is left confused in the middle, driven away, yet attracted and intrigued to all directions at once; disorientated and shaking with icy fever, cold and alone."

Zeuorox shook his head with an apparent superiority of authority on the issue. "That just doesn't make sense. Do not argue with me. You do not understand the crucial structure of how the gods are divided…"

Ruperis could not help but chuckle aloud in disbelief; however, he managed to bring the outburst to an abrupt halt in an attempt to broker a peace agreement before hostilities began. "I'm sorry, but I thought we were not to talk of such things today."

To Ruperis' surprise the cleric was not offended. On the contrary, he seemed relieved at the diversion. "You are right, I am sorry" (though the sorry was awkwardly forced out of his mouth, which had taken on a defensive slit-like shape; consequently the word was spat out like the wrong piece being frustratingly pulled out of the wrong hole in a child's puzzle).

Out of the interruption in the flow of debate came an unsettling, self-perpetuating silence. Ruperis resumed probing the decorations, feeling increasing pressure as Zeuorox scrutinised him with his beady eyes wrapped up in puffy wrinkles. The throat-crushing fear reached an asphyxiating level of panic, causing Ruperis' eyes to jerk in wildly furtive motions, as he sought to avert his gaze from the staring dark orbs. However, it was only a matter of seconds before loss of control meant his eyes were uninhibited in fulfilling their natural impulse to return the unnerving gesture. Once eye contact was locked, Ruperis became transfixed.

Zeuorox furrowed his brow in an attempt at supportive concern. "You seem eager about the future, but something troubles you?"
Ruperis was reluctant to begin, but after a minute decided he would have to proceed honestly and try to decipher where the cleric stood. "I am worried by Juscius' apparent ease in talking of war. We spoke of a great future of prosperity, but I worry he is going to ruin that by bankrupting us with war."

Zeuorox sighed. "His Lordship has a truly great vision, not just spiritual, but also economic. One which you look forward to with expected and justifiable eagerness as it will enable you to achieve the propitious status you desire. We all dislike war, we all want peace, it's just sometimes peace is achieved through war. If Gatan will not agree to the vision *we* share - I say 'we' for our ideals, though different, are not incompatible - then they will have to be encouraged... by force. If they will not agree to our trade agreements then you will always be threatened by them and will have to protect yourself. If they will not co-operate they will allow bandits to terrorise our trade routes (they have already paid barbarians to ravage our coasts and burn a barracks in Gericos)."

Ruperis was shocked. "Have they? The beasts!"
Zeuorox looked deeply saddened. "Yes, our intelligence in Gatan intercepted a message."

"And it will be brought up at the banquet will it?"
Zeuorox shook his head violently. "Oh no! They would deny it, and it would be counterproductive."

"But you have proof."
"Yes, but to allow anyone to see it, or even to hear of it, would put our security service in danger."

"So you do have undeniable proof?"
"Yes, but we can't let anyone see it."

Ruperis realised he was getting nowhere and did not want to offend the cleric. "You say we have compatible ideals, yet if you see war as a possibility then I find it hard to see how - I mean, trade will collapse if that occurs."

Zeuorox gave the entrepreneur a pedagogic look. "Does it?"
Ruperis looked confused. "It reduces desire for luxuries, especially across borders, and increases costs, although I suppose you can make up for it by adding 'risk inflation'. But that won't be that profitable, and is actually risky."

"You will be able to be our national hero," the pontiff declared cryptically.
The merchant, completely misinterpreting, shook his head. "I don't want to die on the battlefield, thank you - honour is purchased through

practical transactions, not mystical associations about physically abusing other men."

The high priest gave a relaxed sigh. "An innovative entrepreneur can make a killing during war... Who arms the troops? Who keeps them supplied?"

"Well, usually coerced and press-ganged peasants."

The pontiff shook his head disdainfully at the idea. "That's the old way... coercion, fear. Now we will hire logistics companies... like your families." He looked shiftily about the room, then leaned in even closer to demonstrate that he was about to disclose crucial information. "I suggest you buy up blacksmiths - then you can go into weaponsmithing too - hire and train mercenaries, build up contacts."

Ruperis nodded, paused, then pondered aloud, "but that would only be brief, it's not a long-term sector."

"Isn't it! The baresarks will still plaque us; we will need to take their lands to end their plaguing of our coasts and ships. Plus our allies will need arming. Then, united, we can create this most prosperous society we desire. We can remove all the stuffy aristocrats, who clumsily exacerbate the totally unnecessary peasant problems by explicitly setting divides between different level of strata, and instead of streamlining their workforces let the countless serfs and peasants run amok. That should free up labour to lower your human resources costs. Also, I am trying to get Lord Latman to deal properly with the Vaca problem; he's getting there, but their desire to stay with the past is hindering any large progress. When it finally does decide to join the rest of civilisation, it should be a very economically viable area."

The entrepreneur beamed, in awe of the mystical advisors knowledge. "You know what; I think I'm beginning to like this new interpretation!"

With that he rose from his seat. "All this time I thought you were a bad influence on Jus, but now I see you for what you really are; a truly wonderful and wise man. I really owe you now!"

Zeuorox stroked the rim of his glass, and shook his head humbly. "How ever I can be of service to you is a service to us all in the household, for it is your kind that are the wonderful people!"

As the entrepreneur left, Zeuorox smiled to himself; the alliance was all but complete.

Chapter 12
The Shed

Rabica lay on his bed. The comforting darkness was patchily illuminated by bright orange embers that skulked in the torch holders, twinkling in a sombre silence. The solemn atmosphere filled the young man with a desolate feeling of charmingly unique isolation. Though the light was minimal, it was essential to creating the correct mood; its contrast to the blanket of darkness surrounding the embers offset the whole room from the rest of the world in an eerily welcoming sign of hope. It was as though the room was a bubble in a sea of darkness. Within it, only edges of items were highlighted. The few patches of wall glossed in sporadic dabs of orange were not parts of walls; they were merely floating collections of matter held in stasis on the outer reaches of the bubble's inner casing.

The minimal lighting stretched shadows out over the whole mini-world; even the slightest crack or wrinkle became a huge gaping smear across objects, betraying lines, as though the result of tectonic faults, emphasising the flaws in once smooth statues. Only in this sombre mien could Rabica really notice the complex contours of his surroundings.

He fingered the pages of the book that lay before him; the dark script swirled across the smooth white pages with an impressive, archaic idiom. The work was an account of a Lewerix adventurer who had lived amongst the Vacarium mountain people. It outlined in excruciating detail their customs, and how they related to their culture of subsistence and balance; an amiably practical and necessary, if uninspiring, way of life. Rabica was torn between admiration and pity for these people. Admiring their caution and quaint beauty, but pitying its cyclical directionlessness that lacked any human ambition.

That said, despite its day-to-day harshness it seemed to provide a sense of unison with the world. However, Rabica recognised that this unison seemed to be the principal force keeping them trapped in the self-perpetuating stasis of a way of life with no route of escape. Every custom built up a responsible social mechanism that avoided large scale tragedy, but at the same time did not allow for any risks from which there could be dreams and aspirations to improvement.

He did not disdain or even pity the people themselves, he had nothing but the greatest respect for their ability to cope with and succeed in such a demanding life, that is to succeed in the battle for survival without being aggressive to nature itself. Though nature often threw them its worst, they did not strive to defeat the force as an enemy, merely reconcile and consequently accept its existence, and in the process minimise its impact. Embedded within nature they could strive in unison; both could blossom with mutual respect, rather than grapple in a polarised struggle. Nature was not their enemy; indeed if anything, their enemy was the spread of 'fellow man', inspired by its own (elite's) creations that it passed off as externally imposed needs. Instead, nature's external needs were the true basis from which humanity could form itself. Nature provided these obstacles for all to overcome, by all, with all. Instead, however, material desires and spiritual recommendations created by the powerful, passed down as unavoidable extra-human necessities, but really just essential to the retention of the social order, have been created to dominate society's goals.

Rabica thought of when Latman 'had' to invade Vacarium because it 'needed' the minerals for itself; the mountain people did not understand this need and so had to be removed. They were the 'subhumans' who did not properly understand 'the true civilisation' and so had to be subordinated to the will of the ambiguous group called 'Latman', so they could be incorporated into the sphere of control of the Latman elite, who in turn ascribed themselves the torch bearers of the will of the gods.

To Rabica, Juscius Latman was attempting to do the same with the other households, with the combined spectre of an imminent baresark invasion and the teachings of the new interpretation. Only the 'progressive consensus' of Juscius Latman could shield Rudia from the alien hordes of savages seeking to destroy civilisation. Never mind that in reality the jealousy of the baresarks stemmed from inadequate homelands and harshness that made forceful acquisition from the more fortunate a virtual necessity. Rabica knew no one was evil for the sake of it: some performed evil acts for their own benefit; others because they believed it would help their comrades. In other words, the only difference between the plundering baresarks and the plundering Latman elite was that the baresarks did it to sustain their people, whereas the elite did it because it made them rich.

Rabica had carefully read the banquet invitation letter sent to Lewerix, and even noticed the second level of devious genius in perpetuating internal fears concerning 'rebels of terror' seeking to keep the various peoples divided. By peddling the internal enemy line they created a homeland human face to the fears they had created to avoid a backlash upon themselves. No doubt an even broader conception of alien was being forged within Latman territory. These terrorists, no doubt Vacarium-descended rebels in Latman occupied territory, would be equated with the external baresark enemy to ensure social tensions within were directed at dissenters rather than at those powerful persons implementing and profiting from the policy.

Suddenly it struck him; it came without warning, without mercy. A single flutter of life in his mind's imagery. She stood before him, only for second, yet it was long enough for her to portray disgust at him, a minimal disgust that seemed overtly bloated with disinterest so as to render it lukewarm, and consequently, ever the more grinding on his withered soul.

Unable to restrain himself, he burst out with the pathetic exclamation, "she must hate me." The whispering sound of his voice sent shivers down his spine. "What have I done for her…" It was rhetorical: "Nothing". He decided to answer nevertheless.

"Except expose her to my crude emotions…"

'She must be haunted by that fateful day; a torturous blimp on her angelic life.' His trail of thoughts drifted from his lips again, much easier to speak aloud now they centred on him.

"The drivel of an emotional peasant, one of the many senseless confessions that she has been subjected to, this particularly pitiful plea standing out not only for its extreme primitive presentation, but also for its significance as a friend's betrayal."

'Could she ever trust him again? Was that why she had not replied to his innocent letter, sent in a vain attempt at reconciliation? No doubt she found it just as repulsive as him; even the sight of his name reminding her of his intoxicated advance. His rudimentary scrawl symbolic of his crude phrasing of his feelings that night.'

"Illegible scratches of ink doodled like a child, yet so unclean that to decipher them would be a form of scatology!"

"Maybe… Maybe she felt a tiny degree of pity, but this was vastly overcast by a fearful distrust and revulsion of *him* as her mind conjured up images of that malignant moment of her life."

'Was she really tortured by him… by me?'

He nodded like a sheep leading itself on with fake reassurance. *'The repugnance of his physical form intensified by his alcoholic stupefaction; no doubt such an inebriated state had betrayed a virility that could not be restrained. This was probably outstripped in its ribaldry status by the content of his blunt incoherent ramblings of admiration both poisoning any attempt to express the honest feelings of admiration that create the desire to treat her with the magnanimousness she deserved. A candour killed by a pestilent plague of acrimonious avariciousness that had distorted his true love for her.'*

Though he could barely recall the offending exchange, Rabica seemed to have created a deliberately distasteful image of the events. Yet at least he recognised that it was not his fault (at least not entirely); caught in the twin pincers of inebriation and fear, his reason had fled, abandoning him to the fate he had irrationally spurred himself into. Anyway, he would have had to tell her at some point, granted he had burst it prematurely:

'Like a balloon' he pondered.

"More like a boil!" he objected aloud.

He knew there was no way of not telling her, merely a matter of short-term postponement.

"Of course it could have been better, both in timing and content... but it would have made no difference... Do I really think that waiting a week, a month, etc, or staying sober... even speaking in a more eloquent way, she would have said yes?!" He snorted and contemplated whether his last sentence had made any sense, concluding that it did not matter; he knew what he meant.

It was futile. A grim blinding cloud of melancholy had drifted over the room. At first it had just been a misty amalgam that buzzed around Rabica's head, soaking into his mind and engulfing it in a deep saturnine slumber. Rabica lay on his back, motionless, as he felt his entire body melt. His head seemed to be absent, mindlessly swimming through the mist, ducking and rising to the undulating current. Yet in reality his whole body lay motionless, rupturing only into an occasional twitch or spasm.

"It all seems too futile." He said dramatically, without truly comprehending what he was implying.

With a sudden expansive eruption the mist had exploded into a thick smoky mien covering the entire room. It clung together and stuck to the various items and walls, sagging gloomily at the bottom and blooming upwards like mouldy cauliflower. Yet to the onlooker there were no walls, merely endless cloud, thick decrepit particles hoping to stand out in the greyish whitewash. There was no fooling the wandering mind of Rabica, however; somewhere there were walls, he just could not see them in his confused state.

His mind raced with thoughts of the present and future, a descent further into madness. From unjustifiable harshness, into a new, darker realm that seemed destined to seal the fate of the islands inhabitants as a factional, divided series of polarised sects fighting for confusing ideas that masked something more sinister and degenerate.

Latman's proposals stank of a crusade to heighten the divisions of imagined communities, polarising the island's inhabitants into two evils each calling the other the epitome of evil. What was worse was that Latman actually believed his own rhetoric; he was not doing it to distract his people from internal issues. He believed in his crusade with so much dogmatic faith that he would stop at nothing to achieve it, even though impossible; the total submission of a spectral enemy. He would proceed with such arrogance that he would actually create the divisions within the islands population by berating the outsiders until they lashed out. It also meant that he would stick to his plan even as the support from 'believers for convenience' (and profit) vanished, and the plan crumbled into an apocalyptic oblivion.

This banquet would be the first peak of pomp and snobbery that would set in place a series of mechanisms to mobilise a new masquerading progressivism of rising elitist ideals. This was no new opportunity; merely an expansionist internal coup aimed at updating the current social order by replacing old ideals and elites, any resistance to it would be driven into the arms of the traditionalists.

The futility of his love was dwarfed by the futility that would soon engulf the possibility of genuine social change. Isolated in the smog, clouded by his own personal failings, Rabica felt powerless, blindly grasping for the means with which to crawl out of the smoke-screened room. Only then could he set about freeing others. But to step out of the walls would render him an external enemy, an alien betrayer of all; and to squeak from within, a mere weak-kneed traitor. At least, it would be easy for him to be branded as such. Then he would no doubt be treated as a traitor by all, hated but ignored by both parties.

The words were on the tip of Rabica's tongue. "Hated and ignored... Hated and ignored, just as I am by her. She who could not understand my love."

She could not understand it for it drifted like a spectre about the room, diffusing through the walls at the will of his imagination, yet ungraspable even by him. One cannot grasp self-conjured ideas.

He felt himself drift off into a reverie, yet he was still technically awake.

The land was bleak and surrounded by thick swirling clouds of all sorts of greys, even near blacks. There seemed to be no sky as such, merely shifting grey patterns with rushing streaks of black that stretched out like deformed limbs. The shapes constantly changed as they thundered by, the swirling black masses occasionally puffed out into balloon-like swollen arms, or constrained and lashed out in an arc with what resembled taloned hands. Despite the swirling array of distant clouds the wind was non-existent at surface level. The surface in question was a square patch sunk deep into the adjoining landscape, adding to the sense of distance to the clouds that whizzed so far overhead.

Down here, well away from the patrolling clouds, the winds of confidence let out not a single sigh. No reassuring nudge in any direction, and no continual stream of a gentle breeze breathing freshness.

Sunk so low down, the surrounding land seemed to have isolated the patch. The soil was a boggy, putrid kind, a layer of greyish-white mould covering vast patches of its surface. Even parasitic life such as bacteria could not find enough sustenance, isolated from the murky topsoil by the layer of dry scum. Under the hardened crust was a peaty mud consisting of anger and fear. The soil was putrefied in a congealed amalgam of non descript hatreds, it seemed to have no true content. The combined anger and fear culminated in nothing but jealousy. Whilst the murky depths oozed and bubbled, the rigid outer shell seemed surprisingly springy. Where the mossy layer had been scuffed off, a jelly-like mud slopped and oozed with no prospect of ever drying, and consolidating; much like dredgings from a river. Such a surface remained intact only because none dared to step near. Its stench betraying the depth of its rotten contents.

In the dead centre of the patch was a huge toadstool, warty and covered in fungal growths and boils. Its thin withered stalk somehow supported the bulging mass of fetid organic matter that constituted its head. This pestilent organism was once a fresh bud; now, transformed over years of nutritional starvation in a desolate landscape, it was a grotesque object of decay. This single bloated abhorrence plagued the landscape like a crown of malignance, its head swelling with veins of putrid cynicism with such force that the flow was visible through its translucent skin. The flowing concoction diffused down the stalk, spreading deadly toxins into the already squalid quagmire, oozing from the mud to form putrid puddles. What little desire that had remained in the deviant monstrosity of parasitic love had been scattered into the marl generating smaller sproutlings of fungi. These sporadic organisms were all that constituted life, and so the only source of nutrients to the beleaguered soil that was sinking further and further down. The chemicals were trapped in degenerating cycles as the behemoth mushroom fed, and, in return spitting out gushes of liquid effluent that acted as a catalyst for the lands descent.

All this pitiful land needed was a single seed; one hope. Yet this degraded eco-system seemed to be self-sustaining; feeding itself somehow, as it festered in its own cycle of degeneration.

Rabica had drifted into the state of semi-sleep; he knew that the images before him represented the wanderings of his mind, the cyclical visions unfolding like mechanically looped fragments of films set to random repeat. He had reached the incomprehensible stage of incoherent regurgitation and recital of confused symbolic skits that changed and drifted meaninglessly, even though they clearly held some deeper significance.

'*The fungi is pestilence... it's pestilence... putrescent... putrescent like love ... love is jealousy...*'

He woke up slightly with a jolt. '*The seed... the remaining seed... the potential to escape... but only if it is... has... something else... No! It is not the seed ... it is a nutrient-feeling... an ideal to sustain...which is... it is... no, it can't be...*'

In his dazed disposition he frowned weakly. *'Or was it the system... the economy... the leadership...?'*

The distraction faded, yet he seemed not to notice that he had shifted topics. *'Love is so fundamental, that is why it is key'.*

He found himself spiralling for what felt like hours:

'The fungi is pestilent... fight it with nutrient feeling... love, that is how the system changes... ideals in love change with ways that change the system... by the sword.

It cannot be done.

Not by the sword.'

In reality the torturous state proceeded for almost an hour, an itchy, blastingly hot and sticky affair. As Rabica grappled with the sheet that clung to him, the burning heat seemed to be emanating from within, asphyxiating him from his lungs. His organs were on overdrive, burning sugars at tremendous speeds, rushing the blood through veins and arteries so the liquid syrup burnt like lava when it struck its destination. His brain seemed to be babbling precariously in its skull shell, like a hunk of mincemeat in a pan of boiling water, the foamy brine froth offering no cushion as it struck against the tin walls that encased it. He twitched with extreme irritation as though thousands of parasites were gnawing away at his skin tissue, empowered by the salty deposits of his sweat.

He scratched and turned. Periodically he kicked out with his feet to send the sheet fluttering upwards in a flurry of ethereal white to allow a blast of fresh cooling air to enter the parched crevice in the bed in which he was entangled; momentarily soothing his body before it was plunged back into the heat.

Distress at not being able to settle down to sleep rapidly by-passed a brief encounter with anger at the futility of dozing off. Instead he found his efforts being increasingly lured into the lethargic promise of sensuality. Being held captive by such sensuality could lull him into physical exhaustion that would shut down the mind, allowing for a senseless drift into sleep.

Yet the rational part of his mind was not willing to conform. No, it needed to find its own pathway, a long winding route that logically led to such activity. Then his mind could be put to rest.

He began to think of her, in all her beauty. His rationality knew what the beast within was attempting to do. He felt drawn to the images; trying, in full knowledge of the vanity of such an attempt, to resist the call of primordial desires that were stimulated by the call of the bestial mentality. Then his mind thought of her, truly, as the person he (thought he) knew, the woman of remarkable intelligence and mental beauty; the baffling internal dynamic of innocence and awareness. Silent but cordial. Reserved but active.

Suddenly the spell was broken. His mental faculties had reasserted themselves over his physical desire. Now guilt flooded his mind, and grabbed the bestial creature by the scruff of the neck. He was shamed, as though caught in the act by some overbearing authority; his own internal judges. Worse than that, was the thought that she was conscious of his current preoccupation. He sighed. Although the rest of his form was frozen, not daring even to flinch, the expression was unleashed with such intensity that it led to the watering of his eyes. As they brimmed uncomfortably with fluid. The phrase resonated in his mind: "He was despicable."

And in all honesty he was. Though so pitiful as well that perhaps one should not despise him.

The beast had been tamed and his mind was humiliated, abandoned as an empty husk. With this repression imposed, he wondered what was left.

★

His mind drifted back to the squalid fungi world. The rotting domain contained only a fetid, corrupt love encapsulated in the huge parasitic organism.

Rabica's thoughts jumped back to her. He imagined her out in the fields at her new home, wandering about the vast lush scenery, her tanned skin emphasising the near perfect toning of her muscles. She was clean and idyllic, just like the landscape. Lively vegetation swayed in the breeze that blew gently over the well-formed mounds and ravines, perfectly moulded and beaming with a beauty only possible by the prolonged efforts of nature.

Dreamily, Rabica transported himself into her landscape; lush green grass sprouting in clumps encouraged by the fertile soil, abundant with nutrients. Fresh sprouts were spread about the territory, tucked away under the overhang of smooth rocks. The teeming wildlife was clearly visible; hopping, trotting and fluttering along in full view.

Instantly, Rabica's pessimistic cynicism led him into wondering how the predators hunted, and what this meant for the accuracy of such a vision of harmony. Surely even on her plains of joy there was killing, even if it was necessary for food? Unable to take the metaphor as it stood, yet refusing any notion that her world was not tranquil, Rabica concluded that all the carnivores must be omnivorous scavengers that only killed the dying in mercy, for, he had decided, there could be no such horror in her life.

Huge beautiful trees loomed gracefully, some grouped together, blossoming and swaying in unison, others were grand organisms of independent solitude, alone but not lonely.

All around him was this world of delight, a world flourishing with precocious endeavour. So unlike his sinking slab of dredged waste; this land had such prospects.

As Rabica blundered through the beauty he tried to tread as lightly as possible, ever fearful that his boots would upset the balanced ecosystem. They could still be infected with the toxins from his pestilent bog, poisoning this purity forever, and bringing about cataclysmic destruction to her paradise.

The sun shone with a hospitable wave of rays. The warmth was pleasant, not overbearing, co-operating perfectly with the fresh breeze that drifted across the land, filling it with a sense of constant renewal. The soothing wind and penetrating rays even seemed to have reached Rabica's soul; revitalising the pitiful organism like a fresh breeze over a previously covered cut. Though it had no long lasting impact on healing, the freshness contrasted positively with the dark dank lair.

The organism twitched, like a severed limb kept in a perpetual state of throbbing semi-life.

'Was it actually alive?'

It possessed only base stimuli for subsistence not requiring the ability to consciously monitor its surroundings; it was somewhere between a plant and a foetus, that kicks for no apparent reason.

Rabica wandered about the picturesque landscape, following a stream down towards a field. The field was perfectly flat and square, and in the centre Rabica could make out a black object; from the distance it was unrecognisable.

Rabica stared at the sky. It seemed to be clouding over, and the wind had picked up. He felt uneasy and stopped surveying the surroundings. As he turned to his right, he was shocked to be confronted by a black shed. It was no doubt the object that had only seconds ago been in the distance.

This man-made construct looked out of place amongst the lush greenery; it was made of wooden planks and coated with a thick black tar. Though dingy, it looked solid.

'But why would someone need shelter in this utopia?' the puzzled Rabica pondered. Despite the picking up of the wind, and covering of the sun, the air was still warm and pleasing.

The shack had no windows; it was a practical construct possessing nothing of particular comfort. To Rabica it seemed to be the antithesis of the world in which it existed; rigid, secret, dark and morbidly cold. The door was bolted shut with a thick solid cylinder of metal; the lock was decorated with slight rust, an orange-brown worn as a badge of its resilience to time and the weather. Bulky chains were wrapped around it, clenched tightly a supportive but distrustful hug. No force could move the shackles even a fraction of an inch. Thick tar magnified the impermeability of the structure to a point that even individual molecules would struggle to drift in, or out for that matter.

Rabica's view seemed to close in on the tar; the glistening black expanded to blanket the entire scope of his vision. As he plummeted towards panels they seemed to stretch before him until it took only one to totally engulf his image. The speckled wood pattern resembled a dried sinewy surface that had been plunged into a prehistoric tar pit. As his vision continued on its collision course with the shed, he began to pre-empt the moment of impact. He winced in preparation for his nose to scrape against the scratchy dry surface, rubbing off small flecks of black powdered residue as he did so. His face would slide down and be soothed slightly as it stroked along a smooth, hardened drop of solid tar. Yet the sensation did not come: he passed straight through the surface like an apparition. Instantly he was inside, the pitch blackness petering out and in doing so revealing an expansive patch of visibility in the sinister gloom. It divulged a mouldy quagmire that very much resembled Rabica's squalid patch. It seemed totally out of place: even though he was no longer in the green utopia, something of a memory of that place had lingered in his mind.

The existence of such a scatological eco-system within her world seemed unthinkable: it was as though another had supplanted their toxic seed into her utopia, or that she had benevolently taken up someone's pain and housed it for containment. Rabica barely cogitated the notion before declaring that she had another's suffering burdened upon her, adopted vicariously in her magnanimity.

A virulent bog, pestilent and fetid, drained of its nutrients like a toxic marl; the soil of stinking decay. A slow stagnant rot stretched out, a product of intense soaking in a pestilent deluge of amalgamated poisonous liquids. Rabica gasped in horror as he spotted the disturbingly familiar fungi: His Fungi, he immediately deduced.

Was this the resting place of his nightmare world? Was this where it had spread to? Infecting her, but in her strong will she had contained it. Shouldering the burden that he had so unfairly thrust upon her? She had to keep it hidden. She could not soothe it, for it was of such potent malignance that it would burn her pure soul.

'Would it spread?'

Though it existed in containment within her, surely its presence must still have some effect: it must be slowly infecting her paradise. It was a throbbing highly contagious boil teetering on the brink of spilling open on an otherwise perfect mien.

Then he began to spread the worry wider; no doubt all who came into contact with him were infected in some way, for it would be naïve to suggest that this was just an issue of his love for her and not a general disposition.

His erratic self-blaming spread into leaps of paranoid speculation as he began to contemplate the notion that if (or to him 'as') he infected them, so it would be logical that he leeched of them too.

'Perhaps that is where the few new nutrients that sustain the ecosystem's parasitic organisms come from?' His ponders were met with approval by his critical side.

As his heavy boots trampled on the soggy layers of mould-encrusted soil, he pleaded for the foundations of the shed to be sufficient to contain the potent melange of evils that simmered in the bog.

Was this really what he was reduced to in her eyes?

This led him spiralling into a paradox as the more repugnant he sketched himself to be, the more idiotic he sketched the temperament of the young lady, for being concerned for him. After floundering in circles he abandoned the solipsistic quarrel.

He found himself drifting back into the world of the shed, and concluded that he was a diseased memory haunting her consciousness. A pestilence perforated with grotesque desire. A plague to test her benevolence. He decided that this was why she had not replied to his letter; no wonder she could not bring herself to do it, just the sight of the ink sprawled out in the scraggy patterns that bore his mark reminded her of him. Even without her reading it and cracking the enigma that hid his affections, the shapes of the letters screamed out his infectiousness. Yet despite this she contained it: in her cordial tolerance she bottled it in her shed and allowed it to with her.

Rabica rolled onto his side and grasped the small goblet by his bed, it was still full of wine. He gulped it down in one, wincing distastefully as he forced it down his throat; its bitter kick was rendered beyond endurability by its luke-warm temperature and a dusty residue from being left out all night.

He let out a sigh and rolled back into the sleeping position, his head to one side so it could see the early morning light swarming out from under the curtain with an absurd, even unnatural, semi-fluorescent glow. Rabica guessed it to be around four in the morning as this was the time this eerie brightness shone on a dead world.

This time of day intrigued the young man; it was as bright as day, yet more lonely than deepest night. It was as though someone had illuminated the night with a phosphorous flash and held it in stasis. The flash scared away all the nocturnal creatures and left a desolate ghost world waiting for life to materialise. The only noise was the occasional dozy bird tweet, which resonated in the silence like a spectre of the previous day. He felt like the only conscious being in a world full of sleeping men and other animals that were totally oblivious to this frozen world around them. Yet strangely, it was this time that seemed the most homely to Rabica. This world was his, as he was the only conscious being awake to construct its functioning. Yes, it was a wasteland, but it was a free wasteland.

For a split second he considered living in this world, dancing in its beauty. But then it occurred to him that he would only plague it with his murky quagmire and corrupt it with his parasitic tendencies. Instead he must sleep and silently adore its innocence.

Chapter 13
Glorified Whores of Violence

Pluvius paced up and down at the crossroads. They had been on patrol for two days. After having a few days 're-education' they had been sent on a trek, no doubt as a test of their new resolve. Apparently a group of bandits were roaming the area; they had had to perform a wide sweeping search across the various backwater paths for tracks. All those miles back at Gorad the priest Vultai and his bellowing sidekick Col. Sgt. Hari had no idea that their efforts were at this exact moment on trial.

The Sergeant was pondering which way to go. Though he should, as a professional, go North East to check the forest of Leira, he felt a growing urge to rebel against the strategic logic and venture south-east to Julia's village. It was midday and he could easily make it by the early evening. Spurred on by a bitter taste that contorted his face in constant reminder of his distrust and acrimony towards the two newcomers to the garrison, he felt the professional remonstrations waning into an irritating chirrup that gradually morphed into an epitome of New Interpretist conformity. He imagined this voice of his as a miniature copy of Hari muttering commands in a boisterous manner that demanded the respect of the supposed listener. Confronted with an increasingly irritating counter-arguer it became apparent that he would defy orders.

It was not just his general feeling of contumaciousness; he had to admit that romance was an incentive. Also he felt that she could help him in the longer term struggle over his concerns at the garrison.

With the decision already made he rubber-stamped it with a vague thought that his men could do with a break after their torturous ordeal in the garrison. This was in fact true, the combined mental, physical and spiritual onslaught that had been inflicted upon them by Vultai and Hari had worn them down completely. No doubt they would be treated as returning heroes by the village dwellers. This would be in stark contrast to the degrading, browbeating sermons of Vultai and bellowing orders of Hari that combined to drive a wedge through their self-esteem.

Besides, that was all they wanted really: the thanks of those whom they really fought for. It was, at least, what Pluvius needed to revitalise his confidence in Latman; to see the common citizen congratulating them and appreciating them for their life-saving intervention. This was not a desire for ego-inflating gratitude; merely to stop himself from hating what he did. Pluvius' soliloquy lapsed and he realised he was staring with a solemn longing down the south-east road.

The path was compacted soil, a heavy smooth lump mass that stretched out over the horizon like the body of a giant burrowing slug-worm. Its carapace was studded with large rock plates worn down like greying organic armour. Tufts of long grass sprouted out of the cracks in its chitinous segments like mole hairs. Flies buzzed around, dancing in the hazy air that created an arid atmosphere to the dry soil creature as though it were its own terrain. The insects landed on its outstretched epidermis and feasted on waste left to decompose on its surface. Like parasitic ticks they sucked at the lifeblood of this mighty leviathan.

Pluvius' survey was brought to an abrupt halt when a sturdy hand clasped him on the shoulder. Just as his heart sought to burst out of his chest and his shoulders instinctively brought him swerving to meet the approacher he heard the calming voice of Heites. This sent his senses back into a relaxed lull.

"Sarge, I know what you're thinkin'. And you're right. We should go S.E.".

The veteran had read his mind, no doubt he knew the reason for his desire to go to the village, and no doubt he was sniggering secretly at him for becoming enthralled by a young strumpet.

Pluvius turned to fully face his comrade and gave him a puzzled look. The returning expression confirmed that Heites was on to the sergeant. He had his 'they always go and get involved with one of them and that's the end...' look.

It changed slightly, into a more approving, pleasant smile (as pleasant as is possible for a far-from-attractive hulk).

"And you can see your lady-friend again. You know, a commitment like that might just salvage you from insanity. Getting a regular is just what you need." He turned as though addressing an imaginary crowd that had gathered, but spoke quietly so the others did not hear.

"An anchor, for our lost (maybe last?) hero!"

"How could I have a regular, especially so distant?"

"Surely that's just better; you have to use your initiative! Go on, use that strategic genius for something other than killing! Use it to spread the love!" Though Heites spoke in a series of exclamations, he kept his voice lowered relatively discretely so the rest of the squad could not hear, and would assume they discussed approach tactics or escape routes.

"Do you have a regular?" Pluvius asked, with the nervousness of an embarrassed boy asking an elder sibling of their personal exploits.

Heites laughed amiably. "No!" he exclaimed, then snorted, humouring himself. "... I have a few!"

They both let out a restrained laugh.

Pluvius stretched up tall, though he was still towered over by Heites. "Ok..." He glanced over his shoulder to his men, who paced and kicked the dirt with growing restlessness, anxiously anticipating his decision. "Let's get cracking, and we'll talk when we get there."

Heites nodded in official agreement and smiled to portray his personal approval. The pair of them set about mobilising the troops.

Arios was appointed to the rearguard, where he quietly assisted the struggling Geric. The young rookie did not even realise they were detouring from the mission's orders. The rest knew very well, and obeyed with a perkiness that suggested they were relieved at the decision; though they seemed gripped by an overarching paranoia that they were being watched by Vultai, not daring to acknowledge that they had noticed the diversion. Despite this, they all seemed to be tapped into Pluvius' psyche, sharing his consciousness and knowing his decision was theirs too: if the sergeant was confronted they would stand by him. Meanwhile, the green Geric merely trudged along in morose silence, occasionally letting out a sigh to relieve the internal pressures.

The pace increased slightly and the temperament of the men became noticeably more vivacious. Pluvius was confident he had made the right decision.

★

As they approached the town they were immediately recognised and jubilation ensued, spreading through the hamlet like a progressive plague of joyous excitement. Sailors and labourers shook hands with the soldiers. Wives waved and blushed with an overflow of impulsive exhilaration that seemed to overcome any ingrained restraint. Daughters ran or skipped over to them, the most impetuous kissing them. Those who had been in a convenient place brought flowers to attach to scale mail carapaces or hair that flowed in fresh relief, having broken free from the sweating enclave of the soldier's helmets. All of the soldiers beamed in appreciation; cracked dry lips broke into smiles as the clamped iron faces of professional restraint dissolved in the atmosphere of celebration. Even Geric's red face seemed to have burst from the internal caging that had sucked his soul inwards.

Something told Pluvius that the squad would not be spending any money at all, even if they wanted company later in the evening.

The landlord waddled up to greet Pluvius with a toothy grin. Overwhelmed by the celebratory reaction, Pluvius could not hear a word that the stocky man spoke. Nevertheless he followed him eagerly towards the tavern.

They spilled into the naturally lit bar. The wall decorations were displayed exactly as before, accumulating dust for added vintage. Even though he had only been there once before, the sergeant felt a surprising sense of familiarity as he entered; a sudden surge of warming nostalgia as though this bar was the site of many 'good-old memories'. Instinctively Pluvius turned to the corner they had sat in on their first visit, protectively scanning it to ensure no others had claimed what he now arbitrarily decided was their spot. Suddenly the homely, soothing feeling reeled back with a searing spasm from his neurons; the statue of Neptus was gone! That item was key to the atmosphere of the room: once he had got over the sinister glare of the statues eyes, Pluvius had found the motherly overwatch calming. Her menacing glare had no longer felt directed at his soldiers as intruders, but instead warding off any who sought to harm the defenders of her village. Without this, the familiarity spell that had comforted him was broken; that deity had been the principal symbol of the entire village to the sergeant, that is, along with his Julia.

'*Where had it gone?*' his mind raced in panic. '*Perhaps the sailors had used it for a new ship because they had run out of hard wood*' Then it struck him, '*They had used it to replace the figurehead on the baresark vessel!*' He laughed aloud as he imagined them hacking away at the sleek alien ship then donning it with an effigy of her most merciful Neptus and a symbol of the village.

He sat down with Heites, and a flock of girls. The landlord loomed over him, awaiting some form of response. Pluvius politely disposed of him so he could resume his conversation with Heites from the crossroads. Both of the veterans were surrounded by young girls chattering and verbally struggling to attract and retain their attention; occasionally they picked at him, prodding him playfully with their slim smooth fingers. Whilst Heites countered and spurred them all on, Pluvius sat perfectly still. Mere polite disregard was not stressing his point enough so he found himself being somewhat frosty in reception, rapidly turning the girl's attention sour.

As the incessant wittering made no sign of dissipating, Pluvius found himself striking into action. With a single slam of his fist on the table he brought the chirruping ordeal to an abrupt close. In a vain attempt to compensate for any possible offence caused by his actions, the sergeant cleared his throat, then in the politest voice he had ever used apologised. "Pardon me, but we would appreciate some time alone for a minute."

The petrified girls slowly backed away. Heites gently removed his arm from around one of their shoulders and winked at her to remind her to return.

Once they were sufficiently distant, Heites turned to Pluvius. "See, I said you needed a regular."

Pluvius was slightly confused by the statement not being made as a half-joke and so shrugged.

Heites turned to the corner where the wooden icon had been on their last visit and nodded at the empty space. There was a lack of dust on the patch where it had been which created a spectral dark patch on the floor mimicking the statues shadow. This patch contrasted with the dull grey around it to create a striking brightness, as though it remained in essence awaiting its physical return.

Heites smirked. "I wonder what happened to that!"
Pluvius was confused as to why the question was posed as an exclamation.

Noticing the sergeant's confusion, Heites continued. "I bet they had to get rid of it, by the order of his holiness." The last word was spat out with vicious acrimony. He cringed as he uttered the name "Vultai" then he paused, embarrassed at the lack of a response from Pluvius.

"Well, you know she's been condemned as well. So they'll be cracking down."

Pluvius was unconvinced. However, insistent on his accuracy, Heites beckoned the landlord over and asked him.

The landlord reacted in a startling way that totally shocked both; consternance filled his pudgy face, vanquishing it of the jovial temperament. His eyes were drained of life and sank with the jolt of profound betrayal. He looked shiftily between the two of them. The acrimony of betrayal seemed to compact into disgust at the two soldiers who sat before him. Yet fearful of his situation he swallowed his contumaciouness and replied with a guilt-tripped saturnine tone, "look, we've got rid of it…" He shook his head in disgust, "…Can't believe they sent you…" he continued, trying to make out that he was muttering more to himself than to them.

Both Pluvius and Heites were taken aback, aghast at the extremity of the landlord's change in countenance, though part of Heites was silently celebrating victory.

Pluvius gave the barman a candid look of confusion. "What are you talking about?"

The barman eyed them cautiously, wanting to believe their ignorance as second best to innocence. The icon around Heites' neck glistened in the light and attracted his attention. As he recognised it as one of Athlye, relief began to resurface. Then he offered a brief explanation.

"Couple of days after you were here, we had a priest and some regulars snooping about, they commandeered the boat and told us to burn the figurehead. They said it had tempted fate and drawn those sea-beasts to us. They said if I didn't burn it they would burn down the whole inn with it inside."

Pluvius was shocked, whilst Heites seemed less surprised and was more preoccupied with trying to hide his beaming triumphalism.

"That's insane, how long has it been here?" Pluvius asked.

The barman snorted and shrugged.

"Surely they could have just threatened to burn the icon itself rather than the whole inn," the sergeant added.

Heites shook his head "Naah, you see you can't threaten someone into doing something they don't want to do by saying if they don't you'll do it for them. It was a bluff. They can't be arsed to do anything, they might as well threaten something extreme to get you to do it."

The barman's face hardened into a resolutely serious posture. Bitterly he spat out a cynical remonstration: "they may not have been 'arsed' but the priest was."

Heites lifted his hand and showed his palm in a submissive agreeable shrug. He showed a concerned expression to Pluvius, before diplomatically returning his attention to the landlord. "Well, what can I say? You were there."

A deep cynical gloom had condensed around Pluvius, a thick cloud of moroseness stirred like treacle by a growing aggravation at the meddling of Vultai. He stared into his tankard as though it was his only hope of consolation. "If that Vultai was involved I'm hardly surprised, to be honest."

Both the landlord and the veteran snorted in agreement. With these gestures constituting the last interaction the conversation subsided and divided into three individuals trying to internally reassert their consciousness by listening to the sea of conversations that flowed and crashed around them. Their concerned faces traced voices in despair, searching for a subject to reconnect with those that stood before them.

"Well, sorry to hear of your misfortune. And we are sorry to have caused you any further unnecessary dismay now," Pluvius apologised frankly.

The landlord nodded, and then excused himself. Immediately he set about ordering barmaids to light the fires and more torches.

Once the landlord was out of earshot, Heites leant into the table and whispered to Pluvius, "this new interpretation stuff is dodgy! You gotta be at least leaning my way now cos you came here rather than continuing on the patrol? And now you've heard about the boat and the figurehead."

The sergeant remained reluctant to break with traditional intuition. "I don't know, we still have our duty and we should seek to carry it out professionally. Let's leave the decisions to those at the top, they know what they're doing and so know what is best for the house. We must let them do their duty, even if it doesn't make sense to us. I mean what do we know of the god's politics? Maybe Neptus has turned on Thelus."

Heites took a large swig of his bitter ale, using the reflex grimace from consuming such a large volume of the intoxicant to mask an expression of dissatisfaction with Pluvius.

The sergeant continued undeterred. "So, maybe it looks wrong to us, but to them it makes sense because they are the masters of all things spiritual or political. And that would include sticking with Thelus."

Heites sat in a thoughtful solipsism, batting his head from side to side a few times, whilst scratching his lower lip with his upper row of teeth. The puffy and bulbous slug of a lip had a wrinkled surface that rippled like an obese slab of fat being forcefully prodded. Then he looked up and stared Pluvius in the eyes with a ponderous look of intrigue. "Hang on. Why do we do our duties? I mean why is it that it is our duty to do 'our' bit for a shared virtue of the house?"

Pluvius replied in a reflex thought mechanism that came out as a virtual chant of a reply. "Because it is the one of the duties emulated by the gods."

Heites seemed to have adopted an amateurish sophist style and tone. "That means all duties are of virtue. Therefore all the gods' duties and all attributed duties are virtuous in their way. Therefore none can be bad. They all have an essential part to play in a perfect whole."

Pluvius nodded cautiously.

"There's no war going to break out amongst the gods – it can't. There could be personal dislikes, or maybe ones that compete with each other. They, like the human finding his virtue, are linked to the whole, but unlike man, being perfect and so holding perfect virtue, must live in the a perfect system, that is, the realm of the gods. So there can be no war. Athlye cannot defect, as there are no sides."

Pluvius felt the itching fear of defeat. "Ok, maybe it is wrong, the whole new interpretation idea," he conceded. "But…"

"Wrong meaning?" Heites interjected uneasily.

"Wrong as in incorrect!" He paused, slightly intimidated. "But it is so that we can understand it. It's simple and unites the people. I mean, that would explain why Gatan has not said the same; because then he would have to side with us and that's not in his interest."

Heites was confused, more due to a fearful dislike of what the sergeant was claiming than an inability to understand. "Ok, assuming that's the case… how can we know it is for the long-term good? Anyway, if the leaders are the masters of virtue and wisdom they should not be deceiving their people."

Pluvius sighed and rested his empty tankard on the table. "But Heites, ultimately you must obey Lord Latman as he is the house; who you swore to protect, even if people around him are deluded, you still shouldn't disobey him. If we did disobey we could cause anarchy, which must mean violence and chaos. We need his power to keep us whole. To not side with him is treason and tantamount to siding with the enemy that seek our destruction. If we weaken Latman we are threatening its survival."

Heites looked irritated, "Well, yes, I have followed, and will continue to follow Lord Juscius; I will obey him through this new interpretation era. But I will not have them changing my lifestyle and telling me how to do my job, only so it can be crammed with their dogma."

"But, we agree that we must obey Lord Latman." Pluvius let out a premature sigh of relief.

"Well, as long as it is strategic-political. In other words they tell me *where* to fight and I, along with my comrades and commanders, choose how to prepare for the fight and how to carry out the fight. Plus it must be for the house as a whole – I'm not following orders to teach Latmans a lesson by killing non-believers or desecrating a temple of any god - I would sooner pick a fight with a priest than a god!"

"Well, we all have principles, don't we?"

"No, *we* both do. You said you wouldn't be surprised at the seriousness of Vultai's threats – that's not just one man speaking, that's the whole new interpretation – it's in the dogma."

"Perhaps," Pluvius was losing interest in what he saw as their virtual consensus. To him all that mattered was that they both agreed to follow the lord. Besides, his mind was drifting off wondering about Julia.

Where was she? Surely she knew he was here by now? Ladies of the night were always the first to know when travellers arrived. Surely she, the princess of the whores, his witty mistress, knew he was here.

Perhaps she was preparing herself especially for him. His mind beamed joyously as he imagined such a scene. Or had she forgotten him? Was he just an infatuated dirty old man, a grizzled, lonely pervert, a clumsy old fool gruffly wanting to grope this vibrant queen?

She had touched him in such a way that none had done before: she had awoken the forgotten youth in him. In fact, it was more than that, she was mothering a new youth, a considerate young idealist totally alien to the grizzled veteran and his hot-headed predecessor. That was it: it felt like a dynamic birth that they had joined and collectively created, conceived in their brief encounter – combining these two 'hims' and adding so much of her richness of character. It was a bastard child of both the grizzled veteran (with newly rediscovered idealism) and the enigmatic whore. Though he hungered for her voraciously the sexual component seemed as an excess deluge gushing over something much more solid; a fiery liquid that sought to catalyse the flowering of their intellect. It was a lively supplement to the complex enlightenment.

Yet Pluvius could not see this. To him, he was an old, lonely soldier finding himself able to transform himself into a young man by forcing a young woman to share his bed (and thoughts) in exchange for much needed currency. Exploiting her company to imagine he was something he was not.

Pluvius glanced about the room in search for his beloved, silently praying to himself that she would appear like a blessed saint. He expected her to appear amongst the joyous crowd like an apparition, dreamily sauntering in zigzags towards him, yet focusing her piercing eyes on a far distant object in her mind so that she stared forwards at nothing in particular. A striking red robe-cloak would swish about her, grabbing the attention of sailors, soldiers, whores and daughters alike. But she would not even flinch in recognition of their awestruck stares, eyes enviously admiring her elegance and intelligent features. Pluvius decided that if she came for him, then he would be satisfied that he had not been the exploiter he thought he was. He longed for her appearance, though this was to expiate his conscience rather than satisfy his desires.

The sergeant was prodded hard out of his reverie. Snapping his head back to the source, his view brushed across the table and up to where Heites sat. He was confronted by two excessively made up, but still attractive strumpets, who were sprawled out either side of the veteran. Heites' hand was still retracting from its prod and back to one of the whore's laps and his back had not quite returned to its relaxed posture sprawling against the spine of the chair. The startling dresses of the two whores fanned out in a shining (if slightly faded) aura of light. It was quite a striking diorama, even when put in perspective against the backdrop of a shimmering yellow-orange tinged bar of vivacious joy.

"Isn't that your regular?" Heites shouted crudely, making a vague point with his left hand that rested on the far shoulder of one of the strumpets.

Instantly Pluvius' head shot up and to his right, surveying the tide like a starved seagull. He felt the outer husk of a heart grind to a sudden halt, the enormous mechanism pumping, struggling and heaving like a beached whale. There she was. She wore a bright red dress equally striking as what he had imagined (though it has to be admitted Pluvius was no connoisseur of garments, so his imagination was limited), with an accompanying bag that swished with exhilarated enthusiasm as she strode. She strolled, zigzagging from side to side like a hunter stalking its prey. The sequin eyes flashed then concealed themselves behind bystanders in a manner that resembled a trailing panther in the dead of night dodging from bush to bush.

Her hair was tied back to expose the maximum amount of her flawless skin that shimmered with a permanent natural tan (even the usually ignorant Pluvius noticed). The toning on her flesh was perfect, an exhilarating concoction of orange-pinkish-browns. This amalgam merged into a golden layer of pure ethereal beauty.

She glided into his personal space, riding the waves of the bar's bustling energy. Gracefully, she slid her long arm forward, offering her hand like a 'true lady'. Pluvius nervously took the hand in his rough stubby equivalent. Unsure what to do he inspected her delicate limb and digits. Unaware of Heites' frantic attempts to point out the gentlemanly reply, Pluvius rose stiffly and offered her a seat.

She looked patronisingly impressed, exaggerated to a level of camp satire. Her piercing dark eyes shot out darts of intelligent sarcasm that betrayed her amused delight in seeing him fumble.

Retracting her hand, she gave him a mock stern look.

"So I don't get a kiss then?"

She deliberately denied him time to interject. "My, you brutes surely know how to treat a lady!" She paused, but only long enough for him to recuperate from the onslaught (and for Heites to make a jibe asking where this alleged lady was, as all he could see was a bunch of whores – to which she smirked slightly with a politeness that showed considerable superciliousness). "So how are you, my dear?"

"I've seen better days… I've seen better years, for that matter." The obstacle of the awkward situation was wiped out by a confidence boost from her beaming face and body language, which revealed her true temperament was that of total delight. He saw her eyebrows flare up as he spoke, this signal in turn causing a reaction within Pluvius that sanctioned the release of his desires.

"Come here," she beckoned playfully.

He obediently threw himself into her arms and she wrapped her limbs around his broad shoulders. Then she brought him in even closer and whispered, "I don't care what the others are up to. You're still paying."

Pluvius clumsily raised his lips to her ear. "I have missed you so much," he whispered.

She smiled with self-satisfaction and widened her eyes to produce a flashing bolt of energy that passed straight into him. Then she spoke in a cold calm voice that merely sought to tease Pluvius' senses. "Well, I thought you would come back. I guess I was looking forward to it."
With a capricious shift she revealed the seductive element by elevating it to an explicit prominence, daintily stroking his stubby neck.

"I've been thinking about what you said," he blurted, awestruck by her presence.

She looked surprised, and equally bewildered. "What did I say?"

"About my life, how I live it. The dilemmas I faced but did not see. You brought me back. I was conceived in our last meeting…" Pluvius babbled incomprehensively, whispering in a disjointed stop-start manner.

She smiled sweetly with a hint of disdain; her feather-light hands stroked his stubbly cheek. The touch felt so light, that though it involved little physical contact it seemed to pass right through his craggy face and cause a warm tingling under his skin. She cocked her head to one side, like an attentive bird perched on a tree listening out and preparing to call out a beautiful song to beckon others to her audience. When she did finally speak her voice was mellifluous. "Really? Well I enjoyed our… chat." She touched his chin playfully, holding it between her longest two fingers and thumb. "Though I didn't find it as uniquely life-changing as you did!" she smiled. Though clients never liked intelligent hosts, even those that attempted to spark up conversations (for these were supposed to be haughty monologues for the whore to listen to attentively with awe), she was secretly relishing that she could finally speak her mind. However, she soon rebuked herself, reluctantly admitting that there was some kind of chemistry between them. She smiled in reassurance that a compliment was coming. "Nevertheless it was insightful… in fact I actually enjoyed it."

A troublesome thought clouded Julia's mind as she began to worry that she actually did love this soldier; that she was being genuine when she greeted him, and that her brutal candour was a defensive mechanism.

Pluvius, who was wrought with confusion, was unsure if this last comment was some kind of private jibe. Clumsily, he gripped her by the shoulders, to his surprise she seemed almost to melt in his grip. He needed to speak to her alone.

"Can we go somewhere quiet so we can talk more..." he whispered nervously.

Julia, who had recovered from her capitulatory response to his hold, frowned bemused, before settling on a solemn nod and leading him off.

Heites looked up from his discourse with the two whores and smiled with relief.

Arios stood surrounded by young maidens, towering over them like a war god, who they worshipped like an idol, feeling attracted to him not because he was actually attractive but because he was an eponym of masculinity in all its brutish form. Upon spotting Pluvius departure he bellowed a teasing jibe across the room concerning his early retirement. Pluvius ignored him. Julia sniggered, more out of pity for the giant's lack of wit than amusement (in fact the lazy snigger was a friendly substitute for a groan) and Heites shook his head in disdain, fearing it could jeopardise the crucial dialogue that was to follow.

They crossed the barroom floor and silently climbed the creaking stairs; Julia led daintily, with Pluvius trudging in his heavy boots behind. Upstairs it was totally silent; the raucous noise from below seemed a world away, distant like a crowd at a stadium. The shouting and singing that filtered through merely highlighted through contrast how silent the bedrooms were. They travelled down the dark corridor (none of the torches had yet been lit), Pluvius following Julia blindly through the darkness.

Julia opened the door to the room and took out a tinder box she kept in the small pouch-bag that swung by her waist. After a few preliminary sparks of tremendous yellow-white, the tiny room was suddenly illuminated in its entirety as a huge spark seared through the room, before dulling to a settled orange flame as the torch caught light. It was just like the room they had stayed in before: a pokey window, sloping ceiling, simple bedside table, and a rack for lodgers to throw their clothes on.

As Pluvius gazed about the room, a warm but wary sense of familiarity rose in him. It was like a scene from his life's history, inducing a collection of images that filled him with reminiscence. Though the room was familiar it did not feel like an intimate environment. It was a distant memory of a unique epoch of his life, but one which he had not yet truly accepted as part of his life. In other words it was distant not because it was so long ago but because it was part of something he had not yet fully realised or lived. However, he feared that he was here just to relive the same hazy experience, and this would become the enactment of a recurrent dream, that hinted at so much, but actually revealed little. This second occurrence would imprint him with a sickening sensation of significance and from this, with further repetition, morph into a nightmarish incident that he would be compelled to repeat again and again.

Julia's voice cracked through the silence. The premonition shattered, becoming an ignored, lingering spectre, as reality revitalised itself through her interjection.

"So you have heard about the Neptus statue?" the statement was lazily posed as a question.

Pluvius just nodded and paced up and down the room.

"So, what've they been doing to you?" she queried, sitting down on the side of the bed delicately. Though still troubled by the realisation that she had genuine feelings for the sergeant, she was enjoying the role of counsellor.

Pluvius sighed and threw his hands up in the air in angered exasperation; he shook his head and tensed his muscles, contorting his already gruff complexion. He looked at her. She sat attentively staring back, loyally awaiting a reply.

Sensing he was still too tense to unleash his worries she patted the bed beside her, beckoning him over and smiling warmly. He paced a few turns before submitting to her request and cagily sat down. As he did so, his hands automatically reached out softly and took hers, which seemed to drift towards him of their own accord. They rubbed each other's hands with mutual fervour. Pluvius' face seemed to have smoothed out, unable to keep up such an abrasive harshness with Julia so close.

Pluvius sighed again, but this time much more calmly. "Oh, just all this stuff about Athyle and re-education." Pluvius mistook Julia's contemplative silence for indifference. "It's not very interesting at all, especially at the end of a long day," he added in an attempt to distance himself from the concentrated boredom he had just spouted.

Yet Julia was undeterred: she overcame her slight irritation that he thought she would not be interested in (or worse, be able to comprehend) man's talk and then leaned into his face with a beaming smile. She motioned as though to kiss him on the lips but stopped as though it was merely a trick for his senses.

With her abrupt halt midway to contact Pluvius found himself in a purgatory position, continually moving between an itching impulse to prepare for contact and the sober realisation that this was a teasing gesture which would end with retraction. The sensual unease was soothed by the taste of her breath as she spoke.

"No, please, it sounds interesting. Why wouldn't I be interested? ... I suppose you just think I'm a silly girl," she teased, with all too obvious seriousness.

Pluvius could not identify the true taste of her breath but it became instantly associated with her and the sensuous aura about them. He could not even tell if it was a pleasant taste as he was so enraptured by the notion that it was from her. Suddenly the impulse became not only dominant but casually acceptable and so he kissed her lightly on the inner section of her lips that were exposed due to her radiant smile.

"Oh, I don't know, they've started all this crusade speak. And tightening the forces with new, paranoid security. I swear sometimes recently I've begun to think… its crazy, I know, that they want you to be a traitor just so they can make you into an example to teach the others."

"Really, what have they been doing?" she asked, stroking his forehead.

As he spoke, her eyes lit up with a darting energy of excitement. "Well, the main thing was about Athyle. Apparently Zeuorox has decided she had gone rogue or something. So we can't get protection from her. And then there was the incident with Heites and the Gatan coin – he got it from the spoils on the baresark raiders and they accused him of espionage!"

Julia burst out laughing, hugging him and nibbling his right ear.

He continued despite the distraction. "They've been trying to convert us to that new interpretation, slipping its rhetoric in here and there; everywhere. To be honest I only noticed because Heites kept sniggering about it."

Julia momentarily stopped kissing his neck and whispered patronisingly. "I'm sure you would have figured it out yourself, eventually."

Pluvius smiled at the apparent compliment and retracted his neck so he could admire her self-illuminating face before kissing her.

As his hand slid down her back inside her dress she whispered. "You're still really tense". She paused, frozen, still gazing at his face that was partially concealed as it made its way down the front of her neck. "We'll talk after… I need some time to think."

The comment was completely missed by Pluvius, who was somewhat preoccupied.

She just laughed aloud to herself, and allowed him to push her onto the bed.

★

Their lovemaking seemed to burn off the remaining itching unease that Pluvius had lingering at the back of his mind: the ever present feeling of being watched by Vultai.

Pluvius lay back, relaxed in the tranquillity of their mellowed state. From this open state of acquiescence he felt he could communicate his dismay without being consumed by it. For ten more minutes they sprawled out on their backs, staring at the seemingly distant ceiling.

It was Julia who broke the silence, twisting her neck so her head rolled onto its side, her untied hair spraying out like a shining array of seaweed. "So, soldier boy, how is all the indoctrination affecting your professionalism?" she asked so casually.

Pluvius was not unsettled by the traitorous implications of an honest reply to this question: he was safe, she was here to listen to him.

"My profession will survive. In fact, if they can get all the new recruits to follow it, they will have a formidable, united, organised and dedicated military force," he answered.

Julia laughed at how the soldier had assumed she was asking about the whole military and not him. "I thought we already had one of them?" she jibed ironically.

"We did..." Pluvius agreed, not noticing the irony.

"... Well, until they started all that new interpretation shit," Julia added, almost ecstatic at the irony of creating something to unite an already united force, splitting it in the process.

Pluvius still hadn't caught on, and in innocent seriousness agreed. "Yes, I suppose."

"Anyway, what I was actually asking was about you personally?" She reverted to a polite correction so as not to cause offence.

"Oh," was all Pluvius could muster, so unused to being asked about his own personal well-being.

Though he stumbled at first, once on track he found it remarkable easy to talk to her. "Well, I don't know... well, I kind of do... the fact that I don't know is the problem. I just don't really get all this N.I. Stuff, and it's always trying to force us to do what it says. I mean, I will fight for the house... I swore to. That is my job. It is why I am a soldier. It's my duty. But it's bad for morale, having all this mind-bullying, and having my personal life controlled too. I hate the way they make our private lives political. That's just not what I've been brought up with; what we do in private is between us and the gods, we should not be judged on earth for it. Our personal duties are our concern, and our responsibilities to the gods. They are private duties that do not affect others."

Julia shook her head. "Private lives are always political; it just shouldn't be formalised in temples and officials."

Pluvius made a puzzled but disagreeable face.

"I'll explain. My job is a profession, like soldiery. We agreed before."

Pluvius nodded.

"So what I do is in the public, or 'political', arena."

"I suppose," he conceded.

"And what I do involves sex."

Pluvius made an expression of submissive acceptance that barely concealed his instinctive smirk.

"Well, that's quite a private activity, isn't it?" She asked.

Pluvius mumbled a weak reply. "Well... maybe not when it's done by a professional?"

"Why not?" she retorted, her whole body jerking back away from him in aversion. Afterwards she was ashamed of her aggressive tone, and moved in close to him again.

"Well, it's not the same as when husbands and wives do," he protested, before continuing. "Like, it isn't the same when I kill someone and when a member of the public does."

Julia looked confused, unsure how this fitted. "But you can't kill just anyone - it is only in times of war... anyway that's beside the point. What I'm saying is that what I do is private and political – I'm filling a hole in someone's private life. At the same time I'm getting money and making a living from it, which makes it public. In fact, to continue on your point - your killing cannot be seen as only a public thing: it affects you personally - I can feel it in your muscles, I could feel it when I saw you, and was sure of it when I touched you. You were so tense, distressed, angry, and anti-social; all of this because of what you are doing in public." She kissed him on the cheek reassuringly. "Of course, now you're more relaxed... perhaps your garrison should pay me for doing them a service..." she added cheekily.

Pluvius was totally baffled. "So what does all that mean?" His tone was awash with an irritated hint of the sense of inferiority.

"It means your public life automatically affects your private life, so they don't need to force their way into your private life as they already affect it through their shaping of your profession. You should be able to act and react to their external influences on your life, and that is your input into your life. This makes you human. They are trying to limit your input to the mere acceptance of their routines; they set all the objectives as well as boundaries and you can merely choose to comply. They seek to turn your actions into habitual reactions so they can use you like a tool." She could see that rather than explain she had merely left him behind scratching his head. "How they run things affects your profession, this has a knock-on effect on your private life. How they bother you affects how you bother me," she added for simplicity.

Pluvius laughed and stroked her hair in admiration. The seaweed became untangled running smoothly in parallel lines like a ploughed field. "Why do I even try and argue with you?"

"Because I love it!" she answered cheekily. Deep in her mind she was worried that this was not just an act. Grabbing hold of him with her slender arms and long pointy fingers in a powerful but dainty fashion, she pushed herself closer to him so she could deliver him a brief but powerful kiss.

Pluvius smiled back sheepishly. "So, what should I do now?" he pleaded of her. "All my life I have been a soldier sworn to protect the household, but now I'm scared it has been hijacked by zealots... but if it is the will of Juscius then I must obey. I signed up to protect him as the symbol of our house and the god's chosen one. Maybe I just don't know the full picture, and this is all necessary."

"Does Juscius Latman have the whole picture?" she asked him inquisitively, like a schoolteacher testing a lost pupil.

"Well, he doesn't know about the morale levels on the ground, but that's not his responsibility, that's mine. I have to work with what he gives me to ensure my contribution works with his grand plan."

"But the duty-responsibility is selective in their philosophy - they condemned my profession as evil! We are demonic seducers - sirens of Angarra. In so doing they condemn some of the cogs that hold this society together."

"But they are not ruining my profession, merely shifting its goals and making it more rigid. Perhaps in the long-run we can better defend the household with such a controlled structure. I joined to protect the household, so I should continue even if I don't get the whole picture."

"Did you really join for that reason? I thought you joined because it was better than being a farm labourer. Remember? You were just like me; stuck in the middle of nowhere - be honest, please, it had nothing to do with duty!"

Pluvius was shocked by the allegations but he could find no coherent retort. "Well... maybe not... at first, but it grew on me," he eventually mumbled.

Julia nodded, accepting his explanation. This worried Pluvius as he knew she could not be conceding; in fact, it meant he must have just bolstered her argument. "I suppose, but you see that will be due to them constantly telling you that you are there for duty. And if that is so, you can outgrow it as well. Especially if it is shrinking and constraining you at a time when you grow."

"But what could I do?" he asked in dismay. "Be a mercenary? There may be no difference in your mind, but I'd have no principles or standards at all - I'd get less pay for more brutal tasks."

"You should do whatever you think allows you to be you," she answered evasively.

"But you said who I am is defined by what I do, and others tell me what to do, so there is no me without them."

"No, now you are the you that has been constructed; you have been different; you could have been different and you can be different in the future. But if you are forced into being something you don't like then you should break from it. Breaking from the conventions of others does not unmake a man; it allows him to shape himself in the future."

"So, should I fight, but try within that to act as I see correct?"

Julia sighed, growing impatient (even though he was finally catching on she had become bored of patronising him and educating him and instead wanted some fun). "Yes, dear." She leant over and kissed him. Then she arose from the bed, making him look up, startled, like a lost puppy rejected by its mother. "Come on, I want to meet your comrades, and more importantly, your friends."

"They are the same" Pluvius protested, rising slowly

She had already slipped her dress on and was adeptly doing up the buttons on the back, her spine stretching tall and proud as her svelte limbs twisted unnaturally to do up each button. As she did so she suddenly burst out in a totally casual way. "Oh, you should probably pay me now, in case you have to rush off heroically and kill some barbarians." Her voice was cool and solid in its matter-of-fact tone.

Once astonishment had washed over Pluvius' mind, he was able to comprehend her comment as a joke; sadly it was his instinctive reaction that was correct. Sensing his scepticism Julia launched a pre-emptive strike.

"What? You think you can get it for free just because I might love you!" She used a loud, mock-angry voice, and could not stop herself from smirking afterwards. Her face turned serious. "If I was your wife I'd expect you to send me money home, so why none for me? Or am I too lowly?" The last question slipped out of her elegant mouth accompanied by a tongue-in-cheek pout; a humorous expression aimed at getting sympathy.

"You'll notice I didn't even try and argue with you there!" he retorted with the half-seriousness that seemed to be the glue of their union.

She laughed and held out her hand, smiling playfully. Pluvius kissed it before standing up, groping into his trouser pocket that lay on the bed and producing some coins. He placed them in her hand one by one. She clasped them in a fist then launched herself forward and kissed him with a brief dominating peck. "That one's for free," she added as she danced off to stash the coins.

★

As they daintily guided each other down the stairs, they heard the raucous noise grow louder. The stair lamps had still not been lit, so they proceeded with caution, groping out into the darkness with one hand each, whilst the others lightly contacted in delicate union. By the sound of things everyone was considerably inebriated, obviously encouraged into rapid drinking by the jubilant atmosphere of reunion. Over the intense background chatter, Pluvius could make out Arios' drunk voice booming. He sounded like a bass drum thundering over the top of a seething mass of cymbals.

The creaking of the stairs went unheard under the crashing canopy of laughter. Their pace increased as they turned the corner and eagerly headed for the blinding light of the tavern. Instinctively, they hesitated before stepping out into the lively arena. As they entered, everyone's gaze casually and conspicuously turned to take a look at them, before returning to their coteries.

They hastily rejoined Heites at his table. He sat sprawled back into his seat with the two whores snuggled up to him. The three of them seemed in total bliss, relaxed and free, cocooned for the evening in their private stasis. Slumped against each other they seemed as one huge resting rapturous creature.

As Pluvius and Julia sat opposite them. The look of tranquillity transformed into one of inquisitiveness.

"You both look troubled," Heites stated.

Heites anticipated their minimalist expressions of confirmation.

"Maybe I was wrong saying you need a regular!" Heites blurted with his unique blunt candour. "Well, at least not one with so much to say," he added. Then turned to his accompaniment. "No offence ladies."

"In fact, quite the opposite," Julia interjected dryly, giving Heites a pouty acidic smirk.

"Exactly!" came Heites' jovial reply.

Julia shook her head dismissively. Then she turned to Pluvius; the Julia Inquisition had begun: "So what's all this about a *regular*?"

Pluvius looked sheepish, and was thankful that Heites offered an answer to the Grand Inquisitoress.

"Well, Madame," Heites began, "I was explaining to our sergeant here that he needed a regular acquaintance... or two... to keep him from going off the rails."

"Or two! He'll be lucky... He'll be lucky to keep one!" Julia laughed in a loud voice, though she was clearly not actually annoyed.

Meanwhile, the two other strumpets eyed each other wearily, collectively calculating whether to move on or endure this conversation. Julia noticed this and felt like laughing at their amateurism. After some silent, almost undetectable, communication they agreed to stay. Julia still saw it as a defiance of the code. She also noted that it was even more foolish in a bar where all the men were taken, and there were locals willing to give the 'gallant heroes' what they wanted, for free.

"Well, you see," Heites continued, seeking to explain, "in our profession it's easy to lose your link to the society you are supposed to be protecting. It's easy to become an isolated maniac with no connections outside the garrison, or even worse outside the battlefields. So, if you have a regular it acts as a link to the real world. In short, with someone to care for and someone who cares for you, you can remain a human being."

"Why not get a wife?" asked one of the strumpets.

Heites laughed "One: the hassle. Two: you are never around long enough. Three: it's more traumatic when you get killed."

"Is it?" Julia muttered morbidly.

Heites either didn't hear, or ignored her. "Four: the prospect of kids.

"We can still have kids!" Julia exclaimed.

Heites gave her a wry nod, "but we don't have to look after them!" before continuing in his list. "Five: pay is sporadic. Six: you can get transferred. So basically it's the same as a regular, only with complications and the impossible expectation of loyalty."

Julia was astonished. "You took the words out of my mouth," she joked.

Before either soldier could object she was off again. "So you've given it a lot of thought? – it's hard to imagine you soldiers discussing it like teenage girls!"

Heites just grunted a laugh.

Julia turned to the two strumpets to lecture them. "See, being a wife is much worse. All that grief and dedication... and for what?"

"But some soldiers are married," one of them protested.

"Yeah, but a lot of them are either just before they sign on to some hometown boyhood fancy.... Those can get quite ugly; when he does go home a totally different person. Or else they are a hasty thing to cover pregnancy. Sometimes soldiers just go through crises around times of fear of war, and marry so they don't go six feet under as a bachelor... and then it will be to their regular!"

"And if she's got any sense she'll take it in case he has any savings!" Julia half joked, squeezing Pluvius' hand under the table.

Heites laughed aloud in shared cynical approval.

Julia turned to Pluvius, who until then had sat like an infant at a family gathering. "You see, wives and regulars are basically the same, it's just one pockets your earnings whilst the other earns them!"

This left Heites in stitches, a state that could only be calmed by draining his tankard of ale.

"You know, perhaps I was wrong... getting our sarge a regular was bad... you're meant to calm him, not torture him!"

"He loves it!" Julia protested and kissed the dazzled sergeant on the stubbly cheek.

It was then that Pluvius launched into the conversation. "She really opens my eyes!"

His voice sounded alien to Heites, like a long dead innocent boy who had taken Pluvius' form in its youth. He took a mouthful of the ale that had been brought to him.

Heites shrugged, pretending not to know what he was on about.

"...But she really means something to me, she makes me happy, actually happy. Not just laughs to momentarily cover distress. She doesn't just add to my happiness; she is its foundations."

Embarrassed, Julia playfully whispered to Pluvius that she was still in the room.

Heites, meanwhile, laughed aloud. "The fact she's got you saying stuff like that proves the point really!" He turned to Julia with a mock (and luckily easily distinguishable) expression of anger "What have you done to our sarge?"

"It's what I need; some time out of all this bullshit," Pluvius interrupted.

"It's what we both need," Julia conceded reluctantly.

"Especially in these crazy times," agreed Heites agreed.

Julia snorted. Though the normally guttural noise was softened and feminised by her sweet nasal passages, yet it retained its inner sharpness. "Yes, I've heard about all the new interpretation stuff."

Heites shook his head as he was reminded. "Insanity, pure insanity... I just hope Lord Juscius comes to his senses and relaxes all this priest-cult stuff."

Julia looked sceptical, even disappointed at Heites for not sharing her cynicism. "What makes you think he will ever do that?" She paused thoughtfully. "What makes you think this isn't him at his senses? ... I mean, he's doing well out of it, consolidating his position by rooting out opposition and controlling people's lives."

"He wouldn't do such a thing, he stands for freedom; the Latman way," Pluvius objected defensively.

Julia ignored that the two strumpets were still drifting in and out of listening, and let out a cruel satirical laugh. "No, he stands for the *new interpretation way of freedom* – slowly coercing us into their 'free' life," she corrected.

"She's right; he is totally wrapped up in that stuff," Heites conceded. "Maybe he doesn't realise..." He was cut short by Julia's disdainful look.

"Come on – when his grandfather got us to invade Vacarium, do you think that helped us? All I recall being told about in my village was the draft, and requisitioning, for the front. We were left with virtually nothing, just enough to survive, if that – the neighbouring village had a failed crop and half the village starved."

"It did get us some iron." Heites found himself in the strange situation of not being the radical.

"Maybe, but I didn't see any! Besides, we could have just bought the stuff off them, maybe that would have cost a lot, maybe we would even have had to provide mining equipment, but it might have saved lives, avoided the enmity and stopped all this terrorist stuff now. Ok, you got your helmets, but you only need them to defend us from the problems people like him caused... they are all the same."

Even Heites was shocked. However, being a cautious man he would not criticise her without thinking about it first. "Well, they are lords who I pledge to; they embody the nation, so we must act on their order. The gods have assigned them to their role and us to ours." He declared his position, though clearly unsure of himself. "They can do as they wish on the political stage as long as they do not try to affect how I live in private."

Julia laughed, though she was obviously disappointed. "That's exactly what Pluvius said... But you see, how they run politics affects where, who, and how you fight, which affects your private life. I mean, if they were to get you to massacre Vacarium children as heretics, that would affect your personal behaviour and would raise moral questions."

Heites nodded slowly in the rapidly darkening room. All around him the seething mass of people were so distant, every crack of blackness that surrounded them spilled out in a grey ink merging into a chattering patchwork quilt of movements. He seemed stranded. Alone, so far from the rest of the inhabitants of the room. An infinite barrier separated even the fellows in his coterie into the spatial gap between him and them. Instead, he was surrounded by the vivacious undulations of a shifting intellectual milieu that stretched out into eternity. It was as though he had finally opened his eyes to a new way of thinking. When he really thought about these things and didn't just accept other's explanations he began to see history was not just about lords. It was people, not houses that mattered. The more he thought the more he got glimpses of this worldview, where people could be seen outside the household, and where such a traditional scope revealed itself as a machination.

"That's true! And of course I would refuse to commit such atrocities, however I fight for the household, and by that I mean its people – they, I have a binding affinity to." Heites declared.

"...And they can be epitomised through the will of Juscius Latman," Pluvius offered.

Julia shook her head, and began to object, but was stopped as Pluvius continued.

"Maybe he is sending us down the wrong path, but he will learn from it. Besides, to disobey his word would be even more damaging."

Heites, inspired by his realisation, led the counter. "But the current events are not a one-off occasion. The Lords have led us through suffering and hardship. Always claiming it is for our good, but it's just been to fill their's and their cronies' pockets. They then claim it is victory for us all." Julia seemed pleased that one had got it. "...And this is just an extremely ambitious version of these ploys the rulers play."

Pluvius was horrified. "But if that's the case; we have been fighting for a farce." He had not accepted the argument like Heites had, but then he had not caught onto the ideas behind it.

"No... well, kind of." Heites, for all his candour, tried to comfort him.

Luckily Julia was at hand. "No... All it means is that you're like me! A vice-boy earning an honest wage to sustain yourself! Tools for the merriment of superior people."

Heites, too jubilant at his new understanding to recognise its terribly depressing implications, chuckled. "Yep, we're the glorified whores of violence!"

Julia turned to Pluvius, then to Heites. "But you can still do good. You can save lives; like when you were here last... it's just it's not a glorious victory for the house, just - I say, just, but it is, at the end of the day, the most important thing of all - a victory for ordinary people."

Heites nodded in agreement, though he was getting considerably drunk now, finishing another ale, and barking for another.

Pluvius was still baffled and upset; his anxiety was visually present in his greying face, his stubble like the post-death growth on a corpse.

"But how can we know what is right? ...The lord has an overall picture."

"You're missing the point. He has the overview, but not the desire; he has more pressing matters, more 'important' people to please than those that need attention most. Helping the poorest is only relevant as far as it keeps them contented. You, however, have human compassion. You should act in consideration of what you think is best for all - after all, you cannot be expected to do any more. You uphold order, but should be prepared to protect the weakest from violation. As long as you can justify your actions and not just accept dictations from others. The gods set us here to emulate them, so we must have choice, otherwise we could never do wrong, and would be merely a minute mirror-image, rather than an aspiring mimic." Julia corrected.

Heites broke of the vehement debate by gulping some ale noisily; once attention was drawn to him he expressed his impressed excitement. "My gods! Sarge, you really got yourself a philosopher queen! I just hope she's as good at her profession as she is at telling everyone else how to perform theirs!" Blatantly inebriated, he continued helplessly. "I mean, she's got looks wits and intelligence, there must be something missing!"

Julia smiled nervously, unsure whether this was flattery. She decided to utilise her newly praised wit. "Like you ruffians care! Or even know what's good in that department! You just count the orifices, drink up and go for it!"

Even Heites blushed. "Gosh, she's a crude one too! Anyway we know our quality... well, some of us do. Why else do you think I'm paying for these lovely ladies rather than getting the free, inexperienced specimens?" He gestured at the two whores, who were dropping off to sleep.

Julia's dark eyes darted across the table at the drunken soldier with impressed appreciation. Heites looked back with a delayed smile. His inebriation meant he was not able to acknowledge the warning as her eyes lit up in pre-emptive ecstasy at her next jibe. "Yes, but do *you?*"
Heites let her down by being too drunk to remember what they had been discussing. "What?" he mumbled.

The gloomy reddish lamplight cast a striking melange of dark shadows and illuminated bright patches with an ominous red tinge. A shadow lazily dropped down from the hazy darkness and enveloped Julia's face in a hood and mask. The whites of her eyes like snow-covered lakes surrounded by reddish darkness, which themselves engulfed pitch black island-orbs that were brought out in striking contrast. Her chiselled features were emboldened by the dark thick lines of shade. The red of the room seemed to bolster her stunning red attire; her dress shimmered with a scarlet halo. It was like a painting; the hazy bustle of shadowy people merged into a moody organic background, whilst in the centre sat this red shrouded angel of the night.

The two whores who had accompanied Heites awoke from their light dreams and stood, swooning like cherubs to their queen, before tempting the soldier upstairs. There they would join their queen's other acolytes in her makeshift temple.

The three of them hovered behind her and she seductively played with her hair and beadily eyed them through the corner of her eye. She smiled dreamily for no apparent reason.

Pluvius sat admiring the diorama, attentatively trying to work out what had amused the angelic queen. He wished he could stare at her for eternity. She sat there, so physically close to him; yet mentally she was soaring past the stars. He could see right into the intricacies of her mind, the red of neurons streamed by as they illuminated and sparkled with stimulation from dreamlike pulses of consciousness. Yet, he could not even comprehend the complexities they contained; fearful and embarrassed he found himself fleeing away from her soaring through the solar system in her reverie. He struggled within himself as he found the invitation to fly with her being withdrawn.

Pluvius snapped out of his cogitation and noticed that Heites had gone upstairs. He turned back to Julia, who sat as though in a trance. She clearly did not want disturbing. Without getting too close and invading her private space, he leant in to her and whispered that he was returning to the room, hoping she would follow soon.

Chapter 14
The Fop Wraith

The goblet let out an echoing soulless bang as it struck the solid oak table. It seemed to boom, vibrating deep within the broad wooden surface in a way that drowned out the faint resonating clang of the upper part of the receptacle. When the noise had subsided, it was followed by an abrupt cough, of the sort to clear a throat not clogged up with phlegm, but the numbness of unease. This time the source of the disruption was Lord Gatan himself. Before him was a meal: Standard Gatanese food of mixed poultry meat and baked potatoes. Both seemed to be competing in being as dry as possible. The accompanying wine was also dry and rich, to the extent that it numbed the senses.
Gatan gazed about the room, fully conscious of the virtual silence.

He eyed the sombre statues of his ancestors and gods. He nodded dutifully to each. Wishing they could accompany him in a grand feast. It would be the antithesis of his current environment. Jovially, they would roar with laughter, tearing great hunks of bronzed avian flesh, dripping in thick gravy, before hungrily devouring it and downing a tankard of ale - the warrior's drink. He was briefly reminded of his last hunt with his sons, when they had done exactly that.

His sons were away on a training exercise near the town of Nepsius, in North Neptus with Hercela, Gatans trusted Commandant. A sparkling smile sprang open on his face as he proudly reflected on his sons, admiring their skill and envying their hot-headedness, especially Maximus.

However, these pleasant images were diluted as they tried to fill the cold and empty hall.

Aside from this, he needed something to take his mind off pre-emptive concern over the foppish bravado that would no doubt constitute Lord Juscius Latman's 'council'.

The room was poorly lit by a distant fire and a solitary candle that dribbled messily over an ornate candleholder, smothering its aesthetic intrigue with a rapidly cooling smoky-grey layer more suited to the mood. Meanwhile, the fire flickered with consistent minimalism, maintaining a drab sprinkling of light on the room. It was certainly far from the roaring, crackling inferno that Adonis would have at a hunting feast. The statues watched the scene; their emotionless faces piercing through the cold with disappointed indifference at the desolate spectacle.

A fly had been buzzing from dish to dish, but had been put off by the extensive distances and minute tufts of steam that were the final remnants of vapour that had survived the intensive cooking process. As each baked potato was opened the billowing jet was like an eruption of steam. For a while it perched on the table a distance from the food, doing what flies do with their sleek front legs and sucker mouths. Now it seemed to be in panic, buzzing to and fro, seeking to escape in epic excursions from wall to wall. Other flies could be satisfied in such a huge room, with its huge meals set out like clockwork. But something had unnerved this fly about this desolate place.

Lady Gatan delicately slipped some chicken into her mouth with a fork and chewed it as silently as she could. What she longed for was gravy; she disliked wine and was thankful that as a lady she was expected to only sip daintily at one glass throughout the meal. Now and again she forced her eyes across the table at her husband. As she did so she managed to retain her stern 'lady of the house' demeanour. It was best when she just caught a glimpse, a quick glance where his striking features shone back; his flashing dark eyes full of excitement, his mighty warrior beard jet black with honourable streaks of white that were, to her, badges of veterancy. But now she looked too long; she saw his eyes were alive as he crudely ravaged the poultry and the beard was littered with flecks of the very same. She tried to open her mouth to speak but could not, cold thick air surged in like a glacier and clogged her voice box. Her thoughts turned to 'her boys', as she was still desperately calling them. She knew it was self-deceit; they were not boys but men. Boys need mothers, youths need fathers, men need fellow warriors, and that is what fathers can become; but as for women they need lovers and maids, obviously Lady Gatan could be neither.

'*Daughters are different*', she thought. '*Women need mothers as guides and council. Mothers continue to assist a daughter in her honour, whereas with sons they can merely strip it by making them mummies' boys. Daughters even need fathers, it's hardly as if Adonis would have lost out, they need protection and so they need brothers, and brothers with sisters have a family honour to protect which brings them closer to the family. So, even Maximus wouldn't have lost out (for it is better for the brother to be elder)... any brothers after that are a bonus.'* Such was the opinion of the lady; the family was quite a specific unit, especially if it is to be perfect and the lord's family should be.

She used to point this out to Adonis, but now she daren't; she knew he thought it too late; but vigilance and piety can achieve miracles, or so she believed. She had even pointed out the political dimensions; it was not mere 'motherly banter' as he no doubt viewed it (one could tell from his jovial scoffs - it was 'woman's talk on a man's issue').

One son and one daughter was best, concise, she had decided. The heir and the alliance builder. More than one son was provided they got on (as Maximus and Claudix did) but, if they become rivals, or the younger more popular, he may seek to usurp. As for the argument that one needs more sons in case the first dies, forgets that if a son is so weak as to die young, the family surely should not rule.

As for daughters, they are emissaries, who, through betrothal, forge alliances with other lords, but never for generals, for once they marry into royalty, the general may expect the throne. Besides, only royalty would be good enough for her daughter. "Maybe Telis," she had told herself resentfully. After all, the son Lewerix, from all accounts, was a bit weird.

Oh, how she wished she had a daughter to nurture. She must have accidentally betrayed her dreamy mental venture with a sigh loud enough for the bearded blackhole to cease devouring.

"What is it dear?" he barked through a muzzle of masticated chicken. Though the tone was not scornful the fact that the usually sentimental word 'dear' was said with such a lack of emotion made it meaningless and therefore hurtful.

"Oh nothing... I just miss the boys," she uttered without even thinking.

Adonis forced a smile of sorts; it was an attempt to warm the room, "Well it's certainly quiet without them about."

Too quiet hung in the air, and dangled precariously off the tips of both their tongues, like aged spiders. The fly buzzed cautiously.

The fire let out a crackle, but it was not enough to disperse the extreme unease that had engulfed the room. Such was the atmosphere that Lady Gatan felt as though her nerves had risen out of her flesh, and now protruded like varicose veins, pushing out of the surface of her skin. She wanted to tense all her muscles at once, screw herself up into a ball of tangled nerves, wrapped tight around a core of tense muscle. Then, just as the pressure became unbearable, throw herself outwards with one huge movement, using all the energy she stored up to lash out in all directions. All her muscles would scatter and stretch, soaring through the tension in the room, the heat exerted cutting through the desolation, turning the icy stiff coldness to steamy vapour.

Then maybe the tenderness could return. She was fooling herself, and deep down she knew it; she was harping back to a golden age of true love that never existed. It had been a marriage of practicality, of tradition, of prudence and ultimately conservation; a union of high politics that made any chance of passion curdle into an awkward stodgy potion. But nevertheless, if she thought really hard she could convince herself. It was ironic that their 'mature-practical realism' could only be made liveable if they anaesthetised themselves with such idealism. Prudence had condemned her to pitiful sorrow and pretence just as flimsy, if not more so, than if she had blindly followed her dreams in the first place. Was it not better to dream of an unlikely better future than lie about a better past?

Sometimes Lady Gatan daydreamed favourably of getting drunk deliberately just to have an excuse for behaving gaily and intimately with her lord. She imagined it now and sat staring at her beast as it cut a swathe through the potatoes. But the stony grim faces of the gods caught her eye, frowning with parental disapproval at the lady thinking such a thing. She sighed and returned to her meal.

Though the stiffness remained. Lady Gatan could not stop herself from glaring meaningfully at her husband, fiercely attempting to repress a wife's (or was it more a mothers?) expression of concern. Yet whenever his beady, watery orbs glanced upwards towards her, her own pupils instinctively cowered in shame, shifting between plates and sections of the table.

This two-way game of blind man's bluff continued for some time, each longing for the other, yet fearing the other's wrath were they to utter a kindly query. With intense vexation they lunged at the food, both concealing the true feeling of woe that hid deep in their contemptuous ignorance. Lady Gatan daintily pecked at the food with an acidic sneer and Lord Gatan savaged slab after slab of crisp flesh, as though his manhood depended on it, only pausing between pieces to steal a sorrowful glance at his wife.

Cautiously they pried at each other, fearing to be spotted by the other, for 'it would not be proper to find oneself doing so'. Yet, with such frustration in the room, we watch on for it is exactly what they dread that can be the only end to their neuron splitting brain haemorrhaging tension. Even I, the narrator (who has kept himself to himself for quite a while until now), has no control over what I see, and as spectator I can only watch as this scene is unfolds before me as outlined by the author.

The awkward silence was already taking its toll on the lord. It was at these times that he was most vulnerable to his haunting sprite, his curse of the living, his pre-emptive wraith torturer, 'The Prancing Lord Juscius'. Already he was beginning to feel the presence of the Jester-Lord, grinning as he peered around the statue of Thelus. Leaning on his shoulder as though the god were an old chum, slapping him playfully on the back while laughing smugly.

'I bet he doesn't go through this every meal!' Adonis grumbled in his mind.

Then the images began.

Ever since the invitation he had been plagued by it. One flippant bitter remark in his head and the sprite sprouted out of the resurfaced bile, bursting out of a gelatinous sack like a tadpole from frogspawn, and straight into a mocking dance. Adonis tried to dismiss it, it said nothing derogatory about himself; but then that was the point, it didn't need too - its happiness contrasted and exposed his glum solitude. Its easy satisfaction, thoughtlessness and youth was the antithesis of his laborious pondering, slow, methodical and traditional.

The fop-wraith danced about the room with his mistress Torian, an overly svelte figure. Flimsy beyond slender, bony to a point of inanely ill; deliberately wasting away; an orchestrated disaster, the body coerced and controlled by a deluded mind. It was not beauty; to admire it would be misanthropic, like admiring a cholera victim for returning to the same well day in, day out. Yet despite all his condemnation, Lord Gatan felt a twisted longing to touch the bag of skin stretched over bones. Despite all the odds, it had retained femininity; indeed, one could argue that that was all that had remained of that self-consumed shell of a being.

They danced with gross sexual satiety; feeding each other with sweetmeats as they did so, in a swirling melee of consumption and exertion that culminated in collective retching. Adonis had to look away at the scene. Everywhere he looked, the newly emerged pot-belly heaved in and out of existence, expelling rich, barely masticated food coated in stomach acid. With each dispensed mouthful the belly shrunk until the rib-cage frame was visible again.

Their laughter had never ceased, and now she had finished her chundering they could return to dancing in duet. The sordid cackling seemed to echo around the hall, bouncing violently off the statues with mocking defiance. The fiendish duo was here, haunting him in his own dining hall.

Surging torrents of anger crashed against counter currents of fear, sending forth the usual impressive spray of despair. He found himself battered and mauled against the sharp and naturally brutal rocks of reality. With a tremendous smack the bulky lord impacted limply against the rocks of impending doom.

Suddenly they vanished, his eyes bouncing off the creases and folds in the chipped statues. The echoes had ceased. Or had they? Adonis surveyed the scene with jerky movements of his neck, repositioning his ears to fan out the search for the taunting joy. He spotted movement and his attention jumped to it.

False alarm.

It was the fly, no doubt intrigued by the surprising arrival of liveliness to the room ('could it see them too?' Gatan pondered). He followed the dancing pest with his beady eyes, and for a moment, lost in its trance-inducing movements, felt a fleck of happiness. It was easily brushed off and he came back to his practical senses leaving a stale-bitterness in his mouth. His eagle-eyed search lapsed into redundancy with a submissive physical sigh. Instead he would listen out; the ear front was given priority.

It was then, amongst paranoia-induced twitches, that the whispering cackles returned; faint murmurs of untraceable scorn. It was all hands on deck as his head swivelled like a dreadnought turret to find the enemy. The order was given out to re-supply the eye front, and the orbs began to search for the target. This was performed, at least at first, with organised smooth sweeps, but as panic rose the movements became more erratic.

Images of the forthcoming banquet-fiasco bombarded his imagination like a devastatingly intense propaganda operation. Leaflets fluttering like dainty wounded birds; dirtied doves. He saw the likely outcome of the meeting. It was worse than having the fop-lord present now. At this banquet, the thespian would maximise his facetiousness with expert skill, viciously but subtly turning the other lords against Adonis, and undermining him simultaneously, before turning on his weak spot: Lady Gatan (this proud traditionalist lord saw, as many of the sagas did, women as a warrior's downfall). He could see her now, being bottle fed wine by the lord as he slithered about her with sly warmth, brushing against her and caressing her into a putty. All along keeping up the pretence of harmlessness. With her as his lap dog, dancing to his tune. This was no congregation of leaders; it was manipulation and segregation - it was a move to deliberately isolate Gatan using this phoney innocent charm.

'It was a masquerade masquerading as a banquet, and so only the host (and his lackeys) would have masks.'

Adonis was too deeply engrossed in his nightmarish reverie to realise what a frightening spectacle he was putting on for his poor wife. She had entirely given up on the pretence of eating and sat staring with a worried expression ably closed with fear. When he began jolting and murmuring she had likewise flinched nervously and fidgeted every so often, daring herself to intervene to no avail.

She heard him mutter something about masquerades. She arbitrarily took that moment as a trigger into action. Yet she had barely even flinched into leaning forwards to enquire when her lord and husband abruptly stood up and with a hazy anger proclaimed that he "would expose this farce" and stormed out.

With a now routine manner of self-restraint, Lady Gatan hid her excessive, gradually overtime overbearing exasperation with delicately dainty fork motion, picking at the wispy streaks of chicken that peeked gingerly from gaps in the poultry bones. Sadly it was only the solitary fly, in its own dance of death, that was present to witness this most remarkable charade of denial.

As her sense of isolation built up in her mind she let out a sigh, partly of relief (at not having to uphold the farce any longer) and partly of despair (that the farce not only existed but was increasingly defining her). Now he had gone she felt free to think of how much she adored him.

★

He was away from her ever-present eye, the beady orb of restraint; it was the beginning of the end of despair. Adonis strode with deliberate attempts to thump his boots in a hasty militaristic fashion, and found the resultant noise comforting. He wheeled speedily around corners in the corridor, for added sense of mission. He passed several guards who appeared to whiz past him in a blur, rendering identification impossible.

In a startlingly rapid passing of time he found himself approaching his office, at the last minute making a right turn to face its solid entrance. In a fit of exasperation he fiddled angrily with the lock - such a pitiful little contraption seeking to emasculate him as he struggled to enter. Eventually, with a little patience, the iron contraption did his bidding. Slamming the door shut, he set about using the metal mechanism to shut out the prancer, in case he still lurked out there. The fire flickered, an eternally burning source of warmth and comfort, which was kept alive by servants with access as they followed Gorax's instructions on how much and when to add fuel to enable ever present enlightenment. As he gazed about the room inquisitively the illumination seemed to spread into every crevice, proving beyond reasonable doubt that the prancer was not present. Indeed, as he was claimed by the flickering flames, he began to remember it was not real at all.

In an attempt to calm himself and simultaneously stimulate thought, Adonis Gatan paced, though in truth it merely intensified his anxiety, like a pendulum whose weight was perpetuating itself with every swing.

He needed to prepare himself for his actual encounter with the lord; then he could simultaneously counter the foppish phantom that haunted him. He needed to use his traditional principles to show he was the bulwark against the masquerade, the honourable warrior of days past. What is more, he needed to prove his grace - not empty showy *grandeur* of Latman, but practical, thoughtful grace. The mailed fist held out for friendly alliance, not a harlequin's foppish glove seeking fiendship.

To Gatan this meant only one thing - he needed to see Gorax. He could come up with something practical.

"It will have to be a gift to justify its presence at the banquet... not a useful gift, an expensive and patronising one! Something frivolous, but certainly possessing; something innovative so it shows off Gatan's potential - a huge diamond is pretty, it is worthless in reality, but crucially it possesses no mechanism, no sense of awe beyond its physical beauty and certainly no proof of superiority - it's mere luck of the territorial draw!"

Just as the Gatanese Lord was achieving gleefulness he heard a faint knock at the door. He paused. *'Was that the prancer?'* he thought absentmindedly.

"Who goes there?" he declared, as though a knight in a fable.

"Where?" came the confusing answer.

Adonis was sure it was Gorax; nevertheless he decided to continue the debacle. "Before this door."

"Before or after? Past or future? Surely now we can only humbly desire the present?"

Adonis was confused and let out an equally baffling noise "g?" He was sure that it was Gorax and so opened the door.

As usual, the eccentric was armed with a collection of parchments. The fire flared up (to Gatan it was a positive sign as the fire spirit welcomed the inventor, whereas to Gorax it was a result of the draft entering the room and feeding the flames) and illuminated his wizened but chirpy face.

He entered, bowed, and rose amiably as the warmth currents from the crackling fire hit him.

"You called for me sire."

"Yes," Gatan hissed ponderously. "... I need something... something to impress..." He trailed to leave the words drifting in the fire's convection current. The hot air barely got to rise before sinking into the cooler air below.

"Well..." The wrinkled prune began to unravel several scrolls at once.

Lord Adonis Gatan waited patiently while the first idea was accumulated into a coherent package.

"This is my favourite," Gorax declared, not realising that its nature would be under such scrutiny.

Gorax took the lord's beaming face as a signal to continue. "Well, the idea is for a system of waste disposal in the city."

Adonis face wrinkled up in disgust. Though he doubted any explanation could redeem this idea, he nevertheless waved for more information.

"This system"- as Gorax blathered through the explanation, he pointed to various points in the map - "would take effluence from the main houses with man-made streams then use a certain type of fungi to remove the bad airs and create a fertile soil which can be spread on fields."

Adonis' podgy warrior nose voiced his displeasure visibly. "Really?" he barked, with disdainful disbelief.

"A most profitable and helpful idea for the city and the masses." Luckily Gorax had reversed his preference of advantages, not that it mattered as Adonis was appalled.

"Use our shit! And I don't just mean our peoples', you mean literally my family... should have our faeces spread out for public display and spread about by grubby peasants! And then be expected to eat such crops ourselves! Why, that is foul! If you were not so respected and faithful I would have you cast out of this house's territory, this instant! You sicken me, plain and simple," he bellowed, barely keeping control.

"But..." Gorax protested, though he soon realised arguing would be futile.

"Besides, how can I take this idea to Latman?"

Gorax had not actually been told of the plan, but now he understood. "My apologies my lord.... had I known... it has been tested - it is sanitary as well - it would clean the streets," he added quickly, before moving on.

"I have another plan, sire..."

Gatan was eager and impatient, "what?"

Gorax produced the next plan, grinning as he was certain this could win his Lord's favour: it was a militaristic design. It was a catapult, much more sophisticated than the cumbersome, temperamental and short ranged onagers that had been tested. This one was properly weighted. Gatan was impressed; however, he was so impressed he worried that it could not be shown to the enemy at the banquet. "Would it not be better to unveil this war engine on the battlefield? Not just for the terror, factor but for fear they may copy?"

Gorax nodded submissively in agreement, his lord was correct; however, he was not disappointed as he had guaranteed funding of these after the banquet gift had been built.

"What I need is something remarkable, totally pointless, but equally as frivolous and expensive. So useless that its genius is almost matched by its uselessness," (to Gorax's mind this was a paradoxical idea as genius had to have practical merit). "For we mustn't give him anything useful, but it must show how advanced and wealthy we are, as we can afford to waste so much and still be better than those prancers!"

"Prancers?" queried Gorax with confusion.

"Yes," Gatan declared, only then realising that he had betrayed to the inventor the name given to his phantom nightmares. Now he would have to use it all the time, to make it an accepted derogatory term of Laterians.

Silence ensued, but was broken by Adonis' mind sketching out an idea. "What we need is a statue of a god; we need to hit him where it hurts: religion, it must relate to that for that is where he claims superiority."

Gorax gave a half smile. He could immediately recognise the genius of the lord's idea, but still felt frustrated, even betrayed for not being able to build his sewer system. He could still feel the imperative of all the lives that could be saved or rejuvenated with better sanitation and crop yield. Then he set to work contemplating the Lord's idea. First, he would listen to Adonis' vague notion.

"It must do something; light up, give off a pungent aroma..."

Gorax was wondering how he would fit it into this: he was no sculpture, and smelling scents was more a priest's speciality. "Maybe it should move!" he flippantly remarked, a grin threatening to explode on his face and replace the serious scholar.

But the lord was not paying attention to expressions. "Could you do that? Excellent!" he sounded so excited, like a child querying an aged uncle who professed to be able to conjure magic.

Gorax could not let him down, and so gave off an equivocal affirmative.

"Excellent. Well, you'd better get planning. I will write a document giving you anything you need without any exception... this must be done," the lord declared with a newly returned gaiety.

Gorax nodded. "Sire, I will need to send notices to the Ateri Sculpture Guild for I will need the finest sculptors in the land."

"Yes, anything!" Gatan declared absentmindedly.

Just as he was dismissed, Gorax suddenly remembered. "Sire, you remember what I told you about the project I had begun in Vacarium? Well there has been a problem; the experimental batch seems to have been delayed on its travel."

Gatan was too preoccupied with pondering the statue's dynamics to properly hear or even be interested if he did and so just waved the inventor off.

As Gorax left all he could think about was the pointlessness of his new 'imperative task' and what a waste it was. However, the scientist was not done for yet, he was already wondering how he could use his newly granted freedoms to amass the necessary equipment for a mini-sewerage-system - who would check, or more importantly who would even have the slightest idea what was for what? Sometimes inefficiencies and monarchist prerogative could work to his advantage.

★

Lord Gatan felt happy, joyous with pre-emptive jubilation. A bemused frown rose over him as he lustfully revelled in his now eminent victory. In the corner of his eye he saw the prancer impotently attempting to degrade and mock him, but it was to no avail. The looming figure of a huge stone effigy of Thelus loomed over the now dwarfed character. For all his prancing, the thespian apparition could not stir the slightest vexation from the proud lord as he calmly shuffled his broad shoulders into his authoritative throne.

The prancer squealed and shrieked as it shrank into oblivion, and Lord Gatan was fully reassured. He was so preoccupied with his personal victory over the nightmarish spectre that the wider implications that would ensue from the banquet had not even begun to twinge in his brain. No, to him this show of superiority would be enough, it would pin the usurping pup to the ground and humiliate him: cut the little weed before it could connect with the other weeds and instigate a rebellion. Yes, a rebellion; for this is how Gatan saw it; not as a rebellion against him, for he was no authority over them. No, he was not so arrogant as to see himself as master. On the contrary, he was a servant of that which the rebellion sought to target. The rebellion would be against that which the lord prized most over all else; the social order.

All the lords were servants in this respect, or more sergeants, those highly respected and practical underlings who ensured the mass bulk of mankind, divided as it was, conformed to the stable order. Oh, he believed in the house, he believed in making it strong, dominant even, but he was not foolish enough to seek total control. It was the law of the gods, and Juscius Latman's belief in the new interpretation proved his desire to upset this social order. It was the desire to retain this social order that ultimately drove people like Lord Gatan, and within this, the expansion of their city state. For, to him, any attempt at complete domination or adherence to particular principles would destroy the hierarchies and societies which existed, and from which people such as Lord Gatan derive their power.

He was confident that this social order would remain, for the other lords would recognise this, whether potential enemies or not. Indeed, enemies mutually benefited and built upon each other's opposition - for without the threat of hordes of Latman or Lewerix soldiers pouring across the border, how else could Lord Gatan find an easy justification for the necessity of his rule and the unity of his people behind him?

Gatan smiled to himself confident he had seen the last of the fop-wraith...

Chapter 15
Forging the Regime

Juscius and Torian lay intertwined in a brightly coloured heap on the soft cloth picnic rug. The lord lay, his body snaking left and right, meandering like a river. Floating on top of this stream was the dainty figure of Torian.

They nestled together in the warm soothing breeze, intermittently listening to each other and the teeming wildlife. Resting by each of their right elbows were crusty baguettes thickly spread with butter and a hunk of cheese.

Torian's handmaiden and Juscius' personal guard had disappeared into the wilderness. Having found themselves together so often, something was gradually and accidentally blooming, a relationship which to the lord and lady was a quaint and cute side-effect of their love. Something that they could patronisingly pat with words as they lazed in the shade.

Juscius and Torian no longer felt the need to hide in the secret garden in these days. Anywhere they shared had become magical, and this magic seemed to increase the further they were from the possibility of being disturbed. They felt the utter freedom to confess all to each other: outside the earshot of others they could finally express all they had to say. Juscius gazed into her eyes. The brown orbs glistened attentively, occasionally darting to a tree or bush in search of some creation of nature. As he twittered endlessly she only half-listened, occasionally exclaiming, "oh look, a rabbit" or such like.

They lay in a space in the dense foliage of a small wood, not a forest, they were too huge and intimidating. This enclave was made up of a small bundle of trees around a pool of water, a mini-ecosystem where everything seemed internally linked. It was not so much a food chain as a food family - close knit - even if hierarchical. A couple of people can sit in a wood and feel part of it, whereas a couple of people in a forest are intrepid invaders exploring a mighty otherworld.

Torian toyed with her hair, but after a while became bored and so began playing with his. Juscius' hair had been cut short to imitate robust masculinity (Zeurox had told him it would go down well with the Commanders, who he needed to appease during the military reform). She worked his hair, rubbing her forefinger in circles all over his scalp, creating momentary crop circles in the brush-like black hairs.

Meanwhile, Juscius waffled about the upcoming banquet. Torian failed to see the point of this banquet, unless Juscius was going to come up with some actual solid proposals, rather than just vague, well-wishing notions of unity and collective self-congratulation at coming so far. Juscius replied that she was entirely missing the point by not understanding that that was exactly its point.

"But what is your overall strategy?" she would demand from him, as though his school mistress.

★

To the returning servants, the duo's banter seemed to float like birdsong in the pleasant breeze, a duet to accompany the chorus of nature's abundant orchestra. They beamed positively - it was when the lord and lady were together like this that they could actually share something with them... from a distance, of course! Their rumoured love affair gave them common ground and reminded them that (despite all the propaganda) they were human too. As soon as household duties resurfaced, both couples had to flee their refuge of humanity and scamper back into the cogs of the machine.

Unfortunately their escape into tranquil paradise had been summoned to an end. But rather than arrive in the opening glum, the servant pair remained gleeful in order to cherish every rapidly depleting moment of their peace together. Juscius' servant knocked on a particular trunk with a series of knocks. The pattern was complex to avoid an impostor striking lucky. There was even a separate one for if he was held hostage.

The duet of mellifluous sounds stopped, the true signal of the end of relaxation and the rebirth of duty and routine. It was then that the servants emerged from the undergrowth to meet their respective masters, both of whom had risen and brushed themselves down, and stood gazing towards the approaching lackeys with the emotionally vapid, steely eyes of the machine. They were already prepared to get back to business.

★

High Priest Zeuorox did not like being visited; he preferred to summon, demand or 'request' council. He told himself this was because he was often busy and so could only meet people at his own discretion. 'The gods,' he said, 'follow the patterns they themselves have fated and placed in the stars. They cannot wait.' And, he, as their servant and celestial link to mankind, could not be delayed either.

Ruperis, however, who had recently had his feathers ruffled into a fine peacock-like display, by being assigned the essentially meaningless, if superfluously impressive, title of 'merchant-prince'. The 'merchant-prince' had not only immediately noticed the High Priest's irritation at being disturbed unannounced, but had pre-empted it, and immediately set about utilising it to help send a diplomatic prod to unsettle (though not dislodge) this overly comfortable mother goose from her heavily feathered nest.

Ruperis' motives were clear, and multifaceted. It was not just a matter of his concern over the priest's unquestionable power, but also, he would have to admit, a childish fun at disturbing and mocking the pomped-up poultry. Finally, the merchant wanted to find out what this feathered behemoth was hiding under all that fluffy deluge of feathers.

This time however, it was a rising concern which he was sure he shared with the tyrant that was the cause of his visit. He believed the High Priest was also worried, but had more at stake (Ruperis was convinced that the cleric had a grand plan - one which Ruperis wanted to either cash in on, or if that was not possible, eliminate, in order to cash in on its defeat).

The room was as gloomy as ever, though the array of speckled follicles of light that swarmed and retreated on the walls kept changing as Zeuorox busied himself with an incense tray. Ruperis hid his inner chuckle as the blue flame was extinguished for the fourth time and the yellow re-lit for the third, the flickering blue gleam wiped away with a swift dropping of a torch cover. The cover clanked abruptly, as though the noise itself was cut short by the steely gaze of the priest.

Within seconds the yellow stain of flame was creeping up the adjacent wall, until it reached a threshold where it remained, its flames panting like an obedient dog's tongue. There it remained until a seemingly source-less breeze began to toss the yellow into a tumultuous pattern of left-right, back and forth movements.

Ruperis sipped the lukewarm wine that had been hastily thrust before him, then looked at his host. "I can see you are busy…" Ruperis began, feigning an apology (and deliberately cutting short of making one), "but I thought with a little collective brainstorming we could resolve a few problems."

Zeuorox did not even pause. He merely threw a suspicious glance at the merchant as he moved from flame to flame, then he uttered with a deadening whisper, "and what problems would they be?"

Ruperis sighed and made a verbal retreat. "Well, maybe not problems…" He fingered the goblet as he wriggled through the choice of words to pick the correct path. "Though they may arise if we do not take the initiative." - He settled on the vague and seemingly clairvoyant knowledgeable warning.

The cleric prodded a green flame maliciously, then put the poker down, and turned to face the merchant in the gloom. With his dark cape and bony facial features, he presented quite a sinister spectacle. The various patterns of coloured flame danced in the darkness, enraptured by it, coalescing with it as though the flame colours were the template, and the shadows dark spectral negatives of the light.

Swooping in close, the priest brought his hawkish beak near to the merchants face. "What troubles you, Mr. Delvinius?" he queried, squawking like a vulture, transferring his worry to the merchant and trying to put him in his place with the mock formality of a title.

But for all his swooning, far from a pedagogic bird of prey, Ruperis just saw a mangy old mother goose, trying to scare off intruders from her nest.

"Haven't you noticed it?" came Ruperis' contemptuous reply, sending a gust at the encircling hawk. It defensively landed by its nest.

It fixed its beady eyes on the intruder; it had mistaken it for a ball of flesh covered in fluff; the usual helpless prey. It was another predator, but was it a friendly one or a threat? The hawisk priest swooped in to the left, paced off to the right, then settled near the table, ready to pounce.

He stood in such a position that fresh red flames caught his hooked nose as it peeped out of the hood, making it resemble a beak. "Look Ruperis, I am very busy. So, no doubt, are you. Will you cut to the chase?" He was clearly losing his temper, gazing at the troublesome boy with irritation.

Ruperis hid his grin. The mother goose had squawked, evidence that it was agitated. The little schoolboy had rattled its cage! Now it was time to plough on. "Are you not worried about this whole council idea?"

"Not at all," the priest declared with evident relief, possibly even disappointment. "It could prove profitable… either way."

Ruperis frowned; the schoolboy was tumbling beyond his comprehension; *'either way?'*

Zeuorox looked disdainful as he proudly continued, "you know, the two possible outcomes - one of which must happen - in fact the other will just catalyse the other." The mother goose sounded like an owl.

Now the little boy was dumbfounded. Was it not a mother goose after all, but a pedagogic bird of prey?

"The theory is for integration, the alternative, if it is resisted, is war - and this will just lead to rapid, extreme integration when we win! Though the conference itself has little to actually offer, that is how Juscius wants it; meaningless but provocative statements to impress people... hence war being most likely." The owl declared in a matter-of-fact tone.

"War! Why, that would be devastating." The little boy was reeling back in shock.

"Don't lie to me boy! There is no point in hiding things; you had a choice; bet on peace and trade or war and arming. You have taken my advice, gambled on the side of war... I do not blame you, I would do the same. It is much easier to start wars than prevent them. All you have to do is make sure you are on the side of those pushing for it and you will get your profits. Only preach that peace rubbish in public. And always remember the barbarians are the perfect indiscriminate enemy to justify your company's existence."

"You see, it is as I said. We can profit whatever happens, as long as we retain our initiative, you can provide for our men and be a hero behind the scenes. Remember it is not just weapons but transport of goods and any other services that they may need."

The merchant prince grinned, revealing himself to be not an intrepid schoolboy but a mercenary magpie.

The priest had left the merchant to contemplate his words of wisdom and decipher the concealed proposition. He absentmindedly played with a strand of his streaky beard. The hawk cautiously eyed the magpie, had it grasped the plan? Was it attracted sufficiently to the prospects of shiny rewards?

The notorious bird-thief cocked its head as though weighing up the argument.

The wise bird of prey had to be sure, but also cautious in its nudging.

"What trades are you in?" it prompted.

"'We' prefer the term services," replied the evasive omnivore.

The cleric smirked; such a look was unbefitting on his hooded wrinkled face, so it just looked sinister. "Services... I like that... after all, we are all servants of the lord!"

The merchant gave him a wry look. "I thought you were a servant of the gods... cut out the middle man."

The Cleric gave an honest matter-of-fact look. "Yes, a servant of the Lord Thelus... so in your crude analogy I *am* the 'middle man', I suppose."

The merchant hid his concern at such a notion, knowing how much his friend and lord had become dependent on the word of Thelus. "You'd better hope they stay on track with each other then and want the same thing."

The wise old cleric raised an eyebrow with confident disclosure. "Ahh... that is exactly what I ensure happens."

The merchant snorted, and leant down to take a sip of wine. "And does it?" he inquired, just as his lips hovered millimetres from the receptacle.

"Every time," echoed the answer in the dark room.

But the wise old bird was caught off guard: just as it expected a lull in the debate the mischievous forager bird was alive, squawking with controlled exasperation declaring a plan of action.

Patience was a necessity, and patience was a virtue in excess on this bird of prey.

"The servant girl," Ruperis began, "it was a mistake. I should never have brought her." He rattled out phrases, declarations and points like a verbal precursor to the Gatling gun. "I am worried she will influence our most knowledgeable and independent lord." The barrels slowed and cooled ready for the next burst. "Have you not seen how much attention he gives her? She is changing him and that could be devastating to us all... I saw him when he first saw her... I saw his eyes, hidden behind a pious man's veil; aside from anything else it could breed a scandal."

With every barrel emptied, the hawk began. He began coolly, with the restrained soothing voice, only paradoxically possible by intense beings, for as it soothed it rubbed in unease.

"How exactly will she influence him?" He paused. "She cannot talk to him."

The primitive machinegun murmured in confusion.

"She seems to hold so much power over him, the potential is there." He skirted around the question, spluttering in a fatalistic misfire. "I know she cannot speak to him but she may use sign language, or just symbolise something to him." He wriggled on. "You heard him in his praise - he sees her as on par with Thelus - 'she is godly' - if she could communicate she could even surpass you... in the long term."

The owl pondered its scepticism. It was as his mind picked over the merchant's sarcasm that suddenly it struck him. '*Forget the long-*

term. Just think, what she poses as a threat now. It is not what she could say. In fact, it is worse that she says nothing - for she may encourage something worse than outside influence - him to derive thoughts from his own mind! She is worse than if she were vocal - if she tried to influence him we could cull it easily, but if she acts as a receptacle for something much worse -independent thought...'

The sour face of the cleric intensified with acute interest. He seemed to join the entrepreneur in mutual concern. "Do you think so?" The priest felt the sudden impact of despair strike his heart. '*Was this true? Had his mischievous merchant brought a too powerful gift?*' Not an object of empowerment that could spur the lord on down the correct path as set by Zeuorox, but an empowered force in its own right, one that could feed him disruptive ideas, or worse still, act as a slate for him to formulate his own independent views.

Ruperis seemed shocked. "Didn't you see him! He was totally awestruck!"

Zeuorox glowered into the coloured torch. The twinkling light reflected off a smooth wooden beam to provide a peachy gleam on the tarred black, a mocking texture that sought to mimic the slave-girl's firm skin. He felt the throbbing in his heart, the advancing footsteps of fear, the resonating vibrations working their way up his spine to his brain. Had the impostor of the gods been foiled by his own plan?

He turned his attention to Ruperis. He would have to be careful. "You know how impressionable our lord is... you also know how he has a tendency to read the gods' will in random events... you may also think that is my work... I can tell you are sceptical, if not hostile, to my operations, but you must understand that using such language is the only way to direct him towards the right decisions. All lords have advisors, it's just I have a unique way of advising a unique mind. If he begins chasing these fanciful religious signs, who knows what will happen. I, on the other hand, use my position to keep him from wandering into this forest of winding paths." He paused, then added, "for example, it was I who persuaded him to fund your excursion." His eyes turned darker, irritated by the merchant's unimpressed expression. "Also, do not forget the favour I did by getting you the Gatanese coin."

Ruperis scowled at being lectured before returning to the diplomatic norm. "Yes, you never explained to me why?"

"So foreigners would not get their grubby hands on our coinage," Zeuorox answered coolly.

"Yes, and one day you should tell me the real reason."

"I don't know what you are talking about," Zeuorox declared decisively. He then turned his attention to the issue at hand. "External influences I can handle... Lords need guidance. Especially young ones, but if she inspires him she might entice him into that most beastly vice of a head of state; free thought."

Not even the gorgon medusa herself, could induce such an expression of petrifaction upon the high priest as had settled on his face now. This sign of weakness was instantaneously shattered and replaced with the hawkish mask.

"So, what do you suggest we do?"

"Eventually we must remove this threat to the lord's integrity. But the solution, well, it's simple isn't it?" he could not help patronising the High Priest. "If we can, for hundreds of years, convince the masses that their next door neighbour is an evil enemy hell-bent on their destruction, how difficult will it be to convince them that a single girl, with dark skin, from a far off land, is an evil alien seeking our entire civilisation's destruction, and has seduced our lord? The world has never known a more easy scapegoat."

Zeuorox seemed unsure. "But there is an entire race out there, would we jeopardise…"

The merchant shrugged his shoulders. "Remember, I'm doing as you say, changing my trade for what is needed in these dark times, we have no need for silk and spices now… we need to defend ourselves from the very enemy I just mentioned… this time we'll ensure it's for real! Besides… after my little excursion they aren't going to be too pleased with us anyway… we did kidnap it." He was already formulating a lucrative plan, one which would probably be enhanced by the spreading of rumours of seductive dark skins.

The high priest grinned, though he was worried about the extent to which the merchant was satisfied with short-term cash flow. "I suppose they are all heathens anyway."

"So when do we act?" Ruperis queried, clearly eager to get the plan in action.

"We must wait until after the banquet. Our Lord, in his infinite wisdom, has been harping on about her to Telis, so if she disappears he may be damaged politically. How well known is she?" the High Priest queried.

"Barely at all." Ruperis muttered with disappointment, much to Zeuorox's dismay, "but don't worry I can get the word out then we can bring her down with rumours, all in the open." When he saw Zeuorox's unconvinced face he continued defensively, "well, there's no point having a scapegoat no one has heard of… The next time something goes wrong and Juscius wants an explanation from the gods you know what to say!"

Zeuorox despised his bluntness. "How dare you? I speak what the gods tell me."

Ruperis just laughed.

"You know, I'm surprised we've been able to achieve so much so quickly."

"It can be surprising for new-comers at how much people such as ourselves have in common. You see, it is much better if we work together in our common areas and ignore those differences, for often our differences are merely different ways of doing the same thing. Division fragments power and may let others slip in. You understand that this slave girl is a crucial issue?"

"Which I brought to you!" Ruperis declared proudly.

Zeuorox, who was one to dislike such glory-hunting, snapped back, "in more ways than one."

This jibe, the merchant could withstand. Now he had shocked the cleric with a threat to his autocratic rule, and proven himself worthy he could press on with the plan. "High Priest, I have a favour to ask of you."

'Ah, so this is why he came' the pontiff noted to himself.

"You see, I have an important package that was lost on its way out of the border forest of Leira... I was wondering if you could contact your friends in Gorad garrison - I hear they have a new priest - and get them to retrieve it for me. Also, did I mention I was looking for veteran mercenaries?... I hear you have new recruits waiting to get on the front line, but they are being held back because their places are filled by old guards ... perhaps you could pass on to your colleagues at Gorad that I am looking for men... and a Captain."

'He's good.' Zeuorox could not help raising an eyebrow. "Why, I will do anything I can in the service of Latman. Now I have things to attend to: his lordship will be returning soon."

★

The previously clear sky was now inhabited by a few large thick clouds that resembled snow covered continents. These landmasses of cotton wool were trailed by various archipelagos of wispy streaks of cloud. Off in the distance high flying clouds smeared across the sky like immovable stains or pallid scars of insipid white-blue, totally motionless.

The road was dry and hard with a thin and sparse layer of dust, which scattered flittingly as the horse's hooves clumped along the path. Heavily manhandled stones were strewn along the path. Unable to get a foothold in the heavily compacted soil, they sat imitating mighty boulders. Nimble beetles sped over them as proof they were otherwise.

The trek back to the palace should have been an adventure. But both parties felt the necessity of restraint in the presence of the other. The expedition ensued in virtual silence, until Torian launched into a sporadic outburst.

"What is it I hear about a beast roaming the palace?"

"What?" Juscius' feigned incomprehension was so enfeebled that it betrayed more than had he remained silent.

"So it is true," she deduced mischievously, before reverting to a serious inquest. "What is this ghastly thing doing in our realm, let alone palace?"

Juscius felt a searing rage, a feeling of abhorrence towards his lover. He was at first disgusted by her ignorant prejudice, then disgusted at himself for feeling so aggressively annoyed at her for her stance.

He wanted to burst into a tirade in the slave girl's defence, then he wanted to reprimand himself for his disloyalty to his love. *'How dare she be so prejudiced?'* He pondered as he began to realise the two were incompatible.

'I must choose, one leads to righteousness,' his panic stricken mind deliberated.

"I hear it is female," she declared with clear derision at the word that was equally applicable to herself being used to describe this creature.

Juscius' eyes bulged in anguish; he felt an agonising pain rise up to his already bulbous eyeballs, searing through neurons. He was lost. His feminine deity was under assault from his female companion and there was nothing he could do to stop such animosity. He wanted to say, 'you should see her before judging' but then he feared she would take him up on his words. *'They must never meet,'* he told himself.

His lover's arbitrary declaration of disgust had revitalised the lord's confusion over the 'slave girl spectacle'. The time he had just spent with Torian had driven her from his mind. She would be a priestess, but nothing more... but Torian's hostility had not only obliterated chances of cohabitation, but had, with her bestial description of the slave girl, revitalised a desire he thought he had put to the sword. This in turn had not only drawn him to her, but also lent some weight to Torian's prejudice as he began to see the slaves darker side. But then on the other hand, would it not be expected that if she were something divine then any sinister unease would be expected as a result of her nymph-like sensuality - a quality expected to be unusually blatant and energetic amongst such a servant of the fire god.

On the other hand, if his pure angel had her reservations, no matter how irrationally based, did this not presuppose Thelus' disapproval?

Was this girl not an acolyte of the fire god, or worse still; was the fire god a traitor? Perhaps Zeuorox could help him, and as usual he rested his unease upon waiting for his priest's judgement.

It was then that he realised an answer was in order. "Dear, judge not what you do not see, and judging by your pre-emptive prejudice I suggest you never see, and ergo you shall never judge."

The snappy 'words of wisdom' were supposed to be concluding remarks to end the torturous ordeal, but Torian had not yet finished and instead decided to tease the lord.

"Why are you hiding it from me... is she pretty?"

"No, and this is not the place," he bit back defensively, using the presence of the servants to cull the inquest.

From then onwards they rode in silence. Juscius' mind was a raging orchestra of debate cut into abruptly by choruses of remonstrations. The symphony rose and fell from surging to whimpering.

Juscius looked over his shoulder at the blazing sun that stalked them as they travelled. The immense orb seemed to throb with pulsating heat and light as though sending out an instinctive signal to the lord. It had sunk low like a hunting cat preparing to pounce on its prey, the bright yellow orange intensifying into a more passionate reddish orange. Suddenly, with a sly bob it skulked behind a cloud, a thick grey plaited knot of grey and white wisps that concealed the mighty deity in its entirety. Still Juscius knew the power and intensity of the omnipotent had not wavered in the slightest behind the fluffy mask.

The late afternoon was clearly in the process of handing over to evening. The birds had mostly retired and the crickets chirruped joyously, eagerly awaiting the inevitable retreat of the sun.

Just below the horizon the wood seemed to bob up and down with the plodding of the horse; an undulating bushy patch surrounded with tangled weeds and shrubs formed a messy series of layers of organic fortifications.

The track was taking them past fields now. Huge stacks of straw remained huddled, bodies of stalks amalgamated into one large hunched figure, a leviathan of cereals. Spreading out into an enormous expanse of earth, the landscape was generally flat. Dips and slight mounds swept across the surface, adding slight but immaculate contours.

He had barely been away from the wood for an hour but he already urgently desired to return to it. Though this time it would be different, he wondered if he could ever take the slave girl there. Oh, how she would learn to love her new country if she visited that wood.

★

The messenger had sped back to the palace to confirm to the high priest that the lord was returning.

The high priest had felt the continual itching irritation of a distant but impending future difficulty. What should be done about the slave girl? Even though he knew he couldn't, part of him wanted to act immediately, just get the filthy business done with, and eliminate the risk before it began to become one. He had to wait until after banquet to avoid inflicting damage on the lord and therefore the house.

Still, he reassured himself of the ease of spreading prejudice amongst the populace, people so miserable in their pitiful contentment that they loved to hear of who to blame, especially if it was some low down nothingness who provided an easy target to enact revenge. Also, Zeuorox suspected the masses secretly loved to hear of ordinary people being so instrumental in causing disaster because it made them think that they had the potential to do something significant. He could imagine their subconscious' at work: 'If a black woman slave can threaten to cause the destruction of the greatest house, then just think what a respectable peasant with my own goat could do?' they must haplessly think. Yes, the priest could not help but smirk. Yes, destroying her would be easy. He was more concerned that destroying her would sully the lord. All he could do for the time being was attempt to catalyse the union of Juscius and Torian. He had truly given up on the idea of uniting Juscius and Telis' sister. Besides, the Juscius-Telis union was no longer valuable, Zeuorox saw much more practicality in her marrying Ruperis. Zeuorox found himself habitually pacing. He paused. He briefly pondered where he should meet the lord, deciding that although the meeting room could be brightened slightly by the wavering sunlight, and so favourable to lightening the lords mood, the priest could not be bothered to adjust his eyes to any new light, praying to keep himself in the dark shadowy temple-room.

The moody multi-coloured torch-light spread forward, swarming across the wall momentarily before lulling and fleeing the encroaching darkness. This eternal battle raged on perpetually in the background, shadows of the priest's figure shrinking and growing to loom over all the inanimate objects and tools that rested awaiting his whim.

How would he deal with the banquet? Zeuorox glowered gloomily for a few moments. After a brief thought he nodded cautiously. "Casual concern," he decided.

★

"What is it, Your Excellency?" Lord Juscius inquired casually as he stepped into the gloom.

A hooded shadow swooned towards him, its dark hazy veil flickering a dancing pattern of advance and retreat in conjunction with the strobe light created by the breeze on the torchlight.

"Sire, I hope I did not disturb you," the silhouette spoke. Its mouth was not visible, its entire jaw and cheeks snugly concealed within the hood line, though the occasional flicker highlighted the figure's wiry beard and moustache with frosty light. The sentence drifted out of the silhouette and into the flickering darkness, wafting away with as many insipid vocal shifts as the priest's monotone contained.

Barely pausing to even give an impression that he cared for an answer, he launched into the subject matter. "Sire," he bowed to gain sentence-building time. "I am concerned about the proposed banquet. I can feel that it will be a crucial event in the world's history, and... though I am sure you are slavishly working on it, I feel that I am not pulling my weight in my assistance."

Juscius smiled candidly. "I am confident that Thelus shall guide me when the time comes."

The high priest's face contorted in poorly concealed horror. "Sire, his mighty lord Thelus will only, I fear, grant us such wisdom, if we put the effort in to begin with. He will reward us for doing his bidding, and for that we must struggle. He will not reward us for blind faith alone."

"Obviously!" exclaimed the lord, clearly offended that he was being accused of sloth. "I do not suggest we do not think about it at all, just that you should not worry and have more faith... besides I have some ideas."

Zeuorox's heart sank... like a stone, which is hardly surprising as it was the organic equivalent. He stepped into a patch of light. "Your highness, beg my pardon, please sit." He gestured at a chair with an air of apology (but without making it). The lord obliged. After a few ponderous paces, and scrabbling for a candle, the priest followed suit. Zeuorox was irritated by the flickering darkness as it was feeding the room with anxiety, which was vexing both of them, undermining interaction. He lit the candle and found the new situation more favourable.

The high priest, in the atmosphere of intimacy, decided candid calmness would get him the furthest. "I just feel that the opportunities here are enormous, but only if we act appropriately, and crucially together - and that is not just you and I, but your good friend Ruperis... and Lord Telis. I trust your judgements, though I feel it is my duty to advise, I also see the importance of coordination in this unique first time gathering."

"Certainly. I value, desire, and even require your advise," beamed the lord with friendly admiration. "I have ideas of unity and of further councils to debate cross-border issues, ultimately to act as a court to deal with outlaw nations and peoples. Security and trade, in short. But I have concerns about Gatan - I mean, they are still a threat and cannot be trusted to follow peace as we do, he could use it against me."

The priest smiled. "Don't worry, we will be the founders, so it will be tilted in our favour... it is also why we need Telis firmly on our side. The lesser houses are less important, and relatively easy to convince to follow our lead. An isolated Gatan is powerless in such a body; it will be nailed into its own coffin by being excluded from our workings with the others."

"So we exclude them?" Juscius queried.

"Not officially, we just talk of how the council should be based on principles like our own and not held ransom to backwards warlords" Zeuorox explained.

"I want it to deal with the problem of Vaca."

Zeuorox looked confused, "You mean this upcoming council not an ongoing council issue?"

"Oh yes, of course, I don't want it dragging on, I want a quick resolution, one where Gatan ceases backing the insurgents and Vacarium ceases threatening us, and we have the right to defend ourselves by combating those rebels and anyone suspected of supporting them."

Zeuorox grinned, it was his day today. "A powerful, resolute message," he complimented.

Juscius looked concerned. "But it will antagonise Gatan. Don't you think that could be counter-productive?"

"No sire, in your considerate modesty you are allowing their biased opinion sway you in your righteous resolve - they are being counter-productive if they oppose your propositions. If they are antagonised by you speaking the truth then you must be prepared to defend your integrity."

"With anything and everything... " Juscius added, "we have already been overly peace-loving by not launching an attack after their barbarous attack on Gericos."

Zeuorox hid his smirk behind a jingoistic bravado.

"What you need to do is ensure you bring the issue up correctly; talk about it in the context of security, just after speaking of the barbarians, something like 'barbarians both seafaring and mountainous.'"

"Cave-dwelling," Juscius suggested.

"I like that," Zeuorox complimented. "Hmm... yes, 'hiding in their tunnels and caves'."

"Then I link it to Vacarium and say how he who supports a terrorist is a terrorist himself."

"Excellent, my thoughts exactly." Zeuorox clapped his hands enthusiastically.

Juscius looked at the unusually ecstatic priest with confused eyes.

"Because it's true, quite obviously."

"Of course," came Zeuorox's overly sincere reply.

Juscius stood, compelled by the energies of dramatic confidence, "and that must be a pre-condition; we cannot even talk of peace until all houses stop their support of brigands and instigators of terror in our homeland. We must begin with such a resolution." He smiled gleefully.

"This really might work – indeed, surely it must for progress is on our side - we will achieve peace. Even if we have to fight to the last man for it."

Zeuorox smiled. He knew now was the time, whilst the lord was worked up on the spiritually-guided idealism, to introduce another plan. "Sire, if I may say so, this most noble cause cannot be won by council and leaders alone. There are a number of things. For one, common ideological ground; it needs to attract and bind the grassroots, the people, and also it needs Thelus' blessing… and the only way to do this is with missionaries - we must give our priests missions to spread the word. This will please Thelus and it will bring people and leaders together. If we cannot get our own New Interpretation missionaries into countries - in particular those that most need them - we may have to use home grown groups. If your lordship desires evidence, just look to our greatest allies Telis. His lordship himself is a convert, as is his sister, and with him swathes of the population are buying into the mindset."

Juscius sighed and waved him off. "Zeuorox… you're not still peddling that one are you?"

"What?" The cleric was not faking, he had genuinely forgotten.

"Trying to get me with Madame Telis!"

"Oh, no… no sire I would never… besides, you have your divine match here."

Juscius' face lit up. "You mean the gods do consent!"

Zeuorox just smiled as pleasantly as his gnarled face allowed.

Now Juscius was sure, the gods condoned his and Torians' union; he must put aside any doubt and be wholeheartedly dedicated to Torian. "Anyway", Juscius beamed with pride. "I think I have found a perfect match for Lady Telis!"

Zeuorox knew the lord was playing a childish game and teasing him into coaxing out his idea, he had no time for such things. "Really? That wouldn't be a certain merchant prince would it?"

"Yes!" Juscius answered, his excitement chipped with a lingering sulkiness.

"Then the unity of Telis and Latman, the twin towers of New Interpretation, could stand as a duo of progress," Zeuorox declared as dramatically as his deathly voice could.

Juscius, filled with religious zeal and marriage prospects was gleeful again. "Is it not a most wonderful idea? We can lead the way in showing how households that behave and adhere to the rules prosper in unity!"

"Like marriage itself," Zeuorox added, rather flippantly, but knowing it would be gaily devoured by the lord.

The pup seized it like a fresh marrowbone. "It is! It is!"

Zeuorox just smiled briefly, then his face darkened.

"The double blessing of Thelus for those unions can only be surpassed by one thing..." the priest prophesised.

"What?"

Zeuorox smiled reassuringly. "Your lordship, we must spread The Word amongst the people; unless we are vigilant, they could turn to the dark side; to Septimo. Never underestimate his power or the insidiousness of his denizens... his agents could be anywhere, dark people with twisted, unfathomable minds..." Yes he would begin to sow the slave girls destruction now.

"Well, that is where you and your followers come in. It is your task to spread the word of New Interpretation. Through that we can keep them on the path of light."

"As you wish," came the humble reply.

"Yes, dear Zeuorox, I will depend on your divine link to keep us all safe, you must continue to use all your resources to spread the word... you were definitely right to begin with the military."

"Begging your pardon sire, but it will take something other than prayer and ceremony to succeed; this is ultimately a battle in the earthly realm, though it is to save the heavenly world. I need your help and resources to sustain a network of priests to espouse belief - like with the soldiers. The word must be spread by word of mouth and practiced by physical example - that takes resources."

"Of course, such a mission of grave importance shall be funded by the household in its entirety. And I shall make it a priority in all speeches."

"Maybe not all of it," the High Priest warned cautiously. "You see, it is not just an internal issue - we may need to be sneaky and secretive and send some across the border."

"Any border?"

"The Border." Zeuorox needed not give utter its name, then continued, "Telis can be above ground, Vacarium is too volatile to notice, Lewerix is too risky, we may unnecessarily turn him against us - that is where I suggest trying to contact allies within the country."

"Would they oppose us in war?"

"No, they would be neutral unless we provoked them... maybe they would voice verbal opposition."

"Is war with another likely?"

Zeuorox knew he meant Gatan. "We must be vigilant."

"True, but I still can't help but think it is not necessary, I mean we have the advantage so wouldn't Gatan avoid war?"

"Yes, we have advantage but that is in war, not avoiding it... they show no reason, their militaristic culture prefers the sword over diplomacy. Our advantage is not large enough to prevent war, it is not enough to mean they will be forced to see sense and join us... and it will be difficult to change the world for the better with people like Lord Gatan in control of such powerful houses." He leaned in close to the lord. "Permit me to use a blunt example; if war was the only way to ensure our aspirations were achieved because of the ignorance of a jealous old man would you back away from military action?"

Silence ensued, allowing the creepy darkness to flicker in. Zeuorox irritably rubbed his fingers. Even if the lord answered in the affirmative now he still wouldn't be convinced, one minute he was declaring they had given Gatan too many chances already, the next he was wimping away. It was the problem with shaping a lord without a spine: even when he was doing what you wanted he still floundered. Of course, once convinced into taking action nothing would sway him from justifying it against all counter-evidence.

Zeuorox rose to conclude the conversation. He turned away from the lord, waiting for him to rise to leave. Then suddenly, with one fell swoop he was back up close face to face with the lord.

"Sire, you do realise that with this plan there stands a sizable possibility that war between us and Gatan will be necessary?" His face showed a deadening seriousness. His eyes bulged, bloodshot and gleaming in the tussling light.

Juscius looked grave, and nodded slowly, clearly troubled. "If need be, but we shall see," he declared and quickly left.

★

Ruperis had been pacing conspicuously in the corridor for fifteen minutes, waiting for his lord and comrade to depart from Zeuorox's chamber and work his way through the passages to the intersection where he lingered. Finally, he heard the hasty footsteps of Juscius Latman approaching. He began a slow and ponderous lurch away from the oncoming feet, anticipating his name being called out at any moment.

The resonating clicking of heels striking stone became suddenly louder and more clear, signalling that the last corner had been turned. Sure enough he heard his name declared in a most surprised and relieved tone.

Ruperis wheeled around and smiled.

"Jus, how was your day?"

Juscius smiled convincingly. "Wonderful, isn't nature so marvellous?"

Ruperis was baffled, unused to such wishy-washy questions. "It has its uses," he grinned.

"I suppose the sea is more to your tastes."

Ruperis nodded, adopting his swashbuckler character. "Yes, the sea is more challenging, volatile. I feel more of an affinity with it."

By now they were face to face, and gave each other a friendly hug in greeting.

"Don't you ever just want to wallow in the tranquillity of woodland? The sprouting of a multitude of flora decorated with a vast array of fauna? Oh, these godly creations, here for our comfort."

The merchant shrugged apologetically. "Sorry, but to me they are just petty indulgences ... or a potentially nice fur coat just waiting to be made into something useful. It's better when they become man's creations, how we cope with nature. Using his own resources against him, huh!" He ranted, totally misjudging his audience.

Juscius laughed patronisingly. "Nature is more than resources and threats!"

"Oh, I'm sure it is... But I'm a busy man."

"So am I," the lord protested.

"Oh yes, sire. I meant no offence. I mean I indulge… just differently." His mouth stretched open like a vast glacier.

"I'm not sure the gods approve of your indulgences,"

"Oh come now Jus, I know who you meet with and why. You have the same needs, same base indulgences, you merely quench them differently, surrounded by furry squirrels, mud and bad odours!"

Juscius, filled with embarrassment, remained silent. In the meantime the image of the slave girl flashed into his mind.

Before an awkward silence could settle on them, Ruperis ploughed on. "I had come to find you, lord." He paused and sensed the formality, reverting to the 'buddy-tone' he had used for years. "Well, I had some ideas for the banquet."

"Go on."

"Is this the right place? Should we not go into your quarters?"

"These are my quarters!" Juscius remarked, gesturing at all around him. "I've just had a gruelling lecture from the High Priest, can't we just have a brief chat here?"

"Whatever you wish, sire," Ruperis conceded. "Well, the key to success in this issue is about drawing the houses together, intertwining them without forcing them into submission."

"Intertwining?"

Ruperis chuckled. "I do not mean that negatively, merely as interdependence. You see, I fear that trying to enforce uniform adherence to principles will lead to confrontation and conflict."

Juscius nodded solemnly. "I know. That is what Zeuorox just warned me of."

Ruperis nodded and snorted, as though he had insightfully predicted Zeuorox would say such. "Ah, yes and he just said 'brace for impact'!"

"Not in those exact words..." Juscius replied defensively.

"...But, yes." Ruperis finished for him. "You know there is another way?"

Juscius' ears pricked. "How?"

"Simple – trade," he answered gleefully. "If we open borders and trade with people they will see no interest in fighting us as it will disrupt commerce."

"Could we trust the others? Wouldn't it jeopardise our security? Couldn't Vacarium sneak supplies to the terrorists?"

"No, no one would foul play us because we have the largest armies, though we would have to demobilise a bit as a sign of good will. Everyone would be in the same boat. Oh, and as for security, obviously we would retain our control of imports from houses that we couldn't trust... that is, they would have to use our trustworthy logistics who would ensure no smuggling occurred. That aside, there would be no taxes on the border. Of course, there is the problem of larger hostile houses, but the worst they can do is stay out of agreements and wallow in their isolation and fall behind until they are compelled to join. The other problem is Gatan. To be honest it may not be a good idea getting it involved, for it may commandeer our mechanisms and use them against us."

Juscius was confused. "How can one use the mechanisms against us? It is just a principle of free trade - the same under anyone."

Ruperis shook his head slowly. "Ah, well you see... no, it's not. You see free trade is relative, and has to accommodate for various unfairness that arise, you see for example Lewerix have developed techniques of cutting trees safely which renders them unfairly advanced over our own fellers. Or Vacarium have more abundant minerals, and stability in the regions with them in, whereas we have much higher security costs - mainly thanks to their brethren who stubbornly reside there."

"Could we not at least push for mutual demilitarisation on The Border?"

Ruperis was rapidly formulating how to shape his advice for greatest profit. "Hmm, demilitarisation is probably not a good idea. If you do, it would be good to ensure you have a large military to act as a deterrent."

Juscius was confused. "But how can we do both?"

"There are ways around it."

Juscius decided he didn't want to know anymore.

"However, it is imperative that we come to some agreement concerning ships, or else they may seize our monopoly of spices" (even though Zeuorox had suggested he focus on the issues at hand he could not help continue with this lucrative scheme, besides if all went wrong he would be able to use his knowledge of the spice route to gain leverage with Gatan).

"How can I say that when I talk of combating the barbarian raiders?"

"Easy, by ensuring all boats are rapid pursuit cutters and not freight frigates."

Juscius looked suspiciously at his companion. "I'm not sure I want to base my diplomatic policy on what will enrich my friends; it's called nepotism."

Ruperis laughed. "Come on, you're a hereditary monarchy which is based on handing power to your son, solely because he is your son - nepotism runs at our core. And that aside, what social order and system of businesses would survive without favours – it's imperative to both of our survival as rulers. That's how you get the foundations of your support - from elitist merchants and aristocrats backing you and funding your pillars of coercion that stop the rabble from taking over. Unless you want to try and get it from the 'power of the people'!" The merchant spat out the phrase like it was a family curse.

"But that's exactly what Zeuorox said!"

Ruperis laughed. "No, he believes in indoctrinating the people and then incorporating them as a fervent posse of zombies queuing up for the next crusading meat grinder. I say leave them be - free and powerless. Don't treat them any different than the rest of us legally. Don't tell them what to do, just let economic necessity nudge them towards doing what we would prefer."

Juscius looked sceptical.

Ruperis felt the need to highlight their common ground. "Jus, we want the same thing - a prosperous household, only that is my end and it is your means - you see I create the foundations and from those strong foundations you can build your principled world. I shall not interfere only provide what I can... but that means you need to let me in on what you are doing so I can stay up to date with your needs. Only you can guide this silent revolution, only you can steer us away from war. But if war comes I will be here to provide for you."

Juscius nodded thoughtfully and reached out to place his hand affectionately on his friends shoulder, then he smirked.

"Look Roo, sorry but I'd better be going."

Ruperis was already taking his leave with an outstretched hand. "Ditto, your highness."

★

Juscius strode down the corridors, passing several servants who courteously bowed as he passed. Outside, the darkness was dotted with patchy patterns of stars. Juscius glanced at them swiftly as he paused at each window. He became enchanted and longed for another look with each space of cold dark stone. A rising desire surged in him to see them all, a desire he decided to respond to just as he neared the door to his chamber.

He turned the last corner to be confronted by two guards. They stiffly came to attention and one turned to slide the bolt. Juscius hastily signalled that he should stop.

"I am going outside for a moment," he declared.

Just as the other guard stretched his limbs and turned to his spear that rested against the wall, the lord called to him to stop also. "No, I will be fine alone," he reassured him. Without a moment's delay he hurried to the nearest exit from the warren of passages.

Immediately outside, the ground was compacted hard into an illuminated stain spilling out two metres from the door step. The often treaded path petered out into an archipelago of compacted dirt surrounded by feral scraggy grass. The temperature was cool, the patchy looming clouds holding little heat in, their locations detectable from the gaps in the studded Braille code of stars: desolate patches of pure black.

Juscius gazed up in awe at the god's windows that lined the sky haphazardly like sequins in an enormous cloak that had wrapped itself around the earth, blocking out the sun. Satrius the moon god shone as he sat overseeing the inhabitants below. Seeing such dark celestial beauty brought an image of The slave girl to Juscius' mind. Her gleaming dark skin was so smooth and sleek, so much more graceful than the dark cloak that had enveloped Juscius' kingdom. No, her dark figure was not like this, more like the shimmering night sky reflected in a pool of water, enticing and mystical. She was the dark side of the moon, the concealed half of the gleaming deity that slowly soared across the sky.

Her svelte figure glided through his mind, swooning as it crossed his mind's image.

She wore a coal black dress-like-robe that flimsily sagged revealingly each side of her cleavage. She began to walk towards him seductively, a thin cord hanging, swinging by her waist. Her perfect lips broke slowly into a smile. Juscius longed to tug on the flimsy bit of string, knowing it would drop away without a sound and reveal yet more of her perfect skin. He was the pale half of the moon, she was the invisible other half, completing him.

Suddenly his conscience kicked in and tried to assimilate the slave girl's sensual figure with the purity of Torian's pale face, but could not. The mesmerising temptress had the limelight, and could not be removed.

It made no sense. Surely Torian was much more suitable, believable, and feasible. "Feasible," he muttered to himself. There it was again: feasibility, calling for a reality check, a compromise, a wake up slap in the face. Though he saw the slave girl as a divinity, such a union would cause outrage and scandal which could also ruin his commitment to principles of purity... he had to cease the temptation and go for the practical path. As well as seeking the approvable unity with Torian he had to take the practical advice of his friend and advisor and adopt the policies of trade and expansionist missionaries.

Spiritualism and economics had to unite, with him as its combining factor to create this new crusading regime. It was not so much compromise as a union, a coalition, bringing together his ideals in the form of the clergy with the social-orders resource power-base.

Chapter 16
Banditry

Captain Dummonius sighed and leant back in his chair, the priest Vultai and Drill Sgt. Hari had been increasingly encroaching on the running of the garrison. Already he was sick of it. He no longer gave orders around the garrison, not that there really were any to be given, in fact that was the point; that orders were streaming from his office by the hour rather than haphazardly by the week showed he no longer had control. However, on this point concerning the bandit problem, he was adamant: sending a single squad of light infantry was the only way to flush them out without embarrassment, and Pluvius' squad had the best experience in this field. Priest Vultai, on the other hand, wanted to mobilise a regiment for the operation. What the priest did not (or would not) understand was that such a thing would be humiliating not just for Captain Dummonius but for the whole Latman military - the notion that several hundred men were required to flush out and kill about two dozen disillusioned vagrants with pitchforks, holed up in a small forest, was disgraceful for the supposed 'world's most potent military force'.

Eventually the priest had stormed out, declaring that he had a sermon to do. Unable to protest on behalf of his men, Dummonius could at least bask in the freedom of refraining from going himself. Ironically, it was whilst the priest was off preaching to the men, no doubt turning them against Dummonius, that he was free to actually get something done.

He had to hurry, as the service was likely to have finished and it was possible round two with Vultai would start at any moment. He had despatched one of his guards to Pluvius' barracks to summon him to Dummonius' office. Even if Vultai came back, he would just let the stalemate play its course and plough on with his own orders anyway.

With his scant reports completed, he set about folding them and tearing off the blank segments and pocketing them. All he could do now was wait, and hope Pluvius arrived first.

★

The barrack's usual cocktail of pungent and familiar aromas had a new addition: sweet sickly incense which the priests insisted on burning every night. No matter what they claimed were its benefits, it was no replacement for ale. It seemed to mix with the leather, sweat, grease and metal smells to glue them into a faint musky sweetness. What was usually a variety of separate aromas was now a faint lingering synthetic disposition of a smell. The consequence was an insipid draining of Pluvius, who was already weary from a long hard day. The sergeant was unsure if it actually caused the vapidity that he felt, or if it merely coincided with the onset of the condition. Heites believed it to be a ploy by the priests to keep the men down and avoid mental discontent, making sarcastic comments about how he felt reinvigorated by the aroma. Pluvius didn't care; to him it was the epitome of his current state.

Whatever the meaning behind it, Pluvius despised the synthetic staleness and so spent each evening as close to the fire as possible. Sadistically he inhaled the wood smoke that speedily fled up the hole in the roof designed for escape. That was where he was slumped now, dreamily lulling in the intoxicating fumes.

"Get any closer to that thing and you'll singe!" came the startlingly close voice of Heites behind him.

Despite the shock of his comrade appearing, Pluvius felt too vapid to even register the surprise, let alone turn to greet him.

In a tone unexpectedly dreary Pluvius mumbled. "Good, at least that'd be a new smell."

Heites had rested his hand on the sergeants shoulder. "Don't let it get you down, sarge," he uttered reassuringly.

"I couldn't be bothered even if it did," he grumbled incoherently. Heites knelt on one knee beside him, looking him in the eyes. "It already has sarge, look at you!"

Pluvius just shook his head wearily and rubbed his brow, which felt smooth and dry in the baking warmth.

The veteran shook his head in bafflement. "I just don't get it, you don't give two shakes about getting a rollicking off Captain Dummonius and Vultai, and almost being demoted for not finding the bandits but now you have a new smell in here your turning into butter," he grinned. "I'd have thought the sweet aroma would remind you of your missus!"

Pluvius tried to smile but a combination of internal animosity and the stiffness of his muscles from the nearby inferno halted any chance of success.

Heites transformed his grin into a smile, knowing he had amused his Sergeant.

"You were... well..."

He was stopped by an abrupt subtle knock on the door. They immediately knew it was not Hari on one of his cronies, as they never indulged in such etiquette, preferring to burst in rattling off a tirade of insults.

The door creaked open and one of Dummonius' guards emerged out of the darkness. He nodded appreciatively to the various huddles of men, then addressed Pluvius. "Sergeant, Captain Dummonius has requested you as a matter of urgency."

Immediately, Pluvius rose and hurried over to join the trustworthy 'old guard'.

★

When he heard the knock at the door his instinctive shock at the sudden noise was dampened by relief as he knew it would be Pluvius (though he could not help having a paranoid fear that it was a trap and Vultai had caught the sergeant on the way).

Therefore he was still relieved to see (only) Pluvius' figure enter his office. He looked weary and anxious. Nevertheless, he cordially approached the desk and stood to attention.

"At ease," Dummonius uttered. His hands discretely covering then removing the scrap of paper he had been writing on.

"Sir," Pluvius responded as he relaxed his posture.

"Sergeant, I need you to take your men out and find those bandits in Leira forest... you are to go at the crack of dawn tomorrow. I am aware it is short notice, but internal circumstances warrant such... tactics."

Pluvius nodded, he at least in part understood.

"This mission needs to be done as quickly as possible... both our reputations rely on it." Dummonius wanted to explain to Pluvius more fully, but knew he hadn't time, nor was this the circumstance. He took a nervous look at the door, then fumbled amongst the towering pile of paperwork for the order for equipment.

"As you conducted the previous search, I do not need to brief you any further..."

Pluvius was rather surprised at the ad hoc nature of the order, but in the circumstances knew better than to request further information.

Dummonius took another furtive glance at the door, which Pluvius misinterpreted as a request to leave. However, just as he swivelled round the door burst open.

Pluvius almost jumped out of his skin as the lanky frame of Vultai strode in trailed by a swishing robe. The theological commissar gave the sergeant an accusatory eyeballing.

"What the Septimo are you doing in here?" he barked.

Pluvius, worn down with fatigue, and especially tired of the jack russel's yelping following the hefty dosage during the sermon, was in no mood for such treatment. In a tiresome matter-of-fact tone he replied, "What any dutiful soldier should be doing; I am receiving orders from my commander."

The priest ignored his insolence and strode into the middle of the room, muttering "heresy," under his breath.

Inspired by his sergeant's nonchalant defiance, Dummonius adopted a similar tone, "Was there something you wanted, priest?"

Vultai scowled, his glaring eyes flashing with fiery rage. "I need you to fill out an equipment order for the 4th regiment."

Pluvius took a few awkward steps back, trying to melt into the shadows.

"There is no need, Sergeant Pluvius' squad is being despatched," Dummonius replied cordially.

Vultai took a dismal glance at the sergeant before returning his fervent eyes to the Captain, taking several steps forward so his robe pressed against the desk. "You dare defy me!" he shouted in an ecstatic cackle.

Dummonius was not intimated by the young zealots shrieks, puffing his chest out and sitting up straight in his chair, he calmly declared, "I defy no one, that is no one *in*, let alone *above*, my chain of command."

"You just wait until High Priest Zeuorox hears of this!" Vultai threatened.

"Are we to wait for his reply?" Dummonius spat, enlivened by his sympathetic audience that skulked in the shadows, hoping that knowledge of this would disseminate amongst the men, showing he was not a willing lackey of the priesthood.

Vultai backed away discreetly, "Sergeant Pluvius can go, provided brother Visuvius accompanies them..." He relaxed his tensed muscles and watched Dummonius' response.

Captain Dummonius shivered at the sound of the warrior monk's name. Far away in Lateria, Zeuorox did not scare him, but the mention of this bulky bulging necked ex-soldier was a clear and present threat.

Dummonius would not verbally concede that he was fearful of him, and so shrugged. "Ok, the squad may need bolstering anyway."

Vultai smirked to give the impression of victory, before turning his attention to Pluvius. "Be sure nothing happens to him... make it your priority."

Pluvius could not stop himself from smiling as he immediately thought of what Heites would say: *'well we'd better leave him here then, it's much safer... then we might as well stay here and protect him if it's the priority.'*

Vultai waited impatiently for Pluvius to depart. The sergeant was far too tired to complain, he nodded appreciatively at the Captain then marched out.

Vultai only followed suit after regarding the captain with a menacing stare.

★

They stood outside the barracks, stiffly at attention, whilst Hari and Visuvius inspected them. The brother was a huge beast with a jutting square jaw and blockish bald head. He rivalled Arios in size, and outdid him with an impressive scar. It ran from his left eyebrow across his nose in a slight gully that was filled with patchy scar tissue, continuing down carving a desolate rootless patch on his moustache stubble before cracking his lip with a swollen pink lump. He was easily as old as Pluvius, if not older. A veteran who had been through many ferocious battles and seen all the sorts of horrors, which had driven him towards the piousness of the New Interpretationists, and done so to such an extent that he had become a most dedicated servant.

He still wore his robe, but underneath studded leather armour peeked out where the hood met the collar in a V-shape. In his right hand he held a heavy quarter staff; it had a large grip area low down for both hands, plus another two thirds up for blocking. The head was a clumpy studded cylinder almost 2 inches thicker each side than the pole shaft. The bottom was decorated with a fearsome round iron bulb, again clearly designed to smash joints with a quick jabbing smash whilst locked in combat.

His robe was tied by a simple piece of rope, but also wound around his waist was a steel chain, from which hung a heavy leather tome backed with brass. The chain was decorated with seals of red wax, stamped with Latman or Zeuorox's crest and fused with parchments with holy scriptures written on them.

The drill sergeant kept pointing out dress faults, which Pluvius and brother Visuvius were taking note of. At the end of the inspection the drill sergeant whispered authoritatively to Pluvius "These men pass my standards... but they have some faults. Most disappointing of all, why is one of the most distinguished soldiers failing to keep his gladius clean?"
He was of course talking of Arios, who still used his broadsword and had a gladius only because he was forced to pretend it was his actual weapon, yet he spent so much time tending to his broadsword he rarely bothered to even remove the dust from his gladius.

"Drill Sergeant, he is much more adept with other weapons," Pluvius protested in his defence.

The drill sergeant was about to reprimand him but the brother cut in. "If he fights better with another weapon then why is he not using it?" Clearly he was speaking from his soldier days.

"It is against regulation," came the inevitable answer.

The brother gestured with his staff, "and this is not?"

The drill sergeant spluttered, "but... you are not under my jurisdiction... whereas I have a responsibility to uphold regulation amongst the men."

"Now they are under my jurisdiction so I decide," the booming voice of the priest commanded.

Hari refrained from arguing, he merely spluttered, "we'll see... don't you go," as rushed off to find Vultai.

As the men were dismissed to get their horses, Pluvius could at least be comforted in the Brother's practicality in war.

★

They had been travelling for a good 5 hours, though the road would soon deteriorate, so Pluvius took the initiative to stop and refresh the horses before embarking on the next segment.

Within a few minutes of stopping and settling the men seemed to perk up to their normal level of talkativeness. They huddled in one large group, except for Pluvius, Arios and Heites who were holding council. The brother also sat apart from the rest, solemnly gobbling his food, then pacing impatiently near the horses eyeing the senior group with caution.

Pluvius and his posse had briefly discussed where in the forest to look; there were three good places that they knew of to camp. One was positioned between the road that ran to the border outpost just south of the forest and the rough path that aimlessly meandered through, it would be ideal for ambushing the carriage. The others were more concealed: one in a valley with a stream running through it, the other on a hill which had a water hole seeping out from below into pools that then ran down almost dead East to the river Neptus.

They agreed it was most likely that the bandits had retreated to one of the latter two, even if they had been at the first spot earlier.

With this discussed, the conversation fell on more informal topics.

"So sarge, when you going to see that lady friend of yours? ...or are you going to look for a new one?" Heites' inquired mischievously.

Pluvius grinned sheepishly and remained silent.

"Naah, sarge is a proper soldier - he's got 'principle'," Arios chipped in.

"Just like our lord!" whispered Heites comically, referencing Vultai's speech the previous night.

Pluvius just looked baffled.

"Come on Serge! Get with the programme; 'what use are principles if you do will not fight for them?'" Heites could not contain his laughter. Pluvius, in complete bafflement, nervously glanced in Visuvius' direction.

Nevertheless Heites continued, dragging Pluvius along too. "What was it?" He turned to Arios. "Ah yes: what use are princes if you will not fight for them?" He pronounced it eloquently.

"What the hell?" Pluvius whispered before casting another paranoid glance.

Heites voice suddenly exploded in a batch of coughing to cover his laughter, using this as a cover to hunch down out of the brother's earshot. "More like; what use are princes if you have to fight for them!"
The three of them laughed, though Pluvius was still not sure of its origins. Heites followed up. "No. Better still: What use are princes. Full stop."

The other two looked at him warily.

Pluvius noticed that Brother Visuvius, who had been pacing nearby, straining himself to pry into what they uttered, had become so full of frustration that he had decided to approach. His deep contemplative expression betrayed nothing.

As he approached, his overbearing presence loomed over and cut off the joviality. His shadow cut out the daylight. His pale bald head shrouded by his dark cape hood, bobbed over their heads like the triumphant moon. He tilted the his head to one side as a gesture of greeting.

The warrior priest bent down over Pluvius.

"We have things to discuss," the warrior priest declared in a booming, yet succinct, voice.

Pluvius nodded vacantly.

Brother Visuvius settled down directly opposite the sergeant and with a tone which was the closest the warrior priest could manage to relaxed informality declared, "now, you know of something and I know of something; we need to exchange information."

Pluvius seemed dazed. "Go on."

"Where do you think they will be?" he paused.

"There are three possible sites, one we checked before, but they may have moved there since it has easy access to the road – which judging by their attack on a cart renders that likely…"

"I wouldn't be so sure," Visuvius warned knowledgeably.

Once Pluvius had realised the brother was not going to elaborate he continued, "… anyway I propose we check the others, they have water supplies and are harder to reach, one is in the valley – a good concealed position. The other is on the hill nearby – it is better defended… but seeing as I doubt if they are looking for a fight I should think they are at the valley camp."

The warrior priest then slowly sank down to his knees and leaned into Pluvius' face. "Now, I must tell you something." His eyes gleamed with moisture, "the cargo being carried was top secret and very important, for not just the Delvinius company, but for the household. I have reason to believe they had been smuggled in across the border, so this 'secret' path is a more likely route for the cargo."

An uneasy silence descended upon them. Without a word the warrior priest wheeled on the ball of his heels and headed for his steed. As soon as the priest had gone the other two were back, swooping in like vultures; their scale mail jingling to signal their return. They eyed him inquisitively expecting at least a hint. He grinned then gave the usual cryptic order. "Right, we all set?"

★

They left the road and moved onto a track that met up with the road to the forest. The path was much more degraded; rough stones had been laid by generation upon generation of shepherds. They clung to the dry dirt in a vain attempt to create some kind of order. All this did was intensify the roughness and consequently the labour for the horses, as they clopped across it flinging rounded stones back and forth.

The track undulated before disappearing into the forest; here part of the path veered off to the south to find the road. The path was now devoid of stones making it easier for the horses. The mud was unusually hard for the season, solidified into whatever intriguing moulded shapes had been plunged into them when moist. Though its direction was north east, it meandered intently and had countless trails stringing off it into the depths of the forest.

Just as the forest reached its standard density Pluvius sent Delis and Juscius, the two best scouts, to cut through the forest on foot to search the nearest possible site whilst the rest of the squad headed for the hill which was further. They would meet just off the hilltop.

As they walked the horses up the path, an air of gloomy silence had returned to the men. Some clearly feared ambush, though Pluvius was quietly confident the bandits were not aware of their approach.

Pluvius was looking to the left for the tiny path that would lead them to the possible encampment site. The air of uneasiness engulfed him and he contemplated waiting back at the nearest waypoint for the other two scouts.

Any qualms were washed aside as he spotted the trail. Pluvius signalled that they were turning down this path. The afternoon was already late, so Pluvius began to worry that if the bandits were at the hill camp it would be too late to attack and they would flee in the night.

They rode on for another forty minutes, the path sliding down the valley, surfing the undulations of the bottom of the valley and vanishing momentarily under the rock fjord in the stream. Here the trees seemed to thin before leaving a space fifteen yards from the stream. This gap stretched up and down the contours following the streams bank, disappearing downwards around a meander and following until the view was blocked by a huge tree which had fallen in a boggy lurch across the stream. It must have been there a long time, since the last summer downpour which would have loosened and washed away the peaty mud. Before crossing they restocked on water and briefly allowed the horses to drink. Whilst they stood by their horses Brother Visuvius approached Pluvius.

Without greeting him he lunged into a piercing question, his deep voice sounding almost scornful.

"Sergeant, it is getting dark. What is the plan?"

Pluvius did not even turn to the priest, uttering with equally cold precision, "there is an opening just at the top of the valley, a kind of steppe before the climb to the hill, we can camp there and await the scouts, whilst sending out others to scout the hilltop. If they do try and flee, we shall be able to follow their trail and run them down. If they stay and fight we defeat them in one fell swoop tomorrow morning."

The priest seemed impressed. "Good," he pronounced, as though distributing a verbal reward in a classroom.

Before long they had set off again. At first the climb was slight, though later it steepened and rocks broke up the greenery, making the climb more precarious.

All the men's eyes were on the top of the valley which was partially concealed by sporadic bushy vegetation.

Pluvius' senses were jolted alive by what he thought was a noise, his eyes focused ahead. Then he saw it. A head popped up from behind a sapling and then frantically made its way up the climb. Before Pluvius could stir himself into action Heites was off, forcing his horse past the sergeant, javelin in hand. With a flash Heites' javelin hurled through the air, but fell just short of its target as the head continued to bob on the skyline. Pluvius saw the frustration in the veteran's eyes.

Pluvius returned his attention to the bobbing head just as it disappeared over the ledge of the 'top of the valley' (it was a ridge roughly equalling the other side of the valley, which smoothed out before rising to the peak of the hill). Instantly Pluvius heard a familiar if unsuspected sound; "bum-bum bsh! bum-bum bsh!" two booming thumping noises followed by a deep solid crash. It was the sound of two spear-to-shield bangs followed by shields pushed forward in unison to lock into a wall. Just from the sound, Pluvius could tell it was from dedicated if nervous amateurs. Though just the existence of such a sound here caused astonishment.

Pluvius rapidly gathered his practical senses, calling the men to dismount. He turned his gaze up the valley wall to Heites. The veteran still stood high on his horse laughing mockingly at their amateurish display. He laughed so hard that the brigands heard him; in retaliation they sent crude javelins hurtling at him. First they rose up, then they plummeted down to rain down upon Heites. Pluvius head stopped, his throat pined with that searing ache of dryness. Most of the javelins fell harmlessly round Heites, but one came down in an arc straight for his head...

Pluvius gasped, feeling the world pass in slow motion just to ensure the imprinting of this set of images in his mind. Then he noticed the lack of glint from the javelin head; it struck the veterans helmet, but rather than punch a hole, it seemed to bounce off. It was no javelin, just a pointed stick! The veteran slowly rode back down to meet the rest of the squad and dismount, still chuckling.

They numbered ten plus the priest. Judging by the noise they were considerably outnumbered. Pluvius missed Delis and Juscius, they were excellent linesmen. Pluvius surveyed the men, they all seemed confident. Even Geric, behind the nervousness, seemed to hold a gleaming smile of pride as he stood between Arios and Heites. All the men listened attentively as Pluvius quickly outlined the plan. It was simple enough, they would advance as nine, with Arios sneaking off to the left, once in range they would hurl javelins before charging, hopefully getting the enemy away from the edge and onto even ground. Once locked, Arios would strike from the flank with his broadsword. The priest would guard the horses as Pluvius was under order to prioritise his survival.

"Sergeant," came the timid voice of Geric. "Why don't I do the flanking. I can sneak up easier as I am smaller?"

Arios chuckled inoffensively. "Yes little brother, you can sneak up like a mouse, but you will also charge like one! Whereas I stalk like a lion." He spoke the words and with one movement slammed one fist into another, "and bam! I charge like one too!"

"Besides," Heites cut in as he tightened his shield straps, "that sword is no use in a shield wall, and we still can't train our resident barbarian to use a gladius!"

Geric laughed boyishly.

"This," Arios bellowed tossing his gladius in the air like a toy and catching it again before making a derogatory exhalation through his mouth, "pff". Then he turned his horse and grabbed his javelin. Wandering over to Heites he chuckled. "Here, take this and make up for your last pitiful attempt!"

The clattering above had ceased and Pluvius looked to see a row of torsos high on the ridge. Their faces were barely even recognisable but their heads were swishing from side to side with anticipation.

The squad milled about for a while so that the rebels would not see Arios disappear into the shrubs nearby, leading the priest and the horses some way before slipping into the undergrowth.

Pluvius' men advanced slightly spaced out so that they would not be such an easy target for javelins. They crouched low and walked almost sideways, holding their circular shields over their faces and torso.

Pluvius took a peek to see a salvo of makeshift javelins raining down. He shouted to his men to brace and either they did or it wasn't necessary as afterwards they all continued unscathed.

He panted and sweated, listening to his heavy exhalations as a life sign. When they were seventy five yards away they formed into a straight line of nine. Pluvius took one flank, Heites the other; the Sergeant had positioned himself and Heites at each edge because it could be tricky and take wits to prepare a defensive arc. This would avoid encirclement. Pluvius could make out their forces now. Most looked like pitiful adolescent commoners dragged by economic circumstance from the farmer's field to the field of battle. They clung onto hastily made shields, pieces of wood: some undoubtedly taken from the cart; their weaponry was equally pitiful, some held onto pitchforks, others poles with old spear heads attached, often crooked. Most of their clothing was typical peasant attire, covered with mud and tears. A few had animal skins piled over their shoulders, or fashioned into caps.

Pluvius could see their watery eyes blearing, seeping liquid. Their faces were all faintly sprinkled with the first traces of facial hair. From this distance it just looked like the rest of the worthless grime that covered their bodies.

He could see them quaking. He hoped they would run after the salvo of real javelins. Pluvius readied the men. "Ready!" he bellowed and the javelins were raised.

"Aim," they swung their arms back and squinted to pick a target. Pluvius spotted a man with a fullish beard who yelled encouragement to the youths and insults on the men.

"Fire!" They threw with one movement and were off straight afterwards, shields locked. As the javelins arced towards the boys Pluvius winced.

Whilst the civilian in him recoiled in disgust, the soldier assessed the damage; the 'commander' was down with several javelins in his rib cage and chest. The soldier in him tutted: *'what a waste of javelins'*. Another was struck in the head, a third had gone a similar way to the commander; pin-cushioned with overly sized needles. Another spluttered as a red fountain spouted from a fresh incision to the neck; the javelin sank deep into the man's neck, probably all the way through. Two more were impaled with stomach wounds, they had crouched down behind shields only to have them split in two by the javelins. Pluvius could just about see pale hands gripping the remnants of their shield, heads slumped over the top, matted hair messily spilling over the wooden wreck while blood seeped to the ground though the crack in the shield. Both must have blacked out in shock, as they would not die of a stomach wound... yet. The adolescent with the javelin in the head had stiffened and dropped as though knocked out by a blow to the back of the head. Pluvius knew he had gone straight out of this world, alive... bang...dead. Here... bang... gone. His body had braced up as his mind jolted to a stop, and it was an empty clothed husk that fell to the ground like a doll.

As they charged, Pluvius heard Geric crying in demonic delight that he had 'got one'. "Did you see sergeant? Look at him, crumpled up clinging to his spear! I got him!" His eyes flared in ecstasy.

Pluvius felt ill. 'Wasn't it supposed to be the other way around?' he thought - he was the hardened veteran. It was like they were on a conveyer belt towards self-annihilation, and he was dropping off the end disgusted, whilst Geric was leaping on the beginning.

Though deeply troubled, he had to remain professional and with his wits about him, his focus returning as they reached the line of spears. The rebels, as expected, held their spears at the end rather than bringing them in close so they could exercise more control over them and ward off swordsmen. Pluvius' squad worked as one, knocking the spears aside and crashing forwards, locking their shields and raising their gladius's above their heads.

Before the rebels could react to their spears being thrust aside, nine fully armoured professionals impacted on them. They jolted back, but those struck by sly gladius strikes could not fall as they were being pushed forwards by men behind them.

As those at the front were shredded, those at the back, unaware of the one-sided carnage, were eager to join. A stalemate ensued.

Pluvius pushed up close to his opponent, who, for all his screams and bellows could not hide his petrification. As Pluvius' senses became transfixed by this boy's torturous plight, he felt his soldierly ways drain from him, he could much more easily drop his weapons and give the boy a hug, and not slowly drive his gladius into the boy's face, as he knew he had to do.

Pluvius lifted his right hand with gladius up, gripping the sword like a dagger, so it pointed downwards and his thumb rested on the ball of the handle. The boy had dropped his spear and was reaching for something at his side.

Pluvius drove the sword forwards. It struck the boy's cheek, piercing it, and spraying a few drops of blood before a trickle began. The boy gasped and stumbled back, impacting on the rebel behind him. Pinned in place, tears rolled down his cheek, attempting to dilute the spillage of blood. It was like seeing a petrified rabbit that had been struck by something, and sat shaking in shock... it would be a mercy killing, albeit a mercy killing to a torture he had inflicted. Pluvius thrust again. It was like splicing a coconut; first it sank through the skin, stalling almost immediately as it forced its way through the skull, pushing and pushing until with one thrust he heard a crack and a cry. Once through the skull the sword slid, almost glided through the brain. Pluvius retracted the sword and winced sympathetically.

He had moments to recompose himself, channelling his disgusted anger into self-preserving lunges. The man adjacent grabbed Gerics' wrist as he tried to imitate the sergeant. In an instinctive follow up Pluvius' gladius struck the adolescent's neck, sinking like a knife into a potato. Its burrowing was carried out in a series of wrenching motions, spraying blood. Pluvius grunted like an ox and drove forward holding their advance in check, but without a reliable adjacent force he could not redress the kink in the line. As he crammed and pushed he could hear the man with the punctured windpipe whimpering for assistance. The grizzled veteran was brought near weeping as his conscience called him to draw back or even push forward and help the adolescent up and cradle him in his last minutes of life. It was the very least he deserved.

The stalemate seemed to go on for hours. But when the breakthrough came, it was over in a flash; he didn't even hear the 'resident barbarian' coming, he just felt the perpendicular force slam into his opponent as it capitulated. Then a seemingly huge blade flashed before him carving a devastating swathe through the enemy line. Severed limbs dropped as through haphazardly flung to the ground, screams escalated and died down to a childish whimper only to be replaced by more intense shrieks of agony from the next batch. Tearful eyes turned blood shot as terrorised rebels fell.

Despite the impending disaster, the rebels fought on, trying desperately to form a defensive 'L' block, though even seasoned soldiers would find making such a formation, in the middle of a battle, near impossible. Still, Arios' advance had slowed, he now battled it out with two rebels armed with axes, hefty iron slotted onto a solid wooden stick. The soldier pushed them back with a body slam then, as though to mock their futility before completing their impending deaths, he slashed their axe poles in two with lightning strikes.

The two clean slashes sent them tumbling into the no-return darkness that was below the waist. Though they were technically still alive, it was a well-accepted fact amongst soldiers that once you had fallen below the darkness line you never came back. Once down there you had a couple of seconds for a helping hand or else you were trampled into the dirt, spluttering in the congealed mud made all the more damp with the pools of blood, that stained the soil as the deathly melee above curdled it with the soil.

The fight seemed to have returned to a deadlock of shoving and close up grappling. Most of the rebels had given up trying to seize their axes and knives and concentrated fully on pushing against the squad. The weapons would be pretty much useless anyway as everyone was hemmed in so close that there was no room to slash. Nevertheless, men on both sides were brazen with cuts from mild scrapes. Being clad in mere rags, the rebels were worst off. Pluvius gazed at the straining adolescents, blood trickling in running droplets down their faces. In places red smears mingled with mud, that hardened into cracked Martian landscapes on their skin. Even their eyes were bloodshot red, adding to the depraved look of feverish plague-ridden delinquents.

It was then that Pluvius realised he had never taken a head count. It was the human in him that wanted to know how many there were, how many had been killed. He felt disgusted that he had taken human lives as such an irrelevance. Not just how many but who? They were people, not numbers, young men fresh from youth, how many had been slaughtered? Who were they? Were all those years of life just an irrelevant prelude to this abrupt and brutal demise? His mind pictured imaginary versions of their lives rocketing through time, live little tunnels being navigated like trapped rats speeding down tunnel vision until they reached the spot they were in now… then blood and darkness.

He imagined how they would look to a third party; an amalgam of interlocking muscle. Crammed into armour and clothes backed up against shields, flat plates separating the components of flesh, Both sides pressed against a steel machine; a meat grinder of swords, the flesh behind the swords taking no pleasure in devouring the opposing meat; it was as cold as mere tools, little more independent than the steel they operated.

An idea struck Pluvius, one both tactically sound, and also humane. He would signal his men back so they could reform, clamp shields, try and intimidate the enemy into retreat. Failing that, they could charge and break their line, sending them into disarray so they would have to flee. Otherwise they would be flattened where they stood in moments.

Just as he prepared to give the order he heard the neighing of a horse followed by horrendous shouts. Suddenly more high-pitched screams began to sound, simultaneously the enemy line buckled and collapsed. Pluvius was thrust forward. Through the corner of his eye he caught sight of a shrouded black figure on horseback swinging a mighty double-handed club-staff with bloodthirsty ferocity. It looked like child smashing a stick down into puddles of red water as with every swing a splash of blood would spray upwards in a brief fountain spurt. As the rebels turned tail and fled, Pluvius lifted up the boy in front of him. The youth stood bewildered, so Pluvius roared at him maniacally, and he turned stumbling off glancing back in sheer terror at the steel demon, expecting it to chase after him.

Instead, Pluvius set about dispatching the wounded rebels; some of his men were doing the same. Others had removed their helmets and rubbed their grimy faces or got out strips of cloth to mop up blood from cuts. None seemed to have any serious wounds.

However, Pluvius was flung out of his focused operation by a demonic shriek:

"What the bloody Septimo is he doing?" The words had come from Heites, who stood staring in disgusted disbelief across to where the remnants of the rebels were fleeing. As Pluvius neared to question him, he merely pointed. The sergeant followed the finger to see the figure of Brother Visuvius. The bloodlusting zealot was chasing after the rebels dodging shrubs along the flattened plateau cutting them down one by one.

"Leave him," Pluvius declared bitterly.

Heites opened his mouth to retort, but was stopped by the sergeant's stern hand.

Pluvius could not bear to watch and found a tuft of long grass to wipe his blade and hands.

Heites continued to watch, the rage rising in him. The rest of the men were silent, trying to catch their breath. All of a sudden Heites was shouting again, though more to himself, "the horses!" and turned to try and find them.

His panic had just spread amongst the ranks when Delis and Juscius emerged over the ridge holding the reins of all the horses.

As Heites jogged over to assist them, Delis smiled. "Don't worry, we got…" he was stopped mid sentence. "Shit!"

Within a second, and without another word he was on his horse and cantering forwards across the ridge. All the men were confused by the usually cautious man's impetuousness so looked up to see what had spurred his action. It was the warrior priest; he had just begun to gallop up the next ascension, darting between wiry saplings. Yet his horse slowed, his normally rigid posture could, even from this distance be seen to be lacking as he swayed left and right. As his whole torso rolled back, they could make out a long javelin protruding. With such an unbalanced rider the horse began to skittishly encircle itself. All the men rushed to their horses, that is, except Heites who just sat down and watched with a savage smile.

Two rebels had turned and were trying to pull the black behemoth off his horse, but due to the monk's extensive weight and the horse's erratic behaviour they were still struggling when Delis arrived. He was upon them immediately, striking them on the head with the edge of his gladius. As the weapon did not have much of an edge it merely knocked them out. He then grabbed the horse's reins and hurtled back to the rest of the men.

Instinctively, the men formed a protective semicircle and faced outwards whilst Arios and Pluvius dealt with the injured priest. The warrior monk was fully conscious but still stunned by the strike. He mumbled something incoherently.

They examined the weapon. It was strange, a combination of a spear and a javelin. Whilst Pluvius prepared to dump a huge mound of cloth on the wound, Arios pulled it out of the clerics shoulder. The head was shaped like a spear; the point was flattened and edged even though it was more sleek and long in the point than a usual spear. Its construction was from one single piece, the pole being all-metal with two padded grips. However what really struck the two soldiers was its colour and weight, it was remarkably light and was a shiny silver colour – though too tough for silver. The weapon looked formidable. Its strength and sharp design meant it could slash through scale mail when in combat, and when thrown it could no doubt punch through. Crucially, it was reusable as a javelin. The rear end had a point, for sticking in the ground, but also to act as a balancing counter weight. Immediately Pluvius speculated in his mind that this must be the 'something of importance', though what mattered to him now was whether the rebels had any more.

Pluvius could not work out why this artefact would be over here in a remote corner near the Gatan border rather than in Lateria... was it being tested? Why had Visuvius speculated that it had come across the border? Was the Delvinius company trading with Gatan?

Arios pointed to the markings on it.

"Gatan," Pluvius muttered.

"What?" spluttered the wounded priest, before inferring, "It must have been given to the rebels by House Gatan."

They tied up the wound with cloth then carried the wounded priest back to the site of the battle. Dusk had set in, turning the corpses into ill-shaped black blobs offset with illuminous white dead flesh. Piles of cloth were strewn across the landscape.

As they passed the recently deceased, Pluvius glanced at the faces of the fallen. Some bodies were sprawled out in the most uncomfortable positions, pale limbs were shattered and lying off in awkward angles. Pluvius bent down over one. The eyes were staring up in frozen horror, the white glistening with moisture like the reflection of the moon in a still lake. Pluvius found it ironic that such a terrorised husk of degraded flesh could so resemble the polar opposite; something so tranquil.

Was this the future of his people? A terror so terrible it resembled a drifting beauty in the darkness, which left one numbed to anaesthetised synthetic tranquillity, the result of an overloading in panicky stupor.

He wiped away the grit dried on with blood, applying some spit to his fingers and running it across each cheek, so a pallid line of pure white was revealed.

These didn't look like greedy men out to rob for profit, just troublesome boys, they had looked like they'd learned their lesson as soon as they saw who had come for them. Watching their families get pushed around for years, now being pressured into faster productivity so they can perform their minute little bit for the nation's cause. Grind themselves into the dirt with all the ants and lice to preserve a colony they were barely even part of. These boys wanted to make a stand and now they had paid for it. Massacred.

It took a good few minutes to compose himself ready to reach his men.

In the meantime, without needing orders, the men had set about making camp and moving the bodies... that is chucking them into the valley. Whilst they did so Pluvius just sat with the horses, staring into space, his memory flooded with the sight of the newly dispatched boys. He tried to stop thinking of them, he even tried thinking of Julia, but could not. His mind was full of so much waste and death that it would be just be a further desecration to bring her into his head when his brain was full of so much brutality. Round and round his brain swam, agonising reminiscing and pathetic anger combined with an excessive, self-despising guilt. If only he could turn back time, but then what could he do? Even if he went back to when he'd volunteered then the same would have happened. Besides, how many years had he done this? Why now? Was it her? He winced as an image of Julia flickered before his eyes before dispersing into a crowd of screaming youths caked in blood and soil.

He was so lost in his thoughts that he did not even hear Heites approach until he started cursing. Pluvius turned his head slowly towards the source of the lewd words. Still lost in thought, in a vague and confused tone, he inquired as to the target of the words.

"That goddamn 'brother'."

Pluvius was even now not fully plugged in to the conversation.

"What did he say?" he asked mechanically.

Heites let out a hate-venting sigh. "He's prattling in a half delirium... but he knows what he's saying... I mean he's arguing back with coherence."

"Arguing?" Pluvius inquired, with a worrisome glance at Heites, as though to argue with the priest was dangerous, even, insane.

The veteran ignored his comrade's concern, disdainful of his sergeant's passive submission to the maniac.

"I asked him what the hell he'd thought he was doing charging off like that. You wouldn't believe his reply: 'the machine was clogged' – those were his words, and so 'the brain' – that's him by the way! (we were the 'machine') had to come in and fix the problem!"

Pluvius shuddered at the analogy.

"Well I said – 'judging by the brashness of your actions, that was no brain – just stupidity.' To which he declared, 'no you are right – it is the heart; the brain is the gods and their earthly incarnations'. Well it must be a black one, this heart. The murdering fool."

Pluvius gasped. "You didn't say that did you?"

Heites laughed. "Of course not! I didn't call him a murdering fool... but I told him he had a black heart for being so merciless – they were just kids! I said you can call them what you want, but ultimately that's what they were; poor kids. He claimed they were 'brigands, thieves and scum'."

Pluvius tried to be clever. "You did say he could call them what he wanted."

Heites had no time to see if the sergeant was making a joke. "I was being sarcastic. He can use any word he likes because they are all interchangeable to him... except that each has a specific connotation in order to influence how others perceive them – one minute they are mere petty vandals, next they are part of some Gatan-based terrorist conspiracy. Soon they will be sign of an internal insurgency that proves the need for suspicion of any within the household who do not wholeheartedly follow them. All that remains constant is the simplistic facade that they are unquestionably evil."

Pluvius was lost, but tried to agree on what he could. "They were definitely not money-grabbing brigands, they wouldn't have stood to fight then – they stood for something."

"Exactly! They had hearts, they believed in something…"

"So does Visuvius, to his credit…. Not like us," Pluvius added bitterly.

"We fight for money, bought as part of the machine," Heites commented.

"We fight for riches – we are the bandits."

Silence engulfed them both and combined with the chill of nightfall causing them to shiver. Both still wore their armour and so felt the cold harshly as the metal cooled.

Pluvius took a glance at Heites, shuddered, then looked towards the campfire.

"We ought to head over, and bring the horses," he declared.

They wearily grabbed the reins and walked slowly toward the glaring orange surrounded by huddled figures.

"Just one more thing sarge?"

"What?"

"What are we going to do?" he stopped and looked straight at Pluvius with a concerned, slightly defiant look that was lost in the darkness.

Pluvius picked up his comrade's anxiety nevertheless and stopped.

"The mission," he barked gloomily before tugging the horses on and gesturing for Heites to do the same.

Heites nodded sombrely. They walked on for a few moments. Heites was agitated, and on the brink of saying something, but they were reaching the campfire and could hear the men's mutterings.

Seven sat around the campfire, the other three were on watch. Arios heard them approaching first and jerked his head lazily towards them in the crackling orange light. "Well hello!" he greeted warmly.
Both of them nodded attempting smiles which failed to crack through the skin of their gaunt faces.

"Did you see my little flank attack?" Arios boasted with excessive pride, unaware of the sickliness it left in his comrades' throats. "Got one sneaking off to tell the others. Then smashed straight through 'em!"

As the two reached the firelight all could see their sombre faces. Heites calmly and politely declared. "Please Arios, not today."

Arios was shocked and looked to his sergeant, who shared Heites' displeasure.

Arios hid his anger though his body language betrayed his dismay. He turned to the men, "better get some more firewood."

He strode over to Pluvius and leaned down so his face was inches from the sergeant. "Look, sergeant, whatever you think about them," he made a gesture with his head towards the valley that was now strewn with corpses, "your men need all the encouragement they can get."

"They are, after all, acting like professionals... and it is our... no YOUR duty to keep their morale up." With that he stormed off. Virtually unnoticed, Geric rose like an obedient jackrabbit and bolted off after him.

The two veterans came to sit by the fire and listened to the uneasy silence. Guilt rose in Pluvius' throat, he knew the hulking warrior was right – he had a duty to his men, even if not to anyone else. Like it or not, battle would come tomorrow, and he had a job to do.

"That was some excellent work lads. I know it seemed a little easy, but tomorrow will be a good test. I am proud of you – I am proud because not only did you fight well, but honourably."

The men nodded solemnly, they knew he was making a veiled attack on the brother's bloodthirsty assault and condoning their humanitarian dispatching of the wounded.

Heites meanwhile sat hunched in a sullen reverie. Pluvius dared not disturb him. He turned back to the fire. The flames licked around a black metal pot full of what smelt like a stew of potatoes, onions and carrots with some unidentifiable meat. Just the thought of the word meat brought back images of seared flesh and bone. He shivered in the hellish heat.

In an attempt to break up his mind's wanderings he addressed the men. "So, how much longer you reckon the grub needs?"

Mateus, the squad's informal cook shrugged. "When I'm too hungry to wait any longer!" he chuckled.

"Well, wake me when its ready, I'm gonna get some kip first, so I can eat then take second watch. Delis and Juscius you can do it with me, then Arios, Geric, Heites and Mateus you can take third watch – Geric's never done it before so he'd better go with someone."

It was then that Arios returned. He only had a few pieces of wood, but he had calmed down and was ready to face his sergeant again. He had the axe slipped under his belt. "I'll go with the kid," he declared as he dropped the pile of wood by the fire before sitting down.

Heites seemed to stir and look across at Arios. "You don't have your sword on you," he noted dreamily. "You should," he added also in a state of malcontent.

"Dunno, might be more fair if I use this!" He lifted the handle of the woodaxe momentarily before returning it so it flopped back down.

Nobody heard Heites' muttered reply. "Hmm, yes, more fair, more just." Then he returned his focus to the fire.

"Is chow ready?" inquired Arios hungrily. Geric rubbed his stomach supportively.

"Not yet," answered Mateus. "Oh and sergeant, your tent is over there, next to brother Visuvius' tent."

Pluvius nodded, as he lifted himself and stepped away from the fire. As he departed from the ring of soldiers, he felt the coming of the late autumn chill as the fire's heat dissipated.

'Hmm, time to try out my new cloak' he thought to himself, speeding up as the thought of the coat enticed him to his tent. He longed to wrap up in its warm fur; it pushed him into a brisk trot – every second out here was a wasted second. He could make out his tent in the moonlight, distinguishable from the others by its smaller size. It bobbed as his vision swayed from his movements – a black triangle standing like a dark beacon in the scraggy grey.

He soon reached the tent and flung the strap open, crawled in and frantically scrabbled for the mystical haze of white that was the cloak. He clutched it, running the silky fur through his worn fingers. As he pulled the cloak around him he sighed, "better go and check on the brother" he muttered tiresomely.

★

In the meantime Heites had sat staring into the campfire in total silence. His mind raced, contemplating an act, the act, third party vengeance.

'If so, when?'

'I must, this is not just for the others; it is for me also –I cannot let this farce go on. I can't stand the enforced silence, the staleness in the air. It has drained good men of their reason.'

'But can I prevent hot blooded massacre with cold-blooded murder?'

Suddenly conscious that he may have been mumbling his words aloud, he took a casual glance at the rest of the soldiers around the campfire. They were engrossed in their own banter and were ignoring him. He also noticed that Arios and Geric had gone again with the wood axe.

Seeing all the men chattering normally after such an event, he wondered if they could be trusted should he take responsibility. *'Arios would protect a comrade surely. He hates that clerical fool, besides he would protect me for the sake of the squad even if our friendship was not enough. As for Geric I'm not sure I can trust him. Sometimes I think he might actually buy that New Interpretation rubbish... but surely he wouldn't dare go against one of the squad? ...And Pluvius?'* he asked himself finally in silent soliloquy.

'What weapon? Arios has taken the wood axe, I cannot use my sword – Gladius wounds are too obvious.'

He paused ponderously, *'So, will I do it then?'* he asked himself casually.

'If I am to do it I need to ascertain why I see the necessity to do it. Not why I want to do it, but why it is morally obligatory.'

His hands shook, as it became more apparent that he was being serious; the build up to the act was beginning its psychological reign of terror. The theoretical consequence of speculation over horrifying behaviour was being put into practice.

'Why do my hands shake? I have killed so many times before, and for much lesser reasons – why just today I skewered a boy and trampled his bleeding little heart into the mud.' Yet he found the trembling intensified rather than dissipated.

'Why?' He begged his hands for an answer.

They continued their skittish defiance.

He began to plead. *'For once I seek to kill for an actual reason, I attempt to use my profession for good, rid our land of an irredeemable idiot, yet you let me down. Do I fear such a task? An assertion of significance? Not much, I confess, but some. Perhaps that is it, yes, finally I am choosing to kill, picking a target, not the stooge of another.'*

He clenched his fists to stop them trembling.

'Can I break from the mould?'

Heites leaned back in horror. *'Is that it? I will kill just to prove I can do other than obey orders?'* He leaned forward towards the fire, resting his chin in the V-shape formed by his hands. He tried reasoning with himself, whispering his thoughts aloud *'It is not from a mere dislike that I do this, though it is a clear incentive, nor is it to save us the disgrace of further massacres. It is perhaps a preventative of such things happening again, as it cannot be justified under the conspicuous idea of revenge. No, it is more than that; it is political. It represents an opposition to the regime (in its current form?), and within that a defiance of the notion that I am just a cog incapable of making significant actions outside the command of superiors. He has chosen to wholeheartedly support this corrupted regime and so can pay the consequences. Also, by doing so, I will give the rebels a slight victory to be remembered by, to provide hope to others.'*

His rant finished, he was irritated by the slight tremble that remained in his hands, and the searing ache of fear in his throat. Sitting upright he gazed at the vacillating red digits.

"Why do you tremble so?" he whispered under his breath.

Suddenly he was distracted by an overwhelming fear that he had been heard, so he quickly glanced over at the other soldiers. They were all engaged in conversation and had not heard him. Juscius soon noticed his gaze and was distressed by the usually relaxed veteran's edgy demeanour. He saw how the alert and quirky soldier's eyes stared, water-welled, in one place before darting with haemorrhaged jerkiness. Warmly, but without sounding patronising he addressed Heites. "Heites, you do not look well." Leaning into the fire, holding a ladle in one hand and a bowl in the other, he served some broth. "Take this and get some rest."

Heites was not hungry, but saw it as an opportunity to excuse himself. He stood, finding the searing heat of the fire unbearable as he neared his comrade. He eagerly took the bowl and scampered off into the darkness.

★

Heites held the bowl ceremoniously in front of him. He knew exactly where to go because he always slept in the tent closest to Pluvius. Heites spotted the smaller tent, next to it was the huge tent where the cleric was, Heites' own being relegated to second closest. They seemed to have been positioned so that Pluvius' tent was between his and the brothers.

With sudden paranoia a terrible thought struck him. *'Had they planned it?'* Was he suspected already? He shook the thought away as he entered his tent.

In the tent it was barely warmer than outside; the wind was so minimal it made little contribution to the cold and so the offering of shelter was quite an empty promise. Heites placed the bowl down carefully just outside the tent then began feeling for his pack in the dark. Once he had found it he fumbled blind within it for something to replace his scale mail. He took off his cumbersome armour, flung on a loose rough tunic and wrapped up in a hooded cloak.

Heites crawled fully into the tent, neglecting to remove his boots, and nestled himself into a comfortable huddle before taking a few awkward spoonfuls of broth. He was in no mood for food, and soon placed it down. He lay back on the patchwork of thin blankets that constituted a floor, the stubby grass poking through. Lying still, his mind floated insipidly, browsing over nothing in particular. His eyes locked on the darkness above, mental inanition coalescing with physical fatigue to give his whole body an aura of numbness. In the chilled desolation he whispered with a hint of disappointment, "why has my anger dissipated so?" He sighed. "I had worked myself up, but now I lie empty."

He clamped his mouth shut and stared intensely at a particular dark patch above him. It soon flashed with shapes and shades as his mind attempted to pick something out of the pitch-black void. Then the notion flashed before him as though a divine inspiration. "No, that is exactly it! Now I can do this and know it is not just an act of irrational vengeance!" He almost shouted these statements in an affirmation of legitimacy.

"I must do this cold, it must be cool, co-ordinated assassination. Call it murder if you must." He declared to an imaginary jury. "But it is the opposite of his crime; I must be calculated and intelligent, not mercilessly indiscriminate like him. Only then can I even begin to consider asserting my correctness. It has to be the act itself that I see as good, not the principles driving me to act – for that is how he and his kind determine their actions. They are filled with such self-righteous fanaticism that they can commit atrocities for an end above us all."

He was slipping into deliriousness as he reiterated the same point over and over: "They can justify any act of brutality as the god's will... The spreading of society by barbarity..."

His rambling faded out and he began to think about the battle, the grinning devilish priest. Before he knew it the rage had filled him again. "Why do I need to justify myself in killing that despicable louse?" he suddenly declared. "I have maimed and killed as a pawn of his kind for years. Spilled the blood of young and old by the gallons, just to obey their every whim! Let them get what they deserve!" He raged, spittle flying unnoticed in the empty darkness. "And I will do this for those boys I killed. They will have their revenge!" His rant came to an abrupt end and he plunged deep into contemplation. The word stuck in his throat like a block of wood, holing up in his oesophagus, keeping his Adam's apple hostage. He held his breath. He could feel his eyes bulge until the strain became unbearable. He let his breath go.

He felt embarrassed at his last outburst. This turned into a sickened anger, directed upon himself. "Revenge?" he spat with utter abhorrence. "If I want to enact revenge for those boys why don't I kill myself? And while I'm at it, burn down the entire camp? If I do this for revenge I am a hypocrite."

The sullen silence that followed gave him the answer – revenge was no reason. Besides who was he, a perpetrator, to enact revenge on their behalf? Once calmed he whispered with slow, precise calculation. "I know I must do something, use whatever skills I possess to combat this abomination that plagues us and confines our lives. It must be separate from what I have witnessed today. For any such reaction would be grudge-based and therefore unjustifiable." He stopped momentarily, thinking of how he could act. "And I am a soldier, a killer, so it makes sense for me to use this in my resistance."

As doubts sank in, he added with calm defiance, "I know I will not end it, certainly not alone. But I can only be judged for my actions. As inaction and apathy are tacit consent, I must do more than sit and grumble."

Almost immediately he posed the question pressing him on into action. "So I must think practically." Before he had even finished the sentence the first hurdle was forming: "I need that axe," he declared.

Countless minutes passed as he lay motionless. Just as he was succumbing to defeat he stretched his arms back behind his head, and his right knuckle brushed against something hard and sharp – it was Arios' broadsword.

"So the weapon is found... I can wipe the blood on a bandage in Visuvius' tent and leave it in there, so as not risk leaving a trail."

The pain in his stomach rested slightly, but not fully. "But when? – I cannot do it while Pluvius is in his tent."

As his mind tried to blank out the images predicting what he was soon to do he whispered to himself, "and now the waiting game."

With his mind cycling he was soon asleep.

★

Heites awoke with a panic-stricken start. Immediately he sat up and with terrified dismay he felt an irrational intuition that he was late. He was in complete darkness and he did not hear a word. He could vaguely remember a dream, which had had an evil priest in it, but was unsure if this was just the repetitive images he had received before sleeping. He decided to reach for the sword; if nothing else it would be an object of comfort. However, as his fingers scrabbled blindly frustration overwhelmed him as he became convinced it was not there.

Reason began to set in; Arios must be on watch. The reign of reason was short-lived; he panicked and stumbled for the exit. Blindly he fumbled in the total darkness, clumsily tumbling out of the tent as though it had collapsed and was trying to suffocate him. As he fell out of the tent he stumbled over a pile of cylindrical objects stacked conspicuously just outside the tent, almost hidden. So used to the complete darkness, he even found the pathetic moonlight blinded him.

The cold cut through his clothing, sending a chill down his spine. He rubbed his eyes then looked around in a daze. To his left, hunched figures sat motionless, huddled around the glowing red embers of a dormant campfire. Heites glared at the top of the brother's tent; like a distant peak it rose high over the top of Pluvius' abode. There was his goal. He stole a quick glance over towards the fire but was immediately captivated by the hill that towered above it invitingly adorned with trees that gave it a nobly cottonwool bud silhouette. Then he thought of the dead flung over the cliff into the valley; Brother Visuvius lay in his way to them.

Slowly and silently the veteran rose to his feet, keeping his neck hunched forward like a stalking cat. He listened: silence. He looked down at his feet; the metal on his boot reflected the moonlight with a dull glint. A smell wafted into his nose; it was recently cut wood. At the same time his eyes caught sight of something that almost shone in the squalid light. The fact that it shone meant it was metallic. He reached into the interlocking maze of fallen cylinders, ascertaining that they were freshly cut pieces of lumber. Amongst the odd shapes he touched the shapely smooth handle of the axe. In contrast to the gnarly pieces of wood, it seemed quite sleek.

Arios must have returned, but where was he now? If he was by the campfire, why was the lumber here, when it was clearly needed? It cannot have gone second watch as he would have been woken up. Heites shook the thoughts off. "Never mind that now," he reasoned. "Be it fate, luck, the gods, demons, my chance is now."

He took a last panoramic survey to check the coast was clear. He took one step, then thought, 'I need some reason for entering'. His mind was truly on the ball and he immediately reached into his tent to pick up the broth.

He took one last peek towards the campfire, observing the ill-formed black statues before ambling towards Pluvius' tent. Within a minute he had reached the sergeant's tent, and whispered his name. There was no answer. "Better check he's not just sleeping." Heites was in that nervous state where one speaks thoughts to oneself in order to pretend one is not alone. Prodding around with one boot he precariously balanced himself on one foot. He went down on one knee and peered in. Not being able to see anything he was satisfied by the lack of breathing and so he set off to the final peak.

He stopped outside the tent opening and as quietly as possible stuffed the axe down the back of his belt. As he reached for the flap his hands began to tremble, making the task ever harder to perform. Broth slopped with cold wet licks against his fingers. Cautiously he lurched forward, the top of the axe head pressing against the small of his back. He peeped in; the flap was only open a fraction when he retracted in horror. A flash of candlelight had flooded out as though he was about to trespass on a divine abode. His heart stopped dead.

'Is he awake?' he pondered, retracting his body, hunching and curling away from the light source.

He shook off his fear, readdressed himself, '*Well, if he is awake, it's too late now.'*

Closing his eyes and bracing himself he stepped inside. Once convinced he still stood on solid ground he opened his eyes. Within seconds his eyes had adjusted. His eyes fixed immediately on the well-wrapped figure of Visuvius. All but a small polished section of his skull lay concealed in thick blankets. The candle flickered as though in futile warning, the flame dancing in panic-stricken fear. A makeshift straw packed mattress elevated the body.

"Our horses go without nutrition so you may sleep sound," Heites whispered, with disgust.

Nothing but the candle stirred, silently dancing as though in a noiseless void.

The tent rose high like a tepee. Each of the four sides rose up like a pyramid to merge in a crease now concealed by darkness. Occasionally adventurous scatterings of candlelight would illuminate it. The canvas itself was plain, slightly grimy beige, providing a near perfect backdrop for the swirling candle to perform a striking shadow-puppet theatre on all the walls. Fading and expanding patches of black coalesced and danced with livid flickers of orange, creating startling contrast.

The brother's belongings had been hastily piled in a corner of the room and a soggy pile of bloody rags lay by the mattress.

Heites stood frozen. Even his trembling hands had ceased convulsing in terror. His bowels felt loose and brimming. The pinkish bald patch so snugly peeping from the warm blankets reminded the hulking veteran of a sleeping baby. Fighting off the tricks of his mind, he declared poetically, "such fiendish mimicking is no saviour tonight." With a wavering whisper he continued his sickened smile. "Sleeping like a baby, yet you are no cherub!"

He remained motionless for a moment, his face displaying the guile of a stalking crocodile or the grin of a hunter that suspects it is being watched. "Do you sleep?" he suddenly snapped in a demanding tone.

Furtively he looked down at his hands. The stiffness had ended and his limbs quivered again, enough to send the broth swirling in waves that lapped against the bowl's edge.

"I must be vigilant, remember," he reassured himself, in a mocking reference to Vultai's sermon.

Heites forced himself into action, placing the bowl on the pile of belongings. All the time he kept a watchful eye on the motionless body under the blankets. Just as he leaned back to the upright position he saw a stirring movement from under the cloth.

"You are awake!" Heites accused forcefully. "... I have your broth, your Excellency," he mumbled incoherently.

With a seemingly natural movement of slumber, the body moved and the fat head surfaced. Heites examined it closely, as a twitching strain momentarily split across the brother's brow.

Without thinking, Heites decided to play along, leaning forward and shaking the brother to wake him. "Your Excellency, you must eat." Rather than perform a ritualistic awakening, the brother just suddenly began to talk, fully consciously.

The candle reacted to the sudden movement, drawing its light back and shrouding the brother in darkness before surging back to flood the oval with brightness. It vanquished all shadow from the mystical warriors face, showing an angry, thuggish demeanour.

"Fool! I have already eaten."

The glassy eyes shot open, swiftly glaring from behind their steely lids like flashlights. Hawkishly they eyed the trespasser. "You are a traitor, Heites. I saw your eyes as the javelin struck, they were so envious of the steel as it plunged into my shoulder. Your hands tremble now for they wish to have propelled that hellish machination." He barely paused to breathe.

"Go on! Murder me! Save your skin! End *another* life; bring us all that little closer to Septimo!" His face cracked into a malicious smile, "... and send me to my peace, my judgement. What about you? When our lords' servants judge you? You have killed for money, and now you kill to avoid execution! For believe me, when I return to the garrison you will swing!" The brother began quietly, rising into a rousing, accusatory spiel. Heites was flabbergasted, his retort confused. "No! You are the heartless murderer, you led me to kill them. You must die before you and your kind ruin us all – you cannot dress up barbarism with phoney principles, but you can stop the barbarism of others with force!"

With this he hauled the axe out from behind his back. The brother started unexpectedly and gasped, whimpering, "no, you cannot!"

Heites, with a fiery glare, whispered with uncontrollable rage. "This is not for revenge. This is not for me. This is my contribution to end this despicable force you represent."

He brought the axe down with one fell swoop, grasping its smooth handle with both hands. Yet he failed to strike, his hands failed him, sweat pouring from his finger pores greasing the handle with indecision. The axe head bumped against the priest's forehead, not even scratching the skin.

Heights gazed angrily at his hands. "Why do you fail me?" he begged of them.

The priest meanwhile lay paralysed in a waning grimace, bracing for judgement. He began to mumble something, a prayer, as though speaking in tongues. Then his eyes opened, burning with a passion of uncontrollable anger. Hawkishly he stared at the veteran as his lips mumbled, "Curse this heathen, this abomination who seeks to sabotage the creation of your paradise... He is no better than Sepitmo's dupes... who seek to hate your freedom... and of whom we must gloriously slaughter... for your name... and for all."

It was then that Heites felt the necessary surge; the anger at the brother's self-righteousness, how he did so much wrong in the name of right. But most of all he was reminded of those screaming boys as they bled and sobbed; it was their image that spurred him to act.

He brought the axe down with exceptional force. A horrific cracking noise resonated through the air of the tent as the cranium split. After the immediate flecks had appeared on the axehead it took just over a second for the trickle to begin. Simultaneously the body convulsed. The trickle rose to a torrent as he pulled the axe out. Gleaming sacks of smooth rubbery yellow organic matter peeped from the deluge of red.

Hastily Heites wiped the axe and removed the flecks of blood from his face. He thrust the rag down on the pile of other bloody rags and took one last glance at the body. Sporadic twitches sent blood spilling out like an active volcano. He grabbed the bowl and fled, fearing the image would be imprinted in his mind.

As he stopped outside the beads of sweat that mottled his face and neck grew cold, adding to the outside chill. It was only now that he recalled the unexplainable warmth of the tent. His torso soon chilled though his brain was still racing almost to a point of overload. The unbearable contrast between his burning screaming mind and his icy surroundings became unbearable, sending his heart pounding into frenzy. It thumped against his empty chest; a trapped animal in a dank cavern. Panicking, he rushed back towards his tent, stumbling and rustling with a noise that echoed in his full ears as though it would be heard in Lateria.

The tent in which he sought refuge lurched closer. Upon reaching it he stumbled on the lumber again and threw down the axe with mental and physical exhaustion. With absent-minded compulsion he poured the cold broth down his throat, gulping it down drastically like a bitter liquid pill. Throwing the bowl down, he wiped his mouth with his arm then clambered into the tent. The darkness comforted him. His mind cooled and he felt calm and alone. Now he must wait. But for how long? When would he be discovered?

★

Heites was woken from a feverish sleep by shouts. He half expected some monstrosity from his last uncountable hours to leap from the indistinguishable shadows that covered his view. Trembling, he stumbled weakly out of the tent.

The fullness of night still ran reign over the sky. A figure came rushing past in the direction of the campfire, evidently not noticing

Heites. He followed. Suddenly it came to his attention that he had no idea what he planned to do. What worried him more, was that he suddenly noticed that he had a lumber log crudely clutched in the fashion of a club in his right hand.

"Surely I do not plan to strike him?" he queried himself.

He slowed to a jog, desperately attempting to rationalise his actions. He nervously tossed the log aside and, without pausing, thundered on.

As he rushed after the figure, he could not help feel a rising mistrust of himself, a troubling spurred by his instinctive grab of the log. "What had overcome me?" he pondered, spitting the words in an acrimonious whisper.

The figure had stopped by the campfire and Heites was soon at the campfire. It was not so much of a fire but a smell, a smoky sodden smell that somehow warms the body just by its association with warmth.

The figure Heites had followed was Hydius. Heites identified him by his voice as he declared that the brother was dead. The men seemed, to Heites, remarkably concerned. They squawked and flapped aimlessly, eventually nominating Delius to go and tell Sergeant Pluvius. From the campfire the watch torches could just about be seen, though they were not where the guards were, as it would make them easy targets.

The men were all muttering to each other, trying to deduce the possibility of the bandits slipping through. Some even queried Hydius about the weapon used. Hunched in the cold and waddling about the circle of the campfire, they were a pack of vultures impatiently awaiting the smell of blood and sweat of violence.

Heites stood quietly to the side of the pacing coterie; his mind was full of fleeting incoherent fears – would they soon turn on him? Did they know? Did they really care? Part of him wanted to flee and never come back. Yet he found himself glued to the spot, petrified by his own gloomy forecast. A sly rationale began to impose a bold dominance. It screamed to him to act, to be involved, as, if he remained silent and shifty, they may suspect him. His body had broken into a cold sweat gluing his joints and muscles, constraining him with lethargy.

Suddenly, without warning he bolted into action, forcing words from his mouth with no prior thought; his head felt overwhelmed, almost dreamlike, away in a slumbering reverie far from here. As he spoke the words it was as though another spoke them and he was merely a passing consciousness.

"How could someone get through the watch… do this and get out?" he heard himself say.

Mateus turned to him, "Did you hear anything, you were near, Heites?"

Cautiously he shook his head. "I was asleep."

Mateus grunted a laugh, one that unnecessarily alerted Heites. "You still look it!" he mused sympathetically.

Heites quickly recomposed himself asked Hydius, "So, what happened?"

"I went in to take him some broth, and found him lying there with a huge axe wound in his skull... plus a smaller graze," he added with proud detective work. He glanced around at the other men who were congregated around him. "Obviously not a professional – he hesitated."

Heites nodded, after faking shock at the horrific description of the corpse he had created. "That would appear to be the impression, at least what they wanted us to see." He cursing himself for allowing the visual disturbance to slacken his regulation of his blathering.

"Well, who else would have done it?" asked Mateus on the point of laughter.

"Well, we did all dislike him... didn't we?" mumbled one of the men. Nervously acknowledging the silence he added, "but surely none of us would do such a thing?"

The white-cloaked figure of Pluvius arrived in the oval stage. He seemed more angry than worried, "Darn bastards must have snuck round behind into the valley and come up through the night. Maybe they're still there?"

"Should we go look for them?" Heites queried eagerly.

Pluvius shook his head. "No... it's too risky. We'd have to spread out too much... it could even be a diversion."

"Where are Arios and Geric?" he asked, directing the question to all even though Heites was clearly expected to answer.

Fear rose in the veteran, causing him to hesitate. He became aware that to answer with the truth might incriminate them. Yet all his mind could focus on was the axe. It flashed before him gleaming as though polished, but remained bloodstained. The flecks shone as proud as the metal, ever present as a badge of (dis)honour.

"Well the axe is here so they must be back," he blurted, secretly proud that he had separated his comrade from the unknown murder weapon. Then he grinned nervously. "Tripped over the darn thing on the way over here."

It was just then that the coterie was distracted by the sound of heavy boots. It was Arios being followed by a furtive Geric.

"Where have you been?" Pluvius demanded.

"Just been showing the young-un some sentry skills, saves explaining the basics when actually on guard – you know how all the stuff you learn is rubbish." The usually short-worded veteran was strangely long-winded.

It wasn't long before Juscius and Delis arrived on the scene accompanied by Cilius, who had informed them. "Sergeant we both heard what sounded like two people off into the western side in the woodland. They were sneaky at first but they stopped for a bit and made noises."

"Probably gloating," Arios commented with inexplicable hastiness. Pluvius looked at the fire. "Why didn't you bring the lumber up to the campfire?"

"Shit," Arios cursed genuinely, "Sorry, forgot... figured someone would go and get it if they needed it," he added. "Got back to get some warm clothes on, had to be careful not to wake Heites, who was sound asleep," he continued apologetically.

Pluvius was already sidetracked with his anger at his own failures. "Should have put a guard on his tent all night!" he exclaimed.

The men had clearly been shook up by Heities implication regarding the priests dislike amongst them. One of them, probably seeking to calm Pluvius, in half jest muttered, "should you?"

Pluvius turned to the speaker with an icy look. "This is no time for laughing – what ever happened. We shall be held responsible for this back at the garrison..." He paused eyeing each man cautiously. "We will have to say he was killed in battle," he proclaimed.

A few men looked shiftily at the others, urging Pluvius to explain. "If we say this happened, even if they don't suspect us of killing him they will probably set an example by trying us for incompetence. You all know Vultai has it in for us and would jump at any chance to turn us into political fodder. We must bank on Visuvius being known for his impetuousness. If one of those men who had pulled him off had had an axe this would have happened anyway."

Heites had shuddered at the words that had implicated murder on one of their parts, and the images had returned.

Everyone expected Heites to chip in, but instead he was silent. It was Arios who spoke, and coming from him, the words touched them much more intently. "Sergeant is right, it's the only way to avoid a show trial."

"So what do we do?" one asked.

"We sleep and then attack at first light. We must kill them all to prove we are not traitors."

Nobody noticed Heites' despair; had he failed? Even exacerbated the problem? He could see the sergeant was right. With the cleric dead they had no proof of success, no one trusted by the High Priest to vouch for them. But then they would have to have killed them all in his presence anyway.

Pluvius looked forwards to ending this. "To bed, we attack at first light."

★

Heites had been relieved from guard duty on account of his apparent oncoming fever and had been left entombed in his tent, alone with his apprehension. Though wracked with guilt for the massacre and hands still trembling from the murder, his mind sought to irritate him by worrying that he would be discovered and denounced. He attempted to wave off the notion declaring, "bah, the thing is done, I have made my stance. Now it is their turn."

But then he would realise that this was exactly the issue that worried him: were the rest of the men with him? In some ways their denouncement would in itself proclaim his guilt, for if they opposed his action then he was guilty – he needed their mandate to prove it had not been a pointless cold-blooded murder. Not only were they his colleagues, but they were a representation of the soldiery he was part of. He found himself wanting to tell them, so they could pass judgement and he could escape this limbo. High Priest Vultai and even the puppet Dummonius could not proclaim his guilt; indeed as his action was against their iron grip over his life such condemnation would only make him more righteous.

As his mind drifted in a stubborn refusal to succumb to sleep he imagined various scenarios, ranging from proclamations of support by the people, to the soldiers betrayal and condemnation of him as a radical lunatic. Even the most optimistic usually ended with Vultai swooping down; a wraith-like Visuvius tied to him with rope and a dark staff.

It was during these reveries that only one person would stay loyal throughout, only one would understand his action: Julia. This set him pondering about what she would think. Would she understand or would she laugh mockingly at his crude reversion to murder?

More and more her opinion grew in importance to him, until he proclaimed, "I should seek her."

He froze, shocked by his own words. He felt a sickening betrayal.

'*How could I?*' he thought as his mind was barged into by a troubled Pluvius. Though his rationale told him he was only seeking her council, a sickly subconscious seemed to plead for more.

Whilst his mind juggled capriciously with such nonsensical abstractions not once did he even contemplate the dilemma he would face on the morrow. He would have to carry out the will of the 'beast' he had slain. Even in death the brother was directing his actions and there was nothing he could do without jeopardising his (and his comrade's) life.

Such practical questions had no place in his mind at this time; the 'practical cynic' had for the time being culled his capacity to consider issues relating to the oncoming reality. What he needed now were abstract thoughts of dreamlike wonder, whether good or bad, at least they were not so closely connected to the grimy filth of the impending situation.

Reality was just an arena of constraint to him, a solid amalgam of brick walls hemming him in and forcing him down a narrow passage. If he could, he would vanish himself away, not to a brothel as he normally did, that is, when he wanted somewhere to drink and get his mind off the swooning cloud of death that followed all soldiers. He needed a quiet room to talk to himself. He could not even touch another being now, he felt too filthy. He would fear to pass on the plague. Even a shoulder to cry on would be an unspeakable abomination, as it would merely pass his guilt into another.

Still, it was not the murder that made him feel so, but the previous day's acts of countless murder that lulled his conscience. Yet, it was the murder that he thought of, it was that which made him feel that he was so involved this devilish tirade. However, for all its degradation and he found it strangely empowering. The murder of Visuvius had elevated him to a position of an actual player in (or more against) the despicable struggle rather than just a tool. He was not a mechanism for the acts of others but a force able to direct its own activity. He reasoned optimistically that this could be the beginning of him as an agent. Larvae stirring within an egg. He had hatched. He may struggle hopelessly and pitifully at first, but in time he would wriggle free and squirm and feast upon the rot. He would eat up the rot on this decaying carcass of society; remove the decay to allow the fresh flesh to flourish. If he could help do the same to others, emancipate them from their cocoons, they could en-masse eradicate this putrification that looked set to spread and reduce all of mankind to foetid waste. He smiled with previously unprecedented optimism.

"I may be but an insignificant worm but if I can set free my comrades we can end this," he whispered.

"That despicable act rests on my conscience, on my soul." He thought of the agonising screams of the dying adolescents. "...and then I was just a tool, but now, I have bitten back at the rot." Then his countenance darkened. "I must be cautious, though," he warned himself. "Impetuousness will lead to demise, perhaps as it did with those young idealists. If I gorge too readily on the rot I will bloat and fall easy prey to the predators who patrol and defend this rot." Heites eyes the darkness around him. He knew he had to remain in the ranks, for only from there could he continue the secret war.

Chapter 17
The Secret War/ Sophisticated Savagery

The pre-sunrise light made the canvas of the tent glow mysteriously, giving the impression that Heites lay on the top of a fog-shrouded precipice. Even without this illusion the veteran would have been confused, as he had just awoken from a meticulously detailed, if now hazily remembered dream. This had, save for a few psychedelic interludes, continued his saga concerning the murder of brother Visuvius.

At first he had expected to see a prison cell. Realising this wasn't the case he panicked and gazed around for an escape from the barracks as they would be after him. Then, as reason crept back into his mind, he inferred that he was not that far down the path to his demise.

'So, I am not back yet... is this before or after the murder?' he thought to himself. He groped about at his body, and found he was wearing his boots and the very tunic he had worn when he killed the priest (or would kill the priest). Rustling around more he found the empty broth bowl and from this deduced it was after the murder.

He stretched and fiddled for a few moments, secretly celebrating his freedom to act without the general shifting direction of a dream dragging him off. He then set about recollecting and separating dream from reality.

As the looming despair of what was to come this day seeped into his mind he defiantly retreated his concentration onto the dream. His memory was extremely patchy; he had been caught somehow, High Priest Vultai had used prostitutes to try and seduce him or something and he had been on the run, Arios and Geric had been pursuing him but that was when he fled from the barracks. There was someone who was meant to be Pluvius but wasn't and he felt a sudden well of disgust as he recalled slight recollections of taking Julia hostage. As with so many dreams it made no sense in hindsight but at the time was totally logical.

Heites shook his head. He knew he'd never do such a thing, yet it resided in his subconscious, and could be built into a logical mechanism of survival. He mauled his conscience with guilt at such an idea. Though, as he knew he would never do it in reality, could he really feel guilty for something his sub-conscience had cooked up but he had never consented to? Could he be blamed? Was it his subconscious, not him?

All of a sudden Heites was distracted from his self-interrogation and his attention was drawn out externally to bear upon disturbances in the physical world. The tent flap rustled for a drawn out moment before being thrust apart to reveal the mighty stature of Arios leaning forward to hand him a bowl of what he could only guess was porridge,

"'Ere get this down your throat, sarge is waiting."

Without waiting for Heites to stretch up Arios dumped the bowl on the ground in the tent. The hulking veteran then disappeared behind the reuniting flap.

Alone again, Heites sank back into a dreamy slumber, feeling totally drained. Fighting desperately against the desire to lie back and let the world drift on without him, he somehow managed to convince himself he was just weak from inanition and would be magically revitalised if he consumed the steamy oaty slop. He scrabbled forwards eagerly, grabbing the bowl and hungrily shovelling the sticky white ooze into his mouth. His concentration focused totally on the act of consumption, blanking his mind of any previous worries.

The bowl was soon clean. Though the meal had merely left him feeling bloated, he succeeded in forcing himself up and out.

★

The morning dew glistened as it clung in heavy drops on the long grass. The sun had risen but was partially hidden behind the dense tree-line that spread off into the distance. As it gradually crawled upwards it smeared the pale blue sky with messy orange-yellow streaks that fanned and faded with the moderate progression of the early morning. Down below the cliff edge, a wet thin mist hovered in the muddy depths as though waiting to skulk upwards and claim the bloody bodies all covered in mud and rags that were strewn mercilessly along the slope.

Though there had been no rainfall the land was sodden and the men clammy. Pluvius had issued the plan and Heites had been dispatched to encircle the encampment. He had been chosen under the pretext that he was the next best after Arios, and Arios, due to his performance yesterday, would be noticed if missing on the frontline. Of course this was only part of the reasoning for the decision. It was a convenient cover to hide Pluvius' apprehension over Heites' mental state and ability to fight.

The trap was set. The steep hill was not easily climbed, but to the western side, rocky ridges made the ascent perilous and slow. The eastern side was cut off by a stream that sank down into an extremely viscous bog as it wound down towards the river Neptus. The Northern side had a secret path, though sadly for the rebels it was common knowledge amongst scouts. This was where Heites would set himself.

A thin thread of smoke wafted upwards from behind the trees that dotted the hill, meshing across their view to cover the whole hill in a layer of bushy dark green. The climb was 70m directly upwards and littered with trees and branches that stuck out of the furry layer of grass like dried grey scabs bulging out of old battered skin.

Pluvius and his squad stood in a single line formation erect and prepared, a thin proud line of blood stained silvery scale-mail that twinkled in the rising sunlight. Pluvius himself stood at the line's centre, the red feathers in his helmet stretching to the west with the sporadic gusts of wind. He stepped forward ceremoniously and turned to his men, nodding solemnly to each. Most returned a sombre acknowledgement of the task at hand. More anxious members gave apprehensive smiles encouraged by their trusted sergeant's concerned gaze. He could not help but smile back, a friendly and authoritative look of elder brotherly affection. Then, as one, they raised their shields high and crouched in a display of preparedness for a cautious advance.

Pluvius' sword flashed out of its scabbard and lunged forward up the hill and they immediately, without a sound, began a steady advance upwards. As they caught him up he fell into line and took up a similar posture.

It was some time before the rebels became visible, though their faces and figures remained obscure blotches.

A voice called down. It came from a bandit who stood high and proud on a felled tree at the edge of the hilltop plateau. It was surrounded by a large phalanx of dark green conifers that rose out of the land perpendicularly like staunch triangular daggers in formation mocking the approaching soldiers. The felled tree pointed its green tip in the direction of the soldiers as though issuing a challenge.

"Where is your warrior priest?" the voice boomed with insincere inquisitiveness, "Has he deserted you?" it added mockingly, but with innocence of the priests fate.

In time the rebel leader became more visible; his face had the sizeable beard of a man past his youth, stumbling into his thirties. He wore the clothing of an old warrior; ill fitting leather armour that had knobbly dull gleaming studs of iron. In his right hand he held a broadsword, in his left a circular wooden shield. From this distance the men could not see that it was a home-made item, built from the frame of a barrel rim and bottom, bolstered with additional wood. Similarly equipped men stood near him. A few held spears, which Pluvius soon realised to be the javelin spears.

Pluvius signalled for his men to halt; they did so immediately, returning to the protective posture but also carefully surveying the scene above. The sergeant took a deep breath then walked back.

"You know the fate of the cleric – a most lowly act. I offer you a choice; surrender your leader and you may go free." Pluvius spoke the words without thinking, shocking himself more than his men.

The rebel leader, though baffled by the claim that he should know the fate of the cleric, assumed the wound given to him yesterday had been fatal, and laughed theatrically. "Lowly! Of what? We are not soldiers! You and your men have murdered men in their youth, massacred young idealists, spoiled the aspirations that sought to free our kind... and yet you call our actions – lowly!"

"I offer you a broker peace; join us and live – for otherwise you shall die – oh, you may kill us but with the resting of our fragile bodies it shall be *your* souls that perish with them. We shall live on in hearts, while your minds rot!"

Pluvius knew it was not feasible. He would be abandoning his fellow old guards at the barracks, endangering Julia, and turning his back on a house he had sworn to protect. He reiterated the deal. "If you want to avoid the untimely deaths of more adolescents offer yourself as forfeit, otherwise let them die for your ambition." As he barked these words he felt rising self-loathing.

A bitter smile rippled across the rebel leader's face. "These men are here by free will, they can leave whenever they wish; they chose to fight for what they believe in. They chose – have you?"

Pluvius signalled the advance. Somewhat surprised but equally relieved that he could not bring himself to answer to the leader's face, he whispered. "So be it."

He swallowed his remorse, shelving it for after the battle. Pluvius concentrated on the immediate concerns; the potential threats to his life.

Soon the threat became real as makeshift wooden javelins rained down on him and the men; this rooted his mind in his professionalism.

The stakes struck his shield and sprang back as they fell to the ground, joining the others in a sporadic mottling of the rugged terrain, accumulating on the ground like the précis to a snowstorm. Pluvius took occasional glances up the hill; torsos would bob up and down like gophers, dropping down momentarily, before reappearing to hurl the next salvo.

Pluvius and his men surged forwards in a creeping advance of inevitable doom. The skirmishers, following their leader's order, took flight, fleeing the tidal wave of shimmering metal.

The human tsunami was soon clinking past their hide holes that were about 10m from the flattening of the slope where the thick band of trees partially concealed the peak. The rebel leader had likewise pulled back with his entourage to the top.

The soldiers were soon over the peak, and were immediately confronted by sharpened posts hammered into the ground at 45 degrees; someone had heard of cavalry spikes and had attempted to fortify the position with them. Pluvius smirked, admiring their effort. Such fortifications were useless against infantry, and only a madman would send cavalry charging up this hill.

They could now see the encampment, a coterie of tents huddled together made from a patchwork of cloths, canvasses and skins. A loose palisade fence had been constructed from bush branches in a tight perimeter around the yurts, though it served more as a windbreak than a defence. The front and back had large openings about 8 metres wide, and the sides had holes, which had been hastily filled with piles of lumber. At the front a low wooden hut, just high enough to crouch in stood with a sinking squatness that deceptively gave the impression it had been there a long time. The wood for the building had been salvaged from the cart and bolted together with second hand nails. It was on this that the leader now stood. A rim of wood covered his ankles from view and when the time came, sword thrusts. His own sword was more identifiable now, an ancient cumbersome broadsword, with the style of the old woodland nomads who used to roam this area until they were forced into settlement, killed, or became mercenaries. He now donned a simplistic iron helmet which pushed his matted hair down until it spilled out underneath in a tangled explosion. He stood awkwardly, anxious that he was not getting stuck in. Next to him stood the four similarly equipped younger men. They had smaller broadswords, probably pilfered from the mercenary guards on the cart.

The peak itself was littered with tree stumps but not a single bush remained.

However Pluvius had no chance to take any of this in as no sooner was he past the spikes then he heard the roaring of a charge. A dozen or so men came surging around the palisade and out the entrance. They came from all three directions.

Though surprised by such a sophisticated assault, his men were well choreographed in action without thinking. They charged, the sides pulling back so to create a defence on each edge and avoid flanking, their swords raised and shields clamped defensively. The next few moments were a blur, as Pluvius watched himself act with expert precision; even his own manoeuvres seemed like an alien invasion of movement.

The men all seemed to strike at once. Sighs, growls and shrieks blended into a haze of disrupted noise, occasionally overplayed with crashes of iron and steel. The squelch of stabbed flesh.

The rebel charge was ferocious. Pluvius' body resonated as the axes and swords clanged on his shield. Their moves were predictable and cumbersome, a weakness exacerbated by poor equipment. Pluvius avoided eye contact and made no attempt to count the number he slew.

The tufty grass seemed to instantly be ground away into mud, soon to be joined by blood that added to the viscosity and left rich patches of colour. To the peasants it must have seemed like an anarchic hell, but to Pluvius it was just a routine chore. In the panic they were so busy fighting to keep themselves alive that they failed to retain a line, which could have allowed them to swamp the soldiers through weight of numbers and pick on them one at a time. Consequently the soldiers cut through the rebels, blades glinting in the sun that now hovered above the horizon.

The soldiers darted to and fro, dodging, twirling and slashing with demonic rapidity that, to an onlooker, would look like haphazard savagery. Pluvius could assure it was not. However, what Pluvius could no longer do was claim knowing this made it an art. After all, sophisticated savagery is still savage.

It all played out so quickly, often seeming to be in different time scales. Pluvius would momentarily slash at one man whilst striking another with his shield before taking a stab at a rebel conveniently engaged with another soldier, and yet at the same time be blocking another who sought to take advantage of his apparent distraction.

Momentary images would flash before his eyes, mingling with each other. He stabbed a young man with beginnings of a moustache, then spun around seeing numerous feet, suddenly an axe would come crashing down, he would side step and the axe head would disappear. It would remain in his mind as a fleeting trail in the universe that could rematerialise at any moment. In the meantime his shield would be pressed against a broadsword. But all he saw was blood pouring over a brown peasant's tunic.

For a professional like Pluvius, time went slow; for a green rebel it was all over so soon, they had barely taken their first breath when they were gasping for the second as blood welled in their throat… it was only then that time slowed for them. Time slowed for them as a final salute before they lost consciousness forever. In these dying moments they would be privileged with the veteran's view, and it would all seem so easy, but frustrating as they lay limp and helpless to act.

The rebel leader stood hesitating on top of the wooden structure. It was clear that his men were losing. After the initial charge had shown some promise his men had become scattered. He hawkishly observed the melee but had not seen a single soldier fall, though he couldn't be sure as the scuffle was so baffling. Whereas his men seemed to be gushing blood, the glimmering splint mail seemed to continue its shine from movement as it was tainted a disturbing silvery red. It was a bloody mess but he saw no way of disengaging his men without them being trampled into the mud in a humiliating rout. Yet all he could do was call the retreat and hope for mercy on the part of the soldiers. He tapped the comrade beside him and he immediately bellowed the sound to call a regroup.

Several men attempted to form a rearguard whilst the others made the retreat, running with the last of their energy towards the wooden construct. It must have looked like a humble yet sacred sanctuary. Their gazes of fear turned to wide-eyed wonder as they saw their chapel of safety standing only metres from this black hole of spinning blades. Like a messiah their leader stood attempting to uphold a look of confident defiance to offer consolation to their terror.

To the rebel leader's astonishment and relief the squad did not pursue. Instead they seemed to let the rebels flee. He counted his men as they fled towards him, naming each in his mind as he did so; there were eleven. From twenty-seven.

Turning his attention to the soldiers, he observed them with the fascination of a twitcher gazing at birds. Some attempted to wipe blood and mud from their faces. With considerable difficulty their dry mouth's spat slimy, mucus-ridden saliva onto hands. Suddenly there was a commotion. One of the soldiers stumbled and fell to his knees. There was silence as speechless warriors ran to his side to examine his punctured carapace for wounds. They fiddled with straps and pulled off the plate. As they did so a row of scales fell out onto the mud-stained ground like discarded glitter.

From up on the barricade all that could be seen was an amorphous red cushion steaming with sticky blood flop out onto the mud, as though it had been floating in a ruby red stream. A hefty axe blade had spliced through the scales and slashed open the soldier's belly. It looked as though the soldier was defecating organs as a continuous stream of misshapen sausage shaped organs stained with red ink plopped out onto the ground as one, still linked together. The soldier's head flopped down. A young slightly-built soldier screamed, The sole noise crackling unexpectedly through an otherwise muted world. Only this piercing shriek managed to cut through the horror, indeed joining it as it sped through the smell of death and thundered into the ears of the rebels. It sounded to the fleeing men as though they had not killed a man but rather wounded and enraged a great beast.

Sergeant Pluvius stood sombre, apparently emotionless, his sword held behind his shield and his helmet tucked under his arm. He gazed straight up at the rebel leader with a morose dry stare that seemed to look straight through him.

'Surely we can stop this slaughter?' Pluvius thought as he stared absentmindedly up at the four rebels on the wooden hut. 'Kilnos *was a good man...*' his thought were distracted by an agonising scream. Stupidly he allowed his instincts to take control and he glanced to his left to see Kilnos' kneeling figure with his head flung upwards, gazing with dilated pupils straight up. He struggled for air as the scream emptied his lungs and the noise sunk from a spine-shattering shriek to a bone chilling groan. Pluvius looked away as he saw Arios stride over to the dying man, sword freshly cleaned and raised ready.

With one fell swoop Kilnos' agony was over. Pluvius could not help wincing even though he hadn't seen the action. To keep his mind off it he wondered how Heites fared.

Heites squatted in the undergrowth a few metres from the path the rebels would flee down. He dreaded the moment but also wished it to be soon, 'the sooner they come, the less they will have fought, ergo less will have died'.

He looked up the path that wound up through the undergrowth that sprouted out, leaning over it in lazy arcs that concealed it poorly. It meandered around a corner vanishing behind trees. Further up and to the east a large rock sat on the side of the hill perched like a natural tower. Heites had passed it as he clambered around the peak.

His mind was pondering a conundrum; would he show himself to the routed men? *'The moral versus the practical.'* Or was it? Did he want to be seen by them just to show how merciful he was being to them? Did he want them to thank him for his delayed hypocritical stand down, his postponed mercy?

'Surely it would do them much good, it would show them they are not alone, that they have a convert amongst the supposed enemy. It would give them hope.'

His mind returned to scepticism bolstered by reasoning. 'W*as this unwarranted hope?'*

'No' he concluded *'all I am saying is that I sympathise, and that I am not a heartless killing machine.'*

Of course there was another problem, what if they still thought him a threat? Didn't trust him, or worse still, shrugged of his repentance and killed him out of spite or revenge?

Suddenly he heard the heavy thumping of panicked men fleeing. He froze still. A mud covered young lad clad in rags sped past. Heites jerked in an attempt to step up but could not. Another went by and he stood, it was then that he saw a group approaching. They were only young adolescents, petrified to such a point he was surprised they could move at all, and mostly unarmed. The panic-stricken group skidded to a halt as they saw the shining metal soldier emerge. He held the sword vertical in his hand, rolling the ball on the hilt in his palm then swinging it so it pointed downwards before letting go. It sank into the soil with a calming squelch. One young boy, no more that fifteen, eyes bulging sprinted past him, panting like a mauled rabbit.

Heites calmly stepped out onto the path, making no attempt to catch the boy. "If they kill me now then all trust between auxiliary and peasantry is lost and we are all doomed anyway," he declared dramatically to himself.

The peltasts clasped knives in their whitened hands, whilst their faces exploded in blood-rush red.

"Forgive me," he pleaded with dignity.

The men were shocked, glancing at eachother with baffled indecision; they stood panting but otherwise silent.

Heites stared at them a while longer with the vacant exasperation of a man whose patience was severely tested. Despite this irritation he was trying to portray his sincerity, an emotion severely battered within him anyway even without the mauling of the last day's events, and the brick wall of emotion that had come scampering into contact with him. He turned his back on them to show his own trust, stepping off the path, then after hearing nothing from them barked, "Go!"

They bolted like jackrabbits, hurtling down the path. Heites heard one or two snivelling, even weeping with relieved fear as they galloped clumsily away.

Heites picked up his gladius and shield then rushed for the rock. *'What would Pluvius do if he found out?'* he asked himself.

'No that is the wrong question – Why did Pluvius send me?'

'Was it a test? Would he want to see bodies?' Heites shook off the fear: *'Surely not?'*

Stumbling clumsily through the undergrowth, taking his frustrations out on the stubbly foliage underfoot, he found himself angered by his own cynicism. His usually sound cynicism was being taken for a ride to the door of paranoia. Upon realising this he was able to re-orientate himself and compensate for the irrationality.

'I do not wish to boast by suggesting that I am probably the best linesman in the squad, (and by far not the best scout), so I must assume I was chosen specifically. Did he send me around the back so as not to compromise the frontal assault due to my condition? or so I do not incriminate myself in front of the men? Both of these are concerned with distrust and lack of sympathy with my situation. Thirdly, knowing my reservations he sent me here to give me free choice of my path, not to coerce me into following the mission. This sounds quite Pluvius, not wanting to get involved in personal stuff and being neutral in my scepticism. Or did he send me knowing what I would do, and so consenting, to what I have done?'

With renewed and justifiable confidence he pondered aloud, "whatever his motives, he will not betray me to the high priest. I shall have to be careful though not to make his job of silence difficult." With this his countenance darkened as he was reminded of his deadly deed: the image of the blood-splattered face of the warrior priest, a ravine cut into his roundish face, brimming with blood which trickled out the end of the bright gash spilling over his facial features and running down his cheeks like war paint. His rough-skinned face all stained with blood, mimicked the bumpy red splattered battlefield.

Fighting to shake off the bloody image, Heites reached the steep climb of the peak. He dumped his shield, and sheathed his gladius. The soil was damp and springy on the slope up to where the rock emerged out of moss covered earth. Shaggy-barked trees arced out of the slope, stretching straight up once free of the overhang. As he stepped up, Heites slipped and grabbed hold of the nearest tree, wrapping his arms around it as his feet scrabbled futilely for grip.

Once at the top he surveyed the scene. His view was limited by the tall trees that surrounded the natural watchtower. They marked out the contours of the land below in waves, sweeping up and down with each rise and fall of the land. On the peak he could see the wooden hut with figures on it, and the tops of the tents that were dotted about in front of it, peeking over the fence. One of the men on the hut was leaning over its front side, evidently the leader giving commands to men below. He reasoned that if the rebels were pressed up against then it must be the prelude to the final assault. He unsheathed his sword and raised it waving it Eastwards towards the hill and the rising sun. The smooth polished metal reflected the sun's rays sending out flashes of silvery-yellow glint. With a brief flash of pink it looked as though the rebel leader did look his way. Its briefness was exacerbated by a disturbance further below; with a flurry of arms one of his guards flung his javelin downwards.

This sudden action brought Heites back to reality as he realised that the target was one of his brothers-in-arms. Immediately he was carelessly stumbling down the rocks like the prologue to an avalanche, not even bothering to re-sheath his sword. As he did so he cursed himself for wasting time with petty symbols that even if seen would not be understood.

The descent felt like an eternity trapped in purgatory. Constantly his mind raced, pouring scorn on his tacit betrayal, not knowing if he had cost the life of his sergeant. He glimpsed the glimmer of his shield, it was unstrapped, and so swayed cumbersomely, yet he could not pause to strap it on. Instead he continued to sprint, whilst gripping the arm straps with his clenched fist.

So jumbled were his thoughts that his mind raced from perception to fact, from sense to experience, juggling them into a conciliatory manifold of memories and fears dressed as fact. He was petrified, trembling like the previous night. The fleshy orb of the dead priest's head hovered before him with its quarried valley, filled with congealed blood and exposed brain. The warrior-priest grinned, then exploded in a spray of blood and splinters of skull bone.

The sudden exhumation of terror from the javelin being thrown had pierced deep into him, releasing all his recently spawned fears. In his confusion they had been able to amalgamate into a bestial monstrosity of irrationality, an antithetical doppelganger to all his reasoning. It was this beast that now dominated him, flinging his mind into turmoil so all he could think of was the savage desire for indiscriminate revenge.

★

Pluvius had been looking to his left trying to direct the men when he was almost knocked to his feet by the excessive force of the javelin striking his shield. The noise was ear-splitting. As he looked down to inspect the damage, he was surprised not to be dead. He was even more surprised to learn he was unscathed: the javelin had punctured through the shield but stopped a matter of inches through, the point protruding so it was merely a barely an inch from his body.

After the initial shock his men had soon realised he was unhurt and had calmly formed up. Arios meanwhile rushed over and pulled the javelin-spear out, simultaneously dropping his broadsword and shouting to the rebels. "Two can play at that game!" he declared, before sprinting forwards and launching the javelin back at the denizens on the roof.

The javelin hurtled through the air with a perfect arc, soaring down gracefully straight at the rebel leader, who seemed transfixed by the glimmering silver that glided at him, the colour intensifying as it caught the sunlight. He had just enough time to raise his shield. Yet it was to no avail; the javelin struck the shield and split it clean in two. It pushed each half out of the iron rim and continued soaring, striking just above the leader's mid-section, burrowing into his torso, sliding past the breastbone and into his heart. The man fell, eyes wide, mouth faltering.

Arios, not even bothering to reattach his shield, gripped his sword in both hands, bellowed a challenge and charged. The soldiers followed, as did the opposing force. Pluvius, who was still shocked by the missile attack, watched anxiously – this would make or break the rebels.

Arios brought his sword swinging down in a diagonal swipe, which cleaved the jaw off his first opponent. In one continuous movement he lunged upwards at an angle in the reverse direction, turning as he did so, catching the next rebel in the jugular with the point. He blocked the next combatant before driving him back with uncontainable ferocity. Soon the rest of the men had reached the point of contact, disposing of the remnants with expert efficiency. Pluvius arrived on the scene too late to take any action.

All eyes fell upon the last four bodyguards who had remained with the dead chief. Pluvius shouted to them with a hint of futility, predicting their defiance. "Have not enough died today?" he pleaded.

They looked at him as one, with such volatile anger; faces reddened around the cheeks, offset by a general pallid complexion of terror, mingled with proud defiance. They would not budge. They would gladly die defending the mausoleum to their martyred leader. They needed not answer, though one did spit over the edge.

Pluvius sighed.

"You want my advice, sergeant," (this was the first time in years that Arios had referred to him thus), "… burn 'em."

Pluvius looked back, more irritated than disgusted at the suggestion of yet lower degrading carnage, though he knew the veteran was right, strategically.

Nevertheless Arios continued to justify his proposition. "From that position we cannot get at them, your gladius' won't reach, and with those light spears they will tire you out and eventually they will get past your shields."

Pluvius knew what had to be done, but could bring himself to it. For some reason he could not face to see them burning to a crisp before his eyes. Also he felt unease at burning this bastion of rebellion.

"No," he declared. "Arios, you can reach them. We can keep them at bay. Meanwhile Geric can go around the back and take them out."

He called Geric over and explained to him what to do. The rookie seemed worried about being given such a job but was secretly pleased to be given such an opportunity to prove himself.

The soldiers advanced slowly in tight formation, shields raised high. Pluvius peeked from behind the gap between his and his neighbours' shield.

The four guards stood motionless, the three with spears holding them in both hands, pointing down so the edge was about head height for someone on the ground. Pluvius could see their hands clasped with a nervous, excessive grip. He couldn't see their faces, only indistinguishable torsos of brown cloth and leather.

They reached the building cautiously, sliding into a gradual engagement with heads hidden under shields. Packed in close their shields overlapped, making penetration into the formation almost impossible. The rebel spearmen prodded and lunged with short sharp jabs, usually in a general thrust, but occasionally at a particular gap that emerged. Suddenly, as though choreographed, they spread out in a hypnotic display of twirling shields, the rebels lashed out in scattered movements at cold mask-like faces behind the shields, but found their spears deflected and caught by gladius's.

It was during this that Geric skulked off around the side and was immediately followed by Arios emerging from behind the dazzling shield display, roaring with an intensity that sent the rebels jolting back. Meanwhile his blade bit chunks out of the wooden rim. The smell of freshly chipped bark floated in the air with a pungent autumn freshness.

As his slashing intensified they all shrank back.

By now Geric, who had ditched his shield, had clambered up, gladius in one hand and a knife in the other. He crept over. His knife took the first with a throat slash before the others could notice. Wisely he had taken out the sword-armed man first as the greater threat.

Shocked by the sudden stumbling of their comrade, they realised what was happening when a cascade of fresh blood began to collect on the hut roof. They spun around, but Geric had one dead from another throat wound before he could make the turn, his gladius piercing through the soft cartilage of the windpipe. Within seconds it was honoured with a deluge of steaming hot blood. The rebel's startled and petrified face flashed then went gaunt as though accelerated ageing had to take its course before he could die. He whispered words with utter terror, though they came out as unintelligible mumbles and gurgles.

Pluvius lost his concentration, marvelling at how the squad's newest recruit had become such an adept soldier. He had made the journey from rookie, to bloodthirsty adolescent, to professional killer.

One rebel tried to strike Geric with the side of his spear, while the other hastily discarded his spear and grabbed at the wood axe that hung limply by his waist. The pole smashed against Geric's knife-wielding arm and he let out a yelp, yet rather than jump back in fright, he lunged forward with his gladius. Just as the knife hit the wooden floor its thump was muffled by a squelching noise as the point of the Gladius pierced deep into the man's upper chest. A shocked gasp was expelled from the rebel's mouth like an unexpected burp. He staggered forward in an attempt to buy time for his comrade. But it was no use; the axe was too unwieldy and this youthful soldier too swift.

He barely had time to flinch; the gladius playfully struck the shaking axe head aside before plunging forward into the rebel's chest. The axe clanged on the floor, a sombre chime for the soon-to-be departed. The rebel reeled back, stumbling as though heavily inebriated. Blood soon stained through the leather, welling before dripping down soaking into his trousers. Probably his only trousers, the very trousers he had used to toil in the fields, now his dying military attire, soaking blood as it once did sweat.

The rebel staggered back further, stumbling over the protective ledge, swaying uncontrollably, tipped too and fro in the balance before falling down onto the soldiers below. They hurriedly withdrew, allowing the convulsing body to drop with a floppy but hefty thud on the scuffed dirt.

The soldiers stood over the boy, staring with sinister intrigue. As the convulsions ceased they were captivated by the waning life in such fresh tranquillity, surrounded by the remains of so much ferocious battle. There lay the gripping reality below all the fancy adrenaline-pumping violence – an increasingly pallid youth ebbing away, drained of life, drugged with fear and drowned in empty hate. As the boy struggled indecipherably to utter his final words a voice cut through the morbid silence of the onlookers. "Here lies the glorious dead!"

Arios could take no more and strode over, just as the rebel began a final fit of convulsions. In a lightning strike he solemnly brought his sword down and struck the man's heart. It slit crudely like a misplaced guillotine, but nevertheless it was all over.

At that moment, just as silence had truly descended, a loud thumping noise resonated across the ground, growing ever louder. The men ignored it at first, treating it as a drum beat for their hearts to thump in unity in honour of the dead.

However it was soon accompanied by words. "Pluvius, Arios, where are you? What travesty of justice have I led us into?" Heites rambled incoherently between exhaustive breaths.

"If they have harmed you I shall spill their blood... no mercy for them now ... I shall reap their souls with my blade... to ensure they suffer the agony they so shamefully inflict upon us men who sought rapprochement."

It was now that he glanced up to see Geric staring down over the far side of the hut where the soldiers now stood transfixed. He called up to him, "Geric, are all well?"

Slowly the soldier turned his golem face towards the approaching veteran. "All is fine – we have vanquished them. How fare you, Heites?" He spoke with an until then unheard confidence, not the eager irritating confidence of his early days. "Your sword lacks blood?" he added with devilish intrigue, as though it were something the soldier had foolishly forgot to pack.

The question worried Heites, not because he feared it would be unanswerable but just it being asked... and by this quivering young pup turned delighted sadist. "No sword 'lacks blood'. Only the body." He made a quick whistle-stop tour of the corpses with his eyes, "except the brain..." He returned the cold look of Geric. "For some it gets too much."

Their mutual stare grew in tension and was only broken by the sudden cry of Pluvius, who had clambered up onto the building; his face beamed as he saw Heites alive. Without even congratulating Geric he rushed over and down to Heites.

Arios was soon up and taking his place beside Geric. He smiled at his unofficial acolyte and patted his back encouragingly.

"That was excellent fighting my boy – but remember it doesn't show weakness to be merciful. You should have finished him off – it is a sign of honour."

Meanwhile Pluvius clasped Heites' sword hand with both of his own and waited in anticipation of a word from his comrade. They moved into a comradely embrace.

"The routed rebels are dealt with; no living rebels are on this hill now," he declared, carefully not lying. Then he added, "we all fought well and should celebrate for the survivors."

As they retreated from the entrance and Pluvius retrieved his discarded equipment, Heites looked into the sergeant's eyes with a look of caution. "Arios is right about morale."

They parted company and the smiling faces of Arios and Geric confronted Heites. The rest of the men were evidently pleased Heites was safe and sound, though were reminded of their fallen comrade. Once away from the battle the cheery relief was replaced with morbid grief as several men began the gruesome task of patching up the body. The organs were scooped back in and a band of cloth tied to hold it in before the scale mail was reattached.

A pair of soldiers had meanwhile hurried down the hill to get a stretcher.

As Pluvius approached they congregated around the body. Several scampered about ceremoniously removing the corpses helmet and tucking the shirt into a knot at the back, evidently anticipating its transit. Pluvius felt a surge of anxiety as he realised the body, if it were to be brought back at all, would have to be strapped into the horses saddle upright (something he had no qualms about doing to the warrior pontiff.)

The soldiers must have sensed his concern and deduced into origin, for they seemed to form a defensive ring around the vacant pale flesh.

'Remember what Heites just said' he noted to himself, then he bit his lip. "Well done men... the task is done." He paused and looked at the expressionless face, his eyes tracing familiar features now drained. Pluvius' eyes misted as his throat hardened. "Kilnos was a great soldier, comrade, and friend. I do not need to share with you my sadness at his passing as it is something we all share. Nor do I need to speak of all those times he was there for me, for you all will have your own memories of him, and I do not wish to disturb them as they drift through your mind now."

Unease rose in Pluvius as he felt the anger of wasted life rise in him, knowing that this must be echoed in his men as their sombre expressions of remorse turned sour. He could tell it needed tackling; "... and with those memories, let this be the last; that he sacrificed himself for us". The words went acidic in his mouth. "I know we all had reservations about this mission, but in these circumstances we have to act in order to survive, and we will achieve this if we are united. He died defending us, and our best way of honouring that is to pledge ourselves to each other."

All the men remained sullen, though they lost their anger; instead creases emerged at the edges of several lips in attempt to show smiles of appreciation. For a minute they all stood in silence looking at the ground. Some glanced at the corpse and surveyed their brethren.

Suddenly the silence was broken by Delis and Juscius arriving with the stretcher. "Sergeant how will we...." The voice trailed off as it became aware of the collective silence. Pluvius had meant to wait for them but the unease amongst the men had driven him into action early.

Pluvius gave a muted smile then calmly and quietly broke the bad news. "We cannot take him back."

There were gasps of outrage.

Arios silenced them with a bark and came to Pluvius' defence. "Why take him?" He eyed the men. "Here he can he buried as a Latman soldier with the blessing of Athyle, like a true warrior. What will he get back at the garrison? Some trumped up speech from Vultai!"

Heites chipped in. "Exactly! Why take him to them? Them that killed him?"

Meanwhile Arios had reached under his scale mail to clasp the idol of Athyle he had been forced to remove and hide. He lifted it off his head and held it aloft. "See – he can get a proper honourable burial here – will they let me place this in his palm? No! They claimed they would punish with lashes anyone caught with one."

The men were now shouting haphazardly in agreement and Arios turned to Pluvius and handed it to him.

Pluvius took it reluctantly, and with a worrisome look asked Arios discreetly, "are you sure? This is yours? Your Talisman?"

Arios shook his head, and whispered in reply, "it is ours." Then louder he declared, "this goes with Kilnos. Then it will be with our squad always."

Cradling the idol, Pluvius declared, "we need a grave for a fallen warrior!"

The men began digging a grave. Heites joined them, his eyes wide, eager to leave this hill. He saw the scattered remains of the rebels being collected up into a pile; here they would remain. Left to rot to complete the life cycle as one indistinguishable heap of drained flesh. Already its pale greyness was reminiscent of the dull rocks that littered the hill. Crustified purplish blood stained the cold listless mound with lichen-like patches. Heites thought, *'This is no longer the refuge of youthful rebels, no! It is part of the rot. This was a hill blooming with life, now it is infected. The kick back against the rot has been struck with a cauterising iron that has maimed it causing oozing puss boils to fester and thrive over it, another nascent society falls down the wayside against the stride of force in a disturbed distorted psyche.'*

Already crows perched nearby, eagerly jumping and jittering as they awaited the feast. Impatiently they squawked, squabbling over the spoils of war. All other life had fled the scene, but the avaricious vermin thrived on the destruction. Every death was not a loss but an asset, potential capital to be fed upon.

Heites saw how they cautiously eyed one another. He found it strange that they seemed to congregate in packs but as soon as the spoils were available they revealed what they really were: self-centred creatures driven by selfishness.

Meanwhile the husk of the leader was un-impaled and his rag-covered body prepared for a separate grave around the back of the shack. Pluvius was overlooking the ceremony, silently respecting the fallen warrior of ideals. To Pluvius, he was burying not a person but a dark episode in his squad's history.

Heites, however, did not see the end of his ills go with this act. It was the death of the priest that held the key to his worry, and the act flashed before his mind. The cold-blooded killing of a being; it was not the gruesomeness that troubled him, but that it was such a personalised affair.

He saw Pluvius re-emerge from behind the shed. He looked solemn and troubled, his rough face a patchwork of vexation stitched with tension. It was from this that Heites found his reason; the act was his act. It was his own personal choice, and yet it had inflicted so much on his comrades', in particular Pluvius. His guilt lay not in the act but the anxiety he had caused his closest companion.

He felt a burning desire to tell someone, but who? Although he knew he could trust Pluvius, he felt that to confirm the sergeants suspicions would only mount up the responsibility on an already stressed man. It would be hard enough for Pluvius to speculate against suspicion but even harder to lie against knowledge of the truth.

Besides Heites doubted Pluvius would understand his compulsion to do it. He would probably dismiss it as impulsion led by dislike for the warrior-priest.

★

With a collective air of woe the soldiers buried their fallen comrade. Pluvius, who was the designated padre, spoke words of consolation much to the same content of his earlier words. His words wavered uneasily with gut wrenching remorse; soon he broke down, and stood in silence, sharing with his comrades the honesty of silent collective catharsis. Once their silence had spoken their emotion, the squad crept sullenly back to their horses and prepared for the journey back to the unwelcome home of the garrison.

Heites, Arios and Pluvius took it upon themselves to secure the flaccid corpse onto a stretcher then lay it across the two spare horses.

The men ambled along on their horses in complete silence, staring at each other with the same indifference as they did when they examined other objects in the surrounding. Clearly the unity of the make-shift funeral had only temporarily overshadowed the unease caused by their actions, and their prospects when they returned.

As they set off the three of them seemed each to be enthralled by the vapid floppiness of the corpse. With each sway Heites was reminded of the convulsions it had made when the priest had ceased to be; its transmutation into dead meat. Eventually Pluvius spoke, "The way it moves there must be something missing."

"The soul," Arios answered with unaccountable authority.

Heites grunted. The corpse flopped and shook from side to side frantically.

It was dead, he had defeated it, now was the time to celebrate. He chuckled abruptly then mused to himself. "The machine really has broken down!"

The other two looked at each other, baffled, before nervously laughing as they eyed Heites' deep smile.

Arios sought to change the subject. "So, are we going to the village?"

It hit Heites straight away. Time slowed. Just the mention of the village reminded him. Like a flash flood his words to himself the previous night crashed into his mind. A thousand thoughts pounded against his heart.

'*Yes, she would understand,*' Heites' found himself being told by his conscience, '*she would mock my worry and... comfort me.*' His thoughts trailed off in terror. Then regret. Then denial. Then renunciation.

★

They had reached the garrison gate anxiously, ambling along like submissive sheep obeying the call of the shepherd and fearing the wrath of his dog. Yet once inside it became apparent that the already bizarre circumstances had taken another, deeper turn. No longer an irritated countenance displayed on the men that passed them. No, even the word 'men' seemed stretched uncomfortably to describe these wandering vagrant-husks. Utter blank faces were being paraded. The garrison troops did not stop and look at the squad, gazing through them in awe as though they were a ghost troop.

Pluvius spotted a fellow old guard sergeant, Maxilies, and smiled at him. The sergeant offered the scantiest of smiles in return before hurrying off to attend to business as though not noticing him. Pluvius turned to Arios. Both held stern expressions, unable to hide both their dislike of being back at the garrison and the general unease that seemed to be enveloping the squad.

"Arios, tell Heites to take over. I'm going to ask Sgt Maxilies what the hell is going on."

Arios nodded professionally.

Pluvius rode towards Maxilies, who was carelessly parading his squad about the courtyard in what looked like an inward spiral pattern. After sending a few worried glances Pluvius' way and realising that he was definitely coming to speak to him he whispered something to the nearby corporal before furtively continuing as though nothing had happened.

Once in the sergeant's vicinity Pluvius dismounted and followed the marching squad, his horse obediently trailing behind. "What's up?" he queried.

Sergeant Maxilies glared anxiously from side to side, then, turning to Pluvius, said in a rapid, barely intelligible splutter, "it's all changed – Captain's gone – they say retirement: Bullshit. Fuckers. Bye."

It was a trail of words crammed into one and they took Pluvius by surprise yet he caught the essential content and the overall gist. He conspicuously thanked him for the update, then led his horse to the stable.

At the stable he met Arios and Geric who stood by the pallid corpse of Visuvius. The rest of the men had gone back to their barracks. Geric's face was stone cold, almost as vapid as the one that lay at his feet; he hovered as close to Arios as possible. His fingers closest to the veteran seemed to twitch.

Pluvius attempted to give them a smile, but his lip muscles failed him. Instead he let out an impatient sigh. "Ok, can you bring the priest with me?" It had meant to be a polite request but in his irritable frustration he sounded demanding.

"Is that an order or a request?" barked Arios in an angered tone which took Pluvius by surprise. Geric meanwhile gazed on lethargically.

Arios came to his senses, realising he was just causing unnecessary aggravation, nodded submissively, and lurched towards the corpse.

Pluvius had a sudden thought, "actually maybe you should take him to the High Pontiff, meanwhile I can go to the Captain". He seemed to have forgotten Maxilies' words about Dummonius' departure but was set on seeing the captain first, and if possible keeping the priest distracted with the warrior monk's corpse.

"Tell him that he died in battle; hit by one of those spears when he rode into the enemy then got an axe to the head. That reminds me, do we have the spears?"

Arios expressionlessly pointed to the four spears propped up against the stable wall.

"Ok, I'd better take them to the captain," Pluvius muttered more to himself.

Arios answered anyway, "Yeah, better Dummonius get 'em than that pontiff."

He grabbed the bundle of spears and headed for the office. When he reached the office he was suddenly reminded of Maxilies words. *'What had happened here? Who was this new Captain? What kind of tyrant would manage to leash Sergeant Maxilies?'*

★

He entered the office to see a petite young man almost quivering behind a mighty desk. Dummonius was no Hercules, but he was sufficiently inspirational to see compared to this aristocratic muskrat. The lean, well-groomed pup was a joke. Instead of the usual piles of scrolls the table was neat, and virtually empty. All the paper, so well placed, was ceremonial.

"Aaaah... sergeant...?" The voice was verging on adolescent, unsure and quiet, though the initial sound implied he recognised the entrant. Something Pluvius knew was a ploy, as he had never seen this 'man' before in his life.

"Pluvius," the sergeant replied modestly, trying to minimise his voice, as even at normal tempo it seemed booming in contrast.

"You have come from which barracks?" The captain asked with what Pluvius mistook for feigned interest. It was in fact a specific bureaucratic enquiry as each barracks was now numbered. The sergeant found this out as he, rather cryptically, tried to explain its location and was cut short by another absent-minded clarification of the inquiry. "A number?"

"Do they have numbers? Sir." The title was added as an afterthought when Pluvius remembered this was supposed to be a captain. The captain just looked irritated as though this sergeant was implausibly ignorant of a most essential piece of information.

Pluvius caught his disdainful glare and explained. "Captain, I have been away from the garrison for a couple of days in search of bandits in the forest of Leria. I had not even been told we had a new commander."

The captain looked sheepish, though tried to hide his embarrassment. "Oh, it is you.... I had expected Brother Visuvius to report... not a sergeant."

It was as though he weren't important enough to report in, as though it were a priest's job to deal in debriefs and military intelligence.

This grated on Pluvius with a burning passion. His gnarled veteran's face tensed and distorted with twitches of below surface responses to such degrading treatment. However, even if he had been about to riposte he would have been interrupted by the Captain's decision to vindicate his meticulous organising. "So which barracks is it?" he asked pretending to care on a personal level.

"The one by the Western Wall, opposite the canteen," Pluvius answered.

"Oh, No. 4," the captain informed him immediately, clearly proud of his ability to memorise them and expecting the sergeant to be impressed.

Pluvius could not help but look disinterested.

Irritated that the sergeant was not impressed, the captain decided to ask a more pressing question. "So, you have returned. High Priest Vultai has told me about it. So how did it fare?"

To Pluvius the captain sounded uninterested. So he answered succinctly. "It was a success... though we had two casualties..."

The sergeant examined the captain's expressions, for one could gauge a lot from a commander's response to such news. It was largely unaffected. A miserable attempt at seeming upset was clouded by an awkward irritation and distress in attempting to create such an expression. He mumbled something about the glory of ultimate sacrifice inconsistently conjoined with the waste of such a life. But then came the crunch:

"... One was Brother Visuvius..."

It was as though a snowdrift had swept through the commanders veins. This *was* a different matter. He looked petrified. "Oh my! By Thelus!" He leaned in towards Pluvius. "Does High Priest Vultai know?" he whispered in terror.

Pluvius retained his calm, trying to conceal his cynical amusement at the captain's sudden change in demeanour. "Possibly, my men are taking his corpse to the temple as we speak."

The shocked captain was flustered further. "What! Do not use such a word. Not when talking of holy men."

The sergeant could not help but smirk at the description of the zealous maniac as a holy man. Luckily the captain was panicking too much to notice.

"How did it happen?" the captain demanded hysterically.

Pluvius retained his placid countenance as he delved into an explanation. "He rode into the battle. I had assigned him to a rearguard, but he charged their shield wall just as we broke it and he rode the enemy down as they fled. However, it was a feint and he was struck by one of these." He indicated the spear-javelins. "And then was pulled from his horse and struck with an axe." He paused momentarily before adding defensively. "We were all on foot and so unable to reach him in time."

"Oh," was all the captain could say for the time being. Once the shock had subsided he ponderously added, "we had better wait for High Priest Vultai."

An awkward silence began to settle in. The captain feebly offered an explanation for waiting. "He will know what to do." His voice turned rather ridiculously patronising.

"You see... neglecting to protect a man of the Lord's holy faith is quite a reprehensible act, some would even call it tacit treachery."

Pluvius had no time for any of this. "If I have done something wrong, then tell me what it is. Why must we, a soldier and his commander, wait for a cleric before orders and briefs are given?"

The captain, still reeling from the onslaught of news, was shocked further by this fiery demand for things to be done in such unofficial ways. "This is not a military issue, it is... theological... we must see what His Excellency has to say."

Pluvius spent all the while trying to work out what theological meant and settled on it being a word made up to confuse him.

It was then that High Priest Vultai burst into the office. Completely unannounced he crashed through the door, robes swishing in shiny bands of undulating purple. His attempts at being a figure to fear were undermined by his piety; the well-trimmed beard seemed to have flared out in spindly twirls of hair; long-legged spiders tied in knots. It sat on a youthful face that had undergone a rapid ageing programme, wrinkled with tensed muscles of fury.

"What is all this?" he demanded in an uncompromising scream. The captain had shrunk further behind his desk. "My temple has been affronted with treachery..." he snapped angrily at the captain, before noticing the swivelling torso of Pluvius. "... Oh it is you!" he added as he redressed his demeanour.

Pluvius, who was already irritated by the cowardice of the commander, was in exactly the wrong mood to have a heated debate with an apoplectic cleric. He launched straight into the mission's success. "Sire, I have these." He handed him the bundle of javelins. "I assume they are what you sought."

"Yes," the cleric hissed, taking the bundle, "but what I want to know is how a mighty brother was killed?"

He grimaced; this was the test. "He was a valiant soldier, but impetuous. Despite my request that he remain out of the battle he rode into their shield wall in order to break a deadlock and as he pursued them he was struck by a javelin, then pulled from his horse in an ambush during their feint retreat."

The high priest eyed him cautiously. "That makes sense," he conceded, "... but does it make too much sense?" he added rhetorically.

"What troubles you, your Excellency?" Pluvius asked, barely concealing his anxiety to demand justification for his being treated suspiciously.

A smirk neutralised the wrinkles, reinstalling the charming face but bolstering it to a point of snide self-importance. The priest allowed for a pause in order to better appreciate his skilful verbal assault. "It merely surprises me that I am supposed to believe that a bunch of bandits could be so adept at tactics – a shield wall you tell me? A feint? An ambush? What next, siege rams, drilling and cavalry?"

Pluvius allowed for his anger to subside. "Your Excellency, was it not your Excellency that suggested the mobilisation of an entire regiment – you thought them a significant threat for that? A shield wall, a feint and an ambush are not hard to attempt, though they are hard to do well. If they succeeded in ambushing a carriage then why not in battle?"

The priest bit back immediately. "As if I would suggest such a thing!"

Pluvius ignored him, there was no point in arguing over that. "What could I have done differently? I put him in charge of the horses and the rearguard, I did not doubt his ability, I wanted to keep him safe. Yet he defied that – he was a great fighter but he was also rash."

The captain eyed them both silently from his desk; his mind was reciting dedicatory prayers to Thelus to guide Vultai in his judgement.

Much to the captain's disappointment the High Priest conceded, "he was of the zealous sort – which is no flaw." His tone suddenly changed from reconciliatory to an acidic bite. "It is a shame your men were not so... for then maybe he would live now."

Pluvius would not allow such an insult to settle unassailed. "My men were on foot; had they had the capacity to keep up with him they would have done. What is more, the primary objective is complete – we killed them all and we got the artefacts. You have the artefacts in your hands and a pile of bodies lie on the hill in the forest if you care to take a look – but do not doubt the dedication of my men!"

Vultai was impressed by the genuine and rousing tone of the sergeant's speech. It impressed him, and whether it had proved his innocence it did not really matter. "You seem to have succeeded in the mission and test of the outing – to prove your dedication and worth to Lord Latman and Thelus. I see no reason to hold you further... Except that you should reprimand your two men who were so crude with their treatment of a fallen warrior. You may leave."

Knowing it was still officially the captain's duty to dismiss him he turned and issued a request.

The captain was confused by such an action but nevertheless stammered an order to leave, which the sergeant did gladly.

The captain still looked flustered and glanced bog-eyed at the pontiff, his mouth gaping open in shock. High Priest Vultai merely stepped closer from his position in the centre of the office by the door and shrugged to hide his sudden change of demeanour towards Pluvius. He rubbed his wrists eagerly.

The captain turned his attention to the javelins, which now lay on the desk, inspecting their design with the look of an inquisitive child. Also with the inevitability of a child he began prodding it.

In the meantime High Priest Vultai hovered closer to the captain's desk. He seemed like a spring ready to leap forward into a plan. And so became irritated by the captain's idle fiddling.

When he finally finished playing the pontiff continued his disdainful look. The captain, without first checking the pontiff's countenance, stretched back on his chair, and shuddered at the thought of that uncouth soldier before uttering. "I'm surprised you let him get away with that your Excellency. What do you want doing with him sire? Shall I call Drill Sergeant Hari for the issuing of disciplinary action?"

The captain's babbling irritated Vultai and so he sighed disdainfully. "No, it would cause an uproar. After all he did what he was asked. I feel he has learnt his lesson, and if not then all the worse it will be for him…"

"What will?" the captain asked.

The priest hesitated, wondering whether it was worth bothering to tell this puppet imbecile. "He is influential amongst the old guard, he is more use if he is used as a great example of new interpretation conformity. We must use him correctly."

"How do we do that?" the captain asked cautiously worried he would aggravate the priest.

"By sending him as the detachment of honour guards to the banquet," he answered with self-pride.

"What!" the captain exclaimed, clearly distressed that his garrison would be represented by a rag tag band of ruffians and not, as he had wanted, a finely chiselled group of dedicated drilled soldiers.

"Calm yourself, he cannot act so impudently if sent on such an honour mission. If he becomes a hero he cannot turn on us, once he is a hero we control his story and consequently others opinion of him. Besides, our garrison will be the talk of the banquet; the grizzled veterans who fought off barbarians both sea faring and indigenous."

"Can we win this stubborn old guard veteran over?" the Captain asked sceptically.

"It does not matter, if he is troublesome after the banquet we can always offer him the redundancy package we offered your predecessor, he can become a mercenary. In short, he is not worth executing."

The captain did not want to ask any more questions, in case he looked stupid. Perhaps he would inquire about this sergeant with his guard.

Chapter 18
The Banquet

Lord Adonis Gatan entered the central plaza of the Lateria Palace on horseback, leading his finest cavalry guard in their historic ride into the Latman capital. Though he had spent the journey in the carriage with Lady Gatan and their sons, he had disembarked and ridden out in the open just as they reached the city gates. Despite qualms about his safety, he had been adamant, proudly declaring that on this first Gatanese visit he would not dishonour his predecessors by being remembered as a lord who hid away in a carriage on such an occasion. He wanted all the Latman people to see him; a brave, wise, soldierly lord, who led his people. With him rode sixty of his heavy cavalry, several carriages worth of cargo, servants and guards plus seventy-two mostly mounted infantry, thirty-six of his legendary spearmen and right at the back his gift: the statute of Thelus.

It was hidden under drapery, but stood fifteen feet tall, sword in hand, a mighty beard flowing down over rippling robes. Such effort had gone into its intricate detail so that aside from its mottled bronze colour, offset by a polished gleam, it could be a real being. Though it was not so large as Gatan had hoped, it was the largest to be transported so far. It amused Adonis how the sculptors had made it resemble him, though he was sure it would amuse him more when the fop-lord was petrified by its apparent moving.

As he had passed through the city, traders and paupers alike had stopped and stared at the spectacle in silence. Some managed to whisper to adjacent bystanders, but overall their faces showed vacant bewilderment at the sight of nearly two hundred of their sworn enemy's elite troops riding through the city in their finest battle gear, headed by an illustriously-armoured general staring forward with a controlled smile and awe-inspiring professionalism.

His own men seemed equally inspired by their grand entry, wearing proud looks. So encouraged was he by his men's impact on the population of Lateria that he was tempted to send word for the spearmen to disembark and provide the masses with a drill parade. But he had been far too eager to get to the plaza.

Now he was in the plaza, and the palace of Lateria sprawled out before him. It was closed off to the public and had squads from each major garrison lining the perimeter. Gatan glanced from banner to banner trying to discern who was from what. He recognised the Neptus banner as well as the Gorad banner from the Neptus campaign. He examined their honour guards. The Gorad squad was kitted as light infantry though several had spears rather than javelins tucked behind their shields. The sergeant was flanked by two giants who dwarfed him. When he stared into sergeant's eyes he saw the steely glare of a hardened veteran. For some reason he suddenly realised that contrary to the other squads, these men had worn armour. That is, except the sergeant, who had a brand new shield that gleamed with the freshness of a newly forged piece of armoury. Underneath their steely looks he could see both the weariness and dishevelled mental-social degradation of the trade combined with more recent specifics of combat and hurried long distance travel.

Gatan was now at the front of the square. Before him stood a wrinkly old man in a deceitfully cheerful white robe. Adonis was immediately insulted that Juscius himself was not present to greet him on arrival. Nevertheless he put this aside and called for the halt before dismounting. It was just as his boots struck the cobbles with a satisfying clap that he remembered he was supposed to go back and collect his wife. Cursing discreetly he signalled for the captain to fetch her and their sons.

Whilst he waited he returned his attention to the aged figure who stood at the top of the steps, partially concealed by the shadow of the overhanging roof, which hovered clumsily above him supported by numerous well-sculpted pillars. In the heavily contrasting gloom his robe seemed to be illuminated, the darkness attempting to conceal his lifeless face, wrinkled by years of dabbling in power.

Gatan glowered at the supreme pontiff as though to say 'come here this instant'. This was acknowledged by a minute glint in the High Cleric's eyes. Gatan knew that with such a man, from such a face, constituted of a myriad of creases and loose tendons, the slightest twinge told a lot. It had to, for such a sombre gaunt mask rarely moved at all.

He turned back just in time to be confronted by his wife's staunch face; she clearly had not donned her diplomatic mask yet, something he would have to summon with a kiss. Her face betrayed not a single fear at this ordeal.

She was before him, so he took her hands, kissed them both graciously, and looked up into her eyes. Did he see a sparkle of youth as they made eye contact?

"My Lady, we have arrived," he declared, with an attempt at the adolescent bravado of those years ago. Clinging to the hope that it was indeed a revival he saw, he leant forward as though in a dreamlike reminiscence. At the last moment he noticed his destination was her lips and rapidly detoured to the side to press his lips against her left cheek. She smiled and kissed him back, warmly. This brightened his demeanour as it felt like so much more than a formality. Then she gazed up at the priest, a wry cheeky smile accompanying the look.

However, the hope died there. As he took her hand he felt it was cold, in a fleeting despair he gave it a squeeze. He quickly realised it would have been more receptive if he had squeezed the bronze statue of Thelus's hand. It was stone cold; a façade, the sneakily passionate kiss a masquerade for prying spectators. With bittersweet admiration he had to admit she was a master at the art. She kept their hands close to their bodies under the pretence of being intimate, but in reality it was to hide the steely grip that they held each other's digits.

As they reached the top of the stairs she swung them apart and simultaneously clasped his hand in a ceremonial manner. He assisted her up the final step as a sign of courtesy, and then they stood upright, awaiting a bow of reception from Zeuorox.

The priest waited a few moments to make them feel as though he awaited their recognition, then bowed with an excessively false humble movement, almost snake-like. "Lord and Lady, I am humbled by your presence, please come into the reception hall. I assume your Captain will dismiss your entourage and Captain Helvinas will assist in barracking them."

Lord Gatan bowed back courteously. "Good day Priest, I have a gift for his lordship." He gestured towards the somewhat obvious statue.

The priest attempted to make an apologetic expression but his wrinkled face was so unused to such uses of his muscles that it just created a minimal, insincere mess. "I am sorry, but the Lordship is busy." "Busy! I come here across the lands, I have the courtesy of bringing a gift, and you tell me Lord Latman cannot come and see it?" Gatan's protestation was a momentary expulsion of angst which soon calmed as he took in his surroundings.

Zeuorox pretended to be taken aghast by the sudden outburst then mimicked calming down before answering with a thin veil of cordiality. "I am sorry, but the lordship does not wish to favour guests. I shall mention it to him as soon as I get the chance."

"When you see him! Won't I see him now?" Gatan visibly fumed. Nevertheless he bottled up his anger and followed the priest into the palace.

The doorway was a huge construct, winged by equally gargantuan solid doors of dense wood. They stood open at 45 degrees, forming a tunnel-like effect as one entered the porch. It was not a room, as such, that they entered, more a grand entrance of solid but barren walls. To the left on the far wall a small door with two guards either side stood slightly ajar. Zeuorox led them to it and through.

Here was the reception hall, a room that had been filled with illustrious depictions of the gods and Latman lords. On the far wall was a sizeable flag of Latman and next to it smaller mimics of the Garrison banners outside.

Two servants came to each of the new entrants and took their cloaks. Adonis nodded in appreciation. Lady Gatan batted her eyelids affectionately and the sons both mimicked their father with attempts at authoritative acknowledgements of thanks.

From here they were hastily taken into a large room which had flags of Latman and Telis held in sheaths. Upon seeing them Zeuorox turned to Gatan and said. "Oh, we will ask your captain to bring your banner so it can be placed alongside these."

Aside from several servants milling about, bringing plates to and from the table to the right of the room, the numerous couches were unoccupied save for four.

In one lay a casual young man in bright pantaloons, a white shirt, red and gold jacket and matching hat with a pure white feather, which flopped out to one side. He seemed to be in the middle of a fantastic story, with foppish gestures and a rolling voice. Though he valiantly tried to pretend that he was addressing them all, it was obvious he was vying for the attention of the young woman opposite him.

Without even considering Zeuorox's words that proved he was not present, Adonis felt sure this was his nemesis. With a surge of anger he muttered under his breath; "and there is my fop-wraith… but in the flesh. What a repugnance! What a pallid little squirt!" As he strode closer his rant deepened. "Look at him banter and squirm for that lady's attention, bah!"

Lady Adonis must have felt the tension rise in him through their connected hands and glanced at him with the pretence of affection to conceal her real concern. He caught her look in the corner of his eye and so gave her a smile of reassurance.

Gatan turned his attention to the girl. Judging by her manner she was aristocratic, probably Telis's sister. She had long hair, black, as usual, and curly. It was tied up at the back into a bun with exquisite lace and held into place with gold clips. Her vivacious manner was encapsulated in her large oval eyes, small nose and rosy cheeks. She had a small face though this made her forehead seem large, especially as her tiny chin receded timidly towards her dainty neck.

Adjacent to her sat a man probably older than the other; he had the vacant smile of someone trying desperately to look relaxed. Though he wore armour it was clear to a veteran like Adonis that the illustrious breastplate was merely ceremonial. It bore the crest of Telis. He had a faint rim of hair sandwiched between his tight lips and small nose, resembling an area of agrarian land between two ridges at the bottom of a valley. His hair was a slightly wavy and in the process of growing beyond his head.

In the final occupied chair sat an old woman. Her face was gaunt and sallow, her large robe in no way resembling that of the foppish sprite who sprawled out on the first couch. Nor did her posture. She was huddled in a long black shawl that seemed to trickle like a black liquid emanating from the fluffy cushions.

It was her, Maritha Latman, who was the first to purposefully look upon the new entrants. She scowled, her sour face drooping even more. So repulsed (and indeed repulsive) was her expression that Adonis half-expected her to leap from her seat, snarling like a ravenous beast. However she had clearly thought the look had been subtle, and so she returned to her own reverie.

The Gatans reached the coterie (Zeuorox seemed to have drifted off through an unknown doorway) and the other seated guests finally looked up to acknowledge them.

Telis stood, quickly followed by his sister. Upon seeing a 'lady' stand, Ruperis then saw a propitious moment to rise up. Maritha remained in her own little world, though failed to hide a skeletal toothy grin that cracked open on her face suggesting she was deliberately ignoring them.

Adonis sized up the lord as he approached. He was slight and surprisingly small, 'Claudix could have taken him when he was just fourteen!' he mused to himself.

Telis bowed, and so Adonis and his family reciprocated.

"Lord Gatan, it is such a pleasure to finally meet you. I hope this historic concourse will be fruitful for us both."

Gatan smiled diplomatically.

Telis turned to his sister; "this is my sister Mistress Elena Telis."
Mistress Telis giggled and smiled, holding out a thin slender arm, she was shorter than her brother, just over 5ft and so her arms were proportionately short.

Gatan kissed her hand lightly, but was preoccupied with a nagging feeling of yet another snub, as Juscius had not done the introductions.

Mistress Telis curtseyed, then turned to Lady Gatan and did the same.

Lady Gatan gave her a motherly smile. "My dear, you are such a lovely young lady – these are my sons Claudix and Maximus."

Gatan had lost interest in this interaction and instead focused his attention on the foppish clown who stood before him. The young man's face was consumed in a wide-eyed stare, which to a veteran diplomat like Adonis was quite a blatant mask.

"This is Sir Ruperis Delvinius, Latmans most propitious and entrepreneurial merchant, and good friend of his lordship Juscius Latman."

The merchant stepped forward and bowed with thespian bravado, even removing his foppish hat and guiding it down in a long sweep out then in to his waist.

"Your Excellency, it is such an honour to be in your presence. I hope that we can take advantage of this day that the gods have blessed us with."

Adonis Gatan merely nodded; his mind was racing at the realisation that this heinous character was not his arch-nemesis. At first he felt relief, for he knew such a false and excessive theatrical character would be impossible to deal with. But then he began to fear that he had been taken in by his own nightmarish anticipation of the lord and in doing so had cast him pre-emptively as a much weaker opponent. Perhaps he was not the childish sprite that Adonis' nightmares had deceptively branded him. However, all of this train of thought was tangled with other instinctive calculations – why was this merchant vying for the hand of Mistress Telis; would this not set him in competition with his friend and master? Why had Juscius Latman allowed such flirtation to take place? How significant was this merchant? Perhaps if Juscius was out of the picture, one of his own sons could offer Mistress Telis a better union than this foppish trader?

Adonis' thoughts were halted by the return of Ruperis' voice into his ears. "I hope that we can utilise this time to open trade between my companies and your nation."

Adonis decided to adopt a cautious optimism. "That would be a desirable advance, to consider. Obviously I shall have to see how political agreements go first." ' *'There, if you want trade you'd better do your bit to keep that pup-lord from messing me about'* he told himself as though addressing Ruperis. He then added, addressing both young men with a smile, "where is his lordship? I would have thought he would be here to greet us all."

The two young men looked at each other, as though trying to subconsciously agree on an answer. Telis opened his mouth to speak, but Ruperis cut over the top of him. "He is not yet ready. He preferred to wait until all guests had arrived to greet them as one so as not to suggest favouring any... Only His Excellency Zeuorox and myself have been able to see him all day."

'The overtones are obvious, the Lord Latman sees himself in a superior light to the rest of us, "not wishing to favour any of us" as though we are servants flocking to seek council with a new emperor. But also there is something else... had Telis already seen him... what would they discuss?' Adonis analysed.

He spotted the old lady Latman again, and was reminded of her presence, so discreetly turned to his wife and whispered to her to engage in conversation with the old crone.

Adonis smiled to himself as he moved closer to Ruperis. Now his sons were left to impress Mistress Telis as he contained the preposterous flatterer. Claudix, who now sported a sizeable beard, manoeuvred himself to converse with Lord Telis, and so leaving Maximus alone with the Mistress.

'Ah... this is it, the whole family working together!' Adonis mused proudly before embarking on an attempt to engage the merchant in conversation. "So... what do you trade in?"

Ruperis rolled his eyes dramatically as though it were not possible to truly answer such a simplistic question without being 'horribly vague'. "Oh, this and that, I have a lot of investment in shipping and transportation of goods. I'm a naval man at heart, you see!"

The word shipping had instantly resonated through Adonis' mind, reminding him of his priest's premonition and the boat building he had ordered then neglected. Was this what the visions had been about all along?

Ruperis again began rambling vaguely, so as not to give the game away, but leave the lord intrigued. "You see, I am a bit of an adventurer – you probably heard me telling Lord Telis a story. Well, soon I will be trading in the most unique things... from exotic places." He spoke in a theatrical way that was supposed to tantalise the audience, but Adonis, who was used to such attention-seekers, just saw it as a pretentious attempt to impress him. "... But that is enough of that, you will hear about it soon from Lord Latman, Jus." He added the nickname solely to allude to his closeness with the lord.

Gatan forced a cordial smile. "Really, well, again we will have to see what 'Jus' has to say."

"I suppose, yet, I'd hate a great opportunity to be ruined by old enmities... or the awkward ponderousness of politics."
Gatan smiled with superior wisdom. "It's all politics my boy."

Ruperis took the patronising tone of the elder man on the chin, then countered, "and that is the problem – politics rules economics, if only it were the other way around." He pondered the final phrase like a small boy wishing for a delightful dream to revisit him.

Gatan laughed. "Then it would be you we were all waiting to see now," he mused.

Ruperis was less amused. With a stern face he countered, "maybe, but then this meeting would have happened a long time ago."

Recognising a need to be serious, Adonis obliged with a more thought-out reposte. "But it would have no order, no foundations."

"It would have mutual order, order because it was wanted, even needed, for commerce to flow. As for foundation, it would be founded on principles of commerce."

Adonis grunted. "Bah, what are these compared to centuries of tested solid rule? Your principles are no more than unattainable clouds in the sky, contentless mist, compared to the robust laws. For they have survived the test of time." He gestured to the palace infrastructure.

"But we have infrastructure too, companies like mine that link small traders and envelope them in these laws. The entrepreneur will use his skill to provide the foundations, and they shall be more sturdy than yours for they shall be flexible – just ask your architect Gorax."

Before Gatan could answer, Ruperis seized the opportunity to sow the necessary seeds for later. "Where is your little inventor? He interests me; I would like to meet him."

Gatan immediately began to fear for his inventor's safety. The merchant would probably try to buy him, and then he would learn that we are far from his utopia, where all can be bought and sold.

Adonis found himself increasingly repulsed by the merchant, who he had found rather irritating from the start. He saw him as an avaricious charlatan. It was then that Gatan knew that he could find no common ground with this entrepreneur; he had no value of pride through honour, only pride from accumulation, gold, and money. He would squeeze Gorax of every profitable invention, and ignore any costly but noble excursions. Such as the statue that stood dormant outside.

"He will join us at the banquet," Gatan declared.

The conversation was halted by the sound of stomping boots entering the hall. Gatan looked to see who it was.

A stout man had entered; he was accompanied by a similarly built man of a similar age. Adonis knew it wasn't Lord Vaca, whom he had met, and guessed it was too young and slight for Lewerix, and so had to be Danite (the current lord, then in his early twenties, had not been present when Adonis had taken Hierda's hand. Hierda had strongly resisted and visits to her former homeland, partially out of disdain, but primarily because she saw herself as wholly Gatan now). He was a lesser lord, his household only having power for three generations, holding the territory together with an iron fist and desperately trying to steer this fledgling House away from disintegration and degeneration into an area like the warlord's domain which lay directly to its north. His House's backwardness was immediately apparent by his armour, which was leather. Even though it was ornately pattered it was nevertheless leather. His sidekick was Faldinite, his right-hand man and likely successor (for Danite himself had no official children – and numerous bastards).

If Heirda recognised her half-brother, she did not show it, maintaining strict diplomatic distance.

Gatan was surprised to see him here, but equally pleased. This fierce and traditional warlord had quite an affinity to the Gatanese style. Gatan immediately saw this as an opportune occasion to establish links with this faction warrior. Even though he was far from Gatan, it was not only a thorn in the side of Latman, but a stable Danite assisted in having a stable Vacarium and gave the lonesome stone mason a vital ally.

Lord Danite clearly had similar ideas, as he headed straight for Adonis. Once in his vicinity he gave him and appreciative nod, and bowed slightly before offering his right hand and giving it a good firm shake. Then he rose to his full height and embraced Adonis. "Greetings fellow warrior, Lord Adonis of the Gatanese people" he declared in traditional warrior's greeting.

Adonis bowed graciously, clearly appreciating the method of greeting. "We meet at last, Lord Danite."

With the mutual introduction completed Lord Danite turned to Ruperis and bowed; however, he addressed Adonis. "Is this Lord Latman?"

Nevertheless, Ruperis replied. "Alas it is not, Lord Danite, it is merely a humble merchant."

Danite hid his embarrassment with a jovial roar. "Well if you are so humble what are you doing here?" he jested, slapping the merchant on the back.

Gatan decided it wise to intervene. "He is Ruperis Delvinius, Latmans most successful entrepreneur and close friend of his lordship."
"Since childhood," Ruperis added proudly.

"Really... don't suppose those two are linked are they?" Danite boomed, chuckling to himself (though the volume suggested otherwise).

"No no, only kidding son. It is a pleasure to meet you."

Danite's right-hand man gave a cough. "Oh yes, how rude of me; gentlemen, this is Commander Faldinite, my military commander, and soon to be my cousin-in-law."

They both laughed. Gatan smiled in acknowledgement, but knew it would be irresponsible to join in. Ruperis, on the other hand, sycophantically chuckled along.

The two burly men stopped and looked at him. "What?" Faldinite queried aggressively. Ruperis was caught off guard and was flustered.

THE SON AND THE HEIR

"Oh nothing, pardon me... I must speak with Mistress Telis."

"I think she's engaged," Gatan declared dryly, with a wink at Danite. Who upon seeing the mistress was talking to a young Gatan, bellowed in return. "Really, already!"

As Ruperis scampered off, the three bellowed in laughter.

It was not long before another diplomatic entourage joined the guests; this time of Vacarium. Lord Vacarium was a wiry, sombrely contemplative old being, the skeletal remnants of a cannibalised, once tough, old bird with a large hooked beak and dark ridges forming a desolate guard to sunken eyes. He had brought with him his son, the inverse caricature of his father. Imagine seizing the scavenger bird-frame of the lord and piling upon it the meat of a fleshy plump pig, stretching its sour glum face with all its blubber into a bumbling grin, then you would have the figure of this jovial imbecile.

★

The fear rising in Rabica's stomach and throat reached a new excruciating level of acidic discomfort. He began tapping his fingers on his knees. But rather than the satisfying hollow sound, all he heard was the rustle of his robe.

He wore a black robe. Underneath he wore a pure white tunic, the round collar peeking shyly from the low cut V of the robe. His robe belt was striking red, cutting across the black and white attire. He wore no jewellery and both garments were plain.

He had left his facial hair to grow for a week or so, his chin roughly pitted with stubble shooting out like the leftovers of cut black hay on arid patchy land.

Rabica sighed then stopped his tapping and instead began to twiddle his thumbs. The tapping had outlived its usefulness at dispersing his anxiety. It had become a steady drumbeat marching him deeper into despair.

Though he loved to travel, he loathed reaching the destination. To him, travelling was a timeless, free exercise where one does not need to worry about practical things and merely dream and ponder. This was the worst part, when he knew he only had a few minutes before being flung into the real world and forced to begin interacting and thinking practically. All of a sudden the carriage stopped and Rabica's stomach churned. Already he loathed to be here, and he hadn't even set foot out of the carriage.

Lady Lewerix briefly fiddled with Lord Lewerix's tunic whilst muttering "I still think you should wear a robe dear, it looks more diplomatic."

"No, it makes me look like one of those darn sophists," he grumbled in protestation. "I've come here to do business, not preach." He declared with an air of finality before standing and giving the knock on the carriage door to signal to the doorman to open it.

As the servant obeyed the signal, a flood of early afternoon light shone glaringly into the gloomy carriage. Rabica dared not look, preferring instead to glance out of the window hole in the other side.

They were in a parade square. Rabica could see the gaunt weathered faces of the soldiers; *'trumped up imbeciles'* was Rabicas silent appraisal, though he then rebuked himself, annoyed that his reluctance to be at the banquet was being vented off in anguish at these soldiers. *'No I should feel sorry for them, they have just been funnelled through into being cogs in the machine.*

Rabica grimaced. Why was he to suffer this farce? *'Jumped up snobs acting like warriors and barbarians dressing as diplomats.'* To him it was a ridiculous idea for ridiculous people thought of by devious zealots. It was a trap. And what is more, his mere presence there would be a betrayal of his principles.

All the way on the journey he had dreamed of causing a ruckus, shaking up the snobs and humiliating the macho-warriors. But now, as he sullenly anticipated, his throat was heavy, and his nerves were searing as though a stream of pins were forcing their way through his neurones.

As he stepped out of the carriage he had to wobble to conceal his shaking legs. With one long panoramic stare he surveyed the mass of troops. He almost laughed out loud at their bulky forms accompanied with resolute, proud faces. Polished armour gleamed with as much macho glee as its wearers.

But then his eyes spotted a squad that was different. Rabica examined these more carefully. Their uniforms were tatters, save for the sergeant's shield. What was more, Rabica counted eleven of them, while he was sure they consisted of twelve. He counted the other detachments to prove this. Although those men looked formidable, they did not hold the zombie-pride of the others. They looked serious but fed up, except the smaller of the two behemoths, who was barely hiding an ironic smirk. Rabica wished he could go and talk to these men rather than the aristocratic scum inside.

Rabica decided to do all he could in the circumstances and nod respectfully at them and smile.

Then Rabica found himself being led off towards the palace; it was a fanciful display of finely chiselled warriors dancing up the columns in melee with demons. Banners and canvasses covered much of its walls, depicting similar dioramas.

THE SON AND THE HEIR

They were led into the hallway, then lounge, by a wiry goat of a man. He had that wrinkled look of twisted wisdom. Rabica, in his already sceptical mood, took an immediate dislike to him. This was reinforced when he deciphered (Rabica had never met a Latman so found his accent difficult to understand) what he had called himself, and realised it was Zeuorox.

Rabica was petrified as he entered the lounge. Banners hung all over the walls. They seemed so distant in this vast expanse of a room, and this conveniently gave him an excuse to spend a long time peering at them. The hall seemed sparse, but this was probably a deliberate ploy to show off its size.

He heard a voice nearby, and turned to see his father was exchanging introductions with a large gruff man in an illustrious uniform. Rabica quickly deduced that this was Adonis Gatan. He watched the Lord, who seemed surprisingly cheerful. *'Doesn't he realise this whole gathering is a prestige boost for Latman to show off his supremacy?'*

Gatan was hastily leading Zenith Lewerix over to two other men who stood nearby. One was a skinny sullen, old man sipping a goblet of wine cautiously. The other was a kind of feral version of Lord Gatan, who stood proud, guzzling a frothy ale from an ornate flagon. With such opposing temperaments they seemed to be finding conversation impossible without Gatan. Ruperis assumed they were Vacarium and Danite but could not place which was which. He had expected both to be bulky warriors with quite a presence, but then for some reason he still expected lords to epitomise their houses.

As his parents moved off, Rabica decided to hold back and survey the scene. *'Remember, stay outside and look from without; observe, be a critical spectator – do not be drawn into their petty debates.'*

Rabica noted the groups. Three brightly coloured young men stood together. One was chubby and loud. A pale, more elegant young man seemed to be desperately trying to overcome the overbearing crude countenance of the fat man, whilst the third, dressed in what was, to Rabica, perhaps the most hilarious minute and delicate breastplate ever made, listened intently to both with the ultimately vacant expression of thinly pasted inexplicable delight. Rabica's face instinctively rose into a sneer as he watched them sip wine aristocratically (except the chubby man who guzzled with crude mock elegance) from finely furnished goblets. He dreaded to think what they were talking about. *'Either fine wine and cheese or gold and trade – either way malignant drugs and mouldy consumption.'*

Rabica looked away with disdain, and turned his attention to two nearby bystanders. One was a few years older than Rabica, clearly a warrior but one that seemed to present himself in a thoughtful way. Rabica detected a slight frown on his face, as though slightly puzzled or bemused by his companion. His companion in conversation was an older man who looked as though he had just fought his way across the island to get here. Occasionally he roared with hoarse laughter.

'*Probably boasting to each other,*' Rabica guessed and turned to the next group.

Rabica's heart jolted in fear as he saw a young woman. He studied her face discreetly with a serious of short shy glances. It was pretty, if somewhat squashed, but he found her blatant 'flirty-young-aristocrat' behaviour repulsive. His petrification turned to disdainful disgust as he studied her actions (he now felt justified in looking at her, his dislike providing mandate for the critical prying of his eyes). '*Look at her giggling haughtily, batting her eyelids and generally utilising what a convenient luck at birth has given to her in order to make her "a person of particular interest."*'

He glanced back to the mercantile triumvirate to confirm that the pale one and the chubby one kept glancing at her with envious pining looks. '*Ha! Suckers!*' Rabica remarked triumphantly to himself, letting his guard slip and allowing a dry grin to appear on his face. With an air of superciliousness Rabica neglected to examine the 'absolute' sucker who now stood in her snare.

Last of all, two older ladies sat in sofas opposite each other. The elder of the two eyed the other with a barely repressed look of scorn, while the other seemed to be trying to converse, though taking discreet breaks to glance at the collection of lords, the two warriors and finally the captivated young man. From this Rabica deduced that this woman was Lady Gatan. As for the old crone, he had no idea, and actually wondered if she did either.

Then a thought came to him, '*how ironic it is that after all these years of telling their people to hate the other's people, the embodiment of these groups, indeed the very advocates, when they finally meet they treat each other like old chums! Far better than they do their own people! And they will go home and tell "their" people to kill trespassers from these other houses on sight. Train them psychologically to hate them*'. A dry smirk slid across his mouth. "*They treat each other like gentlemen, preach to their subjects how much they should hate them and then lament falsely at how their own people are too uncivilised to rule themselves.*'

Suddenly Rabica's train of thought was disrupted by a booming laugh. Instinctively he looked to the source; it was the burly unidentifiable warrior who was talking to one of Gatan's sons. He gave the heir a paternal slap on the back then uttered something which must have been a disengagement as he strode off towards the huddle of lords.

The freshly solitary Gatan prince must have spotted the distant spectator, as he began to walk Rabica's way.

Rabica took a swallow for confidence. Even though this man was scarcely his elder and he had repetitively told himself all these people were no different from any other being he interacted with, he still felt extremely nervous. He forced a smile but it was weak and quivering, barely strong enough to neutralise his face's desire to express a petrified grimace. This was despite the approaching prince having an air of friendliness about him. Rabica decided to move towards him also, pondering anxiously whether to bow. To do so would be legitimising hierarchy and the lordship system, but to not may just be taken as a petty factional snub. Plus it would be rude to do such a thing to someone who was just being friendly.

Luckily the issue did not arise as Claudix entered his personal space with an outstretched hand. They shook awkwardly, Rabica offering a feeble wrist action, whilst the confident young brother gave a sturdy strong shake.

Despite his stature, Claudix's voice came in a surprisingly quiet tone. "Good evening sir, you must be Rabica Lewerix." It was almost a whisper, though in its quietness sure and steady. Rabica gave a small awkward nod and smiled.

"I am, sir." Rabica found the word hard to say, not out of disrespect, on the contrary he found the man's countenance positive, but due to the idea of formalised hierarchy. Plus the similarity in age just seemed to highlight the absurdity. "And you must be the son of Gatan?" he continued.

Claudix grinned, "One of..." he corrected.

"May I ask which?" Rabica inquired, already lost in the babbling grammatical maelstrom that is formalised speech, and thinking in the back of his mind, 'If he says, "That you may" I shall bite my own head off... and if it is not possible I shall never cease trying anyway'.

"I'm Claudix." He paused, "Look, you don't mind if we drop the conventions do you?"

"Not at all!" Rabica accidentally snapped with glee.

Rabica was worried that Claudix would begin to converse about hunting and fighting.

Instead they went through a standardised 'warm-up' conversation about each other's journey. Once this had dried up Rabica found a creeping realisation that here he stood talking nonsensical chit-chat with the second in line for the throne of the second most powerful house on the island. He wasn't sure if he should spit in his face or crumple up into a compressed foetal ball and pray for disintegration. Gradually he began to favour both, and increasingly accepted he would do neither.

All of a sudden Claudix launched into an interrogatory direct prying (though he did so with a relaxed temperament). "So, what do you make of this?"

Caught off guard, Rabica let slip with an irritable reply. "What?"

Nevertheless Claudix persisted. "This, this banquet?"

Rabica was set aback by his own rudeness and shrugged to buy time for the formulation of an answer. "It is a good *show*," he commented subtly.

"'Show', huh," Claudix repeated, but otherwise remained silent, hoping to prise out an explanation.

Failing to fight temptation, Rabica continued. "... It must be for a reason..." he mumbled vaguely.

Claudix leaned in as though they needed more secrecy.

Claudix looked utterly enthralled by Rabica's speculation, as though his words had inspired him to look upon the entire event in an different cast of light.

"So, you think Latman's pulling a stunt?" he queried.

Momentarily, Rabica felt a flicker of paranoia that Claudix was being sarcastic and belittling him. He soon cast such a notion aside allowing it to huddle disapprovingly in the corner of his mind. He laughed nervously as his face contorted uncontrollably into an acidic look of untraceable angst. "Come on, look at the whole thing, even if it has no specific point of furthering Latman and undermining its competitors, it is at least a prestige thing." He felt stupid at not being able to formulate a better descriptive word.

Thankfully the second-heir seemed not to care, and nodded sympathetically, prompting Rabica to continue.

The son of Lewerix wanted to launch into a tirade ridiculing the farcical waste in 'bigging up' an imagined community against another, but refrained, though he was more fearful about failing to express his views correctly than the listener taking offence. In the pause he glanced at Zeuorox, who was swanning about the room like an omnipresent spirit. The cleric would swoon near a group of people, hovering to catch snippets of the conversation before asking some minor question and moving on. Luckily he had, at least so far, ignored the two minors in conversation.

Without even taking his eyes off the High Priest, Rabica declared. "It's that 'New Interpretation' stuff that makes me think there's something more."

Claudix laughed abruptly and simultaneously nodded his head as though he prepared to add to the conversation once he had portrayed his amusement. "You haven't spoken to 'Lord'" (he spoke the title with no attempt to conceal his mocking disdain) "Telis have you?" His pause was brief to ensure his rhetorical question remained so. "Don't bother."

"Oh?" Rabica gasped with intrigue.

Claudix made a mouthing gesture with his fingers and thumb. "New interpretation this, Thelus that. He's a dupe. No thoughts of his own."

"Aah!" Rabica drew out the expression then added cryptically, "but for who?"

Claudix did not understand and looked irritated. "Who do you think?!"

Rabica was equally irritated that the Gatanese heir had misunderstood him and in the process probably thought him stupid, but equally he did not want to offend this 'seemingly sound chap' by clarifying that he was suggesting Zeuorox.

"What other house could do that? Wield so much power? What is more, who would want to? Latman is the birthplace of that abomination."

After this riposte Rabica decided to allude to his actual meaning in the question. "But who within Latman? Which minds?"

Claudix shook his head. "It does not matter, those minds belong to a house. The house is the unit we are dealing with here."

"But the unit is influenced by forces?"

"So what? It's all Latman."

Rabica nodded. "Is it?... they are separate and influence it, they also work with other houses... or between each other... outside the houses... within, outside and between," Rabica's words became muddled in the stop-start sentences.

"This is the inter-house arena, it is no place for such details."

Rabica shrugged disapprovingly. *'Then you are setting presumptions and premises that ignore anything that doesn't fit your model, rather than actually countering their significance... you cannot see the house as a political unit separately – there is no purely political for your model to cover for it is all influenced... even constituted of economics, philosophy, law, history and so on.'* This raced though his mind, and he wished he could say it. However, he became fearful and just mumbled, "I think those details pretty important."

Claudix looked as though he was about to reply but he was silenced by the sudden intrusion of a trumpet being played. This was followed by a servant calling all those present to prepare to enter the banquet hall.

"Prepare!" Rabica whispered so Claudix could hear. "*We've* been prepared for a bloody hour!"

Claudix chuckled.

"Bloody cheek!" Rabica added.

Claudix tapped him on the shoulder in a manner slightly

patronising if friendly, like an elder brother. "It was good talking to you," he declared and took his leave.

★

Each house seemed to be regrouping before entering, so Rabica decided to conform and sought out his father. Once by his side he and his father exchanged identical expressions of bemused boredom but otherwise remained silent.

They entered a most fanciful room; excessive care had been taken to etch and carve every surface with something. Lords, priests, nobles, merchants and soldiers were crammed in and where no space existed perfect idealisations of various products were seen stacked along with flowers and fields of immaculate crops. Banners clung to the walls, pressed up against one another, bending out in strain at being allotted so little space on the vast walls. To Rabica they resembled some nightmarish formation of row upon row of giant playing cards about to do press-ups.

The table was a long thin shape with one seat at each end (these spaces held the most elaborate of thrones) and two rows of finely intricate, if somewhat outdone, chairs. Streaked down the middle of the table was a convoy of animals; a roast pig, several chickens and some mutton joints.

They all took their allocated seats. Rabica immediately set about scrutinising the positioning; however, his analysis was soon disturbed by the memory of that fateful party. Sensing the despairing anxiety of the past overcoming him, he shook it off and returned to his examination of the present.

As it stood, the space at the far end of the table was unoccupied, as was the space to its left. To the right of it was Ruperis, and next to him was Mistress Telis. Opposite her was Lord Telis and next to him was Rabica's father, mother then him. After him was Lord Vacarium and then the lord's podgy son and finally High Priest Zeuorox. On the other side, adjacent to Mistress Telis and opposite Lord Lewerix was Lord Gatan, then his wife, two sons (so the elder brother Maximus sat opposite Rabica). Lord Danite was next, then his brother-in-arms (soon to be in-law). One could see the 'discrepancy' immediately, that Telis had been favoured over Gatan, pushing Gatan level with Lewerix and using both Gatan's sons and Rabica as a buffer between Gatan and the minor houses. Also, all families had been placed in a hierarchical line except Mistress Telis so that she sat next to Ruperis (who found himself above all the other political factions).

Rabica began to ponder who would sit opposite Ruperis – For Latman's mother, the logical choice, was seated down the other end on the opposing throne (presumably to eat in peace away from the discussions up the table.

Rabica's attention returned to the indiscernible person expected to fill the seat beside Telis. His mind raced for a pattern. '*Did Ruperis have relatives?*' he thought hard '*He has a sister I think, but surely she would be lower than him... but then shouldn't he be lower than the lord?... unless a point is being made here... this is his right hand man... so who would be the left hand?... I would have thought Zeuorox...*' his mind was racing through speculations.

Rabica's already stretched train of thought was abruptly called to halt by a dramatic entrance. The double doors virtually opposite swung open and a trumpet blared.

★

Lord Gatan watched the figure enter with cautious intrigue; he fought off fears of the fop-wraith, and sat hunched silently preparing for the phantom to take solid form before him.

In strode an adolescent boy moving in a vague and unsuccessful attempt to look both professional and militaristic. Despite his pathetic form he remained zealously convinced he was making a good impression. Gatan quickly surmised: An overly proud but equally an overly contemplative dreamer misguided and prone to excessive irrationality due to previous exposures in a prolonged impressionable youth.

★

'*He doesn't look so bad,*' Rabica thought at first, '*a bit of a priests eunuch-boy, but...*' his thoughts stopped dead. A smile broke on his face; he desperately tried to remove it, embarrassed that it would be noticed. Immediately Rabica attempted to put a rational and emotionally defunct label on it. She was pretty, though lacking the obvious 'just from sight' evidence of internal beauty of The Young Lady. 'So is this Ruperis' sister?' Rabica pondered.

She was clearly being escorted by Juscius. They held hands daintily.

With a hint of bitterness Rabica declared to himself, ' b*ut she must have flaws if she is with Him... She's probably even a convert!*'

They reached their positions, Juscius was dressed in a pure white robe, with a red sash and a gold sheathed dagger. Torian wore a beautiful dress of pale blue, a calm relaxing colour to dampen her darting eyes and striking dark hair, which was curled in flowing locks that gleamed startlingly in the candlelight.

Rabica was suddenly stunned into self-consciousness and immediately feared that his examination of her had been noticed.

"Welcome guests. I have summoned you here to discuss matters of great urgency. Just seeing your faces here all in one room is a blessing of Thelus. These are great times, and great times offer great opportunities,

opportunities which Thelus has bestowed upon us so we may all come together and fulfill his will." His face beamed with frightening confidence, before suddenly shifting into a serious expression as he regarded the Pontiff. "His Excellency, High Priest Zeuorox shall offer a prayer to the Gods on our behalf."

The priest, who had been glowering eagerly at a slab of pig carcass, started. The grin he had concealed from view with his downward stare was immediately wiped from his face as he rose to mumble some humble words to Thelus before sitting.

The guests sat in confusion for a few moments before Juscius declared, "You may begin."

Servants piled on vegetables. Meanwhile, Adonis Gatan carved away at the pig. Lord Lewerix managed to get hold of a chicken. Juscius was brought some meat, and Ruperis whispered some heroic witticism to mistress Telis.

Once he had palmed enough chicken on Lady Lewerix's plate, Lord Zenith turned to Rabica's. Each house kept to its own.

The silence began building up around them in air as thick as an icy chill. Knives sliced through animal flesh, when they would have been better used to cut a path to each other. A few scant whispers passed discreetly as possible between serving circles.

Eventually, Adonis Gatan broke the ice, by leaning towards Juscius' end of the table and flinging a sizeable slab of pork onto Juscius' plate. It was quite a distance, but nonetheless it was tossed expertly. Juscius almost jumped out of his seat as the pig slab slapped onto his plate with a succulent splat. Adonis hid his grin as his mind relived his nemesis' squeamish reaction.

"So, Lord Latman, are we here to chomp away in silence, or are we here to talk?"

Juscius scowled faintly, evidently irritated that Gatan had taken the initiative to start the proceedings. He was robbed. He decided, with a hint of spitefulness, to make an unrelated jibe at the Lord's manners.
"Well sire, perhaps once you have finished bombarding me with meat." He turned to the girl next to him, then Telis. "Or are you going to juggle some mutton joints to me?"

Torian gave a non-committal semi-smirk, while Telis grinned and was about to make a remark when he jolted discreetly (Ruperis had kicked him under the table).

Rabica looked at his father. He wanted to say something himself. His father remained silent as he eyed the two lords, like a vulture overseeing two bulls preparing for a fight.

Gatan just laughed along, whilst Maximus muttered (so all could hear) "Still, was quite a shot!"

Ruperis laughed diplomatically. Gatan winked at his son, who chuckled; the other brother smiled encouragingly. Mistress Telis giggled flirtily which meant Ruperis then had to scowl. Danite roared with laughter, to an extent that it was obvious it was just to undermine Juscius. Meanwhile Vacarium seemed immersed in the swirling whirlpool that was his goblet's intoxicating contents. Zeuorox just snorted disdainfully.

Rabica was amazed at how they all carefully choreographed their reactions to such a simple gesture. These weren't strangers meeting for the first time, but epitomes of long interwoven trails of entire peoples traceable back through centuries. Each judgement was not one of first sight but of the recognition of years of preconceptions in human form. This was not a 'new start'; it was rather when the weaving threads crash head on, instead of continuing to wind around each other.

Gatan had finished serving, and paused to look at Lord Latman. "So, why are we here? What is your proposition?"

Adonis guessed the young lord would not be able to take the direct pressure, preferring to wriggle his way through the negotiations, gradually sowing the seeds of whatever he clandestinely sought to spread.

He seemed to have been correct, as the lord spluttered slightly before smiling nervously. "Not one for idle chit-chat, are you?"

Gatan had an urge to bellow, 'not when I've travelled half the island' but knew his diplomatic training forbade him. Nevertheless he was entitled to apply the pressure subtly; he did this by giving the lord an intense guarded glare.

Lord Latman took a discreet heavy breath; he glanced encouragingly at Zeuorox, who, unknown to the others, gave the slightest of smiles to signal that the lord should proceed. Before he started to speak he gradually redressed his posture, his innocent choir-boy look became transformed into that of the 'hardworking practical idealist'. His eyebrows arched with an expression that resolutely declared "lets get down to business". His eyes retained their baffled idealistic charm, his hands prepared to lay out some motions to show he was serious and yet his tone was so casual. "Oh this is just a get-together... I have ideas, yes... and we all have something to say... but let us not rush things, we will all have time to speak, but first we need a fresh start."

Most of the lords nodded as though transfixed. Gatan was flushed by the sudden impressive, if nonsensical, diplomatic spiel. Lord Lewerix discreetly sniggered in bafflement.

"What we need is..." Juscius continued, pausing to think of the best word.

"Openness?" prompted a dark sombre voice from the other end of the table.

Heads swivelled, and eyes shot down the table to Zeuorox.

Lord Vacarium suddenly stirred from his reverie with a brief glint of optimism.

Gatan was eyeing Zeuorox suspiciously, then turned to Juscius. "Openness?"

"Yes," Juscius almost whispered.

In meantime Rabica had pricked his ears in optimism, only to sink back down in confusion.

"Well?" Gatan queried.

It was Telis who answered, prompting Gatan to fear that it was too fitting to be sporadic and therefore had been rehearsed.

"I don't think Lord Latman is the one here needing openness. Though he has much to say he has not a single stain of impropriety on him."

Even Ruperis winced at the last phrase, finding it hard to swallow amongst the thick tense air.

Rabica, though missing the sharp end of the statement, could not help but clamp incessantly with his lips.

Gatan was clearly irritated, even angered, but kept his cool. Lady Gatan had tensed up, wracking her brain for a way to mitigate the confrontation. Then Gatan spoke coldly and clearly, making sure the recipients of his words knew they had to be careful if they wanted this banquet to continue. "What is it exactly that you are implying?"

Juscius' lip quivered. Zeuorox quickly realised he would have to lead the way but just as he opened his mouth a sulky angry whine crackled from the far end of the table all the way up to Lord Gatan.

"It's you, you murderer. You killed our men! You got savages to kill our boys!" Maritha flew into a humiliating rage, flailing madly with her hands and glowering red with anger.

"What?" Gatan blurted with disdainful contempt.

"Lady Latman, please," whispered Lady Gatan in an authoritative school-mistress voice.

"Mother," Juscius pleaded.

The rest of the lords and families remained motionless except the two Gatan brothers, who stirred uneasily.

It was Zeuorox who cut in. "What I think," he uttered the word 'think' in the way of all pedagogic theologians to make it interchangeable with 'know', "is that Lady Latman was referring to the raid at Gericos, perpetrated by barbarians but; we have reason to believe, with localised instigation. That is, Gatan coins were found on the few killed barbarians."

There was a collective gasp of shock.

Zeuorox continued. "Our soldiers were burnt alive in their bunks." His dead beady eyes swam in a rim of red skin, as though straining in the intensity of the glare as he stared at the accused.

Gatan was shocked; having no idea what they spoke of, he thought it a malicious lie cooked up out of nothing. Burning with infuriation, he battled to retain his calm. "What! I had no idea – I resent accusations of this sort. Why would I do it? How could I co-ordinate such a thing? No one can communicate with them. Plus if I paid them before-hand, why would they bother to carry it out?"

"Perhaps you did it indirectly, if you gave them gold to leave you alone?" Telis interjected. He seemed shocked at the news.

Zeuorox gave him an approving expression, one that seemed to almost regret he hadn't thought of it.

Rabica couldn't contain himself, was so angered at the vultures circling the lion.

"But that's stupid," he spluttered crudely. He was off to a promising start. "The barbarian raiding parties are separate, aren't they? If he did, then he'd only stop one boat."

When he stopped he was shaking profusely and his eyes were watering over. He looked to his father, hoping for a sign of encouragement. There was none. A beady stare with a fixed slight grin, this meant that even if he agreed with Rabica he could not show it, and so professionally it had been a failure.

Meanwhile Zeuorox thought, *'ah, that must have been why I did not think of it.'*

Gatan nodded at Rabica. "Yes, young man, you are *probably* right."

Telis sulkily remarked, "I wouldn't know. I haven't conversed with the barbarians."

"Nor have you fought them," grunted Maximus, but was ignored.

"Well... maybe we should... perhaps they have stuff to trade," Rabica suggested in broken phrases, taking a look at Ruperis, one which was ignored.

Meanwhile Juscius was livid. "Are you suggesting we negotiate with aliens? It would be betraying our principles!" he declared. His voice rising in pitch and tempo as it did in volume.

Rabica was hooked in now, and bit back without thinking. "That depends on your principles – namely if they are pitted with dogmatic xenophobia. "They take food from us – what does that tell you? If we can trade food for something else... fairly," he gave Ruperis a stare. "Then..."

"Then what?" boomed Ruperis, clearly offended by the accusing stare. "They have nothing we want!" His face was stretching and sinking in and out of sneers. "And before you say ANYTHING, I have been to their lands and fought these beasts man-to-man".

Rabica found himself distracted by the contradictory notion of fighting 'beasts' man-to-man, but managed to tear himself away from this inconsistency to counter. "Maybe their lands have nothing, but why is it that our boats have never caught theirs? I know very little about boats, but they sure as hell do!"

Juscius Latman, Telis, Mistress Telis and Zeuorox all shuddered when he uttered the word 'hell' and glanced at each other disapprovingly.

Ruperis just laughed. "Yes, you're right. You do know nothing of boats." He paused in contemplation then added, "and please do not use the 'H' word, decent people find it offensive." He took a look at Mistress Telis, who smiled at him and then scowled at the heretic.

"My apologies," Rabica conceded begrudgingly.

The whole table seemed to be shocked by the sudden outburst, no one daring to break the bubble of silence lest the same happen again.

Gatan waited for the silence to settle then declared. "So, Lord Latman, will you retract your accusation?"

"I think if we recall what I have and haven't said, I actually made no such accusation," he weaselled out. "... I cannot apologise for what others have said... I mean... mother is mother!" he mused, creeping slowly off the hot spot.

Just as it looked as though the Latman delegation had freed itself from the need to apologise, Claudix Gatan interjected. "I believe, High Priest... your excellency, you made an accusation."
Rabica nodded in support.

A wry smile cracked open on the old wrinkled face. "I think you will find that I made no such accusation; I merely pointed to particular facts..."

"Oh come on!" Maximus cut in, more impetuous than his brother, and with Mistress Telis present with more to prove.

"All I mentioned were known knowns, that is facts. But, there are also unknown knowns concerning why, and even unknown unknowns which we do not know that we do not know, or indeed why."

The word 'bullshit' sat on the tip of Rabica's tongue, but he managed to hold it back. The room was silent in bafflement at the high priest's confusing statement.

It was Gatan who broke the silence again. A puzzled, irritated expression resided on his brow. "So, is there anything else that you feel your paranoid superstitions can muster up to accuse me of?" After blurting this, he turned to his wife apologetically, knowing he had let his emotion get hold of him.

"Well, naturally, we want you to cease your activities in

Vacarium," Zeuorox declared in a matter of fact tone. A tone so deep in his drawl that it felt as though it were already etched in stone.

"Activities?" Gatan spat.

"We all know your history..." Telis began, before being cut short out of fear.

"History!" Gatan bellowed then looked to Lord Vacarium for support.

It was then that Adonis Gatan saw it in those grey features. What was worse, he saw it in the podgy swaying mass of offspring next to the grey husk – Lord Vacarium, indeed House Vacarium was finished. Instantly he was thinking about stone and minerals and about possible coups.

"May I draw attention... seeing as the honourable lord will not." He gave the phantom of Lord Vacarium a stare. "To North Vaca... I hear of turmoil and guerrilla war operating there – in an area that you, Lord Latman, cling onto."

"Ahh," Juscius smiled smugly. "I am glad the honourable gentleman has brought this up," he nodded. "Oh yes," he addressed the shaking heads of the Gatan brothers. "Why is it you know so much about the region? – Because your spies are stirring it up!"

"I am doing nothing of the sort. Yet again you fling unjustified accusations at me... ones I see no reason to bother to deny. I trade with Vacarium, I do not arm paramilitaries."

Juscius grunted dismissively at Gatan's answer and turned accusingly to Vacarium. "Why do you not stop these terrorists?"

Slowly Lord Vacarium looked up at his addresser and stared him square in the face as though he were death himself. "Because I cannot," he declared with morbid carelessness.

Juscius Latman almost leaped up in joy at the answer. "Well, that is where my first proposition comes in – we, that is, House Latman, will provide border control on both sides. We need your expertise, your men's closeness with the population to win hearts and minds to defend against this terrorist insurgency."

Vacarium was silent.

Gatan understood the situation now; it was out of Vacarium's hands. The house was dead and Latman would move in to take the vacuum. He eyed Juscius cautiously. "Are you proposing an occupation?" He took a glance at Danite, who was as worried as him. Even Lord Lewerix had a slight frown on his face. Only Telis seemed unsurprised.

"I would call it liberation, we are securing the area." Ruperis span. A bitter laugh, more like a sigh, came from Rabica's mouth.
He had to point out the twisted logic they were using. "How exactly will

expanding your area of control solve the security issue in your southern province? To put it bluntly, how will occupying the brothers of those who oppose you make them put down their swords?"

Juscius sighed impatiently. "Look," he leaned forward and raised his eyebrows in fake sincerity, moving his hand in a rolling circle as he continued, "we have a security problem, they are a threat to my nation, and so I must act." He spoke in short patronising bursts with long pauses as though addressing children.

Rabica couldn't contain himself. "So you smash everything, hurt more people then wonder why it gets worse?"

His words seemed to have fallen on deaf ears. Only Claudix nodded appreciatively and this was discreet, so as not to be seen by others.

"I cannot allow it," Gatan declared. "I cannot sanction such an expansion under the false pretext of security. If you have internal issues, deal with them yourself."

Juscius was disgusted, though a slight grin implied he knew he could wriggle through. "'Cannot allow' – who do you think you are?" Gatan almost rose to his feet to issue a challenge but was stopped by a stern glare from his wife.

"This," Juscius began again, with a joyous smirk that implied he had won the argument no matter what he said. "This just proves it! You meddle in this, you meddle in that... and then when I try to solve it, you say you 'cannot allow it'!"

This only enraged Gatan further, and so Zeuorox hastily cut in. "Lord Latman means to say that it would be unfair for you to block a security policy for Latman."

Ruperis then chipped in as well. "As well as unwise, if we can secure this area then we can allow trade through."
Gatan shrugged. "We would use boats anyway, as we do now, only not the long way round."

"But with our borders secure we could allow your passage along the coast," Juscius retorted.

Gatan snorted in disbelief. "You expect me to believe that that is the reason for not allowing us passage!"

Ruperis whispered something into Juscius' ear and the lord repeated. "Actually, we could not allow that but we could arrange for neutral, that is private, boats to shift the goods... in return we would expect open trade agreements."

Gatan could barely believe the blatant corruption. *'Oh that cheeky swine... profiting from insecurity'*. However he did not have time to answer before the next onslaught began.

"On the subject of ships... why is it that you, Lord Gatan, are amassing a flotilla in your northern ports? You see I may have to revoke current passage agreements for fear of it arriving in my waters."

He was only then reminded of the shipbuilding operations. He had hoped that it had shut down on its own, as so many things did if he didn't keep pushing them on. He began to ponder why he had bothered to follow his priest's instruction.

He gritted his teeth before launching into a defence. "A number of reasons caused this, for one the barbarian raiders, not only on our homeland but on our trading vessels. The plan is to secure the area before and during shipment. But also my high priest had a premonition that they would be needed," he declared with pride and sincerity.

Rabica struggled not to sink his head into his hands as he heard the latter 'reason'. Telis whispered some repertoire to Ruperis and (he hoped) Juscius. However, it was Zeuorox who spoke up, clearly as the only ordained man it was felt only he could legitimately comment on such a thing. In a stone-dry matter-of-fact way he pronounced that it was "convenient".

"Well of course it was, the gods wouldn't tell us to do superfluous things would they," Lady Gatan lectured in a patronising motherly tone, "you of all of us should know that, your Excellency."

Zeuorox scowled at her, clearly angered at being bettered by a woman. Lost for words he just shrugged.

Telis decided to speak. He would act as a mediator between Gatan and Latman. "Well it seems the best solution would be to agree on a limitation of Household Ships. If we keep building armadas we will cause mutual distrust and so encourage tensions."

Gatan looked at his counterpart distrustfully. "It is not the boats that threaten each of us, but armies… and Latman's standing army is by far the largest."

Juscius stared back adopting a matter-of-fact tone and corroborating emotionless expression. "We have a much larger territory, plus we have the Vaca problem. Besides we are downsizing our military. Voluntary veterans are retiring early from service. Why just last month the Captain of Gorad garrison retired and joined Delvinius' company as a security chief. Indeed, it is your, militaristic system with so many in reserves that overshadows our army."

'The fool! He is purging the military of 'unfaithfuls'' Gatan thought.

Ruperis and Zeuorox sat examining the lord from opposite ends of the table, trying to gauge if he had fallen for the bait or if Juscius had given away too much.

Gatan nodded. "Well, I have no plans to expand my military, I shall monitor influxes… may I also add that the Gatanese system of recruitment merely allows all men the opportunity to serve their House plus be prepared for a defence of their locality. It is not the same as a huge standing army."

He paused. "However, if you intend to carry out missions near the Vaca Mountains I think they need to be monitored."

"Out of the question," Juscius declared simply.

At this point Rabica stirred and kept turning to his father hoping he would offer troops. Yet he did not, he just sat still, staring forwards listening intently but with a nonchalant grin on his face.

"Perhaps," Ruperis declared "Lord Danite could provide troops?"

Danite, who had remained surprisingly quiet during the discussions, glowed a painful red, his cheeks peeping from behind the surrounding clumps of hair like rose mounds. It was obvious that he could not afford to spare troops for such an operation. He also wasn't sure whether accepting would weaken Gatan. He was favourable to Gatan having troops in Vaca, as it may discourage the Latmans from trying anything.

"I fail to see how my troops would address Gatan concerns."

Gatan nodded with a furrowed brow, "Quite, how would having Danite soldiers in Vacarium satisfy me. They are not my troops, nor can I have access to information."

Zeuorox sighed. This was where Telis was supposed to jump in as an independent party to be the monitoring House; however, he had spoilt the illusion of neutrality with his unwavering sycophancy towards Juscius Latman.

Despite the preposterousness Telis attempted anyway.

Gatan just laughed, then he turned to Lewerix. "Lord Zenith Lewerix, could you possibly solve this?"

Rabica's heart stopped, pride was rising already, finally his father would save the day – be the man of reason mediating between the fanatics.

Zenith sighed. "Well, you see I fail to understand what exactly the troops would be there for. Who do they report to? What mandate would they have for action?"

Rabica's pride vanished; the vacuum of emotion flickered in uncontrollable pulses into anger under lied with a constant base of disappointment.

"Exactly," Juscius declared with a smug smile. "There is no point in them being there, we just need troops there to stop the smuggling of weapons and terrorists."

Zenith was clearly irritated with Juscius using his requests for clarity as a justification of his argument; he turned to Vacarium, "Lord Vacarium, do you actually want Latman, or any other, troops in your territory?"

The zombie lord looked up sluggishly. "My side of the border is my responsibility and theirs is theirs…" he trailed off as though retaining the vague commitment to continuing.

Zeuorox was getting anxious. He needed to stop this deadlock before it dragged on and Latman began to look unreasonable. "Perhaps we are looking at the wrong solution. Let us allow our troops to cross each other's borders if pursuing insurgents?"

Vacarium nodded bleakly, not only could he hardly refuse, he knew it did not really matter because it was happening already, Latman troops had crossed the border pursuing insurgents of refugees and Vacarian guards had not bothered to confront them for fear of the repercussions. "Something can be arranged," he mumbled.

Gatan was distressed at the lord's submission, though hardly surprised. He would have to organise stationing troops in either Vacarium or Danite to keep troops nearby.

"Well," Juscius declared optimistically with a grin, "that's one issue solved." He seemed not to notice the irony that after all these disputes the Houses were more divided and embittered against each other and the one agreement was hollow as it would occur anyway. After a brief pause he launched into the next subject. He glanced at Ruperis and Zeuorox first to check all was ok. "The next topic is Barbarians – now I thought this would be easy but we have already had a dissenter who wants to have a chat with them." He took an obvious comic stare at Rabica, who almost leapt out of his seat in fright. This movement was ground to an abrupt halt as his joints seized up with petrification due to the laughter of those around him. He felt the surging heat wave of embarrassment sweep over his face followed by a shiver that ran down his spine like a sweaty snake.

But it was just a passing joke and so attention was soon taken off him and back to Lord Latman, as he continued: "… I propose an agreement for non-negotiation with the raiders. No trades, no bribes, no agreements, only the sword. We should pass on information about their whereabouts. Whatever our differences internally, we can remain determined to protect this land from those who seek to destroy it, and our way of life."

"Perhaps this would be an apt time for Ruperis Delvinius to describe his journey?" Juscius declared.

Given the opportunity to show off, not so much to an audience of important people, as to mistress Telis, Ruperis rambled for a long time, trying to cram in witticisms and 'quaintities' of the peoples he met. He spoke of his daring encounters and the lewd lustfulness of his unidentified 'Number One'. Most of his audience listened captivated, except Zeuorox, who glared about the room impatiently, and Rabica who snorted to himself every time Ruperis generalised a people.

In the excitement, Ruperis got ahead of himself and summoned the slave girl. Both Zeuorox and Juscius were uneasy, and Juscius even jealous that another was to introduce her.

However, before she could be found, another guard rushed in and came to attention next to Juscius. He whispered something into the lord's ear and Juscius glowered in confusion. "What?" The guard repeated it and the look of disbelief remained on the lord's face. "That is ridiculous!" he declared.

Juscius Latman refused to believe it at first. However, the more he thought, the more it made sense – Thelus was trying to tell him something – but what? There had to be some significance as to why now; clearly Thelus had waited until the statue had passed hands as it had no interest in the heathens. But why could it not wait until he was in its presence? Was it so urgent? Did it want to draw him away from the banquet? Was Thelus warning him against peaceful resolutions? It had, after all, included fire.

He took a glance at Lord Gatan and saw him struggling to suppress a rampant grin, and this just further exacerbated the young lord's despair.

★

'The dolled up puppy seems to have fallen out of his monarch's clothes!' Gatan mused to himself, deliberately betraying his grin to spark a reaction from Juscius. Meanwhile he imagined a little lap-dog dressed up so its head popped out of the neck in Juscius' clothes. Suddenly the supports below it vanished and the whole cloth structure crumpled to the ground, the puppy tumbling down until it was left grinning naively, ignorant of its humiliating plight. It seemed to have worked; it had shown up the lord as an easily flustered amateur.

Then came the inevitable spiteful accusations. "What? Lord Gatan?"

Gatan tried to refrain from exposing his glee prematurely. "What, indeed? You are the one who has just received information!" he retorted.

Juscius took a deep breath. He knew he would never get through this evening without revealing it. He contemplated lying, but knew it would come out anyway. "Very well," he declared reluctantly. "Apparently, the statue brought by Gatan is possessed, and moved."

There were shocked expressions from all, even Rabica, though this was more in an attempt to hide his amusement.

Juscius decided to divulge some more. "Apparently its arm moved." He did not want to tell them that it had breathed fire, for fear that it would spread panic.

There were sudden calls to see the spectacle, rising above the general noisome clutter of gossiping aristocrats.

Zeuorox had actually sunk his head into his hands, cushioning the wrinkled orb in a noise-proof padding from the disaster that was unravelling.

Juscius struggled to get himself heard, relying on shaking his head to get across his refusal.

Gatan alone sat in silence, admiring the civil chaos, this lord who prided himself on being a figurehead of tradition smiling with glee that he had turned a collection of rulers into squawking washerwomen.

"We mustn't disturb the council!" Juscius protested pathetically, with the acid exasperation of an adolescent.

Ruperis came to his aid, taking the initiative to deflect the disappointment to a linked issue that could in turn lead to a victory for Latman. In a loud flamboyant voice he interrogated Gatan, "who devised this statue?" knowing the answer all too well.

"Well, Gorax came up with the idea," he answered carefully.

With an expression fit for pantomime, Ruperis looked overwhelmed at the news. "Oh really! I would love to meet this fine fellow. Perhaps we could bring him here and he could shed some light on this…occurrence?"

Gatan's instinct told him something was stirring to undermine his victory. However, pride overcame this hunch, and so he called over the guard who had brought the news to Latman, and politely asked him to bring the inventor. The soldier obeyed Adonis without even consulting Juscius, perhaps it was from fear of insulting him, or perhaps out of personal respect.

After a few minutes the soldier returned, announcing the scruffy genius.

Gorax was quite flustered, as he often was, in his own ponderous way. He wore a workman's robe, though it was a fine garment it was worn in an erratic manner, as though thrown on in the spur of the moment. As he shuffled towards the table, he did not even get the chance to introduce himself to the assembly of superior beings, before Juscius' interrogation began.

"Tell me if this construct was blessed by the gods?" he demanded with an urgency that surprised all the others, no less than the innovator himself.

Nevertheless the reply came almost immediately: "indirectly." A cheeky grin hid under the thin veil of matter-of-fact bluntness.

Juscius cocked his head to request an explanation.

The architect gladly expanded his answer. "Well, it exists due to man's innovation, which must be blessed by the gods as they watch over us."

Any respect that Rabica held for this genius fell to the floor. *'Unless he is just playing along'.*

This sparked a lengthy discussion within Rabica's mind, the topic being, "How much should 'us rationals' concede to irrationality in order to confer influence amongst the ignorant? He soon found himself thinking that one should use any chance one could to end up at the truth. But he then found this unsatisfactory, as truth has to be true, and cannot be founded on lies or half-truths, or as he put it 'any deviation from the truth cannot then end up at the truth, as truth is a process unto itself'.

Therefore the truth was in science, the aspiration to be proven, and never to be found in speculation. Always prepared to be countered but at the time the most defendable – what more could he ask of humanity? The search for truth was, therefore, a perpetual process. This did not mean futile, far from it, indeed if it had an end then what would man do once he reached that end?

During the time of Rabica's little soliloquy, Juscius had explained to those present that the statue's arm had moved and its eyes had gleamed. The lord had set about interrogating the inventor ruthlessly, but was met immediately by a disappointed mumbling completely unconcerned with the lords demands: "so, the flames must not have worked."

Juscius was clearly angered by him mentioning that which he had omitted, and let out an exasperated shriek and began babbling, firing questions concerning what 'black magic' had the inventor 'conjured' and for 'what evil motive'.

Lord Gatan, having had his fun at watching the rival lord discredit himself, decided to intervene to defend his scientist, even though he seemed totally unaffected by Juscius' accusations.

"That is enough, Lord Latman!" Gatan bellowed with an authoritative air as though the adolescent's father. He knew the guests would be comparing the countenance of the two rivals, and favouring the self-restrained competence of the elder lord. Gatan discreetly surveyed his audience. He could see that Vacarium and Danite were with him, even Lewerix's nonchalant (not vacant, merely self-suppressing) face betrayed an unease at the young inquisitor lord. Gatan cared little about the son of Vacarium; he had decided this man's rule would be short-lived, if it occurred at all. When the high priest's face finally peeked from its hidy hole behind his cupped hands, Gatan took great pleasure in noticing the similarity between the beleaguered Lord Vacarium and the now despairing Zeuorox. The high priest's gaunt face had drained its pride; its previously authoritative and intimidating frame now revealed its true form – a frail old man. The only differences were the puffy ringlets of pink flesh that bordered the lord's eyes. They were like rings in the trunk of a tree marking the build up of year upon year of waning resistance in a struggle.

When Juscius finally calmed himself, he put on a restrained and quiet voice in a vain attempt to regain some credibility. "If you have been tampering with idols of the deities, especially Thelus himself, then that is blasphemous and you should be hasty, dare I say immediate, in repenting." He paused and vaguely turned to address Gatan. "I shall not be able to accept such a desecrated artefact in my territory, let alone my city." Returning his gaze to Gorax he glared with a cold steeliness. "If you were one of my subjects you would have to be punished."

Gorax, indeed all the non-New Interpretists present (excluding Lord Vacarium who had heard it many times from reports of 'motives' for Latman activities in the border region), had never heard the word blasphemy but assumed it was something to do with defying the will of the gods. But he did not see why this would mean the lord would punish him, as if he had a quarrel with the gods then they would punish him. This would mean that he was punished twice, and the lord would be trying to interfere with the will of the gods – a defiance (or blasphemy - if that were the new word) in itself. Still, he remained silent and took the seat that had been brought for him.

Telis's face wore a facetious expression, waggling his head from side to side in excited anticipation of the reception he would get for his musing. He spoke aloofly, addressing Gorax, "tell me dear sir" 'sir' was spoken in a mocking ironic tone to establish his superiority over the humble recipient - "What is the secret of your architecture?"

Before Gatan could defensively cut in, Gorax answered. He did so in a matter-of-fact tone that grated on the questioner, as it showed he was either unaware or uncaring of Telis' mocking tone. What was more, the answer came in a simple single and succinct word: "triangles."

Telis burst out laughing, ecstatic at having such material to amuse himself (if no others) with. "Triangles! You know I ought to hire you as a jester! How much does Lord Gatan give you? I'll double it!"

The whole room had been rather amused by the answer. That is, except Rabica, who instantly thought of the Third Party.

Gorax continued, rather amused at how they reacted, as it reinforced their childish ignorance. "Yes, it is the strongest structural shape. A triangle frame is much stronger than the square, and the principles work for so many things. It is a compact robust structure that shares pressure put on it."

Rabica whispered to himself, "of course", and began daydreaming of his political model.

Telis laughed mockingly. "So should I have a triangular house? Shield? Horse? Kingdom? Why aren't the strongest men shaped like triangles?"

Gorax just looked at him with a serious, disdainful expression. "No, that is just silly," he pronounced succinctly.

Deathly silence ensued, as the aristocrats felt collectively embarrassed at their collective ignorance.

Ruperis intervened in an attempt to avoid stagnation. He turned to Juscius, but spoke so that all could hear. "Is it not time to bring out the honour guard?"

Lady Gatan, being the only person present with such highly perceptive acumen for the situation, was the only one to notice Zeuorox's painstakingly concealed grin when he heard the merchant's request. Lord Gatan was meticulously focusing on his counterpart, whereas Lady Gatan had dismissed the dupe long ago and instead focused on the twin pillars of power.

Juscius nodded with reawakened vigour. "Yes!" he declared ecstatically then summoned over the very same guard who had brought both the news from the courtyard, and its perpetrator.

The door opened, and two overly dressed palace guards took up positions either side of the fabulously covered frame. Then a line of trumpeters marched in with proud professional faces. They formed up, great elaborate tunics glittering in the torchlight. As they put their instruments to their lips Juscius stood.

The confused guests, preoccupied by the entrants, failed to notice, except for Telis, who shot to his feet like a trained lapdog. Ruperis and the young mistresses soon joined him. Eventually one by one the rest of the guests stood up, keeping their eyes on the assembly of musicians.

As the trumpets began to blare, Gatan and Rabica instantly recognised the entering unit as the squad that had caught both of their eyes on the parade plaza. They trudged in with the laziness of true soldiery. All their faces were cold and expressionless, indeed, far from a proud marching parade, they looked like a chain gang who had swapped uniforms with their guards.

To Rabica they looked like amateurs, who had just thrown on the uniform. But to an experienced warrior like Gatan, he could see these were men who knew the drill, but had reached that level of front-line fatigue for trivial displays and so lapsed uncaring when pressed to do so. Yet as Gatan looked more closely at their posture he could not help being reminded of images of prisoners after a battle. It got him thinking it was more that the usual fatigue affecting these troops.

Gatan was disturbed from his examination by a gradually intensifying prodding emanating from Gorax and pressing into his left arm. The lord turned discreetly to the inventor and arched his head down so he could be addressed. The genius was unusually disturbed in a peculiar angered manner that was being displayed by a reddening colouration.

"Sire, those spears!" He was pointing with quivering restraint as he attempted to remain discreet at a burly soldier holding a spear.

Confused, Gatan began examining the object. Its design was peculiar for Latman blacksmiths. The Latman army did not have many spearmen, relying instead on heavy infantry and cavalry to blitz enemy positions, rather than to take the defensive – which was why Gatan used spearmen – as a defence against Latman cavalry and to keep heavy infantry at bay while other forces surrounded them. Though the lighting was not good, Gatan was sure the metal gleamed differently to iron, its shine being more intense like that of polished silver.

Once the squad was formed up, the trumpets stopped and Juscius beckoned for the guests to be seated. He was clearly disappointed by the squad's entrance, but glossed over it by launching straight into a speech, "Sergeant Pluvius, Squad XVII Mounted Light Infantry of the 3rd Regiment of the Gorad Garrison. Many of you are longstanding veterans of our proud armies. Sergeant, you are a proud survivor of the Battle of Neptus."

Even though this man had been an opponent at that siege, Gatan could not help but feel a soldier's respect for the sergeant upon hearing this.

"You are here today, in the presence of myself and these prestigious guests to receive recognition of your service. For hunting down and destroying a band of criminals in the Forest region near the River Neptus. In doing so suffering two casualties, one of whom was your Special Morale Accompaniment and Moral Spiritual Advisor..." (he spoke them as though they were official titles) "...Brother-Warrior Visuvius. Brother Visuvius was a proud and dedicated warrior, and honourable soldier of Thelus (peace be upon his eternal soul), who died proudly leading the squad in the final push. Dying only because his dedication to the House and Thelus (may we be forever thankful of his mercy) was so much that he was willing to forsake his life for it. He stopped the enemy from regrouping whilst the hearty battle-hardened warriors reformed for that final push." He returned his attention to the soldiers, having drifting his gaze off to the guests as the flow of the speech bolstered his prestige. "From the account you have given, we shall ensure that this warrior is made a martyr of our cause; a cause of peace and freedom. For years to come this fallen comrade shall be a hero spoken of and his story passed on to children as an epitome of Latman chivalry..."

Most of the soldiers were trying their hardest to look interested, save for one, Heites. He was fuming, his eyes watering and glistening in the light like polished crystals as the restraint brought him close to tears. Juscius noticed the man's evident distress, completely misinterpreting it, thinking he was shedding tears for his fallen priest. Consequently the Lord gave him an obvious look of sympathy. "I see his death has affected you all."

'I hated that fuck, I hated that fuck. I killed that fuck!' Heites' mind was blaring with fury. Curdling with the anger, was a despairing sensation that it had all been in vain. *'I killed him and now look – Have I even made it worse? I have given them a hero. I'm fed up of the lies. If only I could just speak the truth and not taint actions with lies.'* He paused as a new level of despair descended upon him *'If only I could shout now "We murdered boys!" – boys with ideals and principles – they were the peace and freedom... until we came and it all died a messy bloody death.'*

Again the words came to him, *'Why did I have to lie? If I commit myself to act I ought to back them up with truthful words, otherwise they just rot and merge with the rest of the foetid pestilence that plagues us'*. The image of the rotting meat reappeared in his mind, and there he was, the maggot eating off a hunk of rot, only to see that it exposed more clean flesh to the elements, serving to catalyse decay.

Heites began to feel sick, the nausea disrupting his balance so he swayed precariously. In reaction, his muscles tensed, and his fingers dug into his palms, wishing to wrap themselves around High Priests Vultai's throat and throttle him, starve him of air, kill his voice, or better still watch him choke on them. He would revel in forcing those malignant words all wrapped up in pestilent breath back down his oesophagus into his bloodstream. Here they would turn his capillaries a rotten brown colour as the words raced through his circulatory system like a flotilla of pirate vessels in search of the hidden dark artefact; his heart. Upon reaching it they would shatter the stone imitation of the organ of compassion, leaving him dead. As he looked at the rapidly decaying face in his imagination, he saw the bulging round face had drooped and wilted, before melting away to leave the gaunt wrinkled face of Zeuorox's that flopped limply before him.

Heites glowered momentarily with satisfaction as though it had just happened.

'Explain that one in terms of martyrdom! – "Grand High Priest found dead in his office – killed by his own lies"' He grinned at that thought.

At that point Pluvius was summoned forward to accept a medal on their behalf. Unsurprisingly he was nervous, all his life he had been brought up to revere his Lord. Even though his respect was waning, and this young zealot held nothing like the respect that Pluvius had felt for the lord's father, he nevertheless respected the position. It was not the person, the attributes of the particular cog, but the utmost position it held that filled Pluvius with awe. As Pluvius reached the lord it was an unprecedented moment; two distant components meeting in total incompatibility.

Pluvius knelt, it was an awkward task in full-scale mail, but nevertheless he achieved it with statuesque precision. Juscius gave him an appreciative nod (though with his head bowed, Pluvius did not see). Pluvius held himself down until his muscles began to stretch and threaten to shake under the strain. He rose just in time, to rise straight up.

They stood face to face.

A nearby servant produced a medal, which was handed to Pluvius. In a quiet voice, Juscius addressed the sergeant.

"Well done Sergeant, your services in these dark times are inspiring. I hear that it was quite a battle –thirty-plus to just thirteen of you... and with so few losses."

He turned to the guests. "Forty-plus enemies killed, to so few lost!"

Most of the guests sat bewildered, except Telis who positively beamed with joy and Adonis who silently surmised, *'clearly forty peasants got holed up in the forests, surrounded and cut to bits. What bravado!'*

Pluvius was sent back and prepared for dismissal. However, before he could call the order, Gatan suddenly asked, "tell me, Lord Latman, those spears look interesting. May I inspect them?"

Juscius looked flustered, though this coincidentally drew attention away from Ruperis' grin and Zeuorox's shielded smirk.

"They are a state secret," the lord declared nonsensically.

"Then why...?" Rabica blurted before stopping in the face of oral competition.

It was Gorax; he spoke with an embittered tone that Gatan had never heard. He spat just one syllable, "whose?"

"What!" Ruperis accidentally blabbed with irritation.

"Whose secret?" Gorax clarified in a demanding tone.

"What do you mean?" Ruperis replied with an innocent offended whine.

Gorax took a deep breath, gritting his teeth. His whole torso tensed, before exhaling to calm himself. When he finally spoke, he did so with such excessive strain that the whole room of guests were on edge.

"I will explain. Those spears resemble a prototype spear/javelin that several Gatanese blacksmiths and I were developing. Recently the stock was seized from the workshop... I had assumed one of the blacksmiths had pocketed them... how did you come to get them?"

To give the inventor the feeling of being surrounded, Ruperis allowed Zeuorox to fire the next shot, his deep solemn voice striking Gorax unsuspecting right ear like the echo of an avalanche. "So you admit these are Gatanese?"

Adonis felt uneasy. Latman would not have blundered into this; the spears were deliberately brought in to be seen by Gorax. With his inventor sinking into the trap, the lord was hesitating about whether he should stride in to save him, or if Gorax was just the bait.

"Of course, why?" the innovator answered with confusion.

The other pincer closed in on the other ear; Ruperis gave the next retort. "And how did they get into the hands of bandits in our territory?" The prey jolted, more in confusion as to why he stood accused than at the news. "What!"

"Why did you give them to bandits? Unless you expect us to believe that they managed to take them from you!" It was Zeuorox's turn. Before he could answer, the main assault came. Gorax had been a feint, and this was addressed to Lord Gatan. "This is outrageous!" Juscius growled, "you come here, to my peace forum..." (Lord Gatan laughed aloud at the phrase) "... is peace that funny to you?"

"Only your idea of it!" Gatan mused.

This only enraged Lord Latman more. "You came here to this banquet, and in the meantime are arming insurgencies in my territory with prototype mass devastation weaponry!"

Rabica could see this was a case of shouting accusations after speculative 'facts' in the belief that the louder you shout the more it makes the spurious links look solid. "Sorry... Why?" He began, before realising he was being ignored. This was no time for listening to rational argument.

"That is preposterous! I had no knowledge of these 'prototypes'... I believe my architect... *he* is an honest man," Gatan bellowed.

"So now you deny you ever had them!" cut in Telis.

"They were unmarked and untraceable... why is that?" Ruperis accused. It was not a question to be answered but a self-standing indictment.

"That is usual for prototypes – bring in any blacksmith and he will back me up." Gorax countered.

"A convenient, if unconvincing, excuse. You gave them to be tested," Zeuorox declared.

Danite was clearly fed up of this farce. "Why would they give these javelins to random bandits? How would they be able to see the results? You would want them to be used by professionals, somewhere that the makers could see them in use."

Zeuorox was disgusted at such intervention. "Are you suggesting that Gatan should have invaded Latman just to test these weapons?" he retorted with a patronising tone of disbelief.

Danite did not even bother to respond.

Not requiring a counter, Zeuorox went on the defensive. "We are merely basing our assertions on what we see."

Lord Lewerix had remained silent, and followed the raging accusations with interest. Though he found the actual topic rather insignificant, it was the manner in which the competing sides were clashing that raised his concern. He decided to add a drop of rationalism to see how they reacted. "Why not ask these good soldiers where the spears came from?"

Ruperis' look told it all. They had not been briefed, and even if they had, could they be assured to say the right thing?

"Do not bring them into it. They are our heroes. If you even dare to accuse them of wrong doing…" Juscius fumed, genuinely angered.

Worried that Juscius had just undermined the efforts to win over the Lewerix ruler, Zeuorox added as a explanatory footnote. "They cannot be asked for security reasons. It is strictly against protocol for them to converse with foreign military leaders… my apologies."

Juscius, who was still angered, managed to calm his temperament to dismiss them. Sergeant Pluvius tried to hide his look of relief at leaving this madhouse.

Once they had gone, Ruperis tried immediately to stop the talks stagnating. Turning to Telis he asked, "do you recall the story about Porthi[1] losing his tools?"

Telis replied in a mimicking mocking tone. "It was not his tools but the lightning bolts he fashioned for Thelus (may his greatness forever enliven us in our quest to do his bidding). He did not lose them, as such… someone lost them for him!"

Ruperis gave a look of mocking shocked terror. "They were stolen?"

"Steal is such a strong word. Indeed an old Telis saying is that a man foolish enough to leave his wares unguarded, cannot be stolen from, he can merely have his possessions liberated!"

"He who deserves and protects shall keep," Ruperis simplified.

Telis winked, "Exactly."

'*There must be chaos in the streets of Ascelp then!*' Rabica mused to himself.

The two continued, and the rest of the table listened with morbid interest. "It's funny anyway, because… well it turns out the 'thief' is

---

[1] The traditional 'blacksmith' god

Hermes, Thelus' messenger!"

"The cheeky sod!" Ruperis declared.

"Was he punished?" Mistress Telis asked, with apparent innocence.

'*Is she in on it too?*' Lady Gatan pondered, her attention rising momentarily before sinking as she concluded '*probably not, anyway she's hardly important*'. Lord Gatan meanwhile, was anxiously squirming in his seat with a surging discomfort. 'M*ock my own actions and the actions of my council, but do not mock the gods*!'

Telis shook his head. "Only slightly – I mean Thelus had to set an example. But that's beside the point… it was only a minor punishment, he still kept his honourable position. What I was thinking of was that the blacksmith was punished and how no one remembers the name of the god of mining." He gave a deliberate glare at Lord Vacarium as he made the second point.

"He really must have been a *minor* god then!" remarked a clearly drunk Master Vacarium.

Rabica almost reached out to catch the tumbleweed as it rolled down the table like a wicker ball, but felt too drained by the idiotic remark, which was made all the worse by the fact the speaker had apparently not noticed, or cared, that his house was at the brunt of the jibe.

Gatan, who had remained painfully silent, was now on the brink of leaving in a storm of utter contempt for the upstart. He had sat through accusations so preposterous they did not need a rebuttal. However, he had a nagging suspicion that the Latman axis were waiting until the end for the most important issues. Lord Gatan thought maybe Lord Latman was planning to wait until the jackals and vulture had chased him off to begin such talks.

Judging by the performances of the other lords, Latman would be able to rubber stamp anything without Gatan there to criticise. Though Lord Danite had impressed Adonis as a man of true grit he knew he would be powerless as a sole power. Meanwhile Vacarium was surprisingly pitiful. After all the reports about the vigour of the north Vaca resistance and its supporters in the Vacarium house suggested a patriotic and fiercely independent people, their leader seemed a wreck. Whatever the state of the people, Gatan reasoned; this lord would not stand long. Even if Lord Latman hadn't thought of taking advantage of this, Gatan could be sure the vulture would have. Whenever Gatan took a look at Lord Vacarium, he could not help but see the beady eyes and hooked beak of the ecclesiastical scavenger peering from behind its hood, observing its prey with an anxious looming hunger. It would break in its watch only to cast a ravenous eye over the barrel of meat that was propped up in a seat between them. It licked its lips at the discovery of that bumbling prey.

Lord Lewerix fared little better in Adonis' eyes. He remained quiet and distant, under the false belief that he could stay out of it all. Still, Adonis felt that when the time came, the Lord's rationality would lead him to the Gatanese side.

Suddenly, as a great shock to them all Lord Lewerix spoke. His input had a bolstering effect on the diplomatic constitution of Lord Gatan. Though he seemed irritated he kept this to a minimum, preferring instead to try and set example with a cold robust request. "Can we please move onto something more significant. I haven't spoken much, but as far as content goes neither have any of you. Lord Gatan, you have something to say?"

Rabica was filled with joy and pride. He almost rose to hug his father, it was that tone that he really admired.

Gatan was somewhat taken aback, but quickly composed himself. "Well, my concern here - and to be honest, I thought all our concerns were - regards maintaining the inter-house order. That is a balance. Such banquets as these could assist in establishing a stable order; a society of states.

Juscius' mouth was open and he was nodding as though to say 'that is what I have been proposing'. However he was not given a chance to speak.

"That does not mean we have to tie our Houses together, we do not need formal rules and structure, we need only accepted conventions; the P's and Q's of diplomacy. If we all work within this framework, we will achieve a much more successful environment for mutual co-operation between rulers. We do not need to share domestic rules and ideals, indeed we can be totally opposed, even at war... but we have rules of engagement, and a responsibility to try and negotiate and broker deals between our neighbours."

Juscius' lit up face had faded down to the level of Zeuorox and Ruperis. Telis soon joined them in glum dissatisfaction.

Nevertheless Gatan continued. "Now, in order to provide fairness – so no one can be ignored nor claim to have been denied a voice - each house should declare what they think of my proposal. – Lord Latman?" Gatan had wanted to ask Telis first, just to see if he could wrangle out what he actually thought.

"Well," Juscius spluttered immediately, as though to give the impression he was launching into a rebuttal. Then he changed his mind and decided to buy more time by muttered snipes at the lord's forceful nature. "First, can I just say how *unconventional* it is for a guest to act like a host ... I thought I was the one making the propositions. Anyway," he returned to the topic with a refreshing grin, "what has been proposed by the honourable gentleman is not particularly ambitious. I would rather see a close knit community arise, a community based on freedom where nations are not held to these primitive conventions but mutually protected by Houses that share common ideals."

Telis opened his mouth to make the verbal equivalent of an obedient nod, but was stopped by Lord Gatan. "Begging you pardon Lord Telis but I wish to inquire. I do not wish to be insulting but though my idea may not be ambitious, yours seems rather vague... could you clarify? – what does 'a community based on freedom' entail?"

Juscius looked annoyed, as though the mere thought of requesting more information was a grave insult to his doctrine. His voice became startlingly defensive. "Look, we can argue all night about this. But, now is not the time for quick answers to supposed quick questions."

'*So they mean nothing then – that is, except adherence to Latman doctrine.*' Gatan confirmed to himself, "Lord Telis, please?"

"Who made you chairman?" Telis protested.
Danite roared with laughter, before growling, "he's giving you a chance to speak and you try and argue with him... come on lad!"

Ruperis and Zeuorox both covered their faces.

Telis tried to hide his embarrassment, but it only made his attempts to disguise his mimicking of Juscius all the more obvious. "Okay, well, I also see the notion as unambitious – I mean don't we already have all that stuff, it's not really building, merely stagnating."

"Right, fine – any questions?" Gatan fired out impatiently. "No. Lord Danite?... Pardon Lord Lewerix, I am merely circulating around..." He wanted Lord Lewerix to go last.

"...No problem" ('*it is best to hear all the others first anyway*' Zenith Lewerix reasoned).

"Given the choice between vague buzz words, and a loose society my money is on the latter."

Gatan was unsurprised, and slightly concerned about the confrontational bi-polarisation, but nevertheless felt it necessary to give the lord an appreciative look.

"'Vague buzz words' really! Look, we can throw accusations at each other all night but..." Juscius protested.

"Well, clarify then!"

Juscius was totally unused to Danite's in-your-face directness and so became flustered like a chicken prodded from her nest, huffing and puffing before launching into a disdainful rant. "I have said, these things cannot be rushed – I cannot say about such things before they are concluded, we must collate then analyse."

It came to Vacarium's turn. The aged skeletal carrion bird lurched into a deep drawl. "I think that a balance would be good and would allow for my household to reassert its control over its own territory. This would allow neighbouring territories to benefit from calmed borders."

No questions came for Vacarium, so the commentary went to Lewerix.

"Having heard what you both have said, and the following statements, I feel we can resolve this best by first hearing more about Lord Latman's proposal. For, as it stands, Gatan's proposal seems more attractive, though this is because it is simplistic and clear – things which are virtues in one camp and vices in the other."

For all his disappointment at Lord Lewerix's refusal to rule out Latman's proposal, Gatan was admiring of the lord's commitment to reason and diplomatic caution. He was convinced these were attributes that would lean him his way.

Reluctantly Juscius began.

"Well, one issue I would raise would be mutual security – that is, that all Houses co-operate on securing borders and assist in stopping clandestine terrorist activity within each other's lands. Mutual security means not having vast invasion fleets for conspicuous purposes, or dealing with, and arming insurgents. Another aspect is freedom of trade, to allow merchants free rein to reap rewards and provide goods for all…"

Gatan sighed. "You see, this is the problem – to you it is 'freeing trade', to us it is economic subordination. To you it is 'mutual security', to us it is tacit consent to the use of repressive tactics on localised groups and the forbidding of others from assisting those brethren who they have sympathies, all to uphold your House's domination."

"Subordination! Domination! You speak in such old fashioned terms! You see, this polar struggle no longer exists. You can benefit from trade with other nations, cross borders."

"How? I have seen tonight how your friend has a company just waiting to export and replace our own traders, but who will buy? Who will buy, if all they produce in order to make money is produced by you?"

Ruperis interjected in the market's defence, with a tone sounding as though he quoted a prophet. "Each will find his niche."

"But those who dominate will take the most profit."

"… and with that, huge amounts of wealth to sustain their advantage," Rabica added.

Juscius sighed patronisingly. "All benefit, should be seen in overall gains, not comparative rates of gain."

"All the rich maybe, but the people will suffer as they are forced to work for less so their landowners or nobles can compete with more advanced foreigners. Some areas' 'niche' is that they have plenty of pitiful souls willing to work for nothing just to survive." Rabica objected. Most remained silent, ignoring his words, though Telis was cocky enough to mock him. "Since when have *they*" (he did not even want to say the word 'people) "been a concern of ours?"

Juscius decided getting into the details of this issue would be 'counter-productive' and so launched into an impressive spiel about its importance in the grander scheme of things.

"Ultimately it is an issue of principles, of the gods, it is about joining a vision of the future or rejecting it and wallowing in a precarious, unsustainable balance. The principles we espouse need more than a loose notion of convention. They need a body with rules of compliance."

"...and how would we be encouraged to comply?" Danite asked cynically.

Yet it was Lewerix who replied, albeit sceptically, reinforcing the idea that the last question was rhetorical, "such a thing needs leadership."

"Exactly!" exclaimed Telis excitedly, clearly not noticing Lewerix's tone.

"So who?" Gatan asked Telis dryly.

Telis mumbled incoherently whilst taking an obvious glance at Juscius Latman, who in turn made an expression of a denial that obviously meant the opposite, before feeling the need to speak. "Well, we would have to see... if equal collective diplomacy needed leadership... or just a chairman ... that is something to discuss later."

"There would need to be some way of promoting similar ideals and principles. You see it is a humanitarian effort bringing us all together. It is also one of spiritual union, requiring the blessing of the gods." Zeuorox declared with uncanny sincerity.

"It will, in other words, require a degree of conformity – we cannot have rogue states behaving outside the law and ethics of the day," Ruperis added.

It was now that Adonis saw it, whether they meant it or not; they were trundling the whole island towards war. He immediately began seeing his policy in terms of delaying in order to build alliances, though a nagging optimism told him that they were bumbling into this and so not prepared, in which case he should catalyse the inevitability.

Adonis could see how all these 'ideals' conflicted with his 'balance'; it was not just in their specific content, but in the idea of ideals itself. A balance incorporated, or at least left room for competing ideals, whereas they sought a unifying ideal. A unifying ideal does not balance, it exists solo. If it does balance, it does so with the resistance to it, and that is something they seek to eradicate.

He decided to put it to the others as he saw it. "So we seem - and this is not to finalise - to have a choice between a collective society separate and governed by loose conventions and a unified society following specific ideals constrained ideologically but empowered through mutual interaction – even if this leads to submission to one."

It was now that Zeuorox realised that Gatan would not back down, and so war was to happen. He grinned to himself discreetly, taking additional pleasure in no one noticing his slip of the mask. Then he embarked on a little quibbling just to nudge them all closer to the edge, the edge that the gods had just shown to him was their will. "I object to the term submission – it implies forced compliance, we merely wish to establish consensus."

Gatan was ready, and calmly countered. "Well, some force must be part of it, because the establishment of consensus without force is my idea, which you say is unambitious."

Zeuorox decided to lighten the pressure for the time being. "We think it takes a long time to beat out a rigid set of rules. Over some issues certain houses may not truly see the longer-term goals and benefits of unity over short-term protectionism."

"Well, there we go," Gatan concluded. "There it is – the choice. Is it not best to leave it at this for the time being?"

He had decided it was best to stall. He would gamble on the support of Danite and Vacarium over the chance to win over Lewerix. This would be a difficult feat, as Zenith was not the sort to get his House caught up in anything beyond his control, but, with a united opposition perhaps he could convince Latman to back down.

Juscius shook his head. "No, you see, the imperative nature of this has not been properly appreciated."

Taken aback, Gatan was instantly trying to read between the lines. '*"imperative" – what does that mean? That he is ready for war now?*'

"What I have proposed is necessary for the effective defence of the realm. These ideals lie in the foundation of a better system that we need to achieve, with enemies on the doorstep. We must unite and spread our sophistication to the lands that Ruperis has discovered in order to stabilise the world and free ourselves of enemies."

"What makes you think they can?" came a cynical remark from Vacarium, raising his head out of the gloomy shadow, glad to be talking of those more unfortunate than his own people.

"If it is not possible then, then they must be administered by our guiding wisdom... but you must remember it is for *our* safety. It will loosen the grip of restraint and terror that plagues us and replace it with a renewed piety that will better act as a beacon."

Of all the accusations and lies Gatan had heard today this went beyond, into mindless rhetoric. As he examined the faces on the three other non-committed lords, he saw exactly the same images of prediction float behind their eyes. Their expressions pre-emptively echoed the world's response: resistance.

Juscius saw the sceptical faces on his audience's faces, then he lashed out angrily. "Don't you see?" his lips trembled as he paused. "You must side with us in our fight to preserve civilisation; failure to do so is failure of duty. Failure of duty is a moral failure, which puts you in the camp of immorality, from which it is easy to slip into the festering slick of inhumanity: evil - the enemy."

"... and this mission you have set yourself..." Gatan pondered aloud.

Juscius gave a quasi-maniacal laugh, that of someone answerable to higher beings than men only. "I assure you this mission comes from much higher than myself. It shall be carried out with whatever coalition is willing to join us."

Gatan just raised his eyebrows, *'Lewerix surely won't have bought any of that... but is he willing to confront it? Whatever, I am not going to find that out here!'*.

"Is that all?" he asked impatiently, already stretching himself ready to vacate.

The others remained awkwardly silent, not daring to voice their approval of Gatan's request. That is, apart from Juscius, who was taken aback with shock, and Telis who in a baffled whine inquired, "so we are to continue discussions on the morrow?"

Gatan was not going to waste another day. "Do you have anything to discuss?"

Telis looked to Juscius as though pleading obediently silently for approval. "Well... this?"

Gatan looked at him with a tired expression. "I do not know about you, but I need more than forty winks to be able to contemplate the proposals." This was actually a lie – he knew already his own position, it was more a matter of discovering and wooing the opinions of the others. What was more, he could tell their plan was to force this through, so the others would accept it just to get him to shut up, without realising they had bought in and could not buy out.

Telis slouched as though beaten back.

Juscius was similarly irritated, though chose not to speak, that is, until Gatan requested that he spoke. "So, host – what are we to do?"

Juscius lazily hid his scowl after a delay of a few seconds before launching into a jovial declaration. "Well, I thought perhaps we could retire for a few hours then I propose a more relaxed festivity."

Ruperis grinned; he would get to show off his exotic prize after all.

It all ended rather quickly, the guests rising from their seats in silent relief. They haphazardly paid tribute to the host before disappearing out of the room, hiding sighs of relief in muffled coughs.

★

The 'night festivities' had stretched the evening out into a tense tightrope which the lords and sons desperately tried to become enraptured with. Each twirl of a dancer, each note of a trumpeter signalled the slow winding on of time. They sat in silence, trying to convince themselves, and each other, that they were so wrapped up in the festivities they could not spark up a conversation.

Lord Gatan had tried on numerous occasions to talk with Lewerix but always found himself perturbed by the hawkish swooning of Zeuorox, who lingered nearby flitting from place to place observing them like a watchful buzzard. He had managed to extract Lewerix's disapproval of Latman's idea, though he seemed uncommitted to resistance. All of this had been made using extreme use of implicit analogy and so he had found it very hard to point out that neutrality could lead to Latman's victory. He also tried to get across assurances that he had no such ambitions himself, though both knew that such a large conflict would have massive repercussions whoever the victor. Lewerix then insinuated that a prolonged conflict could justify his intervention if it were to tip the balance in a direction favourable to Lewerix, that being one of overall stability.

This took a long time as the two veteran diplomats meandered in and out of this vital topic and other more casual ones in order to leave the lingering spectator none-the-wiser to the content. Their conversing was brought to an abrupt halt when one set of dancers finished and a new band entered with much bravado. This suggested the grand finale was about to begin.

Even Mistress Telis and Torian Delvinius had ceased their previously incessant gossiping. Equally Lady Gatan broke off her 'Lady-like' conversing with Lady Lewerix and intuitively began discretely searching for any hidden event that she should be wary of.

Suddenly all the torches were blown. In the darkness, Adonis immediately feared it was a trap and reached for his sword.

A group of fleet-footed people could be vaguely heard scrabbling onto the dance floor to lay what sounded like a large metal bowl or cauldron in the centre. Once the noises had dissipated two soldiers entered carrying torches. Their flames burnt slowly with a dark orange flicker, flaring up as though seeking to entice and hypnotise the darkness that enveloped them. Riding on the red glow of embers they licked the coal blackness.

Between the two towering beacons of light swaggered a svelte figure; its movement was strangely ethereal and feminine. None of the guests had seen anything like it before. She stood just taller than the two escorting guards; even their plumes failed to rival her hair which was funked out into a near perfect sphere of fuzzy black cotton wool. Her skin was so dark that it hid in its own shadow, though was so shiny (she had been covered with perfumed oil to increase the effect) that patches gleamed with waves of light that rippled across her perfectly smooth skin as she moved.

The audience could trace the shape and course of her body by plotting the movements of these streaks of light, staring eagerly as the light bent and stretched around curves revealing the shapeliness. The males who watched did so hungrily, shivering collectively as a slash of such reflection slid across her smooth stomach, shifting slightly only to caress her belly button; a black narcissus in the centre of a silky shiny plateau.

Her face had striking large white eyes, that eclipsed the rest of her face as it hid in the shadows and was backed by her mighty halo-esque mane. What little they saw of her face was totally alien, and so enticing precisely because of this attribute. Her cheeks were two mounds of bulging flesh resting pertly around her lips.

The music had started the moment she had entered. Various instruments plucked awkwardly to give a strained, eerie, mystical sound. It drew them into a trance, staring at her, drained of all consciousness. Their hearts pounded to the rhythm of the thunderous, deathly slow drumbeat.

As she approached the cauldron she flung out her arm as though gesturing to it (though she actually threw something in) and it exploded into a red fire. Her whole face and supple body was illuminated. An expressionless countenance, utterly enticing for its powerful self-control. The audience could only wonder what passions hid behind the sleek self-styled mask. The darting whites of her eyes hinted at extensive raw power behind these emotions. Her body (and the music with it) had exploded around the cauldron, swaggering towards each of the men in turn.

Her clothing was minimal but (some would say ergo) striking; she wore a gold threaded loin cloth seductively tied at the side with skimpy gold ribbon and a matching bikini top; similarly mere ribbon held it together. It resembled a curious decoration more than an item of clothing, all clinging to the skin so as not to disturb the revealing of the shapes.

Adonis Gatan, like most of the men in the room thought he was dreaming, indeed he was soon totally engulfed in a reverie-like stare as his eyes followed her about the room. His sons were equally seduced, indeed Maximus had forgotten Mistress Telis in an instant. Even Lords Lewerix and Vacarium failed to hide charmed smiles. Lord Danite guffawed crudely, though was outdone in sickening virility by Vacarium's son. The sluggish pig sat drooling, making no attempt in his drunken state to be discreet. Ruperis was grinning, though this was mainly out of self-appreciation at being the provider of the Lord's wonder.

Mistress Telis sat blushing and giggling, pretending to avert her eyes, a brittle façade to hide her jealousy. Torian was having none of it, and sat arms crossed, glaring at Juscius (who was totally transfixed), pausing only momentarily to scowl disapprovingly at her younger brother. Lady Gatan looked on with wonder, admiring the way the 'creature' (*'yes, it is a creature, isn't it dear?'*) had captivated the men (especially her man), but also disdainful of its apparent lack of intellect and finally, and, more honestly, envious of its body.

Lady Lewerix was amused, though this was to cover her embarrassment at the lack of clothing (costumes usually being her priority when observing a performance). She had tried examining the dance techniques (*'they are very... you know...'*), before succumbing to the primordial prejudice and amusement at the strangeness of the girl's form.

Now we come to Rabica (Maritha had not attended). At first he had been intrigued, his eyes desperately piercing the darkness, but as soon as he saw the form in any detail he recoiled, self-repulsion setting in. He wanted to look away, even though he was transfixed. He wanted to run off and stop staring at her, but he also wanted to rush up to her and take her away from this demeaning parade. But his eyes had already become tainted.

Predictably he began to think of The Young Lady. He imagined her in white, an angelic figure, he imagined her normally – just the thought of her face conjured up so many ideals, it was a symbol of such personal beauty.

'*I must resist this abomination, this moral death trap*' he repeated to himself over and over, before adding, '*and that abomination is consequent of my mind and a responsibility of me, not this being who dances before me.*'

He heard Vacarium's son, the blubbery mound of sweaty red flesh flopping out in podgy rings, turn to Ruperis. "Don't have any more of these do you? Quite fancy one myself!... How much for her?"
Then Danite chipped in, "you can take my kingdom," he jested.

Ruperis grinned; the merchant had a sudden thought. Supply and demand resonating in his avaricious mind, his one little iron law had enabled him to grip anyone in his iron vice.

Rabica, if he did not hear, could ascertain from the sickening grin that broke out on the fat lips and undulated through the blubbery jowls, what was said. Utter abhorrence soon overcame him, resonating through his trembling skin. His cursed brain began wandering in self-induced torture as it implanted images into his mind of the repugnant scene that the bloated pig now dreamt of: the svelte beautiful black figure that danced before them being engulfed in a sea of blubbery lord-flesh. The fatty meat seemed to melt as it folded around, slowly restricting and strangling her as it gripped her in place for its glutinous sexual satiety.

He felt a stirring bitter resentment for his gender, his own attraction condemning him to their baseness. His own feelings shied away, shyly shrinking to the pitiful worm that they were, nursing its mortally-wounded confidence. In a vain attempt to compensate he gave the slave girl an innocent smile, an expression neither seen, nor, had it been seen, understood.

With discomfort rising, Rabica's mind wandered onto a tangent to take his mood from the scene.

'*I wonder if She will reply to my letter?*' he pondered to himself.

An air of tranquillity passed over him as he began to contemplate her, and her possibly reply. His mind drifting off dreamily, subconsciously he revelled in his escape from the real world and the perverse chaos that surrounded him.

★

When her dance finally finished she stood pouting with a lust-inducing exhaustion before daintily fleeing, as they all traced her flight from the passage of her eyes, which disappeared half way as her head turned away. Just before her exit the beady pearls flashed in the direction of Juscius.

Immediately all the torches were lit. The entire audience was still reeling from the spectacle they had just witnessed.

Juscius, whose heart had been beating with an excessive intensity throughout the dance (something he attributed to her spirituality), had stopped frozen when his eyes met her glance. He found it hard to look upon Torian, who now squeezed his hand delicately in a request for affection.

Instead he surveyed his guests. In part he was pleased by their impressed faces, but he could not help but feel jealous of them for having seen her. He was deeply disgusted by their barely-concealed lustful expressions. He managed to bury this abhorrence before it became anger by pitying them in their degenerate states, '*Could they not contain the voice of their loins and see the spiritual attraction?*'

Oh how he desired her more than anything... anyone... spiritually, of course!

Vacarium's son mumbled something drunkenly incoherent and was ignored. It was Danite who rose first. "Well, Lord Latman, where do I get me one of them?"

The others laughed. Juscius just glowered disdainfully.

"Forget that, how do I get there!" Telis declared, hoping to mimic Danites machismo.

For once Danite set aside his dislike of the sycophantic pup. "Yeah, bring 'em, all over here – give each of us some, and we'll never have to worry about fighting again – we'll all be too busy."

Ruperis sat quietly, smugly grinning to himself and taking mental notes *'oh this may just be a most propitious venture... still it needs an injection of capital first... from the weapons.'* His mind was racing, formulating his new entrepreneurial plot; *'I will need a partner to run the institutions though...'*

Gatan attempted to retain his dignity. "Thank you, Lord Latman, Mr. Delvinius, that was a most interesting set of dances, it may have even made my trip worth it!" he declared dryly. It was supposed to be a joke but flopped dangerously into truth. He then turned to his sons to indicate that they were to vacate.

Juscius noticed this and quickly declared. "There is one last thing, my scribes have documented our agreements if we could all take one and sign the original..."

"I'll take a copy, we can sign in the morning," Adonis corrected. Juscius' mouth opened in protest but was halted by the echoing totality of Gatan's statement.

"I am leaving terribly early, would it not be easier to..." Adonis had noticed that Zeuorox had given Telis a discreet signal, and so, upon knowing it was part of a scheme, cut him off with an air of finality.

"I am sure we all are... but if *you* will find it easier, then go ahead and sign now. However, I am not signing now."

"But... we should all sign together..." Telis quibbled weakly.

"We are all here as witness..."

"But how will I know if you all have signed?"

"Then you'll have to stay," Gatan growled.

"But..."

Lord Lewerix intervened, clearly fed up of the whinging persistence of Telis. "No, look, I'm not signing now either, nor should we argue about it now. We should look it over ...I highly doubt if you have such pressing matters to attend to as to have to rush this."

Telis, upon realising that he was hindering the cause by irritating Lewerix, fell silent.

Within moments the parchments were brought out. Gatan took a brief look;

Security is a collective effort; united vigilance will be promoted and enforced by all houses against the barbarian threat.

Immediately he noted that the term 'barbarian' was too ambiguous and could be used to include any group (Gatan had in mind the mountain people) and so would have to be replaced with 'Baresark'.

Trade should be free and unhampered, guided by market forces alone.

Adonis could not help shaking his head, '*must be Ruperis' little incentive for support – it should be "promoted" not "free and unhampered"*'

Domestic conflicts remain issues of the given house, and none should interfere directly without seeking council of all the houses.

'Hmm. This must relate to north Vaca... but at least it stops Latman from interfering in Vacarium.'

Houses should agree to a freeze on military expansion – figures to be established at a later date. This includes naval vessels owned by the Houses.

'*Well, I will stop the boat building anyway'* Adonis conceded.

Religious freedom is essential and priests are considered neutral therefore granted special status free to cross borders unhampered.

Adonis frowned, not recalling this being discussed at all. '*This is was clearly a way to allow New Interpretation missionaries to spread into other territories. Yet it was phrased in such a way that it will look oppressive to refuse. By encasing it in the guise of religious freedom, I cannot oppose it. It must be the genius of Zeuorox.*' He concluded before adding, '*perhaps I can add a clause about allowing Houses to eject priests if suspected of subversion or something*'

Under this was a large space for each signature. Juscius had been eyeing the others eagerly, impatiently awaiting their first thoughts. Gatan spoke first, but as he did so rose to leave to signify he would not elaborate. "I can see there will need to be amendments."

Latman clearly wanted to inquire but was restrained by the realisation that it would be improper and, more crucially, unfruitful.

"Well, I think it's fine," Telis announced emphatically.

Claudix, who was just at the doorway, turned and threw him a tired look. "Well, sign now then, your Lordship," he said, before exiting with beleaguered fatigue.

★

The next morning was a hasty affair. Adonis had spent the night trying to ponder over the clauses but as he did so became increasingly indifferent. Only his desire for a free rein and the status quo kept him interested, though he knew realpolitik would continue as normal and these rules could serve only as empty tools for political gain. Only the priest clause worried him, and he was confident his spies would keep an eye on any suspicious wanderers, plus he knew his own people, who were so full of the Latman-Gatan rivalry they would never accept the new doctrine.

Barbarian was changed to Baresark, though Juscius instantly remarked that it was merely academic. The trade clause was weakened though in Ruperis' eyes 'trade promotion' was basically the same thing. One thing remained consistent; the lords left with little idea what this document they now all had actually was.

Chapter 19
Shelob

Despite his exhaustion, Heites could not sleep. Hazy images of Brother Visuvius materialised before him in the utter darkness like partially completed brass rubbings that melted away with eerie disintegration.

The squad had been allowed an extra day in Lateria, to get a taste of its culture and 'absorb its patriotic air' as a reward for their service. They had traipsed lazily around the markets. People stared at them; somehow they knew they were not from the city, even before they spoke. Heites had felt he despised all the city dwellers, they all seemed so unexplainably contented, gossiping and giggling with an air of collective superiority. In their big metropolis they got 'the big picture', because they thought they were the big picture. Everywhere else was somewhere along the line of catching up with them. To Heites, these people would have more in common with residents of Telias or even Ateri than town folk and villagers.

The others had at least attempted to be more positive, trying to haggle over goods that seemed horrendously overpriced, though they soon got fed up of being mocked for their persistent requests for lower prices.

Heites could remember very little that actually happened, just a general feeling of being surrounded by a fine-clothed, fat-pursed rot. Throughout the whole day he was constantly reminded of Lord Latman's speech, and how it sounded just like Vultai.

The confirmation of his suspicions was quite a pyrrhic victory, but at least he knew what he had to do: to continue his rebellion. The only way to save the Latman house was to take out the High Cleric, the architect of the New Interpretation. Increasingly, he found Visuvius' face slip into the shadows and be replaced at the forefront of his mind by

Zeuorox. Somewhere in the darkness lay his comrades, and he was forever fearful that the shabby ghost would materialise within them.

As he tried to assess the likeliness of succeeding, the brass rubbing haze of the split-skull monk was mocking him, that even his success in eradicating its body had only given his enemies a propaganda weapon.
'But they would not be able to cover this one up, and besides, without him the whole machine would break down,' he told himself.

'But can I face another ghoul haunting me?' he asked himself, with a pleading look into the pitch black.

He gave a snarl at the mottled image that drifted before him, before spitting at it. *'I shall not be rendered impotent by phantoms!'*

The image wafted in the stale breeze like a nearby cloud, disdainful in its ignorance of his ranting.

He smelt wax and was reminded of the candles that had lain dormant in the tent. *'Even in death he had squandered luxury items: what a humble servant of Thelus!'* Again, his mind conjured up an image of the new nemesis: Zeuorox. *'How many candles are you burning now? What are they scented with?'* His random speculation became an accusation as he begged the image for an answer, spitting out the question with bitter contempt as though it was the crux of his altercation with the High Priest. Anger surged within him. In order to preserve his free action he must up the stakes.

Heites tried to boost his self-confidence. He had acted as a free agent, he told himself, and felt the guilt that was the accompaniment of such responsibility. This was why it tortured him. It was not that what he had done was so bad, but that it was an action he had actually decided upon. It was the guilt of the first act of freedom.

He groped about under his blanket in search of the knife he had stashed away, knowing tonight was the only chance he would have to do what was necessary to keep his rebellion alive. It was either plunge the knife in further or allow the inexorable tide of the social order wash over what he had done, and turn it into a negligible dip in the ocean. To back down now would be worse than admitting defeat; it would be letting them use his actions to further the very thing he sought to hamper. This was no longer about a battle of morals, but a battle for the recapturing and revitalising of his humanity. Once he had that, then he could use it for good.

Heites suddenly became conscious of his surroundings, which despite the appearance of an empty void, was actually occupied by the rest of his squad, any of whom could be awake and have heard his thoughts as they slipped out in whispered sneers. He did all he could, and froze still, as though his silence now would be distributed back in time to muffle noises of the past.

All the while, his mind raced with a confusing triple pondering; about the task to be done, that already done, and the infuriating outcome of that task. As his hand crawled like a scorpion amongst the blanket and straw mat in search of steel, an irrational panic overcame him. Had it been found? Had one of his 'comrades' taken it off him to stop him? Were guards waiting outside?

He froze still, closing his eyes. Though it made no difference to his view, it did rest his eyelids, spreading a soothing sensation through his skull and into his brain. He focused on the task at hand, reminding himself of the withered vulture who had sat over the table like the embodiment of famine.

Even though Zeuorox had barely said a word, Heites knew Juscius Latman's words had been his. The veteran was unable to blame the Lord for the words he spoke, deciding they were ones put into his mouth in the same way that he himself was commanded to make sword strokes.
'I will be freeing him,' he told himself, with unnoticed delusion, *'and once he is freed from these controlling bodies and the other people who seek to corrupt his power perhaps he can begin to make a difference for the better.'*

His mind was made up, and with a calm slide of the arm he found his fingertips touch the dagger hilt. The feeling of the steel vanquished his fear that it had been discovered, but having such an insidious weapon clasped in his hand made him queasy.

Tightening his grip, and sliding so he sat upright, he paused momentarily to try to detect any noise that would suggest another was awake. All he could hear was the ghostly whistle of a draught squeezing through cracks and winding round passageways to dissipate in the rooms into an invisible chill.

Not satisfied with the silence, he found himself taking the opposite view. *'Is it not too quiet? Shouldn't I be able to hear their breathing?'*

The vacuum-like silence instantly reminded him of the fateful tent and its now deceased inhabitant. He shivered suddenly. For a moment the idea that he was actually in the tent passed through his mind.

"Of course, this time perhaps I shall have to be caught, so they do not accuse someone else..." he told himself in a whisper.

Without another thought he slowly brought himself to his feet, wobbling slightly as the lack of light disoriented him. He held the dagger tucked up his sleeve as he shuffled forwards with cautious anxiety. Now, all he could hear was his breathing, an onerous rhythm of inhalations and exhalations that made him feel unnaturally claustrophobic in the seemingly endless blackness. The darkness swooped in around him, a void of nothingness condensing itself into a thick tar. His every movement reverberated through the globule, shifting momentarily, then returning to its old shape whenever he paused.

Suddenly, Heites was thrust out of his world of lonesome creeping as a hand brushed past, then grabbed his leg. His heart raced and almost leapt out of his body, thumping erratically against his rib cage.

He heard a familiar voice whisper to him. "Heites! Don't!"
Turning to face the direction of the noise, he groped forwards trying to find his sergeant. Pluvius was obviously still lying down as the arm had come out at a low angle.

Reluctantly, Heites let himself crouch down, his knees bending inwards as he sank like a capitulating building. "What are you talking about?" he mumbled, with unconvincing ignorance.

His eyes grappled with mirages of grey to try and make out a shrouded silhouette of Pluvius. His mind toyed with shifting patches, trying to conjure an image of the sergeant's form.

Nevertheless, the actual location of his comrade remained unknown. "Heites, do not start that! I know. I could see how you looked at the High Priest."

Heites lowered his head and screwed up his face dismissively. However, in the darkness his expression went unnoticed. Pluvius continued anyway, clearly not expecting a rebuttal. "I know what you did... to the Brother..."

Heites perked up, startled in an instant, and as a gut reaction spat a doubtful query. "*Know?*"

Pluvius sighed, though irritated by the superfluous question he was at least glad to hear his friend had retained his sharp meticulousness. "Ok, I may not know for definite, but..."

Now paranoia set in again. "Is it that obvious? Who else knows?"

Pluvius gasped and shrugged in the complete darkness, but before he could answer, Heites continued his questioning. Pluvius began to feel he was standing invisible before one of Heites' soliloquies. "Can they be trusted? Can you be trusted? ... Can I? Can I trust you... hmm?"

The sergeant felt that he was not actually being addressed now, and that Heites was talking to a Pluvius in his head. Nevertheless, he could not allow himself to be silent audience to his friend's mental demise.

"Heites, you *know* you do not need to ask such a question... but do not go on with this next stage..."

"Why not? If it is to be my end, then so be it, it is my choice, my reaction to their control... do you not see, do you see this as something so bad?"

Pluvius sensed a quivering uncertainty that was rare in a man like Heites. "Do you?"

With a cold voice he uttered a reply. "For once I shall act significantly as an independent force... so I am wholly responsible, ergo I am guilty. It is a sacrifice I shall make to free another." He spoke speedily as though it all made complete sense and hardly needed explaining.

Pluvius' mind raced to combat the veteran's argument. "But what makes you think this will solve the problem? You want to rebel against their killing, but that is what you are doing."

Heites smiled toothily. "It is not the killing I object to, but the killing of innocents and pawns..."

Pluvius knew he had to be sympathetic. "And that is why you feel guilt for Visuvius, because he was a still a pawn..."

Heites beamed, ecstatic that he was understood without having to mention the gory details. "Yes!" Then his voice turned solemn and pleading, as he was reminded of the guilt that so held his freedom of action to ransom. "But, what can I do except utilise my profession in this struggle?"

"You did what you thought was right..."

"No!" Heites spat with self-disgust. "Emotion pushed me over the edge to do it ..."

Pluvius could not understand why Heites was so disdainful of himself for not murdering on instinct. "So?"

Heites was unusually willing to explain, the pressure clearly getting to him. "So, I was not able to do it as a rational and morally justified act." Pluvius still did not understand and instantly thought of Julia as the ideal counsellor.

Heites could tell he was not being understood, gave an impatient sigh, then decided to move onto the task at hand. "Last time I was freeing myself, this time it is another... it is the only way to get his Lordship out of this madness."

Pluvius still felt uncomfortable hearing people speak of Lord Juscius Latman in such a way, and found himself instinctively burying his own doubts. "We cannot interfere in such a thing. Whatever our qualms, the best we can do is manage our own affairs..." He seemed to be getting uncontrollably irate. "And I think I have given you leeway to do that... but this goes too far... you could just make matters worse. Besides, we need you, and if you step out there you will go to gaol even if you do succeed."

Heites laughed. "I must try... do my bit."

Pluvius shook his head, his neck stubble scratching against his vest. "You will get nowhere. Just listen to yourself, you're in no state to do such a thing. What use is wasting your life on such a hopeless idea?"

"It is a once in the life time opportunity," Heites protested dreamily.

"An impossible plan is not an opportunity, it is a trap," Pluvius declared succinctly.

"True…" he mumbled ponderously.

Pluvius was not sure that Heites was convinced. "It will be a waste of life and effort… even if you must do such things, this is not the time. Don't just charge in there… you don't even know where in the palace to go!"

"But…" Heites began. However, he fell instantly silent as Pluvius grabbed his arm and pushed him around. Surrounded by complete darkness was a slit of orange-yellow light at about ground level. A low-lying beam scattered across the stone floor like rocks lining to a volcanic channel.

Without saying a word to Pluvius, Heites crept towards the side of the door, careful not to place his foot in the light's path. He had the dagger ready, but still concealed under his long vest.

There was a quiet double-knock on the door. They were discreet noises, ones which one could mistake for pretty much any mundane accidental noise if there were not a lit lantern beaming through the crack under the door. Heites crept towards the door cautiously, even though it was pretty obvious that the visitor was not a threat, judging from their lack of stealth. Even without the lingering unease from his freshly abandoned mission, Heites had become obsessively distrustful of anything out of the ordinary.

'*They may be making themselves obvious so we drop our guard, thinking them not a threat*' he reasoned as he unlatched the door and stepped back to allow them to open the door.

Briskly, but unthreateningly, a burly middle-aged man entered and closed the door. He wore studded leathers with an unrecognisable symbol on them; from the design the two soldiers quickly deduced it was for cavalry. He nodded in traditional greeting to them both, then without an introduction whispered in a deep voice. "I have come with a message for Sergeant Pluvius, from Mercenary Captain Dummonius."

Pluvius had heard various rumours about the sudden resignation of Dummonius, but this came as quite a shock. He had almost been swayed by Heites' cynical proclamations that the Captain had been silently bumped off.

"Mercenary Captain?" Pluvius whispered in dismay.

The messenger gave a brief look of confusion before muttering as though taking a personal notification. "So they were not told. A message was supposed to be passed onto you…"

Heites, still suspicious, began firing questions. "So you know Captain Dummonius? How?"

To Pluvius' relief the messenger did not take offence and continued in a calm gruff voice. "I am part of his mercenary force. I cannot offer you any proof, if that is what you require. He had asked a trusted soldier in the garrison to pass on the information, but we can only assume he was *dissuaded.*"

Pluvius immediately thought of Sergeant Maxilies. He had been one of the senior and extremely trustworthy soldiers, but was now tetchy and submissive. It was likely that Vultai would have suspected an attempt to communicate with Pluvius, and coerced Maxilies not to do so. He could read Heites' mind from his expression – he had been right when he had emphasised the 'coincidence' that Dummonius had gone whilst they were away.

"Captain Dummonius... become... a mercenary..." Heites mumbled, astonished, unable to hide his in-built contempt for the dogs of war.

The mercenary flinched irritably at the use of the term, and his equation with it. Clearly uncomfortable with this association, he felt a need to explain his fall. "I was part of the Varyle 6th Horse Archers, they've been offering retirements for veterans if they join company contractors as security. Well a load of us left... for one reason or another, and some went with one of our captains. But your captain was alone and so hired some of us... 'cos there's no point being a mercenary captain without troops." There was a short pause, in which his mind seemed to reminisce over the past days of glory. "Anyway, I can't stay any longer. He wishes to tell you that although he has a contract to leave in the next couple of days he should be back in a month and be ready to take you and your men on under his command should you desire. To be honest I am surprised you were not given the offer of retirement like the rest of us..."

Pluvius wasn't; they couldn't ask the 'old guard' of Gorad because they were most of the troops. Also, he could not help but feel himself being driven into Heites' paranoid ideas of victimisation; that their squad was being singled out.

"How do I contact you?" Pluvius asked.

The soldier was already looking anxious over the amount of time he had been present and quickly answered, at the same time reaching into a pocket in the upper breast of his armour. "You should come and find us at the private security barracks near the merchant quarter..." Having retrieved the rolled up parchment, he handed it to Pluvius. "Take this... if you encounter opposition to retirement or access to the barracks show this to the appropriate authority."

Silently and obediently, Pluvius took the parchment and without a second glance tucked it away in a pocket in his trousers.

Immediately the messenger bid them both good night and departed with a solemn silence. With his back turned and lantern obscured from view his broad shoulders were like a silhouetted plateau adorned with a round squat boulder of a head in the centre. The outline that walked away in ethereal serenity was that of a generic veteran soldier, its silence despite its build merely enhancing its phantasmal aura.

Once the door had been closed and the fading crack of light under the door had dissipated, Pluvius turned to where Heites had been.

"Well I never... a mercenary captain!" Pluvius whispered. Even though he now saw his own profession as merely a mistakenly glorified version of the very same, he could not help but feel ingrained contempt for the lowly occupation.

He heard Heites grunt cynically, knowing that he thought exactly what Pluvius found himself seeking to deny.

"What do you make of the proposition?" Pluvius continued.

Heites grunted again before adding, "we need to see that parchment... what makes their job so important as to mean they can get us out?"

Pluvius began to fumble for a candle he kept stashed for emergencies. In the meantime Heites' mumbling continued in the background. "Its stinks of a trap..." He was saying, drifting between the present and rational and the speculative abstract, "hurry up and find that candle," adding, "I don't mean that Dummonius is part of it, but it's a set up."

There was a flash of sparks as Pluvius grappled with the flints; the spark illuminated their pupils. The flash was too brief to see anything. Within moments the candle was flickering and the room became startlingly well lit by just one tower of light. They both knelt by Pluvius' straw mattress and the sergeant unrolled the paper.

Instantly they recognised one of the symbols as the one on the messenger's tunic. Next to it, and much larger was another emblem, underneath it was written Delvinius Merchant Logistic Security. The words of the letter mentioned something about this company and Sergeant Pluvius' squad.

"Delvinius!" Heites spat, unexpectedly loud. "That's the one with something to do with those spears! This is really fishy... that fishy smell of bait."

Pluvius on the other hand was thinking about how this Ruperis Delvinius was close to the Lord and so to be part of this company would be safe and could keep them from getting caught in the internal battle raging within the military. It could even get them out of fighting in the increasingly impending war. At least, away from the Latman-Gatan border. Plus, he would be under the command of someone he could trust. "I don't know. I mean if it's genuine we could be safe... all of us."

Heites spat in disgust. "I'm amazed, Sergeant, you can do such a thing, just walk out on all that service... all those comrades not in the squad!"

Pluvius immediately thought of Julia.

"I would never walk out on her!" He bit back to his own surprise.

The sliver of the surviving old Heites grinned at hearing his sergeant say such an unexpected thing, but it was short-lived. "I don't think, sergeant, that you comprehend my predicament. I cannot just march out of the garrison and into mercenary work... this is not about military prestige ... something I thought you would care more about... but my own principles. I do not intend to just 'survive'." He paused, trying to control the volume of his rage. "And my principles certainly won't allow me to work for Delvinius!"

Hearing his companion flare up again, Pluvius' main concern was to calm him in case he began to rethink his 'task at hand' so he decided to be submissive and try to get Heites to go back to his mattress.

"Heites, this is no time to argue this, I need sleep, and you need it too." Pluvius had put on his authoritative, 'this is final' voice, one he very rarely used on Heites, and so he was rather surprised, and relieved, when it worked.

★

The day had been long and Juscius Latman was relieved to be in the comfort of his private quarters. The scented torches blossomed with an acrid but soothing aroma that caressed his itching, and numbed his senses.

He collapsed into the soft chair that sat like a motionless cloud by his bed. However, the supportive fluffy hug from this piece of furniture had to be abruptly ended before it could swamp him in an unassailable lagoon of lethargy that would be too comforting to resist. As soon as the Lord had felt the tingling sensation of replenishing strength, he shot upright, stood ceremoniously then took three paces towards the rug that had been placed before a banner of Thelus. He knelt, bowing his head as he did so, with one knee on the rug.

On the rug was a mystical pattern of stars and crescent moons with white and yellow stitched cherubs and nymphs dancing merrily around the edges. The lord took one brief humble glance at the banner of Thelus pinned up proud on the wall opposite him. His head soon shrank down in a lengthy prayer.

The room was exceptionally dark. Torches were placed only where necessary; this was decided upon by strict celestial necessity, rather than for visual support.

Two white candles sat long and thin beside the banner of Thelus. They stretched up tall from a small altar. At their feet a puddle of wax resembled outstretched roots of white wax trees.

The two other sources of light were torches. These were always mixed with substances that Zeuorox concocted. Today they flickered with a red and green smoke respectively, the swarms of colour mingling in the middle of the room in a maroon haze before drifting as one thick miasma towards the chimney.

Juscius took a brief glance behind him, satisfied with what he saw. The torch flames themselves were minimal. Tongues of red or green tinged flames licked around the rim with brief nervous flickers, any large displays of light being hidden in the tainted cotton wool smoke.

In such minimal light, none of the many patriotic portraits and banners could be seen. The fluffy chair was illuminated, its white tainted by the light, but its hair gleamed nevertheless. Its luminous coat made it look like an ethereal mammal-spectre. To Juscius it was his comforting angel. Beside it was the much less impressively lit bed, the white sheet draped over it revealing its form in the darkness. The sheet was distorted into a strange ill-shapen blob as its corners were distorted by the corners of the four-poster trailing. The bronze posts gleamed dully with promise of resolute but unappealing privacy. Indeed to Juscius it seemed like a trap. Why would he want a cloth screen to conceal him from his room, his paternal banner of Thelus and his maternal fluffy seat? That wide motherly guardian floating beside him, protecting him and keeping itself known to him through its illumination.

This was all that the room contained; enough for its two functions, sleeping and praying.

The room possessed two doors. One was situated on Juscius' right, on the same wall as the short end of the bed, and it was adjacent to the torch, level with the middle of the rug. It was approximately two yards from the corner, where the wall met the other wall with the Thelus poster. This door was the entrance. Opposite, but not parallel, was the poorly concealed 'servant's door', which led into the private quarters from the personal servant's quarters, which had just that afternoon been taken up by the slave girl.

The lord's prayers reached their peak, his voice whispering the lyrical chants, the words sprayed out in a frothy stream of syllables, which seemed to slosh about his ears as though in an alien language. His eardrums were so concentrated on blocking any distractions that any other noises became lost in the sea of words as they clashed against the deluge of incoherent utterances. With his concentration so locked, he did not hear the slave girl's rustling; intrigue had led her to peer into the room through the secret door.

Evidently she could not sleep with his mystical noise emanating out of sight but within earshot. She felt the unease develop into an exhilarating prurience towards this estranged lord. Like an inverted snake-charming act, the hissing noise aroused the enchantress into a writhing dance towards the culprit. Ritualistically, she closed down her senses and moved with the sound, swaying her hips with voluptuous power. Once into the rhythm, the dance was in full swing, unstoppable.

In long graceful swaggers she dreamily crept over to him. Her eyes flashed with every stretch of his lips. Her otherwise staunchly-clenched lips trembled whenever his tongue momentarily slipped out of his mouth mid-sentence.

He soon noticed her, glancing from side to side, trying to mask his fearful look at her with similar movements in other directions. As she approached closer and closer she could tell his nerves were frayed.

Then, like an ice-breaker barge she surged forwards, ploughing through the thick shield of air that was his personal space. He sped up, hoping this would send her away, yet the faster he spoke, the more his contorted mouth spat out the words sending his tongue on longer expeditions, heightening her hunger.

She stood in front of him. His bowed head rose up to be confronted by her scant loincloth. Quickly and clumsily he rose to his feet, shifting his eyes with furtive unease, trying to not look at her.

Her long slender arms gleamed with a reflective shimmer; horizontal mimics of the bronze bedposts. They stretched out slowly and clasped him below the armpit. Attentively he turned his head to face her, his eyes setting their sights on her smooth neck. Her concentration on him was undeterred.

Juscius was petrified. She slid her long arm under his tunic, grasping his soft, baby-like, skin, somewhat viciously. Yet her face showed no obvious sign of enjoyment; her facial muscles did not even make the slightest twitch or contortion: She was in control, not just of herself, but of him also. The power was externalised, the enjoyment entirely internalised; none of the fiery heat was lost in betraying it to the world.

Her grasping ceased. His battered and wavering resolve capitulated. Her hands slid out of his tunic. Like a drugged drone, he clumsily fumbled with his buttons. She stopped his bumbling autonomy by grabbing his hands and sliding them around her waist. All actions had to be either hers or under her supervision. The subject could not attempt independent action, for it upset the power hierarchy, and ruined the fluidity.

Whilst he jerked and spasmed in feeble attempts to regain self-control and break off the encounter, she removed her top. The skimpy material fell to the floor, flittering down and lying like a crushed butterfly sprawled out on the rug.

Juscius stared nervously at the spectacle before him, longing to cease his resistance but managing to cling onto his self-restraint and the tattered remains of his dignity. The petrified Lord's hands began to shake and seize-up, meaning they clasped onto the girl's waist even tighter.

Juscius felt the sickening feeling rise further within him. He glanced about the room, seeking out the light to protect him, but the flickering fires were no comfort; their hellish heat served only to mimic the betrayal he was sliding into. Was he wrong? Was this a fiery demoness sent to destroy him? Intent on ruining his love for Torian? Perverting him into a lustful decadence, a gluttonous desire for hellish sweat?

For she sweated most profusely now, and he knew sweat was devilish[2].

He longed for his comforting chair to hover before him and drive her away. Panic overwhelmed his senses and he attempted to flee, stumbling in the half-light. He failed miserably, merely entangling himself more with her; he mumbled an apology whilst retreating nervously.

"Non," she whispered, in an attempt to use his language, stopping him and ravaging his clothes. He shook with humiliation, his dignity torn off with the clothes, and discarded along with his now defunct superiority.

When he finally managed to back away he was naked, a mess of skin, bone and shuddering muscle. His flesh an ethereal white, he seemed unusually frail, as though she had torn away slabs of flesh, to leave a frame of bones wrapped in a stretched-taut layer of skin. As he retreated he shrank into a tighter, compact, more hunched, primate.

---

[2] *"Those of a feverish temperament - A demon has infested you! It seeks to draw out your devilish secretions to further taint the world. It courses through your veins and covers your body with a slick layer which aims to block out the divine rays from Prometos' fiery chariot orb"* – Extract from Zeuorox's *Meta-Physician Handbook*. It notably seems not to be able to explain why one sweated in the sunlight ('Prometos' fiery chariot orb'). However, once asked why it was so, according to a listening trainee priest he declared: *"Prometos, the mighty round shield of Thelus, is drawing out your darkness that taint all our souls for us to then do him service by removing. We should humbly praise Thelus for his mighty deed."* – Brother Beris' Diary.

She strode forwards with a sea of dignity. The contrast crumbled his remaining self-esteem. Knowing victory was hers, she reached for the string of her loincloth. His humiliation reached its peak: in total contradiction of the rest of his body, his supposed symbol of power rose. It might as well have been a white flag hoisted above his waist. For now he truly looked ridiculous. This alleged sign of defiance was nothing of the sort, it was a pitiful submission: a shameful admission deep from his loin that overruled the mind.

What a ridiculous form. Juscius knew it. Whether as a pallid, insipid, white, bloodless ghost set against the near pitch black, or as a black silhouette set against the luminous white angelic husk of his chair, his form made for a truly mock-worthy sight.

She strode towards him; in mid-step she tugged the ends of the bow and stepped over the silent-as-a-snowflake cloth as it fell.

To Juscius, this falling cloth was the last crushed angel that had stood to save him. Quaking, he became delirious; a bestial thing stood before him. It seemed totally alien. Juscius fell to his knees in terror.

It resembled a creature of the arachnid family. The pelvis squatted as though forming a tight haunting pose. The advance rapidly lost its grace, diminishing into an eerie slumber of a degenerate trance, mixed with a bestial charge. A bony ridge formed a sinister horn and below was a sparse patch of unkempt fur. Below this a side-ways mouth quivered.

Juscius was transfixed as though transmuted by petrification. Paralysed in his humbled position his imagination ran wild, seeking to sketch out the advancing beast.

The arachnid advanced through the darkness, the upper torso of a womanly figure dancing in the shadows as though a puppet above the shelob-creature. Beside the head were six hairy black insectoid legs. The redundant mouth was awkwardly placed so as to only be visible when the beast squatted in its advance. His ears seemed to be taking orders from the delusional eyes as he heard the thunder of chitin limbs striking the floor.

Despite the horrific sight, he could not help but feel it had an in-built feminine beauty. He recalled all the mythical female creatures; harpies, gorgons; they were evil, dirty, despicable, twisted denizens of horrifically mutated women. Yet, for all their repulsiveness, they seemed to retain a feminine mystique; something that had latched onto the crude prurience of males and reveal it as truly the most degenerate. The virulence rotted away what little dignity remained.

It bounded towards him, the light from the torches catching and revealing the two slender womanly legs as they scuttled towards him. It was her again; he felt a sigh of relief form in his throat. Then suddenly she disappeared back into darkness.

With a flash, the creature leapt at him, gripping around his sweating neck with the tubes of muscle that was its first pair of legs. Their feeling gave him a soothing piquant feeling, increased as what felt like women's toes dabbed against his back.

Yet it was still the same creature staring him in the face. As he tried to reel back, struggling against the powerful locked grip, he found an eye staring at him with a strange vacant probing. It was morosely vapid in its blank observation, stalking its prey with an emotionless patience. Yet it seemed to be silently relishing his pitiful attempts to resist its inexplicable lure.

Like quicksand, his attempts to resist seemed only to render him more captivated. Juscius shook, totally overwhelmed with vomit-inducing fear. The Shelob's hair was greased into a messy set of locks.

Juscius shrank back in disgust. Two long slender arms reached down from the heavens. Was this his chair manifest in human form to come and save him? He expected them to lift him out of the creature's lair, but instead, to his utter dismay they pushed his head down and lifted his chin up. Startled, Juscius struggled before spotting the seemingly shocked face of Thelus on the banner in the distance.

This, more than anything, sent him into a panicky state of self-revulsion. He struggled and wrestled with the arachnid's face. He attempted to pray for help, but the angelic hands again betrayed him by pushing him towards it.

★

The floodgates of self-control broke, allowing a deluge of avarice to spill over, blinding his senses, setting his body into automation. He gazed up to see the divine form of the slave girl. Her dreamy smiling face shone down as though gazing from the heavens.

This Juscius took as a sign of Thelus' assent; he gave a mental sigh of relief. '*It was all just a test!*'

Had it been a trick of Septimo? Or a test from Thelus? It did not matter... he had not faltered and now he was with his nymph of Prometos. She held him close, wrapped around him like a comfort blanket. But she was much more than mere comfort...

★

The torches flickered uneasily, struggling to remain alive as they sank into the rising ash that piled up around them. His view began to strobe, each period of light being shortened. Less and less became visible; her beaming face disappeared; only the ethereal remains of the whites of her eyes glowed as though self-illuminated. Then her torso vanished into the blackness, replaced with swirling greys that could be alluding to her supple body, or a swirling melting pot for his imagination to conjure up the demon. With the gradual retreat of light, and consequent longer time it took him to make out the figure of the slave girl, he felt the rising fear that the arachnid was lurking in the shadows. That his nymph was transmuting into the Shelob. He prayed for it not to be so. Nevertheless, the swirling grey began to linger in the panicky periods of light, and to make out the form of the beast.

Suddenly the Shelob returned. Its bony ridge and matted mess an undulating black triangle. It was closing in for the kill.

Juscius was struck with cornered-rat syndrome. With a sudden rush of adrenaline-backed fear he stumbled to the fluffy chair.

The lord dived for the floating globule of white, landing on it noiselessly, sinking into its soft fluffiness. He buried his face in its malleable comfort. He sighed in relief, and the mothering chair seemed to breathe back with a gust of cool air that rejuvenated his lungs.

His comfort was however, tortuously short-lived. Before he knew what was happening he was screaming. His screaming made him lose track of events, and before he knew it, he had been dragged, flipped and pushed, so he sprawled over the chair on his back, with his legs off one end, and his head weighing down his neck on the other. The preying blur of greys towered over him and came down. His stomach churned.

Was it the Shelob? Was it his angel?

His sweat soaked into the cushions below, yet the softness was so great that he could feel nothing. This infuriated him into a rampant rage: with so much feeling above; the comfort below became unbearable...

Chapter 20
The Bad Book (A fatal realisation on the part of Rabica)

It had been almost a week since they had returned from the banquet, and Rabica had still not managed to question his father over his lack of intervention in the rising Gatan-Latman conflict. During the journey home his father's indifference had taken the form of a stubborn refusal to discuss it.

The Lord's son was still fuming, though equally distraught with futility, as he found himself being tainted by being drawn into the realpolitik of the crusader and his outmoded opponent. He was angry that he had to side with the status quo just because it was preferable to a warped march of aggressions veiled in a false progressivism. Lord Lewerix had ignored Rabica's doom-laden prophecies over allowing the zealot any breathing space, and merely chided him for his positive comments regarding Gatan's second son.

His father had warned him of his naivety, explaining that Claudix was merely being agreeable to try and win him over to the Gatanese cause, and going as far as to mock him for behaving like a blackguard for the status quo. "I thought you *liked* change! And here you are championing its enemies!"

This deeply troubled Rabica, not for its truth, but as it showed the harsh reality that the only powerful advocates of change were for the worse.

"Didn't you see him chattering and cheering with Felix Danite, the primitive warlord?" Lord Lewerix had remarked.

But no, on this miserable day, with no way to escape into the nearby countryside, he would prepare for the mental onslaught.

With his usual routine, he had laid in his bed contemplating for a good half-hour, trying to motivate himself to get out. His mind resonated with nonchalant despair over the topic of The Young Lady, and, as usual, found nothing to actually soliloquise about. He wondered if she would reply to his letter, as he did every morning, indeed any moment when his mind was not preoccupied with his political aggravation. Haphazardly, he would dream of her replies, capriciously alternating between fantastical optimism and excessive pessimism. All along, knowing all too well that the ultimate negative result was the perpetual torture of receiving no letter, and waiting for it. So in a way, he supposed, it couldn't get any worse than this... unless it remained like this.

With these worries weighing him down, he threw himself out of his dark room (he never bothered to let any light in, and had told his servants 'not to bother' cleaning his room – the amassing squalor comforted him by sharing his demeanour).

The corridor led like a compacted myriad of otherworldly tunnels to the world. As he trundled through, Rabica contemplated how it fitted into his abstraction of his own squalor – jammed into a corner of a world full of so much prettily painted evil.

It was over too soon. He was confronted by the door, its solid constitution only a temporary guard against the endless flood of light that waited on the other side. His hands shook as he reached for the latch, so overwhelmed with irrational fear that he found himself unable to instigate his intended hesitation. He opened it automatically.

The door swung open and the rays engulfed him. His eyes squinted up tight, and his head recoiled fearful of burning. Once adjusted, he was ready to amble through the hall and into the dining room.

One of the alabaster windows had been slid aside to allow considerable light. His father sat in his chair holding a cup of warm water mixed with a dried herbal leaf. Before him was a piece of rough paper and a quill.

"Afternoon," his father paused, without looking up.

The servant stirred in the corner, vacating the room, after taking leave with a bow, to get Rabica's breakfast.

Rabica cautiously sat down on the chair opposite his father. He stared at the great desolate plain of hard wood that stretched out between them. The quill, a solitary tree whose bristles quivered in the breeze. The cup, a chunky totemic monument resting easily within the lord's reach. The paper a dry rice paddy. Rabica went to speak but hesitated, stroking his stubble nervously.

Eventually he conjured up enough courage to launch into the tirade. "Why were you so silent... at the banquet?"

His father did not even look up.

"At the banquet... you just let Latman strut his poison?" Aware that he had already descended into incoherence, he fell silent, staring at his father with fierce intent. Silently cursing himself. "'*Strut* his poison"... and it's not even a question!'

Eventually his father looked up; his greying hair remained motionless in his swift interception.

"What?" he belched out with disinterest.

Rabica glared furtively to each side then stared back at his father.

"You just sat back while he espoused his expansionist doctrine... don't you see, he wants us all to follow him in his maniacal crusade?"

Lord Lewerix shrugged; a look of anger was weakly suppressed on his face.

"We must leave those two to get on with it. If need be, we can get involved, but there is no point in getting needlessly involved in a personal feud. I've told you how master Claudix was trying to recruit your support." By now his voice was booming, "...So if I follow your words I will be playing into Gatan's hands... which I must *never* do. I may assist them, but I will never play into their hands... an ally is not the same as a friend."

"Better to do that than play into *his* by doing nothing," Rabica mumbled contumaciously.

Now Zenith was truly angered. "This is not about his, or theirs! We have our own as priority – that is what you forget! – us!" He tapped his quill on the table for emphasis.

"We are all 'Us'!" Rabica spat sarcastically.

Lord Lewerix's face twitched into a sneer, he slammed the quill on the table; the tree blown over in a gale. The rice paddy rustled.

"That is why you are no lord... and... it seems... never shall be."

The Lord seemed more shocked at his own words than the recipient, who merely nodded as though it merely proved his point.

Had it? He was no use in such an elitist system; the whole concept of seeing people as individuals and not drops of blood in a greater entity made no sense in a world of Houses. A single leader's death is a tragedy, a million peasants is a statistic. A soldier dies in battle killing hundreds of others; he is a hero, while hundreds of others starve to be never noticed, let alone forgotten. How could he rule over a faction of these people when he saw every one of them as of equal worth to any others?

With his entire desire for a better world crashing hopelessly around him, he could only irrationally declare. "Well maybe so; but if so, it is for the fault of the world and not me."

His father merely chuckled as though reminded of some past event in his life, but was quickly overshadowed by a stern expression. "The blame game won't get anyone anywhere. You must face up to facts - the house is your responsibility, its people are yours to serve."

"How do we serve our people?" Rabica blurted.

"We give orders, structure and purpose to their lives, otherwise they would wander the earth haplessly."

"Instead, they are overworked slaves given roles and titles to pretend they are aspiring."

Lord Lewerix gave his son a cynical grin.

"Well what more do you expect? It's the best we can have."

'*Is it?*' Rabica's mind screamed. '*Why don't we just all die now and cut out the automated life full of so much pain, confusion, and tension?*'

Rabica could see there was no use arguing with the lord about this; if he lost he would lose faith in mankind, if he won he would be compelled to be disgusted with his father. Consequently he rose in preparation to leave.

The lord swallowed his anger at his son's insubordination. "Look." He placed his hands on the table. "We have jobs to do, so we do them. Within those parameters we do the best we can, but we cannot upset the balance."

"And it is exactly that 'balance' - a most precarious and unjust set of scales at that - which causes those problems you allegedly seek to solve!"

With that, he set off to vacate the room.

Just as he reached the door, his father's voice rang out. It did so in a tone totally alien to the previous conversation, calmly and as an incidental 'matter-of-fact'. "Oh, a letter came for you."

Rabica jolted. His skin shuddered with a cold tingling while his organs beat furiously, pounding in heated frenzy against the petrified flesh that encased them.

It had to be Her.

The words echoed in his mind; '*It had to be Her*'. His anger dissipated, to be replaced with rampant fear. Immediately he wanted to throw the towel in. He would concede anything for that letter: betray his idealism, settle down, give her 'The High Life'; together they would be The People's Rulers.

Then his dream shattered as the envelope slipped into his hand. '*This is no pass to utopia, it is a death warrant,*' he told himself before scurrying off through the pitch-black corridor-portal to his personal oubliette.

Nothing mattered on his passage. He shot through glaring into the darkness only to be reminded of the probable fatal emptiness it contained.

★

His fingers gently pushed the door closed with one hand. Meanwhile his other hand held the envelope close to his chest, daintily caressing the precious document. The door slammed shut with a surprising crash, following its silent glide through the partial vacuum where the stuffy air of the room met the corridor.

He threw himself onto his bed; his room had retained the darkness of the corridor in his retinas. The familiar hazy black patches of his belongings and the musty air meant he knew it was his. Saturninely he acknowledged that this rancid amalgam of objects represented him just as well as his husk of a body.

"Oh what a dismal state, where those objects that we take into our lives constitute our only connection with life itself," he lamented. Adopting the tone of a poet he continued in a mock thespian voice, "oh dainty chair, how you complete me in my lonesome solitude."

He rocked on his bed, rocking himself into a defensive position. The darkness shrouded him in funereal gloom, rendering all objects distant, but in doing so making him feel immense. This merely fuelled his insecurity; through them he was so exposed, his misery on display in a room-sized diorama. The more he cowered and shrank, it made no difference: his weaknesses and fears were on display. Nor did bathing himself in darkness hide the sensation that he was a caged parody of himself.

The harsh reality was coming to his artificial habitat; his fingers traced the seal on the envelope, delaying its release. Would it be a terra-forming genesis germ?

He caressed the package as though it were some holy relic. He dreamed of her writing it, her slender fingers gliding across the pages as her hand and mind corroborated perfectly to formulate what was now clasped in his hand. This envelope and seal had been in her possession. These objects and the words they had on them were shared between them, documentation of an interaction.

Carefully he pulled on the seal, wary not to damage her creation. As he fumbled to open the letter, he realised that he would need a candle.

Once a candle was lit, it invaded the squalor, gleaming like a lonesome star. The flame remained constant in the stagnant air, giving the impression that it had a solid form, a glistening teardrop bead which inexplicably emanated heat and light.

This lonesome provider of vision cast great swooning shadows which easily rivalled the candle flame for apparent physical form. The looming spectral structures cut dark swathes of black across the room and the objects strewn within. The candle sat low in its holder, the white-yellow bead peeking over the bronze tray lip causing a sizeable blackhole of darkness around the tray.

As he opened the envelope the candle quivered, causing tectonic reverberations amongst the patterns of interlocking shadows and patches of light.

His fingers anxiously pawed the paper; he felt his touch soiled its surface. Nevertheless, conscious of this unavoidable desecration, he ploughed on. As he read the words he admired their apparent eloquence. Still, he was not dumbstruck enough to not notice the lack of depth. Gleefully, she declared her happiness in her new abode, spoke of light-hearted events. Whilst he sought out meaning, the words trundled out like the pressings of a steamroller; the inevitable pondering of a reliable if uninspiring machine.

The only sentence worth his pitiful interest was one that spoke of her 'Bad Book' a book that in which she confessed her deepest thoughts. Just after this, right at the end she merely declared that 'I'm sure things will sort themselves out': This was the speech of someone who knew nothing of his mental quagmire.

It began to sink in with morbid rapidity that he was nothing in her life; a pawn caught in a deadlock against the edge of the chess board.

It was as he reread the letter he began to properly take in the lack of importance he held in her life. Whereas to him The Young Lady was an imperative and integral factor of his continued existence, in her version, the event that had so rocked his life was forgotten, and his role in her life was of little significance: a quaint acquaintance.

An uncomfortable question that had been treading water in a silent struggle at the back of his mind found itself propelled into his thoughts. How could he prove himself to her?

Yet it was not the answer he sought, more a thorough critique of the question itself. Such a question presumed that he could prove himself to her, even hypothetically. The more he re-read her words, the more he saw that the best he could hope for was a vapid relationship on the outskirts of friendship.

He began to see the letter for what it was; a chirpy, vivacious narrative, a sugar coating without a surface below. This set the tone in such a way that the line, *"I hope you can be happy, remember there are good things out there, when I feel glum I write my thoughts in a notebook,"* sounded patronising, disdainful and overall uninterested.

What part of him had been trying to convince the other of for ages, finally slotted into place; he meant nothing to her. She was concerned about him as much as any person, but that fateful day was a forgotten episode, an unsightly smudge not deemed (un)worthy enough of redemption or forgiveness. She had troubles, but ones he could not even contemplate.

The shed flashed before him. His hand reached out and thudded against its hard wood. He peeked though the keyhole. In the darkness, demons danced; prancing figures with green scales and claws, trampling on barren earth. He saw a mighty quill scoop down and crush them into the earth, leaving scaly scabs, surrounded by inky bloody moats on the compacted soil. The scaly beasts' remains writhed, pinned to the ground. Some disintegrated into a molten, glassy puddle before vaporising. Others remained pinned down, squirming, but ever present. Other beings in there were unseeable, except when they distorted his view of others; he could not even contemplate their existence. All he knew was that they were nothing to do with him.

A thick misty cloud surged in front of the keyhole and became recognisable as his ultimate nemesis: emotional impotence, sterility, incompatibility. Hatred was preferable to indifference; at least it instilled emotion. It proved he had an impact, and was reconcilable. Neutral indifference was not the mid-point between hatred and love, but totally separate: a prison with no link to the sliding scale of emotion.

As despair took over, he quaked in fear at the evidence of his irrelevance. He could not cease to continue moping about over a cause lost the day he was born.

It felt like destiny, but destiny implied fate for the sake of an end – it was nothing of the sort. It was only the inevitable consequence of his inherent ineptitude that rendered him not only substandard to her, but also condemned to be attracted to her.

It had become apparent that his whole life was merely the squirming of a severed worm on the cogs of immense structures. He was born to lose. Rabica found this final confirmation of hopelessness hard to take in. His life flashed before him, etched in stone down a narrow path; all the petty aggravation, all the nitty-gritty of living, had been obediently trudged down as the only path for no greater end. All that grief was a build-up to sudden annihilation. Predetermined and futile. 'All that grief' *was* the ride. She might as well have sent a letter that just said: *'game over... Try again?'*

Though, he had, when full of self-pity, declared his hopelessness, now it was an empirical fact (the letter was written documentation) he could not shrug at it bravely as before.

His fingers caressed the paper with a distant longing, a longing for that which now seemed a proven hopeless dream. Nevertheless, here it was; the data, the proof that killed the feasibility of The Idea.

He stared at the words. As his eyes traced over the marks, he recounted that it was not the actual words and their direct meaning, but the collective content, that proved that her indifference was unnoticeable to her as it was ingrained in her consciousness.

His searching eyes bleared with salty water that welled into stinging pools, like two poisoned waterholes in a desert. Equally, they refused to expel forth teardrops, clinging onto their tainted boreholes. The words, so eloquently dancing across the smooth papyrus, blurred into lines of misty black.

"It's hopeless," he whispered. "It IS hopeless," he emphasised.

"You sound surprised!" A bitter laughing voice cut through the darkness.

The gnarled expression remained on his face, forcing it to twitch uncomfortably. He felt a wavering whimper struggle through his vocal chords and escape the bitter intensity. *'Had it not been blindingly obvious? Was this not merely that obvious distant wall that gradually nears without you being able to dodge, then suddenly you hit it? Slam!'*

His facial muscles slackened until they merely sprawled lazily around his skull, resting in a vacant expression – one dictated by bone structure alone. His eyes struggled to remain open. His breath dissipated in intensity. It was almost as though his entire body was imploding around his faltering heart.

"How can such an empty letter contain such a devastating pronouncement?" he mumbled to himself.

THE SON AND THE HEIR

Like a carefully concocted poison, this papyrus vial was exceptional in its concentrated potency. No particular sentence, no single gulp, would betray its toxin, only in its totality; upon reflection, mental digestion, did it do its fatal work.

Rabica felt a twitching sensation in his fingers. He sucked his teeth, drawing in particles to assist in the contemplation. Oh how he wanted to end it all... how he wished it was so simple. He shook his head. Even *that* was too simplistic.

What he needed to do was spend time in contemplation, away from the society that reminded him of her. Into a world free of this, free of her. It did not matter if he never returned. She did not think of him unless prompted, so he had to establish the same in his mind. Remove her entirely from his mind. That was his new aim, and for that he required solitude. He needed his thoughts to match the reality; no potential for relationship existed between them. His adoption of this as a core doctrine was essential to the escape. It would further his political emancipation, if he were to annihilate his feelings for her.

He needed remoteness, solitude; freedom from societal complexities in a world gone mad. His need to escape became imperative, yet he still needed something sudden to spur him into making such a life changing decision.

He scanned the room for an inspirational signal. The barren landscape of abandoned extravagance surrounded him. It all looked too unappealing.

Scraps paper crinkled like mighty fault-line ridden tectonic plates. Clothes hung up like dried flesh, stretched out to dry. Empty bottles stood huddled like abandoned ancient monuments to no longer followed gods.

He thought of taking a quick shot of drink to spur him on. After vainly eyeing the bottles for content he gave up and turned his attention to the heavily distilled spirit that resided under his mattress for emergencies. He took a cautious sip, but was anxious: its consumption was a sign of crisis, and being in such a state was no time to make such decisions.

The bed's position above the rest of the room seemed to reserve it as a place of slight refuge from the decay below; a platform of hope above the lazy chaos.

Rabica's attention was suddenly captivated by the candle's frantic struggle with an untraceable draft. Was it a leak in the corridor-portal? Skulking across the floor, clinging low to the tiles like an amorphous black panther? The flame disappeared with a puff of smoke that rose in a graceful string of plumes, illuminated by the sun's constrained attempt to shine through the tiny alabaster window that was covered by a faded cloth. It was as though the rays had eaten away its substance to gloomily emanate through, creating an artificial moonlight.

Rabica spent a few moments straining to soak in as much of the light as he could, in order to survey the desolate landscape. It was listless; the bottles stood as a horrendous scar on the land, a shard of a blade plunged into the earth. Cloth hills gave off a pungent aroma that plagued the atmosphere. Folds and creases spread unnaturally on the smooth tile-plated basin floor. It was like a diorama of some 'great event' minus the characters; they had perished or fled leaving epic tension as a faint decaying feeling in the air.

In a fleeting thought he was reminded of his barren quagmire. That squalid bog had never supported life. It had rotted itself, broiled and fermented in its own juices; a disaster of its own making. It was an ecosystem doomed to fail before it even began.

In a sudden trick of the mind, something scurried from one mountain to another. Rabica's mind replayed the hallucination and conjured the image of a pitiful blue creature. He focused in on it; it was a lanky-armed, spindly-legged, soft-skinned gremlin with a swollen potbelly. A sparse toothy grin sat back as rearguard to a long pointy nose that was flanked by two yellow eyes.

With the image perfected, similar blobs began to emerge from the fabrics, and scamper from clothhill to clothhill. They hurried from nook to cranny, busying them with a panicky attempt at survival.

"But survival from what?" Rabica pondered, leaning over his bed to gaze down like a god.

Everything was dead; they must be spectres haunting this wasteland.

Rabica began to grasp the insight; these beings, in their crumbled defunct society, had lost hope and prospects of achieving anything.

It reiterated to him that he had to change surroundings. With the bottle gripped in one hand, he forced his feet into his boots, and headed for the door.

He prepared to enter the corridor, taking a cautious glance over his shoulder. The blue gremlins were all gone. In the fake moonlight, the terrain looked deserted, the weak light managing to carve out rough grey patches of cloth-rock. He wanted to see one of the sprites scampering across the floor to remind himself that he was not alone, even though they were mocking him for his pitiful existence in a world of such plenty.

A smile broke over his face like an egg cracked into a frying pan, white lips spreading across his face. "If I leave now, solitude becomes a neutral state to seek, uphold and maintain. Solitude will be purified to be associated with tranquillity and not contorted into seeming negative by its friction with this spurious concept of love."

He reached for the door with a shrug of inconsequentiality.

In such a plodding life, filled with continuity, it did not seem possible for him to acknowledge the notion that his actions could have irreversible consequences. Even his actions on that fateful day felt like the inevitable consequences of his birth.

He felt as though his whole life had been the product of outside forces; a current that drove him into certain actions with differing waves. Even his interactions with others were the consequence of waves pushing him and them momentarily together. Every 'choice' he had made was the inevitable consequence of a sedimentary context.

He could see it all in action now, flashing before him like a film synopsis: A childhood of shyness and physical repugnance. Catching her eye for the first time. Those bungled attempts at conversation (interactions doomed from *his* beginning). The build up. That fateful day. The asking, the crying, and finally, the letter: leading to capitulation.

With all this thundering through his mind he launched himself into the eternal darkness behind the door.

★

Outside it was a dingy day. Huge hulking grey clouds hung over the land like schoolyard bullies. Their mere presence presented a poised threat of rain. Yet, like an ever impending death sentence, it refused to come, preferring instead to spread its aqueous muscle across the sky, knowing this was enough to cause panic below.

Still Rabica was undeterred, exchanging shifty glances with the wisps of vapour towering above. He was like a cowboy entering an unfamiliar town, his measly shoulders defensively puffed up. Suddenly at 15 paces he span around to be confronted by his real adversary: the palace.

No longer was it even intriguing, it was an ugly bloated collection of ravaged stone, chiselled with such sickly savage 'sophistication' that it filled him with contempt. A horrendous monstrosity that drained the landscape, just as it bled the landscapes residents dry. The amalgamated styles displayed all the incarcerated generations that had been entombed, a showy addition, a chronological trophy of a gradually ossified nation. Each patch did not celebrate a style and its generation; it commemorated the defeat of that generation by its incorporation. The statues stood on guard to ensure no stones took flight. Rabica felt a smile crack open on his face when he thought that as these blackguards became more numerous they ate away at the very thing they guarded.

The clouds had backed off, their vaporous existence showing them up for what they were, distant looming inevitabilities to be ignored. People feared them. But to him, they were petty distractions compared to this squatting structure that devoured entire generations just to sustain itself. Really it was this colossal dreadnought, and what it represented, that Rabica knew he should have as the centre of his qualms, not rejected love.

"What a wasted exertion of the energies of youth," he grunted, his attempt at thespian eloquence faltering on the first syllable.

He pondered as to what to do. What could he do? He was born into such a privileged position. Yet, ironically it was this privilege that rendered action out of the question. All those changes he sought to make could not be built upon this: this palace of consumed generations. All this needed to be swept away, but it was the only source of his legitimacy; to sweep it away he would have to sweep himself away. He smirked with despair-ridden irony. "If only I were powerless, then I'd be in a position to use the power no longer had for good!"

He felt the clouds swooping in, casting enormous gloominess over the whole grounds. With this looming over his shoulder he found himself thinking of the 'Bad Book'.

An image of it appeared before him, like a librarian's nightmare. The dark tome, a black bible, the confessions of an angel. A fallen angel, a once-believed-to-be-perfect prophetess whose long lost secrets of menial aggravation, anxiety and anger have been uncovered. With the falling of the exemplar, his principles began to look ever shakier.

In his worship of (his imagined version of) her she had been reified to perfection, and perfection could not doubt itself. But then this conflicted with her attributed modesty, which was a crucial characteristic of his ideal.

Though the shed had been confirmed, it was not a plague created by him, his quagmire overlapping into her life. The fact that it had been mentioned to him proved he could not be its source, for she would not divulge its existent to someone relevant to it.

To demote himself to a position of 'blight' of her life was actually an act of unjust self-attribution of importance within the fable that was her life.

He could see it now, a dark tome, the necronomicon – this was a book of significant anxieties, not mindless qualms about an idiotic prince. This was about reality, not other people's failed fairytales that involved her.

★

Rabica looked around himself. He stood in the wild garden at the back of the palace. Gloomy clouds passed overhead. The vegetation swayed nonchalantly in the wind, like a morbid church congregation, its lively greenery diminished in the dull drab lighting.

Panicking at his own lethargic despair, he failed to see any refuge in the wild. Despair enveloped him, as he realised the tension could not be relieved, except through unconsciousness. It seemed a prerequisite to it all. No comfort could come.

He felt a twitching sensation that affected his muscles, hopelessly seeking physical exertion in the belief it could solve psychological problems. He felt a desire to do something, yet this something was not possible in the physical realm. The twitching unease had spread throughout his body, conquering all the myriad of sinew that controlled it. All his joints begged to be employed, causing tense muscular spasms. He felt like running, but had no destination. Besides, the numbing of the sporadic itches from jolting into action was over in a micro-second. He could see his desire to bolt for what it was: a petty, irrelevant diversion.

Finally, after a long time of looming overhead, the heavens opened. It came without warning; no gradual build-up or preliminary spitting. The air went from a thick muggy sluggishness to a cascading deluge of water.

Rabica, lost in his tumultuous web of tense tendons and itching thoughts, only noticed the rain when he was totally drenched.

His realisation of the water went ignored; instead he watched an ant scurry about, trying to avoid the aquatic meteors. This feat became increasingly difficult as the drops collated into puddles, leaving rapidly decreasing dry safe-havens. He tried to imagine its ant face of panic, its heart (not knowing it lacked one), beating so fast... and in its mind; despair.

Suddenly, smash! It took a hit. It squirmed and struggled. He wanted to reach forward and save it, yet was stopped as he thought, '*I am like a god to it – and if they exist they do nothing. If I am to be judged for doing nothing, then so must they. They nullify their moral goodness, if not their existence.*'

He looked up with a bitter mocking. 'Do not blame me, I only follow you,' he spat bitterly. His bitterness became more demanding as the ant squirmed and struggled in the puddle that was growing around it. "Better still, save it, go on, prove your existence – save it!"

The puddle had become sizeable, joining another, and the ant bobbed up and down in the middle. Its tiny neck stretched its head above the water, only to be submerged by ripples as the drops struck the puddle.

The gods did nothing.

Guilt rose in Rabica, he wanted to save the creature, but knew he could not because he had selfishly staked its life on the existence of the farcical. He leant in to the ant, his head shielding it from the raindrops for a moment.

"After this, little one, I will know they don't exist and are not there to save us, and so will save any of your brethren I see in such peril."

It struggled a while longer before giving up and lying still. Maybe exhaustion had set in on those strong legs. So used to labouring large segments of leaves, but useless in the perilous pools of treacherous water. They call it the fruit of life, but to this pitiful creature nothing was more deadly.

In the meantime, Rabica's robe had become plastered to his skin. Behind him, heavy folds full of water hung stiff, weighted by the rain. The creases waved solemnly, a cautious sullen sway to a death march.

The whiteness had degraded to khaki by the water content. Rain had equally drenched his hair, and accumulated in beads in his scraggly beard. Fake jewels for a fake prince. Nature's christening.

Rabica shook off the markation, and in aggressive reply, the darkest grey clouds swooped in, crashing together in thunderous cackles. Their power was manifested in light and sound as sheet lightening blanketed the sky. It clearly found Rabica's ignorance offensive, yet the more it crashed above him, the more resolute he remained in his resistance. He would not scurry off like his blue-skinned counterparts. The water that remained on him was beginning to cool, exacerbating his twitching neurones. He froze still. The trickling water had mingled with his sweat and began to create icy pin-pricks all over his body. Nevertheless, he would not be coerced into cover, to cower like a defeated hermit. No, he would be defiant to the last, even if it were perilous.

Each flicker, each raucous thunderclap reminded him of an instance of his unravelling story with Her.

As he glanced around at the slushy devastation, he spotted something pink and fleshy. The cascading aerial deluge knocked it about so much he could not see if it actually moved itself. It was a worm, a feeble, blind spineless creature brought unnaturally to the surface by the fear of being drowned by the uncompromising downpour. Instead, so it seemed, it preferred to be drowned where it at least it could be seen. It had no strong legs like the ant, no hard chitin; if the ant stood no chance, how could it?

Cursing the gods for their non-existence, he lurched forward and picked it up. The cold motionless lump sprang to life as its soft skin contacted with his warm hands. No doubt they burnt. Still he could not cast it away in its foolish defiance. No, he would not act like a god; he dredged some soil in a cupped hand and transferred it. It sat there, like him, huddled on a tiny enclave between heaven and earth; a purgatory refuge. Two rejected creatures seeking each other's company for protection against their corresponding destinies.

With sunken wet eyes Rabica saw what it could not, a flower rocking, but undamaged by the downpour. Indeed this flower would revel in this event; to it water *was* the fruit of life. Its roots would grow deep, its flower remain bright, its leaves sprout with a lush green. An ant had crawled up it and clung on for dear life.

He smirked to the worm, pondering if it could see her, smiling longingly into the eyes of a love. Their rosy cheeks and eyes gleaming with the life of love. The fruit of life. Her bad book tucked away behind her back, an irrelevance for the moment.

"Don't worry little fellow, the ant is no superior to you, nor is he your enemy. Luck bestowed him with virtues much more visible to the eye, but you in your blindness and seeming impracticality up here are not suited on the surface. But let us see him dig deep, and below the surface toil unseen so all above ground remain well placed. The flower may never realise what service you do it."

The worm lay motionless on the soil, caked in wet mud. It looked limp and lifeless, yet Rabica saw no reason for it to be dead and so assumed otherwise. Hunched in his defensive position Rabica began to feel cold. His skin was numb and pale. The rain seemed never ceasing and the thunder and lightning continued. He gazed upwards waiting for the heavenly spectacle to reach a finale.

A sudden great flash sent the whole sky into negative colour, dark grey clouds becoming luminous white wisps. It was followed by a stunning rumble.

Rabica tried to admire the striking energy, but all he could think of were all his other brethren; his 'little fellows', lying limp in such destruction. He rebuked himself for ever admiring such beauty and failing to acknowledge its devastation.

He returned his gaze to his flaccid comrade.

"I will take you inside, get you some more soil… what on earth do you eat?! I do not mean to capture you, merely offer you some hospitality, until these deadly rains are over."

He flicked soil at it to remind it that it was still alive, and it squirmed weakly. He took this as acceptance and slowly rose to stand and sluggishly beat his retreat towards the palace, the structure he so hated.

He addressed the worm again, "sadly for now we must seek refuge in this abomination." Returning his gaze to the makeshift path, he navigated through the gleaming lush undergrowth. He added, "yet life is life, and so must be protected as priority. There is no time for foresight, for the will of the non-existent gods and what their charlatan knowledgeable ones seek to profess."

The worm stayed limp in his cupped hand. Teetering on the brink of capitulation, it was unable to even give a response through movement.

The Chronicles of Captain Dummonius
Part 1

Chapter 21
The Chronicles of Captain Dummonius: A (Not So) Spontaneous Revolt

Felix Danite's entourage crossed the Danite-Latman border with a collective sigh of relief.

For the whole journey the lord had been troubled by one question – *why had he been invited?* This was no modesty; it was realpolitik. As an ally of Gatan, it made more sense for Latman to exclude him under the guise that he was just a long-lasting warlord like those in the North.

His suspicions were roused further when, upon reaching Danite territory, he was not met by another contingent of men ready for the march back to the capital. (He had made sure rumours were spread that twice as many men as actually went had left for Lateria. This was to make it sound as though he could afford to send out more troops than he actually could). Instead, he was met by only a squad of 'cavalry', though cavalry was a too prestigious a term for these young nobles' sons; skitty cavaliers with spears and ageing leather armour.

Their three tents were hemmed into a small wood that was in a horseshoe hill. Whilst the ground below them looked decimated and ground into a pulp, their tents looked as though they were being slowly swallowed by the hill's foliage.

An old scout, who led the unit, was brought before Lord Danite. He had a wispy grey beard and woolly locks that sprouted out of a badly dented helm. With the drawling poetry of an old veteran he asked Lord Danite to go to his tent where he could explain free from unwanted ears.

He explained that one of the northern noblemen had raised an army, seized control of the Northern fort of Galexia and then marched on the capital to lay siege to it. Word had spread surprisingly quickly (he added, with the professional paranoia of an aged warrior, 'too quickly'). Consequently, a rebellion in Axia had seized control of the town.

Watchmen fleeing the town had reported that amongst the defenders were mercenaries. The force on the border had left to lay siege to the town.

Danite did not even wait for the 'sergeant' to be dismissed, before exploding in a fuzzy-bearded jaw-jutting rage. It was immediately apparent to him that he had been set up. "That cheat! So that's it! Latman must be behind this! So much organisation." He turned back to the scout. "Tell me, sergeant, have you heard of any other rebellions... say, closer to Danilia?"

The scout shook his head warily as though he was following his lord's train of thought with deep contemplation.

"Latman will have bribed a couple of landowners or merchants to rise up and given them mercenaries, and probably money to buy out the local population. Why, this flies right in the face of what he was setting out at the banquet!"

The lord then turned to the Sergeant who was lingering by the tent flap, eagerly awaiting dismissal for fear he heard what he shouldn't.

"And you said the contingent has left to put down the Axia rebellion? When?"

The sergeant silently drifted into a gentle stroll along his memory bank, before reporting back. "We learnt of it five days ago, then the commander was unsure what to do for a day, so three days ago... about midday."

Danite nodded. "What do we know of the state in Danilia?"

The scout shrugged apologetically. "Sire, I know little, by now they must have reached it. The call had gone out for all loyalists to rally in the capital. We have heard nothing of what they have to defend with, or what they are up against."

"Hanius, take the mounted infantry and head for the capital, stop for nothing, try and get into the city and organise the defence. Tell Captain Julian to command the rest of the troops, pick up as many men as he can on the way and rendezvous with the others outside the capital at Anervil's Hill and set up a defensive perimeter. Neither of you are to attack under any circumstance. Send a messenger to Haji and get the fastest ship to set sail for Atari to tell Lord Gatan what is going on. I shall take my cavalry, and meet the contingent assaulting Axia. Once we have defeated them we shall join with Julian and relieve the forces." He then turned back to the sergeant. "Sergeant, I want you to go to the border guards and tell them what is happening. Then I want you to patrol the border area... try and find where these mercenaries came in from."

With the plan set out, Danite strode out of the tent and told the bodyguard that they were to set off immediately for Axia.

★

Captain Dummonius had seen Axia from quite a distance, a dark brown haze perched on a slight hill. The fields surrounding it were small patches of dismal root vegetables. To a man of Latman, the land of huge landowners, such small patches were a symbol of backwardness. Several packs of peasants nervously worked their fields, giving hostile stares to the passing mercenary foreigners.

The morning frost had only wilted about half an hour ago, even though it was approaching midday.

As they reached the town they felt as though they had travelled back in time. Even though the rain had passed some days ago, the ground between the mud huts was unwelcomingly squelchy. The occasional pig let out a startled grunt from behind rickety wooden fences.

Captain Dummonius was concerned about the lack of military presence. It was hardly the atmosphere he had expected in a town that had witnessed a 'spontaneous' uprising. He caught a glimpse of a nervous-looking adolescent with a gleaming spear. It was quite a bizarre sight, a muddy rag-wearing peasant with his grubby hand wrapped around a finely forged iron spear.

This reminded him of the bag he had been told to give the commander of the rebel army. Though it had been sealed with wax, and been wrapped many times in cloth, Dummonius knew it contained gold. What was more, he had been told that it was essential that he was not discovered by Lord Danite, and that his primary task was to deliver this package.

Open fires smouldered, giving off the smell of burning animal dung. Most of the people seemed to be going about their normal day. Children played in the mud, camouflaged by the grime that was caked over their clothes and skin indiscriminately. They stopped to look at the strange men on horses who had arrived. Their presence out on the streets was troubling, for it was not usual in a town a day away from a siege.

They rode over to the guard and Captain Dummonius asked to be sent to the commander. The guard seemed edgy, making his already thick accent even harder to understand.

"We are the mercenaries from the Delvinius Company," Dummonius clarified.

The guards pointed in the direction they should go, before scurrying off into the shadows of the mud huts.

They headed in the direction that the guard had pointed, but were soon met by a man on horseback surrounded by men in leather armour holding longswords. The man on horseback wore a tunic that in any Latman town would be classed as plain, but compared to the pitiful inhabitants of this town it set him out as a wealthy man. He greeted Dummonius with an accent barely more understandable than the guard.

"I'm Galric, trader in farming equipment." He seemed proud, as though he was declaring that he owned a gold mine. "I know who you are."

The horses trudged precariously through the slush of mud. They passed numerous people, mostly hunched elderly men and women wailing at passers-by for food in exchange for trinkets. He saw some more children wallowing in the mud, one boy was having mud stuffed down his ripped trousers by two other boys, whilst some girls laughed at him between shivers.

Eventually they reached a squat stone structure that peeked over the huts and shacks with tight slit windows. There was nothing grand about this staunch mound of blocks. The doorway was embedded into the structure, so as to have a lip over the top. It housed a small solid door made of oak, buttressed with iron bars that were bolted on in a grid pattern. Its blocky form, solid braced door, and tiny windows made its form seem like a primitive effigy of a man's head.

They dismounted just in front of the keep. The mercenary troop would wait outside whilst Dummonius spoke with Galric. One of the soldiers took Dummonius' horse by the reigns, whilst Dummonius picked up the bag he assumed he was supposed to give to Galric.

The merchant saw the gold and gave it a hungry look. "Ah, I see you brought me a gift!" he exclaimed.

Dummonius just nodded and gave a nonchalant smile.

"Your men can take the horses to the stable around the back and take their belongings to the quarters inside the keep."

Being clearly in earshot, Dummonius did not need to relay the information, though the 'Rebel Commandant' was clearly annoyed that the order did not follow his perceived chain of command.

They headed for the entrance to the fort. Dummonius gazed up at the overhang that stretched out like a stone-golem's upper jaw, the serrated block-pattern its huge grinding teeth, waiting to descend onto trespassers. A small hole had been bored into the roof of its mouth; a salival gland from which boiling oil could be poured down in a steaming deluge of liquid death.

As he descended the dank passageway, he instantly noticed that the passage of the stairway narrowed. He had to confess he was impressed with the defensibility of the building.

Galric had neglected to bring a torch with them so they struggled through the darkness towards the torchlight that flickered in the room below.

Once they had travelled down about one level they reached a sparse guard room. It housed two tables with chairs, occupied by local militiamen. They totally ignored the two entrants, being fully engrossed in some conversation, hunched defensively against the chilling dankness.

They walked quickly through and along a corridor, eventually reaching a more inviting room, which Dummonius guessed was Galric's quarters. In contrast to the rest of the fort, it was well lit and heated with a roaring fire and four torches. Obviously, the merchant was taking advantage of the lavish lifestyle, while he could. In the centre of the room a table was being used as a makeshift desk and against the wall to the left of the door was a chest of drawers. Opposite it was a straw mattress on a wooden board and some blankets.

Galric went straight to the table and sat on the chair. He seemed surprised that the mercenary Captain did not approach the table but instead hovered close to the fire.

"You may sit, Captain," Galric declared, with an air of generosity.

"Perhaps later," came Dummonius' brief reply.

"Well, first, I suppose I ought to take the gift," Galric prompted. Dummonius shrugged, and lifted the bag onto the table with one heave, letting it bang down with a resonance that would ensure he held the rebel leader's attention.

"Why has there been no preparation here?" he declared bluntly.

Galric paused in shock with his arm outstretched, his fingers splayed out like a giant spider suspended in a web over the bag.

"Aside from a few idle guards, this seems like any normal village."

"Town," Galric protested superfluously.

Dummonius breathed out to vent his irritation, and followed it up with an icy stare.

"Who exactly is part of this rebellion?" This time, even though he had actually asked a question, Galric just sat there transfixed. Eventually he mumbled, "perhaps we should wait for your Latman counterpart to arrive..."

Dummonius' tone sank to a deeper icy low. "I am not a 'Latman', I am a mercenary. I am my own captain, and have no 'counterparts'."

Suddenly without prior warning the door sprang open. Dummonius spun around, hand instinctively on hilt.

The man that strode in was somewhat shocked to be confronted by a fully armoured man ready to strike. He was young, very young for a mercenary. However, the way he managed to overcome his shock, reach for his weapon then cancel the manoeuvre, implied he had a considerable amount of experience compressed into his few years in the military. He wore old, but well-maintained Latman chainmail armour with accompanying longsword. His overall look resembled a soldier from the past about to be sent into Vacarium.

"Well, well, is that how you greet people? I thought us Westerners were supposed to be the savages!" He spoke with a Latman-Vaca accent. Dummonius decided to veil his irritation at the impolite entrance with a counter-joke and grin. "We also have doors, which we knock on before we enter!" The man just laughed.

Dummonius' face had already sunk back into one of anxiety as his mind settled back to the task at hand. "Perhaps…?"

"Maximus."

"Maximus… you can explain to me what is going on here?" Dummonius asked flatly.

Maximus gave a smirk. "I assume you are referring to the lack of activity in the village."

"Town," corrected Galric, only to be ignored.

Dummonius nodded to Maximus solemnly.

"Well… we are not sure how supportive the peasants will be, so we are waiting until the enemy are close."

"Waiting to do what?" Dummonius asked, fearful of the answer.

Maximus Aurelius glanced at Galric and winced. "Er… basically… have the rebellion."

Dummonius' heart sank. *What had he got himself into?*

"How close do the enemy have to be?" He asked, desperately trying to hide the unavoidable sarcastic tinge.

"When they are a couple of days away."

Dummonius' heart began pumping erratically. "Have you sent scouts out?"

Maximus frowned in bafflement.

Dummonius took a deep breath then dropped the bomb. "Danite left half his entourage on the border, and they will be arriving tomorrow afternoon."

Galric began shaking. He tried to reach for the bag, but fumbled as his hands, drugged hairless tarantulas, twitched and scurried along the bag's material as though it burnt the tips of their legs.

Nobody replied, so Dummonius continued. "About a hundred and fifty infantry; swordsmen and spearmen, plus some bowmen and skirmishers are on the way, what have you here?"

Maximus looked uncomfortable, swallowing a well of saliva, before shaking his head and coldly mumbling the answer. "About thirty watchmen, several fled as loyalists - one was a plant to make sure the returning army would be drawn here and not defend the capital."

This was clearly news to Galric. He began screaming and pointing an accusative finger at Maximus. "You! You have told them to come here! And you will flee, won't you!"

Maximus spoke on their behalves. "Captain Dummonius must escape so that Latman involvement is not known. I and my men shall remain. This old armour turns up all over, especially amongst brigands and mercenaries."

"How many men do you have?" Dummonius asked.

"My unit of longswords number twenty. We have your eight horse archers... which will be very handy in the early stages. Plus, however many peasants... the population is several hundred, from that about a hundred able-bodied men. Galric has a bodyguard of seven." The tone Maximus used when mentioning Galric's bodyguard told Pluvius they were just thuggish militiamen.

Dummonius, ever the man for action, decided to plough straight into it. "Right, well I don't know who is supposed to be in command here, but these are my suggestions to whoever is: The watchmen must get all the population into the centre of the village, they must be told to assist in building a perimeter wall; rip up fences, cut down trees, whatever. All foodstuffs need to be stashed in this building in case of a siege, as well as water. Then we need to arm the peasants who will fight, and deal with those who won't."

Galric was still shaking and so the words just flew through him. Maximus, on the contrary, had listened attentively, nodding in agreement. After waiting politely he added, "I don't think we have the resources for a wall, we can barricade the roads. That should slow them. Finally, Galric, you need to work out how to get the peasants to support you."

Galric flinched nervously upon hearing his name and the ascription of a task. "What? Oh... yes... I will make something up about a grain tax that the Lord wants to enforce because of brigands. I can use that to get plenty of produce stored in the fort. Plus I will add an economic incentive to fight..."

Both the soldiers were impressed and gave each other wry smirks.

"I had better take Captain Dummonius on a tour of the area," Aurelius declared, gesturing towards the door.

As they moved to vacate, Galric sat motionless staring into space, only stirring from his deep doom-laden contemplation when the heavy braced door creaked on opening. It had finally sunk in what he was actually doing; and an army was coming to get him. He sat silently cursing his ambition for allowing himself to be duped into this escapade. The lure of riches had blinded him; the promises of The Delvinius Company meant nothing now: cheap agricultural tools for peacetime, and to act as a cross-border middleman for Delvinius weaponry in wartime.

★

The Mercenary Captains decided to stay away from the meeting. Galric had all of the guards on show plus a few servants dressed up to bolster their numbers. The masses shuffled uneasily, muttering to each other, impatiently waiting and grumbling, but not actually taking any action to leave.

From his position, standing on a table, looking down on the crowd before him, Galric looked petrified. It felt more like a lynching; his lynching. He stared at the grubby faces. Behind the grime, the tiresome lethargy of subservience lingered.

After a couple of false starts he launched into a speech. "Dear People of Axia," he began, sounding more like a dictation for a letter. "The Lord Felix Danite has proposed a tax on all of us - he wants half of all produce! It is so he can raise an army to try and conquer the lands to the North. He seeks to neglect us even more so he can bribe and coerce new lands into subservience. Your food will be going to barbarians in the north, to satisfy them and lure them into submission.
I, as the chief of taxes here, have refused to collect this from you, because you cannot pay... can you?"

A few mumbled 'no'. Most of the rest were confused; a few shook their heads silently in scepticism.

Remembering what Danite had done at the only speech he had seen, Galric decided to sympathise then emphasise.

"You struggle all day to get enough to survive and already put all you can spare into his warehouse – for you do not give to me, I have to pass it up to him! So he can hoard it all! Give it to lazy foreigners! You cannot afford to give anymore, can you?"

They were more receptive now, but needed something a bit more convincing. Galric signalled for the secret weapon.

Out came the sage, the trusted wise man from the temple. The priest wore a simple black robe with matching simple cap and a necklace with a statuette of Arminus.

"Brothers! Sisters! Children!" he began, in an impressive booming voice that captured the audience immediately. "The Lord Thief descends upon this town now in a thunderous drumbeat of hooves to steal your produce! What will you do? Will you let him? Or will you stand up and fight like proud men? Arminius has blessed us with a worthy harvest; will we just let this robber prince take it from us?"

A sizeable number began to get excited and shouted that they would fight. But it was still not enough. Galric gestured to his bodyguard nearby, who passed him the bag of gold. He knew he had to phrase it in a way that did not sound like bribery. "Obviously, those who fight, will be paid as any town guardsman would."

This caused an uplifting mien in the crowd; some men even began pushing forwards.

"Take't'off me' tithe," one man declared, rushing forwards.

Galric laughed aloud, only to wonder why the crowd did not join in; "No!" He opened the bag and took out a shiny gold coin, "one of these!"

He eyed it with an avaricious love.

To his utter dismay the crowd quietened. Some began to yell, "what the 'ell is that?"

Galric smiled smugly at their quaintness. "Why, it's gold! It is worth…"

"It ain't worth squit! What does it do?" bellowed a wiry peasant.

Galric couldn't believe what he was hearing. They couldn't believe such a useless thing could exist, let alone be valued. "It works… by… if you take this you can give it in as your tax quota for a year!"

The same man looked even more sceptical. "Thought we weren't paying it anymore."

Galric was annoyed at the irritating man's dissent. "No, I said it won't rise."

He shook his head. "But you said the tax money went to Lord Danite, and if we is rebelling, then we ain't giving him any… unless you is thinking of taking it yourself…"

Just as he finished, a guard seized him and dragged him off. Several other men nearby tried to assist him but they were soon overpowered.

The rest stood staring at the glittering metal. *It was pretty* even if they could not understand it.

Galric continued, "or you could barter with it… give it to a street seller and they will give you something in return."

A division rose between the mass of people, those that looked on sceptically, and those that rushed forward to grab their coin.

Complete pandemonium broke out amongst these people; some tried snatching them off others. An old crone began screaming at the guard, as he would not pay her because she was both a woman and too old to fight. Another younger woman waved a baby at the man, saying she could barter it for some milk for her baby. The baby just screamed and screamed at the madness until its tiny throat went hoarse. Its protest became an erratic rocking and flailing of its miniature arms, flimsy tubes of soft flesh pounding against coarse linen. Two men began fighting over a coin and had to be separated by the guards.

The street sellers rushed at the coin holders thrusting junk in their faces, in the atmosphere of the moment, many felt like celebrating by throwing the coin at the beggar-peddlers and taking some useless junk just for the feeling of superiority. They didn't want the thing but they felt elevated.

Those who did not join in stood in complete bafflement. Then one youngish boy from this huddled group wandered over to the queue, waited calmly in line, took the coin examined it sceptically, shrugged to his friend across the square then tossed it away. He completely ignored the cursing rabble of madmen and women who descended on the shiny object with clawed hands.

Those who had exchanged their gold for items were soon itching with regret and a perpetual sense of unachievable satiety. They looked with sheepish envy at the street sellers who were fingering the coins hungrily.

To Galric's horror, one haggard old delinquent, after fingering a coin for a few moments started boring a hole in the top to thread a lace through. The merchants face contorted through many expressions of utter disgust at watching the pitiful, wrinkled, mud-splattered creature jab at the once pure and clean currency. An epitome of a society Galric felt worth aspiring to, being defiled into a primitive trophy to be worn by some filthy degenerate.

It was time to act. For the sake of the rebellion, this rabble needed to be organised. He gestured to his bodyguard leader, who passed the signal on to the head of the watch. The watch closed in on the group who had refused to get involved. Instinctively the few able-bodied men in the group tried to form a protective perimeter to the women and elderly that stood with them.

The leader of the watch tried to calm them. "We aren't going to cause you any harm… for your own safety you will have to be locked in the basement of the fort… as will the families of those who fight."

However those who had chosen to opt out seemed to have subconsciously agreed to remain united, and not try and run for it, or resist, especially as a great number were elderly or women too busy trying to keep control of their weeping children to be able to fight.

With a slither of dignity remaining, they were led like prisoners through the town they had lived in all their lives. The guards were tetchy and forceful, but refrained from any serious offences as they were anxious to get the deed done.

★

It was not long before darkness descended upon the town. As the light waned the terrain became a more dingy grey. The town, a mere black blot on this static, undulating grey sea, became less and less distinguishable from the intensifying darkness around it. In the darkness, the muddy root vegetable fields could only be differentiated from the huts by the solid lines forming near perfect squares. The slit windows of the fort held the inside light captive unless one stood directly parallel. Even then its range was limited.

Captain Dummonius had taken his men out with Aurelius's men's horses to carry trees to be used to barricade the roads. They had commandeered wood axes from peasant hovels, only managing to find two metal axes, the rest were flint stones wedged into crude sticks that despite being stripped of bark still seemed knobbly and branch-like.
They were bringing the last load back when it was dark; they each held a torch, the only source of light in the ghost town. Dummonius found it exceedingly eerie, wandering through a town with row upon row of pitiful mud huts, devoid of life. He felt guilt materialising in his gut and throat. Again he found his unease untraceable, *'I should be glad that a chore is out of the way, and I am closer to returning'* he told himself.

★

The two mercenary units ate together in the guards' room that they had passed through earlier that day. They were served a soupy stew made of root vegetables and some overly cooked non-descript meat. Nevertheless, Dummonius' horse archers were happy enough to not be eating travel rations from tiny bowls in the dirt. The two units kept to themselves, except for the two captains, who sat together in order to discuss the day's progress and tomorrow's problems.
Whilst they hungrily scoffed down the food, Dummonius could not help himself from wondering why Aurelius was committed to remaining behind and fighting to the last. After chewing up a sizeable lump of fatty gristle, he turned to his counterpart. "Are you confident about the plan, then?"
The captain stopped moments away from shovelling a stock-soaked carrot into his mouth. "If they don't wait for reinforcements we might repel them."
"What if they wait?" Dummonius asked.
The mercenary shrugged optimistically. "Then we have partially done our job without even fighting!"
Dummonius looked baffled, requesting an explanation.
Aurelius leant over so he was almost hovering over Dummonius' bowl. "You mean you haven't guessed already? This is a side-show. Our mission is to hold up the returning army and stop them from reaching the capital before the rebellion from the north takes it."
Dummonius looked concerned.
Aurelius beamed with excitement at being able to explain his superior's genius. "You see, it doesn't matter if we win the battle. The best we can do is give them a bit of a bloody nose then hole up in the fort for a couple of weeks. Which reminds me, we need to get all those

'prisoners' out of the dungeons, its just more mouths to feed and more people to have to guard."

Dummonius gave a frown. "More people?"

Aurelius gave a wry expression. "Come on, you think Galric is gonna keep his nerve?"

Dummonius nodded. "I doubt it, his current optimism won't last, then he'll just crumble."

Aurelius agreed. "Exactly…"

Dummonius felt now was the time to ask. "This is what puzzles me… if you know this whole escapade is futile why stay? Why get so involved, you're a mercenary in foreign lands. Just do what you can and get the money! You can't have a contract demanding that you die."

Aurelius laughed mockingly. "Contract!" he mused. "This is not about contracts; it's about orders… yes, they may say 'contracts' but this is about service to the household… I shall do much more for our house now than I ever did in the Vaca regiment."

Dummonius couldn't understand. "But… weren't you… Well, in my case I was asked to leave the military, they wanted me out because I didn't follow their belief system." Dummonius winced as he spoke these words. Even though he was out of their jurisdiction he still feared Aurelius could be a new interpretionist.

Surprisingly he seemed sympathetic. "I don't follow their beliefs… I'm what they call orthodox, but that had nothing to do with my decision. I requested a more significant service. So they told me to go mercenary." He paused, eyeing his counterpart cautiously. "I know some are hostile to what is happening, but it's still the same house."

"I'm not hostile, I just found I wasn't given room to do my job… they offered me it as an alternative occupation and I took it. I am still a dedicated patriot. It's just I felt as though I was being… well I was being overruled by a priest who decided he should command and I should be his puppet."

Aurelius nodded sympathetically. "I have heard this from others too, especially mercenaries."

"Anyway, back to the prisoner's dilemma; can we be sure they will be safe?" Dummonius asked.

Aurelius nodded enthusiastically. "More than if they stay in the fort. They can stay with the priest… we'll lock them in."

Dummonius shrugged. "What's all this about gold? I saw some street sellers with what looked like Latman gold… won't that incriminate us?"

Aurelius thought long and hard about this. "He's a fool for doing it. It was supposed to be for him and the mercenarys' payment. You will have to warn Delvinius about this so they can prepare an explanation…

maybe a plundered carriage carrying taxation gold attacked by bandits or Danite rebels?"

Dummonius nodded with concealed scepticism. He decided it was time for some less probing conversation. "So, how are the barricades?"

Aurelius replied with a less than vivacious tone, "as expected."

"There's just no wood around here! I mean a town without a wall, what are they thinking?"

Aurelius gave him a dry wistful look. "Not *they*... *He*. Felix Danite disallows any towns from having walls... so that something like this doesn't happen! He says walls are for forts, because forts are for soldiers. It's also the reason why he is still in power!"

"I suppose it's also why there are no military people here, just those town watchmen."

Aurelius nodded, "and they took a lot of convincing." He rubbed his thumb and his finger to symbolise large amounts of money, then brought his fist down onto the table to show coercion. "They are pretty loyal because they are temporary guards who, if they do well, will be promoted into the military."

"And those that left will be doing that I guess," Dummonius remarked.

Aurelius smiled. "Yes, even our informant!"

Captain Dummonius couldn't help but see the complete nonsensical way in which this man declared 'our' informant as though it would matter to him... a man who had two weeks, if he was lucky, to live. It filled him with dismal depression to hear this man talk of future victories that would occur after his death.

"Just make sure you get out of here with the gold. That's all he cares about from you, and if you tell him about the fate of the rest of the gold it will count bonus... believe me, I know Delvinius!"

"So I have to get the gold back and you have to hold the town for as long as possible?" Dummonius felt realpolitik had caught him even here. Was there any actual escape? Was there any decision he could make that would free him from its burden? Or was he just trapped, his free will merely a choice of where to be in the machine?

Aurelius nodded.

"But what about if Galric falters? You cannot hold the place yourself." Dummonius inquired.

Aurelius gave a worryingly frank expression. "Oh, he will continue the rebellion to the last, even if we have to kill his entire bodyguard and hold him hostage. He will stay here and justify our occupation. In fact, that would give us even less mouths to feed..." He trailed off, his expression a morbid grin of glorified death.

Aurelius smiled modestly, and spooned his last spoonful, and rose to leave.

Now he was finally alone he felt free to think of his own dilemmas. This was not what he had expected as a mercenary. He had thought he would just be guarding cargo, maybe attacking rival traders, not being involved in covert operations. He had left the military in favour of mercenarydom to escape politics, not delve deeper.

He thought of Aurelius. How terrible it would be to die here, unknown, a dead dog of war. Yet despite what he would be remembered as, he would die a loyal servant of his house. His service frowned upon because he admitted that money was an issue driving his action. It made Dummonius all the more determined not to die.

But it wasn't this he missed; it wasn't this that made him uneasy, it was how he felt betrayed by a false promise of freedom. Instead of liberty, he had condemned himself to solitude. He no longer had his men, people like Pluvius or Maxilies. But even with them he had always had a distance relationship, constrained by the hierarchy.

It was now that he realised who he missed, a young local prostitute, by the name of Pallavi, who he had met one lonely night and from then on frequently. He found himself thinking of her, now he was unable to see her, and he now saw how she had been more than just an escape from the tension. It was with her that he had a character beyond a cold warrior. It was with her that his personality had taken refuge, where he could return to being human, rather than the cordial part of a machine. They were each other's bastion for true comfort; mutual comfort drawn from, and in turn enhancing, the other's.

He had housed her, given her money for food, and on exceptionally rare occasions he had taken her out. Their relationship had been kept secret, not out of shame, but for both their protection (she no doubt had had his soldiers as clients and it could not be known to them that they had such a close relationship). He saw her face that last night materialise in his mind, her sweet face turn pallid and cold when he told her that he was leaving and becoming a mercenary.

She had put on such a strong front, acting so casually; it was like he was just a client again. As he solemnly abandoned the room, she had, with a twinkling well of tears in her eyes betraying her distress, whispered, "drop by... maybe... if you're in the neighbourhood... but I suppose it is really just all over..."

He had thought it a rhetorical question, one he would not answer. At the time he felt as though she was unconcerned, but behind the palisade wall she was wishing it would not be. Later he felt angry that she seemed to blame him as though it was his choice entirely, that she felt betrayed. It was now he could see how to her it was his fault, that he had never truly appreciated her.

He had not seen her wilt and collapse, like a kicked flower, the second he left the room. As he trudged along the crunchy gravel, he did not hear her sob and whisper his name with repentant devotion. Every crackle of stone like crushed glass being ground into her delicate torso.

'*If only the battle could be now!*' Dummonius begged, '*get it over and done with*'. Though he was on a three-month contract with Delvinius he seemed to have a belief that the sooner he completed the mission the closer he would be to returning to her.

It took some time for Dummonius to regain his senses, and when he did he was shocked; it was the first time he had daydreamed in years. At first he felt as though it was a sign of weakness or despair, but he calmed himself by deciding it was better to despair momentarily about a failure than to completely overlook it. All he had to do was make his dream reality; they *would* move to Lateria and they *would* be happy.

★

The next day heralded a virtually cloudless sky. The icy bitter morning gave way to a fresh breezy afternoon made reasonable by the constant presence of the sun. Despite the refreshing weather, Dummonius had spent the previous night silently pining for his mutual bastion and so was unable to appreciate the meteorological incentive.

A scout had found the approaching loyalists earlier that morning, and followed them to gauge how long it would take them to arrive. The scout had returned around midday bearing bad news, but had concealed the worst from Galric. The merchant had been told that a small group of cavalry had joined the force, however the scout waited until after his debrief to inform Dummonius that he had recognised the cavalry from Danite's arrival in Lateria; they were the lord's bodyguard. Dummonius congratulated him for not divulging this information to Galric, who was happily deluding himself with the conviction that they were just some cavalier merchant sons.

As the day progressed, Dummonius saw the enthusiasm of the peasants wane; Galric had locked himself away in his room, gazing over the map Dummonius had sketched, as though it would summon a saviour. He had, predictably, deteriorated into an even more extreme polarised capriciousness. Several times he had raged at Aurelius for betraying them to the enemy, and cursed the remaining watchmen for sabotaging his efforts to win over the population. Things became even more strained when he refused to allow Aurelius to slaughter the horses in the stable as he owned a share in the stock. The captain wanted to deny Danite extra horses that would enable him to ferry men to the capital more quickly.

The moment the scouts returned with news that the loyalists had arrived and were setting up camp on the nearby hillside, Aurelius called an immediate meeting. The three of them stood in Galric's room, though the merchant was still gawping at the map, completely ignoring the two mercenaries.

Aurelius stared blankly at his counterpart, the minimal light (Aurelius had stopped the merchant from wasting vital fuel) making his youthful face look gaunt and solemn.

"Tonight, Captain Dummonius, you must deal with their horses," he declared, as though it were a mere trifle to be dealt with.

Dummonius nodded. Their mobility would make defending the town more problematic, plus they would enable Danite to ride on to Danilia without waiting for the rest of the force, as he had done to get here.

"After striking them tonight, it might be your only chance to escape."

Just hearing the word immediately perked his demeanour. He would soon be on his way back to Pallavi.

"My men will need their packs ready at the first barricade along with the gold, so we can make a hasty exit in case the enemy decides to follow up on our raid. I shall be leaving my chainmail here as well as it will be too noisy and cumbersome for the raid... perhaps you could ask one of the watchmen to donate a more suitable set of leather armour?"
Aurelius nodded. "I shall see to it that it is all ready."

Without so much as a microsecond of stalling Dummonius set off to inform his men.

★

The loyalists had lit campfires before night had fully set in. However, it wasn't until darkness engulfed the town that the peasant militiamen began to look up at the fiery ridge as though it signified the coming of judgement. They had secretly scampered over to the boarded-up temple and whispered unheard words begging assurance from the priest.

To Dummonius' men, it was merely the sign to move out. For the Captain, it was another mental checkpoint to be ticked off in his passage back to Pallavi.

As the pyres flickered silently up on the hilly range, the peasants' whispers seemed to be carried in the wind, trailing after their scampering movements like sonic shadows. The slight sliver of a moon seemed to glide in the smeared grey sky, sprinkling the ground with light. The hills were highlighted with a dry brush of white, offset against the darkness of the fields, the clumpy soil of intersecting rectangles of black. This patchwork of darkness would determine Dummonius' mercenaries' route as they attempted to approach the camp unnoticed. The few trees echoed this darkness with stretched out branches silhouetted against the grey. A few wisps of cloud hovered as sporadic negative patches, contrasting to the definite strips of black soil below. Outside the town everything else seemed still, a frozen landscape crowned with the dancing flames of the campfires.

They rode in solemn silence, a column of lost warriors leaving an inhospitable ghost town: a fragmentary unit of the damned, exiled from their respective garrisons, and now abandoning a lost cause. To these men Lateria was not their home, nor was even their birthplace; home was with their former regiment, the comrades they had left behind.

Dummonius could see it in their eyes, they were like men trapped perpetually behind enemy lines, and cut off from the body they served. He needed to create a new body for them. For this he needed a foundation, people like Maxilies and Pluvius.

They passed the final barricade. Aurelius stood with two longswords flanking him. Several town watchmen stood nearby, in their own enclosed coterie.

As they approached, Aurelius turned; his face was barely visible, a haze of drained white skin and patches of black for features. To Dummonius it looked as though he was passing the spectre of an already fallen man, destined to stand watch in the phantom town that would claim him.

Dummonius could not see if the blotchy haze smiled, but found himself giving one. His men continued riding past, completely motionless as they clung stiffly to their mounts. They were clearly relieved to be rid of this fated place. He, nevertheless, wanted to show his veneration and so led his horse towards the Mercenary Captain.

Even when they were face to face, Dummonius could barely make out the man's features in the shrouding darkness.

"Good luck, Captain Dummonius," Aurelius declared with icy frankness.

Dummonius tried to be warmer in his reciprocal assertion, though found the necessity of using titles an unfortunate scourge to such an attempt. "The same to you, Captain Aurelius. I fear I shall not have much time when I return so I would like to tell you of the deep respect that I hold for your dedication..." He paused, straining visibly as he pushed himself to break through the public-private barrier. He thought of Pallavi, and how he would want someone to ask such a thing of him, though dare not ask for risk of impropriety. "If you have any messages you wish me to pass on to a family member or loved one then write them a note whilst I am gone and have my word that I shall deliver it to them confidentially."

Before an awkward silence could settle, Aurelius replied with a clearly appreciative tone. "Thank you, but I have said farewell to my family prior to this mission… and I have no other distractions."

Dummonius nodded in silent acknowledgement.

The horse archers had not stopped and were approaching the edge of the town. Dummonius nudged his horse into a reluctant trot before falling in at the head of the column. They headed straight for the fields, trying to guide their horses around large clumps that may cause them to stumble.

Dummonius looked up at the campfires set on the horizon surrounded by a black blur of the various tents. Now and again a man-shaped blob would form a silhouette in front of the towering flames. Judging by the size of the beacons they were deliberately being fed excessive amounts of dry wood to make the flames leap high into the air and intimidate the populus below.

As they neared the end of the belt of fields Dummonius signalled to the archers to keep an eye on the solitary trees that sporadically stuck out of the hillside like discarded overgrown ice screws. They held their bows ready so they could strike at the first sign of movement.

The combined trickery of the gentle but inconsistent wind, the swaying of the horses and the occasional stray streaking shadow from the fire's sudden movements, made the operation near impossible. Consequently they stopped at the edge, eyeing the trees with suspicion. With a swish of air and a blur of movement one of the archers leapt from his horse and silently began creeping forwards. Though trying to remain conspicuous, in case they were being watched, all the men tried to discreetly spot where the detected sentry was.

The cloaked shade seemed to merge into the surroundings as though chameleonic, virtually invisible to the mounted mercenaries. It advanced insidiously yet with an eerie rapidity that was almost ethereal.

Suddenly a condensed whizz of air followed by a fleshy thud glided over the top of the breeze. This was followed by a faint whimper and hasty scampering as the assassin-spectre homed in on the wounded victim.

In an instant, the dark haze of the killer merged with the sombre outline of the lonesome tree. The wet gurgling that had ensued came to an abrupt end.

With each gust of wind the phantom scout surged back towards them. Once reunited with his horse, the shade morphed back from the hunched cloaked wraith into an upright, proud horse archer.

As one column they began the ascent. Dummonius felt a rising unease in his stomach. With just flimsy archaic leather armour, and no bow to strike with, he felt impotent and exposed.

They got halfway up the hill before they heard a shout from a distant bush nearer the road. The infrequent mutterings up on the hill went silent as the loyalist soldiers pricked their ears, listening for a confirmation of what they all thought they had heard.

Dummonius kicked his horse into a near canter, knowing the archers would follow. The flames of the campfires flickered over the summit, frantically chasing after the smoke that rushed upwards to escape its fiery tentacles. As there was no time to silence the watchman, whose position was still unknown, the horse archers fanned out behind him ready to attack the camp.

The loyalists must have heard the thunder of hooves, as between the noises of the horses, Dummonius heard confused shouts. The mercenaries veered off to the right of the fires, hoping to circle around to the rear where the horses would be found. As they reached the ridge of the hill range, countless silhouetted figures ran from place to place in total confusion. Like a colony of ants under attack they seemed to rush around a myriad of pathways in organised chaos.

Some of those who had been by the fires, and ready with weapons, tried to chase after the raiders; however, all they did was make themselves ideal targets for the mercenaries.

The mercenaries laughed as the loyalists ran full pelt into arrows hurtling the other way. Bearded silhouettes thundered across the silky grey grass waving great implements for wounding, only to be struck down by thin wooden missiles hurtling against the wind.

As they swung around to the rear of the camp they were veiled in a blanketing shroud, as the flames of the campfire struggled to snatch at air above the tents. The raging fires' lights had blinded the attacker's eyes so the sliver of moonlight became a negligible source of light.

Some of the loyalists had rushed to the rear, their upper torsos illuminated by the torches some of them carried. The others scampered alongside with bows and quivers slung loosely over their shoulders.

The sight of these worried Dummonius as he was clad in the leather armour. He kicked his horse on, trying to ignore the incoming threat and instead focus on locating the targets.

Suddenly, dead ahead, Dummonius could see a misty orange cloud creeping around the edge of a tent, signifying that a torch-bearing soldier was just about to emerge from around it. As the torchbearer appeared from around the corner, the confusing haze of light became a squashed sphere of illumination. In the process, it illuminated a net of hay and a large horse's head. The beams of light stretched out further as he moved, until they revealed the whole body of the horse and the asymmetrical tracing of a slightly bigger horse behind.

The horse archers immediately sped up into a frantic canter, firing arrows at the unsuspecting animals.

The torch holder stood frozen from shock at the horse archers as they rode past him.

The horses were immediately transformed into wild screaming leggy lumps of muscle, dripping with blood. Huge flaring eyes were accompanied by similarly activated nostrils, attempting to portray the psychological and physical anguish they went through.

As the blood was spilled, an oily layer amassed on the grass below, their hooves causing them, in their panic, to slip, knocking each other over in domino run of flailing bundles of legs. This caused them to panic further lashing out with hooves so they struck each other on the back or soft underbelly. The screams became less frequent (but no less piercing), being replaced with frantic snorting and chafing.

Upon hearing these screams, Dummonius could not bring himself to get in close and do the dirty work with his sword, preferring instead to circle round and charge the petrified torchbearer.

The soldier barely moved.

Dummonius' horse brought its own wind with it as it charged at the soldier, blowing the torch flame back and up. Dummonius stopped his horse in front of the man. He plunged his sword at the man, who made a most feeble and belated attempt to defend himself.

The sword caught the man on the forehead, making a solid crack slightly muffled by blood that spurted out. His whole body collapsed, folding in on itself into creases of striped darkness and light. The torch flew up in the air, rolling as it fell to cast its light over his back, leaving a tiger-like pattern.

The mercenary Captain was knocked out of his trance by an arrow striking his leather carapace in the centre of his breast. He jolted in his saddle then looked down to see the crude stick protruding.

With the flames so low and close Dummonius could not see how far the arrow had burrowed; had it cut through the dried animal hide and pierced his skin? Though he felt a throbbing pain, he could not feel the wetness of his own blood leaking onto his skin.

Calming his horse, he brought it around in a 180-degree turn.

With most of them fallen to the floor, the mercenaries decided enough was enough and ceased the carnage. However, when they tried to disengage they found their horses, calmed from the adrenaline rush attack, were intent on approaching their fallen kin.

This was until Dummonius led his still skittish horse full-pelt through them and they, the herd animals that they are, all followed suit, much to the relief of their riders.

Dummonius' face beamed with joy, not for completing the mission per se, but because he had passed a significant waypoint in his journey to Pallavi. Indeed, he had quite forgotten about the carnage, the demonic screams of the horses, and the hellfire. Pallavi's sweet face floated in his mind, and kept him distracted from reminiscing about the atrocities.

As they raced down the hill towards the town, none of them dared look back to where shouts echoed like distraught whispers in the cold air, and fires blazed in a hellish torrent.

Dummonius was so preoccupied with his reunion with Pallavi that he did not even think about the arrow that had snugly encased itself in the leather armour. Nor did he consider the throbbing pain emanating from his torso where it had struck.

As they bobbed up and down on their steeds, the rest of the men seemed contented with the pace, all confident that the loyalists were in too much disarray to mount a counterattack.

Their steeds on the other hand, could not help their bodies twitching in instantly nullified panic with every noise, their ears remaining pricked for several seconds following each interruption. Still they obediently trudged on across the tufty grey, which was becoming more visible as the campfire infernos became increasingly distant pyres.

As they moved onto the dull monotone dark grey of the road they could see the black mass of the town huddled below, the mud huts sprawled out as a dry ossified rock foundation within which the squat fort was embedded. The temple sat staunchly, and the proud merchant houses formed an elite coterie around the marketplace.

He struggled to think of what to say to Pallavi, how to express his realisation of what they (had) had. The exercise was in vain as he found his mind grind to a halt, the emotional cripple that his kind was. Occasionally words would form, as though building a path across this unassailable terrain, only to strike a solid wall. Gradually his mind began to realise that words, building blocks of language, were no way to deal with this gargantuan block that encased his adoration of her. No, he needed action.

Suddenly with a stroke of genius, the predictable male answer came; unable to convey his sentiment as an idiom he looked to more physical methods. *'I should buy something for her in Lateria'.*

'I shall be paid and I can buy her something to show what I mean to say, but cannot.'

'A nice dress, they have many in the markets.'

His horse slowed to a walk when it reached the town. However, this was not a result of this being a place of safety. Indeed, quite the opposite, it crept with an insidiousness unnatural to a muscular warhorse, glancing furtively at every blotch of grey amongst the black. Not that

Dummonius noticed, but since they had entered the town they were surrounded by silence. The horse's ears scanned the surroundings, twitching in single movements to listen in all directions for unexpected noise. In order not to unnecessarily unnerve each other, the horses were careful to move as one. Any clopping of hooves out of time sent the others' ears flicking and heads turning.

Dummonius and his men were hurled into calming action when a dog sudden began barking and almost sent their steeds scattering in flight. From then on they joined their horses in silent surveillance.

Within what seemed like no time at all they reached Aurelius at the barricade. The mercenary captain approached them, guards following lugging the horse archer's kits. As soon as the torchlight hit the arrow, Aurelius hurried over to his counterpart. "Captain Dummonius, are you okay?" he asked with calm sincerity.

Dummonius looked confused at first, then noticed the arrow and without a second thought pulled the arrow out and shrugged. "I guess so," he mused.

He immediately set about the arduous task of removing the leather carapace. Aurelius handed him a tunic which he put on, before wrapping his cloak back around him.

"Your armour is in the pack," Aurelius informed him. He then handed him a bag that, even in the poor light, looked startlingly similar to the one he had given to Galric. He was also surprised at how similar the weight was. It jingled inconspicuously as he lifted it up and attached it to the front of his saddle.

Dummonius took one last look at the empty huts that sat around them like giant crouching beetles as they hunched just out of the reach of the torchlight.

Seeing these empty husks of abodes, despite their being so austere, seemed to fill him with a homeliness he hadn't felt since his departure from the garrison. Even though it was so inhospitable, the attributed sense of purpose gave it a deeper appeal. He felt an urge in his conscience to remain and at least see the beginning of the battle, and only abandon these men when all hope was lost. However, in retaliation, his sub-conscience reminded him of Pallavi.

Aurelius noticed Dummonius' troubled expression. "Do not worry, Captain, you do better service to the House if you leave now... it is imperative that you return and pass on the information and this package." Dummonius made hasty noises of acknowledgment.

"Captain," Dummonius struggled to find the words, feeling even more uncertain as he found himself the unofficial spokesperson for the institution he had left. "Your service to the House can never be fully appreciated."

Though this was supposed to be an emotive piece of rhetoric, it stank of a harsh actuality. Nevertheless, Aurelius mustered an appreciative but modest smile.

"You should make haste in case they decide to attack after all."

Dummonius nodded in solemn acknowledgement, gazing as he did so in the direction of the fort. Yet, so unlike the proud high castles of the Latman provinces, this keep seemed to hide out of view behind the mud huts. It was a dark solid structure, rigid and sombre, burrowing into the earth. Just the thought of dying in that squalid tomb sent shivers down his spine; no need to be buried, that necropolis would stand as a cenotaph to them all. The pallor of his face was masked by the colourful, if morbid, orange glow. Without hesitation he turned his horse and rode off, the squad following eagerly.

Chapter 22
The Chronicles of Captain Dummonius: Shared Dreams

Captain Dummonius had sat in the waiting room for nearly half an hour. A beautiful array of colourful banners and shields adorned the pure white walls. The room bloomed with light, which seemed to have no source, but be drawn in from outside by magic, and kept in as it bounced off the walls.

His scale mail gave off a dull shine in dispassionate tribute to the rooms' vivaciousness. The bag of gold was wedged between his boots, which were still smeared with mud despite a lengthy struggle to bash them clean on a wonky kerbstone. The bag itself, though hardly grubby, seemed lifeless and dull in comparison to the fine cloth adorning the room's walls.

A pattern of leaves danced around above his head in a flowing formation that covered the inevitable crack between the wall and the roof. Huge curtain-like drapes hung down in cloth torrents of colour, each one tempting Dummonius with the promise of being made into a perfect dress for Pallavi. Her petite figure acted as a mental model to each cloth in his mind. Swirling around as the fabric bound around her and slid into place gracefully until it formed a dress; cut, pinned and decorated.

It was as she curtseyed at the end of one of these displays that the picture in his mind was disturbed by the skeletal form of gnashing herbivore's teeth. He jumped back, almost off the bench and thought himself confronted by a muscle-covered horse skull.

His heart was pounding and he blinked rapidly to prevent any image from settling in his mind. His eyes began a slow cautious patrol of the room, all of the lavish decoration mere lines and patterns of potential camouflage.

His search was distracted by being summoned by a servant. He bolted upright, then stood, nearly tripping over the bag as he did so.

The servant looked at him with a professional vacant expression.

He followed the servant down the lengthy corridors of bright colours. The servant then opened an ornate set of double doors that blocked the corridor. They were plated with polished bronze; the wood underneath hidden in shadowy crevices welled with tar, an industrial blood that stained the organic material so that none of it was actually visible.

As the doors swung open, Dummonius felt like a king striding into the domain of the gods. The walls were painted a golden colour. From the far-left corner to the middle of the room was a kind of library. Even though most of the books were company accounts, it was still an impressive collection. Paper was scant enough (indeed, this had been Dummonius' only vice whilst working for the garrison: stealing paper, often ripping corners off scrolls - for a whole blank sheet would be missed - so he could scrawl messages to Pallavi, and then reading them to her as she could not herself) but to have shelves full of whole books to fill was unheard of. This section also had some comfy looking chairs that were constructed as though they themselves lounged, meaning a user would have no choice but to follow suit. These were accompanied by small ornate tables, the surface carved into shield shapes.

Closer to the door was a lounge area with a fireplace and upright chairs.

To the right of this was an area with several chairs and a sofa-chair. They were huddled around a sizeable drinks table. This was the 'family discussions' area, that is, where Delvinius would flatter guests.

The final segment, which was in the far right corner, was the 'official office'. That is, where menials were told what to do. It was here, behind the desk, that Ruperis Delvinius sat. The desk was a solid box with rounded edges; the short legs were built into the main body to form a low arch from leg to leg. This also served to conceal all but Delvinius exquisite boots.

Delvinius looked up and delivered a grand smile. He was covered with clothes extravagant enough to rival the grandeur of the room.

"Sit! Sit! Captain," came the merchant-prince's cheery voice, accompanied by a camp gesture. His eyes refocused momentarily on the servant who hovered by the door. "Julian, you may go! Don't let us keep you!" he exclaimed jovially.

Without shifting a single facial muscle the servant obeyed with a solemn shuffle out of the doorway, shutting the grand doors as he departed.

Dummonius cautiously approached the desk, out of routine from his army days, awaiting the superior officer's order to be seated.

Delvinius waved as though waiting for the order was unnecessary. As he did so he sighed light-heartedly. "You're almost as bad as him!" He gestured towards the door Julian had departed through, then took a self-congratulatory panoramic glance at his surroundings. "This is quite a change from our last encounter! I always like to meet my clients on 'their own turf' for the first time, but from now on we shall meet here."

Dummonius could not hide an appreciative smile. *'Yes, he must have thought I would be intimidated by this place the first time around'.*

'Yes, now you are one of mine I can trust you not to rob anything from my house,' Delvinius thought.

"I see you have the payment... so the mission is complete."

Dummonius made a sheepish expression, questioning himself over whether he had fulfilled his duty.

"I did not remain at Axia for the battle," he admitted guiltily.

Delvinius shrugged. "You have the payment. That was all I asked." Dummonius hesitated before lifting the grimy bag onto the clean table.

"Go ahead," the merchant declared with glee. "My servant will clear up any mess,"

Nevertheless, the mercenary captain placed the bag cautiously on the table, wincing as he heard the soil trapped in the fibres crunch on the polished surface.

Delvinius found the noise pleasing; it was the sound of job-creation.

"I do not know how much you have been told, but Lord Danite and his retinue joined the attack on Axia... Although the rest of his force must have headed straight for Danilia - Danite had left half his force on the border and that is why they reached Axia so soon." He paused and briefly glanced at the merchant.

"That is good. Though the rapidity of the attack on Axia is irritating news to learn, I am sure the Lord will want to retake the capital himself, so the main attack will be delayed as planned." He paused to consider distances and logistics. "Even if he rides by horseback with his retinue, the attempt to break the siege will not occur for at least a week."

Dummonius' face lit up and he proudly announced that the lord had lost his horses due to his unit's night raid.

Upon hearing this, Delvinius was ecstatic.

However Dummonius was undeterred from voicing his concerns. "Sir, the levy militia in the village was abysmal. I fear they will not hold for long. What is worse, they seemed to have acquired Latman style spears which will fall into Danite hands."

Delvinius seemed dismissive of the captain's warning. "I do not expect them to hold, besides they are not my men…"

Dummonius could not help himself from blurting, "but, Captain Aurelius, who is relying on them, is."

Delvinius seemed put aback by the mercenary captain's remark. He calmed himself and with an air of finality declared, "Captain Aurelius took the mission knowing of the risks. I am confident that he will hold the fort for some time." He paused to give Dummonius a fake chance to reply; though in truth it was more a check that he would not. "As for the issue of the spears, it does not matter so much…" He leant in and lowered his voice, "firstly, the Latman army is not interested in such units. Secondly… and let it be known I am only telling you this because your actions regarding the Danite horses has convinced me to give you a related job, we have a prototype spear much superior in the works."

Dummonius was dumbstruck; here he was, after leaving the military, being told of its secrets. Without thinking he began praising his contractor, "I am honoured by your trust, sir and I am more than willing to carry out your next assignment."

Delvinius beamed as he absorbed the gratification being poured upon him. "To be honest I was worried that the assignment would be below you, it is after all merely guard duty for some wagons – you being such a competent tactician. Nevertheless you deserve it. It will not be for some weeks yet… so in the meantime I shall leave the contract open but give you no other duties. You may wish to look for some able-bodied swordsman guards… if you wish to continue with the horse archers it is up to you… you manage your own men." As he finished his spiel he reached for the bag in order to give payment.

The sound of the clinking coins reminded Dummonius of the other vital information to pass on. "Sir, there was one other thing."

"Go on."

"Merchant Galric gave some coinage to the militiamen to encourage them to fight. Though I did not get close to them they looked to be Latman currency. I thought I should warn you in case Lord Danite traces these back to his Highness Juscius Latman."

Delvinius gave a worried look, deliberately aiming it away from the captain. Though the issue Dummonius raised concerned him in the said manner, it also worried him in another. Namely, whether Dummonius sensed foul play, and Latman collusion of the highest level. This he knew he could not trust the Captain with.

He tried to look unconcerned. "Our currency gets around a lot; indeed Danite border areas use it quite commonly. It should not cause any problems... if it does we can dismiss them as it is likely clandestine smugglers had somehow brought them into the Danite market."

Dummonius just nodded, baffled by what clandestine meant. He began examining the room admirably to detach his mind from the tense situation and ensure he did not seem to hungrily gawp at the money as it was counted out.

"Here is your payment, and with it details for the payment of the horse archers. If you wish to hire them again let them know... I will want to brief you on the next mission in three weeks so be in the city so I can contact you."

The mercenary captain was somewhat shocked by the abrupt ending, but upon seeing the bag of gold immediately began fantasising about possible dresses to buy Pallavi, and so departed rapidly.

The second he departed the room the servant Julian scurried past him. Dummonius was too preoccupied deciding which imaginary garment to buy Pallavi to hear the raised voice rattling out orders. Indeed, he only snapped out of his reverie to bow to the robed man who passed him by in the corridor because his sombre gaunt stare seemed to penetrate through the magical veil of his dream.

★

High Priest Zeuorox knocked, then pushed the doors open and strode into Delvinius' office in one fluid movement. It was not his usual system of manners, just one he utilised when he needed to set the scene of his superiority over a rival through flagrant disrespect. Of course, the irony was that for him to regard you as a threat and act in such a way could only be a sign of one's significance.

His beard looked straggly, strands breaking from the goatish column like the early rebellious twigs on an unkempt hedge. The effect was to diminish his grand sorcerer-like look into that of a feral necromancer. His staring eyes still had that captivating deathly stillness, and rings of flesh, like successive bands of age. This combined with his overall sombre expression and skeletal body, enhanced by the great robe that fanned up around his form.

Delvinius was pacing up and down in front of the desk, showing his displeasure at Julian for taking so long to polish the desk back to a perfect shine.

Zeuorox did not even wait for Julian to leave before beginning his tirade. The servant scampered off out of the door and closed it as quietly as he could.

"Have you not heard what is going on over there?" he bellowed with unconventional emotion.

Delvinius just looked at him with a sneer of irritable contempt.

"Danite had split his force, and now his honour-guard, led by Hanius Faldinite, march on the capital!"

Ruperis looked unconcerned and shrugged. "So, Felix will not order the attack until he arrives."

Zeuorox nodded in an 'exactly' kind of way, "but, Faldinite may do anyway. He may do it to thrust himself to the top of a wave of jubilation."

Delvinius was still uninterested. "So? Maybe he will need arming... a civil war would break out... someone will need men to be hired to tip the balance... in fact it sounds pretty beneficial!"

Zeuorox looked flabbergasted, and threw his hands up in the air; the extent of his movement was shrouded by the ethereal flutter of his robe. "You entirely miss the point, what would be the point in replacing one hostile tin-pot autocrat with a just as hostile despot swimming in a quagmire?"

Delvinius chuckled at the ease of the answer; though it came out as a snorting grunt. "Money!"

Zeuorox growled angrily. "But, such a situation would be negative for House Latman, the border would become unstable, and Gatan may support one of the sides, and have an excuse to build up forces on opposite sides of the territory. This would allow spies through that border, or supplies to Vaca rebels."

Delvinius silently accepted the priest had a point, and immediately began thinking of a way to profit from such circumstances. In his world that was called entrepreneurialism.

"So, what do we do about it?" he enquired, eager to hear his new challenge in the ongoing quest for economic satiety.

Zeuorox had calmed, but was no more optimistic. "What is there to do?"

Just as Delvinius threatened to open his mouth, the High priest cut in to prove it was a rhetorical question. "We cannot get any more involved, for fear of being found out... can you imagine the repercussions of that? Gatan would have every reason to send garrisons to patrol the Danite border – a big rapid war would ensue for certain!"

Delvinius perked up another level. "A big war... very profitable." Zeuorox smiled proudly with a dark irony to outdo his avaricious partner and rival. "No... a big *long* war is very profitable. A big rapid one is both low in profitability, and high in risk."

Delvinius grinned as his morbid desire rose in awe to his companion-in-thought. "A long, slow war, needing lots of resources." His face beamed ecstatically at such a thought. Gold coins flashed before his eyes, lavish cloth and statues twirling and rolling as soldiers kitted out in

Delvinius Company heavy armour marched to the sound of the long war. He returned his gaze and focus to the priest. "But how do I ensure that?"

Zeuorox beamed in self-admiration, his normally deadpan face an explosion of emotion. "That is where I come in!" he announced theatrically. "We need a war which we shall certainly win... but I can use my position to... influence things high up, so that victory takes longer."

Though excited at the prospect, Delvinius' scepticism kicked in and demanded to know why Zeuorox would do this. "But, why do you want to prolong the war?"

Zeuorox grinned, moving closer to Delvinius. "I suppose you have not lived long enough, or in the right places, to have learnt that when people are faced with prolonged hardship, they only have one place to turn: religion. No matter what the event, no matter how little concern they show for people, the gods never get the blame."

He sat comfortably on the desk, stroking the hairs above his lip for a moment. When he finally divulged his thoughts, he spoke with an ecstatic emulation of his subjects. "You know, I have always envied the gods, their stranglehold on power is indestructible. Their perpetual grip on mankind is unseverable... I sometimes wonder if they are deliberately trying to shake us from their cuffs, but we go on clinging! They are the ultimate defiance, a smug riposte to the belief that with power comes responsibility. Imagine if the gods had to rule over mankind like human leaders; they would be ousted from power within a year, and forgotten as negligent despots! What leader can claim that his flock are so subservient to his will, that the more he punishes them the more eagerly they revere him!"

"But it's the new gods, of your creation, that fail your plea? The orthodox gods just do their duties as we do... it is yours that are responsible."

Zeuorox shook his head. "The orthodox gods were worshipped and begged for divine assistance, only with them, it was preposterous because the gods were tied to fate, as we were, and so could change nothing. Besides, my religion is set on us proving our worth to the gods so that they will reward us."

Delvinius smirked wryly. "Aaah, there was me thinking you were infallible to profitable gain, but you are doing this to win favour with the gods... bring people into their arms..."

Zeuorox, conscious that he may have divulged too much, decided to go along with this as it was perfect cover for bringing people into his own arms. He decided to move onto another matter. "I passed a man on the way in, was he one of those mercenaries you sent to Axia?"
Delvinius nodded.

"The one from Vaca I hope"

Delvinius shook his head.

Zeuorox looked horrified, "the one from Gorad! But he is an apathetic dog of war! You mean to say you have left the dedicated warrior of Latman to die in a foreign land, and let this disloyal reject continue?"

Delvinius nodded again, and winced as he prepared to defend his decision. He realised candour would be the only escape. "My answer is in your words; an apathetic dog of war is the ideal mercenary. A loyal crusader is not a good mercenary, except in the case where he is being employed in Axia… that is to fight to the last. A man too loyal to the house is dangerous for the company; he has split loyalty. I don't want split loyalty; I want all his loyalty – his loyalty to the House should be via me. And before you condemn me, it is exactly what you want; only you want loyalty to the House through the temple."

Zeuorox shook his head in disgust, so furious that his alliance with this merchant was at times so perfect, and at others utterly at loggerheads. "That Gorad Captain has links with that squad, and my priest tells me they walk a tightrope. I think it would be advisable that you dispose of this heretic."

Delvinius found himself roused into a contemptuous rage. "You have no right to tell me how to run my enterprise!" he bellowed.

Zeuorox, perhaps for the first time in his reign as supreme advisor, backed down and allowed a space outside his bubble of influence. "Delvinius, you are right, I should not interfere in your matters." Of course, he had ruled out direct interference, but should a mercenary be found to be unpious, the relevant authorities would have to be warned.

"Well, Your Excellency, your long war will need good tacticians, and that Dummonius is an experienced man in commanding small detachments."

Zeuorox nodded reluctantly.

"I have sent Dummonius on leave; he will probably seek the employment of that Gorad squad," Delvinius casually declared.

Zeuorox was livid. "What! You should have checked with me first. How can you be so foolish as to get them involved, they already know so much?"

"Exactly," Delvinius countered. "It will not be spreading the knowledge of this any further. It is better to keep this information contained to a few. Besides, with them so close I can keep them under thumb much more easily."

Zeuorox was disgusted at the upstart's tactics. "You fool, it is much better for more to have scraps of information, than a few to have it all. Besides, I had them under my wing through Vultai. You have ruined my plan… let us hope they decline."

Delvinius would not admit a mistake so easily. "One squad knowing is much better, easier to dispose of, and much less costly to replace."

Zeuorox's wrinkled face was an explosion of twitches. "That is your problem; all you think of is economic costs, not the costs of concentrated information."

Delvinius, sick of being lectured, decided to bring up the final issue for them to discuss. "I am sure you are aware of the success with regard to the slave girl?"

Zeuorox grinned back, even his dry old skin and vapid staring eyes, showing a twinge of vigour at the mention of her. "Yes, getting her performing has got the word spread far and wide!" His expression suddenly turned saturnine and serious. "She has fulfilled her role, so now we must prepare for her removal."

Delvinius nodded. "As we agreed," adding, "how does he view her though?"

"He doesn't know. One minute he is praising her, others he is screaming for fear she will devour him. We should act soon…"

Delvinius nodded. "Timing could be key with this one, we do not want to damage his lordship, after all."

In an instant Zeuorox was standing. "Well, Merchant-Prince, I have things to do…"

Without waiting for the merchant to bid farewell, the High Priest took his leave.

★

Captain Dummonius had run straight to the nearest clothes shop in search of a suitable fabric. He was nervous, it was most unusual for a man, especially of his age and status, to do such a thing, even young men wishing to buy for their young ladies would be of a social standing to be able to send servants on such errands. The lady in the shop, though at first rather suspicious of this mercenary buying a dress (especially one for so small a person) soon joined him in his totally uncharacteristic joviality, inspired, perhaps in part by jealousy, by his clear devotion to the recipient. It made for quite a sight: a late-middle aged muddy mercenary and a hunched old harridan rushing about a shop piled high with fabric.

The old crone, resurrected from her zombiesque demise, demanded that she make special exception and make the dress there and then for him to supervise (though in truth his supervision was more a rubberstamp for her ideas). Long hours they had spent, much deliberation and discussion, often sliding into a tangent as he divulged his tragic pageant (of course he did not say the profession of his lady) meant he had to return over several days. Before thanking her and leaving he had learnt of her fateful life as an early widow and her struggle with the business. As he said his goodbyes she expressed a desire to see the lady-recipient and nearly begged him on her hands and knees to bring her to the city.

He thought about his most unusual encounter with the old lady all the way to Fericoa, the fledgling town in which his young Pallavi lived. One may think this rather strange, offsetting the burning desire he had had for months to see his mistress. However, seeing as his whole quest was to see her he was merely remembering a great chapter within his adventure back to his beloved. Indeed she was intertwined in his memory as he recalled his description of her to the lady; in his recollection she was there trying on each dress, twirling it and pulling the appropriate expression.

His horse clopped up the dirt track to the gatehouse of Fericoa. Two urban militiamen stood wearily, hunched close to a fire that crackled in a raised quadruped basin, its rising flames a satisfied grin, smugly wallowing in its own warmth, delighting with snide schadenfreude at the shivering passers-by.

Dummonius passed the guards, giving them as little notice as they did him, and continued on his way past the stone barracks. The rest of the buildings in the fringe were a collection of shacks and huts, lowly squat constructs little better than those that constituted Axia. After passing this band, the road became a channel through two lines of wood. It was as though having passed the soggy bark he now wandered through the grooves in the wood towards a more fleshy, lively centre.

The streets were virtually deserted; the only people he saw were opaque bundles of cloth that hobbled anonymously. Fabric ghosts of serfs, who had left their rural shacks and families during the slow winter months in search of odd jobs in the town. The lucky one would earn a few coins, or at least receive meals for some work, like chopping and carrying the extra firewood the rich folk desired during winter. Others just lingered on streets and in temples begging for coins, or scrounging and scavenging food.

The unassailable wooden walls to the man-made valley were frozen stiff in the moonlight, forming one mass of dead and rotting wood, the night's cold holding their decay in stasis. He passed a tavern that was frequented by soldiers on leave, a rickety building of beams and planks, its open stable an enclave in the otherwise unbroken cliff face. From it came the smell of manure.

As he passed the tavern, his attention was drawn to an upstairs window that was screened by a red cloth that was gloomily illuminated by a candle situated just behind it. The poorly covered window offered alluring scents to passers-by. From within Dummonius could hear sobbing. He quickly shut out the noise.

He hurried on up the path to his usual stable. He dismounted in front of the stable door, and knocked. After some hesitation, he heard the bolt being pulled back, scraping with a rusty sound. The door was opened by a boy he recognised as Theol. The boy looked cold and tired. Sleepily he croaked in his high pitched voice. "Sire?"

The two guards stood rigidly on the spot, hands on hilts. Clearly they had not recognised him in his plumeless steel helmet and strange looking chainmail. Casually he removed his helm and the boy's expression changed immediately. "Captain Dummoius! Sorry Sir, for not recognising you. I shall put her down on the list, and you can collect her whenever you wish." The boy did not ask him about accommodation, as he knew the answer.

"Theol, how are you my boy?" Dummonius asked.
The boy nodded. "Fine Captain, thank you. Yourself, Sir?"

Dummonius smiled, thinking of Pallavi. "Glad to be back."

Theol fought back a smirk, as he knew why (the stable boy was one of the few people who actually knew Dummonius by name who knew of his liaison with Pallavi). "Glad to have you back Sir. I had been worried you would not be back," he added.

"And how are 'the family'?" Dummonius asked (Theol had been 'adopted' by the inn owners, though he was more a resident employee than a son).

"Fine," the boy answered insouciantly.

Dummonius was almost bursting to rush the last couple of streets to Pallavi, so handed the boy the reins of his horse and began grabbing his things.

"Well, my boy, I have to be off. I shall drop by tomorrow as I may have some errands for you, if you have time."

The boy smiled, knowing he would be able to shirk off at some point and earn himself some extra coins. As Dummonius bade his farewell, the boy, red-faced with embarrassment, could not help himself from saying, "she will be so happy to see you sir!"

Dummonius felt the condensed ache in his heart thump in then wane gradually. The boy was telling him guardedly that she had pined for him.

★

He rushed down the dirt paths; the final stretch before reaching her. Once at her cul-de-sac, he sprinted to the small wooden house that he had bought for her. It was tucked away and safe, small and resilient with a petite charm that reminded him instantly of her. His mind was totally focused on reaching it, so much so he did not even hear the drunken shouts of a man slurring a pathetic incoherent excuse to his long-suffering wife, and children who cowered powerless as innocent bystanders, the eldest dreaming of a day when they would be old enough and big enough to stand up to this drunken buffoon.

When he reached the door he hastily removed his gloves. Instantly his hands broke into a cold sweat. No light came from under the door and the window hole was covered with the wooden shutter that that bolted from within.

He knocked, his hands trembling and losing all strength. With a strained expression he jabbed his fist against the door several times, then froze anxiously pricking his ears to listen for noise from inside.

Nervously his fingers began stroking his palms, the moonlight shining down from its high altitude to leave a gleaming shine on the door's surface. Suddenly a bolt slid within. Her petite figure had not betrayed a sound as she had risen to answer the door. Dummonius felt a searing pain in his chest, one so unbearable he looked away in fright. However as soon as the door opened, his anticipation overcame his fear, and he gazed at the widening cavern of darkness.

There came that point when the door was open enough for moonlight to shine in, it seemed to immediately seek out her form in a white nightgown, and upon reaching her stop going any further. His heart froze instantly. The door and all around it disappeared so that all he could see was her set against a black background. Somehow her jet black hair managed to out-black the darkness as it covered the top of her head and ran down either side, half covering her round cheeks before draping daintily over her shoulders. Then all this seemed to vanish as all the moonlight the moon could muster was sucked into her eyes.

Before he knew what was happening to him he felt tears two run down his face. She moved forward, her lips quivering in disbelief. He tried to speak, but found himself transfixed.

They stood staring at each other for some minutes. Pallavi had thought he would never come back, sobbing every night over the loss. When he had gone, her life had evaporated, leaving only the routines that nature incurs in order to manufacture a life.

In one silent movement she flung herself at him, wrapping her arms around his shoulder and lifting herself up to be close to him, locking her neck over his, and her chin where his shoulder became his back.

With her long soft hair in his face and wrapped around his neck like a silk scarf, he finally felt at home. He breathed in and smelt the unique comforting odour of her that had become a familiar homely smell, which he had been denied for so long.

Her soft voice sang out. "You have come back."

Dummonius was too crippled to speak and so mumbled a yes.

"I have missed you so much, I tried to pretend it was nothing, but I could not. It was foolish of me to push you away... please, forgive me," she continued.

Dummonius' mind was still a wreck, too skittish to communicate. "No..." he managed to splutter, getting a mouthful of hair for his pathetic effort.

Knowing he would never be able to get his point across verbally, he prized her away from him and looked her straight in the eyes, repeating, "no," and shaking his head emphatically.

She could see he had made exactly the same mistakes that she had and had suffered just as she had, but she also knew what mattered was that he was back.

"Let's go inside," she whispered, still tearful.

★

The sun was long gone and the stars twinkled in the fresh air that was made all the more invigorating by the scentless mien of the coastal breeze coming from the nearby sea.

There is something about the horizon when near the coast. Even when the sea itself is not visible, there always seems to be a refreshing cleanliness sweeping across the land from its direction.

The moon lit up the flat landscape that opened up before him, a vast expanse with ripples and mounds of earth attempting to emulate the very sea it was a precursor to.

Dummonius was glad that he had managed to persuade Theol to seek out Sergeant Maxilies at the Gorad garrison. The sergeant had reluctantly reported that Pluvius had been allowed leave and had left for Nepli, the small hamlet where he had defeated the baresarks. This meant he had had to leave Pallavi abruptly for fear of missing the sergeant and his squad during this brief period of freedom.

The stable boy commented on how unusually tense and hesitant the sergeant had been. He also appeared to have made no comment concerning a request to join his mercenary unit. Dummonius could only speculate that the veteran was being wise and keeping his head down. As he rode on away from the garrison, the mercenary captain regretted not being able to speak to him in person, and convince him it would be safer to come under his command and be free from the prying eyes of the authorities.

He began to taste the salt in the air, at first unsure if this was a psychological illusion. The taste opened his mind to dreams of freeing himself and his lover from the constraints and complexities that dogged their relation; a calm endless void of tranquillity exempt from restraint and responsibility.

THE SON AND THE HEIR

The descent down to the coast and hamlet came all of a sudden; indeed, the sea had been lurking on the horizon for some time, merely hidden under the ridge that the road followed. Consequently the village, coast, and vast expanse of sea, appeared before his eyes all at once. He gazed down; the torches in the hamlet were negligible compared to the sparkling reflection of moonlight in the countless waves. The buildings were dark blotches intersected with bright orange lights that flickered sulkily in memory of the currently submerged sun. As he looked more closely at the shimmering water he noticed similar dark blotches, fishing boats out delving deep into the secretive abundance below the film of silver light.

This became more evident as Dummonius' horse crunched through the crisp pathway soil without seeing a soul; all the men were out in their boats, the women at home praying for the gods' favour to at least remain for the night.

There was only one inn in the whole village, which stood out as the only structure blessed with noise and internal light. The building had an open stable that was occupied by eleven horses, all crammed around it with their reins tied to the rail and nearby posts. After scrabbling around in the dark shadows by the horse's hooves, he found space on a vertical beam to tie up his horse.

Then he headed straight for the door. A gust of stuffy warm air coalesced aggressively with the chilly freshness outside, and Dummonius stepped in.

A roaring fire danced behind a cage in the fireplace, its warmth and light subtly appreciated by the soldier's relaxed postures. Only the landlord seemed to acknowledge his arrival, greeting him with a surprisingly cordial smile.

Dummonius saw Pluvius sat at a table with Heites, Arios, the new recruit (Geric) and a young prostitute with darting eyes. She gave Dummonius a thorough examining stare, before making some witticism.

Pluvius rose and walked over to the Captain. Out of instinctive respect he stood to attention as he addressed his ex-commander.

"Good evening sir." His voice was dry, but not harsh, implying that the tone was a reflection of a general temperament and not any resentment towards the captain.

Dummonius found the situation awkward. Having always maintained a professional distance from his men he felt that suddenly arriving with a chummy countenance would seem artificial. However, to retain this elusiveness would suggest he was stuffily retaining a now defunct superior social standing. Luckily, Pluvius' saturnine disposition meant retention of the old relation was the most natural.

"Sergeant Pluvius, congratulations on your award. I hope you are enjoying your recreation time."

Pluvius ignored the mercenary's words, and asked if he sought somewhere to stay. Without even waiting for a reply, he turned towards the barman, who must have been watching through the corner of his eye as he immediately shot them a glance.

"A room for the night… and get one of the boys to collect all his baggage and take it to his room."

"And drinks for all the men… and their accompaniment," Dummonius interjected.

Now that their sergeant had risen, most of the men had noticed the old commander's arrival. Though some resented what they perceived as him abandoning them, others were more considerate, either suspecting he had no choice, or saluting his initiative in jumping the boat. A soldier of the latter group raised his tankard and bellowed, "three cheers for the Ex-Captain."

Sympathisers and cynics laughed alike, and put their differences aside, raising glasses in salute.

Dummonius smiled in appreciation. "It's great to see you… honourable soldiers!"

Most chuckled, not offended by his remark, before returning their attention to their conversations, and acquaintances.

Meanwhile, Dummonius followed Pluvius to the table. He immediately felt the tension; it was more like a war committee than a group of celebrating veterans. The normally loud and cheery Arios sat hunched, as though trying to shrink his gargantuan form to that of an average-sized peasant. Heites, the confident wisecracking cynic was even worse for wear, silently lost in some troublesome internal quarrel. The contrast to the other tables was uncanny.

"Heites, good to see you. Arios, how are you?" he turned to Geric and his voice ground to a halt.

Arios looked up and grunted impatiently. "Geric."

Dummonius lowered his head apologetically, then turned his attention to the girl. "And you are?" he could not help smiling in awe at her striking appearance.

"Julia, Harlot of the Hamlet, Prostitute of the Province and makeshift Goddess to the damned." She held her hands out to him seductively.

Dummonius, unaccustomed to such treatment, stood baffled for a moment, before leaning forward, taking her palms and kissing them awkwardly. She withdrew them and laughed haughtily. Dummonius assumed she was drunk. He drew up a seat and sat on it hunching forward, anticipating some form of question from one of them.

Quickly realising the soldiers were going to remain silent, Julia took the lead. "So, you are the former Gorad Commander Dummonius, presumed missing, then found washed up in Lateria!"

Dummonius laughed. "I didn't realise I was that renowned!"

Julia watched him with wide eyes, suggesting she was indeed quite tipsy, this being confirmed by her swaying a few times and snuggling up against Pluvius' rigid, inhospitable torso.

"I'm a practical woman, I am also one who, you might guess, holds little regard for the use of the term honour to congratulate lackeys of our dear leaders."

The soldiers all stirred uneasily, clearly feeling insulted by her candid rubbishing of their hallowed attribute.

"So, I salute your action, if it has freed you from their clutches"

Before Dummonius could thank her, Heites scoffed. "Your breastplate blazon with the emblem of Delvinius suggests otherwise. What talk can there be of honour with that stamped across your torso? Tell me, how is your service faring?"

Dummonius was taken aback. Clearly this sophistic soldier had quite an axe to grind with Delvinius.

"It is just a contract," he corrected, protectively. "I can leave it whenever."

Heites gave him a cynical disbelieving look. "Can you really? And they would do nothing?"

Dummonius held in his instinctive nervous laugh. "Why would they do anything?" He looked to each of the men sat with him to see if they agreed with him in dismissing Heites' paranoid speculation.

He was soon disappointed. "They've not needed a reason to pry into our lives as much as they already have," Pluvius declared.

Arios nodded in agreement.

Encouraged, Heites continued, "I doubt they have you just doing guard duty, not someone with your experience. You'd be ideal for more important operations…"

"Yeah, they could get any bunch of thugs from The Old Chalice to be watchdog," Pluvius interjected.

Dummonius started, and he leant in with worried intrigue. "Why do you say The Old Chalice?"

Pluvius, Arios and Geric began looking at each other knowingly. Julia, who had never been to Lateria, and Heites, who had paid no attention during the visit, sat there as baffled as Dummonius. Eventually Arios quenched their frustration. "The Old Chalice is the tavern of Lateria renown for dregs and bandits willing to do anything, preferably violent, for money."

Dummonius looked down at the table in shame. Overwhelming this cull of dignity was a welling anger as he realised Delvinius had made a deliberate snub on him. Dummonius quickly redirected the conversation. "My next mission is a security one."

Heites looked interested, but not for the obvious reason. "So, your last mission wasn't?"

Dummonius would not have told them anything of the mission but felt his pride injured by Delvinius meeting him in the Old Chalice. He briefly outlined his mission.

The veterans seemed shocked, Heites was the most angered. "That is no escape from their doings – don't you see, you were part of a secret operation to undermine a rival house just for opposing Juscius and his New Interpretationist plans?"

Dummonius sought to salvage some dignity, "but I am just doing it for money... besides someone else would have done it in my place."

This time Julia chipped in to support Heites. "But, what use was your resignation? You still follow orders; the only difference is it is more direct now: from the elite's mouth."

Pluvius felt embarrassed by his lover's wild attack, and so sought to compensate. "To be fair, he is no longer in the clutches of the New Interpretationists."

Julia gave Pluvius a somewhat patronising smile. "Delvinius may not be a priest, he may not even be a new interpretationist, but he is working with them. His orders are from Juscius Latman II. So yes, he is more directly under their control."

Heites gazed at her in wonder as she took the words out of his mouth, rearranging them so eloquently and then sang them out in such a mellifluous fashion. 'She gets it' he thought, instantly reminded of his panic-stricken search for an understanding ear after 'the incident'. Under the table he felt his hands tremble as the horrified temperament made a haunting return. He coughed then forced his hands back into the present by launching them steadfast at his tankard, lifting it to his lips and draining it.

To escape this maelstrom of angst he launched a somewhat premature summary of the mercenary captains proposal. "It seems to me that this 'mercenary opt out' is nothing but a con. No disrespect sir, you have escaped a much different intense circumstance. You had to not only follow all their regulations, but enforce it on others and be part of their schemes. I, however, am neither in your situation, nor can I be satisfied with the position of mercenary – I want more, I need to resist even if it means less personal freedom."

Before silence could settle, Arios addressed Dummonius, picking up on Heites' last comment. "As a mercenary, Captain, do you suffer the same constraints now, in privacy?".

Dummonius, pleased to be asked and not oppugned, was even happier to report something positive. "No, none. The contract concerns my profession only."

Arios' eyes lit up. "Seeing as Heites has made his position clear, I would like to make my own. Our major concern is with their prying into our lives." Geric nodded with him. "So I say we go mercenary..." He turned to Pluvius, who was quite shocked (as opposed to Heites who was just disappointed). "I know this will come as quite a surprise, I am shocked myself. Having been a dedicated soldier for years, I have always been proud of our honourable profession, but I am sickened by what they are doing to it. I also feel that for my service, I do not deserve to be treated with such contempt by the likes of Hari."

Heites was onto his points like a fox. "This New Interpretationist project is much greater than just a shakeup of the military, the military is only the first to come under its supervision, they will gradually rope in others, all we would be doing is jumping this campaign in its latter stages, and into the sights of a later one. What is more, we would be piling suspicion on ourselves – surely someone will ask – why is this honoured squad asking to leave? I say we stay as we are, and slip through the net."

Arios was angered at Heites' desire to drag them all down with his cynical rebelliousness.

"Slip the net!" he scoffed, his voice booming to a level that sent several heads turning in their direction. "Look, Heites. I respect you as a good friend, excellent and proud fighter, but I do not wish to be dragged into your private struggle."

With these two at irreconcilable loggerheads, they all turned to Pluvius for an answer. The sergeant seemed unsure. Though reluctant to endanger his men by attempting some kind of insidious crusade, and tempted by promises of limited freedom, he saw logic in Heites' warning. "We haven't actually been offered the retirement package, so I am wondering if it is possible."

Dummonius, feeling the suspense tried to speak casually. "Delvinius will be able to sort it out so that I can request any units leave."

Pluvius nodded in acknowledgement, but was still undecided; he turned to Julia.

Julia gave each of the onlookers a worrisome stare, troubled and surprised that the fate of all these men was in her hands. The tension and importance seemed to have sobered her up as she eyed each with a daunting look of seriousness. Finally she spoke.

"Well, I agree with Heites. It seems a shallow and uncertain move to be mercenaries." She turned to Arios and Heites in turn, a tingling uneasy feeling of satisfaction as she lectured them rose in her throat, spurring her on. "You need to remember that you do not have to resist if you remain. All you have to do is look after each other, both of you will want your privacy for different reasons, you should respect that and be each other's guard." Then her tone changed entirely as she focused solely on Pluvius, smiling and playfully tickling his chin she declared, "plus, I don't want to lose you… I like you being based nearby. We can save up and escape."

Dummonius seized the opportunity, dispassionately attacking her weakest point. "But, she can come to Lateria, plus the pay is better, you can retire sooner."

Julia shook her head with an expression of distaste; "No, I would hate the city. There are more than enough people here to irritate me. Besides, he would travel so much I would never see him. I prefer to save up and go to Vacarium all in one fell swoop."

Dummonius smiled, clearly happy to hear their dream had not been shattered by all the turmoil, and immediately began thinking how much of a great thing such a shared dream with Pallavi would be.

"That is quite a dream, good luck to you!" he declared candidly, raising his flagon and downing it.

They all joined in the toast, Heites the only to do so begrudgingly. "Quite a cliché at that," he muttered, thinking he was more irritated at the obviousness of Julia's shared fantasy than with whom she sought to have it.

Ignoring Heites' mutterings Dummonius thought out loud. "Where are those drinks?"

As though on cue, the landlord set off from the bar with a tray of six flagons.

"Ah, here they are!"

The landlord waltzed effortlessly with the containers straight to them and placed them down.

Without thinking, Dummonius reached into the pocket of his cloak-coat and placed a gold coin on the table, proudly proclaiming. "This should cover it all."

The dazzling new surface of the coin reflected the orange glow of the roaring fire with a spectacular shine that left all the onlookers gasping.

In an instant Heites bolted up with a troubled expression. He then lunged forward and snatched the coin in a lightning strike, and began examining it, hunching over it like a child with its favoured toy.

"Where you get this?" he asked, not looking away from the object for a moment.

Dummonius was rather bemused at the veteran's actions, believing him to be fascinated by it aesthetically. "Delvinius."

"When? barked his next question, still running it through his fingers, and looking at it like a murder weapon.

Dummonius, who still thought the cynical soldier had an interest its beauty, answered, "well, I was given it two weeks ago. As payment."
Heites made a 'hmming' noise.

"Though it was Galric's (that's the leader of the rebellion) before that – he gave it to Delvinius as payment, and he gave me my cut."
Geites gave him a disbelieving troubled look. "Impossible."

Now all the onlookers were worried by Heites' darkening tone. "This is new... too new, look." He showed Pluvius the coin. "That is the latest batch, it's only just in circulation, probably a few weeks ago."

Dummonius felt a lump in his throat. Something in his mind reminded him of Delvinius' snub and this pushed him into disclosing more. "Although, I took a bag to Galric when I went... and have reason to believe it had money in it."

There was a collective gasp. In the meantime, the landlord muttered something about adding it to the room bill and left the vicinity.

"So you took money to Axia and brought it back to get paid with it." Heites summarised.

"You mean they are subsidising this rebellion?" Julia questioned.

"I don't know. Who knows with the complexities of commerce, taking money here and there, it could have just been a formality," Dummonius answered defensively.

Heites was more certain. "If by 'they' you mean Juscius Latman II and the Treasury then yes!"

He paused before explaining. "This money is too new even for Latman to have paid Delvinius Company for anything. It would have to have been paid before release. When you took it, it was fresh, and had it been recorded in the books as a transaction it would have been suspicious.

"However, if it gets taken to Danite, and comes back a couple of weeks later it can be cashed in with other transactions and go unnoticed. I assume they took a cut, the rebels, as a kind of funding but it was basically a way to pay Delvinius for his services in supporting this rebellion."

"It makes you wonder how genuine this rebellion actually was – if they got paid to do it," Julia commented.

Dummonius nodded reluctantly. "Not much, judging by the difference in weight. But then money is hardly much use... but they also got Latman spears."

Now Arios was angered. "They gave away our spears! To enemies! The traitors!"

Dummonius found himself defending the company again. "Don't worry... I shouldn't say this, but my next job is to guard a shipment of new spears."

However, to his dismay, rather than pacify them this only enraged them more. They eyed each other in abhorrence as the quickly realised that they all thought the same thing. Finally, Pluvius muttered in disbelief. "They cannot have some of those ready already... the material was something totally unknown."

Meanwhile, Julia had switched off, bored by the subject matter (*'huh, men and their sticks!'* she remarked to herself, mocking their boyish obsession). Dummonius, on the other hand was bursting with intrigue. "What?"

The four soldiers exchanged glances. "Did you not know?"

"What?" he repeated, all the more anxious.

"The mission we went on into the forest, that was to recover prototype Gatan spears, ones that Delvinius had stolen." Heites declared casually.

"Well we don't know who had made them, or who had stolen them... but they were a solid unbelievably light metal, useable as a spear and a javelin."

Dummonius nearly choked.

"Well, that makes the large injection of money to Delvinius make more sense, it must have been a payment for the spears," Heites concluded.

Reluctantly, Dummonius conceded defeat. "Well, I suppose you will not be interested in joining my unit."

Neither Heites nor Arios felt they were in a position to answer; such a responsibility was Pluvius'.

"We shall have to decline... at least for the moment," he declared apologetically.

Dummonius was saddened by the rejection, and embarrassed at what they had discovered.

Unable to speak he merely nodded to show he understood.

Heites had been transported to a state of sanguine optimism; together they had uncovered the clandestine operations of the authorities. They knew what the enemy were up to and he had steered them away from a fateful mistake.

Arios, meanwhile, glowered with sombre disappointment. He was not angry with Pluvius for his decision, nor with Heites for opposing him. It was the web of complexities and covert reasons behind everything that made him feel trapped and unable to trust anyone.

Dummonius slipped his hands into his pocket, and began nervously massaging some scraps of paper in his pocket. "However…" he stopped, worried that this paper could endanger her. "… Take this. If you change your mind, seek out this address; it houses my most trusted friend. She can contact me, or take you to Lateria. If you need assistance finding her, go to the Inn, ask the stable boy Theol, he can be trusted." He pushed a piece at Pluvius, Arios and Heites respectively.

They took them simultaneously and slipped them into pouches in their scale mail jackets but said nothing.

After a few moments silence Pluvius commented. "Thank you, it is always good to have options."

Dummonius awkwardly shifted his posture to seem more casual, "So how are things in Gorad?" he inquired.

Pluvius shrugged. "Pretty dismal"

"I contacted Maxilies. He seems to have changed a lot. Is he taking the changes well?"

Heites chuckled ironically. "For himself, very well!"

"He seemed near paranoid," Dummonius commented.

Pluvius nodded with a concerned expression. "He is very… cautious. It worries me how edgy and subdued he is now." Leaning forward into their inner ring of conversation Arios commented. "He's a survivor. He's always been a cautious fighter; now he's threatened in the garrison he's adopting this fighting temperament permanently." "It cannot be good to be in that state all the time," Pluvius proclaimed sympathetically.

"But he's the same old warrior?" Dummonius inquired.

All three nodded warily. "I think so," Pluvius answered, looking to his left and right hand men for reassurance, which he got. "He's guarded. As Arios said, he's a survivor. So he's swallowing any disillusionment and keeping his head down."

"Can he be trusted?" Dummonius asked bluntly.

There was a brief pause as the three veterans assembled appropriate answers.

It was Pluvius that provided the answer. "He can be trusted, just not relied upon." He shifted uncomfortably. "I mean, he won't betray you, if you tell him something in confidence – it's just getting the chance to do so. He's too cautious to allow such an opportunity."

"He operates on a 'if I don't know I can't tell basis'," Heites clarified. "It's not that he can't be trusted now, but as he is a survivor he will look after himself if pushed. At the moment that means he won't get involved in anything suspicious, but if he were dragged into the office and coerced into pointing the finger or losing it, he'd point," he added cynically.

Both Pluvius and Arios resented Heites' condemnation of Maxilies, but remained silent as secretly they suspected he was right. With wary caution Pluvius subtly muttered, assuming he understood the purpose of Dummonius' questions, "he would benefit from being released from duty and seeking a similar profession outside the garrison."

Dummonius nodded. Nothing more needed to be said.

"How long are you staying here then?" Dummonius queried openly.

"We must leave tomorrow evening," Pluvius replied.

"Well, I am tired from travelling, so I think I shall take rest. I shall see you all tomorrow." Dummonius declared.

He rose wearily. The rest of the soldiers at the table made complimentary gestures as he shuffled off, his stiff movements resonating poignantly in the creaking floorboards.

Julia had watched him depart, casually exclaiming, "if you want someone to accompany you, I can get one of girls to come up once you are settled."

He arched his torso round, his feet rolling on their ankle balls to exert pressure onto his toes and consequently summoning an accompanying sound to his movements above. Giving a pleasant smile, he candidly declined. He ambled over to the landlord who gave him directions to the room. All the way up the eerie staircase and equally vocal passageway he imagined Pallavi to be waiting for him.

Once he had gone Pluvius and Julia began a private conversation, whispering and muttering in such a way that made Heites uncomfortable. He turned to Arios and Geric, but to his dismay they seemed just as engrossed in private conversing. Glad to get his mind off other concerns, he began to probe his memory and recalled that Arios was normally a worse womaniser than himself, and yet recently had been much more reserved in such situations.

He sat there silently congealing in his own solitude, before eventually deciding he needed to go and find someone to distract him. With a superfluous sense of spite, he slunk away from the table, making a beeline for a rather aged whore who sat with a sombre expression that almost matched his contrast to the other soldiers.

Chapter 23
A message from Amarrar Hall

The cloudless blue sky peeped through the black webs of tree branches in a cheery expanse of colour. In this light, even the dark twigs seemed to add to the sense of freshness on this chilly winter day. Perhaps they were ossified remains to remind the coming spring of preceded it, of what it would be built upon, and what it did not have to concern itself with.

The sun shone through the elevated black splinters, spreading powerful warmth to counter the natural chill of the season. A gentle breeze caressed the branches and softly drifted through the copse, bringing with it the tapered smells of rural winter. Rabica slowly took a deep breath, drawing in the freshness before exhaling reluctantly. Though his lungs felt the benefit, he could not help but feel guilty that he was taking the coppice's fresh air, corrupting and transmuting it into his stuffy odorous breath. As he wandered through to the far side of the wood and smelled the pleasant air, he felt his guilt wane, disintegrate and blow away in the wind. "There is plenty of it, so even if it is theft and degeneration, it is negligible," he reasoned.

He gazed at the tranquillity with the awe of a tourist passing through a spectacular civilisation. As he took heavy breaths he longed to join it. He listened carefully to the mellifluous birdsong of the natives.

The birds flickered between shadows and branches, leaving him to enjoy the carefree solitude.

His gaze settled on a tree trunk. Its gnarled knobbly texture was laced with moss and toned with patches of lichen. He smiled at the colourful parasitical organism that managed to cohabit with its host, giving the tree life in the desolate wintery months. As his fingers traced over the hard bark he found himself astonished at the complexity and detail that the twisting and turning texture encompassed. He was impressed by the hard resolute cocoon protecting the dormant life in tranquil slumber within.

The damp patches of moss soothed his fingers. When his digits ran over the lichen, the scaly desolate texture served to remind him of how such pitiful scabby matter could subsist on the most majestic of life forms.

He recomposed himself, obliviously stumbling into his own trap as he congratulated himself of not thinking of The Young Lady. He immediately noticed the irony that thinking that he had not thought about her was in fact thinking about her, and that his celebratory thoughts were in fact self-deluding. Inevitably, his mind plunged into the quagmire of contemplation about Her. "Oh how She would love it here," he remarked, with unsubstantiated speculation.

As if on cue, Rabica heard rustling behind him. He turned, starting when he saw someone emerging from the undergrowth.

The first thing he saw was a yellow and green emblem of Lewerix. He hissed and backed away like a vampire confronted with a cross. The life seemed to drain from him; all the placidity that was promising the onset of bloom fled. A rampaging infiltrator had torn through the undergrowth of this peaceful refuge and sought him out to drag him back to the palace.

'*At least sneak into this neutral domain!*' Rabica pleaded. '*Do not barge in as though it were just your peripheral play area.*'

He gave the invading messenger a stern look, but soon found his stalwart posture falter as the foliage rustled around him, and in a fit of paranoia he imagined a whole company of shady forms blazoned with the Lewerix coat-of-arms were approaching. Had they been lurking all this time? Waiting for him to think of Her, for that torturous link to society to become resurgent in his mind.

The messenger saluted and sat, straight-backed, to attention. It was no longer a symbol of respect to Rabica, but a societal malignance manifest in the minds and actions of all its subjects. He was supposed to respond, show the customs of society still had him in its grasp. The man waited for it: a cog awaiting the signal from the other cog to set the machine surging on.

Instead he forced a smile, but the human action failed to compute on the blank face of the recipient.

"Sir, I hope you do not mind the intrusion, but I have a message from Amarrar Hall." The voice was monotone, cold and mechanical.

Rabica's heart stopped: it was the name of The Young Lady's residence. '*So this is how they seek to lure me back from the edge!*' he told himself. Rather than question the logic behind such irrational pessimism, he found himself searching for a viable source of the campaign against him.

'*Is it the gods?*' He felt like cursing them anyway. '*No, it's that irritating sod's-law fate, the seemingly conscious hand of coincidence, conveniently guiding apparent randomness to cause the most inconvenient series of events.*'

He paused in his soliloquy. *'Surely that is the gods!'* he reasoned, with macabre delight.

He returned his attention to the messenger, the anchor that had grounded him just as he thought he had escaped. Rabica staggered towards the mounted guardsman, jerking stiffly as though these were the last steps of a man riddled with arrows.

The man glowed red, shocked at the noble's posture, but nevertheless cordially leant down to hand over a note. To avoid further embarrassment he bid his farewell immediately.

Rabica waited for the comforting silence of solitude to return. He rustled the scroll open and skim-read it, pretending to himself it was out of disinterest and not an insatiable anxiety to know what she had sent to him.

Once he had read it he cursed aloud. It was an invite. Striking the article with his knuckle, he bellowed at it, spitting with ribald acrimony. "You come too late!"

The ink-stained sheet stayed rigid, mimicking a vacant taciturn riposte.

His face screwed up with disgust. "No! You come just right! Just at the right time to destroy my break from compliance, lead me back to them... it!" His mind flashed with an image, not of Her, but of the palace.

"You show me that, you traitor," he accused his memory.

Returning his attention to the paper he spat. "If I renounce that horrific sedimentary entombment of generations I will deny myself any contact with her... You really think it will work?"

He eyed the paper with a deranged steely stare.

Breaking off the confrontation he sank to his knees in submission. "Of course it will! If anything will, She will."

Gazing up accusingly at the sky, he saw a fluffy white cloud looming in a gap in the branches. It seemed to be floating over him, a constant reminder to subtly drive him back the shelter of the palace-cum-oubliette.

He shrugged off the belief that this was an indirect coercion and in the process swallowed the bait.

"But she has specifically invited me. She must want me to come," he reasoned. *"Has my patience finally paid off?"* he muttered hurriedly, not daring to acknowledge he had uttered the words. Feeling disgust at his absurd optimism, the forces of inertia mellowed in order to seize the day. "Well, to fail to attend would be a snub in the face of her benevolence. I should go whatever the reason."

All the time, a deep crevice of his mind was frantically warning him that he should not go as it would only replenish his hazy recollection of her and defeat his attempts to forget.

"Let it be the final test," the mass disposed towards inertia declared. "For she is truly the only reason to stay here."

Resurgent optimism slipped further towards oblivion. "At least it can serve as a final goodbye."

He took in a panoramic sweep of the tranquil view. The breeze continued its endless rolling through the undergrowth. Dry branches and trunks stood solemnly waiting the reawakening of spring. A spring he had longed to be part of. But instead he had to trot obediently back to the system from which he was spawned. He had to cling to the rotten family tree of his House. Clasp its bloody branches with his leeching menial existence, just to remain in her vicinity.

As he looked around him he no longer saw the slumbering freshness of the trees surrounded by a warm carpet of grass, but instead the palace founded on dry dusty mud. Begrudgingly obeying the call, he began to trudge back towards it.

"It seems like too much of a coincidence, on my final days of deliberation. Just as my decision seems to slide irreversibly towards escape, I am hauled back into the grasp of society."

He soon left the coppice and walked along the rough clumpy grass towards civilisation. His mind was simmering with confusion. He could soon see the palace. A contumacious rage filled him and he looked away. Consequently, his eyes settled back on the wood. The sun shone down unhindered, the woody mesh of branches forming a fuzzy mess bedded in grass and moss. The sound of birdsong returned, lightening his mood.

"Maybe she will give me another chance, maybe she won't. But this event will make it final - either I will stay forever and live a compromise, like the scaly patch of lichen, or I shall leave and begin a fresh new start, sprouting elsewhere."

For a rare moment Rabica smiled.

"This will merely reinforce the permanence of my decision... either way."

★

Rabica thundered blindly through the void that was passageway to his room, slamming the door with such a furore as to send the whole building trembling. He kicked the strewn landscape of junk on his floor, desecrating his desolate domain. Bottles chinked as they tumbled to the ground.

His mouth trembled with the rage that he dared not let go of, for fear that it would vacate his body and leave an empty husk behind. Instead, he clattered irritably around his room in search of his desk that he had laden with spirit in anticipation of such a response to the evening. His fingers clinked against a bottle and he soon had his whole hand clasped around the smooth bottleneck. He wrung it tightly. It clicked open with ease, and he soon had a mouthful of the burning liquid in his mouth. He flushed it down with one stalwart swallow, its searing sensation exploding all the way down his throat.

"Well, it is final," he declared. The bitterness coalesced into a sickly smile that slid across his face.

He had spoken to her only once. He had stood around on the periphery, like a ghostly apparition: an antiquated heirloom lost many years ago that now lingered in solitude. She had spoken dismissively to him, negating his attempts at kindness, subtly concerning the bad book. With shrugs and distant words she weaved and meandered diplomatically, telling him not to bother.

"Do not upset yourself with those things. I am sorry to have mentioned it to you. I should not have. Do not trouble yourself," she had told him (only after first listening to him squirm).

It was over. Wallowing in seclusion, he wanted to believe it was part of some divine conspiracy.

"I shall rally here, in this squalid refuge, and prepare to flee this whole abomination," he declared, carelessly sharing his words with the desolate place.

"She has told me that I need to forget her, and this place is where I remember her... so it makes sense to leave. I cannot just defeat my feelings for her. I must break away from my memory of my feelings, if not from my memory of her and the society to which she is integral."

'Was this it?' he pondered deep in his consciousness. A tired, withering, self-critical voice didn't believe he would carry it out. After all, he had declared his renunciation of this life on and off for weeks. He recalled the first serious time, with the rain and the worm. The clouds had been an empty threat to him then, an amorphous distant invasion, but still it had driven him into this stone refuge. Even that rain had stopped him renouncing this palace. It had kept him here, just as the longing for Her had done.

"I must not let this keep me here. I must stick to my decision and leave," he sighed. He stumbled over to the bed and half sat, half lay upon it, lolling uncomfortably in the darkness. "Sitting in here and brooding over the gloom that awaits me is no escape."

As the worm rose to the surface to escape the waterlogged dungeon that his habitat had become, he would have to flee this society. Except, unlike the worm, he would never return.

Chapter 24
A Widening War

The second the Danite messenger had left the room Lord Gatan had slammed his fists on the table and unleashed a rumbling cascade of obscenities.

He had listened intently to what was said, but found keeping his calm unusually difficult. The deceptive and insidious nature of the contents of the report made his blood boil. In his irritable and erratic state he had summoned Xsclepia, deciding he wouldn't be able to face the practical scrutiny of his more conventional advisors. He would come soon, and Adonis was regretting it already.

Though he had not expected the banquet agreement to be adhered to, it was beyond this expected dishonesty to be actually orchestrating contradictory actions, specifically planned prior to that very council, and utilising it as an opportune moment to strike. It really took the hypocrisy of realpolitik to a new level. *'Diplomatic efforts should work with military options, not create a veil for their own defiance.'*

He felt the excruciating irritation of being duped by the upstart, but the fop-wraith no longer needed to taunt him: the real conflict had begun. Indeed the careless trail of Latman spears and coins Juscius had left were far more of a piercing taunt than the phantom could achieve. It seemed a deliberate provocation. He also worried about the ease with which Danite had been destabilised.

Since the banquet, Gatan had had frequent flashbacks of the banquet. Each time, his recollection became more clouded in humiliation; the chuckling images of Ruperis and Telis mocking him, the svelte ethereal figure of the female foreigner, the deep sombre motionless eyes of Zeuorox glaring from across the table; the vacant defeatism of Vacarium, an undead doppelganger to Zeuorox. His son, an epitome of drunken capitulation; a roasted hog splashed with wine. The nonchalant disinterest of Lewerix. Adonis' own sons squabbling with Telis and Ruperis, being drawn into this farcical sideshow. Now Danite, who had been the liveliest ally, was a man with traitors looming over his shoulder.

In this image, his only comfort lay in the steely, watchful eyes of his wife. She was his only hope, his most competent ally, a voice of diplomatic reason, an adjudicatory spectator and extra pair of eyes mysteriously blessed with camouflage so no other noticed her… but what she could not be was a loving wife. Adonis laughed acrimoniously to himself. "Normally that is all people expect from their wives, but it is what I have neglected all these years," he muttered, his voice softening into a regretful tone.

Adonis glared down at the hard surface of his desk. He knew it was too late for any such construction of mutual respect and concern. They had always operated as a practical duo and would never be able to cultivate a dynamic unison.

There was a knock at the door. Gatan shot to his feet, cringing, as his chair scraped on the wooden floor.

"Enter," he bellowed.

The door opened and a wrinkled prunish face, surrounded by a matted mess of hair that cascaded onto a grimy robe, materialised in the doorway.

Xsclepia bowed cordially before entering. His expression was vacant, his eyes ringed with pink bulges of puffy flesh. The eyes themselves were bloodshot.

The acrid odour of incense entered the room with him. It went straight to Gatan's head, leaving him nauseous. He paced up and down, hoping the smell would subside, but on the contrary, it seemed to curdle his thoughts more. Eventually he began ranting at Xsclepia incoherently, vaguely outlining the issue as he did so.

"Latman has tried to destabilise Danite... Felix has crushed the sponsored rebellion, but he had requested our support... Latman may try again or even attempt something in Vacarium... or here."

When he finally stopped, he listened to the High Priest's continued silence before divulging the details much more succinctly. He spoke of the mercenaries, under Latman pay, that had holed themselves up in Axia fort and had had to be cut down to the last man, just so they could hold up Felix Danite's sally to the capital. He even told him that Danite had luckily been able to use a horse belonging to the local noble and arrive earlier at the battle so as to stop Faldinite from disobeying the order to wait for reinforcements, in an attempt at glory hunting; even possibly an attempt to usurp his lord.

Xsclepia seemed unmoved by the news.

"Milord, I am no advisor, I am merely a messenger of the god's. However, the gods have warned of Latman's ambitions. I fear the beliefs that drive him are an attempt to defy the order of the gods. I also recall the warning of the flotilla. Therefore I would suggest the gods will you to support Danite with troops. Maybe it will deter Latman."

Gatan frowned, troubled by the notion that such an action would provoke Latman further.

"If I have a presence there, then I can ensure better cohesion in the need of its defence... but why does he do this?"

Xsclepia, though unsure if he was supposed to answer, did so. His blank expression barely shifting as he moved his lips so the words merely drifted out of him like from an oracle.

"This is part of a wider war the Latmans are waging. I would even suggest Latman is not the primary force behind this, but rather his 'advisor' Zeuorox. He wishes to eradicate all bastions of orthodoxy. I shall consult the gods, but I fear full mobilisation may be necessary... including a quick decisive strike on Lateria, utilising the armada the gods requested."

All his life the warrior lord had expected his head to be held high, and his chest out with patriotic pride, as he declared that the House was on the brink of war. Instead, he felt troubled and reluctant to acknowledge the need to mobilise. Where was the patriotic zeal?

Instead, he just nodded with lethargic acceptance, as though relinquishing his power and scuttling his authority to the tides of war. He had always envisioned, as with all the legends about his predecessors, that it would be a gallant decision. A definitive choice, not something he slid into.

So many leaders say they are the deciders of war and peace, but they are not... and if they are, then the war was not necessary. Those 'deciders' who seek to make war are seeking short-term fixes or manipulating emotions to secure power.

Xslepia stood motionless in the centre of the room. Suddenly his voice boomed out, again his lips barely moving as though a ventriloquist dummy for the gods.

"Lord, I shall consult the oracles and send my orderly when They have spoken."

Adonis nodded in acknowledgment, and the High Priest turned stiffly as though being summoned to return to his lair, and departed without a word.

'I must try to resist this descent into war,' he thought. His diplomatic acumen offered a glimmer of hope through the dark clouds of structural constraint. *'I can try and avoid this so at least I am freed of the accusation of provoking this cataclysm. To do this I must make all my actions and motives clear... for secrecy fuels suspicion and that is the principle cause of actual war. So I will send a message to Latman, making a formal complaint about his breaking of the agreement. In doing so I can explain my actions in bolstering Danite and make it absolutely clear it is not an aggressive act. If he is a true diplomat he will understand and we can resolve this peacefully. That is, by diplomat, I mean a leader of his people and not a crusader for an idea.'*

For some reason, Gatan found his usual confidence troubled by an equally rare cynicism. He sighed, knowing a treacherous political trek lay before him, and it was one that could only be successfully conquered if his old adversary co-operated with him.

★

Rabica trudged along, ignoring the burden of his satchel as it clamped itself tight to his bony shoulder. Its taut inertia stymied any movement, sealing a dank pocket of sweat beneath it.

The fresh wind blew; though itself silent, the foliage resisted its passage, rubbing off noise. Down below, the seething mass of grass rustled with the heaving hiss of the sea. Meanwhile, up and around, branches creaked like the timbers of old shipwrecks.

The bright full moon dominated both the earth and sky as it shone down. With its greater brother gone, it was the unrivalled champion of the sky; the few brightest stars were the only visible ones in the face of the moon's blanketing illumination. Though cloudless, a dispersed mist covered Rabica's whole view, its effect only visible where his view was long enough to accumulate sufficient thickness over a long distance. Here it merged the hazy illuminated sky and ground into a blurring imprecise smear of a horizon.

Rabica heard the crackle of stones under his feet. The precise cracking sounds cut through the wispy musical haze of the wind on the vegetation. To his right lay the rustling oceanic mass of long pastoral fields abandoned during the winter and left to grow into the long clumpy flora that it now was. The gravel path followed the edge of this, and was lined along the left side with a row of hedges and small trees, no doubt planted as an organic boundary. Up ahead, Rabica could see a break in the foliage. He hurried towards it.

Upon reaching it he stopped and leant to one side to allow his satchel to drop off his shoulder. Ignoring the throbbing irritation as the sweat rash was relieved of its sealed cell, he absorbed the scene.

Two saplings stood guard either side of the breach. Between them long grass lapped forwards under the guidance of the wind. However, the pass was barred by a two crossbar wooden fence, two upright posts positioned with near pin-point symmetry, equidistant from the two guardlings. On the other side of the fence, heavily grazed grass glimmered motionless, a placid pool of subdued vegetation that was so uniform it appeared as a fluorescent white sheet. The far side of the field was walled with a dark scribbled line of hedge, its surface broken only by the perfect geometric form of a shed, a black shape whose upper half merged with the hedge line. Its roof was frosted a stunning luminous white, a perfect white parallelogram. Above the hedge line, the mist reached the threshold and clouded the distant fields in foggy confusion.

All that was visible was a dark phalanx of trees clustered together approximately where the horizon would be, the mist being somehow unable to conceal them.

Rabica gasped in awe as he gazed at them. With the mist swirling around them they seemed a world away, tranquil and free from the wind and the creaking of subservient foliage. His heart sank as he saw one tree stood aside from the others; an immediate unsubstantiable affinity arose within him: it was his goal. It stood free, resolute, distinct but not completely alone.

He stared at it for some time before setting off, the inhospitable hiss of the wind as it coalesced with the grass spurning him on.

As the hedge barrier returned to block his view of both his goal and the open stretch of land between, Rabica dreamed of what it would be like to be at that place, a tranquil coppice free from the pressures of the world. Blossoming with life, but none of it coerced into conformity by the demanding structures of society.

Yet even now he knew he could only pass through, hopefully witness it in the freshness of the morning before moving on. He could not stay; it was far too close to society. He would draw from it a temporary emancipation, but then have to leave to search for another refuge on his mammoth journey. It was only a waypoint in a greater trek for a greater goal of personal freedom. Already he accepted he would probably never actually find such a place, but he needed an ultimate goal to spur him on from each short-term goal and not stagnate at one of these minor ones.

"Yes," he told himself with a contented smile. "Freedom is in the process of seeking emancipation just as much as it is actually finding it."

Chapter 25

Divine Perversion

Juscius had already heard from his spies but he had never expected written, signed confirmation from the perpetrator in person. Such blunt 'diplomacy' was unheard of, and so, he reasoned, must be a snub.

Lord Adonis had written directly to Juscius, accusing him of breaking the treaties and in response openly confessed to doing the same by dispatching an occupying force to Danite to keep the tin-pot despot in power.

Not only was he openly backing Latman's enemies, but he was attempting to use it as a premise to encircle the House.

Zeuorox paced up and down with him. "Such disdain for our sovereignty cannot be tolerated," he declared as he waited impatiently for Ruperis to arrive and be a weak 'voice of restraint' in order to provide Juscius with an illogical, and so easily-defeated counter argument.

"How dare he condemn our support of freedom in Danite?" Lord Latman declared.

Zeuorox stopped and turned to Juscius. "We have done nothing; a company operating within our territory had a client in Danite," he corrected meticulously with the coolheaded countenance of any regimes' spokesperson.

"But ultimately his accusation misses the point, we do not have to apologise for helping to overthrow a backward despot and simultaneously defend our ideals."

Zeuorox nodded, turning his face away to hide a creeping smirk. It was the finest music to his ears, hearing Juscius say such things unprompted. *'There truly is nothing better than being able to sit back and play the cautious diplomat whilst another propels your real aggressive agenda.'*

They could both glow in mutual exoneration of each other's guilt.

Zeuorox smiled to himself. He had spent so long covering his true goals he had forgotten that now the time for war was fast approaching, it was time to begin shedding them.

He could see he had trained Latman well; it was him leading the fundamentalisation of ideals over and into real politics. Juscius' self-righteous declaration was a sure-fire way of making oneself seem right: rather than defensively conceal one's clandestine operations, set them out as courageous actions that to oppose would be treacherous. For whilst Zeuorox's proposed tit-for-tat quibbling over responsibility would soon get bogged down with facts, Juscius' assertion that their motives were pure and patriotic would fly over any such criticisms.

"You are right Sire. It is just, should we be accused so... meticulously... we should always maintain that our support did not breach the treaty... it is a minor point, but may win us favour with neutrals – like Lewerix."

Juscius gave a sideways disdainful glance at the unlit fireplace.
"I have no time for neutrals, nor shall I tie my hands with my own treaty when the defence of the Household is concerned," he proclaimed resolutely.

Zeuorox nodded with nonchalant agreement. "But, for the sake of success we must be willing to accommodate others."

"Surely Lewerix would not be foolish enough to confront us or be dragged into an unholy alliance with Gatan?" Juscius asked rhetorically.

Zeuorox stepped closer to Juscius. The window shutters jiggled uncomfortably in their locks, rattling with an erratic exertion of discontent. The sudden gust seemed to have come at the onset of a dark cloud lurching over the area and so sending the room into a sudden state of gloom.

Juscius turned to face his mentor attentively. In a hushed authoritative tone Zeurorox began.

"But you see, sire, if we are too aggressive Lewerix may believe us a threat and so feel the need to support Gatan. I am not suggesting we appease them, just that we are careful and do not push them into the hands of the enemy."

Halfway through his spiel Zeuorox paused as he noticed a sudden, rather sinister, shift in the young lord's countenance. His confident self-righteousness had completely vanished, withered away as a panicky demeanour replaced it.

At first he froze still, then he began convulsing as he gazed in horror at something that seemed to lurk in a dark corner of the room.

Nevertheless, Zeuorox continued, not wishing to disturb Juscius from his troubles as doing such a thing was not considered proper.

Nervously, Juscius looked away from the corner that so frightened him, but only for a moment as his eyes were drawn back to it with a morbid fascination.

He spoke in broken segments of sentences, either unaware or unconcerned at how obvious it was he was not really paying attention to what he said. "We cannot take risks with neutrals. I will not be ransom to their dilly-dallying. Besides, non-compliance renders them dangerous. Untrustworthy." His voice pitched up and increased in tempo, wavering shakily for a few moments before rising further and further into an erratic tirade.

"They may seem gentle and cowed but they are nothing of the sort… It is a most gross snub that they expect us to believe: yet what else do we have to believe? How are we to know that they hide sordid dreams of usurpation," he spat. He then began glancing about the room with hallucinogenic paranoia. "They lie to us, all of them, with their innocent eyes, charming alien looks, but how do we know if they mean good or bad? People are omens, flashing through our lives…"

Suddenly he broke off, crash landing his face deep into his arms.

Zeuorox shrank back in awkward bafflement.

Several moments stretched out lazily and what seemed to be an endless continuum of unpassing time before Juscius finally brought his head out of its limb-based cocoon.

His voice cut through the time stasis, kick-starting it back into measurability.

"Oh, Zeuorox! I should have told you earlier... but I find it had enough even now..."

He ambled towards the high priest, shuffling like a tranquillised zombie, stopping when he stood close enough to embrace the high priest as though he were seeking comfort from his father. However, rather than launch into it, he shrank back ashamedly.

Zeuorox, completely unaccustomed to such behaviour, stood motionless, barely even breathing.

"... The night after the banquet, she came to me.. the slave.. she seemed possessed, yet I did not oppose her. Thelus gave me no sign to oppose, indeed perhaps he willed it. I do not know, at the time I was petrified, but petrified with awe."

Zeuorox glared like a vulture that had just heard the dying squawk of potential prey echoing over a valley. This was just the shocking, unpredictable news he had prayed for. He quickly, and with adept skill, ensured his initial shock was followed up with dismayed abhorrence rather than jubilation.

The hawk-beaked carrion-eater had the sleek black carcass in view. The carcass made a surprising stir as though it sought to renounce its label and reclaim a suitable word for a living body. This merely spurred the gleeful scavenger on, stalling momentarily in flight as it shuddered in sickening greed.

"Oh, my..." Zeuorox trailed, at the last minute remembering not to overdo it.

"It is as I feared..." he began again, before pausing to contemplate for a moment.

He shrugged internally. '*I can always write one later,*' he concluded.

"... She had concerned me and so I had researched and found some old scripture which spoke of Septimo's seducers, and how he would send a mighty queen to try and pervert Thelus' prince. But I hadn't wanted to worry you until I was sure... and now I fear the worst had been spelled out for us."

"It has?" Juscius murmured, unsure and resistant to Zeuorox's condemnation.

"Yes," Zeuorox declared with resolute solemnity. He could barely hide his grin as his scheming brain found a perfect bit of 'rationalising' to manipulate.

"The very fact that you had doubts proves it; would you ever doubt a being of Thelus?" He struggled to hold himself back to await an answer. "'His light shines in his beings, available to the eyes of all willing men, but most of all his lineage of sons – The Lords of Latman.'" Juscius quoted obediently.

"Exactly, you could not doubt her if she were a being of Thelus, as we had supposed. However we are all, including yourself, sire, susceptible to the luring of Septimo."

Zeuorox grinned, proud of his genius.

"So it is true." Juscius gasped in horror. "What is to be done?"

"This abomination must be purged of the land – I shall ensure it is enacted, with your order."

Juscius still seemed to be dithering, yet the more he did the more Zeuorox was anxious to get the whole ordeal over with.

"Does it have to be so hasty? Must she be treated so?"

Zeuorox's voice was calm and commanding.

"I am afraid that we must be vigilant, and decisive when confronted with agents of Septimo. Especially when they are close to us…"

Juscius nodded reluctantly. Taking in a deep breath he solemnly declared, "if it must be done ensure it is done quickly and discreetly."

"I shall ensure your order is carried out and that minimal pain is used."

"Go and order it now, I cannot bear to stand here and debate it, or anything else, now." Juscius declared before adding, "have it done immediately and we shall never speak of it again."

Zeuorox just nodded; as he swivelled to depart a twinkle in his eye showed his relief. Already he was thinking up the plan of execution and was glad to leave and intercept Ruperis on his way to the room. He would get Delvinius to do it, and ensure he was kept out of it; he hated to have his fingers traceably near to bloodshed.

As he closed to door to Juscius' office, he spotted Ruperis turning the corner through the corner of his eye.

His wrinkly bag of skin betrayed a morbid glee comfortably nestled between the creases, one which the perceptive merchant noticed immediately.

"How goes it? I trust by your absence from the room it was a success."

"It went much better than even you thought!"

Before Delvinius could finish his celebratory posy of expletives, Zeuorox cut him short and proclaimed, "but I have even greater news!" He explained the exclusive story.

Ruperis chuckled and began making quite brutal remarks about his childhood friend, all of which Zeuorox overlooked as he was too eager to get the grisly mission completed.

"I need you to hire someone to do the work; it is all sanctioned by his Lordship. However, I am afraid we shall not be able to pay you... at least not yet, it will have to be sneaked into a contract."

Ruperis waved his hand in jovial dismissal. "No no, do not worry about costs. Count it as a favour." He then made the move to head for Juscius' office, though Zeuorox jerked towards him to cause him to stop. "No, he is in no mood. Besides, there is nothing for you to say to him... even if you have other matters, leave them a couple of days."

Ruperis nodded. Clearly annoyed that he would not be able to see if he could wrangle the information from the lord as well. Not just for fun, it was a test to see who Juscius trusted the most.

While Delvinius hesitated, Zeuorox made a hasty departure. Already he was wondering why Delvinius would dispose of the slave for free.

★

With his supplies running low Rabica was compelled to overcome his fearful reluctance to venture into civilisation. To the sombre death-chime of his boots striking stones, he trudged towards the enclosed town concealed behind the stone perimeter wall. Only the hazy clouds of dust and smoke gave any sign of life within.

The road to the town had been relatively quiet. However, the constant grinding sound of wheel on loose stones, heralding the approach of a cart, kept Rabica in a perpetual state of unease that he was not alone.

In his hasty departure from the palace he had failed to acquire a bow, which was essential to survival out in the wilderness. He also had decided to part with his short sword, which he had taken in a moment of childish adventure. The sword was very ornate (as suiting a noble) and so could fetch a good sum, though it would be difficult to sell in a town such as this.

Now he stood before the gates and had been ordered to wait whilst a guard ventured over to check him. Rabica was totally confused, having never been through such a process, fuelling his fear that it would be a humiliating ordeal.

The guard who came to interrogate him was intimidatingly youthful and robust. He wore a superior grin, only slight, but by far enough to skewer what scant scraps of confidence Rabica had left.

"What is your business here?" he inquired with disdainful authority.

Rabica, in a fit of fear, stuttered incoherent noises that were delightful music to the ears of the guard.

"Well?" he postured menacingly.
"Supplies," Rabica shot back in a monosyllabic whelp.
"Supplies for what?" the guard retorted accusingly.
"Food," Rabica pleaded, turning red with inferred guilt.
"For who?"
"Me," he answered, irrationally unsure of himself.
"And what are you?"
"A traveller."
"A spy?"
"What?"
"You heard me." The guard declared, "Answer?"
Rabica was confused. "How?"
The guard moved his hand towards his scabbard slowly, without ceasing eye contact with the delinquent.
"N..No!" Rabica blurted.
The guard laughed mockingly. "You're a peddler."
Before Rabica could protest the guard asked the next question. "What is in the bag?"
As Rabica opened his mouth to answer, the guard shouted him down humiliatingly.
"That was not a question, fool! It was an order."
Rabica froze in utter befuddlement. '*How*...' his thoughts trailed as he stared at the guard like an obedient dog trying to anticipate what its master was demanding.
"Open it," the guard ordered disdainfully.
Reluctantly, Rabica opened it and the guard eagerly bounded forward to rummage. His lips curled up in disgust as he pushed the grubby blanket and clothes aside. Almost immediately he found the hard scabbard sheathing the short sword, lifting it enough to look at the hilt. He almost leapt aside as he saw the beautiful archaic artefact. His fingers avariciously caressed the glistening smooth metal for a few moments before snapping back into interrogatory mode.
Rabica was petrified that he would think him a thief; he began cursing himself for not declaring that he was armed immediately. He was also wondering if he should tell him about the hunting knife he had.
"Where did you steal that?"
"It is mine, it is an heirloom," Rabica struggled to keep his sentence flowing to allow his Delix noble accent to be easily heard.
"And you wish to sell it?" The question was asked with the same inferred guilt as when he was called a spy.
Rabica mumbled to himself, his mind a curdling solution of fears. "Perhaps…" he uttered with flagellant guilt.

The guard looked disappointed; he had looked forward to ridiculing the down-on-his-luck Delixian for claiming he had not come to the town to sell.

"And are you part of the guild?" he asked snidely.

"The what?" Rabica replied timorously.

"You are not." The guard retorted definitively.

Rabica was trembling profusely.

"You must report to the merchant's guild and either pay them for a license, or sell the sword to them - accepting the outsider's tariff."

"Outsiders tariff? But I am Lewerix."

The guard roared with laughter. "So what, I don't care if you're a Sephilixian[3]! You're not in the Guild, that's all that matters. Now look, either you can do that - one of my comrades will escort you there to be sure that you do - or you can pay me now and save you the effort of going there."

Rabica looked confused, '*so I can take this weapon into the town as long as I pay them?*'

"I might as well pay you now then."

The guard gleamed with pleasure. "Good choice, just try to be discreet, the internal guards may not know that you have paid, and do not sell to a guilder, once you pay the inflow tax it is illegal."

Rabica just nodded, glad to hear that his ordeal was coming to an end. "How much?"

The guard looked bemused as he wondered why the peddler had not protested that he had no money. "Twelve gold coins," he declared, his mouth twitching with pre-emptive amusement.

But to his shock the beggar nodded. "Ok," and proceeded to rummage in his pocket and produce twenty golden coins.

The guard's disappointment soon dissipated, he would get some money at least without having to risk meeting his contact. Still it was a waste of so much potential gold; this fool would never sell that without the guild finding out.

"Actually, if you are looking for a buyer, I could find you one…" he began thinking '*I might as well get a bit for this and a cut rather than get no more – besides if he gets caught they might blame me*'

Rabica beamed, '*how nice, I'd better give him something as a kind of thanks*'

"Here you go, accept this as a token of good will." He handed him three more gold pieces.

The guard assumed the beggar was just playing along, and not totally aloof to the complexities of the deal.

---

[3] The name given to residents of the town Sephilix and its surrounding villages.

"Thank you." He mumbled. "Go to the Horse and Buck this evening... they will know who you are."

Rabica nodded appreciatively but was too embarrassed to ask where the inn was.

★

Rabica wandered through the perimeter shantytown. He tried to ignore the ceaseless murmuring, occasionally shooting a glance down a side passage from where he heard the actually traceable sound of people.

People ambled along. Some just stood as though waiting for someone, but really just awaiting the passage of time. Down the narrow alleys between shacks street sellers hid away with small collections of products on rugs small enough to sweep up in one movement and flee at the first sign of authorities. At the end of each was a young person on watch, conspicuously scanning the street with intense alertness.

As he neared the centre he began to see actual shops. All were adorned with a seal that he could only assume was of the guild and were accompanied by numbers. He passed two guards who chatted to each other, their dialogue momentarily becoming separate from the hazy murmur before passing back into the chorus of confusion.

A few moments after passing them he heard a loud whistling noise followed by shouting. He was almost knocked flying by a young man rushing past him clutching a bundle of novelties collected in a rag so that from a distance it took the form of a baby.

★

Between two of these shops was an inn. Its frame was increasingly encroached upon by the adjacent buildings as it went upwards so it loosely resembled a three-dimensional trapezium. Its grimy grey wooden exterior looked to be propped up by the minders either side like the structural equivalent of a drunk. The entire front surface was made from irregular planks of wood. Even the window holes had been covered by thick cross bars of wood that only left tiny crack like gaps which were filled with rags.

A plume of smoke rose from a makeshift chimney roughly in the centre of the building's roof. It smeared the air around it with a grey murky aura, its fluid movement almost untraceable as one patch of smoke was displaced by that which came after it. As he watched particular wisps travel then disperse he saw how one could soon forget that its dilution in the air did not signal the demise of its overall content. It fascinated Rabica that something could be continually happening and accumulating but only be noticed if there was a dramatic increase in its rate.

After a few moments of indecision Rabica forced himself to go and open the door. It had no handle, not even a latch to improvise with. All it had was a minute hole, possibly once resident to a keyhole, the metal lining torn away to leave the frayed splinters of ravaged wood.

Cautiously his trembling fingers reached out and scratched at the uneven surface, trying to catch hold of the timber slats in order to pull it open. The wood felt dry and dead, though not rotten, still hefty and solid. A powerful demurral engulfed him as he attempted to resolve the dilemma. Could he get his finger into the ex-keyhole? Would it give him enough leverage? He doubted it. He began attempting to grip the wood slats, a sulky mood of embarrassment already looming dauntingly over his self-awareness. His hold tightened and he hunched over to intensify his grip throughout his body, before giving a sudden tug. The door shook and gave off a noise that sounded like a stubborn non-compliant refusal to budge.

It was not long before the idea came to him that he should just knock. When he did so it was a light tap, which produced no response. Between cursing and sighing he made increasingly more vocal attempts until, to his surprise, a rather irritated man opened the door slightly, and stared at him with intrusive scepticism. After interrogating Rabica's face for a few moments he mumbled, "well come in," and then stepped back to allow Rabica in. Rabica reluctantly obliged.

Rabica winced as he entered, expecting his entry to be met with deathly silence and contemptuous, swollen-eyed stares from all within. He was somewhat shocked by the apparent indifference the inhabitants had for his entry.

Inside the room was dark, dank, smoky, and rather full. A fire crackled in the middle of the room. A sizeable proportion of the smoke drifted up the hole above it, but much drifted about the room. Consequently the primary taste in the air was a noxious amalgam of stale and fresh smoke. The fire was basically the only source of light for the room, as the hole at the back merely created a mirror image of light on the opposing wall.

The room had many people, or rather hunched rags roughly taking the forms of people, huddled together in disparate groups. The flickering torrent of fiery light cast gnarled shadows that lazily sprawled over the rooms. The smoke wafted about, inducing chesty coughs and occasionally being caught by flickers of light. Rabica found himself morbidly transfixed by the wisps as they drifted like jellyfish, apparently ignorant of the organisms around them.

The doorman barged past him and took a seat near the fire, his back to Rabica, forming a huge boulder-like silhouette that blocked out much of the light. Consequently, he heard grumbles from the table between him and the fire.

Rabica just stood there, wheezing in the acrid air. Being in this enclosed space with so many people had startled his mind, causing it to stubbornly lock like the heels of a goat. With his conscious mind stymied in confusion, fear began to swarm around his body. First he felt a piercing self-doubt strike his heart; it quickly and malignantly spread outwards, through the rest of his body.

As he ambled and squeezed past the people he made a few inquisitive glances to ascertain what they were doing. However, he found the darkness covered all but their faces with a thick shroud, their heads buried deep inside hoods and layer upon layer of rags wrapped together to form a comforting sense of anonymity.

When his eyes finally adjusted to the light and he was able to see the huddled people, he noticed they were doing nothing, just staring at each other, soaking in the atmosphere of shared circumstance. They were the dispossessed, the street vendors forced off their stalls, rural labourers seeking work in the winter and lumberjacks awaiting the next job. Those who were part of families or labouring teams could at least relish the fact that others counted on them, or at least would notice if they did not return.

As Rabica neared the middle of the room his attention was brought to an argument that seemed to be taking place in the murky black haze of the left sideline. Behind the masses of people an orange light stained the musty air, reflecting off the dust and smoke to create a murky haze. At first he could only really make out the shrieks of an old harridan, though a low bark occasionally followed it but was barely distinguishable from other non-vocal noises.

The closer he got the more it became clear. She was pleading for more time to pay her rent. "Just another week," she begged repetitively. She needed to lie low for a few days because the guards had caught her selling trinkets without guild approval and in direct competition to the guild haberdasher (who had taken his rather broad remit to mean he covered anything not already covered by other guilders).

He focused on the two sources of the quarrel; a bald man shook his pig-fleshed jowls in uncaring rebuttal, whilst an old crone, her skeletal figure still evident despite countless layers of rags, wagged a bony finger at him.

'*Ah, so there is the profiteer in this whole debacle!*' Rabica thought, snorting in disgust.

He attempted to approach them then wait politely for them to finish the dispute. They took no notice as he stopped in their vicinity, and began to linger anxiously. Discomfort rising steadily, Rabica tried to look anywhere but at them for fear that he would seem to look impatient. It was so much worse now he had stopped; indeed, he even considered a few pointless laps of the room just to pass the time and try and keep his mind distracted from his self-consciousness.

It was now, now he was surrounded by so many coteries of people, and plagued with a level of self-consciousness only possible when in such a situation, that he truly felt alone. He smiled ironically to himself that one only felt alone, when alone in the presence of others. Otherwise you were in solitude, and to be in solitude, at least to him, was not to be lonely as you had no immediate comparative example to make you realise you were alone. Being alone amongst people showed up the loneliness of being alone, it showed up what you were missing. Being lonely is not a product of being alone but of being secluded.

Somebody barged into him, knocking his concentration and returning him to the situation at hand. The harridan and the proprietor were still remonstrating, though the landlord had clearly had had his fun and was looking to get rid of her. Rabica told himself now was his chance.

"Yes, sir?" the landlord asked.

Rabica jumped and spluttered. He decided his best action was to spit whatever words came to mind before the fear set in and petrified his windpipe.

"Ah… y-yes, I w-w-would like a room," he stuttered.

The landlord laughed aloud. "A room? – How many of you are there?" he took a look behind Rabica as though to greet the horde of Rabicas that trailed behind.

Rabica turned red and sank his head. Already the lump was in his throat, it had risen to his nose and was trying to squeeze tears from his eyes. His head filled with acrimonious rage, *'What an absolute fool! Why, you dismal excuse for a human being! You ignoramus… my gods even these insults attest further to my aloof idiocy!'* he spat at himself with a disgust that caused his head to swell.

"I am so sorry." He paused to cringe at his even more posh apology, "a bed."

"How long?" came the immediate reply.

Rabica shook his head in indecision. "One?" he waggled the side of his lower lip after speaking.

The landlord did not look happy. "Well if you want more you'd better say, peoples are coming here all the time, I can't have 'maybe' beds free."

And so Rabica felt guilty. Then it struck him, though he was unsure how to say it.

"er... that... um.... She" (he pointed to where he thought the old harridan would be). "I have enough to pay for..." he trailed off, not sure if it sounded strange to do such a thing. "...her". He shrugged, he might as well. "I can pay for her too... put me down for just one," he added, believing that even if he did not get all he wanted he'd rather take his luck on the street than go through all this again.

The landlord grinned. "Why, sure! All seven?"

Rabica nodded nobly.

"That'll be eighty pieces."

Rabica looked shocked, immediately assuming it would be in gold. "Eighty!"

The landlord looked angry. "Yes!"

Rabica, with a puzzled expression said, "eighty what?"

The landlord laughed nervously. "Whatt'ya think, eighty pieces of chicken? ...coins, you fool!"

Suddenly it struck Rabica again that he was stuck in his snobbish aristocratic ways thinking in gold.

"Tell you what, how's two gold?"

The landlord looked sceptical, "if it's real."

Rabica gave one too him and looked sheepish as the proprietor nearly danced with delight. "Now sir, if you need anything else just let me know."

Rabica shook his head, and began to turn. He got half way before he realised his fatal mistake. "Actually, can you tell me where the Horse and Buck is?"

The landlord tried to hide his interest at this stranger wanting to go to the notorious hotspot for clandestine transactions, but the peculiarities of the lighting meant the slight shift on his brow was mimicked and exaggerated by the shadows that ran along his face like thick black creases.

Normally he would report this kind of thing to the authorities, but as this time the man had been generous with money he would let it slide, for now.

★

With little else to do except worry that he would not find the place, Rabica set off to find the Horse and Buck within an hour of speaking to the innkeeper. It was only mid-afternoon but he was convinced that his incompetence would shine through and get him lost and confused. On top of all this worry was the added complexity of hunger with its additional concerns regarding choices, interactions and coinage.

As he wandered down the street trying to speculate about the nature and question of the 'guild' he found his mind skittishly clogged with numerous questions and concerns over food. 'What should I get?

Will I have change? Will they understand me? Will I ask for something too exquisite? Or will I try and compensate and sound ridiculous... patronising even, if I ask for something stupid like two carrots and some cheese?' *'Oh it is so complicated, all I want is something to eat. It would be easier to get my own, at least when skinning a rabbit you don't have to worry about whether you have the correct change or that you boil it with the right vegetables.'*

★

It took him a rather long time to get to the Horse and Buck, but that did not mean he did not have over an hour before evening and countless more before they would actually turn up.

He had also had trouble getting in with his state of appearance. The doorman had eyed him suspiciously and questioned him. Rabica had mumbled and stuttered in disbelief and confusion, but the doorman gave up trying to understand him and let him in.

He had been told to wait, then told a table would cost him (he completely missed what was going on). Frustrated and bewildered he had fearfully handed the guard a gold piece and wondered if he'd make any money from this at all.

The tavern was much more pleasant than the inn he had visited earlier. It had a pleasant (and symmetrical) formation of windows. Whereas the other was a dishevelled makeshift shelter for the dispossessed, this was a public house for bottom-rung self-sustainers.

The room was also lit with a candle on each occupied table (though this had to be paid for by the customer). Most of the clientele seemed to be wagon drivers, footmen and cargo guards. Their non-work clothes nevertheless sported insignia and were colour coded accordingly. Rabica wondered if their wives wore dresses blazoned with similar symbols too.

A group of three such men sat at the table nearest him. By the looks of it they were all guards. Despite all his efforts not to be rude Rabica found himself compelled to listen to their banter.

"This lockdown is slowin' trade something terrible," one of them sighed. He was in his late thirties, his beard short as though it grew on his face like a mould.

"Who can blame 'em though, with all this talk of Gatan and Latman troops cropping up everywhere," commented a younger one.

The first one to speak nodded and grinned. "I'm not saying the clampdown is pointless, just wish they'd stop messing about and get into it. All this is doing is slowing down work. You hear about that raid on Gericos?"

"They were saying that Gatan that did it," the younger one exclaimed with a sense of belief.

The third, a silver haired grizzly man who had been listening keenly to their words, shook his head twice, once at each respectively. Then turning to the youngster first he declared, "naah, that's rubbish."

The young man nodded obediently.

The old man turned to the first speaker, "and this clampdown is too! They're just stirring up nothing – even if the others do, Lewerix will do nothing. For one he's no impetuous fool and second he's a coward!"

The younger one looked rather shocked, even offended, by the old man's candid remarks, but dared not question him. The middle-aged one rolled his eyes.

He launched into a defensive retort. "Latman do this, Gatan do that and we are the ones who suffer, sitting in the middle and trying to pull them apart. Well, this time let 'em squabble!"

The elder one, who until now Rabica had felt some empathy for, declared. "Well yeah, best would be to give 'em both a hidin'! First up that little pip-squeak, then the old 'noble warrior' -he's just a scoundrel in disguise. While we're at it civilise those western barbarians and that other pip-squeak. We need something like that to get us all roused up and united – no sense of unity these days". (He spoke as though the dawn of the House was a teenage memory). "And we need to do something like that before that good-for-nothing son takes over – we'll need a boost before we get him."

Rabica jolted in fear as he heard the other two cheer on the old man. In a secretive bout of self-disgust Rabica cheered him on internally too. But this irrational self-hatred was merely a front to hide a deeper abhorrence at the indirect effect he seemed to have had which was, in spite of his pacifism, to drive his people towards violence.

With morbid fascination he listened on. It was the middle-aged one who spoke.

"Well, I'm never one to turn down a chance to serve me house, especially if it means permanent pay, and the odd bit of plunder," he winked. "I'm just sick of all this pondering and posturing, let's get in there and show 'em how it's done."

The old one nodded rousingly. "Bit too old for a fight me'self but you soldiers'll need your supplies guarding. That's what these young'uns need!" he declared.

Rabica was appalled by the old man's words, especially their hypocrisy. He was even more angered by neither of the other guards taking him up on the fact he had never fought in battle. *'It's as though all people over a certain age can pretend to be part of, and have had first-hand experience of, hundreds of years of history, with which they can lecture those younger for spoiling, as though it was all different in 'their day'.'*

The old man was shaking his head disdainfully. "Bah, but he won't do it," he declared with disappointment.

Rabica was fuming; they cared not for fighting to make the world better (or preventing it from getting worse), rather just to keep themselves and generations to come, bound. He was utterly and truly contemptuous of their ignorance, as they bemoaned their leader for not unnecessarily sending them into battle and risking their lives for the sake of what were little more than primordial beliefs of tribal pride. He glanced about the room nervously, trying to vent his anger through his eyes.

As the rage subsided he found himself increasingly uneasy and alone. He worried that he would say something foolish to the buyer. Over and over he kept saying to himself 'I am just selling; take any price... over about thirty... to Septimo with it, I don't care if I break even as long as I can get out of here. No chatter, no buying... just selling. I can get a bow and whatever tomorrow.' He found himself rambling within his mind to stop his nerves from collapsing.

Rabica took dainty sips of his tankard, wanting to do something to preoccupy his mind but also wishing to savour the drink over the next couple of gruelling hours.

The men adjacent to him began chatting about previous jobs. Rabica tried to listen to it just to pass the time. However he found himself preoccupied with fear at things to come, so much so that he could only flittishly be distracted by anything. He felt as though he awaited a prison sentence.

★

He had sat there on the edge of his seat for some time, long enough for him to become so accustomed to his superfluous shadow gazing that he was somewhat startled when a cluster of shapes, rather than wandering past, hovered before him.

Looking upwards, fighting off petrification, he saw a youngish man who was smartly dressed and accompanied by a rather burly minder. The young man was freshly clean-shaven and his hair was cut short. He wore a red tunic and blue trousers that neatly and stylishly clung to his thin, but not lanky, body. Over the top he wore a cloak-like coat of a stunning pitch black.

Whereas the otherwise unassuming young man was transformed into a man warranting respect because of his dress, the minder's clothing had the opposite effect. His brutish face and build, so alien to the frivolous garments, looked clownish.

Rabica nodded to them. The heavy followed suit, while the young man gave him a blank stare before quietly uttering, "good evening, sir."

The words were spoken with the utmost of neutrality to ensure it was made absolutely clear they were just a formality.

Rabica felt it only polite to ask if they wanted a drink. The young man declined on both their behalves. The guard, shuffling irritably, evidently wanted one.

As they sat, Rabica tried to minimise his movements in case they betrayed his fear through jerkiness. Instead he forced a smile, an awkward quivering expression that was counterproductive in covering his timid disquiet. He nervously looked around the room to see if there was a possible discreet place to do business out of public view.

Having failed to spot any side doors or curtained off areas he attempted to speak. After some twitchy spasms of the mouth he blurted, "is there somewhere we can go that's private?"

Even though doubt surged around his lips, declaring his words nonsense, he still felt a wave of relief surge over him as he believed it was now the young man's turn to speak.

The young man was rather taken aback by his words. Meanwhile, the minder began to glance suspiciously around the room.

"My associate had passed on the description... but I shall examine it outside once a preliminary price has been agreed."

Rabica shuffled uneasily.

The young man ignored the bedraggled seller's movements.

"If you would like to put the bag on the spare seat... my buyer is willing to pay twenty-six for it," he uttered in one soothing deluge of words.

Rabica's heart shrank as he heard the number. He really couldn't be bothered with arguing over prices, he was sure it should be a lot more than that, but perhaps it was depreciated by the transaction being illegal.
"No less than thirty four," he stuttered with unexpected bluntness.

The young man looked cautiously at his minder. Rabica thought the negotiator's expressions were a result of him asking too much; on the contrary, it was the cheapness. Either the watchman had lied or the sword brought danger with it. Still, the young man refused to accept it was a trap, mainly because no one would orchestrate it; even rival guildmen knew they would never trace the purchase back to his boss.

The young man gave his colleague a stern look then exclaimed, "thirty-four!", but before Rabica could muster the courage to ask for more, he launched into a probing question. "How did you come across this item?"

Rabica resisted panic. He could try being honest (to a point) and saying he had fled his wealthy home and it was his, or he could say it was a heirloom and his family were paupers. Whilst he decided he stammered out a pleading, "I didn't steal it."

THE SON AND THE HEIR

The young man gave him a stern look. "I do not care if it is stolen, all I care about is if someone will miss it."

Despite the mental disarray, Rabica managed to use this to decide; the latter story would negate the issue of someone missing it.

"It is a family heirloom. One of my ancestors was awarded it for fighting at the battle of Heiphus against Latman in 288. He was given this as a reward... but my family has been reduced to, well... me." He felt a searing pain of truth in his words as he was reminded of the nearby guards blistering words of contempt at the idea of his future reign. "I just need to get money to survive; it's all I've got."

Having heard him say that the young man knew he had him; still, he might as well go for sympathy. Shaking his head slowly and raising his eyebrows with sincerity he declared in his calm tone, "thirty-four doesn't leave me with much; my boss will not be happy..." He trailed dramatically.

Rabica felt an irrational spat of sympathy even though the man was well-dressed and clearly made a lot as a middleman squeezing the poor to enrich the rich. In an apologetic tone he restated the price.

Suddenly the young man's calm tranquil face turned into a sneer. "I also don't believe your story... except the last bit – make it thirty."

He always pretended to himself that he only did this because he was scared the minder would tell his boss that he was being careless with his money, but this time, with the value so good anyway it was hard to justify.

Rabica shook his head, already sick of it and preferring just to walk out. "Thirty-three – no lower," he answered in a nonchalant tone.

It was precisely Rabica's apparent disinterest that infuriated the young man. It was like chasing a wild beast, cornering it, then it just shrugging and trying to barge past you.

"You try and sell it without me! You'll be caught by the guild!" he remarked.

Rabica was taken aback and rather hurt by the man's tone. "I just shan't sell it," he grumbled apathetically.

The young man laughed. "You won't need to, if they catch you with it they'll do you anyway! Come on, twenty-eight, before I lower it further."

Rabica's mind was filling up with numbers: costs and price spent so far, estimations on how much for a bow and a quiver. Meanwhile, in the background as a repetitive chorus his consciousness bellowed 'I thought you didn't care!'

Rabica, in a sudden fit of rage, considered threatening to incriminate him, but instead backed down. "Ok, thirty"

He tried to hide his utter contempt as he spat out "thirty". He noticed the minder was getting agitated by the rising level of Rabica's voice and so made a discreet gesture to the young man.

"Ok, ok," the young man conceded, deliberately not actually saying thirty.

Immediately the young man reverted to his calm voice. "Now the bag..."

Suddenly it hit Rabica that he had no bag to put it in. Utterly embarrassed he stammered as his stomach churned and ached.

The two men looked at him with suspicion.

"It's in my pack... I haven't got a separate bag."

They both scowled with frustration, looking around the room to calm themselves.

The young man gave a disdainful sneer before sighing and looking around. "Wrap it in something," he ordered impatiently, but still retaining his quiet and cool headed tone.

Rabica obeyed, fiddling clumsily under the table, wishing he could disappear beneath the solid structure and into some deep cavern. Shakily he placed it, wrapped in a nondescript rag, on the seat to his left. At the same time he took out a scarf and mopped his brow as a decoy.

In the meantime, the young man had been fiddling with coins and a small bag concealed in the protective canopy of his coat pocket. When he was done he addressed Rabica with a clear voice. "Your twenty-nine will be given to you by my friend here once I have gone. If I am not satisfied I shall return in a couple of minutes – that will be when the candle flame melts where my colleague has just placed a mark. If I have not returned, then he will go, and you may leave any time after he has gone."

Rabica immediately noticed the discrepancy in price, but was too scared to make a fuss, so instead just nodded, allowing a burning irritation to cut through his heart.

Calmly the young man arose and left, the bundle tucked discreetly under his arm. At least Rabica could take some cynical joy in the sight of him wearing his finery but still having to clutch one of Rabica's sweaty under-vests to his breast. Rabica watched the room as the young man exited; no one seemed to notice, most of the tables housed groups like those seated nearest Rabica and were all engrossed in idle banter. The barman gave him the slightest of glances and even the doorman gave such a nonchalant nod that it was only a prying person who knew of the deal that had taken place that would suspect it was anything out of the ordinary.

Rabica returned his attention to the burly man to his right. Part of him wanted to involve the man in a conversation, but he found himself incapable. The minder brought the bag up onto the table and nudged it towards Rabica with expert precision, using his own torso as cover. Once within reach, Rabica snatched it up whilst lifting his tankard to his lips.

His hands were sweaty and felt near weightless, though they were fairly steady. After several unsuccessful attempts to count them in his pocket Rabica gave up; the constant fear he was being cheated (further) plaguing his mind with a gradual surging malignancy.

Time slowed as Rabica found himself in that awkward situation he had managed to avoid all these weeks of travelling; two people forced together. It did not matter that so many others were in the room. It was as though the two of them were hermetically sealed in a vacuous silence, the vivacious expressions of the other tables like tortuous images plastered on the walls of their capsule.

Suddenly, after some time of painfully watching Rabica try to discreetly count the coins in his pocket, the minder declared. "Do not forget to give your landlord a bit extra when you pay him just to keep his mouth shut". His voice was unsurprisingly gruff but it was also well-articulated and pronounced, compared to Rabica's furtive drawl.

Rabica nodded with hasty minuscule movements, much like a quivering mouse. So desperate were his circumstances that he began to dream of being at the inn, where at least he would be alone in his loneliness.

However, just thinking about the inn made him remember that he needed to navigate his way back to it. This set him off in a panic that he would not be able to find it and it was not long before he was thinking of just giving up and getting out. Of course, typically, it was just as he started losing himself in this that the minder suddenly bade farewell.

The relief was short-lived and soon surpassed by a crisis concerning the inn. In his confusion he got up and left, hastily trying to retrace his steps but constantly distracted by constant reminders of his bumbling idiocy throughout the day.

Chapter 26
Another Sermon

Pluvius shuffled uncomfortably on the bench of the Grand Temple of Thelus. Vultai was ranting about the need to be prepared in the face of the Great Enemy.

The sergeant was agitated because he had heard rumour of war. Indeed, if he bothered to actually listen to the high priest's demagoguery it sounded like one had already begun, and if he were to actually believe those words spoken, then he would be under the impression it had been going on for eternity. However, his agitation was not so much at the situation, but rather his inability to find solid information about it. The cautious soldier was one who always wanted to be in the know, certainly before jumping to conclusions. But with Dummonius gone and the rest of the old guard gagged he could not use his contacts to find out.

For all his rhetoric, Vultai's sermons contained no specifics about outside events or their response. He spoke of encirclement and a great stand soon to come, but never even mentioned that Gatan troops had been dispatched to Danite and Vacarium (as the rumour suggested).

All Pluvius could see that there was a rising militarism on the island, which was rather self-evident this side of the border. Plus, even if the rumours were true, they would not be the 'front-line', as was being regularly declared, as they were the other side of the territory to the hotspots. That is, unless total war was being suggested. Pluvius shuddered as he was reminded of Heites' remark that anyone can start a war if they talk about it enough.

He found himself transfixed by the spectacle on the stage before him; Vultai shouted and strutted, taking heavy breaths of the acrid aid thick with incense smoke. His imagination began to run wild with the swirling tendrils of smoke as they curled around the priest's form and the pillars, creating sinister and mischievous shapes. Every time he heard Vultai bellow something about the great enemy he felt the smoky tentacles reach out and nudge them all closer to war.

He took a sideways glance along the bench at his squad members. They were sombre and glum, which was usual during these theological tirades. However, he knew they would remain like this indefinitely afterwards. It was as though their souls were broken. Again he found himself quoting Heites to himself: 'there is nothing more dangerous and volatile than the prolonged inactivity'. Though Pluvius announced it in his mind solemnly, he was puzzled as to why Heites always adopted a vindicated sideways smile when he proclaimed it.

The whole garrison was plagued by an anxious animosity, a kind that had never existed so strongly in peacetime. It was a demeanour Pluvius had only seen so prevalent when the siege of Neptus had set in. Now, just as then, it was a foreboding sense of being trapped and powerless. The tension could be felt all over the camp, swirling around all the men like a transparent aura of tetchy defensiveness and distrust. Men always got like this prior to a war. Pluvius smiled as he imagined what Julia would make of it. She would no doubt giggle with contempt at the 'masculine defect' of insecurity, and macho need to pretend the contrary as they humbly piled responsibility for protecting the entire house on themselves. They all wore troubled expressions as though this global political shift had occurred as a personal affront to their masculinity.

There he sat on his pew, a roosting soldier-chicken perched submissively, petrified by animalistic noises resonating through the hutch. To call the strutting demagogue up front the cockerel would be a grave misrepresentation. They may be cowed, but they were not his flock. Their cockerel had been chased away and now this cuckoo impostor squawked at them.

Vultai's babbling reached a peak, his eyes flaring like glistening beads as he eagerly eyed the meat that would soon be carrion strewn on a field. Then he would receive a new batch to peck at will. Pluvius was stirred out of his bittersweet reverie by the priest's sudden amplified pitch. Though his instincts immediately turned his attention to the noise and its source, he soon amended his senses' directed efforts and began scanning the airwaves for an alternative to the raucous bellowing. Between the muffled voids of noise that were the priest's incessant rants, Pluvius heard the rhythmic crunch of boots on gravel, the beat accompanied by a dirge of constant murmuring. This noise formed grainy silt that sifted between the priest's words spilling a sense of external disarray. Though marching soldiers, even large numbers of them, were nothing rare in the garrison, something made Pluvius feel this was a bad omen. All his attempts to shrug it off as a mere reflection of his state of mind were having no effect. The crunch and clump of boots on gravel seemed to meld with the high priest's words, the marching grinding war machine of his words coalescing in spectacular emotive sound with the drumbeat of militarism outside. With morbid fascination Pluvius found himself drawn to listen to the high priest's words. Was war amongst them now?

★

After his frightful ordeal in the town Rabica had retreated onto more remote paths through the forest. It meant he could avoid the sickening merchants, disdainful guardsmen, and ridiculously contented peasants. In evenings he would sneak onto fields to seize what he could, scrabbling through the dark and fertile soil to grab at potatoes and carrots. Carrots were better, as he could dust them off and eat them there and then, though his favourite were onions, which seemed to have such endurance after liberation from the soil.

But now even the forest was too alive for him, the greenery and fauna constant proof that he remained on the earth coexisting with that malignant society he despised. He still heard the odd group of villagers toiling or wandering with despicable vapidity. The open, far-reaching desolateness of hills were what he yearned for; dreaming idealistically of the vast void of the Vaca Mountains; natural spectacles which were unimaginable legends in his mind.

As he walked he remonstrated with himself about the forests inhabitants and their subsistence lives, at times jealous of their remoteness from it all, other times scorning them for their placid ignorance.

Now the tweeting birds in their joyful celebration of the beautiful greenery seemed to merely echo the pitiful songs of the peasants, so contented in artificial beauty. He did not want vivacious beauty, he wanted wondrous rolling beauty; a real overwhelming beauty of ravines and rocks so remarkable in their grandness and gradual formulation and constant glacial changing. Such landscapes were the earth down to its basics, with no façade of bright fresh fauna perpetuating a farce of painted beauty.

In short, he longed for vision, a long view of miles and miles of landscape; the whole picture not the 30 foot radius of thick trees bursting with life. What were these but nature's mimic of the city? Rabica shook his head. Was he just too cynical?

He stopped to stretch his back, which was becoming slouched and achy under the strain of his satchel.

"Yes I am." He furrowed his brow in passive irritation.

"The animals in nature have every reason to seem so happy." He paused again with distaste at his use of words. "No... contented... yes, contented is the correct word. It is not (by that I mean an animal is, even cannot be,) happy as such (unless it is introduced into society, say by becoming a pet or farm labourer – in which case happiness is a rarity). Even for pets, like, say, a dog, its happiness becomes so base – as with many people, especially the poor – being fed or petted." Rabica sighed as his whispered soliloquy meandered in a confused excursion back to mankind. "And that is why so much needs to change – we dehumanise the poor, then raise certain animals to the same level and feel so pleased with ourselves for apparently elevating the chosen animals to a level, when in fact we are just enslaving them to the same whims with which we cage ourselves."

Without realising, Rabica had begun walking again, quite hastily as though striding with purpose down a busy town street. He had raced on, completely unaware that he was panting with increasing intensity. As he paused in his monologue he suddenly became aware of his exertion, but ignored it and continued hoarsely thrusting out the statements with each exhalation. "We should stay far away from such things." He paused in his respiration, in order to clarify. "We should ensure we interfere with nature as little as possible."

As he marched on, he gazed in wonder at the grass about him, and listened to the trickle of streams enticing him to descend down step gullies in search of them. The occasional sound of birds, the fresh smell of wet peaty soil; moist and boggy, the smell after decay, the smell of renewal, potential for magnificence. "It's so... huh," he sighed in resignation.

"I can see its beauty, but..." He was cut short in his debate by the sound of feet tramping. "Oh shit, this is why," he managed to ventriloquise as the feet came around the corner. Rabica dredged up a smile, but as the peasants came closer he feared he overdid it. They smiled warily and wearily back. He nervously glanced in their direction every few seconds, as though to gaze upon them was forbidden.

As they approached he smelt their sweat. The first scent was musky man sweat, but once they had passed he smelt the pungent but strangely enticing aroma of a woman. Rabica ignored his sense-stimulated instinct and did not even look back, silently cursing his gender and natural impulses. He wished it away, declaring "I would rid myself of it and its sycophantic tag-along love for anything!" before adding, "even this lush paradise... in fact is it not a mere reflection of such ways? Its charm, its beauty, its grace. How it wills you to it, knowing you will only cause destruction of it and the fellow inhabitants."

It was now, predictably that he found his attention turned to The Young Lady. "Oh I miss Her," he declared out of the blue. "... I don't know why..." He scowled with irritation at himself. "How many times have I said that?"

The path meandered and undulated up and down like a perpetual wave of mud, gradually oozing and flattening out over hundreds of years before rising again in the next couple.

"What am I saying by that? Huh..." His tone became aggressive and self-contemptuous. "Huh?" he demanded. "... It's just a slogan isn't it?" he asked himself, the anger rising. "Come on! Spit it out," he bellowed in a whisper, before sighing with self-dismissal.

Sheepishly, he came to his defence. "Well, it makes no sense. I thought I was over her and so why think of her?"

"If I am over her, then why am I here?"

"Oh come on!" He protested sarcastically. "It's much more than Her! Look around you for fuck's sake (not literally though), there's shit everywhere... and its spreading!" He scowled at an imaginary self, though he was secretly pleased with the answer and so cracked the expression open, inverting it into a smile.

"Good," he declared, first confidently, then repeating it several times, driving the stake of its implications deeper and deeper into his mind until he saw it for what it was: submission.

★

Rabica trudged upwards; the foliage was wet, giving it a waxy gleam, almost fake. Even with the casual breeze meandering through the forest it did not flinch. He reached out to touch a tree trunk. The bark felt slimy, as though it was melting. His feet scuffed on stones embedded in mud.

He gazed down at the path that was a gentle climb. So gentle he did not notice it from walking, only when he looked to his left and saw the steep slope off the path below. His eyes traced the earth in silence, the only noise being his breath; like an echo trapped in his brain it continually resonated within his eardrums. On the ground brown leaves lay discarded daintily like dropped hand fans, and round hard berries were like beads from earrings or necklaces, fallen from the bodies of nature's entourage. He imagined he was following such a group of nymphs as a retinue to a mystical lady of nature. These organic items of jewellery and accessories had been dropped unknowingly as they danced gaily to pay tribute to their queen.

Eagerly he trudged on, encouraged by his dreamy belief that he was following the trail of a beautiful, phantom-like oracle of nature. He gazed with wonder at the red beads and natural fans, imagining them swaying and wafting in the listless breeze.

As he strode on in the euphoria, his mind wandered. Every stone became a precious gem of the entourages' decoration. He glanced behind him to see thick mud traipsed by his weighty boots into slush. Hefty boot prints gorged into the serenity. As he scanned, to his horror he saw the consequences of his clumsy steps; crushed desecrated beads, split open and spilling yellow seeds that now mingled with the polluted dirt. No longer were the fans daintily laid upon the soil; now they were ground into the slush, an amalgam of nature compounded by human contact.

He trudged on as daintily as he could, secretly knowing it was to no avail. The path before him became stonier and smoothed out. To his horror, the stones became a more regular; packed together and cemented with a greyish-green moss. They resembled cobblestones.

"No, not the dreaded town!" he shrieked. "How dare it desecrate the path of nature?" It was then that he knew he was doing nothing new, mislead by his dreams and loss of desires.

Rabica laboured on as though in a trance. Lurching from side to side, he seemed on the brink of collapsing. His face was screwed up, braced against some internal pain. His eyes, barely visible as they hid within the crevices of his eye sockets, winced under the strain of keeping themselves perpetually in a partial closure. He looked straight down, not daring to look around him lest he meet the face of a passerby or some decaying miscellaneous waste that seemed to litter the streets. His ears could faintly pick out the sound of people babbling insipidly with arrogant ignorance. He felt like curling up in a ball on the 'street', to hide himself from prying eyes of disgust. "I cannot drop to the ground in front of all these people," he whispered inanely.

Just as he was finding the torment unbearable the cobblestones sunk below a velvety blanket of bright green moss – it was like nature's royal carpet – in fact Rabica uttered these very words to describe it as he sank to his knees to kiss the soft furry sheet.

★

A small trail turned off deep into a generally flat wood with dips. The trees were covered in a sluggish moss. Littered around them were furry, moss-covered stumps, no doubt of old trees. They formed strange shapes of long extinct creatures fossilised on the spot, the moss their endurably furry hide that had clung to their ossified remains and kept it hidden.

Off the trail was a dip down into a gully cut by a long-gone stream. Roots dangled like tripwires down the edge, forming foot holes, each lined with tiny brown leaves and twigs; an assortment of the foliage's discarded components. Such matter lined the awkward path down like shed dead skin forming a cushion to the earth. Moss clambered over the rocks though failed to find a foothold on the underside of each overhanging precipice.

As Rabica clambered down he saw a cave entrance cut into the rock; it passed through under the path, resembling the archway under a bridge. Its bottom was covered with a clay-like mud dotted with rocks that were heavily weathered. Though the edges were smooth, or at least weathered in a series of smooth ridges, the roof had a most intriguing surface. The upside down cratered rock was covered with bubbly rock textures, it was as though it was growing back or the rock had become a crustacean. These anomalies were crumbly and brittle, crushing to powder just with Rabica's touch.

Rabica scrabbled for his solitary candle and after some time managed to light it. The cave had two small tunnels leading off in either direction at right angles to the archway 'entrances'. He eagerly scrabbled through into the mildly damp enclosure to the right, crawling on his hands and knees.

His candle flickered and spilt wax onto his hand, after a brief feeling of painful unease it solidified soothingly. Tonight he had cover.

★

The morning light allowed Rabica to better examine the various types of moss. He glanced with intrigue as he passed the mosses, which clung to everything, often forming animal-like shapes turned to stone or wood, and covered with a thick furry veil, hiding them under a green carpet. Even rock edges were lined from head to toe with often several different competing mosses. They clung to the rocks fearlessly sapping away minerals inside and in return cushioning them from the weather.

The moss covered rotten trees and hardened clumps of peat, spilling beyond in unstoppable surges that locked in close to form one seething mass. It was almost as though they formed a map of the world, each colour staking out an empire; not one speck of land lay unclaimed by the hordes.

The wandering vagrant had stopped to examine a sea of several species of moss that interlocked into tectonic plates forming the crust of the rock. He pushed his finger into several of the species with boyish intrigue. Then it hit him – this flora could grow anyplace – even on his desolate rock. That is what he had though had resided in the shed. His face exploded into an irrational multitude of euphoria. Was this humble yet widespread vegetation his saviour?

The dew-covered moss sprang back to its pre-tampered form after each probing prod. It felt like soaked rodent fur, though slimy in places. Rabica smiled to himself and almost skipped on.

He continued to think about the curious flora as he strode on with a recently unheard-of vivacity. The pale brightest green moss most rapidly expanded and colonised as the competing mosses spread through the image in his mind. Eventually his whole vision became a blanket of furry pallid green.

"So, this easily overlooked plant (is it a plant?) – Oh it is so easily. Whatever it is! What was I saying? – Oh yes this easily overlooked... vegetation." He breathed out heavily as he stepped over a protruding rock on a steep part of the climb. "... Is exactly what I need... metaphorically." He added the final word with some confusion, though he was not really paying much attention to the words, more uttering them as though they were a necessary part of breathing. He rambled on. "It's hope, isn't it," he told himself authoritatively. "You see," he added in a pedagogic tone, "I need to retain some hope and maybe, just maybe, something can sprout from it. Maybe not from the moss... that is, the actual object or person at which the hope is directed, but that it creates a more attractive mien from which to then find, or be prepared for, something... or someone."

His rambling stopped as he sank into deep thought. A frown overcast his face. The blanketing swarm of pallid moss conquering the rock played over in his mind. It spread all over it, engulfing it, sapping all the nutrients and blocking the path of anything else. In a panic he began to scour the sides of the path for a large patch of moss – "Is it not a saviour but a curse? This 'hope' - the obsessive banalities of a crumbling madman. Not the building blocks of mental paradise!"

It was a sinister foliage that warped a desolate land, engulfing it and ensuring it on the path to barrenness. If not, it held it perpetually in a cocoon, hidden away from the multicoloured parade of bustling wildlife that surrounded it.

This moss was exactly the insipid, pointless 'hope-in-hopelessness' he had sought to destroy. It was just a resurgence of his love for The Young Lady.

He saw some and so rushed ahead, throwing his bag down at the foot of the plateau of pallid green. He fumbled through the spotless patch in search of life – anything. Not a single beetle or bug or grub was to be found. Where the moss lay, nothing else dared to encroach. A few pathetic-looking blades of grass or plants thrust out of the furry sheet like a pitiful Excalibur, but these had obviously predated the moss's invasion and grown too high before the colonisation to be swallowed by them. Of course the fight for the front line in the sunlight parade was not the only line; no this was a two front war, and who knows what the conditions were like beneath this green carpet in the root war.

As he ceased being so aggressive with the moss and instead caressed it affectionately he thought aloud, "still, it is beautiful in its simplicity. Pretty fungi." Suddenly, he spun around due to a seething burst of paranoia. He lost his balance and stumbled back, placing his hands palms down on the rock to steady himself. There, pinned against the wall of the moss, he eyed the loose packs of plant life that seemed to be threateningly encircling him, greedily mocking him as an ally of the moss. Panic-stricken, he picked up his sack, and glared evilly at the plants before fleeing onwards up the path. As he did so he cursed the sprouting new greenery all full of promise for its painted vivacity, its mocking silence, sniggering behind twisting leaves.

"It's not what they are but what they represent," he told himself.

The forest thickened again as he descended into what seemed to be a shallow valley. As it levelled off Rabica passed what seemed to be a graveyard of trunks and stumps covered with a dark green moss. As before they resembled creatures cocooned and suffocated by the dank carpet.

About fifteen metres in from the trail Rabica could see what looked like a furry green coterie of creatures surrounded by a larger being. He knew really it was just some thin tree stumps smoothed to have oval tops and a dead felled tree, but it was so enticing for his imagination to run wild and see it as a tribe of gnomish blobs mobbing a wounded dryad. He stared in wonder before hurrying on in excitement.

★

The valley had risen up sharply on the other bank, so Rabica had begun to contour the near-sheer cliff face of cracked, compacted mudstone that constituted the wall of the valley. The path had remained no more than 3 feet wide, but the mudstone wall had backed away so there was a good twelve feet of ridge, covered with undergrowth. On his right the drop descended through the undergrowth to the bed of the valley. Through the foliage he could make out the distance blur of green where the other valley wall rose in symmetrical compliment to the one he now trailed.

Dense plant life was scattered across the valley floor, mighty trees looming like siege towers preparing to press up against the fortress-like wall. Vines were tangled up the wall, scaling ropes hurled for the bracken and other flora to use to assault the fort.

Rabica gazed in wonder at the cracked but sturdy ancient walls, the ingrown trees that stood sentry, mighty watchtowers and turrets gradually built into the structure.

Further on, a pinnacle of the stone stood apart from the wall with a toppled tree adorning it, sprawling down towards the parapet wall: an outpost had fallen.

Palm-like trees stretched out of the ground arcing upwards and outwards away from the wall and pointing menacingly towards the oncoming vegetation. "A palisade wall," Rabica whispered with inspired astonishment.

Rabica traipsed on, soaking in his surroundings. "It's as though a war was going on under my nose and I am just walking straight through it oblivious," he pondered aloud.

He trudged on through the heavily strewn battlefield. He wished he could float away with the humid mist and soar off to distant mountains. Even when he failed to consciously realise it, the woodland, with its life and existent wonder, rekindled his memories and kept alive his link to society. As his pace quickened he declared to himself. "Find me a place of rolling landscape so desolate and remote from these lovely facades that can only remind me of what I futilely seek to flee."

Gloomily he continued, "even the deepest cave down here keeps me tied to that world."

Though he loathed the impairment to long sight that the forest induced, he knew when he came out of it all he would see would be the tamed land of man's permanent domain. So he reluctantly accepted he should be thankful that where he now resided merely reminded him of the outside world and did not keep it always in sight in the distance. In a fleeting moment of resignation he pondered whether to make this forest his abode, travelling around it in a purgatory circle neither free from society nor coerced into it. At least the dirt here was clean, fertile, but untouched by the pestilent defamation of man. But then, it was still close, and to blinker himself so as to not to see how little he had progressed was to resign to defeat. Besides, something about how this place reminded him of the hustle and bustle of society made him think he would only mimic that which he had fled, that is, it would be another compromise dwelling.

As he strode on, he scowled at the beauty he had so foolishly admired and dreamed of a truly wondrous plateau of lonesome tundra with which to join in isolation.

Chapter 27
The Triumvirate Returns

It had been several weeks since Pluvius had heard the departure of half the garrison through the walls of the temple. It was like being in a ghost world, those of them left behind repeating the same tasks each day like spectres destined to repeat the cycle for eternity.

Now they were sparring, as they had for the past countless afternoons. He knew they would then be fed before going to the temple and then finally being sent out for general exercise. As he stood waiting his turn, he watched two familiar soldiers fight a duel he was sure he had seen again and again. With passive acceptance Pluvius followed and predicted their every move, not because of his knowledge of combat rather because it felt like a fight he had seen played over and over. Pluvius was untroubled by the seemingly endless images of *de ja vu*, watching with vapid indifference. It was like watching a familiar dance, one in which if a move was not predicted it was a mistake on the performer's part.

The monotony of daily routine was driving him into a stupor. Each day he found himself shifting between nonchalant indifference and near masochistic rage. One moment he was engulfed in an eerie serenity (made even more sinister when he thought of his actual surroundings) where every action was too much even to contemplate, then the next moment he was anxiously twitching to satisfy an unquenchable lust for violence. The consequence was that he found his obsessing about Julia superseded by a bloodthirsty anticipation of war, or else just smeared onto the mass of worries that piled up before his apathetic eyes.

Bizarrely, the two least affected were Geric and Arios; one would have expected the rookie and the impatient veteran to be petrified and infuriated respectively. Meanwhile, on the other hand, the usually level-headed and adaptable Heites was the most obviously affected.

Of course Pluvius had his suspicions as to why in the present climate this was so, having heard his confession to the killing of Visuvius, although his reasoning over the details was surprisingly off mark. Heites did not feel guilty, nor particularly bothered about being rounded up as a troublemaker. No, he had transcended himself beyond such worries, as he saw his life as doomed now (whether through fate or choice). His concern was regarding his resolute stance in defence of principles, most pressingly, how he would act if thrown into the centre of a huge bloodbath. It was the bandits dilemma multiplied in scale and therefore intensity to a point that even the slightest hesitation at the onset of hostilities could lead to the death of him and his comrades and not even get the point across. He knew it would be impossible to proclaim a 'soldiers truce', indeed he only had to look at the infuriated faces of his brethren to see they would march to war eager to get it done with.. They wouldn't even think of uniting and turning on their rulers with their lackeys, sycophants and machinations of social control which drove them together into an abattoir of reciprocal butchers. Not only would he be killed but his whole campaign would be engulfed and buried in the slash and spray of blood.

To flee the battle would be cowardly (one part of the soldier's code he would not relinquish), to switch idiotic, pointless and probably suicidal. After exhausting all the options he could think of, it became increasingly apparent he would have to adopt Pluvius' scheme to fight as usual for the sake of his friends. He begrudgingly allowed his mind to lean towards such a notion; it was not that he did not care for his brothers-in-arms but that he felt he was blackmailing himself into submission to the whim of the rulers. He still could not help but see it as the defeat of his high ideals, as they were mockingly replaced with the old notion of traditional honour to one's tribe. He had wanted his ideals to supersede such networks and reach out to all, but instead he seemed to be retreating into a depoliticised collective subsistence.

'But surely now, in these times of hardship and pressure in all areas of life, the time is ripe for action?' he would protest to himself, never reaching a definitive solution but often lamenting the unsatisfactory answer. 'It is when the act of defiance is the hardest to achieve that it has the greatest effect, so now it is near impossible to show dissent and that is precisely why to do so would be the most devastating.' This often sent him into a saturnine lull which he would shake off with the unknowingly acute remark that that would mean dissent was the most impotent when it was allowed.

Sometimes he would corner Pluvius alone and witter to him incoherently. Pluvius would just listen and allow Heites to battle out the argument on his own.

"Even subtleties are near impossible in this situation. 'Accidents' can't *happen*, and even if they did, they would still find someone to blame." Heites always used 'They'. He muttered and spat it, his eyes peering around in their sockets suspiciously. "And what is the use anyway?" he would ask. The question was originally intended to be rhetorical, but in a fleeting moment of doubt he would find himself desperately searching his mind for an answer.

"I suppose there is something genuine in your idea – caring for those you know?"

"But what difference is that from before? And why prioritise those who by accident of situation are under your wing of responsibility?"

Pluvius would give a puzzled, apologetic expression, a signal to Heites to counter himself.

"Is that not the injection of practicality? One can only uphold ideals as far as experience allows?" In these dreamy remonstrations, feelings associated with strings of words took preference over coherence; sometimes actual coherent ideas floated in his mind as he spoke the words, but with no real need to express them correctly they seemed nonsensical to outsiders.

"But it fails to address the structural issue, I mean if we do it and an identical squad in Gatan does it we will kill each other when all we need to do is not bother killing and we will both survive, or could unite."

Pluvius was uneasy about his companion's treacherous speeches but dared not say anything because, 1) he would get an earful 2) he still cared for his comrade and did not want to lose his trust 3) he was worried that if this happened Heites would have no one to vent his frustration to.

"But maybe there is virtue in these small mutually protective groups – it is sustainable at least – we can minimise the casualties in the process as it is always safest to only fight as much as is absolutely necessary for survival."

Pluvius would smile as he thought Heites had set his mind at rest... and occasionally he would have done, for a split second...

"But with such a huge battle as no doubt awaits us, how are we to know if we prolong the war by reeling back from delivering a decisive victory early on?"

And on he would go, usually until he either became so disheartened he mumbled quieter and quieter into a silence or broke off the argument because he was so pent up with rage and would pace about outside and alone.

In recent weeks Heites had raised his spirits, during the day at least, doing as he did now and training the new recruits whilst they waited to spar. Pluvius had noticed that he always taught them blocking and evasion, and never offensive moves. This was not just because he didn't want them killing people, but had practical advantages for them too as they stood the best chance of survival in a large battle if they just concentrated on blocking their opponent until either they overran them or disengaged.

Pluvius watched him with interest; his face seemed to return to its proud energetic old self when he did this. It gave him a small quantity of fleeting pleasure to see his comrade behaving normally, even if it were just a momentary distraction. After all, it was a sign he had not lost his old self entirely.

His attention returned to Arios and Geric; they were pretending to be trainer and trainee even though Geric didn't need instruction.

Pluvius left them to it, finding himself reminded of Julia. He could only think of her for a short while because all he did was follow circular patterns that spiralled down and down with the constant driving force being how much he missed her. He dreamed of being with her, that was it. Just them, anywhere, even here. Together they could share it.

★

The fire crackled and simpered, the closest thing to life in the room. The flames stayed squat as though crushed down by the air. The smoke rose upwards in continual waves shooting towards the hole in the roof, a misty dark ring with a black centre. It was like an obsidian doppelganger of the moon barely visible behind thick billowing clouds as they rolled over the night sky.

In the surrounding darkness silent shadows performed their arduous tasks in mechanical repetitive motions like wind toys. Their hunched forms curved cumbersomely over belts, blades and boots as they rubbed them with dingy musky rags. The acrid stench of oils coalesced and mixed with sweat and smoke overpowering the sickly aroma of incense and filling the room with the smell of worn machinery. With eerie repetition they performed these tasks, synchronised like clockwork.

Pluvius' body routinely followed the others. Around him were his men, his brethren, those he had pledged to stand by, those he had promised to protect to justify his prolonged loyalty to the military. Yet here he sat, a capitulated husk of a man, a mere tool; a tool cleaning its additional components ready for its great trial run.

Suddenly in the darkness he thought he saw Julia's darting eyes; intense disdainful beams emanating from two stunning fluorescent white orbs. Though the hallucination was visible for a mere moment the guilt it had mobilised remained. Only through her could it be possible. He had let her down doubly; he could have chosen to be with her now but had attempted to set himself a greater, more honourable mission. At the time he had done so with complete integrity and intent, but he had failed to actually pursue this mission and so had not only turned from her but now he failed to do what he had promised to do instead. Had he subconsciously taken the long-term path just because it put off actually doing anything and now this aim had fallen by the wayside?

'I am just not the kind to lead this, I was caught because the person who could bolster me in doing this thing was the one I had to turn away from at the onset,' he lamented, already feeling a defiant urge to try.

He was a sergeant; it was his job to fight demoralising eras and promote brotherly unity. To claim he needed help from another was either a lie or a worrying sign of his reliance on Julia. In other words it could not be that he was not made of the right material to deal with this, but that his liaisons with her had sapped his determination.

He felt an immediate impulse to try and reassert himself as the leader of a troop rather than one amongst a mob of lackeys. However, so embedded was his routinized non-entityship that he could barely even think of how to interact, let alone how to lead.

Over the past months ranks below that of the Drill Sergeants (two more Hari clones had arrived a couple of months ago) were not so much ignored as superfluous. Sergeants and squad leaders (an informal position below sergeant chosen by the sergeant to take over in his absence or lead part of the squad if split up) were never delegated to, given any responsibility or duties different from the men. Seeing as most sergeants relied on a combination of autonomy and mutual respect, their positions were rendered extinct by never having orders to give. When the mass of the soldiers cared so little about goings on, and had no free time except to sleep, no relationship between anyone could develop. On top of this, the basic soldiers had looked to their leaders to get them out of the mess they were all in; the disappointment ran deep.

Pluvius needed to get their attention, but couldn't think of a viable excuse. He couldn't launch straight into a tirade as they would just see it as another preacher and switch off.

His eyes traced their sombre movements in the moody orange firelight and quickly found his limbs instinctively mimicking their actions.

He had a sudden thought; it struck his brain, startling his lulled mind which was unused to such powerful independent activity. This thought seemed to bypass the stirred organ, pushing him into action as it registered.

'I need to get out of this!'

He had bolted upright and then risen to his feet, his overly polished belt absentmindedly discarded.

Several of the men stirred from their chore-induced slumber. The others continued rocking two and fro in eerie rhythm to their polishing motions.

Pluvius seemed on autopilot as he squatted awkwardly beside Arios. Calmly the hulking veteran looked up from his polishing. Unusually for the soldiers at the time, Arios was neither shocked nor suspicious of the unexpected event. Unnoticed by Pluvius, Geric, who sat beside him, did likewise.

"Fancy seeing you here sarge," he whispered with a humour totally alien to the surroundings for so long.

It set Pluvius off nostalgically reminiscing about the 'good old days' when they all laughed. Rebuking himself for being nostalgic and so condemning those days as a bygone age, he reminded himself that such days were exactly what he sought to bring back.

When he returned to his senses he found a strange expression had settled on his face, which seemed to be cracking and creasing into a strange myriad of tensions. Yet rather than increase his strain (as was the norm) the expression was breathing relief into his face. He must be smiling.

"I've missed those days," he blurted.

Arios' face turned sallow and he nodded bitterly. He knew exactly what Pluvius meant.

Pluvius attempted the face he had inadvertently made previously, but felt uncomfortable.

"That is what I have come to speak to you about."

Arios raised an eyebrow and leant in to show he was listening.

"You remember back in Leria forest you said we must stand together?"

Arios, who had given a fleeting nervous glance at Geric at the mention of the forest, nodded and sighed in relief.

"Well, look at us now." Pluvius invited Arios to take a look around with a sweeping gesture of his hand.

Arios surveyed the scene. He had been so wrapped up in his relationship with Geric and consequent relative contentment, he had not realised how much the others had been affected.

Some of the men had been intrigued by the now unorthodox interaction and were trying to listen. A few even stopped their polishing. In fact, even those who continued with their labour were only doing so as a front, fearing they may be being spied upon, and gave awkward glances through the corners of their eyes.

Heites was one of the latter, his paranoid demeanour plastered over cynical delight at their whispering dissentions (which they had to be, as even to talk at all was frowned upon). He dared not make it visible that he was curious.

Perhaps they were going to orchestrate some kind of resistance. He was somewhat shocked by his ego-centric thought over whether he should join them. For in all his soliloquies he saw himself as a solitary dissident, a spreader of dissent amongst others. It did not occur to him that he could join them wholeheartedly, merely as a side project to be utilised by his own efforts. However, he was immediately appalled at this suggestion: the whole point of his resistance was to join with like-minded men.

Pluvius saw that Arios had realised what he had missed.

"We promised to stand united, this is no criticism of you... two," he nodded respectfully at Geric, "I am pleased you two have formed a brotherly union, I just want to extend such a thing to us all."

Arios and Geric exchanged worried but rather bemused looks.

"Well, we need to need to re-forge our brotherhood," Arios proclaimed in assent.

"...But how?" Pluvius asked.

Arios smiled as he took a sweeping look at the arch-backed silhouettes. "First, you need their attention... which you seem to have already."

Pluvius was rather shocked to see the whole squad was, in various levels of subtlety, listening in. His mind was suddenly a melting pot of jitterish thoughts, accompanied by immediate demands to his limbs to get him into a standing position.

Just as he began to build confidence ready to stand he felt Arios push him forward from his precarious squatting position, forcing him to stand or else he would tumble forward like an eroding rock cascading into the sea.

Once standing he took a sweeping observation of his comrades. Even though he had no idea what to say, he was inspired by the looks on their faces. Though they still wore the gaunt faces of the servitude to Vultai's rule, Pluvius was sure there was something positive trying to break through the thick cowls that clung around their necks like invisible shackles. However, the way in which they were perpetually waiting for him to speak was nerve-wrecking in the current political climate. Besides, before his respect amongst the men had been from day to day initiative, so he had never had need for speeches.

Nevertheless, he found his proud posture returning, and this spurred them into being more attentive and hopeful.

Only Heites did not stop his chores. He clutched the belt buckle like a street urchin does a coin, caressing its near texture-less smooth surface. However, a sly grin made occasional encroaches onto his face, illuminated by the flame-light, evidence that he was listening just as vigilantly. When exposed to the light, his teeth gleamed, mocking the buckle's shine.

Pluvius found himself engaging in a rousing spiel.

"I want you all to think back to Leria forest. Not of the fight, not of our loss, our strains and stresses, but of its outcome: our pledge, our declaration of unity and mutual support." All the way through his speech he shifted his focus from face to face of his comrades. They stared back with awe-inspired astonishment. "This is not an indictment, or if it is, it is of me. I am the sergeant, responsibility for the instigation of our oath lies with me. Well, now I realise we need to act, to act, not to resist," (with subconscious intent his eyes fell upon Heites), "but to subsist. To do this, all it requires is that little extra effort from us all: to rebuild what we had. I know some may blame me for inaction, but I was powerless alone. We must all work together, within our squad, our little community that binds us in solidarity and shared future."

"It is hard, when they squeeze us of every drop of our essence, so we dedicate all our efforts to their programme. We must stand by each other, and to do this we must share. They rely on us being isolated, to battle them alone, but we must not. Instead of drifting apart we must come closer, trust each other." Pluvius felt he was being emotive and so decided he must use the platform of attention he had achieved to lead by example, not just fill their heads with abstract rallying cries.

"I do not know if he asked any of you individually, but Captain Dummonius offered me, us all, a chance to join him. As you all know, I turned it down. Now, none of you have questioned me on this, and although I would like to think this means you all agree, I am certain it is not the case - I for one have often have doubts, and think of life out of these walls."

Most of the men seemed shocked at his candid announcement. Even Heites had stopped polishing and had looked up at his sergeant. The few fleeting moments that his face was partially visible in the light, Pluvius could see from the mildness of the streaky shadows across as they contoured the creases of his skin that he had tempered.

Suddenly Cilius, who had been a close friend of Kilnos spoke up, as he did so he shook with emotional stress. "So, why didn't you get us out of here?" he spat, his rage commendably restrained, but overt enough to leave the question teetering on the brink of rhetoric.

Pluvius felt a sharp pain as he felt the verbal blow of contempt, but nevertheless was pleased someone had spoken out. It was the only way to bring about a collective catharsis.

He had wanted to thank Cilius for his candour, but felt it would seem belittling.

"Heites and Arios, who you all know act as my council on such issues eventually agreed that to go mercenary would have only superficial benefits. It also would not only be a damaging devaluation of our hard work, but could actually open us up to greater scrutiny by making us stand out."

They were all surprised to hear the cynical voice of Heites emanating imprecisely from the vicinity of his shadow-masked face. "Dummonius is working for Delvinius, doing *their* dirty work."

Pluvius, though at first worried Heites would contradict him, was grateful for support, even if it was rather excessive. After all, he did not want to turn his men permanently against the idea of going mercenary, nor did he want to demonise Dummonius.

Even if they didn't know the details, the soldiers knew Delvinius was a rich extravagant aristocrat close to Juscius II and therefore to this whole mess. Indeed, it was widely rumoured amongst the populace that it was these advisors and robber-barons that were driving the whole thing. From this poisonous gaggle there emanated an infectious aura of corruption that swarmed around them all and their associates. It wafted and dispersed with the diffusion of power, soaking into their skin and clothes like a putrescent stench. Just mere association with this loosely categorised coterie rendered one infected.

"But we gotta do something! We're just sitting here like cattle waiting to be marched into a battlefield?" Cilius burst out.

Perhaps it was hearing his despair voiced by another, but for some reason Heites carefully and quietly placed his belt on the ground and shuffled into an attentive cross-legged position. Then, with the succinct cognisance that he had been renown, he declared, "but what can we do? We all saw what my rebellious act did."

Still rather shocked that he had revealed his clandestine operation publicly, he gave a cautious nod, requesting the silent backing of Pluvius. The sergeant returned the gesture. What is more, the silence amongst the men showed they had all known of his assassination.

Pluvius broke the silence with a resolute assertion. "That is why I propose we go back to how we were, survive this drive into battle, then try and get out."

Most of the men nodded gloomily in passive acceptance. Cilius mumbled a garbled set of exasperated noises, wishing to voice dissent and propose some kind of alternative.

"We cannot risk another of my actions… not here," Heites added decisively. "No such action can take place in such an ordered and monitored society."

The men could see their practical level-headed No. 2 was right, though they were unnerved by his casual mentioning of clandestine operations, still finding such insidious methods taboo.

"But if we go on manoeuvres with one of those bastards…" Cilius trailed off hopelessly.

The rest of the men fiddled anxiously.

"… Then it still is no use… such things can only be done opportunistically… in the chaos of war," Heites countered, more to reassure the others he would not do such a thing, than to stop others from following in his footsteps.

"… However, we are not powerless. I propose we reach out to others, especially the young ones who run the highest risk of being sucked into their propaganda. I am not saying turn them into dissenters, just offer them soldierly survival guides. Let them come to our way."

Though he disliked the idea as being meddlesome and too political, Arios could at least agree via practical soldierly advice. "All this zeal they fill them with and carelessness will get them all killed. I will help them if just to avoid slaughter of my brethren," he declared, clearly seeing the rookies as Geric only a few months ago.

Finally, they all understood Heites' actions on the training field, and Pluvius, who had noticed the content of his lessons, was opened to a more politically-motivated dimension to it. It was only now that he realised how dedicated his comrade was to fighting *them*. What he had thought was just a recreational escape from inhuman existence was also motivated by subversion, albeit subtle. Perhaps they could all engage in this; the drill sergeants could not complain.

Heites, who had been studying Pluvius' countenance, must have guessed the sergeant's thoughts.

"My worry is that if we all indulge in this the Drill Sergeants will notice and try and incorporate it. It must not be formalised; even if they assent to it as a formality it is only a matter of time before they subject it to scrutiny. I do not wish to discourage others, merely ask for caution. It has to be something we choose to do."

Arios seemed agitated at the politicising of such philanthropy. "But, we cannot just pack it in just as a spiteful reaction… if they need our help…" His somewhat garbled complaint was shot down by a sneering Heites, irritated at his comrade's naivety and hypocrisy, with a sharp rebuttal.

"I notice the beneficiary of your training is hardly the neediest: to accuse me of dishonesty in politicising an act of kindness and concern when it is far better than for personal indulgence."

It would be untruthful to say Heites had unknowingly launched into a tirade over a delicate issue. He knew it was, and did so deliberately; such was his dedication to the cause. He would not beat about the bush, and it was in his critical nature to use the strongest arguments at his disposal with no regard for sentimentality. What he had not expected, nor desired to rouse, was the rest of the men's antiquated dislike of Arios' relationship with Geric. It was a chauvinism he and his cause could do without. He quickly silenced those who thought they were on his side with a sweeping accusing glare at the culprits, accompanied by a distasteful expression. He then turned his attention to Arios and Geric. "I have no qualms with what you do, either of you, just do not criticise me on an unfounded basis."

Pluvius, who had deliberately remained silent in his two comrades' dispute, sought to end this needlessly public disagreement. "This is no subject for us to discuss. You two are best to argue your reciprocal disapproval in private."

Rather than calming Heites, Pluvius irritated him by misunderstanding him, "I do not disapprove of Arios' activities, on the contrary I commend them both, I do not wish to censor his action. Indeed, I recognise his strains over the issue, and believe that though perhaps he does not know it his personal activity is a similar dissidence to mine. They are nothing be ashamed of, nothing to be hidden, it is that great survival strategy of personal expression. I wish he would respect my methods as much as I do his."

Upon finishing he rose and approached his comrade, who was somewhat embarrassed. He had, after all, thought his relationship with Geric was unknown.

Silence and shock amongst the men seemed to freeze the room, the flickering fire casting eerie shadows on their faces as though they were covered in robes. Heites offered his hand to Arios. The flame's light rolled over the digits, illuminating them as though they were forged fresh from a hearth.

Arios hesitated before stiffly taking the hand in his. The fire-light gradually submerged them in light as they reached Heites' giving the effect of a reverse eclipse. They shook hands and Heites sat himself down with his close companions.

The air in the room relaxed. The coven of dissenters sat attentively with proud expressions: now the triumvirate was re-established.

They sat in silence; all wanting to say something that would propel the reunification, but not daring as to break the silence could nullify their unity. Instead, they preferred to soak up the mutual comfort forged in the knowledge that they were contributing to each other's happiness.

In a whirlwind of commotion the door flung open. The meditating soldiers did not even flinch as Drill Sergeant Hari and two guards strode in. He did not even pause to look at the coven, before launching into his tirade. "Alright men, look lively! We have immediate orders for mobilisation! I want you all packed and ready in ten. Light packs and full uniform. Now! Come on!"

Hari looked down, expecting to see a warren of minions scrubbing his shackle-buckles. Instead what he saw was unusual, indeed unheard of.

"Sergeant, what in Septimo's unholy name[4] are you lot doing?"

Pluvius shot to his feet. "'Ten-sion!" he bellowed, like in the old days.

Immediately his men obeyed, standing as proud and tall as ever. They all knew they were obeying their sergeant's command, finally after all these months.

Hari turned and scowled angrily at the senior of the two guards; they were supposed to shout it on entry, but in recent weeks they had stopped. This was partially because Hari had a habit of storming straight into a bellowing order, not giving them the chance, but also was because such abrupt entrances into the rooms of anxious men meant they stood to attention automatically.

He looked back with disgruntled admiration at the sight; a contradictory expression the result of resenting their autonomous acts combined with an officer's built-in pride at seeing soldiers standing so obediently before him.

Before he could say anything, Pluvius put on his official parade voice. "Drill sergeant, we have finished, sir[5],"

Hari was shocked. "Really!" he exclaimed, with sarcastic disbelief. The men remained motionless.

"Drill Sergeant, if we polish our belts any more they will fade," Pluvius added knowingly.

"So why are you not in your bunks?" Hari retorted self-

---

[4] It was now an offence punishable with lashings to utter the Lord Thelus' name in vain; consequently the NI subtly urged the use of its immortal enemy in place of traditional profanities.
[5] Soldiers were being encouraged to call Drill Sergeants Sir; something they didn't mind as made it easier to see drill sergeants as part of *them*.

satisfactorily.

Pluvius was undeterred. "We were meditating, sir...To Thelus." Pluvius didn't mind pretending to be doing something New Interpretationist, as long as it covered for their dissent, and enabled him to answer back, which would have a much better effect on his men's morale.

Hari contemplated reporting their unorthodox behaviour but realised he could not discipline them for piety. He could mention their disrespect and possible suspicious behaviour, but this would just make him weak. Plus if it came out he had treated strictness as insubordination all hell could break loose.

"Well, you need to be ready in nine – we march to Neptus," he concluded, trying to attain authority.

"Sir, yes, sir!" Pluvius barked, biting his lip afterwards to write off a snigger.

"Good, at ease," Hari replied quietly.

There was a gut-wrenching pause as the soldiers looked to Pluvius, who dared not give the order out loud so instead nodded and they all obeyed.

Hari swivelled on the spot, pretending to not notice their defiance, and marched for the door that was held open by the guard of lesser seniority. Meanwhile, the senior guard called the room to attention, as was custom when an officer left.

The soldiers were already ambling across the room towards their kit and so nonchalantly slipped their right feet in line with their left, and stood rather casually until they had departed. Once the entourage's deliberately loud stamping had dissipated outside, all the soldiers simultaneously turned inwards towards the fire and laughed. Amongst the laughter Heites caught Cilius' eye and they gave each other a solemn nod.

Chapter 28
A Fistful of Warlords

Lord Adonis eagerly entered Gorax's workshop. The inventor had rushed into his office with his usual inadvertent disregard for convention to announce that he had perfected the 'great invention' that he had mentioned frequently but the details of which he had refused to disclose.

Gatan was pleased to go, not just so he could finally see this grand creation, but also to get out of his office, where countless questions bounced in and out of his mind. It had all started with reports of a

Latman patrol crossing the Vaca Mountains in pursuit of some rebels. Having been spotted by Vacarian mountain watchtowers they were followed all the way into the western foothills. Here they were confronted by the local Vacarian force. According to the Vacarians the Latmans refused to turn back and attacked the force. They were beaten back and forced to make a hasty retreat, mockingly trailed by Vacarian scouts who ensured they returned to their own territory. Two weeks ago Latman forces began amassing on the Danite border, intending to skirt through the corner of the household in order to attack Vacarium without sending an army across the mountains.

Danite had been given an ultimatum, to remove all military units from their path or else be treated as conspirators and be attacked. Adonis had heard from his commander of the newly deployed Gatan troops in Danite that Lord Felix was demanding guaranteed Gatan support should he disregard the Latman order.

The Commander had sent a message to Lord Gatan that he had told Lord Danite that he 'regretfully lacked the authority to make such a guarantee' adding that he had advised Danite to 'wait for Latman troops to pass and engage Vacarian forces as it may prove more prudent in the long run.' Though pleased with his commander's conduct, it did nothing to soothe his anxiety concerning the whole debacle. He would have to honour historic pacts with Vacarium and assist them; equally Danite was a good ally and deserved support. However, he had heard reports of troops from eastern garrisons in Latman being moved to Neptus ready to strike against Gatanese territory should he get involved. This meant he would need to immediately mobilise the whole standing army and even some reserves. He was, however, conscious that such an act would rouse suspicions, making full-scale war inevitable. Consequently, he had summoned all the Regional Commandants, who were to meet this evening to advise and (if need be) mobilise.

As he entered the rather ramshackle building, he was filled with a mystical reverence, the kind he got when he first entered the grand temple. However, whereas successive visits to the temple gradually wore down its capability to enthral, this powerhouse of invention only became more and more intriguing with each visit.

Gorax bounded to the double door like a spindly sprite, unlocking a hefty padlock that hung on a thick chain, that was taut with its weight. He tugged the resistant door until it was open just enough for him to slip in, absentmindedly leaving the Lord to heave the door over a rather rebellious clump of coarse grass that had set itself up as a door stop so he could fit his bulky frame through.

Inside, the building was filled with timber of all sizes. In the centre of the crowded room was a squat and rather savaged carpentry table. The piles of clutter adjacent to it suggested its currently clear surface was a rarity. The only object on it was a tiny model that resembled a wheeled weighing device. From the distance he now stood at, Adonis would never have guessed it to be a kind of catapult as previous designs had been compact squat contraptions. This mechanism was tall and lean, almost frail. Its chassis was a triangular horizontal frame with the point at the back. Two symmetrical triangular frames rose from the chassis, their points meeting exactly in the centre with the balanced crossbeam sandwiched between them. At the front of this beam was a bucket full of stones and at the back a sling-like pouch with a comparatively thick piece of rope holding it to a peg at the back of the chassis. The whole contraption was elevated on wheels positioned at the three corners. Lying next to it was a miniature set of pulleys and ropes set out as a kind of winch.

Not bothering to explain what the model actually was, Gorax began babbling excitedly. "I had been experimenting with wheels, to see if it could be mobile but it is very slow." He grinned with seemingly inappropriate joviality. "However, when I came to test it to check that it still worked... you will never guess what! Its range had increased considerably! It seems that the momentum of rocking forward helps propel the rock farther, although it may just be because the bucket falls more rapidly."

Adonis had not been paying attention to the technicalities. Instead he was rather bemused that this fragile cobweb of matchsticks and string was a deadly siege engine in the making. "And this works?"

Gorax ignored the mocking tone, far too excited to be put off by cynicism. "Observe!" He hurriedly scampered over to the machine, loaded the pouch and released the rope loop. It lurched forwards; simultaneously the pivoted bucket swung down, sending the pouch arcing through the air. Two hooks on the front of the pouch loosened independently as it reached the highest point, launching the stone across the table.

Adonis was impressed, but cautious. "And this will work on a large scale?" he inquired.
Gorax nodded assuredly. "I don't see why not... it will have to have some kind of winch to bring the sling arm down... its range then, depending on size, length of string, weight in bucket, etc should be up to 700 yards."

Instantly Adonis perked up. "That is long enough to reach Neptus from the safety of the bank!" he exclaimed aloud.

One may think Gorax would be reluctant to build such an engine of war, and would not be pleased to hear such a thing. However, having actually met Juscius and his cabal, he had realised war would be a necessity at some point. He had also read the account of the siege of

Neptus (an outlawed bard's tale in Gatan) and had been horrified by the atrocious suffering of civilians in sieges. Therefore, by avoiding the need for sieges, he justified his intervention as ultimately humanitarian.

"This is excellent, how much wood do you need?" the lord declared.

"Well, sir, it uses quite a lot, but would be safer and quicker to build on site, if you get my meaning. The wheels would certainly have to be pre built, as would the winch. However for the sake of security, would it not be best to wait until they are needed?"

Gatan nodded, already distracted by a burning desire to try it out. He approached it warily. "May I?" he inquired, neither Gorax nor Lord Gatan noticing the unique situation of a lord asking permission to do something. Gatan tried it, laughing in pure joy as he did so, unable to resist a child-like urge to try it again. Tears streamed down his face as he tested it for the third time.

Once back to normal, he strode over to his gangly engineer and shook his hand admiringly. "Your services are unfathomable! If there is anything you desire just let me know. Really, this is even better than your last invention!"

Gorax tried to take it as a compliment, but found his guilt at such a waste intolerable. He hoped this new invention would in part compensate by edging him closer to creative freedom to pursue his ambitious drainage design. However, it could never make up for those days lost.

"Sire I have no desire for riches, all I ask is that you agree to allow me to pursue my plan for drainage and waste."

Adonis paused to think, finding himself swayed by Gorax's wise inventions to date. "Make a model," he declared eventually. As he departed he lamented to himself that such a plan would only be implemented if he succeeded in the increasingly inevitable war, and even then would be sidelined by political upheaval.

★

Lord Gatan had impatiently gone through the ceremony at the temple. This was not because of any particular contempt for the tradition, though the encounter with Zeuorox had sullied the wise and objective impression he had had of High Priests. Instead, he was just boyishly anxious to tell the commanders his plan.

All his servants, even his wife (who barely saw him now he was in 'war mode') had noticed his sudden reversal of mood. Of course, she hadn't queried him about it, as it was 'not her place'.

Upon seeing his entrance, she had hoped he would be cordial, but instead the meal had been conducted in the usual arduous silence.

Now he was eagerly making his way to the meeting hall, looking forward to the grand unveiling of his solution, a chance to take advantage of Latman's scheming. He would not be led into war with Latman, nor would he be stubbornly attempting to stall it, only to be dragged into it. Instead he would go into it on his own terms: call the fopp-lord's bluff and trample on his plans.

All this time he had been torturing his brain to find an escape from this never-ending march to war. But now, rather than scurrying about trying to stop it, he could seize the initiative and take the fight to them.

For once Adonis had decided to be the last entrant, throwing out his convention of being the first, so he could capitalise on a sweeping entrance to launch straight into his plan. This novel act would certainly get the regional commanders' worked up and worried and so make them more malleable and receptive to their swooping uniter.

As he swaggered hastily towards the meeting house he mischievously thought how his wife would disapprove of his swashbuckling style.

The two guards stood stiff to attention, visibly relieved at his belated arrival. As the door swung open, the torches flickered like hungry digits leaning towards his throne at the far end of the room. The regional commandants all looked up in silence; their bickering had ceased the moment the door latch had clicked.

They all wore doleful features, thickly painted masks that only exaggerated the contours of concern on their faces. Even Hercela failed to meet his lord's entrance with his usual cordiality.

They all sat hunched in sombre postures. The gloomy torch light cast gnarled shadows over the lower halves of their bent, cloaked backs, meanwhile blanketing the upper half in light that was swallowed by the gothic morbid colours of the material.

An adjutant stood timidly in the corner, a rough grey outline and gleaming pair of eyes the only traceable evidence of his existence.

Gatan jolted slightly as he entered. The adrenaline rush was stymied by the disquieting silence. Nevertheless, he launched himself fully into the room, barking as though ignorant of its listless graveyard aura.

"Why aren't the candles lit? It's like a cultists den in here!"

Hesitantly, the regional commanders stood and in a rather disjointed unison welcomed him. "Your Lordship."

Gatan smiled, his lips twisting the straggly wisps of beard that grew in tangled stretches around his mouth. "Gentlemen," he proclaimed as he strode around the table to his seat.

Only once he was seated did the regional commanders return to theirs. Adonis scoured the occupiers of the seats to find one was empty. "Xsclepia is not coming, then?" he asked.

Most of the regional commanders remained silent and somewhat sheepish, clearly even more distraught at seeing their lord act so strangely.

Hercela, who sat directly on Adonis' right, took up the challenge. "Perhaps he will join us later?"

Gatan nodded dispassionately before launching into the issue at hand. "I am sure you are all aware of the problem we are faced with: Latman is to invade Vacarium, something we could not accept anyway, but to make it worse they are to go through Danite. We cannot allow this and so our force will join Danite and engage the Latman invasion once it is in Vacarium. Danite has warned the invaders that their incursion into Danite territory is an act of war. Though our force in the region will help, I have dispatched a message to Latman explaining that this does not necessarily mean we are at war. However, latest reports are the Juscius is amassing forces at Neptus."

Suddenly Meredic interrupted. "Surely sire, if our forces are engaging them then we are at war? I mean this is hardly a small border skirmish."

Gatan shook his head, surprisingly not offended at being interrupted. "It is not the size, but the location; according to convention, it is only war if it happens on one of the House's territories. This is a proxy struggle."

Hercela nodded knowledgeably in assent.

Eager to get to the point, Gatan continued. "As I said, they are preparing for something on our border, which means logically we should mobilise too. Even though this may be interpreted as confrontational, I would say there is nothing more enticing than a comparatively weakly defended border. We basically have three choices: (1) mobilise but take no action and see what he does (2) mobilise and seize the initiative by taking the war to him, or (3) having a limited mobilisation and try and stall the build up to war."

"(1) will just play into his hands; it seems the safest, but it is little short of paralysis, giving him the free hand to manoeuvre as he wishes. (2) is risky and needs something special in order to work – we cannot just declare all out war then spend months sitting outside Neptus whilst Vaca and Danite collapse. (3) seems too much like (1) only more half-hearted, even dreamlike in its belief that if we bury our claws we won't get scratched." He felt a sharp jab in his back. It was the conscience of his wife, the grandest diplomat, castigating him for misrepresenting the diplomatic course.

Before he could continue, an ecstatic Jarius exclaimed, "the boats! We can sail past Neptus, even go straight for Lateria!"

Gatan had tried to forget about the boats, even though Xsclepia had hinted at it in the ceremony, and so was reluctant to comment. Hercela either beat him to it, or saved him the bother: "the problem is that the Latmans have a massive navy. Even if they only sank half our ships that would decimate our ground forces. Don't forget soldiers are no good in marine warfare."

"And a loaded ship is no match for one kitted solely for war," added Gorthan, regional commander for the far Southeast region.

"Why not use it as a decoy?" suggested Meridius, determined to legitimise the prophecy (both he and Jarius had come to the conclusion that even if using the naval vessels was not obviously beneficial, it was what the gods willed and so to do so would bestow their blessing on other actions.)

"A decoy for what?" replied General Perecos.

Lord Gatan, who had been despairing that he would not get around to telling them of his great plan, jumped at the chance to cut in. "Ah well, actually that fits in rather nicely with my plan." He waited for them all to be attentive. "Gorax has just developed a new war engine that can hurl rocks at Neptus from a safe distance away from the river bank."

Perecos and Hercela were the most impressed, both being veterans of the famous previous assault. "It works?" Hercela inquired.

"He has a model, and assures me a full scale one, built on site, would work. It will crush their walls, smash their towers... if they do not surrender in the first few days they will be standing in a pile of rubble!" he exclaimed dramatically.

"And the decoy will divert their troops, allowing for a quicker victory," Jarius added.

Hercela wasn't so sure: "but the more troops we defeat at Neptus the better."

"But what if the machine doesn't work? A sizeable army would have to be mauled in a costly assault," Perecos countered.

"It will also generally spread confusion," added Meredius. "Plus, if the flotilla takes reservists we could have a small force in the territory causing havoc."

Gatan paused thoughtfully before responding to the debate between his commanders. He was conscious of a need to keep Xsclepia happy, but also thought of the wider picture. "What we mustn't forget is that this is not just a war on our border, we mustn't lose sight of our original reason for fighting, and that is the invasion of Vacarium. We may need this decoy as a diversion away from the western front. If we wait to amass troops on the Neptus border they may flood and defeat Vacarium and Danite and then we will have to fight them all at Lateria."

Hercela nodded reluctantly, in a way that showed he was merely nodding solely for the sake of consensus.

With the first tranquil silence of the meeting, Teritus seized the opportunity to make an enquiry. "Have we heard anything from Lewerix or Telis?"

"I have requested assistance from Lewerix, though I doubt he will join in such a large incursion. Sources tell me he has condemned Latman's actions and has ceased primary trade (that is timber and composites). I have requested an all-out severing of ties and requested rights of passage (not that we will use it), but we shall see. As for Telis there is no use, I could request his neutrality, but having met the scoundrel I am sure it would only fill him with self importance when he allies against us."

Teritus clearly wanted to probe further into diplomatic issues and solutions, but knew he would be lambasted. "So war is unavoidable?" he inquired lamely, wincing as he felt the subconsciously imposed rhetorical nature of his question.

Gatan let out a sigh, "so it seems."

Adonis quickly redressed himself to keep the pace going. "This means each province must mobilise its standing army, plus primary reservists[6] with some primaries remaining to guard the region. Each region will have to send some primaries to Gartan, except the Neptus regions who can make their way to Giliad and await pickup. Meridius and Jarius, your standing and half your primary troops will have to sneak through the edge of Lewern forest and make your way to Nepsius. Gorthan, your army for the assault can ride in the ships to Giliad and disembark – discreetly - before making their way to the rendezvous. Teritus, you must load your men onto the flotilla, then sneak them off at night - enlist anyone to make sure all the boats look filled - they can get off later! The central provinces are rather easy, and I shall deal with Ateri. Is everyone clear?"

Gatan finished, his voice booming proudly around the shady room. The heads nodded like obedient acolytes.

"I believe a toast is in order!" he declared. The adjutant hurried about, placing goblets on the thick table, which was heavily overcast by the shadows of the hunched torsos. Their shadows settled over the gigantic desolate timber plain like distant mountaintops, the goblets placed like objects in a surrealist painting, with melted candles and giant's shadows masquerading as peaks.

The wine poured liberally, the sound of liquid cryptically echoing over the otherwise silent plain. Then up where he clouds should be, exactly between the two torches, the timber desert's god proclaimed, "to

---

[6] Those who had left service in the last three years. Secondary would be 4-6 plus any soon to be soldiers. And then, in theory, Tertiary would be 7-9 years.

victory!" and the mountain titans awoke, their round shadows crumbling and rising as they thundered out an avalanche of praise.

★

The traveller nervously paused in contemplation outside the door to the inn. His eyes were bloodshot and watery from a combined offensive of the blustery wind and his emaciation, which was exacerbated by an internal turmoil that was clear to any passerby who bothered to examine him. To the stranger's relief, no one seemed even in the remotest sense inquisitive. In fact the whole village was under a cloud of cowed moroseness, totally averse to doing anything in case it drew attention to them.

Rabica overcame his fearful hesitation and weakly pushed on the door. The solid slab did not budge. He glanced around with embarrassment as he poured scorn on his clumsy weakness. As an automatic coping mechanism he positioned himself in the form of a non-existent spectator. He grunted, stupidly cursing the door's deliberate defiance as part of a greater conspiracy to undermine his confidence, then began fiddling with the latch handle with jerky uncoordinated twitches of his fingers. His drained gaunt face swelled red with embarrassment. In a fit of desperation he pushed his wiry body against the door and it unexpectedly gave way, flinging him into the room.

Consequently he had the tumbling entry of a jester, though luckily this venue had no crowd. Rabica could see three old men hunched around a table sombrely staring into their glasses whilst muttering faint trailing grunts that never seemed to coincide, to give the impression they were not even conversing. They did not even look up. Rabica felt vindicated that the door's victory over him was short-lived.

The bar-room was dusty and dark. A staunch barman drummed his fingers on the bar and stared with slight disdain at the new entrant (he refrained from outright contempt because he feared it may be a disguised official). The walls were decorated with various pieces of maritime equipment. All of these articles were even dustier than the tables.

After Rabica took a few cautionary steps, the old men looked up with blank faces. They did not scowl, they did not need to; in fact, they could not; their faces were ghastly husks, fixed like masks that engulfed the entire face. Hair sprouted out of the top, fusing into the tight bodysuit of skin that had a stranglehold on their entire posture, buckling their bodies into a submissive hunch. These were defeated people.

Instinctively seeking shelter from visual interrogation, Rabica stumbled over to a table and clumsily dumped his pile of rags, kicking a seat out so he could sit. However, much to his dismay the old men continued to stare; now twitching looks of disdain spasmed on their wrinkled faces, tearing through the blank leathery skin that covered them.

They would have spat had they not valued phlegm higher than the intruder.

Terrified by their stare, Rabica glanced at the barman, who had begun wiping a tankard with a grubby rag whilst staring at him as though awaiting his approach. His expression was like that of a sinister executioner when he spots a particularly thick-necked convict. Finally Rabica got the hint and rose from his seat to furtively approach the barman.

The barman put the glass down and stared with minimal intrigue. Nervously, Rabica stuttered that he wanted some ale and something to eat.

The barman requested a more specific culinary choice, grinning cruelly as he expected the emaciated posh-sounding delinquent to ask for something exotic.

But the traveller no longer cared for explanation of such petty necessities. "Whatever you have… anything… enough for a meal … I have money."

The barman shrugged and turned away.

"Whatever is easy," Rabica added, hoping the barman was still in earshot.

He could feel at least one pair of eyes burning into his back, pouring scorn straight into the neurones of his nervous system, spreading discontent and fear up his vertebrae. He turned slowly and saw the old men had ceased their staring. Rabica surveyed the room in search of the feelings source. Suddenly his heart jumped. Sitting solemnly on the corner sat the figure of a youngish woman. Her hair was tied back but unusually straight. It struck Rabica how out of place she looked; she was clean, well-dressed and in a positively dreamy state. For a brief second Rabica became petrified by the notion that she was staring at him, but when he made an attempt at an innocent smile he received no response. Not even the expected frown or turned up nose of disgust. Thankfully she was staring straight through him into some far off dream. He looked away quickly, returning to establish what the landlord was doing.

He had retained an image of her in his mind, not for admiration but to pour scorn onto. He recalled her beauty, her delicate posture, and her dreamy expression. No doubt she was in love, in love with a young handsome soldier – some absolute dunce who now marched proudly on his way to war. This 'darling' would soon be brutally charging across a battlefield to smash the skulls of other idiots and unfortunates dragged through the mud but too stupid to turn on those that actually dragged them. His mind filled with the image of feral mud-clad bulky humanoids being herded like two flocks of sheep at each other by cackling clean-robed nobles and priests.

'*No doubt she loved his courage,*' Rabica thought to himself, his face wrinkling up with a potent combination of patronising pity and jealousy. '*What courage? Isn't true courage standing up for what is right?*' he remonstrated internally, reaching a fiery pinnacle before sullenly undercutting his own righteous rant. '*No, I am just saying this because it makes my cowardly fleeing into a sort of courage. I suppose neither is courageous: I have stood up for nothing and fled responsibility, and they have been herded to make a stand for someone else and in doing so assume they never hold responsibility.*'

He grew irritated with his arguing, '*whatever... it matters not... this soldier-lover had no doubt proposed to her the day before he left as a promise that he would return. How nauseating!*' He was fully aware that he was inventing a story just to infuriate himself.

'*And she sat there dreamily imagining him in a 'utopian-battle' - that is, an unreal dramatisation where he strode at the forefront smashing mud-covered filthy barbarian Gatanese beasts. Purging the land and leaving it cleansed and tranquil; the antithesis of battle. How naïve!*'

As rage rose alongside its common bed-fellow of insecurity, Rabica risked another peek as he became convinced she was staring at him. His jerking movements made her start slightly and to Rabica's horror her focus became fixed on him. Boiling with embarrassment, Rabica turned back to the bar only to be startled again by the gnarly face of the landlord. The landlord pointed to a frothy tankard and told him to sit.

★

Julia had taken a quick professional glance at the bedraggled stranger when he first entered, to assess the potential. On first impression he seemed to be the stereotypical lonely weak boy who could easily be conned into paying just by being friendly. But there was more to it than that. Under the layers of weariness from the elements was a furrowed-brow and a pre-weathered individual jerkiness. In short, there was something internal. Now, while less-experienced or analytical prostitutes (many of Julia's work comrades disgusted her in their lack of interest in classifying and identifying the types of clientele; to her it was part of the profession) may detect this and stay clear, fearful that he was a beater, she was convinced otherwise; this young man was troubled and lonely to such an extent he was emasculated and therefore harmless.

She could easily seduce this husk of a boy, just talk to him, let him drink, carry him upstairs. She wouldn't even have to do anything, he was so tired, she could just say she did and he'd be so embarrassed he'd pay up. But she could see from his erratic and furtive temperament that this young man would crumble to dust and be annihilated.

He was lucky none of the other whores were about, the more predatory ones, they would destroy him for sure. The rest of the whores had gone with the soldiers to rake in the cash. Julia had refused – she had wanted to be selective. She had told the other strumpets they could have Pluvius if they wanted, but if he wanted, all hell would break loose on his return.

Julia had returned to daydreaming about her sergeant, of his return. She had heard he had been sent with the main army. When she saw him, she was going to strike him for not fleeing the army into her arms. For putting a duty he no longer cared for above her. Then she would send him packing, and once he had left she would summon a messenger to trail him all night then tell him to marry her that following day. Then they would travel to the Vaca region and settle down.

At this point Julia was absentmindedly gazing across the room with a gleeful smile when she spotted that the stranger was staring at her again from the bar. She tried to hide her instinctive annoyance with an awkward smile.

The traveller wobbled slightly as he headed away from the bar. Dreamily, it looked as though he was walking towards her but at the last moment he bolted for the table with his bundle.

Intrigued, Julia examined further; he seemed to be sweating profusely despite evidently still being cold. The young man gulped his tankard, cradling it like a child does warm milk.

Suddenly he stopped ponderously. Julia assumed the alcohol was shooting straight to his head because he was so emaciated. His pruned, but normally childish, fingers daintily nudged the cup away from him and he nervously glanced at over his shoulder, eager for food. As he did so he made a sly glance at Julia, his sweeping survey jolting nervously as his eyes passed her.

The barman was bringing a hunk of bread. No doubt the notorious 'fish broth' would be unleashed on the hapless youth some time soon. Julia smirked to herself as she recalled one of Heites' witticisms. 'Is that you or is it the broth?' he had said to a courtesan before responding to the barman's concerned query with, 'barman, my soup is fine but my whore's gone off!"

Our grubby delinquent saw her smirks and plunged into a thick pool of paranoia. The bread was plonked in front of him and he stuttered a thank you, which the landlord ignored. Hungrily his hands descended upon it, tearing it up and forcing great wads into his mouth.

Julia's bemusement turned to concern as she watched him churn the bread in his mouth for a few minutes with increasingly watery eyes. She looked closely, observing his throat muscles push down in an attempt to flush his mouth, but to no avail. The stranger's furtiveness grew into panic as his second attempt at swallowing led to a misfire and he gagged.

By now the bread must have been a doughy pulp, almost glue-like in consistency, yet his throat would have none of it, pushing against his swallowing mechanism in contemptuous rebellion. It rejected his hand's offering, the product of his mouth's manufacture. The fear of his surroundings meant parts of his body could not, or would not, trust other parts. Enemies were everywhere. For a moment he thought his throat could be onto something: had the landlord poisoned the bread thinking he was a deserter? Or knowing he was a foreign 'enemy'? (If Lewerix were enemies – not that it mattered who was at war with whom: in such cases any stranger is an enemy).

Just as he thought it couldn't get any worse and was contemplating just sinking under the table, the young woman in the corner rose and casually walked towards him. The steps seemed to mark time for each tenth beat of his heart. In a fit of desperation Rabica took a swig of beer and used that to flush the pulp down. He did so just in time.

"May I sit here?" she enquired with apparent innocence; her voice had a deliberate tinge of pitying concern.

Rabica could not refuse, nor could he answer verbally, so he nodded weakly and forced a smile from his locked jaw.

"If you don't mind me saying, you look terrible. You need rest," Julia blurted, hoping it would not crush the weak spirit of the boy.

'I wish I could say the same about you,' Rabica thought, adding with an acidic jibe at his stiffness, 'I wish I could say that *to* you.'

Instead, he mumbled something along the lines of, "rest won't do anything to solve that." He had to imagine he had just thought it in order to get himself to say it: she was just an external spectator to his mind.

"You seemed to have trouble with the bread!" she toyed, trying to sound informal and not an interrogator, "... are you ill?"

Rabica just laughed wickedly, checked himself with a rebuke under his breath, before, deciding he liked laughing, stretching it out over a few more moments.

Rather than be deterred by this unpredictable action, Julia darted her eyes to the ceiling in exclamation. "Right... ok."

Then she sighed to herself.

Rabica felt a searing pain that he had been rude, so decided to ramble an apology. "I'm sorry for such an unpleasant sight. My eating, that is (although the contraption I was forcing the bread into is hardly to be surpassed in its hideousness). I am also deeply sorry for laughing now. I have been alone a long time..." Rabica could not be bothered, and did not want to explain, so trailed with, "and so should not talk to anyone." Half way through his rambling his pronunciation became revitalised, though was broken by his confusion. However it revealed itself enough to signal to Julia two interesting developments: one that he was foreign, and two, that he was of higher class.

Julia nodded slowly as though she understood. "Don't worry, I won't pry." But with a gross miscalculation she attempted to comfort him by touching his hand, which lay stiff upon the table.

The hand darted for cover by his chest. Yet Rabica seemed to be more shocked by his reaction than she was, as he found himself doing a double start.

"Wow... sorry." Julia spoke calmly, slightly embarrassed that her profession seemed to be governing her civilities.

Rabica looked even more embarrassed. "Sorry..." He tried to ignore the biting paranoia and self-loathing he felt at his anti-social reaction to her concern. "You see!" he concluded with pyrrhic vitriol.

Meanwhile his mind was racing. 'Come on, what is going on? This must be a trap! As soon as I saw her come over I knew that biting paranoia, which always pays off, was on to something. Why would an attractive woman talk to me unless it was either part of a plot or for her own sadistic amusement? I vote for the latter – I clearly have no riches, unless she is an informant for deserters or infiltrators – no, wait! I am falling for their trap and wilfully doing as they wish by trusting no one! Maybe she wants to toy with me and make me squirm, but I refuse to succumb to their propaganda and be petrified that she is an informer.'

Then a new thought came to him. '*Maybe she's a whore.*' His mind paused, not in disgust but in confusion. '*What do I do? Surely she can't be that desperate... I mean there's some rather unthreatening old men over there and the landlord isn't that...well, actually! But... even that dog outside at least isn't me... although I suppose it has no money.*' He thought with genuine seriousness. However, just the thought and mere speculation had sent his furtive desperation leaping forwards to find potential dilemmas. 'Should I pay her now and leave?' he pondered anxiously, before spitting in disgust. 'No! That's extremely insulting, surely I should continue talking to her... but what if I get tempted?' he added with a naïve shudder.

'It can be a test of my faith to Her,' he declared internally, with some hastily dredged pride that was immediately sifted back into the murky waters. 'Do I have any faith to Her anymore? Aren't I supposed to be forgetting Her?'

Julia had evidently been following his soliloquy in his constantly shifting facial expressions. When he appeared to have stopped she said, "you seem to have a lot on your mind. You also should probably be throwing yourself at the enemy, whichever so happens to take your fancy (you sound foreign – maybe you're a spy, or a counter spy, or even, if they exist, a counter-counter spy... and so on. If so, either way you're wasting your time here, and wasting away as you do so. No, you're not a spy... you're too neurotic... maybe a deserter!" As she spoke her expression was wry and delicately laced with satire. So careful was the acidic icing that Rabica did not even find trace of it.

His response was to laugh, but this time he tempered it. "You could say that," he chuckled with morbid candour before scowling to himself. *'Am I being too cordial? Too idiotic? Am I eagerly trotting to the slaughter?'*

Julia saw the scowl and thought she had offended him or blown his cover.

"I'm sorry," she burst out, baffled and verging on frustrated.

Rabica constructed a solid dry cold composure. "What for?" he inquired with a hint of rhetoric.

Julia gave a frustrated smile, which she turned away from him as it transformed into an infuriated grimace.

Rabica knew such gestures all too well. On the spot he decided that throughout his entire life, every smile targeted at him in time dissolved into such a pitying, scornful expression.

Was she the epitome of everything beautiful that he hated? Happy, aloof, contented, apathetic, sexually free, yet worshipping her subservience to some ignoramus man of muscle. What made it worse was she was probably so nice, so pleasant, and considerate to those that surrounded her but did not need it. Nevertheless, he despised what she represented to him.

Rabica's thoughts were disturbed by the landlord roughly dumping a bowl of brown lumpy liquid before him. He did not notice Julia's instinctive retreat and pre-emptive gag, and so he was caught off guard by the reeking aroma as he inhaled deeply. The odour had not previously penetrated the mucus in his nose, so when he took this first deep breath over it, a gust of foul stench blasted through his nostrils and into his taste buds. At first his famished sensors were excited that it was food, but then they picked up that it was particularly bad food. Still, with hunger and cold stirring restlessly within him, he embarked on the consumption ordeal.

Julia hid her smile the only way possible: with her hands. Ignoring the fact that she was with a stranger (and a particularly peculiar one at that), she pretended it was Pluvius. "Mmm... that looks good!" she exclaimed dryly, as she had to her sergeant weeks before.

"Really? Did you want some?" Rabica hit back with sarcasm so pure she thought he was serious, though he also, on the side, meant it, if she wanted something to eat.

"No! It's disgusting!"

"Really! You're telling me...now!" Rabica slackened his sarcasm. He began thinking about how his previous self would have been able to keep the joke running about the soup with her, but then began questioning if this was just an idealisation of himself in a never truthful golden age. Meanwhile she sat giggling about the soup, and he mustered up pitiful expressions to express that which he could no longer in words. A smile cracked on his face, the unfamiliar feeling of sharing a joke. He glanced up at her just before taking a mouthful and grimaced comically.

But their silent communication was broken by the landlord shouting across at them, "In case you're wondering, that smell is the broth, not Julia!"

Julia turned red with embarrassment, but thankfully Rabica did not get it.

"Is your husband a fishmonger then?" he inquired innocently.

Julia stumbled, not sure whether to explain. "Er... No, and even if he were he'd not be doing that now."

"Not the right season," Rabica reasoned blindly.

"Er no... he'd be at war," Julia answered, rather shocked that it had passed the stranger's mind.

Rabica was embarrassed at being ignorant of the most basic of current affairs. "Oh... yes of course: The War!"

Julia examined his expression with immense intrigue as he continued. "So, if you don't mind me asking, do you have a husband at war?"

Immediately he became paranoid that his interest would be seen as having an ulterior motive.

Julia sighed. "Yes, he's a sergeant... except he's not my husband," she added as an afterthought.

"Really." Rabica pretended to be impressed.

"Don't pretend to be impressed. I'm not."

Rabica was shocked, and impressed at her response. "You miss him?"

Julia was not offended by the implied insinuation. "Of course... but I hate that he went."

Fighting off the temptation to rant, Rabica just sighed and mumbled. "It's ridiculous..."

"What is?"

Rabica sighed, "everything... everything and nothing."

Julia perked up with a sense of intrigue. "Doesn't everything include nothing anyway?"

Rabica nearly jumped out of his seat, his face exploding in fascination. "Exactly! Or is it...? No it doesn't matter, you are right but that is... that is genius... of all the places!"

Julia slyly jibed, "you seem shocked! Don't you expect to hear such profound things from a woman, let alone a whore?" she saw his eyes bulge as she used the 'W' word.

He had already begun his retort, failing to recognise that she was only jesting with him. "It has nothing to do with... oh, you're a prostitute... it has nothing to do with who you are, it's where we are – out here is the last place to expect philosophy."

"Yes, I am a prostitute... and one that thinks," she proclaimed with pride.

Rabica made a comic inhalation of breath, mimicking intimidated authority. "Huh, that's dangerous stuff – a thinking prostitute!"

Strangely there was no need to actually debate the issue. The fact that both parties mused upon the subject was enough to show their understanding, and established a new atmosphere of friendliness between them.

Julia pursued him on a different aspect. "Surely 'where we are' or 'where I am from' is in effect defining who I am?" she queried pedantically.

Rabica nodded, conceding the point by and large, but protesting his innocence by saying, "but where you are from has nothing to do with your gender or occupation. I mean, I was more talking about how I have travelled all this way and come to a tiny hamlet, and now I find an interesting debating adversary."

Julia saw that she had touched a nerve with her jesting accusation, comforting him with a beautiful smile of reassurance.

They both sat ponderously for a few moments, looking in each other's direction but not at each other. This was lucky for Rabica as were they to have eye contact now he would have found all the mutual connection, the friendly joviality, dry up under the intense rays of realising that he was interacting with an attractive woman.

Suddenly Rabica's concentration lapsed and he made conscious eye contact. Her striking form was delicately exaggerated in the smooth material of her plain dress, a perfection veiled under a striking red glacier, her beautifully formed neck rising and spreading out into an exquisitely chiselled face. Beneath the icy exterior a furnace raged; for within this remarkable craftwork throbbed a mighty brain that let out pulses of fire to the beacons of her eyes and lips. These were not of lustful fire, but the enigmatic fire of deliberation. It was the fire of mankind, of knowledge, not fire hauled down by some mystical peer.

He found himself back in the pub and instantly fired out a defensive jest: "so thinking prostitutes remain prostitutes then?"

Julia chuckled and her eyes lit up.

Rabica reeled, back trying to conceal the pain of receiving such a look.

Julia rolled her eyes. "I guess so," she beamed an enigmatic smirk, "... but not for much longer," she added with an inwardly stern expression.

"Oh really?" Rabica interjected.

"That is if the fool doesn't get himself killed," she muttered to herself under her breath.

Rabica felt his old self pressing him to make a reassuring statement, but he knew it would sound feeble.

Julia noticed his confused good-will and reached forward cautiously to tap him on the hand lightly as acknowledgement. This time he did not flinch.

"I shouldn't talk like that."

"No, you should be positive," he answered, already feeling the hypocrisy eating away at his gut. He searched his mind for some reason to be positive, rather surprising himself when he did find something.

"You said he was a sergeant?"

She nodded.

"Well, he must have been a soldier some time, how long?"

She shrugged. "Years... he was at Neptus."

Rabica's face bulged. "So he's fought a lot then? Because, that means he'll definitely survive: it's the new ones that die in battles. Once you've survived a few you survive them all." He swallowed a lump in his throat as he knew he was exaggerating a logical tendency.

Julia cheered up slightly, but then thought of Geric, and could not stop her lip from sinking.

They sat in thoughtful silence. Just before this could stagnate Rabica leant forward and whispered, "what does he think of the war?"

Julia lowered her head, trying to hide the collecting water in her eyes. Slowly she shook her head remorsefully. "He knows..." It was all she could muster, but it was enough.

Rabica loved simplicity of the answer: 'he knows.' Either you know, you don't know, or you don't care. If you do know you are against. If you don't, you are apathetic, but easily whipped up in support, and if you don't care then you know and love it because you are one of its perpetrators.

"So why..." Rabica stumbled. "Sorry."

Julia used her anger at Pluvius for strength. "He saw it as his profession, duty didn't even come into it any more. Well, it did, to his men; he couldn't desert them. I think his pride got him in there too. He didn't want to be a deserter. I told him, 'who cares about deserting, you have no obligation, they use you to keep us all down – they owe you'.

Damn men and their damn pride!" Tears broke from her eyes, though they were more at frustration at his stubbornness than pride at his principles.

"But after this, he will leave?"

"Certainly. He didn't say so, but he doesn't need to. After this he'll be able to slip out with the demobilisation."

"Are Latman going to win?" Rabica blurted tactlessly, then retracted his steps by (even more foolishly) adding, "actually, what does it matter?"

'*Except that my lover's life may depend on the outcome!*' Julia thought angrily. '*Damn they've caught me there – forcing me to want them to win*' she sighed.

"Your sergeant won't endanger himself more than he has to for them, will he?"

Julia nodded and smiled with forced gratefulness.

Moving swiftly on, before any doubt arose in Julia's heart, Rabica pursued. "So what's the plan then? When he returns... what will you do?"

"Oh, go to Vaca," she smiled, slightly embarrassed.

"I know it sounds pathetic," she said. "Almost vile in its cliché... but..."

Rabica shook his head sympathetically. "It's what you want to do; if you actually do it, it will not be a cliché. The cliché is in the words, not in the deed. Besides, it would be lovely." He found himself dreaming of the hills of Vaca, the most desolate and uninhabited place. It would be his destination too, but for totally different reasons.

Julia cocked her head and raised an eyebrow in support of his statement.

"Vaca; the land of subsistence," he dreamily muttered.

Julia gave a start, which Rabica was unsure if it was a mock one. "I hope not!" she expostulated.

Rabica leant in to show his interest so she explained.

"That sounds awfully like the village I fled from: non-stop duty and obedience. Working just to survive: what a pitiful existence."

"But you control your own life; you are independent."

"Independent of other men and the hierarchy, but not of strict family rules and subjugation. What you do not do submit in labour to earn money from others, you submit to nature, and by the gods is it tough."

"I concede your point, but you shan't do that – I can tell – but isn't there a beauty in producing your own food, being in control of it?"

"You grapple to control it because it controls you."

Rabica shrugged. "You are right... it's just a naïve dream." Suddenly the advocate became chief assailant. "And it is divisive to mankind as a whole, centring on a tiny group ignorant of others; isolated in its independence. Furthermore, such independence is not feasible, even if it were desirable – men need each other. Subsistence just leads to nepocentrism."

"What?"

"Like ego-centrism, only for family and people known personally rather than the self."

"Huh?"

"Caring only for oneself and family."

"Never heard of it."

"Nor have I! I think I just made it up!"

"It's mundane," Julia chipped in.

"Oh it is! And no room for improvement, it would be stagnant technologically – unless a disaster happened – technology becomes a coping strategy rather than as tool for the general betterment of man."

"Not that it seems to do that now anyway!" Julia scoffed.

Rabica frowned in thought. "No, but that is not to say it must be used as it is. Technology is a neutral concept; it depends on how it is harnessed. Now it is used to reinforce and enrich the elite."

He spoke with such a matter-of-fact tone, Julia was shocked by his contemptuous temperament towards the authorities. She switched off as he rambled about using technology for emancipation and alleviation rather than dominance and alienation. His words flew over her head, even though she would have understood had he used more common terms.

This was in part due to him never speaking with a lower class person before, but he was also hampered by the weeks of solitude which had made him mutter incoherently to himself, because even if the words made no sense 'he knew what he meant'.

Whilst he was in mid-rant she decided to cut in to salvage the conversation as a two-way dynamic rather than a rambling monologue.

"You see. I desire expression and freedom, but would be denied that in 'subsistence' – one can only express as part of a tribe."

"So it is neither self-expression, nor is it an expression of mankind's unity. All one needs is an accepting society that sees all expressions as individual but each as a part of the human whole, and is not subdivided into tribes."

Julia gave a befuddled look, but ploughed on. "Maybe, but such a subsistence life has no room for freedom and openness – the society functions because of conformity – there are struggles for survival so you have no time."

Rabica nodded, and gazed down at his drink, dissatisfied with himself for previously supporting subsistence. To distract himself from his irritation, he began looking around the room. He immediately began to notice the dustiness, not because he was a tidy person but because, having been in the wilderness where one never comes across settled dust, it was quite a strange thing.

Julia guessed that he was thinking about the dust. "No one cleans it," she began, gesturing vaguely at the seemingly archaic panorama of heavily dust-laden agricultural and maritime tools. These obsolete mechanisms seemed to hold a defeated nostalgia of their own.

Rabica glanced fretfully at the huddled remnants of locals; the drab old men seemed equally grey with dust, insipid but deep down clinging onto an irrational sense of pride, a pride so beaten and alien that it could only rise in them as a bitter distaste of others. Like the tools, they might have well been hung on the wall as antiquated trophies for a bygone age.

Fearing that he had been gazing towards the table of decrepit villagers for too long, Rabica returned his attentions to the room in general. He curiously examined the various utensils, hazarding a guess in his mind as to what each would have been used for. It was as he was performing this visual sweep that he eventually stumbled upon the dusted patch. In the corner was a rectangle of dusted floor, the old durable tar-varnish gleaming dully.

Julia, who up until now had been patiently sitting in silence, noticed Rabica's befuddlement as a consequence of the perfect quadrilateral of dusted floor. "Oh, you've spotted the statue then," she commented, deliberately intensifying his confusion.

He turned and looked at her with an expression to urge her to explain.

She eagerly complied. "We used to have a figurehead of Neptus but the soldiers took it…"

"Latman… Latman Soldiers?"

She nodded in the affirmative. "Who else? So the landlord decided to remember it the only way possible and always dust the spot where it was so we can picture it as still there."

For a fraction of a second Rabica was delighted by their subtle dissidence, but then reality reeled him back. *'But it is quite depressing; clearly that act of 'defiance' - though it merely skirted around the injustice rather than fought it - is all that keeps this society going. Faint reflections on the past, on gods and mysticism, abstract faith in a non-entity is all that unites them and keeps them human. Is there anything more depressing that blind faith in a divine saviour in times of need? They aren't looking forward to emancipation, but backwards to looser shackles… and if they are contented with just their defiance of dust they shan't even achieve that.'*

Rabica kept this rant in his head, which was fortunate because Julia would have felt compelled to defend what she recognised as a pathetic resistance from the criticisms of an outsider. Instead, he mumbled some vaguely positive remark. However, he remained agitated and found it difficult to concentrate, let alone engage in any meaningful conversation.

Before an awkward silence could assimilate their friendly aura, Rabica, spurred on by the intriguing charisma she gave off, decided to learn about her. He asked her about her past. She happily obliged, and he enjoyed listening to another's narrative, a life so different, and so seldom listened to. He took particular interest in her childhood. He was quickly fascinated and enthralled at her spirit, which had guided her through hardships and opportunism without becoming a slave to either. His enjoyment of listening and learning made him fantasise about becoming a travelling listener, hearing the stories their struggles of the dispossessed, their coping strategies and their experiences. However, he knew he lacked the willpower to do it. Remembering his experience in the town, he knew he could not cope. Nor did he have the subtle tact, charisma, or understanding of others and their situations. Such a project needed a much more competent and neutral person.

It also conflicted with his personal mission of escaping society, not shadowing it, learning more of its darkest shades and attempting to find ways of changing it. He knew such a strategy would merely mire him in an even more potent cynicism and disgust.

Even though he had lived both at the top of the society and outside it, both were so extreme they denied him any interaction with it.

It got him thinking of how incompetent and unsuited he was to society. He became so aware of this that his contributions to the conversation began to peter out, and so it ground to a halt. This in itself proved to him that he was unable to sustain a conversation. Rabica felt fatigue overcoming him. Julia could see his discomfort and so encouraged him to rest. Rabica agreed, and thanked her excessively for her time and patience. He gestured upstairs to the Landlord, a silent request for a room, which was speechlessly granted. As he rose to take his bundle upstairs he had a burning desire to ask her to meet him tomorrow morning, but he guiltily felt he would be compelling her to suffer his presence again.

★

Once up in his room, Rabica dumped his stuff on the bed in a state of utter exhaustion. Without even looking at the room he plunged into the bed. As he snuggled down in the damp cold sheets, a cogent notion reinforced itself, spilling out of his mouth in words. "Even if prostitution is no more exploitative than soldiering, or indeed any other worker's profession, that does not justify it, it merely raises questions about the justice of all work in such a system." Having said that to himself he closed his eyes and soon was asleep, drifting in the turbulent sea of dreams.

★

Julia sat opposite the pulled-back chair where the bizarre delinquent had until recently been sitting.

The whole experience had been rather surreal, and a pleasant break from the mundane everyday life in the hamlet. Bedraggled nomadic intellectuals were quite a novelty. She found herself smiling as she thought of him, a pleasant demeanour a result of meeting an inoffensive, pitiable wreck. However, she soon found this perverted by a barrage of instincts. At first she tried to pass it all off as her professional opportunism wanting to exploit his vulnerability to extract wealth off him.

However, she found herself actually wanting to do the act, though she knew it was a result of her circumstances rather than an attraction to him. With Pluvius so far away, and being stuck here with just old men and ignorant lads she had to admit the relative appeal of an educated young man.

By realising this she was more able to stop herself, though she was also conscious it would be disrespectful to the delinquent, piling even more strain onto an already fragile mind. She could tell from his demeanour that he would not be able to treat it as a meaningless action of mutual alleviation of despair. He would probably be overwhelmed with guilt, so much so that he would feel that to leave would be mistreating her.

She was disrupted from her deep thought by the stench of stale ale and nearby shifting shadows.

"So you're not going up there? Or are you giving him a head start, you vixen?" the barman jested with a leery wink.

Julia hid her distaste with a smile, and shook her head gracefully, before returning her gaze elsewhere.

After a few moments of heavy wheezing he began to waddle back to the bar.

She stopped him momentarily with a sharp interjection to his retreat.

"Do not let anyone else go up there… I will pay you… and believe me I will find out if you let anyone do it, and you know who will find out from me!" she threatened, keeping a pleasant smile on her face as she did, loathing to use the power of one of her clients.

With that he continued, knowing he would have to obey or else face the wrath of the local baron.

★

Though Lady Gatan allowed Adonis Gatan full reign over day-to-day running of the household, diplomacy, the high art of politics, was something she saw as a shared domain.

She had, in the past, been forced to rely on servants as informants, or, rather demeaningly, Hercela. However, in recent years, she had acquired a new informant: Teritus. Being young for a regional commander he was not a traditional warrior and so was less patronising (indeed, the dynamic had been reversed). The problem was that he lacked leverage with his lordship, meaning she still had to use Hercela as a conduit.

However, following the recent talks, Lady Gatan was rather surprised when Hercela came to her with concerns. He was still dissatisfied with the boat idea, believing it would only give Latman advance warning of a strike.

Hercela was given quite a shock when the lady began to lecture him with a schoolmarm's austerity about his blind aggressiveness.

"General Hercela!" she had reprimanded, as though singling out a naughty child for the umpteenth time. "You surprise me by your narrow mindset! I thought you were a grand strategist, not a quibbler over technicalities! You have allowed Adonis to neglect diplomacy and consensus building and allowed him to dive straight into the arms of war. In doing so, he is joining that blackguard war enthusiast, the impetuous fool Lord Latman. On they will lead each other, away from sanity and diplomacy to a gladiatorial pit of torment!"

"Lord Gatan should be the grown up, negotiating and rallying against this bully and its insane plot, not rushing into the sandpit with him[7]." She did not pause to let him protest as she ploughed on. "Lewerix is a cautious, but not ignorant man; he would have intervened in the Vacarium/Danite-Latman affair. But he will never join this apocalyptic madness, certainly not in this rapid way. It is the basic principle that diplomats adhere to before transforming themselves into their warlike shadows: build a coalition, then go to war, don't scrabble around for a fist full of minor warlords then declare all-out war in their defence! Perhaps Lewerix would have offered to be a border broker for the sake of avoiding this folly we now are surging into."

Hercela was shaking his head, which only irritated her more, driving her on. "Don't you shake your head at me! I have met Lord Lewerix; he is a prudent man - but his prudence is not of stinginess, but of long-sightedness."

---

[7] Here she is referencing both child's sand pits and gladiatorial rings; both being arenas of sand.

Hercela seemed not to have listened. Chuckling, he declared in a ridiculing manner, "this war was going to happen whatever, and with that fool running Latman what better time?"

Lady Gatan shook her head with the prophetic disdain of an oracle. "What worse time than with a simpleminded zealot? His kind will stop at no lengths. Such a man will raise hell, do any number of self-destructive things just to keep the struggle alive."

Hercela had always seen Juscius II as a weakling, the chink in a long line of resolute leaders. Just as he stood to depart, Lady Gatan demanded to know what he would do.

"Me! I can do nothing, I had hoped you would talk to him."

Lady Gatan was far too worried to celebrate the reversal of the power dynamic between them. "If dissuading him from war is not possible, then I will pass on your concerns. Do not expect any changes, though."

He nodded in thanks begrudgingly and bowed courteously.

Chapter 29
The Rage of a Warrior Chief

Even the relaxed seats of his 'library' could not comfort him. Ruperis Delvinius had heard about the Gatan mobilisation of its flotilla, and was livid. His irascibility had been exacerbated by the gleeful pronouncement on the issue by Zeuorox via his smug messenger. At least that was how Ruperis saw it.

Ruperis knew that his ships would be required to join the Latman navy in its attack on the Gatanese flotilla, totally jeopardising The Company's side project. With a degree of ill-conceived maliciousness he considered making the cleric a member of the company so he would be more careful in future.

It did not seem to matter that the onset of war heralded the coming of great wealth to the Delvinius Company, all Ruperis could think of was that little extra he would miss out on due to his new product being delayed.

However, he was determined to calm himself, and had set about doing this the only sure-fire way he knew: with a new money-making scheme.

'If I cannot make money from an imported minority, then I shall have to look internally,' he had declared to himself.

His mind had ridden through the markets, searching for a vacuum. He was reminded of the pre-war tax session where the regional commanders, supported by Delvinius (because he knew increased budget meant more money to be spent on arms), had called for an increase on tithe payments. He had heard two of the commanders grumbling about Vaca having a privileged position being so low in taxation per capita and high in cost. Pulling favours with a scribe administrator he had got hold of the Vaca records.

Now he sat, in his office, the brand new feather mat on the chair no comfort to the irritable situation. Reading this bureaucratic document whilst potential coinage slipped between his fingers every second was the merchant prince's equivalent of going cold turkey. Impatiently he flicked pages from right to left, he had already skimmed the mining exemption page, ignoring the potentiality for reform as it would only mean he had to pay more for raw resources. He returned to the general taxation rules, tucked away rather innocently in the opening paragraph, he found his clause. He read it aloud for clarity.

"…And those of Mountain Stock, who are tamed into civilisation shall pay a tithe of…" skimming with his finger he returned with; "…the cattle breeders are free to roam, but have no claim to the cattle they follow, nor any right to defence…"

"What imprudent fools!" he exclaimed.

His first thought was to quench his fix with a quick injection of liquid capital by rounding up the un-owned cattle and feast on the fresh beef, whilst the hides stretched in the tannery. However, he soon calmed himself, gently caressing his addiction with the promise of a constant drip of currency, the kind that builds up over time, slowly accumulating like a many-coursed feast. He would force them to be taxed, then offer them money in exchange for hides so they could pay their taxes and he could get cheap leather.

"Aah, a win-win situation!" he declared. He grinned to himself, shutting the book with contemptuous triumph.

Following a moment's pause, he decided it about time to go and see his lordship. On the way he would tell his servant to inform Zeuorox that Lord Latman would summon him in about half an hour's time.

★

Delvinius was stopped at the doorway before the passage into Juscius' room. This was a rather strange measure, as was the guards deportment, but the merchant prince just assumed it was the security protocol now war was all but declared.

The guard was rather bleary eyed, his childish chubby face locked in a sulky grimace. Reluctantly he permitted Devinius' entrance.

However, as soon as the hefty door was opened it became apparent why the guard stood so far away. Juscius was rattling off a frothy-mouthed sermon. The actual words were for the greater part indecipherable through the wall, but for a guard to know that his lordship was behaving so was humiliating enough.

Spurred by intrigue as to whether his lordship was indeed indulging in a rather vocal foaming soliloquy, he rushed to the door to the office and knocked. At first he seemed to be ignored, but after knocking several times with increased intensity the door was answered by Zeuorox. Ruperis was childishly irritated that the High Priest had got there first.

The High Pontiff seemed to rub it in with his greeting. "Aah, I see you received my message."

Ruperis just grumbled.

"...It is a shame about those boats," the cleric declared with mock sentimentality before turning on the merchant with a stern look. "I will speak to you about this later."

In the corner of the room Ruperis could see his lordship, his fist hammering home his points as he spat curses and threats. His usually smart clean figure was bloated with pinkish swollen skin that perspired rather excessively. His smooth features were pitted with a mottled scalded pattern of reds.

"...For to allow such insults to occur let alone simultaneously must be a sign from Thelus that we must not tolerate these warlord dregs. They must be crushed in their entirety. We shall answer Danite's declaration with the burning of those few pitiful collections of hovels that masquerade as towns. Vacarium, for his mischievous ambush, we will have every man skewered, and may Gatan's so-called navy sink to the seabed taking his mighty army with it!"

"First the weak and militarily backwards Vacarium defeated a Latman patrol, then the gruff warlord Danite out manoeuvres Latman with a diplomatic snub, then Gatan threatens Latman naval superiority."

"It is all out war!" Juscius held his hands palms facing his imaginary congregation. He stretched high, filled with the thick tense atmosphere he was creating.

"Let our righteous warriors spread, for our enemy has foolishly begged their release!" His hands waved over an imaginary map, sweeping across its invisible borders and contours to signify the cleansing. "They will sweep across Danite annihilating the criminal's authority and power!" His left hand shot out. "Then Vacarium shall fall. We shall swoop down on that pitiful peninsular of heretics!" His left hand spasmed to sideswipe across the position the peninsula took in his mind. "Meanwhile, we will strike across the border!" His eyed bulged with bug-eyed ecstasy. "Gatan shall be defeated!" With one mighty swipe of his right hand the lands of Gatan fell to their incursion. He gripped the invisible, still beating heart of Gatan then brought it close to his face. He stared at his semi-clenched fist, like a possessed demon clutching a defiled relic, then he spoke unto it, "and who will stop me then?"

"The might of Thelus' chosen will purge the island of these scourges and any petty ungodly bands that seek to stifle the inevitable glory of Thelus shall fall by the wayside and into the dustbin of history."

Whereas Ruperis saw the performance as most imprudent and troublesome, Zeuorox had to marvel in the passionate declaration cloaked in his doctrine. It was like the graduation speech his prize student. He gazed upon his creation with a mixture of fear and awe, marvelling at the politico-theocratic machination he had moulded.

This was no Frankenstein's monster, no dabbling in science, no adherence to laws, tubes and chemicals; such things are the creation of fantasy. Real monsters were forged in the mind. It was the malleability of perception and personality where one manipulates another's mindset to create such an unnatural juggernaut. It is in the realm of the vulnerable mind of the powerful that danger lies, not in the potential power of rods and dynamos.

Nevertheless Zeuorox would have to calm his acolyte, though the opportunity to exercise power over it, and ensure it was under his control, was one he welcomed.

"Your highness, we cannot do such a thing, we need a quick decisive victory against Vacarium before they can organise. We cannot go trampling through Danite without sending out another force, and that would weaken our defence of the realm from Gatan."

Juscius looked upon Zeuorox as though he were a mad man, with the stringency only possible by the utterly insane. "But Thelus is on our side. The greatest God stands as judge over the issue!"

Zeuorox opened his mouth to counter but was silenced.

"I am sorry," Juscius began, with a cordiality that only sought to make his speech more irritable. "But even the greatest voice for the gods cannot overrule the desire of the gods. For I am guided by them, so no matter what our 'rationality', we must be wrong and His declaration to me the truth."

Zeuorox cursed his own genius as he recalled that belief always trumps fact in the eye of the beholder. That meant trying to inject reality would not shift Juscius, rather he had to convince him that his beliefs led to a less suicidal outcome.

"But sire, His Almighty Lord Thelus has only signalled that we must fight, he has not declared that we must fight all at once. Besides Thelus will want us to include our great allies Telis, and for that we will need time. However, having said that, we must act immediately regarding the Gatan navy and force a total mobilisation of all ships capable of fighting..." He turned to Ruperis, "you can volunteer yours, can you not?"

Perplexed by Zeuorox's determination to ensure he had to send his ships, Delvinius scowled. "Are we sure it is genuine?" he inquired.

Zeuorox laughed mockingly; to Delvinius he snapped, "can we really take that risk?" before turning to Juscius. "If Thelus says war is to happen, it is. All I can suggest is that we pull back from Neptus - the castle can hold out until we reinforce it, even if is attacked - ready for a naval strike."

"The other two warnings have occurred because we were not cautious, so I accept your suggestion; tell the forces at Neptus to leave a skeleton force, the rest must fall back towards Lateria. Mobilise Lateria forces so they can engage the enemy when they land. Just the thought of them landing undeterred and allowed to rampage across our hallowed land gives me shivers."

Delvinus did not dare stifle defence policy for the sake of renewing an already postponed expansion. Besides, Gatan victory would end his enterprise.

"So it is agreed," Juscius declared, indicating the end of the consultation rather than ensuring consensus.

Delvinius just nodded. Zeuorox announced that he would instigate the policy, bowing cordially as he headed for the door. Passing Delvinius, he stopped to tell the merchant. "You will wait for me outside... that is, if you have something to say to his lordship now... I know of your plans overseas and you will desist."

Delvinius just laughed nervously before approaching his lordship to press for taxation of the Vacarian Mountain People.

★

The wiry oversized urchin trudged through the mud that clogged up the track, trying not to notice the women who worked in the field to his left. Each furtive glance of intrigue sent a fearful pulse of his neurones straight from his eye sockets to his heart. He feared being noticed; he feared that they would fear him; he feared them, in case they were beautiful.

Yet despite his paranoia, the delinquent was just interested because the sight reminded him of the conversation he had had with the prostitute about subsistence: Did they look happy?

Rabica tried to examine them inconspicuously. They hacked at vegetable sprouts, dug out the roots in routinised fashion, yet as they did so they sang tunefully. Their brittle voices drifted, being broken in the breeze so he heard them only sporadically. One of them laughed a girlish giggle, which startled the traveller. He reluctantly took a peek at the source to see a young peasant caked in mud, flinging severed hunks of fleshy root at a stray cat that had arrived on the scene. Her plain frock draped, sagging into the mud, her craggy hair rustled in the breeze awkwardly. *'Was she happy?'*

Before Rabica could even begin to contemplate the thought, he was suddenly looking down at the mud with embarrassment. With a sudden swirl in his direction it had become apparent to the traveller's consciousness that she may gaze upon him. With this automatic flinch he was saved, glaring down panic-stricken. The terror of eye contact had been avoided, but he could still feel the searing of his flesh from her oblivious eyes. To her naïve mind it was just looking, but to him it was the most sophisticated of 'accidental' assaults.

The only refuge from this phantom onslaught was through immersion in deep thought. *'If they are happy, it is through ignorance. By not recognising the overwhelming pools of evil that swirl about them, curdling day by day, hardening like glue, blocking off paths to condition them into a narrow passage of fate.'*

'Mind you, most of this is from rulers, etc. and subsistence needs no rulers, just family units. Besides it is not about that, that is external constraint, what of internal happiness? Their happiness is mere contentment, like the highest internal state of nature; survival, adequacy. There is no morality in nature – one cannot be condemned or idolised in subsistence, only frugality commended. Such life loses the high attainment of happiness through meaningful action towards others, to notions of justice, improvement and beauty.'

He shuddered. Perhaps it was the last word he uttered to himself, perhaps it was just seeing the peasant girl's figure, or maybe it was because She resided in his mind indefinitely. It mingled with his resentment of how society had turned out, how justice and improvement were so absent from it. In his resentment for this society and its perversion of these notions, he saw her as a key seducer, unwittingly luring him to relinquish his quest and return. She was the perversion of beauty, spawned within the system, totally naïve to the role it bestowed upon her; she was a tool of the machinations that sought to uphold and enforce total compliance to the status quo.

However, his disgust was short-lived. He soon found his anger channelled through guilt and placed firmly on himself for seeking to blame her for his weakness. He remembered he needed to try and forget her. She would have forgotten him, so why couldn't he forget her?

The Chronicles of Captain Dummonius
Part 2

Chapter 30
The Chronicles of Dummonius: Veterans of Vaca

Captain Dummonius had felt an untraceable sense of unease upon reaching the milestone proclaiming that they had entered Vaca. He thought it apt that the dull sign resembled a tombstone, though was surprised that the landscape was nothing out of the ordinary.

He had been expecting an apocalyptic ruin, smouldering on an arid plain, littered with listless gnarled trees, dead but not rotten: ossified with jagged snapped trunks of cracked bone, torn open, the bark stripped off to leave a soft inner carapace exposed to the elements.

Yet it was nothing of the sort. Though its horizon was broken by the undulating hills, the grass was still green and the evergreens lively. Even the deciduous trees wore their baldness with grace.

Yet the province's reputation persisted in this elusive sixth sense, the serenity a mere façade to dampen his more founded perceptions. He looked around at the men (he would not call them his, as he had not even chosen them, rather been given them by Delvinius). They wore sombre expressions, but unlike Dummonius they were not wary, but resolute – like men revisiting a friend's grave. This immediately got him to thinking that they were veterans of Vaca. Even though most seemed too young to be called veterans, he was fully aware of the expression that 'time counts double in Vaca'.

This unsettled him further, making him fearful that they would meet some locals with which they had 'a history'. He would have to avoid any Vacarian villages, which should not be too difficult, they were supposed to go straight to Aurbilane, where they would meet a man named Telgius who would take them to the manufacturing site where a cart would be waiting. However, they would need to rest at some point. One of the mercenaries had suggested they stop at an inn called the Cloak and Coin in Aurelia, on the outskirts of Aurbilane.

Dummonius tried to think of places to avoid, though the only one he could remember was Ferivac. For some reason that name was associated with some kind of resistance. He knew he was building plans on speculation. But these were cautious times, where one had to be extremely careful. His knowledge of the Axia debacle made him a danger to the Delvinius-Zeuorox-Juscius Axis, should he become untrustworthy in their eyes. Binding this to his conscience was a fear for

Pallavi's safety; the authorities would not hesitate to utilise her as a hostage.

They would keep to this central road and try and stay out of trouble.

★

When they reached Aurelia, it was late in the evening. The town was originally a small congregation of warehouses that had spilled out of Aurbilane, though it had grown into a town with the gradual build up of soldiers guarding the wares.

Dummonius was hopeful that it would provide them with a restful night's sleep before an early arrival at Aurbilane.

Dummonius was immediately struck by the military presence. The 'town' was more a village in size but most of its buildings were makeshift barracks. Despite it being a centre for trinkets and other materials, it had virtually no peddlers or stalls, indeed the only metallic objects on display were in the hands of the soldiers. They passed row upon row of barracks and warehouses, only the odd dingy tavern with grotty upper stairs of prostitute's hovels broke the mottled pattern of commerce and auxiliary. These sorry looking structures were sandwiched between the others like lichen on rocks; parasitic life leeching off barren harshness.

The soldiers eyed the newcomers with envy, their faces distorted and made to seem inhospitable by the flickering dancing duet of firelight and shadow on their faces. It was only when he was approached by a group that Dummonius noticed how young they were. Indeed the juniority of his mercenaries seemed comparatively old.

They gazed upon the visitors' Company emblems with reverence, addressing those wearing them with the utmost cordiality. It was truly bizarre for soldiers to hold such respect for mercenaries; normally they treated these dogs of war with contempt.

Still, the mercenaries, overburdened with embarrassment, held their heads low, and did not welcome this reverence. The group of guards invited them to join them at the Goat and Bear (which to locals was called the Vultai and Felix after the alleged resemblance of the two lords to these beasts). It was with unanimous reluctance that the mercenaries agreed, before indicating an impatient desire to move on.

As they walked their horses through the thick mud that was reminiscent of a spring battlefield, Dummonius slowed so Heldius, the squad leader of the mercenary troop, could catch up. Ever conscious of his desire to keep the mercenaries out of trouble, quickly muttered to him, "do not feel pressured to go and meet those hot-heads. I shall make an appearance just so as not to cause offence."

Heldius listened intensely to the Captain, left a considerate pause for thought, then in a monotone voice replied, "on the contrary Captain, it is you who can be excused. I shall go, accompanied by one of my comrades." He then added with a tension leaning towards warmth, "some of us were based here a few years back, though it is strange that I have not recognised a single soldier."

Dummonius silently noted that he had been correct about the mercenaries' past, and was further intrigued by his insistence that he had not recognised anyone, even though the lighting was so poor. He was also sure he would have to accompany them.

"It is only proper that I come along," he declared nonchalantly.

Clearly irritated, Heldius strained to uphold his vacant countenance. "As you wish, sir."

They rode into the darkness. Either side of the dirt street the buildings rose up to form a valley, its walls constituted of dilapidated buildings that completely walled off either side. Tiny alleyways cut under barrack or brothel overhangs like caveats encroaching into the dormant barrier. The only revealing source of light came from the torches of the patrols. The sirenesque window candles of the brothels were mere blips, signalling the residency of fallen inhabitants, holding their light in tight orbs, like corrupted stars.

This all changed when they turned a corner and were confronted by a gigantic structure, where a plaza had no doubt once been. This stalwart building was a temple, illuminated by caged fires that licked the bars around them, eating up the air and sending slick gleams up the granite blocks and columns. Uncovered windows beamed blanketing yellow light that rendered onlookers blind to what lay within, giving the interior a mystical quality.

As they rode back into the shadows it felt as though they had just passed the heart of the town, indeed the only living organ of a decaying organism.

Heldius accelerated to catch up with his unsuspecting captain. His voice contained a restrained anger. "That used to be the marketplace. They'd begun building that temple during my posting here." Luckily his comment was meant only as a personal catharsis and so no reply was required.

Dummonius deduced that the mercenaries were not New Interpretationists, though, amongst all these staunch loyalist Latman soldiers that could be more of a problem.

He was even more unsettled by the growing feeling of unease at how these treacherous times were pushing him into such a way of thinking. It got him thinking that a few years ago he would never have even thought of this kind of scheming. Those days seemed an age of naivety, his efforts dedicated to the external threats, and to the maintenance of order. Now it had all changed, and here he was, trying to read his supposed comrades.

Feeling more and more ill at ease with his thoughts, he slowed so Heldius could advance adjacent to him. "How far is it to the Coin and Cloak?"

"Just on the next corner, Captain," came the vapid reply.

★

The packed tavern combined the impoverished squalor of a peasant pub, with that of a common soldiers' bar. Fusing two ugly eras in Dummonius unfortunate past.

As both an outsider and an officer he was even more out of place than the other mercenaries. Grimy peasant-whores mingled with soldiers who were probably their cousins, the stagnancy of rural living catalysed in degeneration by the pressures of urbanisation.

Sulky fire gave the rancid air an acrid aftertaste and paraded the twisted debauchery with shady lighting. Dummonius' only comfort was that his compatriots, at least in part, shared his unease.

The eager young soldier who had spoken to them earlier had ushered them over to a table, during which time the whole room's inhabitants formed an indiscreet audience, casting sly but obvious glances in their direction. The soldier and his squad-mates were clearly revelling in the public display of their new-found acquaintances.

They were all smooth chinned, shaven-headed men, ranging from teens to early twenties, the only possible form of differentiation being the various degrees of childishness in their faces. They were clad in scale mail armour, that was well maintained given their posting in such a backwater. Something they alluded to with half-jesting requests for Dummonius to smuggle them some Company polish.

"We are so glad to have you people with us again!" the young man declared jovially, much to the confusion of his guests. Adamant that they had never met these young pups during their posting, Heldius' comrade stubbornly replied, "I do not remember meeting you before."

The young soldier laughed. "Don't be silly; the Company's men come here all the time – usually to collect weapons. In and out, honourably serving the House and Company to protect and enrich our territories!" He nearly sang with joy as he praised them.

Heldius was irritated. "We are just mercenaries, any others are nothing to do with us."

Dummonius winced as he realised his fears were coming to life. Heldius, for all his probable honour, was as mouthy as Heites.

Luckily Heldius' comrade was on the ball. "So, what news of the barbarians?"

This confused Dummonius: as a coastal easterner, this term meant baresarks, something an inland area like this would have no news of. It took him some moments to realise he referred to the mountain people (it did not even occur to him that it also included resident Vacarians as well). The young man shrugged. "The barbarians are restless as ever... still they will not yield."

Heldius snorted, then leant forward to give some advice. "To be honest, from my experience, it's probably better to leave those nomads to themselves. As for the Vacarians, I fought them all over – they are more like goats than dogs – the more you flog them the more stubborn they get. Defiance is in their blood."

The young man frowned. "They must be forced to learn." His expression darkened, adding several years of war-weariness onto it. His words were spoken with the utmost seriousness and contempt. "They will only get themselves wiped out if they continue to resist."

Heldius looked puzzled, if only to hide a concerned grimace. "That doesn't sound like it'll get you anywhere," he concluded reservedly.

The soldier's countenance brightened in a way that can only be described as sinister. "Ah, but it is destined, for they must choose between Thelus' light, or Septimo's earthly ways and consequently eradication."

Heldius could not stop himself from rolling his eyes in futility.

Dummonius, who had until then felt lost in the midst of a foreign conversation, was able to identify with Heldius' expression.

The young soldier seemed put out to the point of offence. Adopting an air of self-righteous indignation, he counter-scoffed. "Well, over in your cosy patch in the East it may be of little consequence, but here it is the heart of the battle to ensure the prevalence of civilisation."

Such boisterousness from a young whelp served only to exacerbate his differences with the veteran.

"For one," Heldius began, "the Neptus region is no 'cosy patch' but a bastion against a Gatan incursion – the *real* threat to House Latman – one which looks all the more likely, due to your brashness here, which only serves to infuriate Gatan's ally, Vacarium." He leaned closer to the soldier. "And secondly, I've served in this region since I was sixteen, before that I lived here as a child. I fought rebellions, crushed dissent and brought rule of our great lord to all over these parts for over a decade. And in all my time here, it was the kind like you, so puffed up in superiority and a ruthlessness only matched by tactical uselessness, who always turned our attempts to maintain order into more reasons for them to rebel!"

Rather than cower back and apologise as was the custom for less experienced soldiers, the youth laughed off the comments as though they were archaic ramblings. "Times have changed, my friend. We will no longer tolerate indifference. You remember how even when they swore allegiance[8] their eyes betrayed their desire to rebel, disrupt, betray."

In a surprising move Heldius actually sank back into his seat, his eyes focusing on nothing, as he recalled the disdainful expression he had endured for years. He knew the young soldier had a point, even if his solution was wrong.

The impetuous soldier made a sweeping advance, lurching his body onto his elbows, which rested casually on the table. "Why should we tolerate such tacit dissent?"

Heldius grimaced as he recalled the countless times he had felt the urge to join in with his impetuous compatriots, but had been dissuaded by his dedication to the soldiers' code[9]. And these Vacarians, despite their vagrancy status, were still citizens (another thing the Commandant was adamant to remind his men). Each time the desire to throw in the towel of decency and join in the terror rather than rebuking the others strengthened. It was that urge that had led him to accept the call of mercenarydom.

Of course, now he could see the difference, whether direct or implicit. These new soldiers were either following a new practice, or just not being told otherwise, and so were taking such brutal stances. The truth was no order needed be given, only the circumstances to arise: polluted by the right rhetoric, the cycle began: oppress them, occupy them, disappoint them, dehumanise them, blame them for the result, and with their response the cycle can begin again.

"Look," Heldius began, clearly losing his patience. "I have twelve years of military stories and sixteen more growing up here, I loathe them." He paused quietening his voice in embarrassment, "Sometimes, I wish we could stop them… at my most angry I would want them wiped out, but I would calm and see it is not possible or helpful."

The young man decided it was time to change the subject. "So how did you all manage to come into the employ of The Company?" His eyes glowered enviously.

Bemusement and confusion collided simultaneously in Heldius' and Dummonius' minds.

"Sorry?" Dummonius queried, successfully pulling off the impression he had not been paying attention and was honestly asking for repetition.

---

[8] It was custom to make all survivors of a rebellion and indeed any civilians in the vicinity (of the same ethnicity) to make an oath of loyalty to the House.
[9] Something the old commandant, Hoppolies had always ensured was reinforced.

"I was asking how you managed to get employed by The Merchant Prince himself?" He winked.

Both the mercenaries hesitated, anxious to hear the other's reason for what they saw as a personal fall from grace. Neither wanted to admit they were both, in part, ousted as old guard and in part willing resigners to avoid complicity in sharing guilt in what would come.

Instead, Dummonius subtly remarked, "mercenarydom is rarely seen as a privilege."

Before Heldius could offer his cryptic reply, the conversation was dismantled by an intruder.

"Captain Dummonius?" an aristocratic interjection rolled across the table.

Dummonius looked to the source, and there stood a finely-dressed merchant. His elegant clothing absorbed the firelight, giving its bright red colour a radiant glow. It matched the gleaming metal of the soldiers' armour and easily usurped the crimson of their capes. This was enhanced by its striking difference from the gritty military attire that surrounded it, allowing its flamboyance to steal the limelight.

There was something about military uniforms that no matter how much they were polished they were still tarnished by the grubbiness of their purpose. The clothing of a merchant however, no matter how much they were soiled by a greedy drive, still retained sophistication. It was the same with their respective tools: no matter how polished a sword was, it was still the symbol of killing, whereas a coin, no matter how acquired or how many died as a result of earning it, remained a symbol of civilised interaction.

The merchant did not wait for a reply. "I am Telgius. There is no time for such frivolous time-wasting. You must accompany me to the smelting yard." He spoke in an aloof commanding tone: either unaccustomed to speaking to veterans and so treated them as domestic servants, or he actually believed himself to be their master.

The young soldier and his retinue had shot to their feet and bowed humbly. "Sir, my deepest apologies for delaying your mission," he stuttered, before gesturing to his men to leave.

This irritated Dummonius. As a military man he hated to see uniformed men be humbled by a civilian. It also demolished any chance of him challenging the interloper. Nevertheless, Dummonius wasn't prepared to be spoken to in such a way. "Sire, we have travelled long and hard, are we not permitted one night's rest?"

The merchant ignored the rhetorical question. "Rest is upon completion of a mission. Peasants do not stop half-way through a day for a nap… or if they do, they are flogged." He was clearly attempting to issue an intimidating threat, completely unaware that his local prestige was completely unknown to the captain.

Dummonius was not normally one to answer back; that was how he had made it to captain. However, now he was one, and following the continued interference of commercial and theological leaders in his life, he could not stop himself from retorting.

"My agrarian days are long behind me, but I do not recall harvesting an entire field in one day, nor do I recall working continually for a week until I had done so."

The merchant looked shocked and gave him a menacing look, and was about to rebuke him. Heldius' companion saved both the merchant and the captain from such humiliation.

"Sire, we come with direct orders from Ruperis Delvinius, in his personal consultation with his Excellency; Captain Dummonius was given full jurisdiction over operations."

Dummonius felt triumphant, but rather than cause a fuss declared a compromise. "We shall travel with you immediately, but shall have to rest at the smithy... it has a garrison there, does it not?"

Implication of Dummonius' closeness to the merchant prince clearly knocked Telgius down a peg, and with flustered stuttering, he accepted.

★

The mercenaries had not been happy to be disrupted from much cherished sleep on actual beds. Nevertheless, once awake their anger subsided and professionalism took over, calming their irritation. Though their contempt for the merchant lived on in their silent glances.

They trekked until dawn before reaching their destination. It was a walled-off little place, more of a fort than a smithy. The guards did not wear Latman uniforms, but rather Delvinius cuirasses, like their own. However, what surprised Dummonius was that there were a number of women and children milling about. All their clothing, like the buildings, bearing the Delvinius emblem. It was like an enclosed Delvinius Company colony in the middle of Latman territory.

Telgius hastily took them to the warehouse where the carts were all loaded and ready. Grimy soldiers formed a menacing circle around them.

Telgius brought them to a halt and signalled to dismount.

"Well, here it is, men," he declared proudly. "The cargo is loaded." He gestured to the solid chests that lay stacked on the carts. "And ready to go."

Dummonius looked disdainfully at Telgius for his convenient forgetfulness.

"Good, once we have rested, we can set off immediately."

Telgius smirked, clearly not willing to get on the wrong side of the beleaguered mercenaries by pretending to have forgotten the agreement.

"Of course," he replied calmly, already making jittery backwards steps in order to facilitate his departure.

For some indiscernible reason, Dummonius felt the urge to make his victory decisive. "Before you go sire, we have orders to check the cargo. I am sure it is all here, but Ruperis Delvinius made it absolutely clear…"

He trailed off to allow Telgius to offer a mumbled reluctant assent before starting again. "Actually, he had asked they be counted, but seeing as they are all nicely packed I shall have to take your word for it."

The sergeant of the guard rustled in his knapsack and produced a sealed envelope. He tore it open roughly and lifted out a hefty set of keys. His thick fingers clumsily sorted through them like an ape at an abacus, eventually clasping the correct one awkwardly with his gargantuan hand.

As the chest was opened, all the men stretched up to try and get the first glimpse of the spears. They followed the sergeant movements as he unfolded a cloth and lifted one of the spears, as though observing a religious ceremony.

The spear was long and sleek with a very thin head, more like that of an arrow than a spear. More remarkable was that it was made entirely of what looked to be steel, never before had there been such a length of steel as one piece, nor in such huge numbers.

Holding it with the nonchalant expression of a priest handling a relic, the sergeant handed the spear to Dummonius. He had mixed feelings, though it was surprisingly light for a metal weapon, it was still heavy for a javelin, and rather cumbersome as a spear. Tapping it with his gladius he realised it was hollow.

Allowing it to slide through his fingers he began inspecting the head. His inspection was rather distracted by the messy patch where the head joined the pole, this presentational defect sullying its otherwise magical appearance.

He was further distracted by Heldius declaring, "captain, I am sure the merchant prince asked us to test it."

Dummonius looked up to see a wolfish grin. He turned to look at Telgius who stood like an unwanted statue. After a delay he spasmed into life, opening his mouth in silent tacit assent.

When he looked back, Heldius already had his shield on and was rushing at him, gladius in hand. Rather shocked Dummonius struggled to run the spear shaft through his fingers and up into a defensive position. He immediately felt the weight and retracted it slightly.

Heldius rushed at him, his elbow a rigid hinge between arm and shoulder, clamped at a perfect 45 degrees. Dummonius, who was totally unaccustomed to wielding a spear, lunged it forwards into the shield. The point and the flat surface impacted, but with nothing behind it the spear yielded, sending Dummonius reeling. He almost dropped the spear as resonance set in on the hollow tube. Heldius, though, was given an unexpected jolt as the hefty spear took much of the force.

Heldius stood about three metres from Dummonius. Panting profusely, he childishly nursed the dent in his shield. He began shaking his head with jesting disapproval. "Captain? Never done spear drill? You should dig it in to the ground and let the earth take the force."

Dummonius was thrown into an unusual situation of camaraderie with his men. This titbit of nostalgia perked him slightly as he shook his head to expunge a rare expression of joviality. "Prefer to get stuck in." Heldius' eyes flashed with approval. "I likewise, Captain."

They seemed to have totally forgotten about the spectators, or at least that they were not just any old hoodlums off the street like at an amphitheatre.

"Besides, had I done that, I wager it'd have made a nice soldier and shield kebab!"

Heldius chuckled. "You'll wager, sarge?" He blurted, not realising his mistake until too late. To his surprise, rather than being offended, Dummonius not only overlooked it but even seemed joyful at the blunder as it proved he had not become a stuffy aristocratic officer.

"Delvinius would charge me more for killing you than we could ever earn!"

Heldius laughed again, secretly relieved that he had not been rebuked. In the meantime his eyes glanced over the spearhead that stood upright silhouetted against the misty morning haze of sunlight.

"Ay up," he suddenly declared, advancing on it slowly so Dummonius could lower it.

They both examined the head. The knobbly joint looked as though it had swollen further, but more crucially they were both sure that the head was bent slightly. Heldius looked to his captain to silently ask if they would do anything. Dummonius took a quick decision and shook his head discreetly. Heldius gave a nod. As they backed away, Heldius declared, "phew, nearly left some of me shield's paint on it then!"

It was only now that they saw the blank faces of the guards, the horrified expression of Telgius, and the bemused looks on their mercenary troop.

Dummonius ignored the tacit hostility. "Right, we must rest". He handed the deadpan sergeant the spear and led the way back to the horses.

★

"Sorry about back there captain... it just slipped out," Heldius muttered as they were led to the garrison bunks.

Dummonius shook his head dismissively. "It just takes me back."
Heldius hesitated. "I had heard you were a captain in the military though."

"I was," Dummonius replied

"No disrespect sir, but you don't act like one."

"That's because I wasn't born one... like most the others."

"You're quite a rarity then."

Dummonius shook his head. "No, there are many out there, potentially, they just don't get the chance... to be honest, most sergeants would make better captains than captains."

"So what will you do about the spears?"

"I will just tell Delvinius, it's all I can do. I have no remit to refuse them."

Heldius shook his head dourly. "Shouldn't we report it to them here?"

Dummonius shook his head. "Only report things up. If you report down, you will only anger people. Reporting up is the proper thing to do, so it will mean whatever happens we are absolved of responsibility."

Heldius sniggered. "You really are an officer!"

Dummonius just nodded sombrely.

Chapter 31
Stalks on the Bank

The river Neptus was concealed under a blanketing torrent of mist that drifted with the current. It was as though the sky and the sea had united, coalescing in the form of a gaseous and a liquid snake that writhed through this channel that was cut through the earth. Two endless bodies locked in a ritualistic dance.

There seemed something conscious about the gradual horizontal shifting of the mist whilst it refrained from expanding upwards or widthways. So thick was its sprawling coverage of the river that its movements were only traceable by the wisps that fleetingly strayed onto the bank. Indeed, without these, the gaseous miasma could have been mistaken for a glacial wall of blinding void.

The sun was only just awakening below the horizon; the first few rays that magically bent around the planet were sucked up by this gaseous creature as it drifted off towards the sea. Consequently, the bluish predawn light was regurgitated from it as ethereal luminous white.

Beneath it, the river was smothered out of existence. The evergreen trees crackled as they soaked in the damp air, the solid echoes of the men as they worked on the wood merely sporadic cries of loneliness.

On the Gatan bank weary men shuffled about in a daze, whilst a wiry stick of a man excitably gestured from within the cocoon of a thick cloak. Somehow the padded attire was no deception, even in this light, to Gorax's slight figure. He stood separate from all the others, gesturing with bony fingers that barely peeped from their shelter.

The last trebuchet was almost complete. Those men not on construction duty huddled in circles around the finished machines staring at them in awe, trying to establish how they worked. Many looked upon them with scepticism as they inspected their flimsy structures that rose like stalks on the riverbank.

Lord Gatan sat on his horse with his retinue at what was considered a safe distance from the contraptions, overseeing the construction with frustrated impotence. They watched the ropes and pulleys haul the bucket down so it could be filled with stones. Gorax stood between them and the constructs; the grand conductor passionately mimicking the labours of his minions as he built up to the finale.

Next to Adonis, Hercela sat on his horse, his face betraying unease at his previous unwavering confidence in the engineer. He was considering the feasibility of his men assaulting the fort without a breach, silently glad that the mist was hiding the precarious river below. Even if they crossed under fire they would still have no way of scaling the walls, most the rope would have to be used to make a line across the river. They could not go back, even if they failed to take Neptus, for the marine trespassing deep into Latman waters made the conflict one of full-scale war.

Hercela was annoyed that the decoy had worked for it had made Latman withdraw most of the Gorad garrison from Neptus, meaning Gatan lost an opportunity to eliminate the garrison prior to the invasion and meant less soldiers needed to be fed should Neptus need to be put under siege. On top of this it was rumoured that an army of Telis was to join the Latman main force. He dared not mention his qualms to Adonis, not only because he had warned him from the outset, but because he was sure the Lord was sharing his thoughts now.

Hercela brushed aside his speculation, knowing it only clouded his vision of the present. Instead, he focused on the final stages of construction.

Suddenly the conductor spun around, holding his arms up to gesture a sign of relief to his liege. He hastily scampered over to the retinue.

"Sir, they are complete, once the ground cloud clears we await your signal. Though I will need time to work out the distance."

He turned to look across the river, scowling irritably at the mist stream that still refused to dissipate. It now resembled an amalgam of interlocking clouds rather than the single body it was before, occasional holes appearing in the gaseous patchwork. However these holes were far too small to make out anything except a dark patch.

Adonis nodded. "I want you to start as soon as the target is visible, aim for the towers first."

There was an unexpected noise of dissent. All eyes turned on the culprit; it was Claudix Gatan. "Your Lordship, would it not be better to breach the wall first? It is what we need most."

Adonis paused, his irritable mood swaying him towards feeling he was being undermined. He looked to Hercela.

Hercela, dubious of the mistrustful look in his lordship's eyes, reluctantly nodded in agreement.

Gatan squinted his piggish eyes and let out an abrupt affirmation. "Fine."

★

As daylight engulfed the land it swept away the mist, stirring it up into its component parts of cloud, the swirling segments still coalescing as they cajoled with each other in the mass exodus.

The walls and towers of Neptus fort gradually took form behind it, at first just a few upright spires heavily laden with serrated block work, connected by a thin rim that contoured the layer of mist.

Gorax immediately set about scratching into the dirt with a stick, working out the trajectory, pausing to ponder and lick his finger to test the wind. The soldiers were left to watch these two phenomenon unfurl: nature and man warming up for the sparring.

No sooner had the mist cleared and faintly red specks appeared en-mass on the battlements when Gorax gleefully bounded over to his lord to announce the bombardment could begin.

They were so caught up in the excitement that few bothered to notice the pitiful arrows that thudded impotently onto the bank, a good fifteen yards from the contraptions. As the operators heaved the pulleys to bring the huge buckets up, the Gatan forces, without need for orders, began to form up ready to intimidate the defenders by their comparative number.

Lord Gatan rode forward so he was parallel with the buckets, raising his hand as was custom when summoning a volley of arrows. With one fell swoop he brought his hand down. The trebuchets mimicked his movement; the buckets lunging down sending the war engines lurching forward. Simultaneously, the sling ends glided in a beautiful arch upwards, the canvass pouches releasing the stones and sending them hurling at the walls.

Of the three, two overshot, though they let out a thunderous grumble as they impacted on the dirt below and were accompanied by petrified screams. The third, however, clipped the battlement wall, obliterating the protective toothed section and shattering the wooden walkway. The few nearby Latman soldiers brave enough not to duck were flung backwards by the impact, presumably falling off to their deaths.

Whilst the Gatan soldiers and nobles cheered, Gorax was too annoyed at the inaccuracy of his calculations, whispering an apology to each machine as he instructed the operators to shorten the sling ropes.

Adonis Gatan wondered what was happening on the battlements; all he could see was a lack of Latman soldiers willing to stand up again. In truth, he could not properly comprehend the disarray on their side. Alongside these beastly contraptions and this huge army was the lingering sense that they had been abandoned. The garrison had been told that even if they were attacked, the less of them there was the better, because it would end up being a siege and less soldiers meant less mouths to feed. It was for this reason that the Gorad forces had only left them a detachment of fifty Young Bows[10] and a few squads of heavy infantry.

It took nearly half an hour to reload. The Gatan soldiers were getting restless, whilst the Latman soldiers began popping up like meerkats. When the next salvo was unleashed it was remarkable the perceived difference in velocity. Whilst the Gatan forces admired the seemingly impossibly graceful glide of the rocks as they silently floated over to the wall, the Latman soldiers found themselves with only a split second to comprehend their impending doom. Their hearts sank as the trebuchet buckets rocked downwards, and their senses pricked up just as the sling arms became visible and arced upwards. They barely saw the thundering rough grey rocks before they were upon them. The rocks whined with bestial exhilaration as they neared their prey; some thought Gorax a sorcerer of Septimo conjuring dark spirits to possess the dead rock.

A lucky one was struck on the head by a rock. He had been a labourer from a little village called Fulic, which was only a few miles from the hamlet where Julia lived. Indeed, as a youth he had often gone there with his father to get fish and sell pots that his mother made. When he had joined the army his mother had cried; his father had been proud, but too proud of himself to cry. Now he would finally get to unloose that emotion, now so much more pain would join it. It was supposed to be a new start for Juscius, that was his name; he would earn money and then

---

[10] These were young mostly rookie bowmen, who though adequate archers were rarely older than seventeen and so not suitable for combat. They were often used in sieges because they could be fed less than an adult should.

his father could buy his freedom and they could all make pots. That dream died with him and as quickly as he did.

Others were less lucky; another Juscius, who was also named after the current Lord, who had been born exactly a week before him, had his arm crushed by an impacting rock and was flung off the battlements, breaking his back on the cobblestones that surrounded the stable. Dozens of others fell to slow deaths as the wooden parapet collapsed when the second rock shattered it beneath their feet.

The third rock had impacted on the wall itself. Though to those above it was a relief, to Giliat the stable boy walking below it was the call of Septimo as he was struck by the stones that were flung out by the gaping hole punched through the wall. It was the true sign of the excessive power of the trebuchets; and a sign that the wall could be breached with relative ease.

When the next salvo came all three struck the wall. They all punched through, reducing huge chunks of stone to debris, cascading down in a hail of silty rubble. But they did not just make these lacerations; the impact buckled the whole section of the wall and jolted the ramparts so that most on the battlements were flung off.

Complete disarray in the fort was apparent from the eerie amalgam of shouting and screaming that could be heard on the Gatan bank. In contrast, when the next salvo created a crack all the way down the wall, a cheer went out on the bank. With this gap it would not take much to crumble away the exposed edge of the wall.

As the next volley of rocks slammed either side of the crack, the edges of the wall seemed to disintegrate into clouds of smoke; a breach had been created. A further cheer went out on the bank and Hercela, who had taken up position with his force rode over to Lord Gatan for permission to assault.

His lordship, though ecstatic about their success, was still cautious, preferring instead to give them a few more only with several smaller rocks.

★

Once they had been bombarded with a few volleys of shrapnel the beleaguered defenders had by and large surrendered. Hercela had launched the assault across the river unperturbed and seized the drawbridge. Most of the survivors had already dropped their weapons. Covered in dust they huddled together, shaking violently.

The captain and a few zealous die-hards had barricaded themselves in the temple, but Hercela sent the Gatan brigand marauders to batter down the door, and with the death of the captain and a few ringleaders, the resistance capitulated.

However, it was too late for these men, who were summarily

executed, though this was not for their defiance, but because in a final act of vengeance they had desecrated the Neptu temple. Evidently these troops were New Interpretationists who had relished this final chance to appease their god. Indeed, though no one cared to examine let alone document it, a few orthodox troops who had joined the last stand had been butchered for opposing their comrades' acts.

Other than this act of brutality Lord Gatan was adamant that the prisoners not be mistreated nor the area pillaged. When one impetuous commandant inquired why they were not allowed to follow custom and take the spoils, Gatan replied, "because Neptus is Gatan territory; anyone caught defiling it will be treated as a traitor."

After watching the executions, Adonis housed himself in the keep. This temporary retreat had been stripped of all things Latman. This had left it rather bare as the Latmans, with their stringent belief in property, had an irritating tendency to embroid, carve or engrave everything with the Latman crest. Though in fairness this was more to avoid theft of House property than to celebrate the prolonged reign of the Latman house.

Adonis had summoned Hercela and they both paced about the room, two alpha lions caged in an alien structure. Had any of their men, or even fellow generals seen them, they would have been baffled by the consternation on their faces following such a mighty victory.

Finally Hercela spoke. "Your Lordship, we should not overlook your victory here. It is resounding: Neptus is part of your house now and we took it only losing a handful of men!"

Gatan nodded, but they were both too far-sighted to dwell on the victory with so much hardship looming.

His lordship paced three more steps, his boots thumping with precise sounds on the solid floor.

"I fear you were right about the boats, Hercela," he blurted suddenly.

Hercela froze in his pacing and wheeled slowly to face Adonis, his heart ringing out for his lord's gut-wrenching admission. He gave a frank, but rather indecisive nod, and remained silent.

This urged the Lord to continue. "My soldier instinct tells me that we should be staying here and digging in, waiting for their counter-attack, blunting it then calling for an armistice... but I could not garrison such a force here, they would besiege us and force us out anyway. If I lessen the size of the force here, then the combined forces of Latman and Telis would swarm over this fort. Besides, after all this mobilisation of the troops it would be an awful waste."

Hercela nodded in agreement. "Whatever my qualms before, I stand loyal to your decisions. What is more, now the decision has been taken we must go on as planned. All-out war is now inevitable…"

Adonis' face had remained glued to the same patch of nothingness in the room: "…It was as soon as I sent the boats out… I closed off my options then… if only I had listened to Lady Gatan and got Lewerix on side." He muttered the last statement to himself.

Hercela became concerned for his Lords defeatism. He approached him reassuringly. "Adonis, we still stand a good chance of winning, we have good competent men and some fine generals. Their infantry may look impressive but our spearmen can match them, and keep them in combat while our forces, which are far superior in manoeuvrability, can flank them. Plus there are all sorts of factors; their relations with Lewerix have been so poor their bowmen cannot have decent composite bows. And as for Telis…" he spat "they have never fought in their lives – they even pay warlords to fight the other warlords bordering them!"

Adonis laughed, seemingly perked up, though it was short-lived as his face settled on a mediatory position of decisive seriousness. "I have decided that Claudix should remain here and Maximus should come with us in the invasion."

Hercela was intrigued but not especially baffled. "May I enquire why?"

Adonis nodded, "I cannot risk all of us being on the battlefield… if we should lose, someone must be ready to take command."

"So why not leave Maximus? Surely it would be a grave thing should both lord and heir fall together. Do I detect a mistrust of the competency of Maximus?" Hercela inquired cautiously.

Adonis shook his head. "For one, Maximus would never accept my decision; he is a born warrior. Secondly, if we should win, it is vital that he is present to share in the glory for when he succeeds me."

Hercela bowed his head so as not to tempt fate.

"Thirdly…" he hesitated, unsure on whether to speak his most irksome thoughts, "should we fail, I believe Maximus would be most competent to fight a rearguard, buying the other time, which Claudix could make the best use of." He hesitated again, even more troubled by his final reasoning. "This brings me to the fourth reason: should we lose, the times will change. As I have already said, Maximus is much like me, and so little like his mother. As I should have heeded the Lady's words the new leader needs to be more in tune with her thinking. Claudix combines my militarism with Lady Gatan's shrewdness, and that is precisely what House Gatan will need in such a circumstance."

Hercela felt uncomfortable at the realpolitik that seemed to write off the heir to the throne; however, he also recognised that the arguments put forward were correct. He looked upon his Lord with the expression of assent that meant he need not give verbal seal of approval.

Adonis approached Hercela, putting his arms on his shoulders. "Hercela, I have one request of you. If it should come to the latter you must flee for Neptus and help my sons."

Hercela reciprocated with his arms on his Lord and comrade's shoulders. For the first time in decades he felt a tear well in the corner of each eye. "Your Lordship, Adonis, let us not speak of such things."

They embraced. Finally Adonis declared, "summon the generals and my sons."

Hercela nodded obediently.

★

As Rabica followed the dirt track he spotted a pool of water ahead and to the left. It lay in a drop in the ground's level and was surrounded by a haphazard palisade of fluffy-headed reeds. Immediately, our wandering vagrant decided he would stop by this seemingly glowing pool of water. He looked up at the sky; the sun had either gone down, or was soon to drop below the horizon. Either way, the orange miasma it radiated was concealed behind low-lying thick grey cloud.

Rabica quickened his pace so he reached the designated stop rapidly. As he reached the still water he saw it was a stagnant pool. Getting closer still, he caught a whiff of boggy earth. He clambered over the clumpy straw-like grass of a bank before descending down the other side a few steps. Dumping his bag, he found a place to sit amongst the tall grass that formed an outer perimeter before the reed-based barbican. He ran his hands through the yellow grass, delicately holding clusters of aged seeds that were motionless in the virtually non-existent breeze. Midges hovered between the grass patches and towards the pond, some venturing near him momentarily, before continuing in their journey to what seemed to them a great lake.

In the tranquil dusk the pool lost the repulsiveness that sunlight would no doubt reveal.

The amalgamations of slude and scud seemed as though an intriguing intermediary between the water and the peaty mud that surrounded it. For a while Rabica just focused all his senses on absorbing this visual spectacle, so simplistic on the surface, yet so complex and intricate as a whole. A lazy cog in a gradual machine to which the whole of nature was but a hazy hurried spurt of rushing activity.

Then he listened. At first it was just a faint and occasional dripping, but as he concentrated he could hear the constant trickle of water. It seemed to be coming from the bushes that rose out of the grass on the far side of the pond. Though frustrated at not being able to locate the specifics of its source he found the sound uplifting. Yet the pond seemed not to move. What was more, Rabica wondered where the water from this trickle went. For this pond had no doubt existed for countless years and that eternal influx should be slowly creeping the water level higher and higher.

It was then that the fact that things in nature go on, forever ignorant of what went on around them, amazed him. He thought of how he could walk away and return as an old man, or send his great grandchildren to this spot and the same trickle would exist even though the exact particles he now saw would be hundreds of miles away, and what was seen in that future was now miles upstream or in a cloud, or the sea crushing a rock. Nature was truly beautiful he decided, provided it was left alone.

Rabica gave a wry smirk. 'Just like The Young Lady with respect to me'. He was immediately plunged into a routine mental excursion, pining about how much he missed her; he wished she could see the delight of the pond. "Would she see this? All of it? Or just a stagnant quagmire?"

He gazed up at the sky and was taken aback by its beauty. He lay back, sliding himself down into a comfortable position and nestling his head until it rested on a prominent clump behind him. Dusk was setting in, the sky was cloudy and luminous grey – that sheet grey which seemed so bright, yet was without source of illumination. Perhaps blank would be sufficient to describe this ambient glowing nothingness.

Clouds rolled over this blank film like water-damage. As Rabica lowered his view his attention was drawn to what looked like eagle or a dragon's head gliding across the sky. It was like the spearhead of a cloud, behind the figurehead spread out into an enormous blanket of dark grey fanning out like wings, to blanket all the sky behind. As the cloud swooped on and its dark grey wingspan consumed more of the sky, it was as though the cloud itself was bringing the night. With the sun sinking below, this hawk-headed cape of cloud had swooped down to seize the earth.

At first it made Rabica think of the approaching darkness that Juscius and his minions were threatening to bring to the island, but then he dismissed this and began to think practically; he needed to make a fire.

Rabica glanced about his surroundings. The grass would make a good starter, followed by some thick reeds, and then some twigs from the bush. Then some branches. After that there were no thicker pieces of wood, so the fire would be short-lived. Thankfully, it was not too cold a day so he could just wrap up once he had cooked.

★

He awoke the next morning to see the mountain range standing against the rolling misty clouds that seemed to be encircling its pinnacle. How he longed to be up there – with the clouds, on the desolate pitted surface removed from the bustling below.

Chapter 32
Indirect Logistics

Ruperis Delvinius lounged in his library chair, he was sprawled back like an upturned turtle that has resigned itself to its fate. His fine tunic hung loose off his body, forming perfect folds that disappeared into the cushions below him as though he were one with the chair. A dense book lay open on the small table beside him, open and exposed like a gutted tree. The pallid pages the remains of a once fleshy interior, the scrawl across it the markings of a long gone beetle that had burrowed through.

The merchant prince stared upwards at the ceiling, ignorant of the tome; he was considering the feasibility of having an alabaster roof. *'Would it give sufficient light? Would it be secure? Would it leak or crack in excessive rain?'* he wondered. *'Oh, such decisions! It is greater hassle to work out how to spend all this wealth than it is to create it!'* he remarked, secretly revelling in the concept of 'wealth creation' as though he were an alchemist or conjurer, magically summoning gold.

He sighed. "I am sure one day someone will find a way of telling people what to buy... and no doubt they will make money out of that itself!" he announced to himself, in a rare case of vocal soliloquy.

This was supposed to be free time, but he found himself longing for a meeting, a transaction or scheme. Relaxation was the most arduous task because it was horrifically, indeed inherently, unproductive; it was just a necessary evil between operations. He assumed it was the same for soldiers in peacetime.

He was relieved when he reminded himself that the mercenaries sent after the spears had returned today and so the captain should be visiting soon. This was bolstered by the mental note that Zeuorox would entertain him this evening. It was promising, as it was concerning 'indirect logistics' as the priest had put it. He knew exactly what this ambiguous topic was concerning and just the thought of what Zeuorox would say brought an abrupt childish giggle out of his mouth. Just the thought of discussing such an issue with Zeuorox compensated for the income irregularities resulting from his goons accepting services over payment.

Inspired by this image, Ruperis immediately decided that he would send the captain to be advisor to his old garrison, just because it would irritate the priest further. It was whilst he sat grinning to himself that Julian knocked and entered to explain that the Captain had arrived.

★

Captain Dummonius still found the illustrious mansion of Ruperis Delvinius intimidating. Nevertheless, he strode in with his head held high, trying not to think about how he would break the news about the seemingly shoddy spears.

To his relief Julian immediately sought audience with his master and he was soon sent up to the merchant's office.

The mercenary captain hesitated as he entered the office, its flamboyant furnishing still rather overbearing, though it was not this, nor the status of his employer that resulted in his caution. As a humble man who had risen to be one of rank, he saw through the convolution of rank and prestige, rather it was the issue of the spears that filled him with consternation.

Ruperis Delvinius sat at his desk. He immediately looked up from some papers that were quite obviously hastily strewn across the surface.

"Aah Captain…" He paused to pluck the mercenaries name from his memory. "Dummonius, I trust your mission was successful." His voice was so deadpan and disinterested it cannot warrant a question mark.

Captain Dummonius resumed approaching the office desk, stopping beside the chair opposite Delvinius before nodding.

"The sp… cargo has been collected and taken to your warehouses in the city… but…"

"Good," Delvinius snapped, already looking down and tracing words on the papers.

The Captain continued as though he had not been interrupted. "I am concerned about the quality of the goods you have been sold."

Delvinius jolted, looking up at the Captain as he did so. "What?" The word was near spat.

Dummonius looked concerned. "I thought it only correct to examine the cargo to ensure it was suitable, and I am concerned about the resilience of the spears."

Delvinius clearly was not. "Really? I shall have to investigate this," he declared with an air of indifference, but absolute finality. Dummonius knew better than to press further. He had done his duty and his employer could act as he wished.

"Sir, as I am still contracted to you, do you have any new missions for me?"

The merchant smiled, pleased that the unpleasantness was over. "Yes, I do." He furrowed his brow in an attempt to portray the importance of the new mission. "I do not know how up to date you are on the circumstances, but a state of war has arrived between Latman and Gatan. You are also aware that certain garrisons are lacking experienced officers. I have a contract with his lordship to provide advisors to such garrison commanders. You must travel to Leita and accompany Captain..." he paused whilst he rummaged through a pile of papers, flinging them absentmindedly over the whole table. "Captain Gerial, who is the new commander of Gorad garrison."

He betrayed a slight smirk as he saw the captain fail to repress a widening of his eyes at the garrison's name.

"You are familiar?" Delvinius inquired playfully.

Dummonius nodded, rather suspicious of the notion that Delvinius did not know it. "Yes sir, it was my garrison."

"Excellent!" Delvinius declared, clapping his hands for emphasis.

"And Heldius' squad is to accompany me?" the mercenary inquired.

Delvinius looked down at his papers for a brief moment. "No, you can tell them they are needed in Vaca."

Dummonius was rather shocked. "Oh."

"Yes, tell them to meet Telgius at Auberline, he will instruct them." Instantly Delvinius was cursing himself for bothering to send them back, they could easily have stayed in Auberline, after all it was their presence on paper that mattered with the cargo shipping.

"Yes sir," Dummonius declared.

Delvinius seemed already preoccupied with something else. "Yes, you are dismissed... oh, and both missions are to be enacted tomorrow morning."

Dummonius was just pleased to be out of the office and so bowed rapidly before heading for the exit. He felt rather put out by his brusque treatment at the hands of the merchant, to be summoned here, spoken to with disdain, then shooed away like a servant.

What was more, he was troubled by the merchant's seeming indifference to the spears. Even had he known that the manufacturers were operating within a subsidiary of the Delvinius Company he still would have been at a loss as to why the merchant would not care about Latman soldiers being inadequately equipped. The economic issues of having to shelve the current batch and fund further research were completely unknown to the captain.

Whilst the Captain was making his departure, Delvinius' mind was elsewhere, namely what he would say to the High Priest.

★

Julian had only enough time to bow and mumble 'Your Excellency' before the High Pontiff had strode past him and up the stairs to Ruperis' office. From the brief glimpse of grey lines that coalesced into a dour face within the cape, Julian judged the High Priest to be in the most irritable of moods. He knew better than to follow him.

Zeuorox stormed up the stairs and across the landing, sweeping the door to Ruperis' office open with one of his long outstretched arms so that he could launch himself fluidly into the room. He flung his hood down and swerved towards the desk. However, the smoothness of his journey was disrupted by the abrupt realisation that Delvinius was not seated at his desk, but rather lounging in his 'library'. This totally destroyed the priest's entrance as he had to double take and swerve towards the lounging turtle.

Delvinius lethargically raised his hand in informal greeting. The cleric knew better than to perform as his antagonist desired.

"Ruperis Delvinius, we must discuss certain issues. I shall wait for you in your discussion area, for when you have suitably composed yourself for my presence." He spoke coolly, a slight hint of disdain oozing from his lips. Without waiting for a reply, he strode over to the upright seats and chose one to sit in.

Casually Ruperis stretched, laden with sloth, and rose to approach the high priest, though he knew the seating the High Priest had chosen would make his current composure impossible. In contrast, these rather austere upright chairs suited the stiff pontiff.

"Mr. Delvinius, before I begin do not try and deny your collusion in this abhorrent racketeering."

Ruperis remained silent to allow the priest to continue. "It has come to my attention that someone, that is, someone under your orders, is seeking to capitalise on the vast swathes of immoral ladies of the night that now trail our forces."

Ruperis hid his smirk with a widening of his eyes in surprise.

"Don't give me that!" Zeuorox declared, his voice booming.

Ruperis shrugged. "Ok, so I provide protection for the 'ladies'?"

Zeuorox laughed. It was a bitter, sardonic laugh. "Delvinius." He spoke the name as though it was synonymous with hedonistic avarice. "Your men are taking these girls out, extracting a cut and encouraging soldiers to indulge themselves. Some are even taking services as payment!" Despite his disgust, he retained his cool.

"And you are worried about the moral conduct of our soldiers?" Ruperis laughed.

Zeuorox allowed a slight sneer to resonate across his face, he shook his head disdainfully. "It goes deeper than that, I dislike your profiteering from the moral failings of both parties. It is one thing to tolerate such debauchery, another to profit from it. Besides, though I find their lifestyles abhorrent the conduct of your thugs has to be considered worse."

"High Priest Zeuorox, defender of whores, strumpets, any depraved female! Come to him, he will give you salvation," Ruperis blurted, regret sinking in gradually afterwards.

The gaunt face's muscles squirmed to the surface as the skull that controlled them spasmed. Zeuorox shook his skeletal face, his steely vapid eyes, as serious as the deadly sockets of death himself. "I wonder... I wonder why I care for your soul, when such a self-consumed, gluttonous spirit has deformed it beyond recognition."

Ruperis looked indifferent.

Zeuorox knew, with his doctrine-based argument on the table he needed to explain how this actually affected the merchant. "You may enrich his lordship... I am sure you scam him plenty too, but my gift to him has no bearing on the physical realm and so can be questioned by none, except the gods themselves. On the other hand your contribution to him CAN be measured, therefore it can be criticised. Hence it can be easily demolished."

Ruperis' heart sank (which was no surprise, so full was it of gold). "Just remember, your influence is relative to your economic contribution. Mine is everlasting and unlimited, like the gods," Zeuorox threatened.

Ruperis sighed, and gave a frank (and therefore by his standards defeated) look at the priest. "So will you interfere?"

Zeuorox sighed, before giving the entrepreneur a stern look. "For the sake of the complexities of the moment I will be compelled to do nothing. But let it be made clear; this is entirely because of the circumstances, which are completely out of *your* control. Once this war is over, it had better cease, or else you will find his most pious lord unable to recognise your personal relationship with him as an excuse to ignore your behaviour."

It was a bitter pill to swallow, but the merchant did. "Your Excellency, by then I will be completely shifting my business interests. I can assure you I will have no role in the industry."

Zeuorox nodded warily. "I am glad you agree. Now to other issues; I suppose you have heard of the naval conflict?"

Ruperis, glad the subject had shifted, replied jovially, "yes, we trounced them!"

Zeuorox snorted. "You can save your propaganda. We *should* have trounced them but we only drove them back... their cargo ships were not laden with troops and so they were much more able to fight. I may be no admiral but I have sources that tell me we should have annihilated them. I have other sources that tell me a mighty Gatanese force has taken Neptus!"

Though he had not heard the latter news Ruperis shrugged. "And? Good!" He pretended to raise a glass. "To The Long War! May our troops need new equipment and may they seek guidance in our new priests!"

Zeuorox paused for a moment. Guardedly he replied. "You are probably right, it is just I dislike events unfolding differently to planned." Ruperis shook his head, dismissive of the cleric's concern. "But it is such circumstances that often warrant the greatest rewards... and I have no doubt that applies theologically as well as economically."

The gaunt face concealed itself within the hood again, as a snorting laugh shot out from within. "I shall depart!" it declared. The gnarled shade nodded its hood in farewell and hovered out.

★

The first part of the walk was a level hike across a reddish springy scrub, much like heather, that covered the whole area.

Rabica bounded along the strait, stumbling occasionally as his feet fell down an unexpected hole covered with the plant. As he did so the clouds began to creep in from behind him, the looming grey shadows blanking out the whole sky. As they came they exploded into a puffy interlocking leviathan.

Despite the monotony, Rabica enjoyed the walk. With his eyes set on the goal ahead, the ankle-grinding, bumpy ground was just a necessary evil.

The plant that so hindered his path was curious enough in its singularity, though the entire sprawling patch would be mundane if it were not so sinister. Its complete domination of the land swamped the whole view with a vast array of red, micromanaging the landscape with such intensity. Its roots lodged into the soil, clinging to it in rain, guiding the fallen water into streams and gullies; manipulating one of nature's great powers. Rabica found himself conditioned to follow the water's path to avoid the ankle-deep pits that the sea of red maliciously concealed.

By sticking to the water trails Rabica knew he would make good time.

"Where the water goes, I go," he declared proudly.

Rain hurtled down on the delinquent, who hastily flung on an extra layer of thick wool, that would at least stave off the rain for some time. Still, he powered on, trudging this way and that, splashing through the rising puddles that lay in the channels. Now and again a gust would catch him and he would hastily scrabble for his hood with a flash of red numb fingers that would rapidly scurry back into the shelters in his sleeves.

He busied his mind with petty thoughts to pass the time, occasionally launching into vicious rants against a stone or plant that had attempted to obstruct him, sending him stumbling.

He listened for while, counting time with each squelch of his now sodden boots and feet, though he soon stopped as the ingrained mental monotony began to grate on him and he started cursing the squelches just as he had the obstacles.

Soon he was climbing and the 'red heather' had petered out on the ascent, though a few sporadic incursions were evident. Most were solitary plants, either sheltered behind rocks, or else swaying madly as they wrestled with the wind alone.

Rabica continued walking, but gazed with secret kinship at these red outcasts. He conjured the notion that they, like him, had fled their respective domains and comrades in search of whatever wonder lay above and beyond.

The landscape was more barren as there were fewer floras, but less desolate as it had more variety; yellow long cylindrical grass grew in solid tufty clumps. Greener tufts were also present – more lush-looking than the yellow, but still gaunt and harsh. Some interesting mosses grew like black or orange splotches on rocks. A few bushes had entrenched themselves on the ascent, though they swayed and flopped madly as though they were struggling to hold on to their own branches.

The ground beneath him gradually became more rocky and less muddy, which aside from the more irregular steps he had to take, were a relief, as it ended the tormenting squelch. Nevertheless, his feet were beyond drenched, his boots felt like bags of water crammed with sponges.

Rabica had continued to follow the waterways. Though now the water trickled and sometimes gushed past him, he was undeterred.

"Wherever the water flees: I shall go," he declared comically. "For that must be the residence of desolation," he added in an attempt to salvage some 'serious point' from his ridiculousness.

'*Still,*' he thought, '*at least if I say such things in a comical (by comical I mean "knowing I sound ridiculous" rather than being funny) way then at least I cannot be accused of pretentiousness*'. After a moment he laughed at himself. "Who exactly is going to accuse me?"

"Why, me!" he whispered, with an air of sinister bitterness.

He sighed and plodded on.

★

Hours slipped by and still he trudged up the varying slope as the water trails meandered. Occasionally the gullies would become deep gushing streams and he would have to straddle the banks, or skirt around, clambering over boulders and scrabbling over tufts of grass. He now had no idea where he was going, except up – as long as the water was against him he was going the correct way.

Rabica kept a watchful eye on his surrounding, though with all the cloud he could not soak in the wonder of the vast expanse of rocky tundra that lay before him. The ground below was now fine gravel, constituted of shards from the rocks that dotted the visible span of his view. From what he could see, he had turned left around the mountain as on his left side was a definitive drop and to his right the land rose in a gradual climb which was by and large concealed by the terrains undulation.

All of a sudden he was going down, and almost despaired as he saw the water rushing past him. However, he took a gamble that it was just a short drop or crater in the side of the mountain. Through the misty cloud, behind the pitter-patter of rain, he could hear a roaring noise. Though his subconscious was sent wild, he rationally guessed it to be a river.

Sure enough, as he followed a meander in his trickle-trail, a roaring torrent was gushing down to his left. Now he had a new, more spectacular phenomenon to follow.

★

His route beside the river would be difficult, even without the rain and mist; countless man-sized boulders lined the river bank. Also, those few spaces which were occupied by neither boulder nor the expanding river, usually housed a trickling baby stream summoned to the mother leviathan deluge, so often he had to skirt some distance around before loyally returning to the rivers side. As he did so he listened intently to the continual roaring, finding the noise an invisible companion in his journey. When he was forced to venture away from the mainstay of the river, the roaring became a distant purr, telling him he had not strayed far. By now all he saw were mountains upon mountains of rocks and pebbles mingled with water and virtually no plant life whatsoever.

As hunger set in he declared, "I shall eat when I reach the top – besides I cannot stop here, it's too open." However, within minutes he was retreating from the bold statement. "Ok, I'll stop if I get the chance. If I stop here I will freeze," he told himself. "I will just freeze, get colder at least, and just feel tired, cold and miserable. I'm better off just moving."

After five minutes of fighting the desire for food, he sulkily, and without a word threw his pack on a rock, and scrabbled around for a carrot amongst the sodden blanket and clothing. He hastily stuffed it in his mouth, whilst he threw his pack back over his shoulder. As soon as the carrot was placed in his mouth, his enzymes spurted into action, swarming over the carrot with a sludgy viscosity. Just as the dribble was set to fall from his mouth in its lustful splurge, he grabbed the end of the carrot, took a bite and sucked his juices back in. With the carrot protruding like a comical hook hand from his woolly sleeve, he set off again.

The carrot was demolished in a matter of seconds, though it was enough, psychologically at least, to spur him on.

Despite all the hardship and excessive grouchiness that had befallen him, he was glad to be here. He was as pleased to be free of the seething mass of people, as much as he was pleased to be free of the mass of blood heather, as he had decided to call it.

★

"Have I reached the top?" an astonished Rabica gasped as he struggled against the howling wind. His words shot out and dissipated in the wind so rapidly it was only thought and memory that confirmed he had said anything at all, the words themselves gobbled up the split second they left his hollow mouth. In the cloud he could barely see twenty yards away, but in what he could see he could not detect any overall change in altitude.

Though mundane and empty to anyone else, it was truly spectacular to Rabica; a 20-yard radius of brown gravel with boulders and a few lonesome tufts of grass. Outside of this there was nothing. Everything just disappeared into a misty void. Rabica tried to relax in his new domain, breathing in a struggling gulp as the wind blew the air forcefully into his open mouth. To the delirious vagrant this was a secret place, the mist an impenetrable barrier to the outside world.

He was reminded otherwise by an aggressive shunt from the wind and the return of the rain. The crackling droplets were tiny but numerous.

These two looming weather structures followed him everywhere, and reminded him of the evils back home. One pushing him around with sheer force, nudging him to travel in a particular direction, the other, brooding and hovering over him trying to determine his actions, and drive him away from paths it disapproved of.

Rabica scrabbled along the open terrain, soaking in its desolate beauty. He noticed breaks in the rocky gravel to make way for compacted peaty mud that concealed itself protectively in nooks and crannies between the rocks. He ran to investigate; were these the first patches from where life would flourish?

But his beaming triumphalism was soon ruined – the patches on the ground were not just dark peaty mud, they had a white tinge. He examined closely, squinting and gasping in the vicious wind and rain. It was a fungal mould that stained the otherwise beautiful peat. In places it collected together into craggy clump of what looked like tiny flowers but were actually knobbly dry leaves bundled into a package and sprinkled with whiteness. Dust of some malignant infestation.

"This is a dead place, an aged, desolate, crumbled metropolis left to rot." As he mouthed the last word he kicked a clump of the white parasite. He had to get off the mountain. It was infected. He had decided.

In a feverish state, he fled, panic-stricken by the loss and lies of the promised mountain. He felt dirty, falling for its distant grace, being lured up here only to find a pox-ridden peak. With a sense of urgency completely detached from real danger of exposure, the delusional vagrant stumbled off to find the climb down the other side.

Sure enough, after what felt like an eternity he dropped down rather sharply. This sharp decline, though awkward to traverse, fortunately took the wind off his back. It also gave him some shelter from the rain, though the ground was still sodden and awash with the rain water that gushed down the mountain. The streams were roaring and the gullies, normally just archaic cracked trails, were vivacious brooks of running water.

The terrain remained rocky, though the near sheer drop soon gave way to more levelled ground littered with large boulders that offered some limited protection from the elements. As he stepped down lower in search of adequate cover, the clouds seemed to lift and he could once again see far out. In the distance he could make out the faint silhouette of a line of peaks surrounded by a range of mountains.

A sizeable stream meandered along the near-flat valley towards the mountain range to the left. It was here that he could see the pure magnificence of the desolate tundra, undisturbed by man, ageing and forming of its own accord. It was beyond tranquillity, as tranquillity required something sentient to be tranquil.

He glanced off to his right, away from the vast brown gravel desert, to spot some large boulders with sizeable bushes. He scrambled over to the place, crashing through the undergrowth to find a small dip, virtually surrounded by rocks and bushes. In this haven it was windless, though as it was without overhead cover, if it rained he would feel it. For now he was far too fatigued to worry about that. He flung his bag down and pushed his hands out of his sleeves. They came out as gnarled limbs with curved stiff fingers that seemed only capable of moving slowly as one. His thumb could be operated separately, so, with his fingers and thumb working as a kind of pincer, he clenched them together in an attempt to warm them. To his horror they barely moved, arching in slightly before grinding to halt a good three inches apart.

Letting out a string of curses he scrabbled pathetically to open his satchel, in the end giving up and using his teeth. Once open, he co-ordinated his pincers so they lifted his blanket – though it was sodden, the log within was dry, so was the tinderbox. However, after failing miserably to open the box and knowing starting the flint would be impossible (his mind had slowed to a point that it had not even realised he needed a pile of twigs and dead grass), he took a step back and tried to warm his fingers. It took him a good 30 seconds just to co-ordinate them into his trousers to warm them against his thigh. The icy jab of them against his warm legs was painful.

It was after standing hunched and still waiting for his hands to warm, that he realised how wet he was and consequently how cold he was. The rain had soaked into his woolly fleece and seeped through into his second and first layers. Likewise, the legs of his trousers were drenched.

Though his general temperature seemed to be decreasing due to lack of movement, his hands soon thawed to the point that they were useful, so he set about making a fire. Luckily, a good quantity of the straw he had pilfered from a barn was still dry and he soon found some relatively dry grass to supplement it. He had made so many fires now that with the correct tools and some shelter he could get a fire going, and place his solitary emergency log on at just the right moment.

Just the sight of the fire emboldened his spirit. It was his defence from the evil machinations; wind and rain; it was light, heat and inspiration. The heat that emanated from it warmed his limbs (he had taken his boots and socks off, for they could not have been wetter if they had been salvaged from a shipwreck on the seabed). One can hardly imagine how much of an effect this illuminating construction had on uplifting his morale.

As he gently stirred the water and vegetables he had hung over the fire, he pondered. His mind filled with images of the beauty he had seen, which led him to wonder why men busied themselves with coveting property – most of which was useless with respect to necessity – and in doing so never witnessed the most striking natural phenomena. 'A beautifully carved table may look amazing to a town-dweller, but it is nothing compared to that stretch of forest in the valley from up here.'

"Ok, I have some property!" he conceded, pointing to his kindling and blanket that lay near the fire to dry. "But it is necessity. I treasure it because I need it. And, because I need it, I know others will need it, so if I have excess I would share, for two, as easily as one, can shelter around a fire. What use is more property than you need?" He paused momentarily, then it came to him. "Money," he spat, then laughed mockingly as though to symbolise his desire to reject the concept. "Money means we can sell what we do not need, to use as an intermediary to purchase other things… sometimes other things you need. But it encourages people to take more than they need, meaning others have less. When it itself becomes a commodity, rather than just an intermediary, it becomes an addictive catalyst of avarice. Just like all the other drugs in the world, it is the most useless of its kind; alcohol is the drink which fails to quench our thirst, those mushrooms the priests take, induce vomiting, and money is a commodity with no use beyond passing on to another in exchange for something useful."

"People cry that they want more and more until they want it all – well I say, take it all! Give all the money to one person then they will see its worth – when all they have are mountains of gold shaped into disks and everyone else had intrinsically useful products, who would trade with him?

"It is quite remarkable that something so essentially useless could be so fundamental to society!" Rabica smirked to himself. "Just like religion and nationhood. They are created in society and disseminated so they become imperative – because things that useless and ludicrous must be enforced as imperative to survive! These things have to be ingrained and indisputable, otherwise they would wither away." He paused, clearly pleased with his rant. "And what is more, they inter-link – nation leaders use money to tax and enforce unity, as much as religions do. Religions need nations to police their subjects, and money helps them win power in government and over the people – 'give us money and the gods will shine upon you with mercy,' they declare."

The rain began again, though it missed him as it had changed direction to come down onto the rock behind him. He already had some reasonably dry bush branches and dug up some of their roots, which he had found were thick, woody and relatively dry. As he placed a couple on the fire he moved some more damp branches up to dry.

He rummaged through his bag, luckily the leather had held out and so only the blanket which had been on top had got wet. He quickly got changed, rubbing himself dry with the few dry sections of the blanket. The blanket would be no use as a form of bedding so he set about attaching it to some branches and rocks to construct a makeshift roof, should the rain change direction. Plus, Rabica reasoned, if it did not rain, the warmth of the fire would dry the blanket.

There was little more to do except collect up some more dryish roots and branches. With this complete he returned to stirring the broth, adding a few oats before carefully stashing them away deep in his knapsack.

As he gazed back into the fire his thoughts turned to property again. "What a stupid idea, and trumpeted as a freedom! Well, as they say, one man's freedom is another's restraint – and in their case one man's freedom is everyone else's restraint: once claimed, no one else may touch someone's property! Oh how they love themselves these 'new radicals' with their self-satisfying theories – they speak of freedom then hail private property as their core freedom – one which takes away much more than it gives. By giving it primacy they deny the provision of needs for all. Call it, that which all need, personal property – I agree with that," he exclaimed haughtily. "Only once all have personal property – what they need – then consider private property; the accumulation of non-necessity. If you begin with it then it pushes for currency and profit so the few can dominate that which others need in order to profit from it. It sets in motion inequality, which will always disempower some so that only those with such profit are capable of doing anything with the mere words of the other 'cherished freedoms'. They defeat their own promises of freedom and 'equality of opportunity' with their very first notion." He paused, catching his breath and frowning with a mixture of contempt, bitterness and sadness, before adding, "and to those who assert 'by using money we legitimise this unfair system,' I say – try not using it!" he laughed preposterously. "Look at me! I try, but I still need pots, I still need oats and food. What food I do not buy I violate private property by pilfering. I only live now because I have broken the private property code, and because I started with a huge injection of capital."

He paused in thought. "… Or else should I beg?…" He stopped and listened, as though awaiting an answer. "Oh no!" he shouted angrily, "that breaks your code of honour!"

Just as he finished he managed to fish out a piece of carrot with his spoon. After blowing on it extensively, he popped it into his mouth. It was still piping hot, so he juggled it about in his mouth, flashing his eyes and making comical expressions and noises before taking a daring bite. His teeth numbed, but he could still tell that the carrot was not entirely cooked. He shrugged. To be honest be preferred it that way.

★

The delinquent stumbled on and on down from the rotten peak, glancing over his shoulder with effortless turns of his neck. He had been walking several hours and was already exhausted. The high-flying clouds spat rain down on him, the robust wind spreading the liquid needles over a huge area. Below him, a screen of low-lying clouds blanked out whatever was beneath this desolate place, making the wasteland seem to spread out to the edges of the world.

He felt sweaty and claustrophobic even though the ferocious gale blasted against his frail body as it solemnly trudged on down the desolate descent.

The monotony of walking and the pessimistic mirage over his shoulder, which made the peak look as though it was no further away than when he awoke that morning, were conspiring to raise doubt in his mind as to whether he was actually awake at all. With hazy intermittence his mind struggled to recall the morning to check if he had actually arisen or if this was a preliminary dream. Yet he was so consumed by emaciation that he could barely concentrate his mind for a whole second. Only the sudden searing pain when his ankle buckled over a precarious rock told him that he was awake.

As he stumbled on for well over an hour he dreamed with a longing brashness to just tumble down, rolling and bouncing off the rocks, liberally shedding his blood in exchange for a rapid end to this arduous leg of his journey.

When he finally sank below the lower level of cloud it was some time before his reverie-laden focus registered the greenery of the valley below. A pale yellow-green belt of coarse grass made a near parallel patch around the mountain, acting as a bristly barrier to the thin slither of withered green which followed the river that cut through the valley as it sank down and narrowed off to the right.

He stumbled on like a beetle fleeing towards what looked like a foliage-filled crevice that lingered between the trough of the valley where it narrowed, down and ahead to his right.

The wind still blew across the open terrain like a patrolling banshee; the closest thing to sentient life, forever howling across the desolate landscape as it searched for a force to counter it. In his near vegetable state, Rabica could not even muse whether he was such a counter force as he was blown around like a seed on an endless search for ground to settle.

Having seen how effortlessly the wind passed by the clumps of grass, it was evident how lowly Rabica was when he finally reached them, stumbling over each plant as though it were a mighty obstacle. Now and again, Rabica swayed with a gust of wind to allow himself to reach out to brush his hands, stiffly forcing them from their sleeve-cocoons, against the hard bristles. Yet the numbness of his digits failed to register the tough stems as organic matter, they just felt like an icy pain on the surface of his skin.

The dark green haven was close now. Compared to the drab grassland and rocky wastes it was an explosion of colour. Though not in variety, the few visible colours were striking for their strength of colour.

It was a small, self-enclosed coppice, a bundle of trees creating a resolute canopy of shelter. Rabica used the last of his energy to rush into it. However, when he got there he was so amazed, he could not allow himself to collapse for he stood in utter intrigue.

Inside, the thick trees formed a complete canopy structure, even just a few metres inside one felt as though within a building. The dark pocket soon swallowed him blanking out the rest of the world as though he had entered a separate realm.

The bark on the trunks of the trees was a strong brown, though they, like the branches, were almost entirely covered in a stringy moss, a mess of pallid green with a frosty white tinge. It was as though pixies had laboured arduously to dry brush frost onto each and every strand of the straggly tassels. Drooping over all the branches and hanging shaggily down the trunks like excessive body hair, it dominated the tree line.

Twigs sprouted with fern-like moss at the tips, an assimilation of the role of buds or fresh shoots of the coming year's growth.

The ground was a continuous carpet of moss, so long and lush it seemed like a pre-grass turf, a prehistoric lawn. He ran his fingers through the soft fluffy turf; no longer numb, they sensitively caressed it and were soothed by the silky surface.

The atmosphere was also otherworldly, totally still and tranquil in complete contrast to the howling gale outside. The clouds were nowhere to be seen, replaced by the shaggy dark tendrils of the moss that hung in the upper echelons of the tree's branches.

The whole environment was pure and untouched, at peace with itself, asleep but conscious.

As he gazed in wonder at the base ecosystem founded on moss, Rabica pondered if this was the most advanced stage of his new world. He still could not fully believe that this mini-world was real and not an illusion conjured by his warped mind, still tortured with haunting images of moss. It seemed too much of a coincidence to exist in the real world. He fell to his knees and mumbled an incoherent apology to the flora for accusing it of being a parasitic organic amalgamation that could never be more than a 'glorified fungal leech' on whatever scant nutrients existed in an area. Here it had, independently, created a lush haven in the middle of such ravished bareness. It fed unease within him, a feeling that he had arrived at it prematurely. If indeed it was the goal of his quest, it was too at peace with itself to be compatible with his current state. Perhaps it was not even his dream, but another's that he had inadvertently arrived in during his quest to find his own. Whatever it was, it was not for him now, though it was ideal, as though waiting for someone like him to colonise. It was a domain lying dormant, unoccupied and waiting for a lonesome traveller to take up as his or her home.

Despite his extended exhaustion, he could only stay here as a brief visitor. Even if it were somewhere for him to reside, he felt he needed to know more of it before he settled. If indeed he could ever settle. He had become so accustomed to his quest being a perpetual venture that he felt it was only the continual search that kept him going. He had a feeling that something was missing, at least in his understanding of it. He felt it could not have arisen out of itself, spontaneously, in this crevice crammed between rotten peaks. It was from this that he began to establish that whatever he sought had to be on the other side of the valley, on the peaks beyond. Up there would be something spectacular, something he had to see; something that had contributed to the gradual birth of this place. But which had not had the power to stop itself being perverted on the peak he had crossed, where it had rotted and decayed as the feted lichen had formed in place of the delightful spectacle he saw before him now.

He promised himself he would return here when ready, but for now he knew his perpetual mission would drive him on to seek a more kindred land.

Chapter 33
The Lethargic Eye

Dummonius had only spent the first night in a village; the villagers' speculation concerning the unfurling of events spurred him into hastier travelling. They had spoken of all-out war. One had said Neptus had fallen and that Gatanese forces were surging across the territory for Lateria.

Though he refused to believe such rumours, he was eager not to be subject to them again as they only worried him.

This all changed when he reached the hellish Latman encampment around Leita. A grey-brown ring that smouldered with campfire smoke surrounded the small village. Judging by its size, Dummonious could immediately see that this was not just the Gorad garrison. Just off to the south of the scorched-earth perimeter was a box-shaped blur, which totally baffled the captain.

He had wondered if it was for the officers, but it was far too large. Instead he settled on it being for mercenaries, and in a way it was.

He was relieved that no one rode out to meet him. Even the checkpoint guards allowed him to pass without so much as a word. Their leader took one lazy glance at him, saw the emblem on his chest and returned to mumbling to his men.

As he entered the camp, he received ever more disdainful looks, people eyeing him with suspicion. It reminded Dummonius of the schizophrenia that had set into the military, the convergence of professional reverence and personal animosity. As a member of The Company, he held special status, but as a mercenary he was a lowly dog of war and servant of that avaricious merchant.

Aside from this, he also read lethargy and hunger in their demoralised faces, eyes ringed with thick circles of grey wrinkled skin.

Each pair reminded him of the encircled village, that shadowy patch beneath the ring, the mysterious southern box.

What had once been lush pastoral ground had been scuffed and trampled into a brown belt of slush, made all the more unsavoury by the stench of faeces and urine that coalesced in brimming ditches. The soldiers seemed to be huddled around the smouldering ashes of fires in gangs of about twenty-four - two squads. They would stop mid-sentence and stare at him with grubby eyes as he passed. Yet, still, no one bothered to question him, let alone give him directions.

Dummonius soon tired of this and waited for a particularly burly soldier to come wandering past along the 'path' (the particularly thick stream of sludgy mud that ran all the way around the camp). He had waited for a burly soldier so he could show he was not scared, as many officers were.

The soldiers' forced cordiality faltered into being genuine when he heard Dummonius' voice was not one of stuffy aristocratic breeding.

After telling Dummonius how to get to the Gorad officers' cabins, the soldier suddenly added in a hasty blur of noise, "so when's the grub coming?" He winked, accompanying the gesture with a slovenly grin. His grimy, stubbly face creased, sliding into place seemingly lubricated by sweat.

'This is the other reason for asking such types; you learn things,' Dummonius thought. He could only guess that The Merchant Prince was meddling with supplies.

His thoughts on the matter were disrupted by a shifty snarl of a voice inviting him to *"see something spectacular"*. In confusion, he gazed down to see a gangly man dressed in a once rather fine, but now shabby, robe. Sprouting out of the top of the robe was a ratty face with straggly, greasy hair, centre-parted, making him resemble a bathed and combed rodent.

Dummonius instantly thought of Pallavi and he stiffened. "No," he grunted, with repressed eloquence.

The pimp was undeterred, or at least felt the uptight manner was a front. "You must be weary, sire?" The last syllable seemed to ooze over his lips, curling out as his chin buckled lewdly.

Dummonius had already looked away and kicked his horse on, but the dissolute being began pleading, "come on Sire! Me boss only pays me on commission… and the ladies (for they are!), sir, they must get a quota to be fed… please sir… just come and take a look…" His weasely voice became more frantic. "Just come and take a look… that's all I ask… that's all I need… Sir? Sir!"

Having never come across such an industrialised form of prostitution (though it was rife in the city, rural areas and towns had, at most, brothels run by 'mothers'), Dummonius was appalled. The encounter had conjured up the image of women locked away like sows, lying limp, rocking to the whim of the clients and continuing to do so between them with perpetual motion.

He was actually glad to hear a new heckler, who disturbed him from this nightmarish vision. "Course, Company men get a discount," a sleazy voice declared. A smooth grin spread then cracked on the grubby young face, contorting it into the composure of an old crone.

He stirred his horse faster, clinging onto his good faith that Pallavi would not be among them. However this reminded him that, though further to the south, Pallavi was between him and the Gatan army. His hope was that they would be in too much of a hurry to reach Lateria to venture down there. *'Besides,'* he comforted himself reluctantly, *'she has important contacts. She will be safe.'*

As he rode on through the squalor, debauched invitations, and misery of lonely soldiers, he began dreaming of an exit strategy. His train of thought was obstructed by the rapidly solidifying notion that it was too late; the cataclysmic battle was just around the corner, and it would suck entire generations into a seemingly endless conflict.

He tried imagining Pluvius and Julia's dream, only for himself and Pallavi. But he could always hear the hungry cries of the zealots rushing over the Vaca mountains to seek them out. *'Whatever our fate, I shall go to her after this'*.

★

He had seen the cabins from a long way off, these wooden structures so comparatively solid in appearance when surrounded by the flimsy tents. They had already nestled comfortably into the mud, suggesting they had been a priority construction. A compacted mud path ran off from the main mud road, with branches off to each cabin.

A nervous young guard had politely asked for him to dismount and leave his horse at a tying bar that stood at the point of intersection between the main track and the officers' cul-de-sac. As the Captain had proceeded to do so, he was asked with a sharp abruptness attributable to fear of his reason for visiting the officers. Again he had gladly obliged, if for no reason than to present his status.

★

Now he stood in one of the cabins, Captain Gerial's to be precise. It was like being trapped in an overturned giant crate; all sides were made of wooden panels and it contained no windows. The centre of the room had a metal stove, with a tin chimney jammed though the top (for it was not a roof). A makeshift desk-table had been hastily constructed, and had two stools. Behind it sat a (in the circumstances) unsurprisingly youthful captain. He had the vapid look of a zealot.

A priest paced up and down pontificating, whom Dummonius immediately recognised as Vultai. The padre attempted to feign non-reciprocity to the Captain's recognition, but was forced to when the Captain made a rather theatrical reunion with his old adversary.

Already irritated that his intense hypnotic pacing had been disturbed, Vultai was further enflamed when Dummonius bypassed him following their brief reunion and walked over to Gerial's desk. Captain Dummonius had actually felt physical pain at being so abruptly reminded of the existence of Vultai, who he had successfully forgotten. Or at least cast into the pit of the past.

Already the priest was trying to intercept him. "Mercenary Captain" (he pronounced the M-word with the utmost of contempt, spitting it out as though casting it out of his brain.) "... We are dealing with sensitive..." (He paused to allow Dummonius to wheel around impatiently with the grace of a rebellious school child), "... material... if you would excuse us..." he indicated towards the door with a discreet finger.

Dummonius stared at him blankly. "Your eminence," - he revelled in speaking 'eminence' in the same way that Vultai had 'mercenary'. "I am Captain Gerial's advisor. How can I advise if I do not know what is going on?"

He sealed the message as rhetorical by immediately spinning around to address the Captain. "Captain Gerial, first could you confirm for me the reports that Neptus has fallen?"

The Captain looked to the side of Dummonius, who was unaware that Vultai had moved so Dummonius would not realise that Gerial now looked to him for a signal.

Vultai furrowed his brow then raised an eyebrow to tell him to give Dummonius the spun version.

Gerial obliged. "Neptus has fallen; we suspect treachery on the part of heretics. Now Gatan seeks to rampage across the land, surging from town-to-town wreaking havoc, heading straight for Lateria."

Dummonius swallowed his fear for Pallavi. Once it had been sufficiently suppressed, he thought about what had been said. Just as he was detecting inconsistency, he remembered that he was now free to speak his mind. "Surely if they are making their way to Lateria they do not have time to go from town to town?"

Vultai answered definitively, "these are a dark people, they know they are defeated and so wish to cause as much damage as they can."

Spurred on by resurgent frustration concerning Pallavi's fate, Dummonius found himself testing the limit of his autonomy by slackening his instinctive self-restraint. He slammed his hands palms down on the desk and leaned towards the captain.

"I have close friends in the region, are they just following the main road, or not? Have there been orders of evacuation?" His voice rose in tempo, and as it did so it catalysed the intensity of his concern.

Gerial nearly jumped out of his seat, before cowering back into it. Tremulously, he looked to his theological advisor.

Vultai had pricked his ears at the news that Dummonius had 'vulnerable assets' in the area. "Evacuations have been instigated, but you know people, they seem clouded by the evil descending upon us, and unable to see the refuge of the wilderness as our great prophet once did!" For a fleeting moment his countenance completely changed, roughly resembling genuine concern. "Was there a settlement in particular?"

He was still worried about the pandemonium that Pallavi would be caught up in; he struggled to wrest control of his mind from horrific images of her surrounded by a bestial grubby army of conquerors. She was so petite and pretty, exactly the kind they would seek out. His only hope was that she would use her contacts to escape, Theol had promised to protect her and get her from harm's way and he could be confident the young ragamuffin would be able to do so. But still, just the thought of his little angel being surrounded by such malaise was an affront to the decency that the whole species aspired to.

What was more, he knew he would learn nothing from Vultai, and to divulge information of his acquaintance with her would only endanger her further.

Dummonius had calmed himself and shook his head in resignation. He sighed to give himself time to recompose himself. "At least that gives us more time. What are your orders, Captain?"

Candidly and calmly Captain Gerial replied, "we are to wait here, more reinforcements shall be arriving from Lateria, and possibly our allies Telis."

Dummonius nodded. "That's fair enough. Now what of logistics? How is our food situation?"

Gerial and Vultai looked at each other; their expressions were hard to decipher, though Dummonius thought they seemed bemused. Vultai spoke on their behalf, "we had hoped you could tell us!"

Dummonius was surprised. Even if he had guessed the reasoning behind the riposte, he would rather hear it from another to show he knew nothing of it. Vultai gladly obliged. "Your new employer is responsible for such things and was supposed to be sending bread for the troops and grain for the town to build up a stock ready for the army. None has arrived and so the men are forced to buy what they can from the adjacent black market camp... it makes me wonder if *your* employer is doing this deliberately, for we all know he runs the vagabond cartel as well." The high priest was making the most of the enjoyable moral high ground, grinning with self-righteous glee as he tarnished the mercenary with the entrepreneur's brush.

Dummonius was still reluctant to cotton on. "Are these the same as those that wander the camp selling other wares?"

Vultai snorted in disgust at how the implicated dog of war was so vague in describing the crime he shared by proxy. "Do you mean the immoral lechers who seek to pervert our soldiers with offers of a woman's flesh?" His voice boomed with righteous indignation.

Dummonius found himself dipping his head sheepishly.

The high priest stood tall, ready to launch into a spiel. "Officially, they are stragglers, thugs and criminals following the army like a plague riding on the back of that other vice, the whores." He paused to eye his accused. "But we all know they pay commission to The Merchant Prince, like homage to a dark prince of hedonism, and so are protected. They began by assimilating the first moral malignancy and reaping the rewards of these pitiful sinners and their weak prey."

Gerial chipped in, "we have tried our best to defend our warriors from this plague, but few go to our sermons and spend all day indulging in sinful activity, or inactivity."

This reminded Dummonius of his other point. "What of training? I saw no troops out on exercises..."

Gerial looked at the mercenary as though he had not been paying attention. In a shocked voice he declared, "we can barely get them to temple, let alone to run about a field!"

Vultai added the dogmatic backing. "What use is physical training if it has no mental-moral bedrock?"

Dummonius was filled with sudden rage, having tolerantly sat through their accusations; he now heard how their incompetence had led to the spread of this problem. "You may find that getting them to do things they are used to, will at least stop them from indulging in such malpractice... it may even make them less apathetic to your sermons."

Vultai eyed him cautiously, evidently weighing up whether to lambaste his moral flexibility or guardedly acknowledge his sound advice. He looked to Gerial and quietly declared, "we should see if the Drill Sergeants can at least get them to do some basic exercises."

Gerial nodded.

Dummonius was already thinking, '*why not the sergeants? They can do it, they will motivate the men better and keep them under closer control*' but knew he should not push himself onto them too quickly.

Instead he turned to the most pressing issue, "the bread issue must be resolved as priority," he declared.

Gerial nodded in assent, but looked sceptical. "I have sent envoys to report it, but nothing happens…"

Dummonius smiled cunningly, "not you, Captain." He turned to his former nemesis. "High Priest Vultai, you must have contacts with His Most Exhalted Excellency Zeuorox, I trust he will apply pressures, if you so request. Failing that, the Regional Commadant must be told…"

Vultai snorted. "Fat lot of good! That heathen is on the Delvinius Board!"

Dummonius didn't even know what that meant, but continued anyway, "so what! It is his responsibility to look after his men, so he must act!"

He stopped abruptly to see if his words had sunk in.

Gerial nodded nonchalantly. "Advice taken," he declared with an air of finality.

Dummonius was glad. He needed to get out and find someone who would tell him if Pallavi was safe.

★

Dummonius left the cabin to be confronted by a faceless servant who informed him that his horse had been taken to the stables and a room made for him in a cabin near the Captain's. The gaunt young man had that uncanny servile ability of talking to someone whilst fully conscious that he himself did not actually exist in the same realm as the master. His eyes were like glass beads pushed into sunken sockets solely for the sake of imitated completion, and stared blankly off to a slant.

He spoke again in a monotone that bounced off various cabin walls, making his voice untraceable to its source.

"If you wish, I can guide you to your cabin, sir?"

Dummonius found himself unable to focus on the phantom manservant, instead nodding into the wind.

The servant set off, his lightly-soled shoes shuffling across the mud in slight movements. Dummonius followed the willow-the-wisp from a distance. Overwhelmed with a baffled unease, he decided to seek Pluvius, but first he would give the impression that he was resting in his cabin.

★

Captain Dummonius had wandered for over an hour in search of Pluvius before finally bumping into one of the sergeant's squad members. He was directed (rather vaguely, thanks to the lack of notable landmarks) to their domain.

In the meantime, he had not been approached, or even acknowledged, by a single Gorad soldier. Either they hadn't recognised him, or (as his growing cynicism inclined) they refused to acknowledge their recognition. In the case of the latter, it was unascertainable as to whether it were from fear of attracting attention, or a deliberate shunning of their traitor-commandant, who had abandoned them.

The constant reminder that Cilius did not offer to accompany him fuelled his paranoia. However, when he approached Pluvius and his men he was immediately taken pleasantly by surprise by their high spirits. He was even more surprised by Pluvius' complete reversal of the coldness of their last encounter as he perked up further upon seeing his old commander. The stocky bear gave his Captain a comradely pat on the back.

Meanwhile, the rest of the men who were present sat around a smouldering pile of ash that had been built up into a smooth sloped cone of white and grey silt. Several prodded wizened potatoes into the remnants of the fire, smearing them with chalky grey ash and black soot. Nevertheless, they seemed relatively jovial, given the circumstances.

Pluvius invited him over to join the rest of the men (who sat on bundles of kit piled together and suspended only by the play-off of various points of compression). They all greeted him with warmth.

As he took a seat beside them, he took a panoramic survey of those present, noting that Heites was absent.

A jabbing pain of paranoia irrationally spread up his spine, malignantly filling him with unease. He was especially worried by the absence of the resident cynic. Knowing direct questioning would be useless, he attempted subtly.

"I bumped into Cilius and he directed me... but there are others missing..."

Pluvius' deportment did not change, which caused a shoot of hopeful optimism to sprout in Dummonius.

"Cilius went to find out about the grain situation, Mateus has gone to find some firewood, Juscius has gone to request that we do some exercises, and Heites is training his acolytes."

Dummonius suddenly felt guilty for asking such serious questions. "It is good to see you all!" he declared candidly. "I am glad to see you in such high spirits..." He tried to pacify his erratic expressiveness, "and as for manoeuvres, I am encouraged..."

Delis laughed a brief snort, "to be honest, it's more an excuse to hunt for potatoes!" He gestured discreetly towards the small, wrinkled lump on the end of his stick.

Dummonius swallowed his anger at what the men had been reduced to. "Resourceful too!" he remarked, with a joviality that almost became lodged in his throat.

Pluvius' expression suddenly became a ponderous frown. "So why are you here?" he asked suddenly.

Dummonius was not at all shocked by the blunt question, indeed he was glad of the candour. "To advise Captain Gerial, though I feel I am just brainstorming for Vultai!"

Pluvius nodded, knowing better than to press further. "So how have the gods treated you? Has work been better?" He leaned forward, "and your lady friend?"

The mention of Pallavi was enough to destabilise his contented demeanour. Thrown into a state of malaise, he stuttered before blurting, "have you heard of the Gatan advance? I fear they are rampaging…"

Pluvius' smile instantly vanished, not from displeasure, more as a self-chastisement for raising a contentious issue. Slowly he assured, "from all believable reports they are marching straight for us and are not even stopping on towns on the way."

Dummonius knew what he meant by 'stopping on', and was relieved. He gave a gratified smile.

"It is most comforting to hear these words, especially from you, sergeant," he commented, with the utmost of seriousness.

"So you have not seen her since our last encounter?" Pluvius asked, only briefly giving the mercenary the opportunity to answer before continuing, "nor I Julia… though I am thankful she did not join the troupe."

Dummonius consolidated his solemnity into a sharp melancholy. "So, you have encountered those those crass sellers of company?"

Pluvius nodded with sullen shame, not for his own actions, but of the kind when one sees the less fortunate embroiled in debauchery. The mottled red cheeks of some of their compatriots betrayed that they were more than acquainted with the process.

Both mercenary captain and sergeant sunk their heads to inspect the ground constitute of inverse archipelagos of stagnant pools formed in the myriad of footprints.

Over the buzzing noise of the soldiers Dummonius heard the word "Captain". Instantly, his face shot up, inferring a reciprocal action on the part of Pluvius. He whispered, "listen Pluvius, I shall have to head back to my cabin." (A few of the men pulled faces at the comparatively exotic abode) "But I must warn you – do not use the new spears."

Rather baffled, Pluvius nodded, but before he could say anything the captain was bidding farewell to all and hastily skulking off.

★

The climb was in batches, it was the gradual sum of ups and downs. Now he knew why the bottom of a mountain was called the foothills. It was like climbing over a giant's feet. He passed many streams, alive with algae; streaks of it clung to rocks, resembling the beard hair of an elderly man who is swimming, except these were a reddish orange. The water itself seemed to meander and creep around the huge lumpy boulders of a deep black. Colonies of moss were strewn across the land, along with patches of lichen.

The vagrant looked up ahead. Before his glance could even reach the rise of the mountain peaks, he was enchanted by what looked like snow up ahead, though immediately he knew it was not. For one thing, it was too warm. Despite his previous exhaustion, he found a sudden spurt of energy, eagerness driving him to this enticing phenomenon.

He passed over boulders that looked as though they had been discarded haphazardly by an army of ogres. They too were mostly of a deep coal-like black, though they also had smudges of thick red. Indeed, they were quite remarkable spectacles themselves.

When he reached the sea of white he recognised it instantly as lichen; the puffy mounds had interlocked into a pure-as-snow layer. The layer followed the earth in a long gulley about a foot deep that ran off to the side of the direction Rabica was heading. Nothing got in its way, except for one red/black rock, a fiery hard coal that seemed to lie on top of the layer as though lobbed by some mighty force all the way up from the summit to where it now lay, surrounded by serenity.

Rabica gazed at this spectacle a good five minutes before continuing on along his somewhat arbitrary route.

He passed many delightful streams that flipped lazily off rocks as miniature waterfalls. And yet being exposed to such joys unleashed a mightier deluge of thoughts of Her. Her image would flash before his imagination and with it attributed perceptions of Her; compared to this angelic ideal these accidental beauties were nothing. He could not admit to missing her as to do so would imply a desire for his presence in her vicinity, something he could no longer tolerate. Instead he imagined himself as the 'gaseous spectator' again, able to ensure she was safe and revel in her perfection without causing her ill. Just the concept of him existing in her world was abhorrent enough, let alone any kind of interaction. Solitude was his only salvation; the unspoken moral obligation for the dispossessed and unworthy.

★

Rabica had clambered over many small peaks, driving himself on to a point of exhaustion, forcing himself to stop over momentarily. He found that when he stopped his pulse raced, heating erratically. He would swig a few mouthfuls of water that seemed to work like magic, revitalising and calming his body.

When he stopped he would survey the scenery behind him, the varying drops all leading down to the smooth ground level. However, often clouds would drive and engulf him so as he turned back all he saw was the deleted-film-like nothingness of hazy mist. It seemed so thick in substance, yet, at the same time, like a weightless layer, no thicker than light itself, a pure mystical blanket both endless and non-existent.

★

Rabica awoke the next day to see the early stages of the morning. Though he could not actually see the sun, a pale yellow was beginning to spread from behind the peak off to the East. Above him there were no clouds, just the fresh cold blue of sky. He gazed down the climb he had made the day before, and saw streaks of clouds drifting like continental phantoms passing by. Up higher was a thick blanket of roaming, icy cloud that rolled over the far mountains like a wave, striking and engulfing cliff rocks. Their progress was glacial, making their approach seem like fate.

Off to the West, streaky lines of varying red/orange found parallel layers of colour gradually fading into the blue sky.

Rabica pondered, *'what is the colour between the yellow and blue? – There is no way of getting from yellow to blue and if you mix them you get green, then perhaps it is a negation? Where they crossover it seems like a hazy blur where tints of both mingle and cancel each other out – Although what you see if you look closely is blue next to yellow, but on the whole it is neither.'*

Chapter 34
Firewall Shield

Lord Juscius Latman II had no idea that the spectacle down below him on the road had been carefully managed by an assorted cabal of underlings. To him the only sentient beings exerting any pressure on him were the divine.

His arrival had been choreographed, divinely or otherwise, to occur in the darkness of midnight on the full moon.

The relatively static lights of Leita managed to retain their visibility, primarily due to their permanence in the face of the multifaceted flickering of the ring of fires that ran around them. It was a small patchwork of lights, pulsating like a compact constellation contained within a circle of flame, and beyond this, a shimmering mass of still water sprawled around the firewall.

Juscius peered out of his carriage in awe. "A mighty firewall shields the universe, and beyond it lies a mighty moat of divine tranquillity that is further energised by the fires!" he remarked, his eyes lighting up with glee.

As the carriage trundled on down, he proudly thought of his Warriors of Thelus, standing by their beacons waiting for the Eastern Hordes, who were approaching in their ignorant drive across the land.

Having made such a proud declaration he was rather disappointed when the pungent aroma reached him (or more accurately, he reached it) and he learned the 'divine moat' was actually an overused ad hoc latrine system.

Once he actually reached the encampment, the stench was so wretched that he was forced to close the carriage windows and instruct his servant to light some incense. What was more, the sight of the grubby soldiers ruined his powerful imagery.

Juscius then turned to his servant. "Inform the driver that we and the convoy shall camp a mile to the east. Dispatch the messenger boy to pass on word to the others."

The servant obediently nodded, took a deep breath and in one movement opened the door, swung out, leapt onto the roof and closed the door.

Juscius wrinkled his nose at the hint of faecal pungency that seeped into the carriage. In response, he delicately took the incense and wafted it below his nostrils. The smoke rose towards the twin ducts of flesh, filling them with powdered ash that stung and burnt. He quickly retracted the sticks as the smell of singed nostril hair replaced that of the incense, somewhat embarrassed that his great lord was watching him (as he frequently did) and seen his blunder.

He began uttering a prayer of apology to Thelus, but as he did so Septimo inspired a fleck of burning ash to maliciously disrupt the prayer by leaping off the incense stick and onto the bare toes of his sandal-clad foot. He yelped, flinging the possessed stick to the floor. "Be gone and expire, foul creature of Septimo!" he spat.

★

Rabica had sheltered just before the top; he quickly packed his things and clambered up over the rocks with eager anticipation.

Over the peak he was almost blown away by what he saw before him; the black and red boulders continued for about 200 metres of virtually level ground before sweeping down into a mighty oval sand crater that had to be nearly a kilometre in diameter. He raced over the rocks, briefly observing the passing flora.

A startling variety of low-lying plants existed, always in clumps. Though Rabica had had once been to the coast and seen the sand, this smooth oval dust bowl looked totally alien, like a giant's sand pit that had been compacted down like a seabed abandoned by the sea thousands of years ago. Dust blew over it creating a mystical hazy atmosphere, trailing the floor no higher than a foot. This thick band of misty miasma added further to the ethereal aura of the place.

Save for a few sandstone rocks that looked as though they had been hurled from the edge of the crater and left to wallow in the sand for eternity, the crater was empty.

Some clouds drifted in, concealing the edges and making it look like an eternity of flat sand disappearing into the vaporous void. Then the clouds drifted in lower, skimming across the sand, hovering a yard above it and drifting along in small split-off clouds, floating across the sand like lost souls.

Rabica spent a long time soaking in the extreme void of undesecrated desolation. Had he found his domain?

★

After wandering across the basin the vagrant clambered away from his new declared abode up over large boulders. These were similar to previous ones though they were covered with ink blotches of lichen as well as some orange, red and a beautiful velvety black-purple moss. He was soon up over the edge and above the sleep-drifting clouds – here he found desolation. A pure barrenness spreading out for eternity, rising up and down in mounds of rocks and tufts. He gazed at it like these were his first images after twenty years of waiting. Despite its remoteness and unique reclusive inhabitable situation it was, surprisingly, populated with several types of plant.

He gazed at each in detail. Most numerous were the patches of a pale green, sometimes yellow little plant with almost perfectly oval leaves (they had a slight point) that measured no more than 7 millimetres at the very most. Rabica stared in wonder at each leaf, remarking in utter bafflement as to why some had a red tinge and all had darker green to highlight the veins which seemed to be indents or wrinkles. The top of each stalk bunched into tiny pointy buds.

There were numerous others, less abundant but still plentiful. One, for example, was a comparatively large plant with thick hard leaves that were white on the underside. Another was like a tiny fern that also took refuge amongst the rocks, rising up with layers of minute leaves until it fanned out into a tower of pale yellowish green.

After clambering over boulders and habitually stopping to gaze at the wonders of the desolate terrain, Rabica found the most remarkable thing. A tiny dainty little white flower, it was kind of like a snowdrop only less shapely and even more frail looking. It rose out on a thin stalk from a clump of other stalks with near identical flowers. What was more, it was so beautiful. Rabica dared not approach it lest his presence in its vicinity cause it to wither. It looked as though it would disintegrate if he touched it, making its survival in this harsh highland even more remarkable.

Later he found another clump similar to this though less spectacular, mostly because it seemed sturdier, its stalk had tiny red leaves and it was encased in a pocket of such leaves. Still, it added to this growing excitement of what Rabica felt was a remote land on the brink of rebirth.

He became convinced it was a renewal; this was the beginning of life. Even the rocks with their hard but torn look and their intense blacks and reds swirling through the surface seemed to emanate a waning energy. They were like encased obsidian coal capsules with the fire that burned with them as they were flung to the earth. The swirling patterns and velvet coats made them truly remarkable. His mind filled with intrigue about what would cause such a spectacle. Casting aside speculative fantasy causes involving fire golems and ancient civilisations, he found himself hungry for a real explanation.

A profound realisation came across him; he had been treating nature as a mystical phenomenon just as he had of Her through his idealisation. Consequently, its physical embodiment sought to constrain the extent of its aesthetic beauty, meaning it could not compare to her infinite reification in an unrestrained abstraction. This had meant he was not focusing on the real beauty of the phenomena around him, which resided precisely in the wonder of its physical realisability. He should not be mystifying its beauty, but rather, establishing its beauty through the knowledge of what constituted and caused the spectacle.

★

Lord Adonis Gatan's forces had stopped on the western edge of the Solvius Plateau, a vast raised area of agricultural land that ended with a ridge that rolled down a couple of hundred yards over the first mile before sinking down more gradually into the pastures below.

In the far distance, a grey ring visibly encircled the hazy blob that was Leira; a blotched globule of Latman civilisation stained into the rich boggy pastoral land; the ring of encamped soldiers a shock wave to this droplet of poison.

The previous night Adonis had seen a ring of fire nestled in a veil of darkness, this adding an elusive mysticism to the settlement. Now, however, it was revealed as the malignant pox on the land. It brought a smirk to the beleaguered face of the Lord; like sighting a voluptuous woman after an irksome missed opportunity who, in the light of day was revealed as an unimpressive charade now that her seductive veil and striking makeup was removed.

★

Lord Juscius Latman found the squelchy ground an affront to his divinely authoritative demeanour. It filled him with unease that this boggy land was an agent of Septimo and Neptus, the coalescing of these squalid anti-deities. In a fleeting thought he dreaded the unsavoury swamp that his Warriors of Thelus were now encamped on.

His fleeting thought snowballed into an irksomeness that determined that his mighty crusaders must press on. The Gatanese army had been sighted just up on the hilly plateau and from all reports were determined to remain there.

Just the notion of these barbarians residing on his hallowed high ground was an affront to Thelus and so demanded immediate rectification. He returned to his tent, where his servant hovered. The drone's vapid face of weariness Juscius took for cold determination. *'Such willing servants are just the thing a righteous leader needs'* he thought to himself.

"Tell the Commandants I am ready to see them."

The servant nodded, bowed and immediately despatched himself to the task. Luckily all the commandants, bar Commander Gilius of the Northwestern province (who was arriving with his forces later), were already in the new encampment, having been in Lateria with him.

He began to daydream of a victory this very night, mighty box formations of heavy infantry marching across the plains and up onto the plateau whilst hail upon hail of black arrows impotently struck their resolute armour. They would crash through the ragged black line and route the heretics!

The commandants entered as one, ambling in with tight stomachs, further compressed by stiff breastplates. They lined up, then bowed awkwardly.

"Gentlemen," Juscius began, only to be stopped by a flicker of morning light as the tent flap momentarily opened. The tall, looming form of Zeuorox swooned in and hovered behind the Generals, his full-length cassock arching over his wiry shoulders before shooting down to the ground as though he had sprung up from within it. Despite his hunched posture he still towered a head above the tallest generals.

The High Priest said nothing, prompting Juscius to lower his head in reverence. "Your Excellency."

The gaunt skeletal face seemed to glower in response, exaggerated by the flickering fire's attempt to penetrate the hood's shadowy domination of the facial landscape.

Juscius returned his attention to the commandants.

"Gatan awaits us on the hill tops; we shall march forth and engage them; with one multi-faceted fist of shimmering steel we shall puncture their lines and rout them once and for all," he declared.

The commandants clearly wanted to look to each other to ascertain if they could muster any support if they spoke out, but they were so conscious of the looming presence of the High Priest behind them they felt trapped. They glanced around at the various inanimate objects in the tent hoping to glean some motivation. The silence thickened the air like a pressure chamber.

With a stuttered start, Commander Pholius of Gorad and Gericos muttered, "sir, it will take some time to mobilise the encampment... You do not intend to fight today?"

Lord Latman swallowed hard. He had imagined just that, but did not want to seem to be tactically deficient. Luckily, he was saved by the booming voice of Zeuorox.

"I thought the whole purpose of your men being where they are was to be an advance party to be ready to stall the Gatanese hordes should we be delayed. Though I do not doubt your assertion of their unreadiness, I am troubled as to why they are not the most ready of all."

Commander Pholius shrank in dismay, he knew his men's current state was not his fault, indeed, he had been unable to rectify it by being summoned, rather unnecessarily, to Lateria. But with the blame placed on him by such an authoritative figure, he had no option but to remain silent and swallow the slingshot.

With a viable excuse for delay already established, the more opportune (Lord Juscius would say pious) commandants joined the bandwagon.

"It worries me that if we had been attacked, then part of our force here would not be ready," Hericius, Commander for Central Latman, commented vitriolically, fully aware that his own detachment in the encampment was in just as much disarray.

Then Mercenary General Arcius of the Delvinius Company Detachment declared, "my veteran Auxiliaries can be ready to march within the hour. I can have some scouts, horse archers and light infantry ready to keep the Gatan army busy whilst the Regulars organise... though I shall need some reinforcements."

Pholius saw this as an opportunity to redeem himself. "My Gorad Light Infantry are some of the best in the army, I am sure they can be ready in just as much time. Captain Gerial can command them within your command structure."

Mercenary General Arcius smiled to himself, "Captain Gerial has an advisory Mercenary Captain, does he not?" He had been told of the infamous captain's name, but also not to reveal that he did. "It is essential that he comes too – I need quick thinking and experienced captains such as him."

Juscius was pleased by the result. "So, the Light Forces can harry the enemy, allowing us time to move up and begin the sledgehammer assault."

Arcius nodded in approval. "Better still, my lord, you shall know of the enemy's deployment; strengths and weaknesses by the time you arrive."

"So there it is!" Juscius exclaimed with self-congratulation. "All commandants are to order their Captains to break camp immediately and begin forming up. Arcius, get that Captain...?"

"Gerial, My Lord," Commander Pholius prompted, rather tiresomely.

"...Gerial to mobilise his light infantry and join the mercenary detachment," Lord Latman continued, as though he had never needed assistance.

"Your Lordship?" came Pholius' voice in defiance of the lord's air of finality.

"Yes Commandant." The tiresome reply was not even posed as a question.

"My Captains have spoken of a lack of food, would it not be advisable to first allow the Light Infantry to feed from our resources first?"

"I thought you said your men could be ready?" Arcius sneered superciliously, before adopting a more progressive tone, "my forces have plenty of food, the attached force can join them for breakfast."

"There you see Commander; you needn't worry about such things," Juscius commented casually, clearly not concerned with the incongruity between mercenary and regulars rations.

"You are dismissed, Generals," Lord Latman made clear that he wanted Zeuorox to remain.

They shuffled out, preparing to ignore the muted but evident qualms of their Captains.

Zeuorox strode through the fresh vacuum not waiting for the obvious question to be asked. "Lord Telis has split his force so his cavalry shall arrive later today, he and the rest will not arrive until tomorrow. Gilius will probably be later than that." He deliberately emphasised that the Lord would not be present in the first and crucial wave.

Juscius nodded silently. His mind soon flooded with glorious images of his divine triumph over the dark forces of Gatan in a historic victory.

Yet there was something missing; he felt the righteous fire within him but it felt so mundane, so human, self-conscious piety and dedication. He had expected some mythological sensation of transcendence to bring him into communion with the gods. He had imagined that the divine words of Thelus would roll off his tongue or at least take up residence in his mind ready to stream past his vocal cords when he came to rally his men with a speech.

Zeuorox must have noticed the lord's dismay and deduced its cause as he declared, "we must prepare to link with Thelus, only then can he truly guide us."

'*Of course!*' Juscius exclaimed internally. '*One must seek such a direct link and not just expect it to seek you out!*'

Zeuorox had ensured one of his orderlies was waiting for the commandants to see when they departed the tent so the necessary equipment could be fetched immediately without the High Pontiff having to risk leaving the Lord to his own thoughts. Consequently, the orderly promptly arrived, entering with remarkable silence, considering the clunking chest he brought with him.

Just the sight of the archaic oak trunk and the intrigue of the mystical equipment inside were enough to enliven the lord's senses towards transcendence.

★

Captain Dummoius awoke unsurprisingly early, however he was rather confused by the darkness that enveloped him in the cabin. The past few days of sleeping in the open had meant he was used to being greeted by the early morning haze of light and not the noxious stench of human waste.

Outside, the ethereal glow of the sky was a strain on his eyes and he squinted with a screwed up brow as he dizzily navigated the muddy rut that was the path towards Gerial's cabin.

The door was answered by Vultai, whose pasty face, already prepared for a disdainful scowl at being disturbed, intensified into one of utter contempt when he saw Captain Dummonius.

"Yes, Mercenary Captain?"

Dummonius was not awake enough to be able to meet the priest's steely stare. Instead, he stood vacantly staring through him. Though this blank response worked better than any confrontation as the priest soon backed away, allowing him to enter.

Captain Gerial sat up on his straw mattress, so low down and tucked away in the corner he looked tiny. His night shirt was mottled with grubby stains that formed a grey archipelago on the map of white.

"Ah... Captain Dummonius! You missed His Eminence last night!" he spoke with genuine sympathy.

"Oh, I was not told," Dummonius replied, too tired to muster any real regret.

"Really?" Vultai interjected with his own brand of being genuine.

Dummonius ignored him, stepping into the room towards the desk and chairs.

Gerial took the hint. "Captain, please be seated."

Dummonius approached the stools, and sat sideways to face the Captain, leaning his right elbow on the table.

"So, I presume the Lateria reinforcements arrived as well?"

Gerial replied in the affirmative.

"So are we to advance soon then?" Dummonius inquired.

Gerial's face turned grave. "The Gatanese hordes are reported to be nearing the Solvius plateau, they could be swarming down into this quagmire tomorrow."

Dummonius stiffened at the prospect of war so soon; he was worried they would not be ready. This soon subsided as he realised that it would mean he would see Pallavi in a few days. When he considered the situation, he realised, war was likely to be even closer.

"With all our forces here they will not relinquish the high ground. I should think they will form up on the edge with their spearmen and wait for us."

Gerial chuckled dismissively. "You forget, dear Captain, that we do not face Latman, indeed not even those cautious, cowardly Lewerix!"

Vultai, though probably no more informed than the others, must have known that his acolyte was wrong and so interjected rather viciously. "The Captain seems to forget that this is our land and they are occupying it. I doubt Lord Latman will tolerate their presence on his territory."

This brought Dummonius back to his primary concern: mobilising the garrison for imminent assault. "Captain Gerial, I am here to advise, may I suggest to you a possible course for action?"

Gerial nodded. "Of course."

"The drill sergeants must prepare the garrison immediately. We would not like to be a delaying factor in his lordship's plans."

Gerial still seemed oblivious to the impending battle. "Naturally, I had wanted our troops ready for inspection for Lord Latman."

In the absence of vocal reservations Gerial addressed Vultai, "how long would it take to get the troops formed up on the perimeter ready to march to his lordship's encampment?"

"We have still not yet instilled the piety that was lacking when we took command, it could take some time," Vultai replied with a thinly-veiled swipe at Dummonius, meant as a threat to him, indicating he would be the scapegoat in any failure.

Gerial fumbled to get up in a rather embarrassing attempt to emphasise the urgency. "Well, you'd better give the order then!"

Dummonius watched Vultai's chameleon face with a sense of morbid justice. His long steely stare at the Captain followed by his riposte through gritted teeth was perfect and filled with an irony that even Dummonius found amusing. "I do not give the orders... I merely pass on yours... Captain."

The tempo, tone and timing was perfect, as was his dismissive swivel to depart. It was, however, ruined by a knock at the door that made his manoeuvring just a pre-emptive movement to the demeaning task of being the doorman.

A rather nervous messenger wearing a leather cuirass adorned with the Delvinius Company emblem entered. Visibly flustered and near blind in the darkness, he addressed Dummonius, "Captain, you have orders to accompany your light infantry to form up with the Delvinius Battalion. The rest of your garrison is to be commanded directly by Commandant Pholius. Sir."

Mutterings came from the corner; Gerial was offended at not being addressed, spitefully exclaiming, "what is this? Is it demotion?"

The messenger stuttered without actually intending to speak any words.

Dummonius calmly looked back to the messenger. "Does that include me? The Delv... merc... Company Advisor?" 'Company Advisor' was the least undignified description

"Yes," the messenger blurted before adding, "Captain... His Excellency too." He did not even dare look upon the priest. Instead, he stared forwards avoiding all eye contact and twitched nervously awaiting permission to leave.

"Thank you, you may go," Dummonius dismissed him philanthropically.

Once he had left, Gerial let out a huge sigh. Vultai, clearly revelling in the shock to Gerial, decided it was poetic, if not divine, justice.

"So, shall I give *your* order Captain?" he inquired, not bothering to conceal his smirk.

Gerial sighed and gave a brief nod.

★

Pluvius sat on the muddy barricade of clothes that had gradually dilapidated into a crusty ruin. Solemnly, he ground the charcoal from his breakfast against his teeth. The others, bar Heites, had gone in search of provisions, hopeful that his lordship's convoy had left them some food as it trundled through. Pluvius had missed the procession, though others had gone, trailed by Heites, who had returned silently with a self-satisfied expression.

He looked to the cynical veteran, who now lounged in the muddy turf, delicately prodding the ashes of the fire with a long thin twig. Pluvius was surprised that he was not desperately trying to cram in a few more training sessions with his acolytes, yet since the events of last night his intense concentration had dissipated.

The demeanour of all his men had changed since last night; however, in reverse to Heites they had undergone a transformation into serious professionals. Like them, Pluvius felt the same tightening of his chest, knowing the battle was soon to be upon them. With the flagship force now with them, it was time to ditch the lax attitude and adopt a more robust countenance. It was as though the arrival of Lord Latman had awoken them from an anaesthetised dreamworld that had lain on the brink of all-out war, waiting for the rest of the island to catch up with them. And now that it had, they had to knuckle down extra hard as they had recklessly become contented and so unprepared.

Sparked by the sudden descent of impending strife, Pluvius seized the moment to try to put a fear to rest. "Heites, come over here," he requested cordially.

The veteran began to stand, although the promptness by which he responded showed he had been awaiting summoning and was not lost in thought. He tried dusting off the wet mud, to little avail, instead just smearing his clothes and hands with sticky earth.

Towering over the hunched figure of his sergeant he responded, "Pluvius?"

Pluvius stared at the trampled mud, struggling to phrase his request carefully. "Heites, you know the big fern tree by the east wall at Gericos?"

Heites, rather confused, nodded cautiously.

"I have buried my savings and a note there... if I don't get out of this, will you take it all to Julia?"

The veteran was visibly dismayed at the pessimistic premise. "Sarge! Don't start getting all negative. Saying things like that'll bring bad luck... which is the last thing you, we, or anybody needs right now." Pluvius was adamant and defensive. "You of all people should understand the situation and respect my practicality."

Heites scowled, something he rarely did, usually because it denoted that he knew his opponent was right.

Pluvius continued. "I really care for her. I need to know someone will look after her if I don't make it."

Heites nodded soberly, resting his gaze on the ground.

Still unable to shake off his sombre demeanour, Pluvius tried to bury the subject as well. "So, you saw the convoy?"

Heites' face shot up, beaming with an ecstatic grin. "Yeah," he chuckled, unable to contain himself. "Dunno which I love most; that we were too lowly for his lordship, or the sight of all the hookers trailing after them; the priestesses of Angarra come to pay homage!"

Pluvius issued a restrained laugh.

It was then that they both became aware of an increased tempo in the blurred noise around them. However, it was not until the others arrived, notably empty-handed, that they first heard the shouts of the Drill Sergeants.

"Come on, get a fucking move on!" came the booming screech of Hari, accompanied by tired groans and mumbles, which mingled with the sound of squelching mud against their boots into a sloppy squalid sound. Amidst the shuffling people, the drill sergeant emerged, striding towards the bewildered squad.

"Pluvius, get your grunts moving!" he bellowed as he approached menacingly.

Pluvius did not move, bolstered by his men's resolute protective stance. He waited until the Sergeant was close enough for conversation.

"Drill Sergeant, what is going on?" he asked amiably.

So unused to being questioned by lowly soldiers, the drill sergeant accidently responded as though addressing a fellow Senior NCO. "The Lights are being mobilised to advance with the mercenaries." Once he realised his mistake, he attempted to re-establish his dominance as he continued on his rounds, not daring to confront the burly sergeant and his retinue. "Now get your fucking act together!"

Pluvius took a few moments to realise his men were obediently awaiting his command. He nodded quickly before setting about breaking camp himself. The rest of the men immediately assisted him, except Heites who stood watching the drill sergeant sweep through the ranks.

Hari suddenly stopped his general shouting and turned on a youthful novice who stood petrified. "Oi, laddy! What you waiting for?" he screamed as he grabbed the boy by the scruff of the neck. His brethren cowered whilst scrabbling blindly for their kit.

Without any of his comrades even knowing he was not assisting them, Heites strode over to the drill sergeant, his voice began booming in a deep voice that made the sergeant's roar seem like a squealing pig.

"Hari! Get your Effing hands off that boy, or I'll give you some much needed battle training!"

Hari kept the boy close and, turned trying to hide his shock at being addressed so. "What the..." he began.

However, by now Cilius had abandoned his kit and was striding over to stand by his comrade.

Heites had already cut the sergeant short. "Anything can happen in the turmoil of this camp, and I'm sure you want your squads to look like the most disciplined."

Hari let go of the boy and gave Heites a steely stare. "I have work to do... as do you..." With that he strode off and began bellowing at the top of his voice as though nothing had happened.

"Porthius, everything ok?" Heites asked.

The youth nodded appreciatively.

"You'd better get on with it kid," Heites declared with a smile before returning to the squad who were engrossed in breaking camp.

As he did so Cilius muttered to him, "that Sergeant is gonna get some 'sudden justice' I wager."

Heites ignored him, but he felt a tingling desire to grin.

★

They had been marching for a couple of hours. The plateau ridge was dotted with a hazy line of black that was the enemy line. The Gorad Light Infantry held the left flank. Behind them were two units of twenty archers, followed by two units of light cavalry, with Gerial's retinue sandwiched between.

All the light infantry had been ordered to relinquish their horses at the Lord's camp as they had been commandeered by the bands of young turk nobles.

The rapid pace kept their bodies warm in the chilly breeze without tiring them. Still, Pluvius' breastplate was beginning to chafe with the accumulating sweat on his stomach. He glanced to his left. Through the ranks of his own detachment he could just about make out the assorted array of 'Mercenary Lights' on the right flank. He could see the light infantry and swordsmen[11] keeping to their opposing flanks pace. Behind them, ranks of 'spearmen' struggled with their hulking weapons; though he had not got close enough to realise they were shoddy imitations of the javelin-spear he had encountered.

---

[11] These men used 'traditional' wargear; large broadswords and shields but minimal armour.

In the centre marched a huge block of mercenary heavy infantry; unsurprisingly they had fallen behind. This was something which did not trouble Pluvius as he would rather them be out of line than so tired that they were no use.

Returning his attention to the hilltop, Pluvius began assessing the terrain. Directly ahead of him, a patchy wood spilled over the edge and down towards the valley and his advancing troop. Here, the slope seemed reasonable, or at least passable. Meanwhile, the Gatan left flank (where the Mercenary Lights sought to assault), a hazy gravel patch before a rocky lip betrayed a near impassable last ten yards.

Pluvius was already planning to subtly wheel his squad as far to the left and behind the treeline as possible in the last moments before they charged. Gatan archers did not bother him so much, provided he and his men were not clambering over boulders with their shields all over the place. Rather, it was the last few yards clambering up the lip into a line of spears that worried the sergeant.

The black line had grown pink faces. Wrapped in bronze helms that glimmered yellowish-gold, reflecting the sunlight that shone down in a glorious haze. They stood casually, the spear poles now visible so the tips of their spears no longer mystically floated above them.

Just before the ascent began, Pluvius heard a shout that wavered in the breeze. Its origin was ascertained when a galloping horse, trying its best to cling onto Drill Sergeant Hari with its, rather preoccupied, backbone. *'Well at least he is going to lead us,'* Pluvius thought, noting the lack of Gerial, or indeed Dummonius.

On they trudged; every tuft of grass a waypoint to destruction. It was only now that Pluvius realised he was part of something more significant than the Neptus skirmish; this was a war for the whole island.

Pluvius almost laughed aloud when he saw the first hail of arrows leave from behind the Gatan line; he had located a notable feature that marked out when they would begin to be effective, and it was a good fifteen yards away. Indeed, he doubted they would even reach them now. But, it was lucky that he had kept an eye on the volley anyway, as he soon realised the swarm of black needles were arcing much later.

Time slowed. Heites, who marched beside him, had noticed too; his voice stretched out in the stasis sounding like a dying wildebeest. "Com-po-site's!"

Pluvius heard his own voice bellow something incoherent. Luckily his men, and some other squads nearby, heeded the inchoate warnings, raising their shields protectively. The missiles clunked like solid hailstones on the shields, shards of shaft wood splintering and pinging as they disintegrated on impact.

There were a few moments whilst the ranks buckled, though, the seasoned regiment immediately began rectifying its mistake and reforming. Pluvius fought the temptation to look behind him, fearful of seeing any fallen comrades. Instead, he returned his attention to Hari, who, despite being such an easy target, had somehow managed to reamain unscathed.

This was short-lived, as his attention was ripped away by the sound of a bugle from behind; it was the order to shift into attack formation. As they ambled into formation the bugle went again, signifying another volley was about to rain down. Raising his shield in front and above his head six inches, with his elbow forming a solid V with his limb, Pluvius braced himself. It was in the few moments whilst he awaited the swarm of long arrows that his mind caught up with events and began wondering how superior Lewerix bows had got into the hands of the Gatan army. He brushed the geo-politics aside and began thinking about how it affected him and his men. Such bows could penetrate their scale mail, and, it was said, through their shields at a close distance. This meant they could not press their shields close to them as was custom for the last volley (usually the fear was that one arrow would knock the shield out of line allowing another through, rather than that one would punch through).

As the hailstorm of arrows pattered against the Latman shields, Pluvius' mind was ablaze; how could he warn the less experienced soldiers? He hesitated, moistening his lips ready to shout a warning. But, before he could say anything the bugle sounded for them to advance. Agitated, his fingers wriggled in the shield grip.

He heard Heites attempting to shout over the resonating instrument, but this momentary rallying cry was no consolation to the grim reality. No amount of soldierly solidarity could ameliorate for the terrifying chaos that was beginning to envelop them. These swarms of arrows were just a preliminary excursion of the pitiful waste that was to come.

Despite the onslaught, the Gorad Light Infantry kept their nerve, the standing having courtesy to avoid trampling on the fallen, but all knowing better than to be distracted by their humanity as training buddies spluttered and clutched feathered twigs. On the right Latman flank, the swordsmen's unarmoured bodies made unsightly squelching noises as arrows thudded into them; the spearmen's cumbersome weapons made using their shields difficult so they too fell foul to many arrows. For them, dispersal seemed the only defensive mechanism, the physical representation of the anti-thesis of solidarity.

In contrast the Gorad Lights fused together into a mass of rounded shields. They sank into a routine, getting used to when the volleys would come, and, being seasoned soldiers, no longer needing the bugle.

Instead, it rang out to signal for the Latman archers to prepare to return fire. Pluvius' heart sank further. Engagement was less than a minute away and he felt a collective surge to the left, a mutual action no-doubt enacted by all the veterans who, like him, had noted their best chance stood in the tree line.

Over the carnage a mighty roar sounded; the archer-captain had ordered the Latman volley. Seeing a swarm of arrows hurtling in the opposite direction was quite a heartening spectacle. It was hard to gauge the actual impact on the Gatan lines but the psychological effect on the Light Infantry was phenomenal.

However, it was the counter-volley from the Gatan archers that provided Pluvius with the most satisfaction; Hari tumbled from his horse, his red cape swishing dramatically as the horse stretched its muscles now it was free of its load. Yet still, Pluvius felt remorse as his nemesis met his fate. A darkness seemed to loom over the battlefield, though it was in fact a hefty cloud, Pluvius looked up to see an ethereal bust of Julia had formed above the hilltop.

Her delightful darting eyes looked down on both lines playfully. They were thousands of toys ready to crash against each other. Yet Pluvius was not disgusted by her amusement.

He could not criticise her, she, who had been exploited by such men, often in response to their aggression towards other men. His only regret was that he found himself compelled to be part of this mess.

After all, that was what men needed when they were engaged in such testosterone fuelled destruction: the ridicule of an attractive young woman. Indeed, it set Pluvius thinking, if such a woman was to materialise between the two hordes and be so derogatory, would they cease in the carnage?

Bring in Torian, bring in Pallavi, and every wife and lover on the island. Could they stop it? Let the Maritha's and Hierda's stand either side and call their sons and husbands to peace. Could they?

But he, like them, knew it was all futile. Pallavi wants to see Dummonius again. Julia doesn't want to admit it, but seeing Pluvius again will make life worth living. Arios doesn't want to march alongside Geric; he wants to hold him tight.

But alas, the gold jingles, the priests plot, and the ghosts of the past linger, whispering the word vengeance. This war could not be thwarted by petty emotions.

Pluvius passed the first scraggy shrub. It was only a matter of time before they would charge. As the regiment flanked right, Pluvius skirted his men straight ahead at a quickened pace to make a flanking manoeuvre. The rest of the squads either did not dare question, or saw the utility of a flanking squad.

They could now ignore the timing of the volleys of arrows. Though the saplings were of little protection, that they were no longer part of the whole, meant they were not targeted. He heard the roar of the rest of the Gorad Lights as they charged, the noise spurring them on, so they could break the line.

★

The moment a scale of Latman armour glimmered in the morning sunlight, the brigands sprang their trap; each piece of foliage symbolising a split second of time as they charged at the flanking unit. They were impressed by how quickly the Latman soldiers had their gladius' in their hands.

Yet, the mighty barbarous weapons crashed through the short sword's defensive postures. Several were felled immediately, stumbling in incongruent staggering as they spiralled down like spiders down a plug hole. The sergeant and his adjacent minders managed to dodge the blows where their swords had failed. The burly one with a hefty bastard sword was immediately on the counter, slashing forward with mighty swathes that opened up gruesome incisions on the brigands' bare flesh.

★

Pluvius, baffled by the sudden appearance of marauding feral barbarians, thought this was a reverse re-run of the coastal encounter. It felt as though everyone was siding with Gatan; first Lewerix bows, now barbarians. As he slew them, he found himself intrigued by these creature's origins; they were not blond, like the baresarks, indeed they looked like unkempt Rudian's. He could hear Julia mocking him for his brutal masculinity forcing him to slay that which he did not understand, and have the audacity to label them barbarians.

A hefty double-handed axe came swooping down at him and his shield was raised to block it. However, its impact was phenomenal, knocking him off balance and onto the mossy floor. Dazed, he struggled like a beetle. The plumes in his helm splayed in the slight breeze, marking him as a prime target. For some reason he thought of the white fur cloak he had pilfered from the baresark raiders, which he had left at the encampment, caked in mud.

He had just enough time to look up and catch the eye of Heites who was buttressed up against a burly adversary, his yellow teeth bared like a wolf. What he did not see was the old veteran falter as he witnessed the sergeant's demise.

It would be comforting to describe a melodramatic montage to summarise Pluvius' life, even more so to claim he thought of Julia as his life ebbed away. But the brutality of reality has no time for such emotive dwelling.

Rather than enact his revenge on the feral troops, Heites realised it would be better to save the rest of the squad from a similar fate. Besides, it was not the fault of these warriors; it was the generals and lords sitting on their horses testing their prestige with others' lives. He swore to get his revenge on the real perpetrators: Vultai, Gerial, Juscius, Ruperis and that vulture Zeuorox. That parasitic theologian owed his life to the sergeant, for he had stopped Heites from slipping a dagger into his wrinkled throat.

"Fall back!" Heites bellowed, lunging and leaving his gladius in the thigh of his adversary. Cilius turned immediately and fled. The rest disengaged more slowly. Heites, assuming command, looked around to assist anyone caught in combat. He saw Arios slashing wildly keeping several at bay. As he blocked with his shield and backed away, Heites called out to him.

It was then that he saw the reason for his delay. His helmet buckled, Geric emerged from Arios' feet. He seemed in a daze as he tugged Arios to pull back, stumbling forwards as he did so.

The remnants of the squad thundered down the hill; luckily their opponents' hefty weapons meant their advance was ponderous and slow.

Cilius, who was by far ahead of the others, led them towards the line of archers who were raining death down on the centre of the Gatan line.

★

Captain Gerial flapped helplessly as he saw Pluvius' routed squad sprinting out of the shrubs. Vultai sulked under his immense robe; he was sure the gods had told him in his sleep that they would be victorious. The assault on the flank was not going anywhere, which meant it was a failure. Though it had fared better than the mercenary assault; the bank of the plateau was far too steep to traverse and the regiment had been forced to wheel round and fall back towards the mercenary heavy infantry that had taken up position in the centre.

With their backs exposed, the volleys of arrows from the composite bows were lodging deep into their bodies. The fallen squirmed like crushed beetles, as they continued to struggle towards the shimmering fortress-square that was the heavy infantry. Under such fire, they had fragmented into a disparate mass of routed individuals; those lucky enough to survive each salvo leaping over those that fell.

Exasperated, Captain Dummonius hesitated before usurping the dithering commander. "Call the retreat!" he finally bellowed to the buglist.

The young boy hesitated then looked to Gerial. His fingers tapped the instrument nervously.

"Captain Gerial, get the cavalry to hit the marauders when they come out of the forest. And get the rest of the infantry to disengage before they are cut off!" he shouted.

Captain Gerial jolted nervously, and twitchingly looked around. His mouth sneered like an upset child as he spoke.

"Those heavy infantry should be moving up! They can plug the gap." He waved his finger accusingly at the solid formation to the rear.

"They are the only solid unit on the battlefield! If they move towards us then the right flank will have nothing to fall back to, and will be ridden down by a Gatan excursion."

Captain Gerial ignored Dummonius and began shouting at the heavy infantry.

His heart pounding with rage, Dummonius brought his horse close to the bugler. The boy cowered. Dummonius ignored the reprimanding bark of Vultai and snatched the bugle. In a moment he had kicked his horse into a canter towards the light cavalry.

He fumbled with the instrument, pushing the buttons in a clumsy ad hoc fashion. It let out a muffled screech, which at least caught the attention of the cavalry. As his horse broke into a gallop he thrust his arm through the bugle's strap and let it swing beside him. He drew his gladius and waved it at the bulky black forms that were emerging out of the woodland in pursuit of the squad from the Gorad 3rd. The cavalry obeyed his order and charged. The thunder of hooves and accompanying roar of the men a defiance of the screeching of the soaring Gatan arrows.

When Dummonius reached the remnants of Pluvius' squad, the cavalry had already swept through the advancing Gatan marauders, lunging their lances into their enemy without engaging them and already circling around to re-engage. He rode over to Heites, the sombre expression on whose face meant that he didn't need to ask of the fate of their sergeant.

Instead, he called to his surviving comrades, bellowing, "on me!"

Delius and Hydius were immediately at his side, their shields held high to stop any arrows coming their way. Cilius continued running towards Vultaim a maniacal grin twisting his face into that of a gremlin. Arios, pulling a wobbling Geric along with him, soon reached them. Though he bore no sizeable lacerations, Geric had suffered a hefty blow to the head, which meant he swayed weakly and collapsed onto the hulking bulwark of a soldier.

Dummonius looked down pitiably at the young soldier. "Is he wounded?"

"Just a bit battered, Captain," Arios barked defensively.

Dummonius gestured at the back of his saddle. "Get him up here."

Reluctantly Arios obliged, dragging Geric over to the horse and, with the assistance of Delius, hauled him onto the horse's rump. It nervously trotted forward a few steps, but soon settled.

Geric slumped forward, resting his head against Dummonius' shoulder, his hands weightlessly fumbling to get grip of the Captain's torso. His eyelids flickered, struggling to stay open, finally capitulating as his head sank down.

Dummonius looked up to see that the rest of the light infantry had disengaged. Their opponents slowly advanced towards them; the cumbersome line of spearmen wary not to break their line for fear of a counter attack. Meanwhile, the Latman cavalry were forming up ready to charge the impetuous marauders, who had ceased advancing and stood stranded from their line. Dummonius smiled to himself, knowing their hefty weapons would be no use in another lightening strike from the cavalry: one shallow victory in an otherwise unmitigated disaster. He didn't even dare look at the shambles of a force that was the remnants of the right flank. Without another word he tugged on his horse's reigns, signalling the retreat. It was only now that he remembered that Cilius was still fleeing. "Soldier! Form up with your unit!" he bellowed.

The infantryman took a brief glance over his shoulder and grinned contemptuously at the captain and continued running. He wouldn't take orders from any of them; especially treacherous deserters to mercenarydom.

As acting squad leader, Heites tried to shout to him, only to receive an equally dismissive glance. To Cilius he was another whipped cow. Heites shook his head in dismay; even before the new interpretationist takeover, this was cowardice, and punished accordingly. Still, he was surprised when he heard the order relayed to the leader of the archers, who acted as conduit to the death warrant.

"Cilius!" Heites shouted.

The bows raised in perfect synchronicity. As the strings were pulled back the shafts creaked like chewed bones, a teeth-clenching groan. It was a calling to death that Cilius sought to cheat, putting a final spurt of energy into his now aching muscles.

The volley of arrows honed in on their target like a swarm of hornets. They whined as they descended. Numerous arrows struck him, sending him sprawling to one side. A second later, blood began to seep out of the holes, collecting around the arrow shafts, before trickling down them and soaking into the feather tails. Cilius squirmed stiffly. Those that had missed had sunk deep into the mud, small wells of water accumulating around the shafts, a mocking mimic of the leaking lifeblood.

The squad bowed their heads solemnly. Heites felt a resounding guilt wash over him; he had been the one who had made a rebellious acolyte of the soldier. He had seen Cilius' deterioration as rage against the powers that be had consumed him. It was such a waste, to make a negligible stand of defiance with such definite consequences.

Heites glanced over his shoulder, the rest of the Latman Light Infantry were falling back unpursued. This was mainly on account of the Heavy Infantry advancing in a reformed block that stretched out across the line. The handful of survivors on the right flank sprinted for the Latman line, clearly deemed too few to risk pursuing.

Dummonius lead them in a slow trudge towards the command unit. Heites could see the exasperated expression on Gerial's face, even from this distance. Vultai must have muttered something to him as he turned to him and nodded, sending a flash of reflected light from his helmet at the approaching beleaguered squad.

As the retinue began to advance towards them, Heites felt a throbbing pressure in his throat. This irksomeness was confirmed when the burly retinue, rather than stopping in front of them, encircled them. Their heavy horses snorted and stomped their hefty hooves anxiously. The grim faces of the guards gave a sign of what was to come. This was further confirmed by them drawing their swords. Gerial breathed heavily, calming himself ready for his declaration. "Mercenary Captain Dummonius, you are under arrest for disobeying orders, usurping authority, mutiny, undermining morale, causing our forces to rout, and theft of Latman military property."

Dummonius' jaw swung open in shock. He opened his mouth to ridicule the accusations, but was shouted down by Vultai.

"Dummonius, you will answer when and what asked! Any further deviation from protocol will add to your crimes!" The priest's beady eyes flashed with righteous pleasure at finally being able to say such a thing to the Captain.

Dummonius knew better than to answer back. However, Arios, never one to be bound by such convention, angered by the death of his brother-in-arms and such treatment of his commander, spat on the floor.

"You lay a single scrawny finger on him, you rat, and I'll snap it off." The shocked High Priest, still celebrating his victory over Dummonius, was in no state to counter. Turning his attention to Gerial, Arios continued, "as for you, you incompetent whelp! This Captain is all that was standing between you and the annihilation of the whole regiment." He turned and pointed a tarantula finger in the direction of the remnants of the mercenary force. "That could have been us!"

Gerial breathed in slowly to try and hide his fear. He did not address Arios; turning to Heites he addressed him coldly. "You are now acting sergeant. Sergeant, you can save your men from sharing their fate with this mercenary captain if you form up with your regiment when it returns."

No one noticed Vultai scowl. He had planned to rid himself of the troublesome squad.

Heites was torn. Still plagued by the sight of Cilius' arrow-riddled body, he did not want to condemn the rest of the squad to a similar fate. However, he felt a pressing obligation of solidarity with the Captain who had saved their lives. His mind was awash with arguments over how far he would compromise his ideals in order to survive. He turned to look to his brethren; each in turn gave a brief shake of their heads. Spurred on by their counsel, his rebellious mind declared that now was the time to make a stand. They could not just execute a Captain on the spot, nor his 'accomplices'. The circumstances were totally different from Cilius; the whole regiment, if not army, would witness their defiance. They would see soldierly solidarity and loyalty to a true worthy officer, and they would see it punished in cold blood.

Furthermore, to his surprise, the usually quiet Delius spoke up. "Captain, you do not expect us to carry out another assault do you?" His calm voice bolstered by genuine disbelief.

Both priest and commander gave expressions of disgust at a lowly soldier speaking out of place, but it was Vultai who spoke. "We have a duty to keep the enemy occupied until the rest of the force advances."

Arios spat again and shook his head. "Well, you'd better lead the next wave! At least Hari and Visuvius did that."

Vultai gave a look of fake surprise. "Ahh, it is that squad is it... I should have known." He paused as though piecing something together, giving Dummonius a wry smile that chilled him to the bone. "Drill sergeant, strip them of their weapons, search them, and arrest them. Dummonius, dismount immediately," the priest declared, doing away with the facade of Gerial's command.

Several of the retinue dismounted and began pulling the daggers out of the infantrymen's sheaths. Only Arios resisted, slamming his shield against his arrestor. Heites cringed, but was thankful that Arios was soon surrounded and gave in. They all unbuckled their shields while Dummonius cautiously dismounted, keeping hold of the partially conscious Geric as he did so before lifting him down to the ground.

The guards began rummaging through the soldiers pouches, throwing half-eaten hunks of bread onto the ground disappointed. Suddenly one of them shouted to Gerial, a tiny slip of paper held between his hefty fingers.

"Bring it here," screeched Vultai, like a crabby child.

By this time the guard searching Arios was holding a similar parchment.

Vultai stretched a wiry arm down to take the paper and opened it. "Aha!" he declared, primarily to himself, but fully aware that he had an audience of minions. Again to himself he whispered in delight, "an address! And if we compare this to parchments in Dummonius' office..." his voice trailed, overwhelmed by his perfect detective work.

Gerial, who did not want to seem to have lost control then interjected. "That address must be searched..."

It was only now that Dummonius realised what the paper was. "No!" he shouted. "She has nothing to do with anything!"

"With what?" Vultai retorted accusingly.

Dummonius was silent.

"Captain Gerial, keep the prisoners under guard. This will require higher authorities to deal with." Vultai declared. He immediately turned his horse around and without another word, enraptured by his success, rode off to find Zeuorox who would be with the advancing army.

Once he was out of earshot Dummonius looked up to Gerial. "Captain, do one last thing. Do not send the Gorad 3rd out again. They have taken punishment enough for today."

Gerial said nothing. Still dismayed by the priest's sudden departure, and lacking any guidance, or people to blame.

★

The rocky path brought him around a small mound of rock sprinkled with boulders and tufty grass. There it was. Rabica gasped. Off the pass, a smooth shape of fine black powder was littered with boulders; huge chunks of reds and greys, each sprouting an ecosystem of velvety black-purple moss and black lichen. The moss was splattered on the rocks like a negative impression of polar ice caps on a globe; a pitch black that radiated a silky purple-maroon shine. As Rabica charged down the hill the ground resembled rubble; small chunks of red rock like chipped bricks as though this was an ancient building site. Where it smoothed out, he saw what looked like a mini desert, much like the dust basin he had seen before: perfectly flat, desolate sand. A river of rocks meandered towards the centre. Rabica's eyes traced the path of the rocks until he saw the spectacle in the centre; a black mound of bumpy rock. It was truly stunning; a near perfect circle like a coral reef made from a knobbly black rock. It was completely surrounded by flat compacted sand, save for the sporadic rocks that rested like tombstones in the open plain around it.

Behind it rose a range of hills of sandy brown. There were four peaks in all. The first two were studded with bumpy rocks and ridges. The third was smooth and seemed to slither down itself with cascading winding contours. The fourth split open; its far side rising above the nearer, to partially expose the red rock of its crater peak. It resembled a monster's lips; grey sand spilled over the left corner as though the monstrosity was dribbling. Rabica squinted and focused on the gaping mouth. To his utter surprise and delight he saw smoke rising. He couldn't believe it. At first he had a horrible thought that others had come here before him. Then he feared crazed local inhabitants of unheard barbarity had an encampment there.

Rabica rushed to the coral reef. As he neared he saw that it was not just the sand that came surging down the third peak; a legion of grass tufts were spilling down onto the basin, some had even reached the coral rock.

The reef itself was not one lump, but of countless weather-beaten clumps resembling pre-processed coal soaked in the salty seas until it became wizened and knobbly. Rabica picked up a small piece; it was surprisingly light, as though just the essence of rock.

The white flower lichen was also part of the tufty grass's assault. "But why attack?" Rabica pondered in bafflement.

As he clambered past the grass-lichens' furthest advance, he looked across the 'coal-reef', but just saw endless mounds of knobbly black ravines and peaks. He stepped up onto the coal-reef plateau and crouched down low to gaze over it as though it was its own giant world, a mass of volcanic rock. Suddenly, Rabica's heart jumped – he saw, tucked away in a ravine, a dainty little white flower, virtually, if not exactly, identical to the frail flower he had seen on the other peak.

"Was this what the invasion sought? – this seething mass of life he had once seen as beautiful was rampaging across this alien world to destroy a petal so delicate?"

Rabica decided to press on. He wandered towards the gully, which he had designated a path.

This path was a hard climb obstructed by countless boulders in a sea of rubble. Nevertheless, determination drove him on. He only stopped once on the thirty minute climb to guzzle some water. It seemed as though some mighty palace had collapsed under its own grandeur and showered down the gully in a hail of debris. His mind filled with glee as he instantly thought of the Lewerix palace.

When he reached the top of the gully, he was perched on a trough between the third peak and the rocky cone of the fourth. The latter rose high into the sky; by rough estimation he was barely a quarter of the way up. The slope gradient must have been over 45° and the ground was loose gravel. All he had done so far was clamber up the now extinct stream between the two peaks, but this fourth, with its crater, was so enticing, rising way above the others. Rabica knew he would have to ditch his pack and attach a small water skin to his belt.

Once ready, Rabica sprinted forward, grinning with manic anticipation. The slope was made of tortuously slippery gravel. The cascading avalanche of grey stones that jingled down behind him only spurred him on. Indeed, to an onlooker it would look more like he was a beetle trying to burrow into a giant mound. He made a beeline for larger rocks, pushing them in with his white and red mottled hands, before hauling himself onwards.

Rabica glanced upwards, spotting a formation of sturdy-looking rock that protruded out of the shingle like a desolate island jutting out of the high seas. He paused, panting as he clung to a small boulder, perched behind it in a hunched, goblin-like posture, greedily eyeing the new found haven. Between him and the rock was a stretch of fine gravel. He squinted at the obstacle, counted to three then lunged forwards. Each step slid back down a good eight inches, yet he powered himself upwards, sensing his advance in altitude was being thwarted too easily. Filled with an uncontrollable desire to soldier on, he sank down to all fours and bounded upwards, flinging dusty grit in all directions.

Rabica finally reached the rugged rocky formation of the mountain itself that protruded out of the shingle. Panting manically, he stopped momentarily to take in his surroundings. The clouds had swept in, engulfing the delinquent in a purgatorial haze of blank white. It was an endless void of weightless nothing, filtering out the rest of the world and giving the appearance that what he progressively saw was being constructed as it became visible.

As he neared the top, the rock briefly turned a black colour, then a faded red. It resembled red hot coals the morning after a fire, but without the emanating heat.

Finally, he reached the top and was looking down into the crater. He almost fainted, not from exhaustion, but from love. Nothing could compare to this magnificent descent into scorching reds. Nature was the mightiest creator. He dropped his water bottle from his belt, and ventured closer. Rabica gasped in shock. There opposite him was an opening just like an oesophagus – the orifice down to the creature's heart deep below. It had two prominent walls that protruded out, down to a lip at the bottom, meeting in a U-shape, which had a solid cylinder, like spliced cartilage, at the trough. The upper lip arched in like an upside-down V, the walls retreating back as they moved closer. Directly above it the ground was a fine pitch black – the kind artists dream of. Its stunning colour was matched only by the red rock around and below. It was truly the most striking pure essence of natural red in existence. Rabica poetically suggested that from the orifice nature's eponym red had gushed out, staining the nearby rocks with its pure shade. He looked at the rocks adorning the crater rim; here a more dull, greyed red, the same red as before, only exposed to the elements for several thousand years.

As he stood staring at the beauty of the crater's bright red, its surrounding sub-layers of reddish browns and yellows, and the looming presence of the black, Rabica, for a fleeting moment, found himself thinking of Her. It came as quite a shock; he had become so wrapped up in his own solitude he had almost forgotten about Her. She who had been so crucial to spurring him into this self-imposed exile. Though he was sure he missed her deep down, it wasn't just Her he now missed. He missed the him that was continually longing for Her. Now he was so far from the society in which they had coexisted, he could see that he had drifted out of the paradigm that rendered them even the slightest compatibility. Yet he still cared about her, and saw her as a force of good in that ugly society.

He quickly realised he was speaking of his own conjured impression of her character and not the 'Her' of reality. Nevertheless he shrugged dispassionately. "So what? That imaginary version of her is who I fell in love with, so it makes sense. I can never escape that idealisation of her who I worshipped, nor the real one I adored. For both played such a crucial part in the unfolding of my life," he declared, as though confessing candidly to the crater. "Maybe I sound harsh, or self-centred, but I know not about her, though I am sure her life is no worse without my presence... that is, after all, what I established that final night before my departure," he explained defensively.

The image of Her face floated in his mind. He thought of being with her, the warmth radiating off her and comforting him with a warming sensation. Consequently, it reminded him of his solitude and coldness. He was remote and alone; seeing a remarkable spectacle of nature. Her angelic form floated before him; he knew, but did not care, that this was just an idealised image of Her. She always would be part of his psyche. Both the actual Her and the Her he had conjured, were intertwined with the fundamental epochs in his life, and could never be discounted. With remorse he acknowledged that she was both a major cause of him being here now, and a, if not the, reason for him wishing to be elsewhere. Had his whole mission been in vain, a hopeless task of escaping Her?

He shook his head. There was so much more to it; he had escaped the world he loathed, and besides She was now free of him. Surely that was more important than his own fancy? Besides, he now knew that though he could never escape his feelings for his reified ideal of Her, there was a greater beauty that resided in the understanding of the spectacle of nature.

He returned his gaze to the crater, focusing on the oesophagus. From it had spewed the material that had created those patterned rocks and moulded the land he had trekked these last few weeks. The 'head' of the mountain had been blown off, but it had not ascended to the heavens, it had been scattered in the form of the rocks he had seen at the foothills. Just attempting to imagine the raging energy that had caused that outstripped his initial explanation that ogres had cast the rocks down. That eruption of energy and material had no doubt brought much destruction, but at the same time opened up an opportunity for renewal, its relative impact on what existed before creating all the different phenomena he had witnessed in his travel over the mountains.

He found himself thinking of the forest he had named the latter haven. Was he now ready to go to it? He had seen the source, and on the way many stunning things. He knew he could walk no further; there was nowhere to go from here. If he wandered over the hills he would find nothing more stunning than what lay before him now.

Looking intently at the oesophagus, an erratic inkling in him wanted to believe the top of the mountain had blasted away to escape the world that had held it captive, but this was a pathetic fancy, seeking to mystify a natural event in order to justify the urge to dive into the chasm to join it in its escape, purging all his fears and qualms. He knew he needed to accept there was no mystical escape from the past.

He began to stumble back down the slope from where he had come. As he did so he increasingly felt the cold. Now he had reached and passed the climax of his venture, he was beginning to feel the weary emaciation and true extent of his extended exhaustion. The blinding adrenaline rush that had silenced his inanition for the past weeks was fading rapidly. He found himself not only reeling at the excruciating pain he had unwittingly forced himself through, but also he was awakening to the bleak practical prospects that lay ahead due to his ignorance of such issues for so long. It was like waking after an anaesthetic has worn off; during which time you had beaten your body to a bloody pulp. He was cold, exposed, exhausted, hungry, and had virtually no resources.

★

The mainstay of the Latman force did not arrive until the onset of dusk. This had put the already distressed Juscius Latman in a foul mood. He refused to see anyone, even Zeuorox, much to the dismay of the High Priest, who was anxious to get the traitors 'processed'.

The Grand Pontiff paced up and down his tent. His acolyte Vultai hunched in the corner, stroking his well-trimmed beard nervously, not daring to speak lest he upset his Holy Eminence.

"It is entirely that foppish-cur Ruperis' fault! If he hadn't been too cowardly to join the battle he could have spoken to his Lordship!" he expostulated to himself.

He stopped pacing and gripped his lower lip between his teeth, allowing his wiry face to contort into a wrinkled mess of fleshy irrigation canals towards his pinched mouth.

"I have a good mind to reveal his whole behind-the-scenes scheme!" he spat acrimoniously.

"No, that would only add to my worries," he countered.

Vultai shuffled nervously, scratching behind his ear where sweat was beginning to collect.

Zeuorox gritted his teeth, his translucent skin stretching over his skull, the wrinkles bunching together like lifeless veins meandering across his skeletal face, snakes waiting to pounce. He turned to bring this frightening gaze to bear on the priest, who stood furtively in the corner.

The onlooker nervously stroked his immaculate beard, his young flesh glistening with life in the torchlight. His wisps of facial hair were slick and waxed, a greasy wave that momentarily switched directions with each stroke.

As Zeuorox's gaze intensified, he felt forced to comment. "Perhaps, Your Excellency, you should consult Thelus, he often..." He was cut off by the skull uttering a mocking snarl.

"Who are you to talk of Thelus, boy? You know nothing! Get out of my sight and make sure those prisoners are secure... who is guarding them?" he added with sudden paranoid clairvoyance.

The priest stuttered, taken back by his holy leader's dismissive rebuttal. "The Gorad 3rd, Your Excellency... they were arrested by them so..."

The skull creaked, its dry teeth stretching out of the thin purple lips. "Fool! At least get another Gorad regiment to keep watch."

The priest shook, petrified to the spot.

"Now!" Zeuorox barked.

Vultai fled the room immediately.

★

Darkness had engulfed them rapidly. They were surrounded by a crude pen and were bound tightly at the wrist and only slightly more loosely at the ankle so they could shuffle about. Most of the men had managed to sit with their backs to the fence, albeit awkwardly. Arios squatted beside Geric. Geric himself was sprawled out, his whimper the only sign of life from his crushed body.

Only Heites and Dummonius stood, the Captain scratching his digits behind his back with anxiety for the sake of his beloved Pallavi. No matter how much he tried to not think of her unwitting wait for capture, he could not. His mind seethed with anger, knowing that to act, even kill himself, would only incriminate him further, and so her. His only hope was that Theol would hear them ask about her at the inn and warn her in time. But he knew this was remote, that even then, it only gave her a slither of a chance. Worse still, he would never know.

Heites, meanwhile, attempted to stand proud, but could not help but feel his stubborn defiance of his fate only sought to infuriate his condemned men. His posture sank.

"Sarge..." Hydius began.

Heites shot him an angry stare. "Do not call me that!" he snapped.

"You are our new leader; it has nothing to do with what that priest said..." Hydius protested.

Heites shook his head. "I could never replace Pluvius; he was the only man to have respect from all of us. He united us, he made us a collective."

"We all made the collective. We all still do." Delius commented.

Hydius nodded in support. "And we have our captain back," he added.

Heites, feeling the burden of collective responsibility collect around him as the newly designated leader, recognised he needed to accept the post, even if it just meant passing it up to their returning officer. He turned to Arios, who must have sensed the acting sergeant's gaze, as he turned to face him. He gave Heites a nod of assent.

Heites approached Dummonius, calling his name to gain his attention.

"Captain Dummonius, will you rejoin your old regiment? Join it in its final act of defiance?"

Dummonius snapped out of his troublesome trance. His face lit up as the collective consciousness enraptured him. "Heites... Arios, Delius, Hydius... Geric; we are the remaining loyalists of the Gorad family. We are all brothers; do you accept me as elder brother?"

"Captain," the men uttered in unison. Even Geric mumbled something that sounded like assent.

Though he felt comforting warmth from the reasserted solidarity, Heites could not help but feel frustration at not being able to avenge the death of Pluvius.

He shook his head in dismay. "Julia will never know his fate..." he uttered, his voice trailing as he thought of how his comrade had been cheated at the last hurdle.

They heard noises outside the makeshift cell.

"Adeptius and Hidius will be joining me in a moment. They just got stuck in the chow queue. If you go now you'll get there before the next batch. Don't worry, I won't tell."

The prisoners listened for the sake of a distraction. They heard the sound of hefty boots clomping on sodden earth. Moments later the gate was open and a weedy soldier stood before the downtrodden men.

The sight of this youth was only uplifting for one of the men: Heites. It was Porthius. "Heites!" began the boy.

"It's sergeant to you!" cut in Hydius.

Before the squad could react Porthius was already behind the bulky veteran with his knife out as he spoke. "Quick! You don't have much time... I checked the roster; they haven't included the wounded one... I'm sorry I can't let others go... for they will notice."

The rest of the prisoners soon caught on and so remained silent so as to not attract attention from outside.

Heites was soon free and turned to face the boy.

"Heites, your training saved my life; it is only fair I return the gesture."

"Bu..." Heites began, ready to protest, looking to his comrades.

"Go!" they all whispered.

Heites hesitated. As the champion of solidarity, he felt he was betraying them.

Arios looked up from nursing Geric. "Heites, get out of here. You were the first to see what was coming. Remember, when Kilnos was killed, we buried my idol, because death only solidifies our unity; we have our collective grave, but as long as one of us lives we all live on."

Heites nodded slowly before turning to Dummonius. "I will go to Fericoa. I do not remember the house but I remember you told me of Theol; a trustworthy boy, he can lead me to Pallavi."

Dummonius nodded ecstatic thanks. Even if Heites failed, he could die believing he had succeeded.

"Hydius, your wife, she lives near there does she not? I will seek her. Delius, your family is in Promthius. I know that town, I shall find them."

"A hamlet called Gerd," Hydius responded.

"If you can, go to Hius; Geric's parents live there," added Arios, who had no relations of his own.

Heites nodded. "And I shall tell them that he was in the good care of a trusted friend to the last. A mighty warrior by the name of Arios."

"Now go!" Dummonius ordered.

Porthius led the soldier out, and they embraced briefly before sneaking out.

With that, Heites was gone, and not a sound ensued. The prisoners and solitary guard remained silent, fearing the sound of his capture.

★

Heites crept along the latrine ditch. Though sheltered from the chilly breeze, his nostrils filled with the nauseous stench of faeces. Either side, he heard ghastly groans of wounded soldiers from inside the tents. The roofs peeked over the ditch like giant toadstools. In the darkness his vision filled with the face of Brother Visuvius, blood trickling from the gash in his skull. He gazed up at the sky to see streaks of cloud stained an orange-red in homage to spilt blood.

Startled by the chaotic sounds and sight, Heites flung himself down low onto the bank, burying his face in cold earth, trying at least to shut out the visions. The words 'cold murder' seemed to emanate from the earth, sending a chill down his spine. With no actual objects to see, his mind conjured its own horrifying imagery, spurred on by the sounds. In this visual plateau, more tent-mushrooms sprouted from the ground; inside each came the groans of all he had slain in his gruesome past, murmuring in agony. These bulbous organisms cannibalising the claimed souls of Septimo, spreading their rot, it was as though Sepitmo's lair was spreading and encroaching onto the earth's surface, taking advantage of the tumultuous times to claim the land in anticipation of the blood sacrifice that was to come.

Heites fought off the trembling fear, and took a glance up, half fearing to see the reanimated corpse of Brother Visuvius glaring down at him, a captain of the dark legion. After his initial relief, he soon regained his wits, rebuking himself for such irrationality. The oncoming carnage and shameful execution of his comrades were terrifying atrocities enough, without the need for mystical apocalyptic imagery, which would only shroud the real crimes. It was for these reasons that he needed to get away.

Chapter 35
Fragments of Uniforms

Deep beneath the heavy winter clouds the sun was on the verge of rising above the horizon. Light that found its way around the curvature of the earth was refracted, then re-fused into a fiery red blanket that bleached the sky with hellish grandeur. The thick clouds refused to yield, tinged blue silhouettes of igneous rock floating on the lava backdrop.

Lord Gatan stood staring over the previous day's battlefield. Corpses littered his left flank, pinned specimens strewn out in wait for heavenly inspection. Shields and helmets caught the fiery light that lit up the pre-dawn sky, reflecting an oily purple haze like the shells of stag beetles. These cracked and buckled carapaces were the most solid remains of once living beings. Between these glimmering items, fragments of uniforms lay tattered and ripped, soaking up the blood that still dripped from lacerations in the luminous white flesh of the dead. Blood that refused to dry in the chilly squalor. Matted hair, twine transmuted into congealed hemp by the fusing adhesive of amalgamated sweat, blood and dirt, these grimy substances losing all their glorious propaganda properties when seen in morbid reality.

The previous afternoon, Gatanese soldiers had hastily attempted to separate their own losses from the Latman dead, before darkness rendered differentiation impossible. When darkness fell, the soldiers cursed the similarity of purple and blue in the setting sun.

As light threatened to return, Lord Gatan anxiously awaited the point where they would be able to see if any of his own had been thrown down the ridge into the bloody squalor. No attempt had been made to retrieve the corpses of the barbarian marauders; even drafted Gatan militia were deemed above these bestial outlaws.

Lord Gatan cursed their feral impetuousness, wasted on a handful of Light Infantry when they could have led a decisive flanking manoeuvre in the coming day's onslaught. Nevertheless, he was pleased that the militia spearmen had taken the charge of the enemy, a hopeful sign that they would stand today.

He halted the drifting of his mind over the strewn dead, and focused on the day at hand. The previous day's skirmish had shown that the rocky segment of the climb rendered the bulk of his line left of the road impassable. This meant he could leave a gap in the line, place a unit of regular spearmen and veteran swordsmen on the far edge of the ridge, and consolidate the rest of his forces on the gap between the woodland and the rocks. A spare unit of spearmen could be placed behind the woods at an angle to protect his right flank from a flanking incursion.

He could picture his deployment in his mind: it seemed formidable. Yet he could not help but feel a rising unease as the fresh sunlight illuminated the mass of Latman infantry as they emerged from their tents with glimmering sets of armour.

With this spectacle unfolding before his eyes he could not help but allow his mind to drift back to Lady Gatan's misgivings. Though he had marched unstopped into Latman territory, the thought of inaction unnerved him. Up on this high ground he had mustered the best odds he could; all he could do now was sit back and wait for their attack. All his cards were on the table; it was Latman's turn to show initiative.

★

The orderlies had arrived at daybreak to strap Juscius Latman into his armour. They fastened the carapace like a straightjacket, hindering his boyish desire to flee responsibility. In a quivering rage the lord had dismissed the servants once the task was completed.

In these moments of fear he had found himself thinking of the slave girl. He did not for a moment think of Torian; only the resolute but undemanding figure of his dark temptress could instil him with the requisite vigour to calm his nerves. He longed for the comfort of her soft smooth skin and towering body to smother him in matriarchal warmth.

Yet, in this manly domain of war, the best support he could muster was Zeuorox. The icy high priest was summoned and arrived promptly, greeting the lord as though it were any day. His gaunt face betrayed no emotion in the probing illumination of the crackling fire.

As the cleric began performing various rites, no amount of incense could counter the raw stench of earthly waste; the noxious aroma of soldierly faeces gave a stark realism that no mystical scent could overcome.

Juscius perched on the edge of his seat, awkwardly encumbered by his fixed breastplate. His lips quivered, trying to follow the priest's chanting. When the priest ceased, he strode over to the lord, his tall stature casting a looming shadow over his acolyte. His voice boomed with a succinct coldness, completely immune to the intensity of the moment. "Have you learned the speech I gave you?" he asked, following the query with a beady stare.

Juscius looked up, a humbled choir boy before his master, and nodded irksomely. The priest's emotionless, commanding voice continued. "You may deviate from it, should you desire."

The lord just repeated his cautious nodding gesture before shrinking into his steel carapace like a turtle.

The high priest showed no sympathy for the monarch's furtiveness, indeed he seemed to relish the relative superiority in which it placed him. "I have given the orders out. The commanders will be able to form up the force immediately afterwards. The Telis cavalry will join the Latman lancers on the right flank, they should be able to circle right round the Gatan line." He revelled in the strategic militarism he was able to espouse. His eyes lit up with fiery excitement as he spoke of the flanking manoeuvre.

As the moments of silence that followed stretched out into a tense stasis, the high priest began to pace anxiously. The trapped vulture was soon relieved when the orderly arrived to announce the men were ready.

★

Lord Adonis Gatan had watched the speech by his adversary in the morass. The tenseness down in the quagmire wafted up with the breeze. Though he could not hear the speech, the roar of the Latman soldiers when the lord finished resonated up the hill, sending a chilling sensation up his spine. His men were already formed up, he wanted them to witness the Latman deployment; this meant they would be able to see where the various enemy units went and so would be conscious of the whole Latman army and not just the section that marched on them.

Only once the sea of silver had formed up and begun its advance did Lord Gatan ride through the elites that guarded the road to make a snappy speech. Sat tall on his horse, with his son and close advisor, Hercela, either side, he knew it bore a stark significance for his men to see him turn his back on the advancing horde. He hoped the image would stay with them and they would see his image as the Latman charge descended upon them.

"Men, we have marched side by side to stop this upstart and his dreams of domination. But it is not just a young pip-squeak's fallacious dream that we have come to quash: for too long we have allowed these pretenders to act as a law unto themselves. That too dies today! We fight now to restore a much needed balance, a balance that the gods have willed, and that this upstart wishes to demolish. It is here that we, not just as protectors of our great land, but as defenders of balance, shall make our stance. We are this island's last bastion of sanity against a tide of madness; a tide that seeks to invade, to bully, to control. Here, on THIS day, WE SAY NO!" his booming voice finished in a short sharp salvo of words.

The whole line of spearmen roared. Spear shafts bashed shields in a crashing maelstrom of passion. Lord Gatan raised both fists, roared, upturned his wrists then brought his hands in to bash his chest. As he did so his men fell silent, awaiting his gesture. Melodramatically, his kicked his horse forward and the bellowing began again.

He trotted through the ranks with the clatter of steel on steel clashing all around him, ready to take up position with his cavalry bodyguard. Once amongst them he kept watch of the advancing enemy, the patchwork of square regiments resembling the scales of some mighty beast. The light infantry and light lancers, backed up by yellow-caped Telis cavalry, advanced on each flank like pincers.

THE SON AND THE HEIR

For all their polished steel and regimented formation, to Gatan the advancing horde was exactly that: a rabblesome horde encased in a carapace of metallic false sophistication.

When they came within range, the archer captains gave the order to begin volley fire. As the first salvos thundered down on the regiments, Gatan saw a look of dismay on the faces of the Latman captains as the superior Lewerix bows punched through their men's scale mail. But they did not falter, merely reform, trampling on their fallen brethren indifferently as they did so. As the glimmering sea of Juscius' followers unflinchingly marched on from the aerial assault of the longbows, there was something spine-chilling about their vacant expressions; they seemed entranced by the noise of their own marching, like automatons, not one stopping to lift a wounded comrade.

When the next volley came, a most peculiar thing happened. As though mimicking the orders of the archer captains, the Latman captains ordered the men to halt, then, when the order was given to fire they barked a second command and in one lightning movement, they all crouched and simultaneously brought their shields together, forming a roof over their heads and the sides and front forming walls. The contrast with the previous volley was staggering; Gatan searched their ranks for fallen men, hoping some arrows had sneaked between the roof and the wall.

As the metallic organisms trudged on, Gatan saw that less than a handful of Latman soldiers had been hit, several rocking as they tried to pull arrows from their ankles. He saw the creases on their faces as they fought the excruciating pain of lacerations in such tender places.

The archer captains called for their men to free-fire, hoping this would stop the Latman infantry from forming this bulwark. However, the Latman soldiers merely began to keep their shields locked in formation and advanced slowly in the crouched position. As Gatan observed their gradual trudge towards his lines, he felt he was merely prolonging the inevitable. Nevertheless, the archers were able to take more careful aim and a greater proportion of arrows were guided into the shadowy gap between the front wall and the room created by the curvature of the shields.

Gatan glanced at the flanks. The Latman and Telis cavalry had taken a wide encircling path and looked set to engage the spearmen and veteran detachment on his left. He sent an order for a detachment of archers to be reassigned to the flank to try to disrupt the cavalry charge. On his right flank, the Latman light infantry were about to enter the wooded area, stopping him from moving his spearman line into a concave formation so as to envelop the advancing heavy infantry.

Within minutes the heavy infantry were preparing to charge. The Gatan spearmen were nervously flexing their muscles, ready to take the onslaught. The Latman infantry stopped, and crouched low, carefully sliding the javelins from behind their shields. Behind them, a line of archers were summoned to fire a volley, which was cleverly disrupted by the Gatan archer captains, who had anticipated the move, firing a volley prior to the order. As the swarm of black arrows cascaded down on the young archers, Gatan looked away, wondering where the one youth who deserved to be on the receiving end, Lord Juscius Latman, was. Off in the distance an entourage of mounted men sat observing the scene. Gatan knew Juscius was among them, a fallen cherub seated between that foppish entrepreneur and the insidious vulture; both showering him with praise so they could better leech off the rewards these men that now faced him would sacrifice themselves for.

His attention was disrupted by the bellowing of the heavy infantry as they rose and began jogging forwards. The Gatan spearmen braced, crouching low holding their shields high and at a distance from their bodies. In one fluid movement, the heavy infantry launched their javelins, drew their gladiuses and accelerated into a full charge. When the javelins struck, Lord Gatan winced. Gatan could immediately see that the reservists were not replacing the fallen, some looked from side to side nervously. Deep in his heart, Gatan knew what was going to happen.

The heavy infantry charging up the road struck first, but the elite spearmen were more than ready for them. Those lost or wounded by javelins had been replaced and the phalanx was a horizontal trap of spikes onto which the front rank of heavy infantry had no option but to launch themselves into. Having marched such a long way in heavy armour, and now unable to alter their pace for fear of being trampled by the ranks behind, they could do nothing to avoid the carefully placed spear-points of the elite spearmen. Virtually to a man they fell, sending their following compatriots tumbling down over them. As the elite spearmen cautiously advanced to drive them back, Gatan's attention was drawn elsewhere. The regulars had held, though were now locked in an uneven close combat with their heavily armed adversaries and so would need support. But the militia spearmen had crumbled, still in shock and confusion from the salvo of javelins. Their trembling hands had been unable to hold their spears properly, let alone keep them in a phalanx formation. The disordered front ranks sought to flee, pushing their compatriots behind them into a fully fledged rout. But, the heavy infantry were soon upon them, stabbing them in the backs mercilessly, not bothering to finish them off as they trampled over them to slaughter those behind. The few spearmen that valiantly tried to put up a fight were unable to defend from all sides and so were quickly dispatched, though buying vital fractions of seconds for their less steadfast brethren.

The vapid faces of the Latman heavy infantry exploded in bloody vivacity, stabbing and withdrawing, gleefully feeling the warm blood spray across their faces to coalesce with their own perspiration. They set about their work like foxes in a chicken run, a frightening bloodlust conquering any compassion or doubt about the necessity of slaughtering a defeated foe.

The archers behind the routed spearmen began to flee, their captains trying to control the retreat so they could rally once safe. As the heavy infantry that had punched through spread through the Gatan lines the regular spearmen became anxious of their unprotected flanks, subconsciously giving ground to their adversaries.

"They must hold!" bellowed an anxious Gatan, signalling to the swordsmen behind the regulars on the right flank to prepare to try and plug the gap. However, the gradual retreat of the spearmen between them and the Latman infantry that had broken through disturbed their path to their target.

Suddenly, the regulars on the right flank fell into a fighting retreat, the second ranks, who still had their spears, holding the heavy infantry off whilst those on the front line fell back. However, the spearmen with the swordsmen behind stood their ground, knowing the swordsmen would stop them from being outflanked. In response, the spearmen guarding the forest pulled back close to the swordsmen.

Gatan turned to his messenger. "Get the woodland spearmen to send a detachment around the side of the Latman line, we need to hold the right flank. Get the swordsmen to charge their infantry as soon as they pass the spearmen line."

The elite spearmen had ceased their advance, anxious of the Latman infantry that were open to encircle them. The regulars to their left had held, no doubt bolstered by their closeness to the elites and his lordship, but also aided by the detachment of archers behind them, who were free to rain down arrows on the rear ranks of their adversaries.

The retreat of the regular spearmen in the centre was leaving a chasm filled with shimmering devils between the two flanks. Gatan's bodyguard drew their swords, knowing it would be up to them to stop the Gatan line being fractured into two.

With chaos unfolding around him, Gatan turned to his son, gripped his sword by the blade and thrust the hilt towards him. "Maximus, you must flee. My reign is coming to an end; my era has tried to stop this upstart, and has failed. Now you must lead our people."

Maximus gave Adonis a stern look before shaking his head sincerely. "Lord Gatan, father, we are one of a kind; if your days are over then so too are mine..."

"You are my son, you are the Heir..." Lord Gatan declared.

Maximus shook his head. "Don't you see father, all around us the lineages are broken? They say Juscius is the son of Thelus, not Octavius. Zenith Lewerix's son has disappeared, Vacarium's son is the death of his house, Faldinite will usurp Danite. There is a schism in the lineage, a new era is upon us, whether we like it or not. Our house must adapt, it needs a suitable leader for such times. I have no acumen for the path that lies before us, I am a warrior like you, and should die a warrior with you; Claudix must succeed you!"

Adonis Gatan stared into his son's eyes. He had a horrible inkling that Maximus spoke words of wisdom, something he gallantly refused to accept. He felt emotive pain in his chest. Though he had always been proud of Maximus, he had evidently underestimated his son's dedication to being an honourable warrior, and also the depth of his self-understanding. He truly was his heir, and for that reason unsuitable to the future of guile and compromise. He knew Maximus' words were not boyish posturing; they were a warrior staying pure to his path.

Maximus took the sword from Adonis, then turned to Hercela. "Commander Hercela, it was you that had foresight on this plan. Furthermore, you are a great strategist, advisor, mentor and friend to us all. Claudix will need you by his side, he will need a staunch experienced warrior to guide him in the art of war. You must take it."

Lord Adonis sat proud on his horse as his son took the words out of his mouth.

Hercela looked shocked, and uncomfortable in taking the sword, but knew time was short. However, he could not refrain from making one correction. "My reservations were insignificant compared to those of Lady Gatan. Where war will be my domain of mentorship, let us hope the great advice of her Ladyship will steer Claudix away from needing my advice."

Father and son solemnly looked to the ground when Lady Gatan was mentioned. Visibly pained, Gatan eventually spoke, looking directly at his companion. "Hercela, I wish I could say nothing needs to be said to my wife, that she will instinctively know how much I have adored and respected her, but I fear it is not so. She has been my finest companion and advisor, my greatest emissary, my most perfect counterbalance, and the nurturer of two of the greatest royal sons to inherit the earth. Her service to this house outstrips us all, her dedication manifold, and so wholesome that it has been self-sacrificial. My only regret upon my passing is that I leave this world so indebted to her." Adonis reached

forward and drew Hercela's sword from its scabbard. "Hercela, my most trustworthy friend and commander, knowing you are by my son's side when he succeeds shall bring me much comfort. Now go!"
With that they turned their horses in opposite directions and launched themselves into their respective missions.

As Hercela galloped off down the road, Adonis, Maximus and their guard gave a mighty war cry they charged into the seething mass of heavy infantry. High up on their steeds, facing fatigued infantry with short swords they would be hard targets for their adversaries. But it would be only a matter of time before the small unit of Latman spearmen joined the fray.

Lord Gatan slashed down with Hercela's broadsword, cleaving through the exposed necks of his opponents. Their blood sprayed in vivacious fountains, splattering on his horse's fur and barding, but never reaching his torso. In a whirlwind of a moment he saw his trusted bodyguard Alledic pulled from his horse and stabbed by a huddle of sweating bloody Latman soldiers.

After a few minutes he heard the bellow of a bugle, a messenger calling for him to disengage. He kicked his horse forwards, pushing through the exhausted Latman infantry, his guardsmen following suit.

Many Latman soldiers vainly sought to follow him, their ponderous advance making them easy targets for the archers on the left flank. The bugler was from the far left contingent the other side of the rocky unassailable section of the hill. He rode over to Gatan to tell him that the cavalry had been repelled and the soldiers were on their way to reinforce the main line. Gatan paused momentarily to survey the battlefield. It was a disordered maelstrom of clattering iron and steel, and one that did not count in his favour at all. The right flank was entirely cut off from the left. Sending another contingent into this mess would be like feeding them into a meatgrinder.

He returned his attention to the messenger, "No, get them to form a defensive perimeter against the rocky cliff edge. There we shall make our last stand." He turned his attention to Maximus. "Maximus, go with the messenger and organise the defence."

Maximus hesitated, "Lord Gatan..."

Adonis cut him off. "You *shall* be lord, Maximus. Be it only a short while, that final defiance shall have you as its leader." He clasped his sword in his shield hand and lifted the royal necklace from his neck. "I could not bestow both regal symbols to just one of my sons, for they are both worthy Lords. Take this... you are Lord Maximus Gatan I, the lord that combined the virtues of a Lord with that of a Son and a Brother."

"But father..."

"The elite spearmen have fought valiantly today, but they will never escape this onslaught. The least they deserve is to die alongside their Lord."

With that he was off, deliberately giving no order to his bodyguards, letting them chose who they fought with. Only one rode out with him, Malki, for to him, more than any of the others, it was the man and not the position that he defended.

As Maximus watched his father, and his trusty bodyguard ride into the carnage of oblivion, he knew Adonis primarily did it out of loyalty to his men. But he also knew the old warrior did so because he feared that great terror of all men's lives; to outlive one's son.

And so began the shortest, if not bravest, reign of a Gatan Lord…

★

It was now that the trembling pile of rags realised that there was no conspiracy against it. At least, if there had been it was the construct of its very own subconscious: a deliberate trap set by intrinsic mechanisms silently toiling away to destroy the conscious being that was Rabica.

This whole journey had been the result of this project; She had not driven him, nor had the terrifying realities of the world; he had driven himself into seclusion and self-destruction.

Only now, in such a desolate place, with the consciousness and body of Rabica waning, could this subconscious feel at home, finally ready to assimilate the consciousness and physical body it inhabited.

It had latched onto primordial attraction, attributed the concept of love to her, and let it settle in the contradictions of a vile political reality. Allowing these two to combine into a powerful engine of conspiracy against the conscious being.

She was not a problem, merely a tool of this self-disgusted spirit. That it was her and not another was mere coincidence. Had he survived the ordeal that was affection for her, he would have only found another, then another, and so on, until he was worn out and accepted the inevitable.

As consciousness drifted away, seeping through the pile of rags that vainly attempted to withhold the warmth needed to sustain it, the subconscious triumphed, consciousness losing out due to its intrinsic link to the inadequate body it inhabited.

Was it a pyrrhic victory on the part of the subconscious? Had it not realised that it was tied to the body too? Does the subconscious live on? Or did this subconscious resent the body it inhabited so completely that death became the only escape anyway? Or were the few moments free of this inept body and incompetent consciousness worth death afterwards; seconds of bliss worth an early eternity of oblivion?

We shall never know. Rabica; the young man we began to know, is dead. Perhaps, for all true purposes, he always was, a husk slavishly mutilating itself for the whims of a disgusted subconscious.

If so, then maybe we should celebrate the demise of Rabica too: a consciousness, so at odds with itself, so dominated by a party that loathed it. A third party, one that watched the struggle of the ideal consciousness and necessary (but defunct) physical, with despair and frustration. It had ended the dualism; killed them both, and perhaps sacrificed itself in the process. If this was the case, then it had done precisely what the consciousness of Rabica could not; sacrifice itself for the ending of a greater perpetual pain.

The mound of rags was rendered incapacitated, the vitriolic subconscious finding itself confined to the waning power of the brain. It had finished the cycle. Recognising that capitulation was the final act of anything, had it been able to express its sudden realisation, its words would have been:

"Everything destroys itself."

Lightning Source UK Ltd.
Milton Keynes UK
01 August 2010

157714UK00001BA/3/P